THE EXPANDING UNIVERSE

VOLUME 3

An Exploration of the Science Fiction Genre

28 Science Fiction Stories by

Bestselling & Debut Authors

Compiled & Edited by Craig Martelle

TABLE OF CONTENTS

8 - A Language Barrier by Craig Martelle

Language isn't the only thing that can bring humans and aliens together.

41 - Weaponized Math by Jonathon P. Brazee

Staff Sergeant Gracie Medicine Crow, United Federation Marine Corps sniper guards a well-known secret to her success.

65 - To Catch a King by Mike Kraus

One ship, one crew and more trouble than they bargained for.

88 - Skeleton Crew by Mikey Campling

It takes a million moving moving parts to send a starship across the galaxy, but only one mistake to bring it crashing down.

112 - Epiphany by Andrew Dobell

Dain's first mission as a special forces Wraith isn't as simple as it sounds.

135 - The Achanean Reception by Richard Fox

Security for the wedding of a merchant prince and his mysterious fiancée grows complicated as the bride's family has a very different notion of matrimony.

154 - The Trophy by B.C. Kellogg

Private Pyrros Eav is a foot soldier in the invasion of Rhitec. Nothing can stand before the might of the Empire...or so he's been told. When he's stranded in the middle of an alien forest during the annexation, he encounters an unlikely ally that threatens to destroy everything he believes in.

178 - Blood and Treasure by Terry Mixon

The Terran Empire's best brings the hammer down.

201 - Dreadnought by Yudhanjaya Wijeratne

What would an AI think of war? How would a vastly superhuman, yet slaved intelligence, bereft of fear, anger, hope, envy - all the things that drive us - ever understand its masters?

224 - Save the Scientist by J.A. Cipriano and Connor Kressley

When a research vessel crash lands on a bug-infested planet, only Infinity Marine Mark Ryder is close enough to save them in time

250 - Severance by C.C. Ekeke

One brutal act of sabotage throws a day of celebration between two star-spanning governments into chaos.

276 - Across the Galactic Pond by Christian Kallias

Kevin's encounter with a dying alien propels him into the midst of an intergalactic war.

306 - Catalyst by Lisa Blackwood & S.M. Schmitz

When Catalyst sustains heavy damage from a rogue AI attack, the Spire warship's only chance for survival lies in an outlaw telepath with the power to destroy him.

333- Wrenching Free by Zen DiPietro

Wren can fix anything mechanical. But can she fix her own life?

349 - Fugitives' Gamble by T.M. Catron

An imperial inspection, a pirate raid, and a spacewalk... and that's just before lunch. Captain Rance Cooper prefers being called *anonymous transporter* instead of *smuggler*, but the heiress-turned-fugitive has a knack for finding trouble. Stranded inside a battle zone, Rance must decide which is worse—turning herself over to the authorities for protection, or fighting off a horde of angry space pirates.

391 - One Last Job by Amy DuBoff

Out of money and options, Thom takes on a risky delivery job that's far from legal.

415 - Maybe Now the Stars Will Shine by Michael La Ronn

Agent Devika Sharma's mission is simple: stop three criminals from transporting kidnapped humans to the next galaxy. Stuck on an ice planet, in a warehouse, with nothing but her wits and a few bullets left, the fate of twelve innocent people rest on what she does next.

443 – Ice Field by Scott Moon

Lieutenant Colonel Reginald Humann must evacuate a mixed team of civilians and soldiers before nightmare creatures drag them below the ice.

462 – The Next Level by Thomas J. Rock

A three-man digital insertion drop team is infiltrating a deep space Russian weapons R&D station, when a malfunction cripples their ship, leaving the team stranded, and the ship's A.I. goes missing. Reed Wilson is the only equipped to look for the A.I. The problem is, he's not a soldier. To save the ship and the team, he'll have to take himself to the next level.

487 – Save the Queen by Emily Walker

Spence has the chance to prove he's a real hero to the galaxy, but the Queen of Pop won't make it easy. Along with his daughter Mary, the transport mission to deliver the queen to a safe house turns into the adventure of a lifetime with danger, strange enemies, and hot dogs.

510 – Alas, Thudonia by Bill Patterson

To whom does she owe her allegiance her ancestors or the man who would take her away from a future disaster?

530 – Exiled by Chris Fox

Mankind's outer colonies are quietly disappearing and Commander Nolan is ordered to find out why.

566 – Voyage of the Dog-Propelled Starship by Robert Jeschonek

Dogs are man's best friend, but dogs' best friends are something else entirely.

584 – Assault on Tarja by M.D. Cooper

Venus may stand, but Tarja must fall.

606 – The Piayan Job by Laura and Daniel Martone

Take one conniving high priest. Add a handful of ornery pirates. Toss in a couple dashes of deceit. And you've got a recipe for mayhem and misadventure in the galaxy.

630 – Final Intelligence by Kevin McLaughlin

Investigating a derelict starship turns out to be anything but what it seems.

658 – In the Shadows by Danny A. Brown

Helen and her followers seek sanctuary deep in the void on one of the countless rogue planets out there, worlds lost in interstellar space. But what happens when that planet is not empty?

683 – LZ New Birth by J.R. Handley

No one's ever found glory hiding in a bunker.

FOREWORD: BY CRAIG MARTELLE

I love science fiction.

We escape to new and different places, but we find that futuristic or alien cultures will have many of the issues we also face. It's safe to talk about issues of the day painted on a science fiction backdrop. Isn't that what all scifi is, in one way or another?

We can look at a variety of worlds through a lens that helps us escape. The stories in this collection are military science fiction, or space opera, or space adventure. We like our heroes, whether they are driving a mech and firing a railgun or like in my story, where they have no weapons whatsovever.

How do you fight without weapons? Sun Tsu told us how millennium ago. Pulling the trigger to kill an enemy is the same whether one is using a flintlock or a plasma rifle. The emotion of the act, the reasons behind it, the consequences of doing it – that is what we get to address in science fiction. We make it futuristic with crazy aliens, red skies, and multiple moons shining in the night sky with a backdrop of unknown stars.

Science fiction is freedom to do as we wish. The megalomaniacal dictator must be removed! He's evil. Or the conglomerate, or the monarchy, or the alien overlords. We oppose oppression and seek freedom and liberty. The hero's journey. We want to take it, and we can.

Because of science fiction. I love the characters and the stories. An escape from the trials and tribulations of real life. Even if only for a short while.

Twenty-eight different stories follow where thirty-one authors bare their souls for you. I guarantee you'll find something you like within these pages, and thank you for taking a look and seeing what there is to see.

Let's fight the good fight together. Join me among the stars.

Craig Martelle

11/24/17 – Waikoloa, Hawaii

A LANGUAGE BARRIER

By Craig Martelle

Language isn't the only thing that can bring humans and aliens together.

The windswept plain looked the same as yesterday, as it had the day before that.

The weeks before. It was always the same. Magenta-hued grasses, like an ocean's waves, cresting and dipping. It reminded Doctor Franklin Berens of his native Kansas, where the wheat grew a beautiful gold. Brown to the untrained eye.

He stood outside the shelter, nursing his coffee. Supplies were waning as the survey party approached the date of their pickup. One standard month of surveys would determine the planet's fate, whether the conglomerations would mine or not. Their methods resulted in a minimal footprint. In many cases, the congloms would have their crews in and out in six months.

No sense wasting time or resources digging anything that wasn't a target mineral.

Brandon Ellis left the shelter, pulling his collar tightly around his neck. "Hey, boss. I set the rover to core sample the area of x-ray seven. We got some promising results from yesterday's deep scan. I want to take a look at the ore, touch it. The last sample was crap. Can't trust that sonar system. Gentry says there's nothing wrong with it."

Franklin looked at the other man, similar in age, always unhappy until he ate his first Snickers bar. Franklin reached into his pocket for one of the single-serve food packs. He always carried them, just in case he broke down away from the shelter. Calories were life. Water was life.

Never leave without them. Brandon kept his pack in the jeep. As the group's mineralogist, he said that he had no intention of ever carrying rocks around—they were always heavy. He would not stray far from his ride. And he hadn't, even when Franklin tried to coax him away.

The doctor held out the bar.

"Snickers! My favorite." Brandon chuckled in response. Taking the offering, ripping it open, and devouring it in two bites.

"Those taste pretty good, if you give them a chance," Franklin said as he watched his bar get choked down.

"Did someone take my name in vain?" Gentry Race strolled outside, jacket open, seemingly immune to the cool of the morning air. She was slight, almost a full-head shorter than the two men. Her specialty was systems, keeping them running as needed, and that meant reconfiguring them for purposes no one had contemplated before the mission arrived.

Every planet was different. Every survey had its own unique challenges.

"Your sonar doesn't penetrate this ground, so you have to do it the old-fashioned way with a pick and a shovel," she taunted.

"You pronounced 'core sampler' wrong," Brandon replied.

"Do you have any more of those?" she asked, pointing to the wrapper. Franklin pulled the last bar from his pocket and handed it over.

"Coffee pot is shut down!" Doctor Jimi Johnson, the team's microbiologist, called from inside the shelter. "It looks like one of my petri dishes in there."

"Hang on, Satan!" Brandon yelled before rushing for the shelter door.

Franklin and Gentry watched him go. The doctor drank the last of his coffee while it was still warm. He smacked his lips when he finished.

They heard a crash from inside the shelter. Gentry took a step, but a firm hand gripped her shoulder, holding her back. "Sometimes, it's best to let things work themselves out." He let go and shrugged, turning back to watch the wind flow through the prairie grasses.

***

The ship came from deep space. It slowed quicker than the Terran vessels before settling into orbit. The beacon that was left behind for the survey crew's use had already noted and transmitted the arrival of the alien vessel to the planet, as well as the long-haul communications array at the edge of the heliosphere.

The ship changed course, arrowed toward the beacon. A laser reached out, soundlessly burning a small hole through the beacon. The lights on the system went out as its circuit boards were fried. In an instant, it had become a lifeless hulk, a derelict piece of space junk.

Most of the planets in the explored systems had trash circling in a decaying orbit, to burn up in the atmosphere, if the planet had an atmosphere. Some, like this, had only one human-made object in orbit. Its loss activated an automated signal.

***

"We just lost orbital comms!" Gentry shouted. She waited for a response.

Nothing. When she went outside, the jeep was gone, along with the other three members of the survey team. She returned to her station and cycled the point-to-point system.

"You slimy worms abandoned me again!" she called into the microphone, tapping her toe impatiently as she waited for a response.

"Did we do that again? I must take full responsibility for that breach, Miss Race," Doctor Berens apologized.

"Uh-huh," she replied, unhappy with being forgotten. She had wanted to go along to watch the core sampler work. She'd repaired it when it broke, but she hadn't seen it in the field. And she still wouldn't.

"I called to tell you that we lost orbital comms," Gentry said coldly.

"Atmospherics?" Brandon asked.

"No, Rock Doc, the sky is clear and magnetism is low. Let me check the last data burst and I'll let you know." The team had dubbed Brandon the Rock Doc. He didn't have a PhD, but that didn't matter.

Not out in the middle of nowhere.

"Guys," Gentry said in a low voice. "There's a ship in orbit, and it isn't one of ours."

"We're on our way back, and then we'll figure out what to do."

***

Franklin signed off. Brandon looked left, then turned the wheel that way. He floored it to spin the back end of the jeep around, let off the gas for the wheels to regain traction, and then gunned it to launch the jeep toward their shelter.

"What do you think it is?" Jimi wondered.

Brandon screwed his face up as he wrestled with not delivering a sarcastic response. *A spaceship,* he thought. He settled for shaking his head.

"An incursion. Probably someone doing the same thing we're doing—a little exploring, some prospecting, you know, seeing what the galaxy has to offer," Franklin suggested.

"I don't like it," she replied.

Franklin and Brandon couldn't argue with that. They remained silent, absorbed in their own speculation as they drove on, retracing their tracks through the grass.

Brandon slowed their headlong rush when he spotted the shelter ahead. Doctor Berens thanked him for slowing down.

"Why didn't you say something?"

Jimi Johnson piped up from behind the driver. "Because you get mad when someone complains about your driving. Especially if it comes from the backseat."

"Do not!" he replied, trying to keep the banter light, but no one laughed. There was too much to think about.

As they pulled up, Gentry was standing outside, waiting for them.

"Took you long enough," she snapped.

Franklin breathed deeply and listened to the breeze whip across the shelter and into the grasslands beyond. He stepped casually from the jeep.

"Be calm, people. I ask that everyone put on their best face. They may not come to the surface at all. Once they see we're here, they may move on," Franklin told the others, trying his best to sound hopeful.

Gentry cleared her throat and pointed over the doctor's head.

He followed her finger, turned, and saw the dark mass of an approaching ship. "Well, crap."

He stood transfixed by the sight. There wasn't anything in the procedures to deal with visitors. It had never happened to an exploration team before. Teams had disappeared on two occasions over the course of the previous fifty years, and those had never been resolved. People speculated, of course.

Doctor Franklin Berens did not want his team to be the third. He felt like his mission was no longer in his control. He hoped that he could hang on when the ride got rough.

"What are you thinking, Doc?" Gentry asked as she chewed the inside of her cheek.

"I think we need to remain calm," Franklin said in a shaky voice. Gentry walked up beside him and took his hand. Brandon took her other hand. Jimi stood on the other side of Doctor Berens, taking his free hand in hers. They stood, holding hands in unity, something they would have never done before.

Jimi whispered a prayer to Shiva.

"Amen, sister," Brandon added.

They watched together as the ship slowed, hovered, and descended to settle gently into the grass. A hatch popped and a short staircase unfolded.

"Moment of truth," Gentry whispered.

No one blinked. They stared at the hatch as one, fixated on the next moment. Their hearts hammered in their chests, pulses pounding in their hands.

A shadow darkened the doorway and a tall woman wearing a sleek spacesuit stepped out. The material reflected the sun with a pastel iridescence. The woman walked down the stairs gracefully. She was followed by two men, dressed similarly. No one carried weapons.

Not that the survey team could see. Franklin breathed a sigh of relief.

"Hello!" Doctor Berens called, pulling his hand free to wave at the newcomers.

They froze in their tracks and started speaking to each other. Franklin looked at his team, from one to the next. Everyone shook their head.

When forming the team, he had not cared about their linguistic backgrounds. It had never mattered before.

"Good morning," Franklin said, speaking slower and louder. Gentry rolled her eyes. "I am Doctor Franklin Berens. Who are you?"

The doctor stepped forward and held his hands out in what he thought looked like the universal gesture for peace. He wasn't a threat to anyone. He hoped the newcomers understood that.

The woman walked boldly forward, followed closely by the men. She walked up to Franklin and stopped when she was well inside his personal space, about six inches away. She was slightly taller than the middle-aged doctor. She leaned down and sniffed his face.

He tried to point to himself, but brushed her breast with his hand. "Oh geez! I'm sorry. I'm Franklin. Frank, if that's easier for you."

She cocked her head as she listened, furling her brow.

He tapped his chest with a finger. "Frank."

"Foerank," she struggled to say.

"Frank, yes!" the doctor exclaimed. He noticed her eyes. They were a deep magenta, a color he'd never seen before. Doctor Berens pointed toward the woman, taking great care not to repeat his earlier mistake.

"Afzelius," she said, tipping her head back slightly to look down her nose at him. He raised one eyebrow. She said her name again.

"Ass Feely Us," Brandon said.

Franklin closed his eyes and gritted his teeth, before turning and pointing to each member of his team.

"Gentry. Brandon. Jimi."

"Jen. Boran. Jimi," she repeated.

"Good enough," Brandon replied, nodding. "Maybe we could offer them some coffee. No, wait..."

Jimi reached past Gentry and slapped Brandon across the arm.

"People," Franklin cautioned. "Brandon and Gentry, please, put some water in glasses for all of us. Bring some fizz sticks just in case they like their water sparkly."

Brandon and Gentry turned to go into the shelter, but the woman stomped her foot on the ground and said something harshly, gutturally. The two members of the survey team stopped and slowly faced the strangers.

The woman pursed her lips. Frank leaned a little closer as he studied her eyes. She moved toward him until her forehead almost touched his. He didn't mistake her move for flirting. Her eyes were narrowed as she glared at him. He took an involuntary step backward. She followed him, holding her distance.

"I'm at a loss as to what to do," the doctor stammered. He finally stopped moving and closed his eyes. He could feel her breath on his face. It was hot, much hotter than it should have been. She grunted and he could feel her move away.

When Frank reopened his eyes, the woman had moved past him and was in front of Jimi. The microbiologist was arching backward as the woman leaned in closely.

"I guess we're all going to get our turn, huh?" Brandon asked, but it wasn't a question. Franklin knew that the Rock Doc was right.

The two men took their turns sniffing Franklin's face before moving toward the other three members of the survey team. They all turned their backs on Doctor Berens as they "inspected" Jimi, Brandon, and Gentry.

This is where the little man rises to the occasion and frees his people from the aggressors, Franklin thought. *At least that's what the movies teach us.*

A boot scuffed behind Doctor Berens. He turned and found a small woman standing there, watching him closely, studying him.

"Where'd you come from?"

"She came out of the ship while you were ogling our new guest," Brandon replied. Frank rolled his eyes, before returning his attention to the newest visitor.

"Foerank," he said slowly, pointing at himself.

"Frank. Yes," the small woman replied.

14

"Thank the Blessed Virgin, you speak English," Frank blurted. "Who are you and where do you come from?"

"Frank, Yes," she repeated.

"Well, crap," Brandon said from behind.

Afzelius and the two men finished their review.

Franklin pointed to the tall woman. "Afzelius," he said. And then he pointed to the two men and the other woman.

"Torel, Shelina, Jens," Afzelius said, pointing from one to the next.

Franklin said their names one by one, bowing his head in their direction respectfully each time. He had to turn around to nod to Jens, the short woman.

"Where are you from?" he asked, knowing he would get no answer. The group stood in a rough circle, looking at each other as they shifted uncomfortably.

"I feel like a freshman," Gentry whispered. Brandon chuckled. The tall woman said something and the two men snorted.

"I don't know about anyone else, but I need a drink. A good stiff one, but no alcohol on mission. I'll request we change that next time. Until then, it's water and fizz sticks." Franklin headed toward the shelter.

The tall woman stamped her foot.

"I know. You don't want us to do that. I'm sorry, but how long are we going to stand out here and look at each other?" he tried to explain.

She stamped her foot again.

He held up his hands in frustration. Franklin stepped aside and motioned for her to go inside. He opened the door and held it for her. She crossed her arms and tipped her head back.

"Now there's body language I understand," the doctor admitted.

"Ex-wives?" Brandon asked.

"Two." Doctor Franklin shrugged and waved for the others to follow. He walked slowly through the door, expecting to be stabbed in the back at any moment. No one else moved. He kept walking, letting go of the door as he entered.

Afzelius rushed ahead, grabbed the door, and jumped inside. She hit the floor of the shelter in a crouch, eyes darting back and forth as she took in the space. She straightened, and said something loudly. The other three members of her group filed in, leaving Jimi, Brandon, and Gentry outside alone.

Brandon held the door open and called through, "Want me to check out their ship, boss?"

Doctor Berens sighed heavily. "No. Just come inside. All of you, please."

Jimi and Gentry walked through and squeezed past the strangers. Brandon came in last, shrugging as he wedged into the last free space in what passed for a living room.

"Good idea, boss. We're doing the same thing we were doing outside, except that here, we have no room to do it."

"We came in to get water, thank you very much!" Doctor Berens shot back. "Excuse me."

Franklin worked his way past the newcomers, noticing that they all had the magenta eyes that sparkled seemingly with their own light, more pronounced in the dim light of the shelter.

Franklin poured a glass of water and offered it to Afzelius. She looked at him without moving. She refused to acknowledge the existence of the glass.

"As you wish," he said and drank half of the water. He dumped a fizz stick into it and then refilled the glass. It bubbled. He drank it down halfway.

The tall stranger watched him carefully before reaching out and taking the glass. She sniffed it, raised her eyebrows, and then drank, slowly at first, but finished with a flourish.

She handed the glass back and pointed to the counter.

Franklin smiled as he filled his glass and three others, dumped the fizz sticks in, and then handed them to the newcomers, one by one, saying their names as he did so. "Afzelius, Torel, Shelina, Jens." The strangers drank what they were given as if they'd just been rescued from the desert.

Brandon raised one eyebrow as he watched. "The good old days. I remember my first fizz stick," he said, nodding.

Afzelius said something in their guttural language and all four of them snorted together.

"Is that the way they laugh?" Gentry asked softly.

"I think so. I prefer that than, let's say, getting kicked in the groin?"

"There's a lot I prefer to that. I think maybe everything," Brandon pondered, stroking his chin with one hand.

"Would you look at that? We killed ten whole minutes. When is pickup?" Jimi asked nervously.

"Emergency signal activates. Nearest ship is notified. Begins transit through interstellar space. Two weeks start to finish. Minus ten minutes, of course," Gentry replied.

"It's going to be a long two weeks," Brandon said from where he stood, wedged against a cabinet between Torel and Gentry.

***

The survey party had enough of standing within the shelter and after an hour, they'd gone back outside. The strangers joined them, where they resumed standing around and looking at each other.

"Screw this. I have work to do." Gentry waved as she returned inside.

"Me, too. Coming, Doc?" Brandon asked as he headed for the jeep.

Franklin shook his head. The tall woman watched the survey crew return to their work. Brandon climbed in the jeep and started the engine. She stamped her foot and said something. She ended with Brandon's name before nodding to Shelina. The man looked at the jeep. Brandon pointed at himself and how he was sitting.

Shelina climbed in cautiously and sat down. Brandon pulled out the seat restraint, showing him how it worked. The stranger looked at him but didn't move.

"Take it easy and don't kill our guest," Franklin said loudly enough to be heard over the jeep's engine.

17

Brandon waved an arm over his head as the jeep spun its tires, throwing dirt as he headed toward x-ray seven and the core sampler.

"Do you think they'll let me take some tissue samples? I don't think they're human," Jimi said softly, smiling at the strangers.

"No. We're not going to rip pieces off our guests so we can make slides and study them under the microscope. Don't you have something you're working on that doesn't involve assault and battery?"

"Well!" Doctor Johnson exclaimed, before starting to laugh. "Since you put it that way. It does sound kind of bad. If you'll excuse me, I have some cultures to attend to."

"While you're at it, can you take care of the coffee pot?"

She gave him the thumbs up. He wasn't sure what that meant, but didn't bother to ask. He hoped a cup of coffee would simply appear in his hand. Thinking those things but not asking had helped expedite his two divorces. Being gone all the time was not an added benefit. He had married professionals with their own careers. They had no interest in waiting on him when he returned home for brief stints before going back to space.

So they moved on. He couldn't blame them. He still sent them Christmas gifts. They sent cards.

Doctor Berens and the tall woman watched each other carefully. After a few moments, she turned and gave directions to the other two in her party. Torel and Jens headed into the shelter.

"What do we do now, Afzelius?" Franklin asked. "I wish you understood me. I'm sure you have a great story to tell."

She looked at him and they stood, shifting uncomfortably as they tried not to look at each other. Franklin closed his eyes and sighed again. He tried to look at the situation as a scientist should.

Two weeks and the ship would arrive. They had a month's worth of experiments to run. They had guests, who weren't in the way. They'd have to work with the strangers watching over their shoulders.

"I can cut out one week worth of work and compress three weeks into two. We'll be finished when our support ship arrives, and we'll be able to leave with them. That works for me," he said. Afzelius cocked her head as she watched him talk with himself.

18

Her shuttle sat in the grass. He wasn't an engineer, but he appreciated what went into making a ship fly. He wanted to take a closer look so he could write a more substantive report on the encounter. He tried to signal to Afzelius that he'd like to see her shuttle. She watched him dispassionately. He started walking toward the ship, moving slowly away from the open hatch. He saw that she was following a few paces behind.

He walked around the ship, looking at its surfaces. He was at a complete loss regarding the metallurgy used for the skin. It had an iridescent sheen, like their spacesuits. The engines looked different from what he was used to, but seemed to rely on Newton's principal of thrust out the back to propel the ship forward. It had stubby wings, but those seemed to be surfaces from which vertical thrusters protruded.

Thrust to hover. It didn't appear to burn anything. There were no scorch marks or other signs of combustion.

When he made it back to the stairs into the ship, he looked at them, then to Afzelius, and back to the stairs. He moved at a snail's pace toward it. The tall woman brushed past him, hopped up the steps, and held out her hand. He took it and she yanked him bodily up the stairs and into the shuttle.

There were four seats with instrument panels across the front and to the sides. All four occupants seemingly had systems they needed to access during flight. The space was tiny, reminding Franklin of the historical footage from Earth showing people in bulky space suits, strapped into oversized seats within a capsule.

There was a door behind the command section. The tall woman brushed past him as she opened the door and went in. Franklin followed. Bunks, a cabinet that was probably the kitchen, a small one-person bathroom. He saw a cubbyhole that looked to contain something similar to a mass spectrometer.

It had all the same things as the survey team's shelter.

"I'll be damned. I was right. You are just like us, explorers and prospectors. But we're going to need to learn how to talk with each other if we're going to move forward. We can't both mine the same planet. Well, I guess we can, but it'll go a lot more smoothly if we knew each other's intentions," he said.

Afzelius replied with a monologue of her own. He listened carefully until she was clearly finished. Then he held up his hands and shook his head. "I don't understand."

She twisted her mouth around for a few moments before motioning with one hand and leaving the shuttle. He was alone on the ship.

Clearly you are as trusting as I should be, he thought as he hurried after her in the hopes that she would not think her trust misplaced.

***

Brandon and Shelina watched as the core sampler carefully removed the stone between the ground level and the ore sample below. When the sample made it to the surface, Brandon clapped, startling the stranger.

"My man!" Brandon exclaimed as he leaned close to the deposited sample. The machine went back to work reinserting the non-sample core rock into the hole. "This looks like Ytterbium. That's what I'm talking about. I have never seen a sample like this. You know what I mean, Shelly?"

The stranger looked at him without comment.

Brandon bundled the sample into a small bag. "Let's get this back where we can take a closer look, but this is what we came here to find."

Brandon slapped the stranger on the back. Shelina jumped and dropped into a wrestler's stance, arms and legs wide apart, eyes wary.

"What the hell?" Brandon started to say as Shelina rushed him and wrapped him into a bear hug. Brandon tried to twist out of the man's grip, but it was rock solid. The magenta-eyed man bounced Brandon up and down before turning him loose.

The Rock Doc didn't want a repeat of the episode so he stood where he was. Shelina snorted, then slapped Brandon on his shoulder hard enough to send him staggering. The stranger turned around and walked toward the jeep, climbing in and sitting patiently in his seat.

"Don't go all weird on me, Shelly," Brandon said as he threw his sample in the backseat. "I'm cool with a man-hug, but not the

20

bouncing stuff. I think it's best if we don't mention that part to anyone. Ever."

***

Gentry tried to focus, but Torel's hot breath was on her neck as he peered over her shoulder. "I've punched guys for less," she told him. He didn't move. Jimi was having her own issues with Jens, who was shorter than she first appeared. Her eyes were shoulder level as she tried to watch everything that Jimi was doing.

"Do you want to look?" Jimi asked, stepping aside and motioning toward the eyepieces of the microscope. Bigger labs had everything electronic, but for the survey teams, they found that mechanical systems fared better under the harsh conditions of remote worlds. Jimi tipped the eyepieces down. Jens stood on her tip-toes to look in. She moved her head back and forth, then settled into the view.

She moved back from the microscope and started chattering excitedly, drawing pictures in the air with her fingers. Jimi pointed to a whiteboard and handed Jens the input pen. The stranger looked at it. Jimi took a second pen and drew a rough picture of the microbe she was looking at on the slide.

Jens started drawing, on a larger scale, detailing the microbe, then breaking it down with exceptional detail. She added a list to the side. Written in a different language, it meant nothing to Jimi. She casually pressed the button that would store the information captured on the whiteboard within their computer's data storage.

Jimi looked closer and then looked back through the microscope. "You can't see some of that detail here. You've seen this microbe before?" Jens didn't respond.

Jimi went through a series of charades using her image as the basis of what could be seen through the microscope. After ten minutes, she gave up. Jens had lost interest and was looking at some of the other petri dishes stacked within a streamlined vertical incubator. She pointed to one.

"Sure, we'll look at that one so you can show me what I can't see," Jimi said, disappointed that she didn't understand the stranger since Jens appeared to be a colleague, a fellow microbiologist.

***

21

As the sun headed toward the horizon, Franklin found the strangers seemingly attached at the hip of each survey crew member. He had his own, and despite the phenomenally difficult process of communicating, he couldn't say he was unhappy with his fellow team leader.

As the eight of them gathered outside the shelter, Franklin was first to speak. "I think we have guests for dinner?" he said/asked.

Jimi was the team's microbiologist, but she also doubled as the supply chief. "We have a month's worth of food. There are double the number of us, but we only need it for half the time. Company is welcome for dinner."

"Hang on. I'm still doing the math..." Brandon joked.

Doctor Berens ignored him and started pantomiming eating. The strangers looked at him.

Strangely, as it were.

He gave up. "My turn to cook. It'll be ready in ten." He left the others as he went into the shelter. Afzelius followed him, standing aside as he dug through the cabinets and set up the various food packs for dinner. Each pack provided a portion of a meal, perfectly sized for four people. He microwaved each pack separately, then combined them onto plates. There were only four plates and four sets of utensils. Franklin squeezed past the tall woman to get to the door where he called outside, "Jimi and Gentry. You, Jens, and Torel will eat first." They entered the shelter and took their plates.

The strangers watched them. "Don't tell me you don't like roast tofu, snap peas, and tubers?" Franklin said with a grin.

Gentry didn't wait. She dug in. This was her favorite meal pack.

Then again, they were all her favorites. She had a fast metabolism and it needed fuel. Which reminded him that she'd eaten his last Snickers bar.

Jens and Torel cautiously tried their meals. They didn't bother with the utensils. They dug their faces in and inhaled the food. Their tongues were wide and almost prehensile. Franklin watched closely as they used them like a spoon and tongs.

"Isn't that something," Franklin said. As they handed their plates back, he inserted them into the cleaning system and started on the next dinner pack.

Jens and Torel pointed to their mouths.

"I'm still working on that math for you, boss," Brandon said. Jimi shook her head.

"What did they intend to eat?" she asked.

"I am positive that tomorrow, they'll have us over for dinner!" Franklin said with a big smile. He wasn't happy at all and was curious if they were going to watch him and his people as they tried to sleep.

When the next meal was ready, Franklin served the four who hadn't eaten. "Gentry. Why don't you dig out a Snickers for the newcomers."

"Good idea! Can I have one, too?" she asked, having already squeezed past him, opening the cabinet and removing five bars. Franklin shook his head.

The group ate in silence. Gentry was successful at getting the strangers to eat the Snickers bars more slowly, so they didn't finish too quickly.

When Shelina and Afzelius finished eating, Gentry handed them each a bar. The tall woman talked briefly with Torel and Jens before wolfing the bar down.

Gentry took the wrappers from all and stuffed them into the recycler.

The group proceeded to stand around and look at each other.

Brandon huffed and went outside. It was getting cooler, as it did when the sun set on this planet. Franklin encouraged everyone to go outside, where they stood in uncomfortable silence.

"I don't know what you want from us," Franklin said. "I wish we could talk. We need some time for us to work out our way forward, hopefully suiting all of us. With that, I'll wish you all a good evening."

He bowed to Afzelius. She watched him expressionlessly. He ushered the other members of the survey crew into the shelter and remained at the door, holding his hand out when Afzelius tried to follow.

"No. We need our time alone, as I'm sure you need yours. Enjoy your evening." He closed the door and latched it from the inside. He watched through the window. She stood motionless. After a few moments, she said something to the others and they headed for their ship.

When Franklin turned around, Jimi was bouncing with excitement. "Out with it," Doctor Berens said in a tired voice.

"I got an eyebrow hair, a hair from her head with the follicle, and some skin cells!"

Franklin threw his hands up. "I thought I said no ripping chunks off the strangers?"

"I didn't rip anything off. It was all left behind, where a discerning scientist could find it."

"And?"

"Oh! I didn't have time to analyze it."

Franklin motioned toward the DNA sequencer and microscope. Jimi went to work.

"Brandon?" Franklin asked, leaving Jimi to herself. She wouldn't have any results for a while, and bugging her would not expedite the process.

"Shelina seems a good sort. He watched, as they do. I couldn't tell if he recognized the Ytterbium or not, but he was fine with leaving after we found it."

"You found a deposit of Ytterbium?"

"I didn't mention that? Sorry. It got lost in all the excitement. We found it. The vein. In denser quantities than I've ever seen before. I think the gold miners used to call such a find 'the motherlode,' if I'm not mistaken. It's what we were looking for, and as the crew's official Rock Doc, I'm declaring one hundred percent mission success."

Franklin held a finger to his lips as he thought about the mission parameters, before finally conceding. "Mission success," he said, smiling, "as long as our shadows let us have it."

"Gentry. What do the language programs have to say about the strangers?" Doctor Berens asked. He knew that she would have run every program at her command.

"Nothing. Not a single recognizable syllable, Frank, Yes," she replied, mimicking Jens.

"How can that be?"

"You can't just press a button and know another language, despite what you see in the science fiction shows. Their language doesn't seem to have anything in common with any known language in our databases, which are rather extensive. Thousands of languages across all mankind and not a single hit. We need them to provide context. They need to tell us their words for objects and then we start building a dictionary. Phonology, syntax, morphology, their grammar, as well as their social usage of language. I think that will take longer to develop than the time we have left here."

"You drop that on us just like that?" Brandon replied. "We can't get there from here. Simple as that, if I heard you right."

"You heard right." Gentry stood tall, confident in her assessment. A trace of chocolate from the Snickers bar lingered around her lips.

"Write your reports, people," Franklin requested while they watched Doctor Johnson and her equipment work.

***

"Aliens," Jimi stated firmly. "I've run the tests twice. There isn't anything human in the samples."

"But they look like us..." Franklin said, his statement trailing off.

"Bipedal. Head on a swivel. Two arms. That commonality was predicted eons ago. But that speculation didn't matter because we've never run across aliens. Until now, that is. We are not alone," she added in an ominous voice before chuckling.

"Aliens. We're the first humans to ever meet aliens." Franklin pursed his lips. "It seems anti-climactic."

"I know, right?" Jimi said.

"They're just like us," Gentry added. "Quirky, but the same."

Brandon held his tongue as the vision of getting bounced up and down by the alien Shelina reverberated within his skull.

"Let's get our reports ready. Gentry? Could you build us a shared space on the server so we can recount everything we think we know about them and add to it until the pickup? Be careful with your words, people. The public will be reading these words for a long time to come. They will be studied ad nauseam."

"Buzzkill!" Brandon retorted.

Franklin rolled his eyes. "I doubt that, Brandon. Note your observations and let's see if we can start building a dictionary, along with a cultural reference. They're trusting. They keep turning their backs on us. Afzelius left me alone in her spaceship! They get close and sniff. I suspect they can smell our pheromones, but what does that mean to them? Do they know anything about humans? Damn. I better get these questions documented."

Doctor Berens hurried toward a corner where there was a computer interface. He nestled into it, put on a headset, and started talking, watching his words fill the screen.

Jimi archived her findings, including copying them to a small removable data storage device that she tucked into her bra, for securing at a later time. It was strictly against policy to take anything from a survey world without first giving it to the conglom and then filing the paperwork to get it back. But this was raw data and that was never released to the public.

But earth-shattering news like aliens was worth the risk.

 Wasn't it?

**

After three hours of fitful sleep, Doctor Franklin Berens woke up, climbing from the top bunk carefully to not disturb Doctor Johnson in the lower bunk. Brandon was snoring in the top bunk, but not too loudly. Gentry was curled into a small ball, nearly invisible beneath her covers. He wondered if something had happened in her past that made her afraid. He wouldn't ask.

His job was to make sure that she was safe with them. And she was, because he was a good survey team leader.

He yawned and rubbed his eyes. It was going to be a long day, and he wasn't ready. He stumbled to the door and looked out.

"Hey!" he yelled, startling the others awake. They were as groggy as he was. None of them got out of their beds. "They're gone."

"Who's gone?" Doctor Johnson mumbled, before rolling over. A second later, she shot upright. "What?"

The mad scramble to get out of bed began, with the three other team members bumping into each other and bouncing off the walls as they hurried to the window. Franklin stepped back so they could see for themselves.

"We have our hard data, thanks to Jimi. We have our notes. And most importantly for the mission, Rock Doc found the Ytterbium in what looks to be a commercially viable quantity. You will all be memorialized in the history books."

Gentry leaned away from the window, lifted the bar, and opened the door. A cold wind blew in, but she went outside as she was dressed. Brandon grabbed their coats, not bothering to put his on as he headed out after her.

She walked to where the ship had stood. The grass was still matted down from the weight of the shuttle's landing skids. "We probably need to take measurements from all this," she said, pointing.

Brandon handed her a coat, and she put it on. Franklin brought the laser tape and a bunch of stakes. Still in their pajamas, wearing their coats and untied boots, they put the stakes at the key points of the crushed grass. Franklin dutifully recorded the measurements, then they removed their markers and put them where they estimated the edges of the shuttle had been. Less precise, but it would give the rocket scientists something to contemplate.

Jimi stood next to Franklin as he mapped and measured. "If it weren't for the data, I'd think it was a dream. Did we really see aliens?"

"Yes, we did," Franklin replied, looking at the numbers on the screen of the laser device. "We've got work to do, people. Time to get back to it. So much to do, and not enough time to get it done."

The crew recovered the stakes and returned to the shelter where they started their morning routine, in a weak attempt to return to normalcy. No one said anything.

It was like a dark cloud hung over them all.

***

The next thirteen days passed without incident. The first day after meeting the aliens was slow, but the crew picked up the pace with the imminence of their pickup. They finished what they had to, packed, and waited. Gentry sat in her chair with her legs on the desk. She watched the screen, waiting for the report from their recovery ship.

She still jumped when the message appeared on the screen, the automated message that reported the ship entering orbit. Gentry sat upright. "Ride's here. Tighten the screws and tie everything down. We're going home!" she cheered.

A second message popped up on the screen. "Large foreign ship in orbit has engaged us with lasers. We are responding with missiles. Stand by."

Franklin's mouth hung open. Jimi unconsciously clasped a hand over her breast, where she'd sewn the data wafer into her bra. Brandon leaned close to reread the message.

Brandon stood up straight and turned to the others. "What does that mean?"

No one answered.

The screen showed the first part of an emergency distress message before going blank. Franklin hung his head. He put his hand on Jimi's shoulder. She covered her face and started to cry. Brandon looked back and forth between Franklin and the blank screen. Gentry leaned forward with her elbows on the table and her head in her hands.

Franklin left the stifling confines of the shelter. He needed to breathe fresh air. Outside, he opened his collar and gulped the cool air. Winter was coming. He could feel it.

Even though he had no idea what a winter there looked like.

The sky was clear. Above, flaming trails of small debris reentering the atmosphere suggested that he and his crew would not be rescued. A second set of debris burned its way into the upper atmosphere.

Both ships destroyed? he thought. The others joined him to watch the fireworks. No one spoke.

"I guess we better figure out our food situation. The quickest anyone can get here is two weeks, but I doubt that, not after the message our ship sent. When they come, they'll come in force, a force that will take time to build," Franklin said sadly.

"What's that?" Brandon asked, pointing to the sky.

A dark spot appeared in the distance. It was coming for them.

The alien shuttle.

"What do we do?" Brandon asked in a panic. Franklin looked at the younger man. If any time was appropriate for some of Brandon's humor, it was that very moment. Franklin filled in for him.

"Maybe we can spell out 'take us to your leader' in a crop circle?" Doctor Berens asked. Jimi shook her head, not understanding what he was saying. Gentry hurried back into the shelter, slamming the door behind her.

"Maybe a petroglyph of a peace sign?" Franklin added. Neither Jimi nor Brandon found it funny. "I'm sorry. Brandon, you let me down, my man. We need a laugh right about now because there isn't jack-all we can do about this. I personally think we're going to die in the next few minutes. I don't want them to find my corpse and determine that I was curled up in a ball and crying. They're going to find me giving these bastards the finger!" Franklin thrust both hands in the air, middle digits upright as the ship approached.

"Damn straight, boss!" Brandon agreed and joined him.

"When all else fails, revel in the absurdity of it all," Doctor Jimi Johnson added and held one hand up, giving the finger to the approaching alien shuttle.

It slowed, aligned itself with its previous landing spot, and descended into position. The hatch popped and the tall woman rushed out while the stairs were still extending. She stormed up to Franklin, who had dropped his arms in expectation of getting beaten.

She stopped close, inches from his face. Afzelius sniffed him. Her eyes glistened, almost as if she'd been crying.

Jimi's face was still red and streaked from where her tears had trailed down. The tall woman looked from face to face, then wrapped her arms around Franklin, hugging him tightly as she sobbed.

"So, we're not going to die?" Brandon asked.

Franklin stroked the alien's hair as he held onto her, like a drowning man hanging onto a life-vest. She finally pulled back. He had no idea how much time had passed. Jimi had gone back inside and Brandon was sitting in a chair outside, simply watching. Torel, Shelina, and Jens stood patiently behind Afzelius.

Franklin and Afzelius held onto each other, even at arm's length, as if afraid to let go.

"Food?" Franklin said, pantomiming eating.

"Foerank," Afzelius replied, pointing to her mouth. "Food." She looked back at her shuttle and started walking, yanking Franklin with her since they were still holding hands.

"Brandon," Franklin called over his shoulder. The Rock Doc jumped up and hurried after them. Shelina slapped him on the shoulder as he passed, propelling him forward until he stumbled and landed face-first on the ground.

Franklin ignored him as he followed the tall alien into her ship, through the door into the living space, and then stopped as she opened a cabinet packed with cartons. She popped one open, licked out some of its contents, and handed it to Franklin.

He hesitated for a moment, calculated the distance into the carton, and decided that his tongue wasn't up to the challenge. He reached two fingers in, scooped some out, and stuffed it into his mouth before thinking too long about the smell. He forced himself not to gag.

"What's the verdict, boss?" Brandon asked over his shoulder.

Franklin smiled and nodded to the alien leader. "You try. I think it tastes like a goat's ass."

"Why would I try it, then? Damn! You'll eat anything."

"How much food do we have left and how long before we're rescued? Just eat it and smile. It's probably an acquired taste." Franklin heard Brandon gag, but to the younger man's credit, he did not spit it out.

Franklin pointed outside and Brandon led the way from the shuttle. Together, the six of them went to the shelter, where they crowded inside. They stood looking at each other as they had done two weeks earlier.

"I think you are just like us," Franklin started, speaking softly and looking into Afzelius' magenta eyes. "Explorers. Scientists. Whatever started that stuff in orbit that got our carrier ships destroyed had nothing to do with who we are, or why we're here. We lament the passing of our people, each and every soul, no matter which ship they were on.

"For us to survive, we need food. We have shelter. And we need a purpose. In whatever time we have together, we need to learn to communicate. Without that? Well, that's how ships get destroyed and people die. I don't want any more of that."

The aliens didn't respond to Franklin's words. They couldn't understand. But Afzelius gripped his hand firmly, squeezing it until it hurt. When he winced, she lessened the pressure.

***

The group had little time for pointing and naming. Winter was coming quickly and they didn't have enough food, even when they consolidated everything between the two groups.

With much pointing, drawing, and showing, Franklin convinced Afzelius to move her party into the small shelter. They had to do some reconfiguring, but the extra bodily warmth would help heat the place. All they needed was food.

The Rock Doc became the tuber hunter because core sampling and the mineral search were put on hold. Shelina followed Brandon everywhere as the two became odd friends.

At the end of each day, Brandon would join the other humans inputting the words they'd learned into the system. They reviewed them together. The Chreons, as they learned what the people were called, started doing the same—keeping track, reciting the words, and building their vocabulary. Grammar would come in due time.

But first, food.

Franklin, Afzelius, Jimi, and Jens started harvesting the grain that was similar to wheat. They dumped all their rock samples and filled those containers with anything that could be food. Jimi examined each item and declared it good or good enough.

Franklin's plan was to mix the good enough foodstuffs with the more nutritious items. If they ate all the good items first, he feared for their long-term survival.

"Six months," he said. Afzelius repeated the words and pointed at various objects. Frank pointed at his watch. She shrugged, a mannerism she'd adopted from Doctor Berens. He waved at her to follow him to their ship. After much pointing at displays, she powered up the instrument panels. He studied them until he found one that looked like it was counting. He held his watch next to it.

Chreon seconds were slower than human seconds, which were arbitrary measures in any case, being planetary dependent. The light bulb went on and that was when they each learned to count to ten in the other's language.

Frank was relieved and considered that a monumental breakthrough. For him, as a scientist, the numbers always mattered.

Afzelius moved close as she did, but she kept approaching until their noses touched. Franklin didn't stop. He planted his lips on hers as he wrapped his arms around her. She pulled back with the wondering expression on her face that she used to convey a question.

He didn't know how to answer. He liked her—an exotic scientist, beautiful in his eyes, but an explorer first. A person that he could go on a lifelong adventure with and never get bored. To answer, he only smiled and traced a finger down the side of her face. She smiled back and pulled him to her, where they kissed again.

"I want to live," he told her. She didn't understand. "I want you to live."

They returned to the shelter where there was always work to do. The solar power array needed cleaning daily. Meals planned and cookware cleaned and readied.

The area around the shelter needed to be built up to protect it from the winter winds, but there was too much dirt to move and only two shovels.

Torel suggested using the shuttle to move the shelter to a more protected location within the shadow of a rocky outcropping. With their shovels and their bare hands, they leveled a spot. With the clamps raised on the shelter, Afzelius flew the shuttle with Jens at her side. She hovered over the shelter while Shelina and Torel rigged a lifting harness. The small spaceship seemed to pull the shelter off the ground effortlessly. It flew at a turtle's pace until it was almost in position. The humans manhandled the shelter to keep it from spinning as they yelled commands to the aliens on the roof, who relayed those into the shuttle.

The shelter settled with a thump and the shuttle landed, its stubby wing nearly touching the shelter. Everyone gave each other the thumbs up. Afzelius and Franklin kissed.

Probably far more often than the others were comfortable with.

The group sat together as arctic wind blasted the shelter. They thought they had some time left. The original mission would have been wrapping up. The original survey crew had properly guessed the weather patterns almost correctly. Had a carrier ship been in orbit, the recovery shuttle would have had to wait until the winds died down to land.

No one was happy, especially with the topic at hand.

Food rationing.

Frank used the white board to detail how much they'd consumed in the past three weeks and how much they'd added to their stocks. To make it to the spring, they'd need to cut their consumption in half.

Or they would die of starvation. At least the humans. Frank didn't know how long the aliens would last without food. Winter meant rainfall, so water wouldn't be a problem. They set up a catch, but the wind knocked it down. It needed to be set up each day. They found that it was best to do it two hours before dawn, and then pull it down halfway through the morning to avoid the worst of the winds.

It reminded them of the price of survival.

Or the old adage that the early bird gets the worm. Too bad there weren't birds or worms. They were left with the wheat-like grain, some root vegetables, and each other.

It didn't make for a great diet.

"We'll keep searching for food. Whenever the weather breaks, we'll go out. In teams, never by yourself. We will survive because the alternative is unacceptable," Franklin said, looking into the magenta eyes of the tall alien. They held hands, as they always did.

"Whatever it takes," he added. The others nodded.

"We go food," Afzelius offered.

"Yes. We'll find food, wherever it may be. And just for reference, your food still tastes like a goat's ass. I thought I'd get used to it, but no."

Brandon started to laugh, and Jimi too. The aliens joined in. They toasted with plain water. The fizz sticks had already run out.

Frank was taken by the moment. The group was laughing in the face of death.

"I love you," he blurted as he looked at Afzelius. The humans froze.

"Holy crap, dude!" Brandon said before starting to laugh. The others chuckled to themselves. The aliens continued snorting. *Revel in the absurdity,* Doctor Berens thought.

***

The winter hit with a vengeance. And the aliens got sick. Jimi dug into her systems and microscope to figure out why.

It didn't take long for Jimi to figure out that the Chreons couldn't metabolize the grains. "Who would have thought that humanity was the universe's garbage disposal? We can eat any of what we have, but they can't."

The aliens could eat their own food, the tubers, and some of the processed human meals. The humans were left with scraps of their own and all the grain.

Bread and water. Prisoners were punished with that diet. The planet was expressing its displeasure with the intruders. Human or Chreon. It didn't care.

Maybe it was a test. Franklin stood by the side of his bunk where he and Afzelius slept each night, wedged against each other, bundled in their clothes and blankets as they tried to stay warm. Her skin was ashen as her eyes fluttered weakly. He clenched his jaw in frustration.

"Brandon! Grab your coat. We're going to find food and we're not returning until we have something."

"I'm going, too!" Gentry yelled.

"I'll hold down the fort," Jimi said, looking at the aliens. "With a few good meals, I hope they are back on their feet by the time you return."

The three grabbed gear, water, the only extra blanket available, and loaded into the jeep.

Brandon drove because he was the best behind the wheel. Franklin and Gentry watched the landscape, unsure of what they were looking for.

It sure as hell wasn't snow, but that was what found them. Two hours of driving later, they sheltered behind a small tree on a small rise as the snow started to fall. They wrapped themselves together within the blanket. Not running the jeep to conserve juice. Its small solar backup power was useless without the sun. Their energy module was already mostly depleted.

None of the three had anything to say. They shivered together in silence, each praying in their own way for a resolution that didn't involve any of them dying.

***

Afzelius stood at the door of the shelter, looking at the blowing snow. She said something harshly in her own language. The other Chreons remain stone-faced.

"Foerank?" she asked.

"He's looking for food. Food," Doctor Johnson said sympathetically. She stood close to the tall alien, peering out. She wore her coat and all her clothes. It was barely warm enough to keep water from freezing. That was all they dared of the heater.

Afzelius opened the door and went outside. Shelina and Torel joined her. It tore at Jimi's heart to hear the alien yelling Frank's name. Shortly, they returned, shivering like humans, with pots filled with clean snow. It would melt and they would drink it.

And the shelter would get colder until the snow melted.

Jimi was wearing down. At half rations of only grain, she was blocked up. She needed to drink more water, but barely had the energy to do so. She wasn't getting the right nutrition. Man cannot live on bread alone. And neither can women.

Jimi closed her eyes for a moment. When she opened them, she found herself in bed with four emotionless faces looking at her. Had she not felt so bad, she would have laughed at the throwback to every alien movie she'd ever seen. At least they didn't have probes sticking out of her. She smiled.

"I hope they find food," she whispered before passing out again.

***

The storm passed, and they found themselves snowed in. A meter of snow stood on the ground, light and fluffy snow, the type that fell in a desert climate.

"We can't walk all the way back," Gentry suggested, tipping her chin toward the jeep.

"Who said we're going back?" Doctor Berens replied. "We still need food."

Gentry pulled her smart-pad out, pulled up the map, and oriented it. "Looks like the river is that way." She pointed. "In the desert, a river is life."

Franklin squinted against the brightness of the newly fallen snow. The jeep came to life behind him. Brandon sat behind the wheel and waved at them to get in.

When they started moving, they found that they could drive with little problem through the snow, but their three-dimensional vision was impacted. Brandon couldn't tell what was in front of them, so he drove slowly. Twice they rolled into ditches and had to push themselves out. It was time-consuming and draining. The more they moved, the more exhausted they became. Their clothes hung on them as they had already lost weight, losing more with each day.

But they powered onward until they reached what the map showed as a river. It was well away from any deposits, so they had never considered putting the shelter there. Judging by the snowfall, that would have been folly.

Rock Doc parked the jeep and they slid down the bank. Brandon used a rock hammer to check the ice. It was already ten centimeters thick. He chipped away until he was through. The water that surged through the hole was dark and smelled funny.

"Dammit," Frank said softly. "Take a sample, just in case. Maybe there's something in there."

Gentry stuffed a small sample bottle into the hole, shivering at the cold. When she started to pull it out, a pair of jaws clamped onto her hand. She screamed and yanked backwards. Brandon swung his rock hammer into the side of the creature and dragged it from the hole. He hit its head until it let go. Gentry rolled in the snow, groaning in agony as she held her hand. The puncture wounds from the creature, a cross between an eel and a fish, had cut deep into her flesh.

The murky water stung. Doctor Berens tried to clean the wound with snow, but the cold was making her skin red. He hoped that was all it was.

"Dinner!" Brandon declared. Gentry grimaced and held her hand.

"Back in the jeep with you," Frank told her. She stumbled up the bank and climbed in.

"Look here. Bite marks." Brandon pointed at the creature's side.

"Are you thinking what I'm thinking?"

"Bait." Brandon pulled a knife and cut the head off and gutted the creature just like he would have done with a fish from Earth. They wrapped some of the guts around the end of the hammer. Frank checked that his gloves were tight and kneeled next to the small hole. Brandon dipped the end of the hammer in and waited.

After a while, he chipped out a bigger hole. Gentry gave them the thumbs up from inside the jeep. Frank waved back.

"One and done?" he asked. Guts on the hammer didn't appear to be working. "Get ready."

Frank took his glove off and stuffed his hand into the hole. There was no doubt when the fish creature grabbed on. He yelled and struggled to pull his hand out. He braced himself beside the hole, fighting against the intense pain. He straightened his back and lifted with his legs. The head appeared, and Brandon buried the pointed end of his hammer into it.

He wrapped his arms around it to keep the massive creature from falling back into the hole. When it let go of Frank's hand, he stepped back, then dove forward, ramming the creature and trying to drive it sideways onto the ice. Brandon back-pedaled and finally pulled the creature free.

"My hand is on fire," Doctor Berens cried.

"That took some monster balls, Frank."

Brandon cleaned the creature while Frank cradled his injured hand. Brandon dangled a string of intestines over the hole and a creature's head appeared and bit off a chunk. "I guess we hadn't tried all our options," Brandon said softly as a way to apologize to Franklin.

Frank joined Gentry in the jeep with a small bowl of snow. He started the engine and maxxed the heater. They took turns washing out their wounds. They had broad-spectrum antibiotics back in the shelter. They only needed to hang on until then. The fire in their bite marks suggested they would need the drugs to fight off whatever was in the water.

Brandon cheered. They looked up to see him with two more of the creatures. The one that had bit Gentry was a relative baby compared to the others. "Thank the gods," Frank sighed.

Brandon was on his own to clean and load the sixty or seventy kilos of fresh meat into the jeep.

"I hope we can eat that crap," Brandon lamented.

"You make it sound so tasty." Gentry smiled and shook her head. "I feel horrible."

"Next stop, home and a warm bed," Brandon promised. He backed away from the river and turned the vehicle around, aiming back the way they'd come. He was able to follow their tracks to the hill, avoiding the ditches, but they were on their own to cut a new path after that.

Brandon drove even more slowly. Frank and Gentry had deteriorated to where they would be no help to get him out of a ditch. "Slow and steady wins the race," Brandon repeated to himself. He jerked the vehicle often as he jammed the breaks, got out, checked the way ahead, and then climbed back in where the heater was keeping his fevered companions warm.

He turned the heater down until only the defrosters were keeping the windshield clear. He shivered against the cold, removing his glove occasionally to stick his fingers out the cracked window to help keep himself awake.

Every step they took risked their lives. If he crashed the jeep, Gentry and Frank would die. It was sobering, but he was exhausted. He banged his head on the steering wheel and yelled into the night. The snow didn't care. The planet had decided that interlopers weren't welcome.

"We're bringing home the bacon, ladies!" Brandon yelled at the windshield. He gritted his teeth and accelerated, thinking he knew where he was—the broad plain below the shelter. Once he saw the dim light, he jammed the accelerator to the floor for one final run. The jeep screamed in protest, but raced through the snow and up the long hill.

Woodenly, Brandon lifted his foot off the pedal. He turned the wheel to avoid crashing into the alien shuttle, then stomped on the break. The jeep slid sideways and he shut it off. He wanted to go for help, but that was all the energy he had. His head fell sideways against the window as he passed out.

***

Frank blinked against the bright light inside the shelter. Magenta eyes watched him closely. "Hi there," he said.

"Hi," Afzelius replied.

"It is about time!" Jimi bellowed. "Those nasty-ass fish you brought taste pretty choice when cooked right."

"I'll be. Maybe this place didn't want us dead after all," Frank mumbled.

"Or maybe this place wanted us to earn it," Brandon replied from the bunk across the shelter. Gentry was squeezed in next to him, sound asleep.

***

Five months had passed since the ships battled in orbit, destroying each other. Each group's scientists had escaped the conflagration. The eight of them had joined together to fight their own battle against a hostile planet.

They sat around a small fire listening to the sizzling pan.

"More, pulease," Afzelius said in a raspy voice.

"Of course," Franklin replied, using the spatula to scrape some more of the deep-earth grub's meat from the pan. The grubs were a relatively new find, while some of the vegetables they were cooking had survived the winter. They'd cultivated some of the roots to establish a garden while they ate the rest. They had learned what to look for. They had learned to survive.

The group ate in relative silence as they usually did, each to their own thoughts regarding what was happening in their universe. They didn't know if an interstellar war had started or if both sides withdrew, creating an ad hoc neutral zone in which neither traveled so both could avoid conflict.

The real reason didn't matter. The only thing each crew knew was that they had been abandoned, left to their own to make their existence worthwhile. On a remote planet in the middle of nowhere, alien and human had learned to communicate and come together to fight a greater foe than each other.

"I love you, Foerank," Afzelius said after he gave her another grub.

Edited by Craig Martelle

Author Craig Martelle

Craig is an Amazon bestselling author and writes the Free Trader series (a cat and his human minions fight to bring peace to humanity), the Cygnus Space Opera series, the End Times Alaska series, and the Terry Henry Walton Chronicles, co-written with Michael Anderle. See more at www.craigmartelle.com where you can find all of Craig's publications and join his newsletter to get the latest updates and sales.

WE4PONIZED M7TH

By Jonathan P. Brazee

Staff Sergeant Gracie Medicine Crow, United Federation Marine Corps, accepted the cup from Rabbit as she scanned the almost-deserted village below. She blew on the coffee, then took a sip, nodding in appreciation. She thought she recognized the brew as Cushington Blue, and she wondered where her new spotter had scored it. Lance Corporal Christopher Irving—"Rabbit"—had only been assigned as her spotter for a week now, and she hadn't formed an opinion as to his skillset yet. He'd had good grades at Triple S, the United Federation Marine Corps Scout-Sniper School, but school performance didn't always reflect performance in the field.

Still, if he can shoot as good as he can scrounge up a good cup of Joe, then he might have potential.

"Take the west side," she told him in dismissal. "Let me know if anyone takes an unusual interest in the library."

"Roger that, Staff Sergeant," Rabbit said as he scurried, as much as a two-meter tall, 120 kg Marine could "scurry," to the other side of the roof.

Gracie could sense his eagerness. Like all snipers, he'd proven himself in combat as a grunt before being accepted into Triple S, so technically, he wasn't a newbie. Despite that, he still had that new-sniper smell to him, straight out of the package. More than that, he was still only a PIG, a "Professionally Instructed Gunman." This was their first live-mission together and, for once, Gracie was fine with

41

the fact that it should be a cold mission. As part of a routine security element, she would have the opportunity to observe him in a field setting while the stakes were relatively low. Scout-sniper teams had to depend on and trust each other, and that usually meant months of training before going in hot, but after Saracen had been killed three weeks ago, her previous spotter, Sergeant Halcik Sung, had been pulled from her to fill Saracen's slot. Forty-one confirmed kills made Gracie the most accomplished sniper in the platoon, so she'd had to take the newbie.

She took another sip of the coffee. Five floors below on the ground, Sergeant Rafiq exited one of the shops surrounding the small square. He and his squad had been conducting a sweep before the rest of his platoon escorted the major to the meeting with the local commissioners. He looked up and caught her eye, then nodded. Gracie acknowledged him with a half-salute.

She really hadn't expected Second Squad to find anything. Tension Gorge—why "Gorge," Gracie still hadn't figured out as the area around the village was as flat as a rugby pitch—was not in a high-risk area. The last incident, an IE attack, had taken place thirteen days prior, eight klicks away. But with a field grade officer coming from division, all precautions had to be taken, and the village had to be swept. So, instead of pursuing the FLP commandos in the Mist Mountains, she and Rabbit were here, glorified security guards.

They hadn't even set up a proper hide with overhead cover and concealment. They were meant to be seen. Gracie felt exposed to the world, making her nerves crawl. Every instinct told her to get into a hide from where she could deal death unseen, but orders were orders. Not many fighters, even FLNT commandos, would choose to take on a Marine sniper. She was there as a "Warning: Attack Dogs on Premises" sign.

The slightest bit of movement caught her eye. Gracie raised her Windmoeller, scoping the spot. About a klick away, at the western edge of the village, a woman shifted her weight behind a window, looking out. She stood there for a moment before stepping back out of sight. Gracie pulled the map of the village onto her helmet display, noting the two-story house, then running a line-of-sight to the library. She didn't think the women could see the library entrance, but she could have a sightline on several of the library's upper-story windows. She ranged the building, getting 984 meters, then entered it as a "C-level" target in her data book, joining the 44 other potential target positions she'd identified since arriving early in the morning with Second Squad.

She ran through the target positions again, seeing if she could remember the range for each one, starting with the A's. She got 39 of the 45 correct.

Come on, Crow. Get them down! she chided herself before going over the list yet one more time.

It would only take a moment to pull up the range on a specific target, but even a split second could make the difference between taking out an aggressor or allowing the enemy to engage the Marines. Some fellow Marines thought her anal-retentive insistence on memorizing details was over-kill, but none of them had notched 41 kills, either. Gracie believed in leaving nothing to chance.

This time, she got 42 out of 45 correct. Better, but not good enough. She'd wait twenty minutes, then try again. It wasn't as if range was the only parameter that went into making a good shot. Her angle to the ground, the temperature, wind speed and direction, humidity, the planet's rotation, gravity—those and more would affect her round's trajectory. The constants were already entered into her scope's firing computer, but the variables had to be measured or determined at the time of the shot. The more variables she could enter into her scope AI, the better her chances of success, and the quicker she could do that, the quicker she could fire. If already knowing the range could slice off even a microsecond, it could be worth it.

At Triple S, a wall plaque proclaimed: *Snipers aren't deadly because they carry the biggest rifles; they're deadly because they've learned how to weaponize math.* This hit the nail on the head. Some people, even fellow snipers, claimed that sniping was an art, but Gracie knew it was pure physics, pure math, and ever since she'd become a sniper, she'd dedicated herself to making her math the best possible.

"Staff Sergeant Medicine Crow, your package has been delayed. He's still at Hornsby. Call it 80 minutes late," Lieutenant Diedre Kaster-Lyons passed over the platoon net.

"Roger that," Gracie passed back. "Any idea as to why?"

"That's a negative. We just got the word. I'll keep you posted."

Gracie took a deep breath, letting it out slowly. She wasn't surprised. Nothing seemed to ever go according to plan on this planet. Part of it was normal Marine Corps operating procedure, but more seemed to be because of the local government's maneuvering factions. Everyone agreed that the *Frente de Liberación de Nuevo Trujillo* was the enemy to all that was good and just on the planet, but none of the various political factions seemed willing to cooperate lest they cede some sort of advantage to another. She should be used to it by now, but the thought of sitting up on the roof for an additional hour-plus made her want to scream. By the time she got back to camp, she'd have spent at least 14 hours doing absolutely nothing.

"Did you hear that?" she passed to Rabbit on the P2P.

"Roger that. Uh . . . is it always like this? I mean, the changes?"

She suppressed a chuckle. As a junior grunt, he wouldn't have been kept in the loop as much as he was now as a scout-sniper. This wasn't even the first change: the meeting had originally been planned for yesterday, and this was now the second delay for today.

"Hurry up and wait, Lance Corporal Irving. You know how it is in the suck."

"Yeah, I guess so. It's just so . . . well, you know."

Yes, I do know, Rabbit. Boy, do I know.

Gracie could bitch with the best of them—usually just to herself and not aloud, though. But she still wouldn't change her profession for anything. She was meant to be a Marine. A member of the Apsaalooké Nation from Montana on Earth, she came from a long line of warriors, and her lifestyle was embedded into her DNA. She might chafe at the delay, but this was her life. Without conscious thought, she reached under her collar and rubbed the "hog's tooth" hanging from her neck between her fingers, a recovered round from her first victim's magazine, but more importantly, the symbol of being a HOG, or a "Hunter of Gunmen."

She continued to scan the area below her, working quick firing solutions in her mind for various locations, almost on autopilot. Sitting in a hide for days on end waiting for that one shot, there wasn't much else to do, and she'd done this tens of thousands of times over the ten-plus years she'd been a designated scout-sniper. Tens of thousands of calculations, more than a year of combined time in hides, all for 41 kills. Civilians used to the Hollybolly war flicks

44

might think it a lot of effort per kill, but some snipers never even registered a single kill. Never became HOGs. Gracie's total was now the fourth-most among active duty snipers.

"Dingo 3, Charlie-Two-One, we've got a cargo hover approaching your position from azimuth Two-Zero-Five, range two-point-three klicks. Looks like it's got agricultural products in the bed. There are a few anomalies in the scan, but within accepted parameters. Just keep an eye on them," an unnamed voice passed over the command net.

"Roger that," Gracie and Sergeant Rafiq said in unison.

"You got that?" Gracie asked Rabbit over the P2P, but turning her head to see him.

Two-Zero-Five was to the south west of their position, and her spotter should have a straight line-of-site to what they had designated as Route Bluebird, the road leading into Tension Gorge from that direction.

Rabbit swiveled his body to glass to the south-west before shouting "Got it!" ignoring the P2P.

They might not be in a concealed hide, but Gracie winced. In the open or not, snipers didn't shout like that, giving away their positions. It was a bad habit to start, and she'd have to remind him of that.

"Looks like a typical hauler, one of those gas jobs."

Which was to be expected. Nuevo Trujillo relied heavily on methane for ground transportation, methane extracted from agricultural waste. She ran a scan through the available feeds before picking up a micro-drone that had the hovertruck in its sights. The truck, three-quarters loaded with cargo pods, was making its way north down the road, the secondary north-south thoroughfare in the sector. Salinas, another small farming town, was twelve klicks south along Bluebird from Tension Gorge.

Gracie wasn't overly concerned about the truck. Tension Gorge was not a restricted town, and while it had been largely abandoned during the fighting of two months ago, some people still lived there, and there were still crops to be harvested and transported to the processing plants. Still, Second Squad would have to stop and search the truck as it reached the village.

"Keep your eye on the truck as it gets here and Second checks it out," she passed to Rabbit.

She was tempted to move to his side of the roof and do it herself, but he needed to get his feet wet. To her side in its case was her Kyocera, her hypervelocity sniper rifle, and with any other spotter, she might have told him to take it. Rabbit, however, had not snapped in with it, and without being able to key in the cheek weld and eye position, he wouldn't be very accurate. No, better he keep his standard-issue M99. It had more than enough range to cover Second Squad, and he had it zeroed in for his shooting position.

She turned back to her area of responsibility. The Navy and Marine Corps scanners hadn't found anything suspicious about the truck, but using something so obvious as a decoy was not unheard of. With short quick movements, she covered the mental grid she'd constructed, using both her prime focus as well as her peripheral vision to spot anything out of the ordinary.

One of Second Squad's four-man fire teams was moving to where they could meet the truck. Gracie shifted her focus to the two local security standing outside the library door. They'd arrived with the first three commissioners. Casually sucking on stim sticks, flare-barreled Munchen 44's held at the ready, the impressively lethal-looking men didn't watch the fire team as it left. If something was up of which they were a part, they were hiding it well. Gracie didn't suspect the two guards of anything, but she had a firing solution for them already locked in, and her Windmoeller's WPT-331 rounds had the penetrative power to defeat the Cryolene body armor they wore. Better safe than sorry.

She was more concerned with the young boy, who she'd nicknamed Space Dog due to the brightly-colored image on his t-shirt. Perhaps ten or eleven years old, he sat on the stoop of a home a block off the square. He wasn't armed, the best she could tell, but he'd been sitting there for half-an-hour, seemingly interested in the goings on. That could be merely normal adolescent curiosity, but he could be acting as a lookout, feeding information to the bad guys. Gracie had zoomed in on him several times with her scope, but she hadn't seen any signs of him communicating with anyone.

"The truck's almost here," Rabbit shouted across the roof.

"Use your comms, Irving. You trying to paint a bullseye on us?" she passed.

"Oh, yeah. Sorry Staff Sergeant," he said, this time over the P2P.

"OK, then. Just keep an eye on them."

She pulled up Rabbit's feed, reducing it and sending it to the top left of her helmet display where she could monitor it but still have a full view of her own area of responsibility. She quickly ticked through her known potential target list. Silver Hair was still in his garden, Red Shirt was walking along Calle Jones from where she'd gone to the lone store still open, and Limp Man was no longer in sight. She shifted to the right where Route Robin led into the town and from where the major would arrive. A local policeman still stood at the edge of town, ready to hop on his scoot and escort the major and the rest of First Platoon to the library. He looked bored out of his head, something Gracie completely understood.

Closer in, she checked Space Dog, then Gollum 1 and 2, the two security guards at the library. Shifting her view farther to the fight, she—

What's with Pot Belly? she wondered.

The older man, his protruding gut hanging over his belt, had risen from where he'd been sitting on a porch for the last hour, supposedly reading a novel. The reader was now on the small table beside his chair, the screen dark, and the man was standing, looking with poorly disguised interest to his left. Gracie followed his gaze's direction, but nothing jumped out at her. That wasn't a comfort— something was tweaking her instincts.

"I don't have anything for certain, but something might be up," she passed on the local command circuit, keyed into Rabbit and all the Marines from Second Squad. "Keep alert."

"What d'ya got, Staff Sergeant?" Sergeant Rafiq asked.

"Nothing for certain, but Pot Be . . . the man at building 23," she passed, using the number Lieutenant Diedre Kaster-Lyons, dual-hatted as the battalion intel officer and the scout-sniper platoon commander, had designated the house, "seems a little too interested in something."

"The fat guy? Eric?" the sergeant asked. "I spoke with him. He seemed OK, happy to see us. Tired of the fighting and all."

Maybe, but something's up, she thought as she continued to watch him. *I can feel it.*

Pot Belly—Eric whatever—was now looking in every direction except to the left, which could mean something, but he sat back down, picked up his reader, and started to read again. Gracie wondered if her nerves were playing with her, making her see things that didn't exist, but something still nagged at the back of her mind. She zoomed in on the man, and something hit her. The reader. The display was off. Pot Belly was "reading" a darkened screen.

"Stop the truck!" she passed. "Something's wrong!"

From Rabbit's feed, she could see the truck, now a mere three hundred meters from the village's edge. Corporal Ben-Zvi, the fire team leader waiting to search the truck, didn't wait for orders from his squad leader. He stepped out in the middle of Route Bluebird, weapon raised while his amplified voice called out, "You, in the truck. Halt!"

The truck sped up.

Gracie bolted across the roof before conscious thought registered what was happening, yelling for Rabbit to take her place on the roof's east side. Ben-Zvi's fire team had spread out and was taking the truck under fire, but it was a big, hulking thing, and their M-99s weren't having much effect on target. There was a whoosh as a Marine launched a Hatchet, but the missile hit high on its right side with an impressive but ineffectual blast, missing the engine block and anything vital.

Firing at a moving vehicle, through a windshield, and from a high angle, was one of the most difficult shots a sniper could make. Gracie had spent countless hours in simulators and on ranges from Tarawa to Alexander, but still, this was no sure thing, and she both hadn't pre-calculated a firing solution and didn't have time to calculate one now. She'd have to go with her gut.

Firing from a height meant the round drop would be less, but firing through the windshield meant that the round would most likely deflect downwards upon hitting it. The WPT-331 rounds she'd loaded to take care of the security officers armor had more punching power than the standard WPT-310 Laupa sniper round, so the deflection would be less—*but how much less?*

Gracie hit the roof's edge, flipping off her helmet as she brought up her rifle and laid it across the top of the low retaining wall. Her scope was zeroed at 300 meters. She had already ranged the edge of the first house where Route Bluebird entered the village at 445 meters. The truck was still 150 meters or so away from that, and the wind had been blowing north to south at a slight eight-to-ten KPH. She didn't have time to enter any of that; it was pure Kentucky windage time. Unable to see through the windshield's glare, she put her crosshairs slightly high and to the right of where she thought the driver would be. Just she started to squeeze the trigger, she saw the slightest of cracks from the driver's side door.

He's not suiciding! He's going to try and get out!

The car that Gracie had taken out on Jericho had been driven by a suicide bomber. This driver was either not as dedicated or was still needed. If the latter, then this was just the initial act in a larger assault.

With a last-second shift to the right, figuring the driver would be scrunched over to be able to bail out, she squeezed off a round, then shifted lower and to the left before firing off a second. The flower blossomed on the windshield as the 285-grain jacketed round punched through it, and the truck started to veer before the second round hit.

"Axel-Three, this is Dingo-Three. We are under attack. Cancel the mission," she passed on the command net before adding, "But send the rest of Charlie-One. We're going to need them."

"Roger, Dingo-Three. Understand you are under attack. Axel-Three-Five is being recalled. Will get back to you on Charlie-One."

The major had to be pulled back, but Gracie thought they'd need the rest of First Platoon here in the village. She scanned for more fighters as the hovertruck left the road and slowed to a stop in a field of knee-high, green, leafy crops.

On Jericho, the suicide VBIED had exploded as the driver she'd killed released the suicide switch. This truck didn't. Gracie looked over her scope at it, wondering if she'd jumped the gun on declaring a full-out attack.

The truck erupted into a fireball that roiled into the air.

Of course. It was on a timer so the driver could escape with his skin.

Gracie was half-listening to Corporal Ben-Zvi was on the net with a quick sitrep when the sound of firing from the center of the town reached her. She bolted back to where Rabbit, who had taken her place, stood, peering over the building's edge.

"Get down. You can see just as well if you're prone, and you won't be exposed," she told him, jerking him down by the collar.

"I'm hit, Sergeant," someone passed on the net.

Without her helmet, Gracie didn't have her display to see who it was, but she swung her scope to the two security guards. One was crouching, weapon ready as he scanned for a target, while the other was running forward. Gracie put her crosshairs on him, ready to take him out if needed, but he reached the wounded Marine and dragged him back to the base of the library.

Guess they're not part of this.

Someone was, though, and Gracie's job was to take them out.

"I've got someone. Looks like he's got a Halstead," Rabbit said.

"Where? Give me a location."

"Uh . . . Building 38, second floor."

"Building 38, 185 meters," she mumbled, then "Take him out."

Such a close distance was child's play to a Marine with an M-99, much less a trained sniper. She could leave the target to Rabbit as she searched for more. She heard the whisper-snap of darts as Rabbit fired, then an excited "I got him!"

"Well, HOG, go find your number two kill," she said, wanting him to focus on the task at hand.

"A HOG, really? But that was with my 99."

He was right. A kill like that wouldn't be tallied as a sniper kill, and she'd jumped the gun on anointing him a HOG. Now wasn't the time to get into technicalities though.

"Later, Irving. We don't have time to discuss it now."

"Roger that," he said. Gracie heard him quietly add, "Shit, a HOG."

A string of automatic fire opened up, but with the sound reverberating between buildings, Gracie couldn't pinpoint its origin. Putting that weapon out of her mind for the moment, she shifted back to Pot Belly. The man was gone, his reader abandoned on the floor of the porch. She kept scanning the direction where he'd been looking. Tension Gorge was not a very densely populated village, but still, there were enough buildings to intermittently mask her view. She was dead sure, though, that there was somebody there.

A flash of movement proved her right. Two people, pulling an ancient but effective looking crew-served gun that she didn't recognize but looked like an anti-tank weapon of some sort, passed between two buildings, moving out-of-sight before she could aim and fire. She swung her barrel left to the other side of the house that now masked them and waited. Automatic fire still echoed in bursts throughout the village, but she slowed her breathing, letting her sight picture become her world. A few moments later, a head peered around the corner. At 210 meters to the home's front door, she could easily drop him, but she wanted the gun in the open.

Come on out, the coast is clear, she implored him.

He turned back, said something, then disappeared for a moment, reappearing holding the crew-served gun's controls, leading it forward. He pointed towards the square, saying something to his companion, who followed him into sight.

Gracie and Rabbit were not exactly in stealth mode, and their position had to have been noted, but the two FLMT fighters didn't even look her way.

Your loss.

Five meters out from the house's protection, Gracie squeezed the trigger, going for center mass. The man dropped as if poleaxed, and Gracie cycled her action, swinging to take the second man into her sights. With cat-like reflexes, the second soldier bolted back into cover. Gracie snapped off a shot, but she was sure she missed.

"Staff Sergeant, do you got eyes on whoever is on our asses?" Sergeant Rafiq asked between heavy breathing.

"Where's it coming from?"

"Through the fucking wall, from the north. It's chewing the shit out of the place, and we've got no cover."

"Lance Corporal Irving, we need to find that automatic weapon. Move to the edge over there and see if you can spot it." She keyed back to the command net and asked, "Rafiq, what's the status on your platoon? I'm not hearing anything. When's their ETA?"

A round pinged just below Gracie, taking a chunk of cerocrete off the wall.

So much for them ignoring us.

"As soon as the major's lifted out of there, they'll break free. We've got a Minidrag on the way, though. ETA in six minutes."

Gracie half-expected the delay in the platoon. They couldn't just leave the major out there on the road, cooling his heels. The Minidrag was a nice piece of news, though. The Marines had two "Dragon" drones. The "Mini" was the smaller, but depending on its combat load, it could still pack a decent wallop. It would have been providing overwatch for the column bringing in the major, and she was frankly surprised that the S3 had cut it loose to support Second Squad and her sniper team.

As Gracie watched, chunks of the closer wall of the store in which Rafiq and two of his fire teams had taken cover blew out into the square. The enemy gun was shooting all the way through the building.

"Fuck! Can you get them off our ass, Crow?" Rafiq passed. "If we weren't hugging the deck, that would have cut us in two. I don't think we can wait for the Minidrag."

"I think I have the position, Staff Sergeant," Rabbit shouted, forgetting her earlier admonition. "I saw a flash."

"Wait one," she passed to Sergeant Rafiq on the P2P. "Let me see what I can do."

"Hurry up, Staff Sergeant. I've got one down, and I don't have anything to engage.

Gracie slid back behind the retaining wall, then crouched, scooted to where Rabbit hunkered behind his section of the low wall.

"Give me your helmet," she ordered.

She should have put hers back on—then she could have simply downloaded his feed. But it was still 20 meters behind her, so she threw his on, then reversed his feed 60 seconds, and started it up again. Her image appeared first from what looked like just after she dropped the FPL fighter.

Don't look at me, Rabbit. Look out at the bad guys.

She heard her voice telling him to move over to try and spot the shooters, then the herky-jeky image as he ran to the roof's far corner. He was scanning, back and forth when there was a flash at the corner of his vision immediately before the burst of automatic fire could be heard. Gracie made a mental note of the building from where the flash originated: Building 14, the Ag Co-op, a two-story office made from the same cerocrete as the bank on which she now perched.

She gave Rabbit back his helmet, then did a quick turkey hop to orient herself before dropping back out of sight. From her adjusted position, the window on the building would be about 465 meters, still an easy shot. Gracie's longest kill to date with the Windmoeller was 2005 meters, so this would be child's play—if she could acquire a target.

She entered the data in her Miller, then eased up, bringing the window into her sights. The sharp report from behind their position startled her for an instant, but the cracka-cracka-cracka was from a Marine M110, the standard automatic slug-thrower for a fire team. Corporal Ben-Zvi's team had engaged, and she hoped they'd taken out the soldier she'd missed. She acquired her sight picture again, and immediately, the muzzle of a barrel edged out before firing off another string of 15 or 20 shots. This was their baby, but the gunner hadn't exposed himself. She was pretty sure that whoever he or she was, they knew exactly where she and Rabbit were, and they didn't want to become targets.

"Can you get them?" Rabbit asked as she slid back down to sit on the deck, back against the low wall.

"You didn't happen to bring a Hatchet, did you?"

"No, Staff Sergeant. You didn't tell me to."

She hadn't expected him to have brought one of the little personal anti-armor rockets, but it didn't hurt to ask. Semi-smart, the rocket could take out most armor and would blast its way through any civilian construction.

She shrugged, then half-turned her torso to reach up and touch the wall's rounded top. It was about 10 centimeters thick. Only three buildings in the entire village were made of cerocrete, and she had to figure that they were probably made in a similar fashion. Cerocrete was more expensive than the pressed vegaboard that was used for most of the village buildings, and not surprisingly, it was more robust. The walls of the building in which Rafiq was taking cover might as well have been paper for all the protection they were providing, but the cerocrete was different.

How different? she wondered, dropping her magazine and checking the rounds inside.

She had one of her remaining WPT-331 jacketed rounds in the chamber and two in the magazine. The WPT-310 Lapua was a much better round for long distances, but the 331 had more punch. She didn't know, however, if it could punch through 10 centimeters of cerocrete. Once again, the math of sniping had raised its head, but this time, she didn't have the numbers to plug into the equation.

Only one way to find out.

More firing was erupting from around the village. With Sergeant Rafiq pinned down, only Ben-Zvi's fire team and maybe the two civilian security officers were returning the fire. That had to change. Marines took the fight to the enemy, not let the enemy take it to them.

"Sergeant Rafiq, if I cover you with that automatic crew-served, can you make it to the library? It's made of stone, and it'll give you better cover."

"If you can get some rounds to the east, too, I think we can. We're taking small arms from there, and we've got to carry Parker."

"Can you let the two security guys know you're coming? I don't want to see them take you out."

"Roger that. They pulled Omato out of the line of fire, and she's fucked up, but she's on her comms now."

Another heavy burst from the crew-served gun tore through the building, and Sergeant Rafiq passed, "With you or without you, we've got to go now!"

"Irving, on my go, I want you to put rounds downrange to the east. No one-shot, one kill. I need volume."

He nodded, his hand squeezing and relaxing on the pistol grip while Gracie checked her scope one more time.

"On three," she passed on the command net so every Marine could hear her. "One . . . two . . . three!"

Gracie swung her barrel over the top of the wall, set her cross hairs on the wall about 15 centimeters to the left of the window's edge, and squeezed the trigger. She shifted lower and slightly to the right and fired again as Rabbit started sending hundreds of hypervelocity darts across the square and in amongst the buildings.

"Go, go!" Sergeant Rafiq shouted over the net.

The muzzle of the enemy gun disappeared, and Gracie put her last 331 into the wall. She wasn't sure if the rounds had penetrated through it, but she'd certainly gotten their attention. With a WPT-310 now chambered, she swung back to the square, looking for a target. A flash of movement caught her at the edge of the scope, and she brought the crosshairs to bear, but realized that it was the boy, running away from the square, not toward it. A door opened ahead of him, and a panicked-looking woman came out, wildly beckoning the boy to her.

She didn't bother to see if the boy made it. Rounds started to impact around her, and she looked over the top of her scope, trying to spot a real target. She immediately picked up an FLNT soldier running full tilt towards the square, firing up at her as he went. With a smooth move, Gracie acquired the man through her scope, adjusted high, then fired. The round hit him just below the throat, and Gracie knew he was dead before he hit the ground.

There was a thud next to her, and Rabbit grunted before spinning around and falling to the deck.

"You OK?" she asked.

He gave her a weak thumbs-up, then rubbed his upper chest, saying, "My bones stopped the round, but shit, that felt like someone hit me with a club."

The "bone" inserts that acted as body armor would stop most small arms rounds, but while darts might barely be felt, larger caliber slugs could still beat a Marine up pretty good.

"Where was the shooter?"

"Over there," he said, pointing past Gracie. "I was turning to you when I got hit."

"Show me."

He picked himself up, and with a grimace, popped his head up and pointed. Gracie followed the direction, then both dropped as another round zipped past where Rabbit's head had been an instant before.

He can't be, she told herself as she tried to analyze what she'd seen.

There had only been one structure higher than their building in that direction, the water tower. While water towers seemed to be the platform of choice for snipers in Hollybolly flicks, they pretty much sucked for the job. A sniper on one was completely exposed with no route of egress. Not only a suicide position, but a stupid one because a sniper perched there would get taken out immediately.

But this guy's already proven himself to be pretty dumb. Why try to take out Rabbit instead of me?

Gracie knew that she didn't look much like a Marine at times. At 1.4 meters and 38 kg (and that after a Harvest Festival Banquet), she could look like a little girl playing dress-up in daddy's gear, especially when she had on her full battle rattle. But any soldier should have realized that since she was carrying the Windmoeller while Rabbit had his standard-issue M99, she was the threat, not him.

Being a sniper, despite all the advances since the Evolution, was still pretty much a man's game, and Gracie had run across misogyny more than once. But this was ridiculous, and she was going to enjoy taking advantage of it. If that cretin didn't think she was the threat, she was going to prove him wrong—and enjoy doing so.

"You ready to play Rabbit, Lance Corporal?"

He looked up at her in confusion. Gracie wasn't one much for nicknames, and she'd always kept military discipline in her professional relationships.

"He doesn't seem to recognize that I'm the sniper here. You're twice my size, so you must be the threat. So, if you're up to it, can you pop up for a moment and run a few steps while I disabuse him of his notion?"

A smile crept over his face. He nodded, saying, "My chest still hurts, Staff Sergeant, so yeah, I think I owe him this."

She held up her hand while she entered the range and the height differential. More math, lethal math. At 884 meters, this would be a longer shot, but the calculations were done the same way.

"No matter how good he is, it'll take two seconds minimum for a round to reach you, so no hero stuff. I want you back down in two."

She muted her earbud to the sounds of Sergeant Rifiq directing his squad and took three deep breaths, calming her pulse, then nodded. When Rabbit bolted up, she rose, rested her barrel on the top of the retaining wall, and only had to nudge her scope slightly up and to the right to have the enemy sniper in her crosshairs. She'd just acquired him when she saw him fire.

"Down!" she shouted at Rabbit as she started squeezing her trigger—just as the man picked up his head to look over his scope as if trying to see if he'd hit Rabbit. Gracie raised her point of aim to take advantage of the larger target and fired. She could see the trace as the round pierced the air, and she immediately knew she was on target. Long range sniping might be math, but it was almost art to see the round arch up, then come back down and slightly to the right to impact with his throat. Blood splattered the white paint of the water tower behind him as his weapon fell forward to tumble to the ground.

"Did you get the bastard?" Rabbit asked.

"What do you think? Of, course, I did."

Firing below them was intensifying. She keyed her earbud back on. Second Squad was getting in it deep. At least now, from inside the library, they were dishing it out as well as taking it in.

"Back to work, Irving."

She started scanning with her scope, trying to find targets and take the pressure off of Second Squad, but while she caught a few shadows, she was having a difficult time. The Marine Corps Miller was an outstanding scope, its targeting AI second-to-none, but snipers usually engaged at over 1000 meters at a minimum. Even with the scope at its widest display, she just wasn't getting the field of vision she needed to be able to spot the enemy as they maneuvered below her. Rabbit had fired four time since she'd taken out the sniper, and she'd yet to engage.

"I need the Kyc," she muttered.

Gracie was more attached to the slug-throwing Windmoeller, but at 45,000 credits each, she only had one Miller Scope. On her hypervelocity Kyocera, she had attached a normal combat scope, something quite a bit less sophisticated, but with a much wider and higher contrast field of view. Normally, she wouldn't even have brought the Kyc on the mission, relying on her Windmoeller for sniping and her Rino .358 for personal defense. Since she had an eager Rabbit there willing to hump it, however, she figured it wouldn't hurt to bring it. And now that might have proven fortuitous.

Keeping low, she scurried alongside the wall to where Rabbit had left the weapon. She powered it up and checked its readouts. Power was at 98%, and while the Kyc didn't carry the 1000-round dart mags of the M99, she still had 150 slightly larger 3mm darts ready to throw and another two mags ready to use. She brought it to her shoulder and looked through the combat scope. As if a gift from the gods of war, she immediately picked up two soldiers hugging the wall of a building that was giving them cover from Marine fire.

Not all Marine fire, buddy.

The combat scope might have brought her back to her time as a regular grunt, because instead of squeezing her trigger in the best Triple S fashion, she snapped off five shots in quick succession. With negligible recoil and semi-automatic action, she could fire three darts per second, which beat the 1.8 seconds per round for the Windmoeller. The first two darts punched through the head of the lead soldier, both probably hitting the second soldier in the chest. He didn't drop but lunged back as the next three darts chased him. He fell out of sight, only his legs visible as they churned to push him back, so Gracie fired two more darts, at least one hitting him in the left leg.

The FLNT soldiers had layered plate armor on their torsos, but their legs were unprotected, and the man left a smear of blood on the ground as he pushed himself out of sight.

"Dingo-Three and Charlie-One-Two, we have two armored vehicles, Kuang Fen 10's, approaching your position from three-four-niner, two klicks out. We are diverting the Minidrag to intercept, and Charlie-One is on the way. ETA for the platoon is 45 mikes, so hold on."

Gracie glanced over the Rabbit, who met her eyes. Kuang Fen, an Alliance-registered company, was a new supplier of relatively cheap military equipment. While nothing they made could match up to Federation, Brotherhood, or even Confederation equipment, they were a match for what Gentry, the major supplier to local governments and mercenary units could put out. More importantly, a KF-10 was more than capable of taking out a lone Marine squad and sniper team. Intel hadn't caught on to the little fact that there were KF tanks in the sector.

"Hope the Minidrag can take them out," Rabbit passed on the P2P.

"That's out of our hands for now, so keep firing."

Over the next five minutes, Gracie dropped three more FLNT fighters, one as he crouched to fire a shoulder-launched missile at the library. She picked up the Windmoeller again to put a round through the missile as it lay in the dirt so no one else could pick it up and use it. As she searched for more targets, her mind was on the Marine drone as it closed in on the KF-10s.

The fight, more than a klick-and-a-half away and within sight of them on the roof, was over in seconds. The lead KF-10 erupted in a ball of flame, and moments later, the Minidrag was knocked from the sky. That left one tank still in the fight, and it looked huge as it pushed forward.

"Now what?" Rabbit asked, firing off another burst of 20 darts.

"Keep firing."

There was whoosh, then a boom as a missile crashed into the side of the library, blowing a hole through the stone. Gracie tried to spot the gunner to no avail. She could almost feel the enemy close in though. The hammer would fall when the KF-10 arrived.

"You still with us?" she asked Sergeant Rafiq on the P2P.

There was a pause before he answered, "We're down to three effectives. That last one, shit, I'm down hard, bleeding like a stuck pig. I'm not going anywhere. I just gave Ben-Zvi the order to retreat to the west, and I'd suggest you do so, too. We'll try to give you some cover, and when that fucking FLNT tank gets here, well, we'll see what happens."

A death sentence, Gracie knew. The FLNT didn't see the value of prisoners.

She tied in Rabbit to the net, then said, "I don't think so, Sergeant. We can keep them off you."

She looked over to Rabbit. He nodded his agreement.

"You can take out a KF-10? Don't think so," Rafiq said with a groan of pain.

"Lieutenant Hjebek and the rest of your platoon are almost here."

"Look, Staff Sergeant, I . . . we appreciate the sentiment, but this time, the dice rolled against us. All of us here, we talked about it, and we agree. Get out of here. Semper fi," he said before breaking out into coughs and cutting the net.

"Keep at it, Irving," Gracie said, snapping off another round, not hitting the running soldier but making him dive for cover.

The enemy tank was getting closer, and Gracie pulled up a threat assessment. The KF-10 would be vulnerable to any Marine anti-armor, but the two teams, or whoever was left of them, had used theirs in anti-personnel mode to push back the assault. A few antennae and the periscope were vulnerable, but not to her when armed with only a Kyocera.

What about the Windmoeller? she wondered.

She didn't have any more WPT-331 rounds, but a WPT-310 would still be better than her 3mm darts. She changed weapons, then shot a range to the tank. It was about to enter the northern edge of town, 1,245 meters away from her. She took a few moments to enter the environmentals. Gracie was an excellent marksman, but hitting a 4cm-wide periscope lens on a moving tank at that range was going to be a task.

"You can't take out a tank with that," Rabbit said as he realized what she was doing.

"No, but maybe I can blind it," she said as she took her three calming breaths.

The tank was still advancing, and Gracie had to estimate what that would do to her sight picture. She made her decision, then fired. A moment later, she could see the round ping off the periscope turret, four or five centimeters low.

She immediately adjusted, but the driver juked the tank to its right just as she fired again, and she never saw the impact of her round. Now, with an almost side aspect, the shot would be almost impossible, but she held the target in the hopes that it would turn back to her.

There was an explosion behind her. Gracie spun around as three figures burst through the door to the roof that had been blasted right out of the frame, hitting Rabbit hard on the head. Gracie swung her Kyocera around and fired an un-aimed shot which took one soldier in the thigh and dropped him, causing the man behind him to stumble. She fired again, hitting that second soldier on the top of his head. The third soldier, however, fired a three-round burst at her, one hitting her in the left arm and causing her to drop her Windmoeller, her entire arm aflame with pain. while another hit her square on her left knee.

With a smile of . . . satisfaction? . . . scorn? he lowered his rifle and pulled out an enormous boarding gun. Probably over 100 years old, it fired a short-range rocket that had the power to blow right through her body armor, something it had been designed to to. He was slowly raising it to bear down on her when a string of darts hit him in the side where his plate armor deflected them. He spun and fired, the rocket crossing the ten meters to where Rabbit lay on the ground, the muzzle of his M99 wavering as he tried to keep it on target.

Rabbit never had a chance. The rocket blew apart his upper torso. The man stopped, looking at Rabbit's body for a moment before turning back to Gracie. That small delay was enough to give her a chance to pull her Rino from her thigh holster. His eyes widened in shock as she fired, double-tapping the trigger, the first .358 hollow-point hitting him in the forehead, the round expanding and lodging ten centimeters deep into his brain.

Gracie felt a pang of loss, but she couldn't stop to mourn Rabbit. She stumbled to her feet, arm numb, and picked up the Kyocera again. Below, the final assault was about to kick off, and she intended on taking out as many of them as possible. Heedless of how exposed she was, she leaned over the top of the wall, firing round after round. She thought she dropped at least four of them, but she wasn't sure. All the time, the sound of the KF-10 reverberated between the buildings as it made its way to the square.

She heard Sergeant Rafiq ask the lieutenant how far out the platoon was. She didn't bother to listen to the reply. She knew there was no way they could reach them in time.

"I'm still here with you, Dylan," she told him. "Hang in there."

"Shit, Staff Sergeant, you're as stubborn as they say. But you sure the hell ain't no Ice Princess like they say, though. You've got balls, sister."

"And so do you."

And then KF-10 rolled into the square, big and mean, blue-diesel engine pumping out smoke. She knew her Kyocera would be useless against it, but she fired off 100 rounds, more a statement than anything else as the tank gunner raised the 80mm gun to take her under fire.

She knew she should do something, but there wasn't much left in her box of tricks. The big gun was going to take off the entire top of the building, and her leg was already swollen and immobile. Math worked for snipers, but also for tanks—80mm trumped 3mm.

Gracie kept firing, though. The gun was halfway up when there was a loud whoosh from beneath her, and a smoky plume raced across the square to hit the tank right below the commander's cupula.

The gun stopped moving. No massive explosions, no turret flying through the air. The tank just stopped.

"Scratch one tank," Corporal Ben-Zvi passed on the command net.

"Fuck, Abe, I told you to take your team and get out of here," Sergeant Rafiq passed.

"Ah, I've always been a fuck-up, Sergeant. You know that."

The cracka-cracka-cracka of an M110 sounded below her, the rounds shooting across the square to disappear out of sight.

"I'm still effective up here," Gracie passed. "And thanks for taking out the tank, but this isn't over. We've still got a job to do."

But it was over. With the KF-10 gone, the will of the FLNT fighters seemed to slip away—that or the fact that they knew a Marine platoon was minutes out. Gracie fired one more shot at a retreating figure, but that was it before Lieutenant Hjebek led the rest of the platoon into the village.

The fight was over.

"Corporal Ben-Zvi, can you do me a favor?" she passed on the P2P as the new Marines swept the area.

"Sure thing, Staff Sergeant."

"Go find one of the dead FLNT fighters before they get policed up, one who looks like he was taken out with an M99. Get a round from him and bring it to me."

"Uh . . . Staff Sergeant, you know we can't take trophies."

"I know the regs. But just do it, OK? It's important."

"Shit, if you say so, of course. We owe you."

"And I owe you. Thanks."

She moved back to the wall, her Kyocera at the ready. Her arm and leg were aching, but at least she could move them now. She could go down to get one of the docs to check her out, but she was a sniper, and two squads of Marines were clearing the village. Her job was to cover them.

***

A day later, after the Heroes Ceremony, the members of Third Battalion, Seventh Marines' Scout Sniper Platoon held their own ceremony. Gracie took the round Ben-Zvi had scrounged up and had attached to a piece of parachute cord the night before, and with Doc Rhymer turning off the stasis chamber for a moment, she slipped it inside with Rabbit's body. The corpsman turned the chamber back on, then left the snipers alone.

Technically, by rules developed over centuries, Rabbit had not become a true Hunter of Gunmen. He hadn't used a sniper's weapon to make a kill at distance. Just as Gracie wouldn't get a kill credit for dropping Rabbit's killer with a handgun, Rabbit's kills with his M99 were considered merely part and parcel of being a Marine. Gracie had asked that he be put in for a medal, and the battalion commander had agreed, but that didn't make him a HOG.

Gracie was a dedicated Marines, and as a habit, she didn't lie. She'd never made a false official statement—until the night before. She hadn't been sure of what kind of Marine Rabbit was, but he'd proven the quench of his steel. Without him, she doubted anyone would have made it out alive. So, she lied. She said she'd given her Kyocera to him, and from the enemy bodies recovered, five had died from the tipped 3mm darts. Gracie didn't need the kills on her record, but he did.

Gracie was sure that Gunny Adams, the Scout-Sniper platoon sergeant, didn't believe a word of it. He knew how possessively she treated her weapons. But after staring into her eyes for a full 30 seconds, he nodded and accepted it.

As the other stasis chambers were being loaded for a return, either for resurrection or burial, each of the snipers in the platoon made their way past Rabbit's chamber. Each Marine quietly made their goodbye. As his sniper, Gracie was last. She wasn't much for long talks, so she kept it simple.

"Fair winds and following seas, HOG."

She gave the chamber a little slap, then turned to join the others.

"Do you need a day or two?" Gunny asked her.

She gave one last look as the loading crew came to take Rabbit, then said, "Nope, I'm ready. What's my next mission?

The End

Author Jonathan P. Brazee

I am a retired Marine colonel now living and working in Thailand. I was born in Oakland, CA, but have lived throughout the US and the world, and have traveled to over 100 countries.

My undergraduate degree was earned at the U. S. Naval Academy (Class of 1979), and I have attended graduate school at U. S. International University and the University of California, San Diego, earning a masters and doctorate.

I am a lifetime member of the Disabled American Veterans, the Veterans of Foreign Wars, the US. Naval Academy Alumni Association, and the Science Fiction and Fantasy Writers of America.

I have rather eclectic tastes. I have won awards in photography, cooking, and several sports, earning national championships in rugby and equestrian events. I love reading, writing, exercise, cooking, travel, and photography.

I published my first work back in 1978, a so-so short story titled "Secession." Since then, I have been published in newspapers, magazines, and in book format in fiction, political science, business, military, sports, race relations, and personal relations fields.

I write because I love it. I only hope that others might read my work and get a bit of enjoyment or useful information out of my effort.

TO CATCH A KING

By Mike Kraus

One ship, one crew and more trouble than they bargained for.

Chapter 1

King's Fall – Command Deck, Bridge

"Shut off those damned alarms!" Captain William McConnell clung to the arms of his chair as the *King's Fall* bucked hard to the left. Red lights flashed and loud klaxons of no less than five different pitches came from various sections of the bridge. The hull of the ship groaned as she unexpectedly dropped out of slipspace before her crew had time to react. The ship's emergency shielding and inertial fields kept her from breaking apart or turning her crew into a pink jelly on the walls but she wasn't happy about the situation.

"Tom!" Captain McConnell braced his legs against the floor to keep from sliding forward. "Shut off the alarms!"

A heartbeat later the bridge descended into relative silence though the alarms were quickly replaced by the shouts of the crew as they struggled to figure out what was happening to the ship.

"Somebody tell me what's going on right now!" McConnell sat up in his chair and watched the forward monitor. The stars outside were like streaks across the screen, indicating that the ship was in a violent spin. Those inside felt nothing thanks to the inertial fields but the disconnect between the motion on the screen and the relative stillness inside made McConnell feel sick to his stomach.

No idea, captain!" Drake O'Neil, the navigator and flight officer shouted back as his hands worked the controls at his console. "Something knocked us out of our slipstream!"

"Really? No shit, Sherlock!" McConnell's voice was layered thick with sarcasm. "Rut'kor, how's it look?"

"Hull integrity holding and the main shields are coming back online now, captain." The Andarian glanced down at McConnell and frowned. "We appear to be suffering from micro-fractures in the lower cargo bay and along the length of the port side, though."

"Tom, get the automated repair systems on those fractures."

A disembodied voice came from speakers on the bridge and from inside his left ear. "Already on it, Captain McConnell. I also took the liberty of re-routing power from the main shields to the inertial field stabilizers to keep them online when we were knocked out of the slipstream. Releasing the power now."

"Nice work, Tom." McConnell shifted in his seat and glanced around the rest of the bridge. The rest of his motley crew was hard at work diagnosing what was going on and he found it agonizing to sit still while he waited to hear what was going on.

"Captain!" Lindar called out from his station behind McConnell and the captain swiveled in his chair. "Sensor sweep shows a dampening field starting several thousand klicks behind us. It appears to be the reason why we were kicked out of slipspace."

"A dampening field?" McConnell got up from his chair and ran around to the science station to look at the readouts. "Is it artificial?"

"Absolutely." Lindar's spindly body quivered next to McConnell and his large eyes blinked several times. "A large grid of emitters surrounds this sector of space. Anything passing through would be knocked out of their slipstream and unable to jump again until their engines were recalibrated to account for the dampening field."

"Why the hell would someone put a dampening field out in the middle of nowhere?" McConnell turned to look at the screen then glanced at his first mate, his eyes wide with realization. "Federation?"

She nodded once, repeating the word with a tone of finality. "Federation."

As if on cue the forward screen lit up with the flash of half a dozen ships dropping in out of slipspace. Unlike the King's Fall's awkward and near-disastrous exit from FTL travel to sub-light speeds, the ships that appeared in front of her all exited their slipstreams with poise and grace.

"Rut'Kor! How are those shields looking?" McConnell ran back around to his chair in the center of the bridge and sat down, his eyes still glued to the ships on the main screen.

"Eighty percent, captain! I'm still dealing with power surges!"

"We need them at a hundred as soon as possible before these assholes decide to open fire on us!"

While the *King's Fall* was nearly three hundred meters in length, she was dwarfed by the six-hundred-meter Federation cruisers moving into formation around her. The cruisers were slow and ponderous compared to the *King's Fall* but they had clearly been planning their ambush for quite some time.

"They're moving into position on top of us." Evie Walker—McConnell's first mate—worked her controls and spoke in a calm and steady voice as she watched a three-dimensional representation of the ships around the *King's Fall*. "Brace for impact!" Evie shouted just a few seconds before a loud clang accompanied a gut-wrenching shudder. McConnell felt the ship move several meters in the relative downward direction and not even the inertial field dampeners could fully compensate for the unexpected movement.

"What was that?" McConnell instinctively looked at the ceiling of the bridge before turning to Lindar. "Give me something here!"

The response came not from Lindar but from the disembodied voice that filled the bridge—and McConnell's head thanks to his neural implant—with a soothing explanation. "We appear to be caught in the lead Federation vessel's docking clamps. I am showing unauthorized access in the main docking and cargo bays."

McConnell glanced at Evie again and shook his head. "How did they find out about the shipment?"

Evie shrugged. "How would I know? It doesn't look like they're interested in talking, though."

McConnell sat down slowly, considering his options. A group of six cruisers would be impossible to break through when one of them had used a pair of massive docking clamps to hold fast to the *King's Fall*. Only by breaking the hold would they have a chance to get away, though that depended entirely on if they could jump back into slipspace.

"Hans! Andre!" McConnell shouted to the mass of muscle in the corner at the security and weapons station. "You two with me. We're going to work with Tom to repel the boarders. Lindar and Rut'kor? I need a miracle. Get the engine's tuned to match the dampening field so we can jump back into slipspace the second we're free from these assholes."

"Captain?" Lindar's bulbous eyes blinked open and shut rapidly. "That'll take at least twenty—"

"You were going to say twenty minutes instead of twenty hours, right?" McConnell stood up and started walking towards the lift at the back of the bridge with Andre and Hans following close behind. "Because if it's more than twenty minutes then I hope you can breathe in outer space."

Lindar's mouth opened and shut several times in rapid succession before he nodded and looked at Rutkor. "How can I be of assistance, chief?"

Evie stood up as McConnell got into the lift. "Captain? What about the clamps?"

"Figure out a way to break the hold, Evie. We'll keep them away from the shipment as long as possible but if they get impatient then they might just crack open the hull and sift through the wreckage."

Evie watched the lift doors close and turned back to the forward screen before glancing at the other crewmembers on the bridge and muttering under her breath. "Shit."

Chapter 2
King's Fall – Main (upper) cargo bay

McConnell, Andre and Hans ran down the corridors of the *King's Fall* as they wound their way to the main cargo bay. Situated on the top of the ship a short distance aft of the bridge it was—thankfully—a short distance to travel. The bridge and the main entrance to the cargo bay were both located on the top deck which had windows looking out to the sides and up out of the ship. Instead of the light-dotted darkness of space or the spectral hues of a slipstream, though, the view was completely filled with the black and grey colored metal of the Federation cruiser's underbelly.

"Where's the closest weapons locker, Andre?" McConnell didn't bother looking at his chief of security as he asked the question.

"Twenty meters ahead, outside the door to the cargo bay. Full complement of weapons." Andre's response was short and to the point, delivering the exact amount of information needed with no frills.

"All right then, boys." McConnell slowed as they neared the door. Hans punched in the security code for the weapons closet and flung open the doors. "We're going weapons free here. Take whatever you need to keep them from getting past us. We're the only ones standing between them and our shipment and you know what they'll do to us if they get their hands on it."

"The same thing they'll do if they don't?" Hans Beike, a native of the Ketmar-9 colony had a thick German accent and McConnell swore that the man liked to both state the obvious and make his accent as difficult to understand as possible. He and Andre worked together on the weapons systems, general security matters and moving heavy things around when the need arose. McConnell knew he could count on both of them no matter what.

Andre stepped up to the security panel next to the door to the cargo bay and tapped on the screen. A view of the interior of the top floor of the bay flared to life and he shook his head. "This is not good."

"What is it?" McConnell stepped up next to Andre and winced. "Holy Toledo. There's got to be a couple hundred of them in there. Why the hell hasn't Tom engaged them yet? Tom?"

"I was awaiting your arrival, Captain McConnell. Would you like me to engage them now?"

"If you don't mind, yeah, that'd be great. Well, no. Give us a thirty-second silent countdown, please."

"Confirmed."

McConnell turned to Andre and Hans and looked them over. "Joking aside, this could go very poorly in there. It's a huge open area with very little cover and a lot of guys who want to kill us. We need to take out every last one and seal their entry point up, okay?"

"Where are they coming from?" Hans asked. "Aren't the main doors still sealed?"

"Indeed." Andre grunted as he tapped on the panel next to the door. "They appear to have blown open one of the four loading doors and moved down from there. The interior security seals are keeping them from moving farther into the vessel but they will not be contained for long once they realize that our shipment is not located in the cargo bay."

"Great." McConnell slapped Andre's arm. "So here's the deal." McConnell was about to tell them exactly where he wanted them positioned so that they could move through the cargo bay, up the lifts at the back and then repair the loading door. The sound of weapons fire inside the cargo bay made him realize that Tom's countdown must have ended.

"Shit!" McConnell reached past Andre and hit the button to open the door into the main cargo bay. "Go, go, go!"

Chapter 3
King's Fall – Command Deck, Bridge

An experimental craft developed by the Federation years ago, the King's Fall was a test to see if it was possible to carry dreadnought-class weapons inside of a destroyer-class vessel. The key to the test was twofold: miniaturizing dreadnought-class weapons and providing enough energy to power them while still retaining a small form factor. The Federation ultimately declared the test a failure and ordered the King's Fall—at that point named some long-forgotten combination of letters and numbers—to be scrapped for salvage.

The vessel was unlike anything the Federation had built before or since and while she appeared ungainly with her odd angles and scooped cross-section she was, in the right hands, a thing of beauty. Her hull was twice as thick as the most protected part of a Federation carrier, she had cutting-edge engines that could power a fully-armed dreadnought and she was designed for a crew complement of two hundred and fifty with ample room for hundreds more.

Aside from her unique design, massively overpowered engines, thick hull and reinforced shielding she could have passed for a destroyer-class vessel from some obscure world. The thing that made her special, though, and the reason for her very creation was contained in the two thick winglets positioned near the aft of her body.

Two miniaturized dreadnought-class plasma cannons were housed within the winglets, close enough to the engines that they could draw power directly from the King's Fall's twelve fusion reactors that took up most of the space behind the main cargo bay. Mounting dreadnought-class plasma cannons on a destroyer-class ship had been an insane idea that hadn't worked out at the time of the ship's creation. Upon her "liberation" from the salvage yard by Captain McConnell, though, he found the right group of people to both acquire two plasma cannons, refit them into smaller housings, solve the heat and energy distribution problems, install them and figure out how to make them actually work.

It took two years and every resource to his name but the first time he saw the cannons pop out from the bottom of the winglets, rotate to track their target and vaporize it all in less than a second's worth of time he knew all the trouble had been worth it. And that was before he found the *King's Fall's* true greatest secret: Tom.

"Evie?" Tom's voice cut through the noise on the bridge and she replied without looking up from her console.

"What is it, Tom?"

"They've engaged Federation forces in the main cargo bay. So far I've killed thirty-eight individuals using the security systems but that's not going to be very effective for much longer."

"And you're telling me this why?"

"We may have to consider more drastic approaches if the Captain is not successful."

"We'll talk about that later, Tom." Evie's fingers danced across her console and she looked over at Drake O'Neil, the *King's Fall's* helmsman and navigator.

"Drake, you ready with a jump solution as soon as we've got the engines tuned?"

"You get us free and give me engine power and they won't know how to begin to find us."

Evie nodded and looked back at her console as she muttered under her breath. "I'm more concerned with how they found us in the first place."

The bridge speakers came to life and the sound of distant shouting was followed by laborious breathing and a haggard voice. "Bridge! It's Jakob! We've got the tuning frequency figured out thanks to Lindar. It's going to take time to get everything reconfigured, though!"

Evie pushed a button on her console and replied. "How long, Jakob?" She could hear him talking to someone in the background before he responded.

"Another twenty, maybe twenty-five. It's not exactly easy to retune a dozen engines on the fly, you know!"

"Dammit." Evie pinched the bridge of her nose in frustration. "Make it fast, Jakob! If we get free and can't jump they won't let us get very far." The only response was the sound of more shouting as Jakob ran to help his fellow engineers with their work.

Evie manipulated her console as she started work on figuring out how to break free of the clamps that held them in place. With all three of the ship's engineers engaged in retuning the engines she lacked the input she felt she needed to make an informed decision so she turned once again to Tom.

"Tom, what options do we have for breaking free?"

"Give me a moment, please." Evie's screen changed as Tom brought up a three-dimensional view of the *King's Fall* and the ship that had clamped them in place. "Based on preliminary sensor scans we do not have any secondary or tertiary weapons in place that could open fire on the clamps."

"Could we launch the *Tempest* and use her to shoot them out?"

"Negative. The Federation vessels are too many in number. The *Tempest* would certainly be destroyed almost immediately and even if it were to somehow survive there's not enough room between the cruiser and the *King's Fall* to open fire."

Evie stared at the three-dimensional representation of the *King's Fall* and the four massive clamps that held her in place as an idea began to form in her head. "Lindar?"

The Ketarian's body segments rotated to face her. "Yes?"

"Do a low-level sweep on those clamps. Not the whole cruiser, mind you. Just the clamps. I want to know what they're made out of and how strong it is."

Lindar's face was incapable of showing emotion but after spending enough time with the Ketarian, Evie had developed a sixth sense. At the moment it was telling her that Lindar was confused by the request. "Are you sure? Just the clamps?"

"Just the clamps, please. And hurry."

Chapter 4
King's Fall – Main (upper) cargo bay

McConnell, Hans and Andre crouched behind a stack of metal boxes as they tried to plan their next move. The Federation troopers had spread themselves across the main cargo bay after taking out several of the automated turrets. The turrets—controlled by Tom—had eliminated a decent number of troopers but McConnell could see that there weren't nearly enough of them gone to tip the odds in the *King's Fall's* favor.

Every few seconds one of the three would pop up and fire off several shots at one of the troopers before ducking back down amidst a withering hail of fire. It didn't take more than a few minutes for the troopers' energy weapons to burn their way through one side of the metal boxes and before long McConnell noticed that the side they were one was starting to heat up and glow a dull red.

"All right, you two. We need to flush them out so that Tom can use the remaining turrets to bring them down. Our cover here's finished so we need to move across to that cluster of support columns." McConnell pointed at a location roughly fifty feet away, trying to sound encouraging so that his doubts about whether or not they could make it wouldn't filter through to his crew.

Before McConnell could do or say anything else there was a loud "RAGH!" from next to him. He turned to see Andre tear off the side of one of the metal boxes and hoist it up, carrying it vertically like a shield. "Let us go now, Captain!" The Luxon wasted neither time nor words as he thundered forward. McConnell and Has glanced at each other as they stood and ran after him, keeping their bodies behind the piece of metal.

While Andre kept their temporary shield up the other two fired blindly around the sides. The action didn't cut down on much of the incoming fire but it was enough to keep the metal from heating up too badly. When they finally reached the support column McConnell turned to see a group of Federation troopers waiting for them. He raised his rifle to fire and hopefully take one or two of them out when a dark piece of metal soared over his head. The side of the box hit the three troopers square in their chests, breaking their ribs with the initial impact and then their spines as they fell to the ground and were crushed to death.

"Damn, Andre." Captain McConnell grinned as he patted Andre's back. "Well done with that little maneuver."

Never the one to do anything but talk business Andre peeked around the column before pulling his head back just in time to avoid having it shot off. "Captain McConnell. While we appear to be in a somewhat safer location we still have the problem of getting the troopers out into the open. What is your plan for this?"

"Plan?" McConnell laughed and reloaded his rifle. "Hey, Hans. Andre thinks I have a plan." McConnell couldn't help but laugh and his human colleague soon joined in. Andre merely stared at them for a few seconds before shaking his head.

"Now is not the time for amusements, Captain."

"Andre, we've been working together for long enough now that you should know there's *always* time for amusements." McConnell's eyes twinkled with thoughts of death even as a smile still played around the edges of his lips.

Andre sighed and shook his head. "If we don't do something soon they'll overwhelm us, Captain."

"Yeah, yeah." McConnell waved his hand and peeked around the corner. "We still need to get them up here, to the main level, right, Tom?"

"Correct." Tom's voice buzzed inside McConnell's head. Most of the destroyed turrets are on the second level. If you push them back to the first then I should be able to finish them off."

"Do we still have that shipment of Landarian gas on board?"

"Yes, sir. On the second level." There was a short pause before Tom spoke again. "Are you seriously considering... *that*?"

"Oh no." Hans groaned. "No, no, no. That's not a good idea, Captain. That stuff is incredibly toxic!"

"Which is precisely why this is actually a fantastic idea." McConnell took another peek around the corner. "It'll spread out and fill the second level, driving them back up to us."

"And what'll we do when it starts eating through the door and vent seals?"

"We'll have to make sure we vent it out into space before then."

"You will have seven minutes, Captain." Tom spoke again. "Any longer than that and the seals will degrade to the point that the gas will escape into other areas of the ship. There will, of course, also be a week-long cleaning process required to ensure the residue is disposed of before the cargo bay can be used again."

"It's either that," McConnell said, "or we die at the hands of the Federation." He looked at Andre and Hans. "Either of you want to take the second option? No? Great. Now let's figure out how to do this."

Chapter 5
King's Fall – Command Deck, Bridge

"Captain!" Evie stood over Lindar's shoulder, shouting into the intercom.

"Little busy here, Evie!" McConnell's voice was interspersed with heavy breathing, shouting and weapons fire.

"I think we found a way to break free from the clamps!"

"Oh? Marvelous! Why are you calling me about it? Just do it already!"

"Well..." Evangeline looked over at Lindar, mouthing 'are you sure' at the Ketarian. He nodded several times in rapid succession. "Well, Lindar's run scans on the cruiser's clamps and they have several weak points. If we spin the ship with enough force I think we'll be able to break the clamps."

"They'll snap off? Just like that?"

Evie watched Lindar as she talked, still unsure about the efficacy of the proposed solution. "They should, yes."

"And what about us? That sounds incredibly dangerous. Dammit, Hans! Cover left!"

"I already talked to Rut'kor. He's pissed but he thinks that if we route enough power into the structural field then we'll be okay."

"Ugh." Evangeline could hear McConnell's hesitation and weariness through the intercom and knew that he was rubbing his eyes and forehead as he tried to make up his mind. The answer came a few seconds later. "Fine. Do it."

"Just... do it?" She was somewhat surprised to hear him agree so readily to such a risky plan.

"Either we get free or we die. I vote we try to get free. Just give me eight minutes to get these troopers taken care of, though, okay?"

"Eight minutes. Got it." Evie cut off the intercom and looked at Lindar. "You're certain about this?"

Lindar's eyes blinked rapidly and his spindly body quivered. "Absolutely. As much as I can be, that is. There's always an element of risk involved but I believe this to be the only course of action with an appropriately high level of—"

"Okay, okay." Evie waved her hands. "You've convinced me. Figure out the calculations and let me know when you're ready."

Chapter 6
King's Fall – Main (upper) cargo bay

"Tom, are you sure you can't target the gas shipment?"

"As I explained already, Captain, the majority of my turrets that were destroyed were on the second level. The same level where the gas is sitting. If I could target the gas containers then I could just kill the troopers instead."

"Lovely. Okay then, we have to get down there on foot." McConnell looked at Hans and Andre. "Any suggestions?"

Hans pointed across the bay, past the destroyed crates where they had been taking cover originally. "There's an access hatch in a side room over there with a ladder. It leads down to the second level."

"So I'll run over there while you cover me, head down the ladder and shoot one of the canisters."

"The ladder Hans is talking about is in full view of the troopers downstairs, Captain." Tom's disembodied voice rang through McConnell's head. "You will need some type of distraction to keep them from noticing you."

"Tom says we need a distraction. Thoughts?"

"What about a cargo loader?" Hans turned to look through a nearby doorway at a maintenance area. "We could strap some makeshift armor plating to it and send it on an automated run. If we cover up the driver's seat then the troopers will think someone's on board and focus their attention on that while you go down and destroy a gas container."

McConnell nodded, smiled and slapped Hans on the shoulder. "Nice thinking. I like it. I want you to get an automated sequence ready for it. Andre? You're with me. Lay down cover fire so I can get to the ladder then I want you to collect up pieces of that cargo container they destroyed and get them back to Hans. Use some mag clamps to fasten them onto the loader. As soon as you get done you need to get it rolling. We don't have much time before Evie and the others try to break us free."

Andre and Hans both nodded and got to work. Hans darted into the nearby maintenance room which was, thankfully, out of sight of the ramp leading down to the second level. Andre picked up the piece of metal he had used as a shield previously and ran out toward the broken cargo containers along with McConnell. The troopers started firing on them almost immediately and the pair didn't dare to stop until they reached the ladder.

"I'm good here!" McConnell panted and pointed back at the cargo containers. "Get some more metal and get it over to Hans. Hurry!"

The Luxon nodded at McConnell before turning and heading back. Built like a tank he barely fit behind the piece of metal that was slowly starting to disintegrate due to the level of incoming fire it was sustaining. He dropped low to the ground once he reached the pile of scrap and pulled a few large pieces of metal from the pile and placed them on the ground. One by one he turned around, placed his feet up against the pieces and braced his arms on the floor. He then used his massive legs as springs to rocket the pieces across the floor towards the maintenance room, sending up an awful screeching that had Hans and McConnell both reaching for their ears to try and block out the noise.

Once a total of six pieces had been slid across the floor Andre picked up his makeshift shield and ran for the room, barely making it into cover before the shield finally became too hot for him to hold. He grabbed the edge of the metal and slung it out towards the cargo bay ramp with one hand, smiling slyly as he heard the distant *thud* and immediate scream of at least two troopers who hadn't been able to move out of the way fast enough.

"Damn, Andre. Did you get enough scrap?!" Hans looked out at the pile of metal sitting outside the maintenance bay and shook his head. "Nice job!"

Andre grunted and picked up the nearest piece. "Hurry. Time is running short."

The two men worked swiftly and in less than two minutes they finished attaching the pieces of metal to the front, sides and top of the cargo loader. The loader looked as though a demented child had come up with the design but both men were confident the shielding would fool the troopers long enough for McConnell to do his part.

"We're sending it out now, Captain. Get ready." Hans spoke into his intercom.

"Locked and loaded. Get it moving!" The reply was immediate.

Hans reached through a narrow slot in the metal covering the loader and pressed a button on the control panel. The loader sprung to life and Hans had to jump back to avoid being run over. It dashed off of its charging dock and went forward, heading out of the maintenance room before taking a sharp right turn that nearly toppled it over.

"I think you made it drive too fast." Andre's voice was flat and matter-of-fact.

"I think *you* made it too top-heavy." Hans shook his head. "It doesn't matter. It'll make it."

A hail of weapons fire made both men peek around the corner where they saw the troopers leaning up over the ramp as they started firing on the loader. Hans and Andre grabbed their rifles and started firing at the troopers, killing a few and wounding several others. The extra distraction helped buy time for the loader to continue moving into position while also helping McConnell.

A few hundred feet away, McConnell hurried down the ladder, cursing under his breath each time the rifle on his back banged against the metal of the ladder shaft. He was certain that the noise would alert the Federation troopers until he heard weapons fire coming from the other end of the cargo bay.

"There's my cue." McConnell took the rungs of the ladder two at a time until he reached the second floor. He hopped off and turned around, half-expecting there to be a group of troopers waiting for him. He was relieved to see that while there were troopers nearby they weren't looking in his direction but were instead firing at something above. "Nice work, boys." McConnell mumbled to himself as he slunk forward and began to read the labels on large crates and containers sitting on the floor, trying to find the shipment of Landarian gas.

Heavier than air and extremely corrosive to organic and many inorganic materials, Landarian gas was useful in certain types of mining where it was used to eat away at rock formations while leaving minerals intact. Because of its corrosiveness, though, even the smallest amount was fatal and most types of suits and filtering masks couldn't deal with the substance for more than a few seconds.

"Is this it?" McConnell dropped to his knees as he read the label on one of six cylindrical containers to confirm his suspicion. "Yes it is." He stood back up, looking back at the ladder. "Perfect. Now all I have to do is not kill myself."

"Captain?" The voice in McConnell's head was Hans'.

"What is it, Hans?"

"The loader's about to go up in flames. How's it going down there?"

"Nearly done. I just found the gas. Give me one more minute."

"I'm honestly not sure if you have that long, sir."

McConnell looked up from the grenade he was trying to rig to the side of the container with a short fuse timer and glanced over the top of the cluster of canisters. Several troopers appeared to be falling back and heading in his direction. "Damn!" McConnell cursed under his breath and picked up the grenade. It slipped from his hand and clattered to the floor, making a loud *bang* on the metal before he could scoop it back up. He glanced up over the canisters again, hoping that the trooper's wouldn't notice the sound.

The crack of an energy weapon passed by a few feet from McConnell's face and he rolled backwards, taking cover behind another crate. "So much for that!" Throwing subterfuge to the wind he stood up and ran for the ladder, weaving his way in between crates to make it as hard as possible for the troopers to hit him. Their gunfire tore past him, nearly striking him several times, but thankfully none of them appeared to be able to hit a moving target.

When McConnell reached the ladder he took cover behind a crate and pulled the pin from the grenade. He glanced around the crate and saw that the troopers were about to run past the gas canisters. "See you later, fellas!" McConnell shouted as he stood up, pulled his arm back and threw the grenade in a tall, slow arc.

The troopers spotted the grenade just before it hit the ground next to them but by that time it was too late for them to do anything that would make a lick of difference. The grenade bounced one time before it exploded, sending shrapnel and flames in all directions. McConnell had managed to land it just feet away from the gas canisters. The troopers were initially concerned with their injuries from the grenade but once the green gas began to fill the air they realized that they had far bigger problems to deal with.

McConnell watched them for a second as they panicked, trying to hobble and crawl away from the thick gas as it slowly expanded across the cargo bay. Their screams quickly faded as their vocal cords were eaten away and they stopped moving shortly thereafter. Once he was certain that he wasn't going to be shot at McConnell lunged for the ladder and headed upwards as quickly as possible. He was near the halfway point of the ladder when he heard a secondary explosion from down below.

"Captain?" Tom's voice burst into McConnell's head. "You might want to move faster. There's... a problem on the main floor." A panicked look crossed Will's face and he increased his speed, popping out of the ladder and turning to look for his crew.

"Captain!" Hans yelled at him from behind a large piece of metal that Andre was holding in front of the remains of the cargo crates near the door they had entered from. "They're scattering!"

McConnell ran over to hide behind the shield but stopped short and stood in the open staring in wide-eyed horror at the sight at the other end of the cargo bay near the ramp.

"Captain?" Hans looked at McConnell questioningly before peeking out from behind the shield. "Oh no. Oh no! Andre, run!" Hans slapped Andre on the back and the giant dropped the shield, took one look out where McConnell was staring and began thundering toward the exit.

"Let's go, Will!" Andre reached out and snagged McConnell's arm as he passed by, dragging him along behind. The trio ran for the exit out of the cargo bay while, behind them, a cloud of green gas continued to quickly spread across the main floor. While the initial explosion had released gas only on the second floor the secondary explosion—a nearby container filled with ammunition—had not only dislodged one of the other canisters but sent it rocketing towards the ramp. There it bounced off of a wall and came to rest in the middle of the main floor of the cargo bay where it began to leak.

The troopers, caught between two clouds of gas, were dead before they realized what was going on. Once Tom saw the canister on the main cargo bay floor he hadn't bothered to engage the turrets, instead monitoring the situation to make sure none of their enemies managed to escape. When Hans, Andre and Will reached the exit for the bay Tom opened the door and sealed it behind them.

"Purge the bay!" Will spoke hoarsely and rubbed his aching shoulder as Andre pulled him to his feet. "Don't let that shit get any farther!"

Hans punched a series of numbers into a control pad near the door and the lights around the door flashed red. "Done, captain!"

"Good." McConnell leaned over, putting his hands on his knees as he took in deep breaths of air to make sure he hadn't sucked in any particles of the gas. "Tom, watch for any stragglers. They should all be dead but I don't want any survivors sneaking in. Keep the main doors open until the gas is gone, then seal them and flood the bay with a neutralizing agent. We'll do a deep clean and get rid of the remains later."

"Will do, Captain."

"Nice work out there, you two." McConnell stood up and patted Hans and Andre on their backs. "You're both okay?"

Both men nodded and McConnell smiled. "Excellent. Let's get to the bridge. We're going to be breaking free any—"

As if on cue the ship shuddered and McConnell could hear the distant scream of metal being twisted and rubbed together. "Second. There it is." He gave Hans and Andre one final glance. "Let's teach these assholes a lesson."

Chapter 7

King's Fall – Command Deck, Bridge

McConnell ran onto the bridge and dashed for his center chair. He looked at Evie as he sat down. "Hull still good?"

Evie nodded. "She's dented but holding. We're free for now, but they might have another cruiser with clamps so we should jump as fast as possible."

The confirmation that his ship was not only intact but also flying free brought a grin to McConnell's face. He turned back to the main screen and called out over the intercom. "Rut'kor! Do I have sublight power?"

The answer was swift, coming back over the intercom as it echoed through the bride. "Yes, Captain! Full sublight at your disposal!"

Captain McConnell jumped back out of his chair and headed for the helm, still wearing a maniacal grin. "Drake, move aside please!"

Drake O'Neil jumped out of his seat and moved to an auxiliary station as McConnell sat down. Will's fingers flew over the controls as he brought the sublight engines online, pushing them to fifty percent power. The ship groaned as she punched forward, flying beneath and away from the cruiser that had been her captor.

"Lindar!" McConnell shouted over the groan of the engines and the rattle of the hull plating. "I need constant readings on the distance and bearing to the nearest cruiser. Feed them through to me and to Hans' station. Hans, get ready to deploy and engage the twins on my mark."

"Will!" Evie shouted from the other side of the bridge as she realized what he was doing. "Are you insane? We still don't have full shielding back yet! They'll destroy us before—"

McConnell waved his hand dismissively at his first mate. "I don't think they know exactly who we are. If they did then they wouldn't have pulled us out of slipspace and boarded us. They would have pulled us out, destroyed us then and there and sifted through the wreckage for what they want." He shook his head. "No, they don't know who we are. We'd be floating through the vacuum right now if they did."

"If you do this and they report back, though..." Evie trailed off.

"We're in a fringe sector. It'll take them months to correlate the data." McConnell glanced over at her for a second. "Trust me. It's either this or we all die." Evangeline shook her head and sat back in her chair, resigning herself to McConnell's plan.

Will's eyes darted across the displays on the console, watching and managing the massive amounts of data that poured in. He rolled the ship sharply as a readout showed an increase in radiation output from the closest cruiser, narrowly dodging an array of energy beams as they lanced out from the cruiser's forward cannons. He rolled the ship again in response to a second blow though he wasn't quite fast enough and a portion of the beam caught the *King's Fall* in the rear.

"Captain!" Rut'kor shouted over the intercom. "Can you try to keep the shooting to a minimum? We're trying to lock down this final set of adjustments!"

"Sorry about that!" McConnell didn't take his hands or eyes off the data displays as he replied. "By the way, you're going to see a massive power drain here in a minute. Just a heads up!"

"A power drain? What?" there was silence for half a second before a loud string of curses came through the intercom that were creative enough to make a sailor blush. McConnell grinned again, ignoring the cursing as he pushed harder on the *King's Fall's* sublight engines.

"Come on, baby." McConnell whispered as he watched a three-dimensional display of the position of the King's Fall in relation to the Federation cruisers. He had already pulled a few hundred kilometers away from them but knew that they could easily overtake the ship at any moment. She wasn't as large as the cruisers and her top sublight speed wasn't as fast as them, either. She was, however, extremely maneuverable. With Tom's systems augmenting McConnell's already lightning-fast reflexes he was able to keep dodging most of the fire coming from the cruisers.

"Will... I don't know how much longer we're going to avoid the inevitable here." Evie gently cautioned McConnell, hoping he would listen to her.

"Good. It's time." McConnell's eyes remained glued to his screen. "Tom? Execute maneuver 'Will alpha' in ten seconds."

"Yes sir." The disembodied voice called back in response.

McConnell looked back at his weapon's officer. "Are the twins ready?"

Hans nodded. "Ready to rock and roll, Captain."

McConnell's grin returned and he turned back to face the main screen at the front of the bridge. "Good. Let's have some fun."

Two seconds later Tom engaged maneuver 'Will alpha." One of the many pre-programmed maneuvers devised by McConnell the alpha maneuver was his standard go-to whenever facing a group of enemies that needed to be shown a lesson. It was as dangerous as it was flashy, providing the enemy with the perfect opportunity to close in for the kill. Or it would have if the *King's Fall* were any other ship.

She leapt forward, her sublight engines pushing her several hundred kilometers forward in the blink of an eye. When she reached the preprogrammed distance the engines cut out and the side thrusters engaged, sending her into a spin that turned her around as though she were a 1960's muscle car pulling a bootleg turn. As the *King's Fall* spun into position the twins—a pair of massive plasma cannons built into the *King's Fall's* winglets—were already halfway through their deployment.

Each of the main cannons contained a projectile that generated its own magnetic field. The cannons, drawing power from the reactors, generated plasma fields that were shunted into the projectiles' magnetic fields. Once the plasma fields were created and stabilized the projectiles were fired, either conventionally at sublight speeds or through slipspace rifts created by the guns.

Using such rifts would cause the projectiles to emerge directly on their target but using them at short ranges had a tendency to cause violently unexpected results. Unlike controlled slipspace jumps the rifts were limited in their usefulness since they were one-way and had restrictions on how much mass could pass through them. Their advantage, though, was that dampening field had no effect on them and they couldn't be avoided in most situations. Despite this advantage McConnell decided to fire them traditionally at sublight speeds just to ensure that the target vessel would see them coming.

With the ship now stable as she continued moving away from the cruisers and the twins fully deployed and locked onto their target the time had come. McConnell roared, his voice thundering across the bridge. "NOW!"

Hans slammed his hand down on his console and the plasma cannons energized, drawing unimaginable amounts of power from the dozen reactors housed in the heart of the ship. The energy drain was so powerful that non-critical systems blinked out and the main lights flickered. Blue and green flames licked outward from the twin cannons as the plasma-encased projected fired forward at roughly eighty-five percent the speed of light.

The tenth of a second it took for the projectiles to jump the three-thousand kilometer gap between the *King's Fall* and her target gave the commander of the cruiser just enough time to recoil in horror at the sight of the bright plasma fields barreling through the blackness of space. Before he could speak, turn or react in any other way, the projectiles hit home. McConnell had wanted to fire the projectiles through normal space instead of slipspace just so that the Federation cruisers would have an extra bit of terror added to their day.

Terror, as it turned out, was in abundance.

The two projectiles tore through the targeted cruiser's shielding and into her hull, releasing the stored-up energy of their plasma fields into the vessel. The energized gas clouds ripped through emergency shielding and the deck plating like a trillion hot knives through butter. Explosions rocked the cruiser, sending fireballs swirling into space as flammable gases ignited. The fires lasted only for a brief moment, though; they were quickly snuffed out as their fuel dissipated into the vacuum.

It took under fourteen seconds for the cruiser's reactors to finally fail. The antimatter containment fields ruptured in a glorious display that caused the main screen on the bridge to flare white for an instant before slowing fading away. McConnell glanced between the main screen and his console as he worked his controls.

"Lindar? How are the other Federation vessels?"

The Ketarian science officer had been monitoring the ships ever since McConnell arrived the bridge and instantly provided an update. "Target is destroyed. Five cruisers remain." Lindar's large eyes blinked rapidly. "Two of the five are heavily damaged. The ones closest to the target. The three remaining have fallen back and broken off pursuit to lend aid to the damaged ships."

"Good. Hans, line up another one and—"

"*Captain!*" Evie stood up and stalked halfway across the bridge toward McConnell. "I think we made our point with them." McConnell started to rise from his chair, his face twisting into a masque of anger when Evangeline cut in again. "Besides, we have a rendezvous to make. For our delivery. Remember?"

McConnell froze and glanced over at the main viewer. The remains of the destroyed cruiser were slowly scattering outward. The two damaged cruisers' lights were all dark and one of them looked like its hull had been heavily breached. McConnell shook his head and sighed before trudging back to his chair.

"I don't like leaving them alive out here, Evie."

"I know." Evangeline stepped closer and sat down in the chair next to McConnell. "None of us like leaving them out here alive. But we need to make that rendezvous. Our outlay on the data was—"

"Yeah, yeah. I get it." He tilted his head slightly toward the ceiling. "Engineering? How are my reactors?"

"Ready to go, Captain!" The answer was accompanied by a pair of shouts in the background and Rut'kor had a touch of panic in his voice as he continued. "You can jump whenever you're ready! Rut'kor out!"

McConnell shook his head. "I really don't want to know what's going on down there, do I?" He glanced over at Drake who was moving back in front of the console that McConnell had been occupying only a moment before. "Helm, get us out of here. Hans, retract the twins. All hands prepare for slipspace."

The *King's Fall* turned smoothly as her twin cannons retracted smoothly back inside her wings. In the final seconds before the jump to slipspace Evie leaned over and whispered so that only McConnell could hear.

"You'll get your revenge one day, Will. We all will."

"Not today, though."

"No." Evie's eyes lit up and she gave him a devilish grin. "But when you do? Ha! It's going to be *glorious*."

Author Mike Kraus

Mike Kraus started writing when he was a child and has had a passion for making up stories for his entire life. He started publishing in 2012 and came out of the gate with a bestselling fiction series called Final Dawn which sold over a quarter-million copies. He then went on to write a non-fiction "how to" series of books under a pen name that sold another quarter-million, proving that his ability to connect with readers was not just limited to the fiction realm. He's since returned to writing primarily fiction and main genre is post-apocalyptic. Mike has, however, recently started expanding into the urban fantasy and space opera genres as well. You can find him online at http://www.mikekra.us or www.facebook.com/mikekrausbooks.

SKELETON CREW

By Mikey Campling

Aboard The Pharaon, Pantechnicon Class Transport Ship, Galactic Resettlement Corps

Chapter 1

Technical Bridge Assistant Nathan Joffe glared across the virtually deserted bridge. The Captain had called almost everyone else into the executive office, so Joffe aimed his scowl at the only other person left: Reserve Navigation Assistant Simon Parkins. The jerk was wearing dark glasses, but he wasn't fooling anyone; the snoring was a dead giveaway. Joffe plucked an empty paper cup from his workstation and crushed it in his hand before hurling it at Parkins. The projectile connected neatly with the man's left ear, and Parkins sat up with a jolt, his head swiveling from side to side. "What the hell?"

Joffe tutted. "Seriously, Parkins? You've been out of the sleep pod for three days and you're taking a nap?"

Parkins grunted and leaned over his console, his fingers hovering over the controls but never quite making contact. "I was just...running through some figures. You wouldn't understand."

"Is that a fact?" Joffe sat back in his chair, his hands behind his head. "Tell me—how the hell did a grunt like you get to serve on the bridge?"

Parkins sniffed. "Drafted. Same as you."

"That may've been how you wormed your way into the Corps, but how come you wound up in here with us qualified officers?"

"Qualified? You? All you have to do is watch the scoop monitors all day. You could train a chimp to do it."

"The gas collector array is damned important," Joffe insisted. "The GCA data is part of our scientific mission."

"Scientific my ass! We're glorified bus drivers for these settler types, nothing more."

Joffe rested his hands on his workstation and leaned forward. "Shut up, Parkins. I outrank you, and don't you forget it."

Parkins pursed his lips, and no doubt, behind those glasses, the bastard was rolling his eyes.

"Go back to sleep," Joffe snapped. He'd wanted to point out that Parkins was only on the bridge because the last guy had stepped into an airlock and opened a vein, his blood boiling away into space. But he bit back the words, returning his attention to the monitors. And his eyes went wide. For the first time in months, the GCA display showed a stark warning:

SENSOR CONTAMINATION ALERT - FOREIGN OBJECT DETECTED.

Chapter 2

Captain Alistair Coverack drummed his fingers on the glass tabletop, and although the XO was crammed with senior staff, the rhythm he tapped out was the only sound. Chief Navigation Officer Owen Taylor coughed, and Coverack fixed the man with a penetrating stare. "We're off course? How could that happen?"

All eyes went to Taylor. "The nav system disregarded the beacon and locked onto an incorrect target."

"The system?"

"Yes, sir." Taylor stiffened his spine. "But...I should've noticed it sooner. I'm sorry."

"Right. So what target *are* we headed for?"

"A marker buoy in orbit around planet V536."

Coverack frowned. "And what's on V536? Anything we can use? Could we resupply?"

"Doubtful," Taylor replied. "It's been explored and designated as habitable, but a supply run would take days, and aside from water there's nothing of value."

"I see," Coverack said, his voice tight. "And how long will it take to get back on course?"

"At current speed, thirty-two days."

Coverack clenched his jaw. *Four years and eight months to get this far, and now another month just to get back on track.*

"Shall I program in the course correction?" Taylor asked.

"Yes, goddammit!" Coverack snapped. "But I want it double-checked by the first officer." He set his mouth in a grim line, his gaze sweeping across the anxious faces of his senior officers. "No more mistakes, people. Not one. Dismissed."

Coverack sat motionless while the officers shuffled out the room, but when the door closed behind them, he pinched the bridge of his nose. Something was wrong—he could feel it in his bones. He knew this ship, knew her crew, and something, some damned thing he wasn't seeing, was not right.

"Something rotten," he whispered, and a thought came unbidden: *The Terran Alliance.* They'd fought against the galactic resettlement program, calling it a colonial invasion. They'd carried out a slew of cyber-attacks against the Resettlement Corps' HQ and caused massive disruption. But had they gone further this time? Had they targeted his ship?

Coverack swiped his fingers across the tabletop to activate the visual interface for Cleo, the ship's computer. "Cleo, show me the navigation logs for the last two months."

"Complying," a voice answered, and the air above the table was suddenly alive with a web of intersecting lines and glowing icons.

Coverack ran his hand over the mesh of data, rotating the three-dimensional display to inspect it from several angles, pinching any icons that interested him and then drawing his fingers apart to expand the web of data further. But after a few minutes he was rubbing his eyes and shaking his head. This was slow and clumsy. "What am I even looking for?" he wondered. But he knew the answer. A ship like *The Pharaon* didn't just lock onto an incorrect beacon by accident; its core systems were bulletproof: designed to run with minimal intervention. In theory, the ship could cross the galaxy with the whole crew sleeping in the pods, and still arrive at its destination on schedule. A navigation error of this magnitude couldn't be accounted for by simple human error; there were checks in place, and multiple warning systems that should've been triggered. So that left Coverack with only one possibility. "And I know exactly what I'm looking for," he murmured. "I'm looking for a saboteur."

Chapter 3

A runnel of perspiration trickled down the back of Joffe's neck and crept beneath his collar, but he could do nothing to wipe it away. It had taken him thirty minutes to squeeze into his hazmat suit—thirty minutes of mismatched gloves and fastenings that refused to cooperate—and now the damned suit clung to his sweat-slicked skin, entombing him in an impenetrable shroud of crinkling plastic.

He trudged along the corridor that ran below the engineering level, his respirator dangling from his hand and his tool belt jangling at his waist, the reassuring weight of his tools knocking against his hip with every step. As usual, the place was deserted and his footsteps rang out on the metal floor, the sound echoing across the empty space ahead and behind. This stretch of corridor was so long that the upward curve of the floor was clearly visible, and it reminded him just how huge *The Pharaon* was. Maybe that was why nobody ever came down here.

They're quick to send me though, Joffe thought. *No good deed goes unpunished*. He snorted, remembering his encounter with the science officer. Joffe had been standing beside the main entrance onto the bridge, waiting for her to return so he could report the sensor contamination straightaway, but she'd breezed past him without a glance. Feeling his moment slipping away he'd chased after her like a whipped dog and explained the situation.

"Well, go and clean it then," she'd snapped. "You know the access code, don't you?"

Joffe had tried to hide his scowl. Of course he knew the goddamned code; he checked the GCA bay all the time, didn't he? The hatches, the vents, the cables and connectors: check, check, check. That was all he ever did. Every damned day.

Now, he stopped in front of the GCA bay door and stared at the keypad. When was the last time he'd had a change in routine? *Three months ago*, he decided. That time there'd been condensation in the sensor tubes: moist air from the ship leaking through a damaged hatch seal. After replacing the seal, he'd tracked down the source of the damp air and found a fault in the bay's environmental controls. He'd fixed the problem himself rather than wait for the grease monkeys from engineering. It had taken him hours, but so what? There'd been a principle at stake.

"My bay, my rules," he muttered, and he jabbed at the keypad, tapping in the access code without thinking about it. But his gloved fingers were clumsy, and he must've got it wrong because the keypad buzzed, and a light above the buttons flashed red.

He tried again but accidentally double-tapped the third digit. "Goddammit!" Joffe pulled off his glove and in two seconds he had the door unlocked. The light on the keypad glowed green, and a recorded voice split the silence, its stern tones reminding him to wear his protective gear.

"All right, all right!" Joffe grumbled. He donned his full-face respirator and tightened the straps, checking that it sealed against his skin. The mask smelled like someone had barfed in it, and the grease-smeared visor blurred his view, but it was the best respirator he'd been able to find, and he was damned if he was going to go back and change it now.

He pulled the suit's hood into place and sealed it around his mask, then he tugged his glove back on and heaved the bay door open.

The GCA bay was cloaked in darkness, but when he stepped over the threshold the ceiling lights flared into life, their harsh glare reflected by the rows of circular hatch covers lining the far wall. Each cover was two feet across, three inches thick, and crafted from a single piece of gleaming stainless steel. Joffe closed the bay door then walked the length of the room, counting off the hatch numbers as he went.

The contaminated sensor tube lay behind hatch seventeen-C, and thankfully he wouldn't need the stepladder to access it. Joffe stopped in front of the correct cover and tapped the small display screen mounted above it. Five rows of digits flashed onto the screen, and Joffe read them off, taking his time. He'd shut this tube down from the bridge, so there was no danger of depressurizing the bay, but even so, whenever Joffe had to open a hatch, his stomach squirmed; the idea that he might be sucked into the tube and out into space was hard to shake.

Don't be a jerk, he told himself, then he pulled a wrench from his tool belt, his fingers finding the right tool from habit. The cover was secured with twelve sturdy nuts, and Joffe set to work, loosening them in the correct order. After a full turn of the wrench he could spin each nut free with a flick of his fingers and catch it in the palm of his hand. There was a knack to it, especially when you were wearing gloves, and Joffe smiled as he warmed to his task, pocketing the nuts one by one. Nobody could say he didn't keep the place shipshape and the locking nuts properly lubricated.

When Joffe removed the final nut, the cover shifted on its hinges with a metallic clunk. "There she goes," he whispered, and he took hold of the hatch control lever and pulled it downward. With a gentle hiss of escaping air, the cover swung open to reveal the circular sensor tube. Joffe peered inside, staring into the void that seemed to go on forever. In reality, each tube was only twenty yards long but they hadn't been fitted with internal illumination, perhaps because they'd been designed to need no maintenance. The tubes were equipped with automated cleaning arms, and each tube's intake was protected by a screening system, but the long journey had taken its toll. The chief engineer hadn't admitted that the screens were beyond repair, he'd just issued Joffe with a set of cleaning tools and a bundle of carbon fiber extension rods, along with a stern warning not to damage the sensors.

Here's hoping I don't need to use the damned things, Joffe thought. *I'm a technician, not a chimney sweep.* He pulled his flashlight from his tool belt and shone it into the opening. Countless rows of sensors glittered as the flashlight's powerful beam passed over them, their polished surfaces reflecting the light like the eyes of some strange swarm of nocturnal animals. Each sensor was powerful enough to detect a single atom, and each one gleamed: pristine.

"Looks fine to me," Joffe said, and his shoulders slumped. He'd had a wasted journey.

But as he swept his flashlight around the tube one last time, something caught his eye. *What the hell?* Slowly, he traced the flashlight's beam back, and there, about five yards from the hatch, a dark shape was pressed against the tube's upper surface. The object was the size of a man's fist, and it was lodged between two banks of sensors.

A frown creased Joffe's brow, his skin tugging against the respirator's seal. How had he missed something so large when it was right in front of his eyes? *And more importantly*, he thought, *how the hell am I going to get it out?*

Chapter 4

Captain Coverack woke with a start, his head snapping back against his chair's headrest. A warning sound was jangling from the computer interface, and a notification flashed red in the air in front of him:

ACCESS DENIED - FILE ENCRYPTED.

Coverack stared at the blinking message, his fingers curling tight around the chair's armrests. *I fell asleep?* he thought. *That just can't happen*. But he'd been trawling through the navigation logs for hours, finding nothing. Eventually, he'd set a diagnostic utility to run through the data, tasking it with a search for patterns of illicit activity, and then there'd been nothing to do except wait. Until now.

He touched the red icon that denoted the encrypted file and set it aside, then he massaged his eyes, rubbing some life into them. As captain, he didn't get to use the sleep pods, and despite the carefully regulated environment on the ship, the long years in space had played hell with his body's natural rhythms. Perhaps it was time he visited the medical officer again and stocked up on Stim pills. "Got to do something," he mumbled. "Can't happen again."

He took a breath then studied the red icon, twisting it around to reveal the locked file's properties. It was a log entry, a personal journal kept by one of the crew. Nothing unusual in that; the crew had every right to a little privacy, and the logs gave them an interest and a way to blow off steam. But the diagnostic routine must've had cause to red flag this particular journal, and for some reason, he couldn't see who'd created the file.

"Cleo, whose log is this?"

"I'm unable to provide that information," Cleo responded smoothly. "You have insufficient clearance."

Coverack sat up straight. "I'm the captain, for God's sake."

"Identity confirmed," Cleo replied. "You have insufficient access to interrogate this locked file. It has been encrypted locally by its owner."

"All right, so who owns it?"

"You have insuff—"

"Forget it," Coverack interrupted. "You say it's encrypted locally, but it must be on the network somewhere, so just tell me where the file is located."

"The file is stored on a personal device which is currently in quarters assigned to Reserve Navigation Assistant Simon Parkins."

"Parkins!" Coverack scraped his hand down his face. Parkins had only just been allowed onto the bridge and his access level was the lowest possible. He was no saboteur; he couldn't alter the navigation if he tried.

Coverack grabbed the red icon and started to swipe it away. But something stopped him. He let the icon go, leaving it hovering in midair. "Cleo, how long has Parkins been using his current quarters?"

"Three days. He was reassigned at his request."

Coverack's mouth was suddenly dry. "I remember. And those quarters...they belonged to..."

"Simon Parkins' quarters were previously assigned to Navigation Assistant Stephen Tibbs."

Tibbs. Captain Coverack thought about the man he'd worked alongside for years, picturing his smile, remembering his air of professional certainty, his dry wit. But those pleasant mental images were quickly corrupted by darker memories: a ruined face, its pale skin frozen solid. Empty eye sockets staring out into space. A body, slumped and lifeless in an airlock, tethered by a tangled strap wrapped around one arm and knotted many times over.

Stephen Tibbs hadn't wanted to let go of the ship, hadn't wanted to drift out into the endless darkness. But he'd been very thorough in making sure of his suicide, jamming the inner airlock door and disabling the alarm. They hadn't found him for hours.

"What's in that log, Stephen?" Coverack whispered. "What in hell have you done?"

Chapter 5

Joffe held his breath and squeezed the trigger on the carbon fiber rod, watching the foam-lined, plastic jaws of the cleaning tool close around the fist-sized foreign object. A switch locked the jaws closed, then a gentle tug was enough to pull the offending article from its resting place.

He kept his hands steady, but even so, the rod shook, and the object wobbled and threatened to slip free. Joffe froze. If he dropped it now, the damned thing might roll farther away. "Easy does it," he murmured. He rested his arm against the edge of the open hatch then resumed his task, drawing the rod through his fingers inch by inch, settling into a steady rhythm. And slowly, the mysterious object drew nearer.

"Got it!" He stepped back from the hatch, his prize dangling within his reach, but he did not take hold of it. Instead, he made his way across the room, holding the rod and its cargo in front of him. The object looked like a hunk of metal, its edges worn smooth, and it glistened under the bay lights as though damp. *Condensation*, Joffe thought. The object had been floating in the deep cold of space, and there would be moisture in the bay's air despite the environmental controls; all the more reason to seal his find safely away.

Joffe had prepared well, and a mobile containment unit sat open and ready, its sturdy wheels locked into place. Carefully, Joffe eased the object in through the doors, then he worked his way back along the rod and released the trigger. The object fell into the container with a dull thud, and he smiled. He withdrew the rod, placing it on the floor, then strode up to the containment unit and flicked the red switch on its side. With a faint hum, the thick metal doors drew closed then sealed with a series of staccato clicks. A blue light flashed on the unit's control panel: it was ready to begin its decontamination cycle.

Maybe I should report this first, Joffe thought. But he could do that later, couldn't he? He tapped the control panel to begin the process, and immediately the unit whirred into life, vibrating beneath his hand as the cycle began. Joffe exhaled noisily and rolled his shoulders, but the plastic suit hampered even that movement. He had an urge to pull the damned thing off, but he looked back at the open hatch; his work wasn't done yet.

He patted the containment unit, then turned away and took out his wrench.

***

Something beeped while Joffe was tightening the last nut on the hatch cover, and he glanced over at the containment unit. It beeped again, insistent. "Give me a second," Joffe complained. He gave the nut a final check then stowed his wrench in his belt and crossed the room. The unit beeped a third time, and the display panel showed that it had completed its decontamination cycle.

Joffe flicked the switch to open the doors, but an error message flashed on the screen:

CONTAINMENT UNIT LOCKED - ID CONFIRMATION REQUIRED.

Joffe hesitated. He'd forgotten that once it was in use, the unit needed his name and personal passcode before it would open. Maybe he should leave this to someone else, someone who was paid to deal with this sort of thing. But his lips curled in a wicked grin, and he began typing.

On Parkins' first day on the bridge, he'd left his passcode on a slip of paper at his workstation. Joffe hadn't meant to pry, but the code was in full view and somehow it had stuck in his mind. Unlike some, Joffe wasn't the kind to play pranks, but this was an opportunity to teach Parkins a valuable lesson about security. *No harm, no foul*, he thought. If using Parkins' code caused trouble, he'd own up. Eventually.

But he must've made a mistake because another message flashed up:

PASSCODE NOT RECOGNIZED.

The unit beeped.

"Don't start that again," Joffe said. He pulled off his right glove and typed the number again, and this time he was rewarded with a satisfying clatter as the unit unlocked. It took only a moment for the doors to open, and Joffe reached inside—making sure to use his gloved left hand—and took hold of the foreign object.

He weighed it in the palm of his hand. It was definitely metal, perhaps an alloy, and aside from a few scores and scratches it was smooth. It didn't appear to be damp anymore—the decontamination process would've taken care of that—but it was stained with patches of a blue-green color.

"Some kind of corrosion?" Joffe asked. But metal needed oxygen to oxidize, so where had it come from—another ship? "A planet, more likely," he decided. The metal seemed too shapeless to be from any formal structure. It was more like a chunk of magma, perhaps ejected from a planet after an asteroid strike.

He placed it back in the containment unit and closed the doors. He'd see what they made of it in the lab. And he might as well take it there himself. He had no reason to hurry back to his station on the bridge.

I guess that's the excitement over, he thought. *Job done.*

He removed his other glove then peeled back the hood from his hazmat suit. Finally, he took off his respirator and took a gulp of air. "That's better."

He laid his mask and gloves atop the mobile containment unit then bent down to unlock its wheels, but he caught sight of the cleaning tool and rods on the floor. "Goddamned mess," he sighed. It would only took him a few minutes to dismantle the carbon fiber rods and stow them in the cabinet, but the sooner he headed out, the quicker he could get out of the hazmat suit. *The hell with it*, he thought. *I'll tidy up tomorrow.* Then he unlocked the wheels and pushed the unit toward the door.

Chapter 6

Captain Coverack sat on the small metal chair in the narrow cabin that had once belonged to Stephen Tibbs. In his hand was a small tablet computer of a type that was popular with the crew. Strictly speaking, no one was supposed to attach a personal device to the ship's network, but the rule wasn't enforced; the tablets could deliver a range of games, books and movies, and they helped the crew to pass the time.

Tibbs had personalized his tablet with a few colorful stickers on the back, and when Coverack tapped the screen, a photo of Tibbs appeared, his arm around a young woman. The photo must've been taken a few years before *The Pharaon* left Earth. Tibbs was young, his expression full of hope, and he was sharing a smile with the woman—a smile full of warmth and carefree affection.

Who was she? From the look in her eyes, she must have been his partner, but Tibbs had never mentioned her. Coverack studied the photo and noticed the young woman wore a badge on her sleeve: the distinctive silver emblem of the Galactic Research Division.

She must've been something else, Coverack thought. The GRD were an elite; only the brightest were accepted into their ranks. No wonder Tibbs had looked at her with such pride in his eyes.

Coverack pushed the thought away and swiped his hand across the screen to activate the interface, half expecting the device to be locked, but the display responded, showing him the main directory. He raised his eyebrows and opened the journal folder, then tapped the first entry.

Tibbs appeared on the screen, fresh-faced, excited, and self-conscious all at the same time. "We're on our way," he started. "It's so great to be part of this mission. *The Pharaon* is an awesome ship with a crew of over eighty men and women. Plus, we're carrying five hundred passengers—settlers bound for a new home, whole families traveling together. They'll spend most of the journey in the sleep pods aboard the twin landing craft, then when we get to—"

Coverack stopped the playback and skipped forward to a more recent entry.

In this recording, Tibbs looked a little paler, but otherwise much the same. "Hi, Catrina. I was thinking about the day you set off on your mission and left me back on Earth. In a way, I've been following in your footsteps ever since. But it's time for our paths to diverge, my love. While you go ahead to explore new worlds, my route will take me to a planet that's already been—"

Again, Coverack stopped the playback. This stuff was hardly worth encrypting. He scrolled to the most recent entries then picked a file that was about a month old.

This time, Tibbs looked more familiar, his hair slightly tousled and the suggestion of stubble on his chin. His skin had that greasy sheen that developed during a long tour of duty, and his eyes glittered not with hope, but with anxiety. "I hope everything's all right, Catrina. I haven't...I haven't heard from you in a while. I guess it goes with the territory. Even so...it's difficult. Send me a message as soon as you get this. Please."

99

The screen flickered, then the next entry began playing automatically.

"I don't how much time will pass before you get this message, my love, but here I am." Tibbs sniffed and dabbed his eye with the back of his hand. "It's been months since we lost the signal from your ship. Comms said you were out of range, but I know different. Something's wrong, I'm sure of it, otherwise you'd have found a way. But I'll keep looking for you, my love. There must be some trace, some sign that will tell me where you are. I'll keep searching. I'll get this message to you somehow, no matter how—"

Coverack closed the file, unable to look any longer at Tibbs' pathetic expression. What had the man expected? He must've known that he wouldn't see his partner again for many years. Her mission would certainly be longer than his, and fraught with danger. Only a fool would hold on for so long; a fool or a man driven by some dark need, some deeply buried vein of desperation. And who knew what such a man might do?

A chill crept across Coverack's skin, and his finger hovered over the tablet's screen before touching down on the most recent log entry.

The man who appeared was a ghostly parody of Tibbs' former self; his face drawn and lined with worry, his mouth twitching, and his dark eyes empty, devoid of all emotion.

"He was a wreck," Coverack whispered. "Why didn't I notice?"

As if in answer, Tibbs' voice echoed from the tablet's tiny speaker, "I wonder who's watching this. Perhaps it's the captain. I hope so. I need you to hear this, Captain. I want you to know how sorry I am." He paused, his eyes darting from side to side. "By now, you've probably discovered what I've done, but you won't understand. So here goes." He took a breath. "I found a signal, a distress call from my wife's ship. I should've reported it, but I didn't. I took a different course of action, you might say. I couldn't leave her out there, and there was no one else who could help, no other ships in this sector. So I reprogrammed the navcom. I switched out the target, ignoring the beacon and locking onto the distress call instead. It wasn't easy, but I knew what I was doing and I covered my tracks." Tibbs closed his eyes for a moment, and when he opened them, they glistened with tears. "All for nothing. When we neared the source of the distress signal, I finally understood the truth. Her ship is gone. Nothing left but debris and empty space. The signal came from a buoy, perhaps launched as a last resort. And I've dragged hundreds of people across the galaxy for no reason, perhaps endangering them all." Tibbs hesitated, his red-rimmed eyes staring out from screen. "After all, whatever happened to my dear Catrina's ship may still be lying in wait for you. I hope not, Captain. But whatever happens, I'm sorry."

Then the screen froze, leaving Coverack to stare at Tibbs' final, sad smile.

Chapter 7

Joffe scooped up a lump of egg with his plastic fork and shoveled it into his mouth. He chewed slowly, trying to recall the taste of real eggs. This synthetic stuff wasn't right, he decided, but it wasn't bad. The bacon too, was kind of spongy, but he'd gotten to like it. A little hot sauce on the side of his plate, and his day was getting off to good start. He scratched the palm of his right hand absentmindedly as he looked around the room, and decided that breakfast in the officers' mess was pretty much the highlight of his day.

"Hey, Nathan, how's it going?" Parkins sat down next to him and placed his tray on the table, knocking Joffe's arm.

Joffe grimaced and rubbed his elbow. "Watch it, you jerk!"

"Sorry, man. I'm starved." Parkins picked up his fork, then his face fell. "Shoot! I forgot my drink." He stood and offered Joffe a hesitant smile. "Can I get you a cup of something?"

Joffe considered this for a moment, then his expression softened. "Sure, I'll have a cup of brown."

"Okay. You want creamer?"

"No way," Joffe said. "That stuff gives me cramps. I like my brown, black."

"Got it."

He ate another lump of egg and watched Parkins retreating toward the drink dispensers. The guy wasn't so bad really. He was a fish out of water, promoted beyond his competence, that was all. *Was I like that once?* he wondered. But when he watched Parkins return with two paper cups and a hopeful smile on his young features, he pushed the thought away. Some people were eager to please; Joffe had never been one of them.

"There you go," Parkins said, sitting down and sliding a cup toward Joffe. "One cup of brown, almost hot."

"Thanks." He took a sip and Parkins followed suit.

"Tastes like tea, today, doesn't it?" Parkins asked.

Joffe shook his head. "No idea. Sure as hell isn't coffee, I'll tell you that."

The two men studied their drinks until Parkins broke the silence. "You're early today. I'm usually done by the time you show up."

"Ever wonder if I do that on purpose?" Joffe replied, but when Parkins' face fell, he relented. "Just kidding, Parkins. I'm a heavy sleeper is all. Well, usually, anyhow." He let out a grunt and scratched at his hand. "Not last night, though. Didn't sleep worth a damn."

"Stress?"

Joffe almost laughed. "In my job?" He looked away and carried on eating, but Parkins persisted.

"What then?"

"Nothing really. It's just…" He showed Parkins the palm of his hand, and he couldn't help but scratch at the red, flaking skin. "It's just an allergy or something, but it itches like hell."

Parkins' eyebrows drew together. "Did you show that to someone?"

"I just showed you, didn't I?" Joffe rubbed at his right forearm.

"No. I mean, someone in medical. You need to get that looked at, man."

"Maybe later." Joffe picked up his cup. "Right now I need to finish my brown. I'd hate for it to get slightly less tepid." And the two men shared a smile.

***

The bridge was quiet again and Joffe looked over at Parkins. "Looks like it's just you and me again, huh?"

"Yup," Parkins replied. "Skeleton crew, that's us."

Joffe drummed his fingers on his console then inclined his head toward the XO. "Any idea what's going on in there?"

"Maybe something to do with this new course correction."

"Yeah, I heard about that." Joffe frowned. "What's the problem?"

Parkins glanced over his shoulder before replying, then he lowered his voice. "Between you and me, we're way off course—I mean, seriously headed in the wrong direction." He paused, his eyes twinkling. "The captain's mad as hell. He had Taylor and the first officer pull an all-nighter to put it right."

Joffe let out a low whistle. "This ship's going to hell."

"Tell me about it." Parkins shook his head. "You know what? When you were out, the captain hauled *me* into the XO. He was just about ready to lose his shit."

Joffe raised his eyebrows. "Really? He wasn't trying to pin the nav problem on you, was he?"

"No way. It was some bullshit about a power outage in the lab. He was blathering on about some kind of container, and didn't I know the protocol for foreign objects."

Joffe gave a guilty start. He'd meant to set the record straight about the passcode and the containment unit, but when he'd arrived in the lab, there'd been no one there, so he'd just left the unit for them to find.

"I told him I hadn't been anywhere near the lab," Parkins went on. "I was at my station all day, and the logs prove it."

"About that," Joffe said, but Parkins wasn't listening.

"Look, Nathan, it's here in black and white." Parkins tapped his console, and his face fell.

"Listen—" Joffe began, but Parkins cut him off with a look.

"My console's dead."

"What?"

"I think..." Parkins said, "I think we just lost the nav system."

Joffe stared at him; the man's face was white as a sheet. "Relax. It's probably just another power outage. Give it a second."

But Parkins was already out of his seat and heading to the navigation officer's station. He tapped the main nav console. "This one's dead too."

"Let me see." Joffe stood and went to Parkins' side. Sure enough, the whole console was dark. Joffe ran his hands over the control panel, but there was no response. He grunted. "Must be a loose connection or something." He knelt down and opened the access panel, then touched each module in turn, checking they were pushed home.

"I don't think you should do that," Parkins said. "I'll go fetch someone."

"It's fine," Joffe replied. "And you heard what they said—they don't want to be disturbed."

"But this is an emergency." Parkins' voice was high and unsteady. "I really think we should—"

"Stay calm," Joffe interrupted. He replaced the panel and stood slowly, his brow creased in thought. "Sometimes it's the simplest things that get overlooked, like a module coming free from its socket." He tried the control panel again, but as before, the console remained stubbornly dark.

"Aw hell!" Parkins moaned. "You left dirty fingermarks all over the screen. Taylor will know we touched it." He set to wiping the panel with his sleeve. "What is this, oil? It won't come off."

"Sorry." Joffe rubbed his hands on his uniform. "It's this thing on my hand. It makes me sweat."

"Still? Didn't you see the MO? Man, I told you to go this morning."

"Yeah, I know. I'll go in a minute. We just need to figure this out."

"No, you'll go now."

"But, the nav—"

"Forget it," Parkins interrupted. "I'm going to call the XO. I won't tell them you opened the panel, but it'll be easier to keep your name out of it if you're not here when they come back."

Joffe heaved a sigh. "All right. You win, Parkins. I'll see you later."

Parkins acknowledged him a nod, then Joffe turned and headed for the door.

Chapter 8

Coverack looked around the officers assembled in his XO and saw pain and confusion. "Tibbs let us all down," he said firmly, "but we need to move on. We're experiencing system failures and power outages across the ship, and disturbingly, we've found inconsistencies in our audit trail that suggest someone covering their tracks. If these issues are connected, there could be someone aboard who intends, for whatever reason, to disrupt our mission."

A murmur ran through his audience, but he quieted them with his raised hand. "We've suffered problems in the lab, the officers' quarters and the mess, even on the bridge, so we must all be on our guard. If you detect anything suspicious, bring it to my attention immediately."

A notification sounded on his console, and he tapped the screen. "What is it?"

"It's Parkins, sir. Sorry to interrupt, but you're needed on the bridge. There's something wrong with the nav system."

Coverack looked up and barked, "Back to your stations. Now!"

Chapter 9

Joffe watched Doctor Giadrini hurry into the medical bay and take a seat opposite him. "Sorry to keep you waiting," she said. "I was in the XO."

Joffe shrugged. "No problem."

"Okay, how can I help you?"

"It's my hand." Joffe showed her his hand, and his cheeks flushed. He shouldn't be embarrassed, but his palm and fingers were raw and inflamed, and the sight sickened him. Giadrini studied his hand. "How long has it been like this?"

"Since last night. It itches like crazy. Kept me awake."

"It looks like an allergic reaction, but before I start running tests, have you any idea what might've caused it?"

Joffe scratched absently at his forearm. "I got kind of sweaty yesterday. Maybe that set it off."

"Unlikely," Giadrini said, "but tell me more."

"I was in the hazmat suit and—"

"What?" Giadrini interrupted. "A hazmat suit! Why didn't you tell me that in the first place?"

"Sorry, I didn't think." Joffe shifted uncomfortably. "I was real careful. I decontaminated everything—"

Giadrini held up her hand to cut him off, then she looked him in the eye. "Why were in a hazmat suit? What were you handling?"

Joffe swallowed then recounted the essential points of his time in the GCA bay, being careful to explain how cautious he'd been.

Giadrini stood slowly. "Are you okay to walk? No dizziness? Fainting spells?"

"I'm fine apart from this damned itch. Just tired."

"I want you to follow me." Giadrini took a step back.

"All right." Joffe stood and rubbed at his upper arm and shoulder. "Where are we going?"

"I want you to rest for a while. We have a quiet room you can use."

"I don't need to rest. I don't understand."

"It's just a precaution. But I need you to stay for a while until we figure this out." She backed across the room, keeping her eyes on him. "And I want you to think about everywhere you've been since you went to the GCA bay."

Joffe took a step toward her. "There was breakfast in the mess. Before that, I was in my quarters. I visited the lab yesterday." He paused to rub at his neck, his fingers clawing at the skin. "And the bridge."

Giadrini's eyes went wide as she recalled the captain's words: *problems in the lab, the officers' quarters and the mess, even on the bridge.* She stepped back again and came up against the wall, almost stumbling in surprise. She yelped and Joffe hurried to help.

"No!" she cried, and Joffe stopped in his tracks. For a moment, no one spoke, then Giadrini put a hand on her chest, regaining her composure. "I'm sorry, but I don't need help. I'm fine." She reached out to open the glass door next to her. "Go inside and take a rest, okay?"

Joffe nodded slowly. "All right, but I still don't see what this is about."

"Probably nothing, but please do as I ask." She ushered Joffe into the room and shut the door behind him.

"Thanks," Joffe said, but when he turned around and peered through the glass, the doctor was already hurrying away.

Joffe stared into the empty medical bay, but he soon tired of waiting and crossed to the bed to sit down, running his hands over the crisp, white sheet. The itching was worse now, like a thousand hot needles piercing his skin, but the sheet felt cool, and he swung his feet up from the floor and laid down, resting his head on the soft pillow. *That's nice*, he thought. *But what the hell got into the doc?*

He closed his eyes, thinking back over their disjointed conversation. She'd freaked out when he'd told her about the GCA bay, about how he'd gone back yesterday to tidy up. He'd hoped to impress her with his professionalism, his attention to detail. He'd wanted her to know that he wasn't the kind of man to leave his workplace in a mess with tools lying on the floor.

The cleaning tools!

Joffe's eyes flew open. When he'd stowed the tools away, he'd noticed that the plastic jaws had been damaged, the foam lining degraded and crumbling away. The jaws had held the foreign object so perhaps... He shook his head. He would've worn his gloves to tidy up. Of course he would. He was careful. Professional. He always wore his gloves.

And as he stared up at the ceiling, he scratched his hand.

Chapter 10

A shudder ran through the bridge, and Coverack's chair bucked beneath him as if attempting to throw him from his seat. The first officer cried out, but Coverack simply sat back and opened a channel from his console. "Engineering, report."

The only reply was a crackle of static, then a distorted voice broke through: "...an organic growth. We can't stop it. It's spread into control systems, comms, navigation, propulsion. Main engines are heading for critical overload. We can't shut them down. There's nothing we can—" The message cut off abruptly, and when Coverack looked around, every officer was staring at him in silence.

"My console is unresponsive," he stated. "As of now, we have lost control of the ship." He paused. "If our main engines go critical, *The Pharaon* will be destroyed, but the landers can make it to V536. I'm about to give the order to abandon the ship. If you have some reason to disagree with my assessment of the situation, now's the time to say so."

No one moved a muscle nor said a word.

"Very well," Coverack said. "Our first duty is to get the landing craft underway. Separation takes ten minutes. In that time, we must get as many crew aboard the landers as we can. Any remaining crew will take to the escape pods. Is that clear?"

There was a chorus of agreement.

"Good luck, everyone. Do your duty." Coverack paused for a split-second, then, "Abandon ship."

Chapter 11

Joffe sat up with a start, the alarms loud enough to pierce his skull. "Oh my God! Abandon ship!"

He hurried to the door and tried the handle, but it was locked, and there was no one on the other side of the glass. If he was going to get out, he'd have to do it himself.

He scanned the room. There was a chair by the bed, but it was plastic and looked flimsy. The bed though, had a metal frame and he knelt beside it. The frame was complex, made from a series of adjustable sections bolted together. He selected a steel tube held by only two bolts and tried to loosen the nuts by hand, but they were fastened too tight and his fingers were slick with sweat. If only he had his tool belt now! *Focus!* he told himself. *Use your brain.*

He jumped to his feet and went to the wall cabinet. It wasn't locked, and he wrenched the door open, almost ripping it from its hinges. Bandages and bottles spilled to the floor, but Joffe paid them no heed. He rifled through the cabinet and his hands closed on something solid: a set of stainless steel scissors. Did the bed's bolts have slotted heads, or were they plain?

Joffe knelt beside the bed, scissors in hand. "Yes!" He was in luck. Hands shaking, he found the correct bolt and inserted the scissors' blades into its slot. They fitted well enough, but as soon as he tried to turn them, they slipped free.

Cursing, Joffe gritted his teeth and tried again, pressing the scissors home until the metal bit into his hand. "Come on!" he growled. And this time, when he turned the scissors, the bolt began to move. *Almost there!* With his other hand, he reached around and held the nut, but it was still too tight to loosen by hand.

He adjusted his grip, reapplied the scissors and turned the bolt again until he felt the nut give, then he held the bolt still and spun the nut free until it fell onto the floor. He turned his attention to the second bolt, and a moment later he yanked the steel tube from the frame.

Joffe leapt to his feet and ran to the door, then he swung the tube with both hands and struck the glass with all his strength. "Shit!" His blow bounced back harmlessly without even making a scratch. *Toughened glass*, he thought. But he wasn't beaten yet. The door's lock was mechanical: an assembly of rods and levers. And what had been put together could surely be smashed apart. Joffe went to work on the lock, his arms a blur of frenzied motion, unleashing a barrage of blows as steel rang out against steel.

The handle gave way first, bending beneath his onslaught then coming free from the door, but still Joffe carried on. The lock's housing buckled and distorted, the tortured metal giving way with agonizing slowness.

Joffe was exhausted, his arm muscles on fire, but he would not give in. "Come, on, you, bastard!" he yelled, his words keeping time with his relentless assault on the lock. And then, with a sharp crack, the battered mechanism surrendered, its housing shattered almost beyond recognition.

Joffe let out a cry, and when he shoved the door with his shoulder, it shuddered open.

"I've done it," he breathed. Now all he had to do was make it off the ship.

He staggered across the medical bay then let himself out into the corridor. The place was empty, but in the distance he could hear shouts and the sound of running. He was not alone.

I can make it, he told himself. *I have to. At least, I have to try.*

Chapter 12

The landing craft lurched from side to side as if shaken by a mighty hand. The cargo bay was crammed to capacity, officers and crew standing shoulder to shoulder, and Chief Navigation Officer Owen Taylor stumbled into the man next to him. "My God! That was *The Pharaon*," Taylor said. "Her engines must've blown. She's gone."

His neighbor shuddered, and Taylor said, "Hey, are you okay?"

The man's head was down, his arms wrapped tight around his chest, and when he mumbled something, Taylor had to bend down to hear him. "Did you say Parkins? He stayed on the bridge, trying to help. Maybe he made it to the pods."

The man buried his face in his hands.

"Don't worry," Taylor said. "You'll find him when we make planetfall."

The man looked up, his face pale, glistening with sweat.

"It's you!" Taylor breathed. "I didn't realize. You look like hell. What happened?"

But Nathan Joffe simply hung his head. And a bead of perspiration dripped from his brow onto the floor, where it seeped between two panels and disappeared.

Author Mikey Campling

Mikey has been a financial systems programmer, a website builder, a full-time dad, and a primary school teacher. As a teacher, his particular interest was in encouraging children to love books, and his lively readings were always popular. His proudest moment was when the parents of a boy with a learning difficulty told him that their son was begging for bedtime stories for the first time.

Today, Mikey writes stories with characters you can believe in, and plots you can sink your teeth into. His style is vivid but never flowery; every word packs a punch. His stories are complex, thought-provoking, atmospheric and grounded in real life.

Mikey has always read widely, and his work spans many genres, but all his books have one thing in common: respect for the reader. His motto: Amateurs strive until they get it right; professionals strive until they can't get it wrong.

The best way to sample Mikey's work is to sign up for his readers' group, which is called The Awkward Squad. You'll receive free books and stories, plus a newsletter that's actually worth reading. Learn more here: http://mikeycampling.com/freebooks/

 EPIPHANY
A 'Space Magi' Prequel

By Andrew Dobell

'That's it, what are you standing there holding your dicks for? You're dismissed. Head to the hangar bay and get yourselves over to that Aether ship before I kick your asses,' Sergent Morton barked at them.

'Yes, sir,' Dain Lambi and his squad chanted back with a salute before they about turned and filed out the room, falling into a more relaxed group as they navigated along the corridors of moon base Canis towards the hanger bay. Dain stayed towards the back of the group and attempted to adjust his armour which was digging into him a bit. He'd rushed and maybe panicked a bit when the call came through about the briefing.

It was to be their first mission as a Wraith Squad. They were fresh out of training, and the rest of the squad were eager to get out there and kick some Nomad ass. While Dain was equally keen to contribute and wanted to serve in the Wraiths just as much as his teammates, he felt sure he was probably the most nervous of the group and wanted a more gentle introduction to the rigours of fighting the enemy.

His heart had been pounding when he'd walked into that briefing room. He'd imagined all kinds of horrific scenarios where they would be sent to some distant frontline somewhere in the ass end of space to fight and die.

As it happened, he needn't have worried, as it looked they were going to ease them into things with a simple escort duty of a low-risk VIP called Dasha from the Sol based Ormond family.

To say that Dain felt relieved would be an understatement. He was no coward, and he wanted to serve as much as the rest of his squad, but real life combat was a scary thought.

'I can't believe it, fuckin' escort duty on some no-name family ship heading to Sol, of all places? Fuck me. I wanted some action, not this boring ass shit,' Braydi said, spitting everywhere as he complained to the group. Of everyone in his squad, Braydi was the one Dain probably liked the least. All of his teammates were typical hard-ass soldiers in their own way, but Braydi was a straight up bully and was prone to mouthing off way too much. Dain did his best to keep his distance from him whenever possible.

'You'll get your action soon enough,' squad leader Griff answered him. Dain liked Griff the most. He was a tough and hard as nails soldier, but he was also fair and level-headed. He often stepped in to keep Braydi from doing something stupid and had stood up for Dain a few times. Griff understood that everyone on the squad was valuable, no matter who they were. Dain appreciated this.

'Yeah, sure. I bet lamby-pie here is happy, though, hay?' Braydi said to him.

Dain looked up but didn't react. Braydi had been calling him names since the first day they'd met, so he was used to it now.

'Got yourself a nice easy mission, haven't you? Just what you were hoping for, I bet,' said Lexi. She was easily the most glamorous of the three girls in the squad, but also the one he liked the least. She often sided with Braydi and thought nothing of berating Dain whenever she felt like it.

'It might not be as easy as you think,' Dain said, answering her back. He felt confident that every member of this squad could kick his ass if they wanted to, even Lexi. He worked hard, exercised and ate the right stuff, but he was never going to be a muscle-bound mountain like Jaik, the biggest man in their squad. True, he could get one of the Magi to enhance him, but he didn't. He just wasn't keen on the idea, and preferred to get there himself, through his own hard work rather than cut corners.

Lexi wrinkled her nose at his reply. She probably wasn't expecting him to answer her back. Usually, he just ignored their comments to stop things from escalating, knowing he'd get beaten to a pulp if he started a fight. But even with the good news of the escort mission, his nerves were still on edge, and he just wasn't having their crap today.

'The kid's right, this might not be the easy ride you think it is. Who knows what could happen on the trip from Sirius to Sol. That's a lot of void to travel through,' Elva said. She was Griff's right-hand woman, as tough as any of the men and not someone who took any shit. When Braydi got out of control, she was just as likely to step in as Griff was.

'No, it's not,' Braydi said. 'We're still inside the Sol protectorate, what the hell's going to happen to us with such a short jump?'

'Well, we'll have to wait and see, won't we,' Griff said.

'Sure, boss,' Braydi answered Griff before turning to Lexi and addressing her in a lower tone. 'Shit, girl, this is bullshit. When we gonna see some action?'

Dain ignored him and concentrated on fixing his armour, and by the time they reached the hanger bay, he was starting to feel a little more comfortable in his suit. They'd picked up their weapons along the way and walked into the cavernous space of the hanger bay. Aetheric craft were spread around, some on the ground, others hanging in space, waiting to embark on their latest mission. Dain always found it fascinating walking in here and seeing the huge array of ships and the various designs that were employed. You could always spot the Magi ships as they were always the most outlandish and crazy in design.

A deckhand directed them over to a ship sitting on the ground. It was a small transport designed for ferrying people around between ships and planetary bodies. Dain had been on one of these plenty of times before and followed his squad as they marched over towards it.

As they'd made their way over here, Braydi had given up complaining all the time and had settled into a grumpy acceptance of the mission they were given. Dain had breathed a sigh of relief at this as the incessant moaning was becoming annoying, not that he'd do anything about it. Standing up to Braydi was asking for a beating.

Instead, Dain did what he usually did and kept quiet. He just followed along, only speaking when it was strictly needed and went through the drills he knew so well by now. Their training had been intense and had lasted for several years. Half the people he'd joined up with had dropped out, but Dain had been determined to make it. He wasn't the strongest, or even the most capable, but he made up for it in pure grit and determination.

He was desperate to serve and to make a difference. He'd idolised the Wraiths since he was a boy growing up on Sirius Alpha.

He'd heard about their exploits and their heroic deeds, and it just sounded amazing. A life of adventure and heroics fighting against the enemies of mankind, what more could a boy want?

Of course, as he'd grown up and lost the innocence of youth. He'd realised how dangerous it really was, but by then, he'd already made his choice, and the threat to life and limb would never be enough to put him off.

He remembered playing with Porsha, his best friend growing up, pretending to be Wraiths in the woods near their homes, hunting down Nomads in the bushes. She was older than he was, and when she had her Epiphany in her early teens, the Magi arm of the Wraiths took her in for training years before Dain joined up.

Dain, like most humans, was an Initiated Riven. He knew about Magic and the Magi, but was Riven from it, separated from it and was unable to use it. He wasn't a Magus. He was in his early twenties now, and most people had their Epiphany and became a Magus in their teens when their body was already going through changes.

Dain had come to terms with not being a Magus a long time ago, but he often thought about Porsha and wondered what she was doing now? She'd been in the Wraiths years before he'd joined, so she'd be on active duty by now as a Magus. But the galaxy was vast, and she could be anywhere.

Dain sat in one of the free bucket seats in the transport and watched through the window as their transport rose up and flew out of the docking bay and into space, leaving the moon, Canis, behind.

The trip over to the Ormond family ship was short, and as the transport banked around the frigate, Dain looked out the window beside him to look at the craft that would be their first mission.

The ship was long and sleek with sweeping lines of white and gold. It wasn't a huge ship, but was big enough to have a docking bay that their transport could fly into. Opulent ships like this were not uncommon amongst the fleets of the powerful families, and the family member that was aboard this ship wasn't even that high ranking within the Ormond family.

Their transport swept around and floated silently into the docking bay at the rear of the family ship. As it slowed to a stop and softly alighted on the docking bay floor, Dain could see three people waiting for them, one of whom he recognised, even though he hadn't seen her for years.

Standing just outside the ship was Porsha, his childhood friend. She wore black and deep red robes that had a Magus feel to them with her long dark hair falling about her shoulders, framing her soft features.

She looked all business today, though. Dain wondered if she'd recognise him and what she'd say to him. Shit, what would he say to her, for that matter? Was she going to be their Magus for this mission?

'Who's the hottie?' Braydi whistled as he looked out the window as well. He was clearly referring to Porsha, as the other two people were men.

'Who?' Jaik asked and turned to look as well. 'Oh, yeah, she's a babe for sure.'

Dain grimaced at the comments of his squad mates, why did they have to be so crass?

'She ain't all that,' Lexi muttered, apparently unhappy with the guys ogling another girl.

'I believe that's our Magus,' Griff said, peering out the window as well. 'Let's find out, shall we?'

'Sounds good to me, boss,' Braydi said to Giff, before turning to Jaik and speaking to him in a low mutter. 'Let's go and probe her depths, hey?'

Jaik chuckled. It was all just a load of macho bullshit, of course. They wouldn't do anything to Porsha, not least because she was a Magus and would be able to rip them to shreds with a thought, but Dain didn't like it. Porsha was his friend, and he hated hearing them talk about her like that.

Dain scowled at Braydi, but they weren't paying any attention to him as they walked out of the transport and down the ramp at the back. Dain huffed, picked up his rifle, and fell into step with this squad, his heart in his mouth as he went. He'd thought about this moment so many times. How would he say hello? How would she react to him? He'd built it up into something much bigger than it should be, of course, but he couldn't help it.

He supposed he'd always had a bit of a crush on Porsha. Even as a young boy, he'd enjoyed her company. She was someone he had just loved being around. He probably didn't know what it was he was feeling back then, but he was well aware of what it was now. But that was a long time ago, and they had not parted company on the best of terms.

Dain stared at the floor as he walked down the ramp and fell into rank beside Lexi on the end of the row.

'Welcome, Wraiths,' said one of the two men. He was a slightly more mature man in an officer's uniform. He looked like he had probably seen service with the Wraiths for a long time, but Dain didn't know who he was. 'I'm Sergeant Major Malax, and this is the Zephyr, one of the Ormond family's ships. I know this is your first mission, but I also know you will do us proud. Your Magus for the trip will be Porsha,' he said, looking her way as he spoke. Porsha, who had been looking intently at the floor, listening to the Sergeant talk, looked up and smiled with a nod. Suddenly, her eyes fixed on Dain and widened slightly as she saw him for the first time.

Dain gave her a nervous smile and felt his breath catch. He caught some movement to his left and glanced at his squad, some of whom were sneaking looks at him.

Shit, he thought. He suddenly remembered that they knew about Porsha. He'd told them about his childhood friend, who had joined up as a Magus several times. They'd poked fun at him about it before, but now here she was, stood before them.

'And this is Assistant Pervik,' Malax continued, referring to the other man there. 'He's part of the family's staff on board this ship, and he will be your main point of contact. You know your mission, and Pervik will deal with any questions regarding the details of the mission. Good luck, Wraiths,' he finished and backed away, only for Porsha to move in towards him and whisper something.

The sergeant answered, and Porsha's face fell. She'd been denied something. Dain pressed his lips together in consternation. If he had to guess, he'd bet she'd just asked to be reassigned and been refused the request.

'Good day to you, men,' Assistant Pervik said as he stepped up while the other two spoke in hushed tones. 'It's a pleasure to have you aboard. Dasha Ormond is grateful to have you along as his official escort security force. We have a room ready for you, which I'm sure will be suitable for the trip,' he said.

Dain looked over to Pervik and raised his eyebrows. A room? He'd assumed they would be patrolling the ship, not stuck in a room.

'A... err... A room?' Griff asked, voicing Dain's thoughts.

'But of course,' Pervik said brightly. 'Only the best for the Wraiths. It has all the amenities that you will need, you will be quite happy in there. Trust me,' he said.

'Okay, men, let's go,' Porsha said as she walked back up to the group. The sergeant was already walking over towards a portal that Dain could see a short distance away, flanked by a couple of Wraiths.

'Of course, Magus,' Pervik said, with a slight bow. 'This way,' he said, and moved off. Porsha led the way, keeping pace with Pervik while the squad fell into pairs behind them. Lexi was next to Dain where he stood at the back of the column, with Braydi and Lana in front of them.

'That's your girlfriend, isn't it, Lamby-pie?' Braydi muttered back to him.

Dain looked up at the smirking face of Braydi and felt his stomach tie itself in a knot. He hating giving leverage to anyone, and this was something that Braydi would relish.

''Oh, it is, isn't it. She's your childhood sweetheart, isn't she,' Lexi said, suddenly catching up.

Dain sighed. 'Friend. Childhood friend,' he clarified, no longer feeling like he could just take it as they dished it out.

'Yeah, right. As if you wouldn't bend her over and give her a good...'

'Shut up!' Dain said.

'Oooh, touched a sensitive spot, I think,' Lexi said.

'Quiet back there,' Griff called from the front of the squad.

Lexi and Braydi smirked but fell silent. Dain cursed to himself silently and shook his head. Fuck, he thought. That was all he wanted. This was meant to be an easy mission, something to ease them into active duty, but it had already turned into a cluster fuck before it had even started.

He now regretted talking to some of his squad mates about Porsha, wishing he'd kept it to himself instead. But everyone seemed to know everything about each other in the squad. It was surprisingly difficult to keep secrets from each other when you lived in such close proximity.

Pervik led them from the docking bay, along a gently curving corridor made from graceful sweeping lines of gold on white panels. The ship was beautiful. Their squad looked very out of place in here in their black utilitarian armour. As they walked, they passed a few of the crew. They all looked like graceful models in their perfectly pressed stylish uniforms of white and gold. Body modification wasn't uncommon, and there were lots of options available, not least of which were cosmetic procedures to modify your looks, skin, and hair. You could change your appearance to anything you desired, although most humans didn't stray too far from the ideals of beauty. There were exceptions, of course, and there were plenty of people who chose not to undergo such modification.

Dain himself had so far opted not to go through such a change, as he felt perfectly content for the time being and didn't like the idea of not looking like himself anymore.

Although, if he'd been through such a procedure, maybe Porsha wouldn't have recognised him and things might have been easier. Well, whatever, these were all pointless what-ifs.

Pervik led them out into a large central area of the ship that had several small groups of people stood about, all of them in the most stunning outfits Dain had ever seen. He knew the families, like the Ormonds, were extravagant, but this was amazing.

He wondered if their client, Dasha, was out there in that room.

Pervik led them away, down another corridor to a T-junction, and to a door just across from them. He opened it and led them inside.

'So, as you can see, you have everything you need for the trip in here. Comfortable seating, refreshments, and hygiene facilities at the back,' he said as everyone walked in.

'Assistant Pervik, may I have a word with you?' Griff said to the man once everyone was inside.

'Of course, what seems to be the issue?' Pervik asked.

'Let's walk, shall we,' Griff said, guiding Pervik back outside.

'I'll go with you,' Porsha said, stepping up to them and following them out the door.

For the moment, the team were preoccupied with investigating the room and checking out the food and drink that was available, so with Griff and Porsha gone, Dain went and sat on one of the soft, but stylish seats with his rifle across his lap.

Well, this was turning out to be a bit of a stressful first mission, he thought to himself.

When Porsha had become a Magus in those last few weeks before she left for the academy, their friendship had become a little more strained, and in the end, they hadn't been on the best of terms, he remembered. The reason was simple enough, looking back. He'd been jealous. Porsha was going to join the wraiths before him, and not only that, she would be a Magus rather than a grunt. She would outrank him from day one. At the time, he'd found that tough to deal with, and when she'd finally left, they weren't really speaking much.

Well, he thought to himself, that wasn't strictly true. The truth of it was that he wasn't speaking to her. Porsha had insisted that they would always be friends and that her being a Magus wouldn't change anything, but Dain hadn't been so sure.

After she'd gone, he'd eventually come to regret what he'd done, but by then, it was too late, and the lines of communication between them never really opened up again. He'd never stopped thinking about her, though, even now, years later, he had always wondered what happened to her. As it turned out, she'd followed the path she'd always said she would. She wanted to serve and to be on the front lines in much the same way that he did.

They'd taken very different routes to get there, but that was the only real difference between them.

'So then, short stuff, you going to introduce me to your lady friend when she gets back?' Braydi said, walking up to him and perching on the arm of a nearby seat.

'And why would I do that?' Dain asked, looking up at the smirking brute.

'Because she's hot. Hey, I bet she can do some sick shit in bed with her Magic. What do you think?'

Dain sighed and tried to keep his anger from bubbling over as he took a controlled breath.

'Don't worry,' Braydi said to him in a low voice. 'I'll teach her a thing or two.'

'Fuck off, Braydi,' Dain blurted out, his anger finally getting the better of him and he started to see red. He'd had it with this motor-mouthed idiot.

'The fuck, you say?' Braydi asked, standing up.

'You heard me. You'd best not get shot on one of our missions, cos I'll just leave you to bleed out,' Dain spat.

'Not if I smash your face in first, you little...'

'You little what?' Griff said from behind Dain.

He hadn't heard the door open, he'd been so focused on Braydi. As Dain watched, Braydi pressed his lips together and backed up, looking up towards Griff.

'Nothing, sir,' Braydi said.

Dain turned around to see Griff with Porsha standing behind him, both of them looking over towards them. Dain locked eyes with Porsha for a moment before she broke the shared gaze and walked away to one side of the room where she poured herself a drink. Griff walked up to them.

'I won't stand for any shit on our first mission,' he said in a low tone to them. 'I want this to go smoothly and without upset. This is a nice easy mission; let's not stuff it up before we've even got underway.'

'Yes, sir,' Dain and Braydi said in unison.

'I don't want to see you anywhere near each other for the rest of this mission, got it? Now, get your ass over there, Braydi, and grow the fuck up,' Griff said.

Braydi nodded and slunk away quietly. Dain watched him go while still standing alongside Griff.

'You alright?' Griff asked quietly.

'I'm fine, sir, nothing happened.'

'See to it that it doesn't, soldier,' Griff said before he walked away. Dain looked over and saw Porsha watching him. She looked away and focused on her steaming hot drink. Dain sighed. He wanted to go and say hello to her, but he wasn't sure if she wanted to speak to him again after all this time. The way he'd been with her when she'd left was ridiculous, but then, he'd only been young and he'd not known how to cope with it.

Those feelings had stewed inside him for years now, and putting them aside would not be terribly easy.

'Okay, listen up, everyone,' Griff said to the room. Everyone stopped to look. 'It looks like we're confined to this room. They don't want us wandering around the ship making the place look ugly, so, we're to stay in here. The ship is about to get underway and is apparently due to make a scheduled stop part way to Sol before making the rest of the trip. Unless directed otherwise, we are to stay in here. I know, I know, it's not what we wanted or would like, but there's nothing I can do about it. I've spoken with our point of contact within the family, and he would not give on this issue at all. So, settle in, enjoy the hospitality of the Ormond family, and we'll be on the battlefield on another mission soon enough,' he said.

Dain could hear the muttered grumblings of his squad, like Griff, no doubt could, too, but there was nothing they could do. They were stuck in this room. Dain slumped back into his seat and decided to make the best of it.

The missions would only get harder from here on out, so why fret about this one?

He stared up at the ceiling for who knew how long, listening to the sounds of the ship. It was quiet, and he barely knew they were moving. They eventually announced they had entered flux, but Dain had failed to notice the moment they had made the jump to FTL travel. But, that wasn't unusual. They might now be skipping across the galaxy on their way to Sol at speeds many times faster than light, but it was impossible to tell unless someone looked out the window.

Dain looked over towards one of the few small windows and watched the stars streak by in lines and the bluish mist that surrounded and zipped past them as the flux drive propelled them through space.

'It's amazing to watch, isn't it,' said a soft voice close to him. He looked to his left and saw Porsha lowering herself down into the chair next to him, looking out the same window that he had been fixated on.

'It is,' he answered, unsure what else to say.

'You know, you never actually said goodbye to me,' she said.

'Yeah, I know. I was...'

'An idiot?' she finished his sentence for him.

'Something like that.' He felt bad, but she was right. He was an idiot back then. He really should have known better, but he was young, his emotions were all over the place, and he didn't know how to handle it. He was losing his best friend, and she was going to be doing the very thing he wished he was doing. Of course, he'd been upset.

'You didn't answer my messages,' she said.

'I was pissed, and when I eventually got over it, it was too late. I didn't know what to say to you, so I didn't reply, and as the time passed, it only got harder,' he said, looking up to see Braydi looking over at him with a furrowed brow. Dain looked at the floor. He wondered what the big idiot was thinking. But then, he didn't care, not really.

'Your friends seem... interesting...' she commented.

'They're not my friends, they're... my squad. There's a difference.'

'Of course,' she said.

Dain sighed. 'I'm sorry,' he said, finally plucking up the courage to say those two words. He didn't look at her, though, he couldn't do that.

'Don't be, what's done is done. We're soldiers now. All that is in the past, and we have a job to do,' she said.

Dain nodded. 'You're right.'

'We're stopping.'

'What?' Dain asked, looking up. Outside the window, the lines that were the stars streaking past at mind-blowing speeds shrank back into points of light as the blue mist faded to nothing. 'Oh.'

'Sir?' Elva said to Griff.

'We're not at Sol yet, we've not been in flux for anywhere near long enough,' Griff answered. 'This must be the stop they said they might make, so, everyone relax; we'll be setting off again soon.'

Dain sat back, doing his best to relax and looked over to Porsha. She was frowning to herself and concentrating. She was probably using Magic.

'You know, I've not really thought about it much, but I can't believe you're a Magus, you know? After all those games as kids pretending we're using Magic to beat the bad guys?'

Porsha looked over to him with a frown. 'Huh?' She suddenly realised what he'd said and lost the stern look, smiling at him. 'Oh, yes, I remember.'

'What's it like?'

'Sorry?'

'Being able to use Magic? What's it like?'

'Well,' she said, her eyes searching for a response, 'I'm not sure how to answer that. It's incredible, but it's also scary. I mean, terrifyingly scary. It opens up such an incredible but dangerous world that I'm not sure I really grasp the full reality of it, you know?'

'I can imagine,' he said. 'So, do you know what's going on out there?'

Porsha looked at the door. 'Not really, they've put an Aegis around the room so...'

'A magical shield,' Dain said. 'Is that not suspicious?'

'Not really, the families are secretive by nature so, no. I'd be more surprised if there wasn't an Aegis in place, to be honest.'

'Aaah,' Dain answered.

BOOM!

The whole ship shuddered, and suddenly the room was bathed in a red light as a warning alarm sounded.

Porsha leapt up, her robes flaring as she leapt from the chair. Dain jumped up also. The shock of the explosion had sent adrenalin pumping around his body, sending his heart rate soaring.

'What the hell was that?' Dain asked, but Porsha wasn't next to him anymore. The staccato sound of gunfire echoed through the ship. Were they under attack?

'Lock and load, Wraiths. Looks like we'll see some action today after all,' Griff called out as he strode across the room.

'Yes!' Braydi whooped as he armed his rifle.

Dain hefted his own gun and checked it. The sleek looking gun was black and still fairly new looking, with some small glowing lights along its body. Like all his weapons and armour, it was enchanted. His rifle fired slugs which had been infused with Essentia so that they might damage a Magi's Aegis, but there were also many other bullets with a range of effects enchanted into them. His guns were linked to his mind, and with but a thought he could select the round he wanted and fire it.

With a mental command, he brought the active effects that had been cast upon his armour online. An Aegis sprung up around him, and as he turned on the Heads-Up-Display in his vision, he could see the magical effects of his teammates appearing as well. Each squad member had a faint blue bubble of energy surrounding them as they marched across the room.

Griff was standing near the entrance to the room next to Porsha, who was already there and concentrating hard. 'Anything?' he asked her.

'Nothing. The Aegis around the room is still there, so I can't sense anything past it. We have to go outside,' she said.

'Copy that,' Giff answered while the background noise of gunfire and explosions rang out around them. 'Squad, our objective is to find Dasha and secure him and take out whoever is attacking this ship. Understood?'

Everyone made noises of agreement.

'Okay, lock and load, Wraiths,' he said, banging his fist against the switch on the wall, making the door slide open.

The noise from outside doubled in intensity the moment the door opened. Dain watched as Griff stepped out, his gun up while Elva watched his back. Griff fired, his rifle unleashing a glowing stream of shells filled with magical energy.

Half a second later, they moved again, and the whole squad left the room behind. Dain craned his neck to see where Porsha was, but he couldn't see much. She was upfront with Griff and would be leading the squad into battle. Dain brought up the rear with Lexi, and as they stepped out, Dain looked down the corridor to where the body of a man in spiky black armour lay on the floor. Suddenly, several more people dressed in similar outfits ran around the corner, brandishing weapons.

'Contact,' Lexi called and fired at the men.

'Aaah, crap,' Dain said and followed suit, aiming his gun and squeezing the trigger. The weapon bucked in his hands as a stream of glowing blue death flew at the men that were approaching them.

'Lexi, Dain, do you have it under control?' Griff called through the mental link they all had access to. His voice also sounded through the mundane tech headset Dain wore. They all had one as a backup in case their magical communication lines faltered.

'We got it, sir,' Lexi said. 'Ain't that right, short-stuff?'

'Dain?' Griff asked.

'I'm good, sir, you go on, we'll handle this,' he said. Although he wasn't averse to the idea of an easy first mission, Dain wanted to serve and pull his own weight as much as anyone else in this squad. He wanted to show them all just what he was capable of.

Dain tracked the next man as he moved, let out a slow, steady breath and squeezed the trigger of his rifle. The figure dropped to the floor, much to Dain's satisfaction. He could do this, he could fight as well as any of his team. He might not have the physicality of Braydi or Jaik, but he could shoot a gun just as well as they could.

Keeping to cover, Dain calmly fired at another, and then another enemy combatant, dropping each one without issue with his cool, precise shots.

'Awesome shooting, short stuff,' Lexi said as the last man fell to the floor.

'Who are these guys?' Dain asked.

'Fucked if I know,' Lexi said as she looked down the corridor. 'Okay, we're good to go, come on,' she said.

Was she being nice to him? She was usually always mean and always had a smart comment or clever insult for him. As far as he could remember, that was the first compliment she'd ever given him.

Dain shook his head to clear his thoughts and sprinted after Lexi. Up ahead, the corridor opened up into the large central area of the ship and Dain could already hear the gunfire intensifying and growing louder as they approached.

Shots slammed into the wall at the end of the corridor, bringing them both to a stop as they peered into the room.

The rest of the wraith squad were shooting from behind cover at several groups of these black-clad shock troops they had already fought. Griff was close by and on the floor next to him was Porsha and a man who was wearing some very ornate clothing.

'Porsha? No!' Dain cried as emotion rose up within him on seeing her laying there motionless. Was she dead? In a panic, Dain brought up the scan data in his HUD and looked at Porsha, allowing it to get a reading on her.

Her heart was beating, she was alive but unconscious. Dain let out a breath and choked his emotions back. For a moment there, he'd thought he'd lost her before they'd spent any time together. While he was at it, he checked the man, who he guessed was an Ormond family member from his appearance. He was alive, too.

Griff looked up and saw them standing at the entrance to the corridor. 'You two, get over here and get these two to that safe room over there. We're in the shit here,' he yelled.

'Yes, sir,' Lexi answered and ran forward, only for a barrage of gunfire to slam into her Aegis. The energy shield fluoresced as the rounds hit, knocking Lexi to the ground. Dain swung around the corner, spotted the shooter, and unleashed hell. His Essentia bullets hit the trooper full-on, disrupting his enemies Aegis and dropping him to the floor. Dain looked over. Lexi was back up and basically okay, but Dain's readout put her Aegis at below thirty percent.

Dain checked the coast was clear and ran over to Porsha. Lexi joined him and they crouched down behind the cover Griff was hiding behind.

'What the hell's going on here?' Dain asked. 'Who are these guys?'

'If I had to guess, I'd say they were Nomad affiliated troops. As for what they're doing here, I have no idea. But, I saw at least two Nomad Magi fighting each other over there a moment ago.'

'Two Nomads fighting each other?' Dain asked. 'Shit, this is a mess.' Dain knew that the various groups of Nomad Magi often didn't get on with each other and would just as readily fight each other as they would the Arcadians. Dain looked down at Porsha and the man. 'And who's this guy?'

Griff followed Dain's gaze to the man on the floor. 'That's Dasha, the family member we were here to protect. He was knocked unconscious at some point, I guess. I dragged him into cover.'

'Okay. Lexi, have you got him?' Dain asked as he picked up Porsha.

Lexi easily lifted Dasha with her boosted strength and nodded to Dain.

'Then go, I'll follow and watch your back,' he said. Lexi moved out and headed away from the firefight towards the doorway that Griff had mentioned. Dain followed on behind, getting his gun ready in one hand while hefting Porsha with his other, holding her under her arms. The stealth suit that he and the rest of his squad wore boosted his strength, making picking someone up really easy to do. As they pressed on, movement and the sound of footsteps to their right caught Dain's attention. He looked over, following the noise to see two more troopers exiting a corridor and raising their weapons.

'Lexi, duck,' Dain shouted as the troopers fired on her. She dived for the nearest cover as the shots slammed into the remains of her Aegis, which had been recharging. But the Essentia charged rounds of these troopers made short work of it, and her Aegis failed moments before she reached cover.

Blood erupted from her leg as she finally found cover to shield her from the barrage of gunfire.

Dain raised his gun, switching the rounds to explosive with a thought as the two men came into view and fired. Essentia laced explosives erupted on and around the two troopers sending them sprawling. Dain didn't wait and moved up to Lexi, who was holding her leg and hissing.

'You okay? Can you move?' he asked.

'Shit, yeah, I think so,' she said and pulled herself up, favouring her good leg.

'We're nearly there, come on,' he said as they lifted Dasha between them and walked the rest of the way to the door. Moving inside, they placed Porsha and Dasha on the floor. Looking up, Dain saw Lexi perch on the edge of a table with her gun in her arms.

'Get back out there and help them,' she said.

'Are you sure?'

'I can look after these guys here. Go, now,' she yelled.

Dain nodded and ran to the door, checking his corners for any hidden troopers before be moved outside. His heart was pounding, his adrenalin was pumping furiously around his body, and he felt like he was at the end of his tether. He'd had enough of these guys hurting his friends and his squad mates. He already hated Nomads, as did most right-thinking people. Ever since he was a child, he had heard of the atrocities that they committed in the name of their dread masters, the Deep Ones. Seeing them today for the first time only cemented his hatred of them.

Looking out, he saw the greater numbers of Nomad troopers advancing on his squad mates. He saw several of them getting shot and knocked back with their Aegises failing. As he watched, he could feel the anger rising within him. He could feel the emotion grow, so he ran. He sprinted in towards his squad, running as fast as he could while still being able to fire his gun. As he approached his team's cover, the world moved in slow motion. He watched as the force they were facing started to overwhelm them, with each of them taking fire.

The Aegises of his squad mates flared as they were hit, knocking them back. As he ran in, the Nomad troopers saw his approach, and several of them fired at him, too.

Dain fired without finesse, without much care, and sprayed magical death at the shock troops as he took fire. The integrity of his Aegis faltered under fire while the rage within him grew. It felt like he could feel an up-swell of emotion or energy within him. It grew almost in parallel to his faltering Aegis, and as the shield from his suit was finally overloaded and powered down, the energy within him, the emotion and anger, erupted from him in a scream and shout of pure emotion.

Light flashed blue all around him and suddenly blinding white energy burst from his hands and lashed out at the troopers, smashing into them, ripping through their Essentia shields and then tearing their bodies apart.

It felt like a dream. A violent one to be sure, but a dream all the same. He felt almost like a spectator, separate from the events that were unfolding around him, except that he wasn't. This was him. He was doing this. He was shooting powerful magical energy in a hundred different directions at the advancing troopers and killing them like they were nothing.

As the gunfire from the troopers stopped, Dain felt the rage and energy fade as he dropped to his knees. He watched the energy he'd been throwing arc along his arms, hissing and popping as it faded away.

Dain looked up to see Griff and Braydi, both of them nursing wounds, staring at him wide-eyed with shock or maybe even fear.

What the hell was going on? Looking up again, just beyond the cover they were behind, she spotted two people still standing amidst the many dead. One was a woman in black with light brown hair. The second girl was standing tall, her right hand gripping the first woman by the neck and squeezing tight.

This second girl, who, Dain noticed, was protected by an Aegis, looked like a Magus to him, going by the energy signature his sensors were picking up. She was a strange one, though, wearing a revealing outfit that he'd never seen before. She had on the tiniest tartan skirt and a white shirt tied up just under her bust to show off her midriff. What was she trying to look like? It was sexy, sure, but so out of place that it looked incongruous, weird even. Was this an Earth fashion he wasn't aware of?

She was looking at him, her striking face framed by light blonde hair that fell over her shoulders. She cocked her head slightly sideways before she looked back at the woman she was strangling. Essentia flared all around them, centred on the girl, and the woman in black's body tore itself apart, spraying blood everywhere as it fell to the floor in bits.

The girl with the tartan skirt then turned her attention back to Dain and started to walk forward, approaching him, her hips swaying and her thighs wobbling as she walked.

Dain felt fascinated by her, captivated, when Essentia suddenly flared around her again.

Could he see Magic now?

Suddenly, he was yanked from where he was kneeling and launched across the room towards the girl. The throw by an invisible force snapped him out of the fascination he'd been caught in as he flew through the air, the ground swiftly approaching. Half a second later he crunched to the floor with a grunt. It hurt, but it wasn't as bad as he had thought it would be. His armour had protected him.

The sound of approaching footsteps forced him from his momentary funk, and he pushed himself back and up as he caught sight of the patent leather heels that this young woman was wearing walking towards him. He looked up, his eyes following her shape as he scanned up her legs and the over-the-knee socks she wore, up to her face that smiled down at him. The smile wasn't one he liked, though, and his mind was filled with visions of being ripped to shreds.

He looked at his hands and clenched them, trying to focus and bring back the energy that had saturated him just moments before. If he could just summon it again, maybe he could save himself and at least scare this Magi off.

But try as he might, nothing happened.

'What the...' he muttered, before looking up at the girl again.

'Awww, can't summon that Magic back again?' she taunted him.

Was it Magic he'd summoned? Was he a Magus now? If only he had a moment to think about this calmly, to think it through and figure out what had just happened.

'Well, too bad,' she said and raised her hand as Essentia in the form of the faint glowing blue mist he'd been seeing gathered about her again.

Suddenly, more Essentia flared to Dain's right, but this effect was massive. He'd barely turned his head to look when a huge section of hull plating on the side of the spacecraft was ripped off. Electronics sparked, gases belched forth as Dain got a clear view out the side of the ship into deep space. There was no rush of air into the vacuum outside the ship, though, meaning a force shield had been put in place to stop that happening.

As the hull section floated sideways, it revealed a figure in white hung in space behind it. Hovering outside the ship, her white robes flowed about her as she looked inside. She was beautiful with her long bright red hair standing in stark contrast to her white outfit and pale skin. As he watched, he could see another Aetheric ship out there behind the redhead as well.

The woman floated into the ship and stepped onto the floor, Essentia crackling about her, her attention focused on the girl who was standing next to him.

'Anastasia, yeh little Nomad gobshite' the redhead said in a melodic Irish accent.

Dain looked up at the girl in the tartan skirt. She was backing off and looked quite on edge. Was she scared of this women?

'Amanda, that was quite an entrance,' Anastasia said.

'Not a bother, glad yeh enjoyed it,' she said sarcastically. 'Now, kindly feck off.' Essentia flared, and in the same instant, Anastasia was hit by an invisible hammer blow that sent her flying across the room into the hull plating.

She dropped to the floor, landing on her feet in a crouch and looked up.

'Catch you later,' Anastasia said, and Essentia flared about her once again. With a whip crack of moving air, she was gone.

Dain relaxed and took a breath, looking at the floor as he tried to relax. A shadow fell over him, and he looked right to see a pair of shiny white heeled boots. He looked up to see the redhead. She crouched down beside him and smiled.

'Are you okay?' she asked softly with a warm smile. Dain looked up into her friendly face.

'What the hell is going on?' he asked. Then suddenly a thought occurred to him. The girl, Anastasia, she said this woman's name. 'Hang on, is your name, Amanda?'

'Mmm-hmm.'

'As in, *the* Amanda, the one who founded the Wraiths?'

She smiled. 'Guilty as charged.'

'Holy shit. What are you doing here? I'm... wow. It's great to meet you. This is crazy,' he said.

'Here, let me help you up,' she said and took hold of his arm, lifting him to his feet easily. She was strong. Once on his feet, he looked around at the carnage and saw the rest of his squad standing up with grunts of pain. Griff was already walking over to them.

'You're, Amanda, right?' Griff asked.

'Nice to meet you, Lance Corporal. What's the craic?'

Dain saw the flicker of surprise at her familiarity. For the founder of their organisation, she was not at all what Dain had expected. It looked like Griff was put a little off balance by her demeanour as well.

'Well, it looks like the ship was attacked by Nomads - two groups of Nomads by the looks of it - and we were caught in the middle,' Griff said.

'You're half right,' Amanda said. 'Dasha was dealing with both groups of Nomads, betraying Anastasia's group by starting to deal with another group. Anastasia was sent here to teach him a lesson.'

'So, how come you're here? Did you know about this?'

'I've been following the Dark Knights, the group Anastasia's a part of for a while now, and I was aware of Dasha's dealings, so, I kept watch,' Amanda said.

'So, why didn't you kill that Nomad girl just now? You had the perfect opportunity.'

'She's too useful to us alive, for the time being,' Amanda explained.

'Oh, okay. So, but, hang on, isn't Dasha a part of the Ormond Family, they're...' Dain began.

'The good guys?' Amanda finished.

'Well, yeah. They're Arcadians,' Dain said.

'There will always be those who make deals with the devil for more power or other such things. Dasha was one such person, and he won't be the last,' Amanda answered.

'Are you okay, Dain?' Griff asked.

Dain looked over at Griff. 'Um, yeah, I think so,' he said, looking down at his hands. They were still tingly from the energy that had been surging through them.

'He's fine,' Amanda said. 'He's just gone through his Epiphany, that's all.'

'My Epiphany? You mean...'

Amanda nodded. 'That's right, welcome to the ranks of the Magi,' she said.

'Holy crap,' Dain muttered to himself.

Andrew Dobell

A UK based author, Andrew Dobell has written an Urban fantasy series, a Cyberpunk series, and has stories available set in the Genre's of Space Opera and the Post Apocalypse.

Andrew is currently working on expanding his Magi Saga universe with a spin off series set in space, which this short story is a prequel for. He has many other ideas to expand it further as well.

You can learn more about Andrew and his fiction at his website www.andrewdobellauthor.co.uk where you can get some free Short Stories by signing up to his mailing list.

THE ACHENEAN RECEPTION

By Richard Fox

Security for the wedding of a merchant prince and his mysterious fiancée grows complicated as the bride's family has a very different notion of matrimony.

Whoever thinks weddings are magical moments has never organized one. And they've definitely not had to do so on a backwater planet for a trade prince whose fiancée wants things just so. And in three days. And the days on Achenae are *very* short.

As consigliere to the Diodanna trade family for the last eighty-eight years, there were some challenges. Drive malfunctions on the *Sky Dancer* that left us stranded in a nebula for a few lean months. Credit issues that were worse than living off of nutritional yeast in a nebula and volatile cargo. Even more volatile trade partners...issues with the family patriarch. None were unsurmountable, but these last few days have tried my patience more than I cared to admit.

Not that I'd ever admit to them. I am the consigliere. Everything was under control. At least, I had to appear that everything was under control.

While several hundred leaders of the sector's trade families, chaebols, conglomerates, zaibatsus, triads—and whatever airs these merchants put on this week—made small talk and enjoyed the hors d'oeuvres, I remained on damage control duty. That we held the wedding on neutral ground and forbade all electronic devices made things a bit harder for me, but relying on analog means kept me sharp.

The guests seemed to be having a good time. The normal cliques had formed around existing trade agreements and shipping lanes. One could almost map out the sector by where business men and women gaggled. Reinhart Fashion traded jokes with Omni Vat Goods. Gochu Armaments glared at Krupp Munitions, both sides were competing to supply the latest tyrant on Godall. Oh how I wished I could work the crowd and perhaps scrounge up an easy charter or shipment for the *Sky Dancer*. We needed the cash.

I checked my watch and the small note pad in my hand. The platters of tigiack spiced soufflés should have left the kitchen two minutes ago. They'd lose their fresh-from-the-oven puffiness soon and I would not be known as the consigliere that served mush soufflés. It was bad enough Prince Aric was hemorrhaging cash for his wedding, but to do so *and* be remembered for poor hospitality...

A shudder ran down my spine as I made my way to the kitchen doors. They burst open just before I arrived and a quick stop saved me from a broken nose. Waiters hurried out, trays gripped in both hands in front of their stomachs. The soufflés looked marvelous, at least.

"Stop," I hissed at the waiters. Well, not waiters. Crewmen from the *Dancer* repurposed at the last moment to be waiters. No robots on neutral ground and I didn't have to hire locals. Though I did have to promise to reimburse them for the tattoos that were erased. Longshoremen. Don't get me started.

"That is not how you carry the food," I mimed holding a tray almost up to shoulder level. "Work your sectors. Don't come back until your tray is empty and no smiling Gersh, what did I tell you about all those gold teeth?"

"That they made me look like a pirate..." Gersh looked down and scratched a foot against the ground.

"And that you clean up so well after we got the clan tats off your face. No talking either, Gersh. Chop chop, men. Guests are hungry," I waved them on once they held the trays like they were moderately civilized, which they weren't, but they put on a good show.

I ducked my head into the kitchen, a mess of steam and clattering pans, looking for the one responsible for the delay.

"Where is Maurice?" I asked one of the cooks.

"Oye, Master Sebastia. Mo, he out front, said big big trouble with the bubbly," the cook said. Her dreadlocks were looser than normal from the heat. The environment in an analog kitchen was always rough on the staff, which was why I stayed out. The steam would upset the fabric in my overcoat.

My left eye twitched and I spun around and screamed internally as I hurried across the reception hall. Why was the bar on the other side of the hall? All food and beverage potential problems should've been collocated so that my assistant—and by extension, me—didn't have to ping back and forth across a crowded room. I knew the answer, Prince Aric's fiancée, Ella. She had to have the ceremony close to the ocean, and the building had to match some old book she had. Prince Aric wasn't particularly adept at trade, negotiations or spacefaring, but after his fourth engagement he'd figured out that appeasing his future wife on most everything was the smart way to go.

Sending a fabrication crew down to the spot she wanted wasn't hard, robots could build a future spot designated for neutral ground, they just couldn't be there when the party started. But the architecture was so...archaic. Why would a woman about to marry into a merchant house and spend most of her life on a deep space trading ship insist on getting married in something from the 19th century?

But since Aric's shuttle crashed off the coast a few days ago, and his rescue by Ella, the young man had done everything she'd desired. Ah, to be young...

The sky darkened through the stained glass windows behind the stage at the far end of the hall. Odd, weather satellites promised a sunny day. Were sudden storms a problem on Achenae? I shook the concern off and went to the bar. It was stocked with every ounce of spirits from the *Dancer* and all the expensive bottles I could buy from the locals—and nick from other consiglieres from arriving ships— and given the crowd and the smell of alcohol in the air, this part of the reception was going swimmingly.

I stepped around the bar and slipped into the back, where Maurice and a pair of sailors poured sparkling wine into tall flutes. The smell stopped me dead in my tracks. The aroma from the 2899 Ryukyu was unmistakable. Faint notes of orange and mulling spices. A tingle to the sinuses that promised a euphoric effect to the imbiber; Ryukyu didn't brew alcohol, they distilled pure serenity. We'd kept the cases locked away in the ship's vaults for decades, waiting for just the right moment to finally imbibe.

God knew I could use a drink of that right then. But no, I had to stay sharp.

The case lay broken, plasteel splintered and the stasis field sparking on and off.

"Couldn't use the cipher," Maurice, a pudgy man with a drooping face, said. "Not on neutral ground. Had to use a crowbar and molecular wedge to get it open."

The code ciphers. I knew I forgot something.

"The case should've disintegrated when you tried to break it open," I narrowed my eyes at him slightly.

"Well, Master Sebastia, the older Feingold cases won't trigger if you open them just right," Maurice said with a shrug. I'd picked him up on Colaria years back and never did get a reason why he wanted off the planet so badly.

"Just get the toasts prepared," I looked at my watch. "You are seven minutes behind schedule, Maurice. Seven."

"Normally takes me eight minutes to get into a Feingold...I mean, if I did that sort of thing. Boss, you wanted to know when the in-laws arrived, yeah?"

Oh no. How long had they been wandering around, displaying their yokel ways to the other guests? Achenae was known for its oceans, superstitious populace and little else.

"'Cause they just walked in," Maurice pointed over my shoulder.

Crisis averted? Maybe.

"Very good," I straightened my jacket and gave myself a quick once over before I left the back room. The future in-laws weren't hard to find. They were tall, gangly limbed and their hair had a slight tinge of sea green, a local mutation that had crept in to the gene pool while the planet was cut off from the rest of settled space for hundreds of years after the Great Schism.

Three Achenaens stood behind the rows of seats facing the stage. All watched the party with apparent disinterest. They all wore the same simple tunics with overlong sleeves that extended past their knuckles, which I'd seen in the nearby fishing villages. One held the holo chit with the wedding invitation between his fingertips.

Ugh, Prince Aric you could have fallen for a girl from a people with a sense of style, I thought.

"Welcome honored guests," I opened my arms wide and approached. "I didn't know Ella's family would attend...she told me

138

that wouldn't be possible. I am Consigliere Sebastia of the *Sky Dancer* and what an—"

"Where is Ella?" the man in the middle asked. His voice was high and raspy. The two shorter men on either side of him didn't seem to be aware of the conversation.

"She's indisposed at the moment," I said. "Isn't it the local custom for the bride to be alone for the few hours before the ceremony, Mr..."

"Shondark," the middle said, "we are her un-cows. Knuckles. Uncles. Your tongue is difficult." Shondark, the only import-export company based on the planet, I'd seen the name most everywhere during the whirlwind wedding preparations. Perhaps Prince Aric had proposed to a girl with some wealth and taste after all. Or Shondark was the local equivalent of Smith or Jones. Probably the latter given how our stop on the planet had gone so far.

"Basic is a bit tricky depending on your base language, but you've hardly an accent, Mr. Shondark," I flipped the pages of my notebook over to a seating diagram and rubbed out three names from a table. The storm outside had grown darker and faint booms of thunder echoed against the hall. "You'll be on table four, right next to the happy couple once we break for dinner. Is there anything else I can do for you?"

"Food," one of Shondark's eyes meandered to one side, the other stayed locked on me.

"Yes," I swallowed hard. The eye thing wasn't the worst mutation I'd ever seen on a backwater world. At least Ella had escaped that genetic hand me down. "We've a variety of off world delicacies making their way through the crowd. We have a table behind me where—"

Shondark walked off toward the spread at the back of the hall, the other two right behind him.

"Father of the bride perhaps send a check with you?" I muttered.

"Sebastia," came from behind. I turned and found Prince Aric behind a curtain next to the stage where he was about to be married. Or not. I'd seen that look on his face before and began thinking of contingency plans.

Aric wore a fine suit of local spun sea silk done into a tuxedo with an archaic tail. I couldn't help but roll my eyes as I went over to him. He

139

should've been in the same raiment his father and grandfather wore every time they got married, but that's not what Ella wanted. At least the tailor had managed to compliment the prince's frame. He had his father's countenance, they looked so much alike before the glimmer dust had ruined the older's mind and body. Aric had his mother's demeanor, and that had saved the Diodanna family business.

"Your hair is a disaster," I said as I hustled him away from the curtain edge. "Where is your cousin Ferdinand? Does he have the rings?"

"He's still hungover," Aric pointed to a dressing room behind him. "But I need to talk to you, old friend. This time…I…"

"I understand completely," I looked for an exit with a straight shot to the air car I had waiting just beyond the neutral ground perimeter. "There's no shame, sire. You met her only a few days ago and while she's lovely to look at this sort of—"

"No, this isn't like the last time. Times. Ella is incredible and I must marry her," Aric said. His words carried one meaning, the look on his face and shaking legs said something else entirely.

"Aric, my boy, are you certain you've met the right girl? This time? I will remind you of the trouble we got into when you almost wed that chieftain's daughter on Tonagra. Yes, you were supposed to fight her cousin to the death first but that," I shook my finger, "was a formality. We spent days pulling arrows out of my favorite air car but I'd rather you make the right decision," I leaned back and looked at all the merchants and shippers enjoying the reception, "than make a tremendous mistake."

"No, you don't understand, Sebastia. I'm in love."

There it was. The words that signaled anyone was beyond rational discourse when it came to the opposite sex.

"Then you're in the right place and wearing the right clothes. Just remember to say *her* name and 'I do' when prompted. Easiest day of your life," I said. "Now, go mingle with your peers and see if anyone has an easy charter for our ship."

Aric's jaw worked from side to side.

"How much will this cost? Did we dip into the emergency funds?"

"We spent the emergency funds months ago. You may notice some jewelry missing from your quarters so go out there and find us some work...and say hello to Uncle Shondark, your future in-law. You can't miss him."

"In-laws? But she said—"

I gave Aric a pat on the shoulder and pushed him out into the open with a fair amount of force.

Maurice stuck his head around the edge of the curtain.

"Boss, they're here," he said.

"I know that, Maurice, didn't you see me talking to them? Did you get the puff pastries into circulation yet? Thirty seconds," I rapped a finger against my watch face.

"Not them. The other them. The them we're not supposed to mention," Maurice frowned.

My hands balled up, and I cursed my sense of decorum.

"Two of them's at security," Maurice said. "They ain't happy neither."

"I told you to lose their invitation!"

"No you didn't."

"No, I didn't, but I should have. And you should've known I should have and lost it for me without me asking. What do I pay you for, Maurice?"

Maurice looked up at the ceiling. His lips moved and his fingers tapped like he was doing complex math in his head.

"The puff pastries," my voice went an octave higher than I would've liked and he ducked back behind the curtain. Damn them for being so polite. A 'so sorry' card and cookware as a gift would have been perfectly acceptable, but no they just had to warp over for the event.

I strode along the edge of the hall, noting that the Lingus delegation was rather inebriated. It wouldn't take much for an incident, such as the Gruffudd Corp remembering that their vendetta against their drunk rivals was not enforceable on neutral ground, to send things south. But weddings were sacrosanct. Any party that stepped out of bounds would face immediate sanctions. While I would have loved for Don Buello to commit a faux pas, I knew he was far too clever for that.

I hurried down a covered walkway to the security station. Thick drops of rain smacked against the awning. The sky roiled with dark clouds and the promise of more rain. Just beyond the wedding hall was a steep cliff that ended in crashing waves of the ocean. Or what should've been crashing waves. The water of the bay was oddly tranquil. Now, I'm a sailor by training. Void sailor, not the kind that gets wet, but I'd spent enough time on planets that this weather struck me as odd.

The security station was just beyond the neutral ground, and my lead man-at-arms and one of our scanner bots stood between two people and the path to the wedding.

Don Buello was just as I remembered him, uglier than an alley cat with a penchant for losing fights, still wearing the same leather get up as the last time I saw him. With him was a woman too unattractive to be anyone but his daughter, the poor thing.

"Sebastia," Buello sneered at my droid. "Your junk's malfunctioning. Let us in already," he tossed his invitation chit at my chest. I plucked it out of the air and tumbled it across my fingers.

"Don Buello, what a...surprise to see you. We're holding the wedding on neutral ground for the sake of everyone's—"

"I know what neutral ground means," Buello flicked his fingers at a stasis box the man-at-arms carried, a plasma pistol and wrist needler inside.

"Then you won't mind leaving that neuro toxin injector inside your pinkie ring in the stasis box," I said. "You'll get it back at the end of the day. Diodanna doesn't like such methods."

Buello smirked at me and took the ring off.

"Forgot I had that on," he said.

"And the monofilament garrote in your chest pocket. The inner pocket," I gave him a big smile.

"Oh, thought this was my good suit," Buello dropped the weapon with a clatter in the box. "I should've hired you away from old man Diodanna when I had the chance." He clapped once and pulled his sleeves back.

"We'll begin shortly," I stepped to the side and half bowed.

Buello kept pace with me as we walked to the wedding hall.

"My my, Aric's finally getting married this time," Buello said. "He's got my hopes up a few times. He does understand the contract between our houses, doesn't he?"

Leave it to Buello to bring up settled business at a wedding. I wasn't surprised, the man was known to send flowers to his enemies' funerals.

"Prince Aric is well aware of the terms of the loan. I take it you're prepared to make us whole once the ceremony ends?" I asked.

"Aric weds outside of the Buello clan before he turns twenty eight and the interest on the dowry I promised is forfeit. His father got quite the sweetheart deal from me. With compounding the amount is...substantial," Buello looked at me.

"Aric's father was not in the best mental state when he made that deal," I said. "He had no right to negotiate such a merger, since we are a free will ship." I didn't add that the former captain of the *Sky Dancer* then leveraged the money Buello agreed to put up for the dowry into massive loans...which the family was struggling paying the interest on. Payments we made most months.

When Aric got married in the next hour, Buello would repay the principle...which would cover the wedding expenses. Almost.

"Well, if Aric gets cold feet again," he motioned back to the woman following two steps behind, "I'm prepared to pay the entire amount once he and Desdemona are bound."

I glanced back at his daughter. She raised a bushy eyebrow at me.

"And as Crytex Securities has a collection force on the way to Achenae...I hope Aric chooses wisely and quickly," Buello said.

Crytex. Blast it. Their cyborg enforcers were immune to reasonable solutions and had no qualms about seizing assets in arrears with force, and the Diodanna family did owe them a substantial amount...that Buello's dowry would cover and then some.

"Did you mention to Crytex that this is where they could find the *Sky Dancer?*" I asked.

"My good man, the entire sector knows about this," Buello said. "My offer of employment stands, though your salary will be an awful lot less if you come asking for a job after your Diodanna paycheck bounces."

Not a denial, I thought. *Though let's not pretend you let slip about Crytex by accident.*

"Do enjoy the reception," I said as we entered the wedding hall. A bolt of lightning broke overhead, though no thunder came with it. "I'll seat you next to the Lingus."

"Boss," Maurice pulled me away. "There's an emergency."

"What now?"

"We're out of shrimp," Maurice swallowed hard.

"That's the emergency? Get the after dinner plates out. Do I have to make every decision around here?"

"That's the thing, they ate that too," Maurice said. "The bride's kin, the Shondarks, ate every last bloody one of the little blighters and they're asking for more."

"I ordered almost a hundred kilos of shrimp from the...all of it?"

"Yes, boss, damnedest thing I've seen since Gersh tried to eat a whole cockatrice rotisserie back when we stopped on—"

"Go put something else out. *Not* the Nipponese prawns, those are still cooking. Oysters. Put the oysters out," I rolled my eyes and found the three Shondarks back where I'd last seen them near the pews. All had a decent bulge to their midsection.

I made my way over, wondering if they'd stashed the shrimp in their robes to save for later. The main export of Achenae was shrimp—a pitifully small number of shrimp—why steal any? I knew this was a backwater planet, I just didn't think it was *that* backwater.

"Uncle Shondark," I touched him on the back and God as my witness his flesh felt almost spongy beneath his clothes. He looked down at me and licked cocktail sauce from the corner of his mouth. "Enjoying...everything?"

He put one hand on the back of a pew and his thumb writhed from side to side, boneless like a tentacle. He slapped his other hand on top of it.

"Your catch is bountiful," Shondark said.

"Yes. Well if you don't eat too much at a wedding you might as well have stayed home, yes?"

There was a gurgle from his distended stomach that made mine lurch.

144

Now, I've been in trade—licit and illicit—since my early teens. Been in every kind of deal you can imagine and dealt with characters on the entire savory spectrum. I'm still alive because I learned to develop one hell of a poker face.

So when Shondark blinked, and by blinked I mean membranes on the side of his eyes moved from left to right, I held my composure. Humans had changed slightly on the many new environments of settled environments since the great diaspora from Earth. But the mutations Shondark had were far beyond anything I'd ever even heard of.

"Is there more?" Shondark asked.

"Oysters," I smiled. "Bay, mountain and otherwise coming right—oh look at the time," the speakers in the ceiling began a new song, much louder than the background music that had been playing. The crowd began to wander away from the reception area and into the pews.

"You're in row two. Left hand side. Excuse me." I moved away with purpose to my steps and found Aric behind the curtain, looking almost green. His cousin, Ferdinand, fanned a handkerchief over his face.

"I can do this," Aric said. "I love her. I can do this. I love her."

"Aric, is there anything about her that's..." I looked back at her uncle, "unusual?"

"What, Sebastia? Now? Unusual because she's the most beautiful creature I've ever seen? How her laughter makes me feel like Mom and Dad are still alive? How when she sings it's like I'm a kid playing in—"

"You're stealing lines from my toast," Ferdinand said.

"No, Aric," I held up my palms to him, "anything different...different. Like she's not entirely—"

"Seriously?" Aric went pale and dry heaved slightly.

"Pretty obvious that she's got very poor eyesight," Ferdinand gave Aric a gentle punch to the ribs.

"You've made that joke already," Aric said. "Just pretend you've lost the rings and shut up."

The priest came out from the other side of the room and walked onto the stage. Behind him and waiting in the wings was Charlene, Ferdinand's sister and the only bridesmaid, waving at me frantically.

Maybe Aric's not the only one with nerves, I thought. Don Buello and his daughter were in the crowd. There was an option, a distasteful and depressing option, to save face in front of the sector's business elite.

"Boss," Maurice, his face red and sweat beading on his forehead, "Ella...she says..."

Aric turned around his mouth agape.

"She says she's ready now," Maurice said. "She's on her way out and—"

The music changed to the Bridal Chorus.

"Oh my god," Aric said. "What do I do? What do I do?"

"Stand there and follow instructions," I grabbed him by the arm and pushed him out past the curtain. Ferdinand followed, the stench of whiskey in his wake. Guests hurried to their assigned seating and turned around as I caught sight of the bride's gleaming white headdress just over the crowd. The bride's family kept their gaze locked on Aric.

I waved Maurice over and snatched the Diodanna crest pin off of his lapel. I pinched it against my pin and felt a thrum between my fingers.

"Boss?" Maurice asked.

"I'm suspending neutral ground for a few minutes," I said. "Need to see something." I slipped a monocle out from a tiny pocket inside my jacket and tapped the edge against the two lapel pins. A screen flickered on the glass as the device charged up.

"Boss, what are you doing with that?"

"I seem to have forgotten to inspect myself for electronic devices during the preparations and left my unpowered spy glass on my person and dual charge batteries in our crests...oops," I said.

"But won't the other hoity-toity types get upset? Maybe even get violent if they know neutral ground is off?" Maurice's hand went to a sleeve where he kept a knife.

"Then we better not tell them," I angled the monocle toward my boots and saw the bones of my foot through the small glass.

"Tell them what, sir?" he made an over exaggerated wink.

"You've come so far, Maurice," I said.

Ella turned down the aisle and my breath caught. They say every woman is beautiful on her wedding day, but no one would ever hold a candle to the vision I saw. The green highlights of her red hair caught the light perfectly, tiny jewels in her wedding dress sparkled like sea foam as she moved. Sculptors would strive for a thousand years to match the beauty of her face without success.

I shook my head to clear it. Aric was the one infatuated with her. I had a job to do.

I raised the monocle to my eye and ran a finger along the edge to zoom in on Ella. Her body temperature was perfectly normal, I changed the spectrum analyzer to peer beneath her face...and found nothing unusual. Perfectly human.

"Stress, old man," I mumbled. "The stress is getting to you."

The three Shondarks were still looking at Aric. None had even glanced at the bride-to-be, which I took as an insult. I turned my head toward them and held up the monocle.

"Mr. Sebastia," the man-at-arms from the security check point bumped into me and the monocle slipped out of my hand and slid beneath the stage. I looked over at him, my eyes burning with anger.

"Mr. Sebastia, we picked up a neutral gr—" I put two fingertips on his lips.

"Thank you," I over enunciated.

"And the guards say they saw something weird in the water," the man-at-arms said.

"Is it a tidal wave come to wreck this celebration of love and impending financial ruin?" I asked.

He shook his head quickly.

"Then just keep an eye on it," I shooed him away.

Ella finished her promenade down the red carpet and joined Aric and the priest on the stage. Aric had the biggest, dumbest grin on his face. I couldn't help but feel happy for him.

The Shondarks' faces, on the other hand, had soured considerably.

"Psst," I hissed at the priest and got his attention. I touched my watch and then made a rolling forward gesture with my fingers. He looked confused. I mimed putting rings on fingers and pointed at my watch. He shook his head slowly. I repeated myself, then pointed at him, then rubbed my thumb against my fingers to remind him of his pay, then threw that imaginary money away.

He nodded furiously. Even on backwater worlds, some messages could get through cultural differences easily enough.

"Ladies and gentlemen," the priest began. "We are gathered here today to see Aric and Ella joined in holy matrimony. On this day let us remember—"

I stomped my foot against the ground.

"Do you have the rings?" the priest asked Ferdinand. He passed the box to Aric.

"Traditional challenge!" Shondark raised a hand into the air and I buried my face into my palm.

So close.

"There is nothing to challenge, Grishilak," Ella said. "This is my choice."

The crowd murmured and I hoped, pleaded with Caishen, Saint Homobonus, and Plutus that they'd write this hiccup off as a bit of local color.

"The Mother did not agree to this. You cannot give up your birthright," Shondark said. "Not forever. Not for a land walker."

Land walker?

"I made my decision." Ella took Aric's hand in hers and looked at him with those beautiful green eyes. "I do not care what the Mother wants."

The three uncles looked to the ceiling, then started gurgling. Not a rinse your throat sort of gurgle, but a deep sonorous noise that no human throat could ever make.

The ground shifted, like a shuttle had made a hard landing just outside the building. There was a cry from the crowd...then silence.

A shadow moved across the stained-glass windows and something huge and shapeless pressed in close to the glass. The smell of brine and low tide filled the air.

"Maurice," I grabbed him by the shoulder, "trip the fire alarms and open all the exits."

There was a rumble and shadows ran down the side windows, like arms had just wrapped themselves around the wedding hall.

"Cancel that." I let Maurice go.

"Mother!" Ella shouted at the darkness on the other side of the stained-glass depiction of a barefoot girl sitting next to the seashore. "Don't do this!"

The window shattered and a deep green barnacle-encrusted tentacle broke through the glass. There were shouts, screams, and a reasonably justified amount of panic from the guests as more tentacles ripped out the back of the wedding hall.

A mass of dark flesh replaced the wall. Hundreds of eyes in many different sizes and colors blinked at me. The smell of the ocean was almost overpowering as a beak the size of the front double doors emerged from a fold of skin and snapped in the air. Heaven help me, I swear there were smaller beaks inside the big one.

Aric grabbed Ella by the waist and pulled her aside, putting himself between her and the monster.

"My child," the words boomed out of the sea creature, rattling the unbroken windows, "what has happened to you?"

"I went to the flesh shaper." Ella wriggled out of Aric's grip. "I wanted to walk the other world and there I found the one I love. Give me this, please, Mother!"

As Aric's consigliere and de facto master of ceremonies, one would think I would know what to do in this sort of situation. But you have a wedding interrupted by a creature from the abyss and we'll see how you handle it.

"Maurice," I grabbed my second, "more alcohol. Now!" I pushed him away.

"He cannot love you," the Mother boomed. "You have lied to him."

"No, this is who I truly am!" Ella shouted.

A tentacle pointed at her and a thin black tendril lashed out and touched her arm. Ella fell to her knees and all of her skin darkened almost instantly. Her fingers lengthened and suckers sprouted along her arms. Her eyes widened and went pitch black. Her hair went full green and thickened like kelp.

Aric backed away, his jaw slack.

"He sees you," the Mother said, and a tentacle the thickness of a firehose snaked around her waist and lifted her up. "Time to come home."

"No, Aric please!" She reached back to him.

Just let her go, I thought. *Please be smart about this.*

Then, Aric—who I've known since the day I was born—surprised me. He ran after his fiancée and grabbed her by the wrist. Ella's hand morphed into a tentacle and wrapped up his arm. The Mother pulled Ella towards her, dragging Aric along.

He really was in love.

The Shondarks were still in the same place in row two. The rest of the wedding guests were huddled in the back of the room, screaming and shouting the ransom they'd pay to get the hell out of the hall.

I ran over to the uncle in the middle, who was still gurgling, and snapped my fingers next to his ear. He looked at me.

"You're talking to that big one, right?" I asked. One of Shondark's eyes blinked, the other rolled over, and a cat's eye stared at me.

"You tell the Mother that she will never get her daughter back if she takes her like this," I said. "Ella will never forgive her. She will never forget Aric. He loves her, even though she looks like—not what she looked like earlier. That's love. True love! Let them be together."

The uncles on either side of Shondark stopped gurgling and looked at me.

"And if he mistreats her?" the one on the left asked.

"And if she is unhappy?" right asked.

"You have my word I will bring her back home if she so desires," I said.

"Aric is...true?" Shondark asked.

"He's a good man. I promise," I said.

Ella's cries stopped. I turned around and the tentacle had released her. Aric held her alien form against his chest.

"He must commit now," Shondark said.

"Yes! I have just the thing." I flipped over a pew and found the priest in the fetal position. "Not what I'm paying you for." I grabbed him by the robes and hauled him toward Aric and Ella. The priest babbled and tried to wiggle out of my grip.

I set him down next to the couple. Even in her...more natural state...I could still see Ella behind those eyes. Those many many eyes.

I pointed the priest's face toward Aric. When the priest managed nothing but baby noises, I slapped him on the back of the head.

"Do you?" the priest stammered. "Take this-this-woman to be your only begotten wife? Don't eat me. Please don't let it eat me. I'll never touch seafood again I swear."

"I do," Aric said.

I angled the priest toward Ella.

"Do you—It's looking at me!" I slapped him harder. "Do you take this man to be your only begotten husband through sickness and—"

"I do," Ella said, her voice just as lovely as ever.

I let the priest go.

He ran off, shouting, "By the power invested in me by the state of Achenae, I now pronounce you man and wife!" He switched to screaming as he found another pew to hide beneath.

"Rings." I looked up at the Mother...and God as my witness, I swear I saw a tear coming out of some of the eyes.

Aric pulled the box from his coat and removed a jewel encrusted ring. He slipped it onto the tip of Ella's tentacle...and it morphed back into a hand.

Ella laughed as her face returned. She put the other ring on her husband's finger and the two kissed.

"Be happy, my darling." The Mother pulled back from the gap in the wall. The three Shondarks followed as the creature slipped over the cliff and back into the ocean. A tentacle scooped them up.

Aric and Ella huddled against each other, foreheads pressed together, speaking quickly. The guests stormed out the now clear doorways and rushed towards their waiting air cars.

I walked over to a pew and sat down. Maurice showed up with a bottle of open Ryukyu champagne and some empty flutes. I snatched the bottle and a glass away and poured myself a tall drink. I swirled it beneath my nose for a moment, then drank it all in one sip. Maurice left the tray with me and jogged away.

"Sebastia." Don Buello sat next to me. He looked at the empty glass, then to the bottle. I poured myself another drink.

"Buello," I said.

"I'm a man of my word." He handed over a credit chit. "Payment in full for the loan his father gave me. No interest."

I turned the chit over in my fingers, then slipped it into a pocket. The money might buy us enough fuel to get to the next star. Might.

"My ship's leaving in an hour. I suddenly have the cash for a hostile takeover in the Naginana system. You interested?" Buello asked.

I held up my drink to the wrecked wedding hall and heard the whine of air cars leaving. The happy couple's conversation had devolved to kissing.

"And leave all this?" I asked.

"That's the one thing about you, Sebastia, can't buy your loyalty. The shrimp on this planet is top tier. I bet there's a market for it on Ione, what with all the food tourism they've got going on. Ione's not too far from here." He gave me a pat on the shoulder and left.

"Ione..." I looked over at the kitchens, which weren't too badly damaged.

"Sebastia," Ella said. She had her arms wrapped around Aric's waist as they walked over to me. "Thank you. I don't know how you did it, but thank you."

"Nonsense, my lady." I finished another glass. "You did it for each other."

"So...what happens now?" Aric asked.

"You're married. Now the work begins," I said. "In the meantime, we have some pressing issues. Ella, how much do you know about the local commodities market? Specifically, do you know where we can get a good price on shrimp?"

Author Richard Fox

Richard Fox is the winner of the 2017 Dragon Award for Best Military Science Fiction or Fantasy novel, and author of The Ember War Saga, a military science fiction and space opera series, and other novels in the military history, thriller and space opera genres. He lives in fabulous Las Vegas with his incredible wife and two boys, amazing children bent on anarchy.

Sign up for his spam-free mailing list and receive a free copy of The Ember War HERE (http://eepurl.com/cmo7S1).
To see the rest of his books, click Author.to/RichardFoxBooks

THE TROPHY

By B.C. Kellogg

Private Pyrros Eav is a foot soldier in the invasion of Rhitec. Nothing can stand before the might of the Empire...or so he's been told. When he's stranded in the middle of an alien forest during the annexation, he encounters an unlikely ally that threatens to destroy everything he believes in.

It should be easy, they told him.

But when was war and conquest ever easy?

Private Pyrros Eav tasted the salty tang of blood as he ran his tongue over his teeth. He'd hit the ground hard when the first blast hit his transport. Save for a few loose teeth and that goddamned ringing in his ears, he was alive. Which was more than he could say for the other troopers on his transport.

He staggered to his feet, his hands reaching for his lasgun by instinct. He was completely and utterly alone.

This wasn't the way it was supposed to go. Rhitec was going to be the perfect way to start his career in the Empire's ground forces. It was just an annexation of a single world, inhabited by a people that hadn't yet fledged to the stars.

A low boom sounded in the distance.

Well. The bastards turned out to be trickier than they looked.

He cursed the planet, the stars, and the Lords-damned Emperor himself as he stumbled off into the bushes. The ruined transport lay in pieces before him. Crimson splatter surrounded it.

Lords of the Dark, he thought to himself. *Where did that blast come from?*

He leaned his back against what seemed to be a twisted, spiky tree. He was still swaying. He had to pull himself together before the Rhitecci found him.

Crouching down, he tried his comms. There was only silence. His transport had been heading toward the Rhitecci capital; there should have been *someone* on the line.

He'd been stuck inside the hot, dark transport for an entire cycle, crowded in with the other soldiers, his armor smelling of sweat and *shiroppu*. Their officers hadn't told them much. All he was supposed to do was hit the ground running, lasgun blazing, and do as much damage as possible so that the wave of soldiers that came in behind him could storm the Rhitecci palace to secure the planet's leaders.

He swallowed another mouthful of blood. He knew he was cannon fodder, but he was cannon fodder with a brand new, top-of-the-line lasgun among a people so primitive they hadn't even made it to the moons that orbited their planet.

It should've been fast. Simple. Easy.

Catching his breath, he took stock of his surroundings. Whoever it was that targeted his transport had to be close.

Time to go. Now.

The Rhitecci road before him was worn and broken, made of ancient stones. It cut through a forest that looked to be just as old. Its trees were going to be the best cover he could get.

Best thing to do was to stay here, he decided. *If I'm anywhere near the capital there's bound to be another transport coming through.*

He raised his lasgun and hacked through into the tangled brush. Rhitecci sunsets were fast—the sky was already shading from green to purple—and he had to find someplace safe.

Lords only knew what could happen here in the dark.

***

His tongue went to his loose, wiggly teeth again. The copper taste of blood filled his mouth as he teased a damaged one. It was hard to ignore. The human body seemed to like picking at its own wounds.

What am I doing here anyway, he thought, over and over. *I was supposed to be traveling the galaxy. Seeing things. Getting the hell away from Oyruta.*

The Eavs had lived on Oyruta for generations, but it had all dwindled down to just him and his sister. Pyrros and Osma. Once Osma died there was no question of staying on the farm.

This was supposed to be the beginning. He scanned the starless skies. Clouds had gathered above—was it going to rain on him too?

Maybe this is more like the end.

He turned his gaze to the dark forest. There was a mound of rocks ahead. As he got closer, he realized that it was the entrance to a small cave.

Good a place as any to wait things out, he figured. *When it's light out I'll get back on the road—see if I can find a Lords-damned transport.*

He touched the top of his lasgun, turning on a small light. Crouching down, he edged into the darkness. It smelled like rotting plants and fungi inside. He was on full alert—what if some native soldier was inside?

There was a distant rumble and growl.

There's an animal in here.

He hefted the lasgun up, his muscles tense.

That's when he saw it—a strange alien creature about the size of an Oyrutan dog, its body covered in feathers, small conical horns on top of its head. It lifted its head and bared its teeth. Long, pointed fangs glinted in the dim light of his lasgun.

The light—it saw me!

In the span of a nanosecond, Eav took aim and fired. The force of the first blast slammed the animal into the wall. It dropped its jaws open and screeched, leaping toward him. He shot another blast at its chest as it launched toward him.

It let loose a bloodcurdling cry as the blast burned into its innards.

He had to be sure. He fired one more shot into its twisted body. When it was silent and no longer twitched, he approached it with caution. It was dead, its body contorted on the ground—but something else caught his attention.

The small, soft body of its pup lay in the far corner of the cave. He stepped over its dead mother. The pup was no larger than the length of his hand, with stubs for legs. It had a small mouth and sealed eyes.

He picked it up. It weighed just a few ounces.

Bad luck. He groaned. It was an old Oyrutan superstition that killing a mother animal meant that you'd be killed by another animal of the same species in time. The only way to lift the curse was to raise its offspring.

Besides, he had no time to skin its mother. Imperial custom was that a soldier could take a trophy from each annexation. Traditionally, it was a body part from the conquered alien sentient. His uncle's trophy room had been full of them—shriveled up skulls and severed limbs, alien skin flayed from corpses.

You'll have to do for now, pup. He dug through his pockets until he found his emergency vial of shiroppu. The syrupy-sweet drink was full of stimulants and could sustain a soldier for a full cycle or more. He squeezed open the pup's mouth and dribbled in a few drops.

He tucked the pup in behind his neck, next to the back rim of his armor.

Time to get back on track.

***

"You know why I'm here, pup?" Eav grunted as he climbed over a mound of brambles. "'Cause I can't go home. The Vehn took my sister Osma and left nothing. I should've been there. Was irresponsible of me to leave her with the neighbors. The Vehn swooped down and took 'em all. Left bloodstains, and nothing else. She was six. The monsters ate her alive."

The pup shifted against his neck. He reached back and scratched it—it was warm, and curled into him.

"Farm was no good after that. Joined up the day after. Osma always did want to see the universe. Figured I'd do it for her. Besides, the Empire's the only thing keeping the Vehn under control. If they gave me a chance to kill a few of 'em, I'd do whatever they wanted."

Of course, instead of killing Vehn, they dumped me on this sorry excuse for a planet.

The sun was rising. It was a white sun, quite different from Oyruta or Albion Secundus, where he'd gone through basic training. It lit up the forest. Rhitec's star was fast setting and fast rising.

"There," he said, the fresh light revealing the full length of the road. "Tracks from some other transport. Now I know which direction to go." The pup pawed his skin as he picked up his pace. No doubt he was drenching it in his sweat.

He stayed off the road itself, traveling a few feet to the right. It was too dangerous to be seen walking directly on the road. The risk of being seen was far too high.

As he walked he continued talking. He wasn't used to being alone. The barracks on Secundus were always full of boisterous men arguing, gambling, and trading stories.

"Osma wanted to join the corps of engineers," he continued. "Or become a shipwright and live in orbit around Albion Secundus. I've seen Secundus. It's no place for a girl like her. Too much testosterone and not a single garden. She wouldn't like it."

He was dimly aware that he was talking about his sister as if she were still alive. He knew she was dead but couldn't shake the habit.

"The whole planet's just one big military installation. Women aren't even allowed on the planet, 'cept for doctors, or officer's concubines. The shipwrights who lived in orbit—half of 'em are prisoners from Cadero, anyway. Not a place for my Osma."

The pup let out a soft yowl. He stopped in his tracks—it was the first sound he'd ever heard it make.

A flicker across the road caught his eye.

Someone's there.

He grabbed his lasgun and shifted back into the cover of the brush. He thumbed the energy discharge level to high and stood still, watching.

A gnarled old man emerged near the road, misshapen armor covering his shoulders. There was a glimmer of movement behind him, the reflection of light on armor.

Natives. More than one of 'em.

Something sailed across the road and landed ten feet away from him. It exploded.

Hells. They saw me.

He took cover. Then, he exhaled slowly and aimed his lasgun in the direction of the natives.

The first shot hit the man across the jaw, burning into his throat. The next shot disappeared, but the agitation of the bushes behind the man suggested that he'd made a hit.

Eav didn't wait. He charged across the road, firing indiscriminately into the forest.

Leaping over the body of his first victim, he saw a woman's body lying a few feet away. There was the sound of a third person running.

Can't let 'em get away or they'll come back for me. He took off in hot pursuit, his heartbeat thumping in time with his footsteps. Through the narrow slits between trees he could see the figure of the frantic native zigzagging through the forest.

Eav was big and lumbering in his Imperial-issue armor but he had one advantage—that brand-new, top-of-the-line lasgun.

The man slowed just slightly. Eav shot smoothly between the trees and hit the man in the gut.

As he approached, the man spasmed and went still. Eav frowned and nudged the body with his boot. The blast to the stomach was enough to kill him, but not immediately. The native must have suicided.

He knelt down and searched the man's clothing and makeshift armor. There was what appeared to be an explosive device in his belt. Eav fished it out and checked to see that it was disarmed. As far as he could tell, it was.

"Should've just surrendered," he muttered. "Empire's not interested in killing humans." Indeed, even when human populations fought back viciously against Imperial annexation, the Empire did not permit trophy taking. Only alien sentients were fair game for the hunt.

As he stood up he felt his comm vibrate on his collar.

Finally.

"Private Eav," a flat voice said. "Are you injured?"

"I'm fine," he said. At that moment he felt weary for the first time. He took out his container of shiroppu and sucked it nearly dry. Who knew how long it would take before they came for him.

"Transport XJ-130 will collect you within the next subcycle. Maintain your current position." The comm line closed.

Eav looked up to the turbulent Rhitecci sky and reached back to touch the warm, squirming body of the pup. He held the creature in his palm and fed it the last drops of his shiroppu.

"Guess we're safe, then," he said, not quite believing his own words.

***

"You got 'em all?" The disbelieving trooper gaped at him. "They've been blowing up a whole string of transports going through this forest. Dunno how some pre-spaceflight primitives managed that, but the whole battalion has been on alert 'cause of them."

Eav shrugged. "I killed three natives," he said. "Didn't know who they were."

"Pity they turned out to be human," the man added. He lifted his visor to reveal a deep scar across his face. Judging by his age, he was a veteran of many annexations. "I'd have sawed off something memorable. I was hopin' for a couple of horns or jawbone with some pretty canines. And this being your first annexation—by rights you should have something to remember it by. Better luck next time."

He patted Eav on the shoulder. He flinched, knowing that the pup was inches away. Thankfully, the thing had stayed silent since he'd come on board the transport. He could feel its weight against him—it seemed to have gotten heavier. But maybe that was simply the consequence of carrying the pup for so long.

Eav moved toward one of the thin window slits in the interior of the transport and looked outside—the landscape was blurring by as the vehicle flew. He sat down on the narrow slab that served as a seat and ran a hand through his damp hair.

Another trooper came over and offered him a ration bar. "Ignore Gitto over there. He always picks on the young ones like you. Way I see it, we should be thanking you for keepin' us from being blown portal high," he said. "My name's Berton. You ever kill anyone or anything in combat before?"

160

Eav shook his head. "Only in simulations."

He took a bite of the thick, waxy bar. The trooper sat down next to him and handed him a flask. Eav took a sip—it was shiroppu mixed with something stronger. *Much* stronger. The trooper grinned at his reaction.

"It gets easier," Berton assured him. "Feels good, once you figure out that they'd kill you if they could. And that you're doing right by the Empire. Those natives don't know it yet but they'll be civilized soon enough. Be like any other group of humans in the rest of the Empire. Hells, we're even going to hand them spaceflight and tech that would take 'em another thousand years to develop. As far as I'm concerned, what we're doing is charity."

"I'm new at this," Eav mumbled.

"Thought as much. Well, stay close to me when we get out there. You clearly have some talent with a lasgun. You'll get through this alive."

"Not talented so much as . . . trigger happy." It was true. He had been functioning on pure adrenaline when he'd killed the natives— and the animal in her den before that.

Berton continued, undaunted. "By the time you've been through a few more annexations, you won't be able to tell 'em apart, except for whatever trophies you take home. Don't worry, boy. Get your strength back. We'll be entering the outskirts of the capital within two subcycles."

Eav took another swig of the spiked shiroppu. He could feel his exhaustion fading despite his lack of sleep, and his mind coming to full alertness. There would be hell to pay once it was all over— overusing shiroppu had some nasty side effects—but he didn't have time for anything else.

He felt a sudden, sharp pain at his nape. The pup *bit* him. He sucked in his breath and muffled the curse that rose to his lips.

Don't do that, you little beast. I'll feed you when I can.

"One thing's for sure," the trooper mused aloud. "You never forget your first annexation."

***

The transport dropped them into pure chaos.

They surged out into the bright Rhitecci sunshine with the walls of the capital before them. The walls were old, and should have been an insignificant obstacle for Imperial troops and guns, but there seemed to be mass confusion within the crowd of soldiers.

The capital was surrounded by miles of empty suburbs, charred by Imperial fire.

"Hold your position," came the voice from his comm. "Await further instructions."

He exchanged glances with Berton. The older man pointed up.

Hovering above the capital were atmospheric assault vehicles— they were firing down, to no effect. There was something protecting the capital.

Berton spoke quietly into his comm as Eav looked on, nervous. The man had more contacts with other troopers than he did. He beckoned to Eav.

"Smart little bastards," he whispered to Eav. "Things seemed to be going well—troops were entering the capital. Then halfway through this shield comes outta nowhere. Locks half of us in, and half of us out. Now they're slaughterin' the men inside, I'll bet. And the rest of us are trapped out here 'til the diggers get us in."

A rumbling sound behind them heralded the arrival of the diggers. Eav turned and watched the crowd of soldiers part for the massive machines. Diggers were actually multipurpose war machines—a sophisticated battering ram. They could be reconfigured to climb, dig, or even run across a combat zone.

Eav watched as the digger near them began to bore into the earth, at the exact same moment that the other diggers began to delve underground.

He was so mesmerized by the machine's action that he was startled to hear screaming and weapons discharging behind them.

The suburbs!

They were under attack.

"I thought those Lords-damned buildings were empty!" Berton growled.

"They're back, somehow," said Eav, tensing as orders poured in through his comms. "They infiltrated those buildings again. How're a bunch of primitives this coordinated? This organized?"

Berton merely grunted as he ran away from the wall, toward the heavy fire. Eav followed him, unwilling to let the man go alone. The pup jostled against his shoulders, heavier and sweatier than ever.

The narrow streets of the capital suburbs were deserted—or seemed to be. It was eerie to run through the whitewashed buildings, sunlight reflecting brightly off them. The sound of the occasional explosion was the only hint that something was terribly wrong.

They're clever, Eav thought. *They divided our forces a third time. Those diggers better work fast, or we'll need replacements rather than reinforcements.*

A heavy crash behind him caught his attention.

"Eav." It was Berton's voice. "Heard from the lieutenant. There's a bunch of 'em holed up a few paces to the south. They've got some kind of grenade launcher. I'm going to take 'em out. Get up high if you can and cover me."

"Got it," he said. Berton peeled off, and Eav climbed the nearest stairs to run in parallel alongside the trooper. From his vantage point he could see the Rhitecci as dark specks, moving through the white maze of buildings.

He kept his eye on Berton.

There—

He breathed slowly and squeezed the trigger. A Rhitecci who was chasing Berton collapsed to the ground an instant later.

Eav adjusted the targeting mechanism on his lasgun. He had to move quick—no doubt there were threats that he hadn't seen.

The closer Berton got to his destination, the more Rhitecci targets there were. Perspiration dripped down Eav's face as he took them out, one by one, as many as he could.

How's Berton going to take out a grenade launcher? He cursed under his breath as he dashed to take up a new location. *One man against a whole crowd of crazy—*

A teeth-rattling series of booms went off in the distance. He grabbed at a nearby wall to catch his balance.

"Shield is down," a voice announced over the commline.

Eav exhaled shakily. The blasts had to be the diggers exploding. The diggers were programmed to finish the tunnels and then detonate, making as clean a path as possible for the soldiers who followed.

That means—

Out of the corner of his eye, he saw a group of Rhitecci dressed in makeshift combat fatigues scattering. Then he saw Berton running after them, mowing them down with his lasgun.

"Berton," he said urgently, switching to the direct commline with the trooper. "Did you hear?"

"Yeah, I heard," the man panted, pausing at the body of one of his victims. "That's why the natives are runnin'—this place isn't worth it anymore."

"We'd better get back," he said. "The wall—"

"What's this?" Berton murmured.

"What's what? I'm coming down to you." He was close enough already. He crossed the deserted street in search of the trooper.

He found Berton kneeling at the body, a dagger in his hand. The body was a woman's, with a head of thick red-gold hair. She wasn't quite dead—Eav could still see her chest heaving.

Berton looked up at him. "Time to take my trophy," he said.

Eav's heart was thrashing inside his ribcage. "You can't," he said. "She's human, and she's still alive—"

"She might be alive, but she's definitely not human," said Berton. He yanked her hair back and the woman's eyes opened and closed. A nictitating membrane showed—a third eyelid.

At that moment the pup sank its teeth into his neck again. This time he couldn't help but to wince. *When did this thing grow teeth?*

There was a malevolent smile on Berton's face. "This whole time we thought they were human," he said. "But they're not—or at least some of 'em aren't. Maybe they been crossbred with humans. That's even worse than a pure alien. This one's fair game."

Don't, he heard the woman plea.

Eav automatically lifted his lasgun. Had she spoken?

The woman's eyelids blinked again. She looked at him and spoke despite her mouth being closed.

She's in my head, he suddenly realized.

Let him kill me, she said. *You need to stay alive to keep Rhi alive.*

Rhi?

The pup stirred against the back of his neck. The woman closed her eyes. *The . . . pup. It's one of ours. You have to get off the planet with her. It's the only way our people will survive.*

"You best not point that lasgun at me," said Berton.

He lowered his lasgun. Not at Berton's demand but for the woman.

"Good," said Berton. "Don't let their looks fool you. They're not human. That means they're fair game for the hunt. As for this one, I'm going to take the hair—"

In a flash, Eav raised his lasgun, aimed, and shot a blast through the woman's forehead. She died quickly. The pup twitched.

Berton let the body drop to the ground. "You little bastard," he growled. "It went through her skull—through the hair."

For once in his life, Eav didn't blink. "Plenty more where that came from," he said. "We need to return to the wall. You should've heard the same thing I heard from comms. They're bombing this place. We don't have much time."

Berton looked at him with suspicion. "You stole my trophy from me," he said, advancing on Eav, kicking aside the dead body.

Eav held his ground, his fingers tightening around the lasgun.

"Only a traitor would do something like that," said Berton, advancing. "A sympathizer. You *feel* for these aliens, I'll bet. You do know what's going to happen to them once this annexation's complete—the hunt. It's tradition. And once we're done here on the ground, they'll kill 'em all. With a bioweapon or something else. Clean the whole planet for human settlement. They were dead the minute we landed." A feral gleam appeared in Berton's eye. "I'd be within my rights to shoot you where you stand."

"Don't make me defend myself," he said, his voice taut.

"Traitor," said Berton. The trooper's hand moved toward his weapon.

You don't have to kill him, he heard a voice say in his mind. It sounded familiar . . . painfully familiar. *Pyrros . . .*

He recognized the voice. He made the decision in the moment he heard it.

I've got to protect her, he realized. It was the clearest thought he'd had in days.

With a flick of his finger he turned the lasgun and shot Berton in the chest. The man crumpled to the ground.

His stomach lurched at the sight of what he'd done. He lowered his lasgun as he straightened slowly.

That voice, he wondered. *Is it really you, Osma?*

***

Overhead, the roar of the atmospheric assault vehicles was deafening. Eav found cover in the threshold of a dilapidated house and watched as they sped toward the capital. He was breathing hard. They should have left the moment he'd gotten the order to evacuate the buildings, but now he was a marked man. If they found Berton, they'd discover the discharge signature of Eav's lasgun on his corpse. He was the worst kind of murderer, in the eyes of the Empire.

The first bomb hit the outskirts of the settlement, the white buildings crumbling under the force of the blasts. Another bomb came nearer. He didn't bother moving. There was no place to go.

Orders were pouring through the comms nonstop. With the shield around the capital finally down, there was no obstacle to the invasion forces now. Eav grappled with the comms with clumsy fingers, debating whether he should rip it out of his collar.

Berton's dead eyes stared up at him from a few feet away.

I killed him, he thought numbly. He'd killed those Rhitecci natives first, sure, but they were enemy combatants. Berton was just like him, wasn't he? He was officially a traitor now.

He was a criminal.

Pyrros.

The voice was crystal clear, and feminine.

"Osma?" he muttered, his voice rough. *I'm going mad. I'm imagining things. That's definitely her voice . . .*

Not quite. I'm right here with you, though.

With his heart thumping, he reached behind him and touched the pup's warm body. It *had* grown since he'd found it. He pulled it out of his armor and stared at it. The pup had more than tripled in size. It was growing even as he looked at it, its body changing from formless blob into something more familiar.

Something more *human.*

Put me down, it said.

It was speaking in his mind.

"You're telepathic," he said in a state of mild shock. He laid the pup amidst the rubble strewn on the ground.

It grew before his eyes, stretching its limbs. They changed from white to pink and then tan, each appendage resolving into a hand or foot. Dark brown hair cascaded from its head, past its shoulders.

It was Osma, as he remembered her. She was a small child, intelligence in her wide, coffee-colored eyes. There was even a small, healed scar above her right eyebrow. She was exactly as she was before he'd left the farm and the Vehn attacked.

"Pyrros," she said aloud. This time, it wasn't in his mind. "I'm cold."

It shook him out of his shock. His mind buzzing, he kicked down the door to the house and searched. He found a tunic.

She'd followed him when he turned and offered her the tunic. She tugged it over her head and smiled at him. She blinked, and he saw the telltale blink of that third eyelid. She was not quite human.

"Thanks." Her childish voice was small but bright.

"What are you?" he demanded.

"I am the Rhi," she said. "But you can call me Osma."

*　*　*

"Osma died," he said, his mouth dry. "Years and years ago."

167

"You're right that I'm not quite human," she said. "I'm not completely Rhi anymore, either."

"What's that supposed to mean?"

She looked down at her hands, and opened and closed them. "Hands," she observed. "Opposable thumbs. They really are as handy as they look." She glanced up at him and gave him an impish smile. "Get it, Pyrros? Handy?"

"Osma . . ."

There was a loud crash above them. Eav automatically wrapped his arms around the creature that was Osma, shielding her from the dust and debris that fell.

"We need to leave this place," she said, studying their surroundings. "It won't stand for long."

He clasped her shoulders. "Not until I know who or what you are."

She wrinkled her nose, a familiar habit of Osma's when she was annoyed. "Fine," she said. "I'm not Osma Eav. I'm the Osma Eav that exists in your memories."

"How is that possible?"

"It's the nature of Rhi," she said. At his confused look, she continued. "The Rhi were here before you bipeds came. We are . . . one life form. One organism, really. We exist in symbiosis with other life forms. Our offspring mimic the first animal they encounter in life. One day, a long time ago, humans landed on this planet. At that time, we were not sentient. We were just an animal like any other. But when a Rhi mimicked one of you . . ." she shrugged. "We gained sentience. And over the millennia we have become a sister species to the humans on this world."

He shook his head, stunned. The Rhi named Osma continued. "When I encountered you, I was already connected to the other Rhi on this world. I took your memories of your sister—she was at the uppermost part of your mind—and formed myself in her image."

He took a step back and raised his lasgun. "You're a fake."

Osma lifted her head. "I'm an original," she said, sounding slightly offended. "And I know that you won't hurt a child, Pyrros. Even a nonhuman one."

He didn't lower his weapon. He stared at her for a long moment, worked his jaw in agitation, and finally gestured with the lasgun. "Get out of here, then. This is no place for you. If they find you, they'll kill you for not being human."

He couldn't bear that thought, even though she wasn't really his Osma.

"You're lonely," she said, not backing down. "You miss her. And now . . . you're afraid. You have no place to go."

The building trembled again, bathing them in dust.

"Get out of here," he said, taking a step toward her to intimidate her.

"Not without you, Pyrros," she said, extending a hand toward him.

***

He ran with her arms wrapped around his neck, her body heavy on his back. All around them, buildings were crumbling. The bombing had stopped but the damage was done.

"Left," she said. "And then a right, when you see the metal grate on the ground. We'll go deeper from there."

"You've gotten heavier," he groused.

"Not since I came into this form," she replied. "You're imagining things."

He grunted. Beneath the surface level of the city there was a maze of underground tunnels. He realized that this was how the Rhitecci had appeared in the suburbs so suddenly. He didn't know where she was guiding him, but what other choice did he have?

She winced above him and buried her head against his shoulder.

"Hey. What's wrong?"

"So many of us are dying," she whispered. "They're killing us."

Pyrros's lips tightened into a thin line. It was all going exactly according to plan, now. They'd penetrated the capital and were slaughtering any nonhuman sentients. He thought about the trophy that Berton was planning to take and suppressed the sick feeling in his stomach.

"Not all of you," he said. "They can't, can they? There's more of you on this world—"

"I saw your mind. They'll kill every last one of us if they can. We've defended ourselves the best we could. You killed three of us before I bit you. Imagine what an entire army of soldiers like you will do to the Rhi. If they kill all sentient Rhi, then the next generation of Rhi will lose its sentience and be like animals again." Strangely enough, there was no bitterness in her voice.

"I'm sorry about that," he said. "I didn't know."

She hummed softly. "Keep going. Don't think about that now, Pyrros."

"Where are we headed?"

"Deep into the dens."

They ran on in relative silence. The only sound in his ears was his own ragged breathing. It was quieter underground, and the soft earth muffled his footsteps.

He was still running when he felt the first bolt of exhaustion hit him like a thunderbolt. The shiroppu was wearing off.

"Lords," he muttered.

"No swearing. Mama wouldn't like it."

He felt an ache manifest in his legs. He'd forgotten how heavy Imperial armor was, and then to have the weight of a six-year old on top of all that . . .

"Don't slow down," she said to him. "We have to escape."

"Can't," he grunted. Each step was more difficult than the last, as if a weight was in each boot and it was getting heavier with every passing second. His mind was churning, fighting against the overwhelming pain and exhaustion. "Sorry, sis."

The last thought he had was a wish for this Osma to live, despite it all.

***

". . . can he do it?"

The whispering floated above him. It didn't sound right, like normal human conversation. He could feel the weakness in his body

170

and his shredded muscles, and he wanted to sleep forever. Still, he let his consciousness rise up toward the sound of the voices.

"Osma?" he rasped.

"I'm here, Pyrros," the familiar voice said. He focused his blurry vision on the face that appeared above him.

"Where am I?"

"Down deep," she said. "With us. With me."

He hauled himself up to a sitting position, struggling to ignore the stabbing pain in his skull. "Isn't that all the same thing?"

"You're right. Ever since I joined with your mind all of the Rhi have been watching you. Protecting you, when we could."

"I killed you—"

"Many times," Osma finished his sentence. "But you didn't know. And if you want to save the Rhi, you still can."

Another figure lowered down next to him, in a kneeling position. "Osma is young," it said. "Take her off this world, and out there." It gestured above them. A long time ago, the humans who gave us sentience came from up there. We know that there are innumerable worlds and peoples there. Take Osma, and whatever happens to us, the Rhi will survive through her." It was an older man. *Rhi,* Eav corrected himself. *Not a man.*

"You're manipulating me," he said grimly. "Using the memories of my sister to trick me." The Rhi gathered around him shifted at his words.

Osma leaned in, her expression earnest. "You don't believe that, Pyrros. I could have been anyone, you know. I could have looked like you, or anyone else in your memories. Do you really know why I chose to manifest like this?"

He shook his head.

"Because . . . she was so alive, in your mind. So clever and colorful. She had so much hope. I loved her like you loved her, so I chose to embody Osma over anyone else. I have no regrets."

"You saw all that?" he finally got out.

She nodded. "I know it's dangerous up there," she said. "But Osma would have wanted to go, and so do I."

He closed his eyes and leaned his head back against the wall.

"There's not much time left," said the other Rhi. "And there are only a few of us left here. Will you help us?"

Eav looked at Osma and at the crowd of Rhi around her. He looked at Osma again.

"I will," he said at last.

***

They raced toward the capital, deep underground. He carried Osma on his back again.

"Are you in pain?" she asked.

"No," he said, lying.

"You always were a bad liar. Set me down." She slipped off his back and down to the ground. The Rhi path terminated at a larger tunnel—a tunnel made by a digger.

The three Rhi behind them made a disapproving noise. "I'll be fine," Osma assured them.

He forged ahead, Osma running as fast as she could behind him. The digger tunnel angled up to the surface. He exhaled sharply and primed his lasgun. What would be waiting for them within the capital?

"There's still some of us left in there," she said. "Not many—but some."

"And once we're in there?"

"We find a way out. The capital's surrounded and we can't wait them out in the tunnels. This is the only direction we can go."

His heart was racing as they approached the surface. The tunnel opened into a blast zone, the ground and surrounding structures charred black. There were bodies in the distance—or body parts. The Imperial troops had come through already.

He began to move cautiously into the open when he felt a hand on his shoulder. "Step back," the Rhi said. "We'll go ahead. You protect Osma."

Eav let them move in front of them, their bodies crouched and tense. There was a certain coordination to everything they did, he realized. The consciousness of the Rhi was linked.

He scanned the horizon. There were transport ships hovering above every sector of the city. They'd have to stay low to avoid being seen—and pray that they wouldn't run into any troops.

"Our people are there," Osma said behind him, pointing at a gray plume of smoke twisting up from a building in the distance.

Eav stared hard. "They're fighting there," he said. "That's why there's smoke."

"I know," said Osma calmly. "It's all on purpose."

"Which is?"

She then pointed to a sector on the far side. "We've secured a ship," she said. "A small one. If the annexation forces are focused on killing us, then they won't notice you and me."

He shook his head at the audacity of the Rhi. He held out a hand to Osma. "Come on, bean," he said to her. Calling her by Osma's old nickname felt strange but right. She let him lift her onto his back again. Together, they moved through the ravaged city.

***

The ship was damaged. The Rhi at its gangplank ushered them on board. Osma dropped off his back as he made for the cockpit. Eav was so close to escape that he could taste it.

But this was the most dangerous stage.

"Not much in the way of weapons," he muttered. "The engines are good . . . warming them up now."

Osma appeared at his elbow. "Hurry," she said darkly. "They're coming . . ."

He glanced behind them. "We have room. If any of the other Rhi want to—"

"No," said a sharp voice behind them. It was the Rhi that had traveled with them. "We stay here. This is our home."

Eav glanced at Osma. "This is her home too."

173

"No," the Rhi said. "She embodied one of *you*. She is ours, but she'll carry us all up there." He pointed up.

Osma made a soft little cry as the Rhi stiffened. "They're close."

The ship shuddered as a bomb went off nearby. The Rhi turned and ran.

"This ship's weapons are almost drained. I can't—"

Osma rested a hand on his arm. "They've gone."

Eav's eyes widened when he saw troopers heading toward them like a swarm of insects. "Hells," he said.

He moved faster, the ship beginning to hum.

The ship rocked again. This time, it was a sharper movement. They were being fired on. He switched on the shields, and powered up. He grabbed hold of the piloting hologram and brought the ship around.

Osma cried out again in pain as the troopers swarmed the last of the Rhi.

"I'm sorry, bean," he said. "But I won't let them become trophies."

Eav gritted his teeth. His jaw ached.

I gotta do this. This is the right thing.

He aimed the nose of the ship toward the fight. He plowed the ship forward, firing the last of the ship's weapons stores.

It destroyed troopers and Rhi alike, their bodies convulsing as their flesh dissolved into formless black ash.

"They're all dead," Osma said shakily. "Every Rhi in the capital . . . I can't feel anyone . . ."

He jerked his hands up, yanking the ship up toward the sky. His flying was unskilled, and he prayed that his technique wouldn't give them away when it mattered.

The ship lurched, but lifted. He dared to exhale as he throttled the ship toward the bright Rhitecci sun.

"Say goodbye, bean," he whispered.

***

Osma was plastered against the viewport, her hands and face pressed against it as if she wanted to be one with the darkness on the other side. She was looking down at Rhitec.

Eav switched on the autopiloting program. They were floating amidst the annexation fleet, a vast contingent of ships of every size, from fierce dreadnoughts to single-man fighters. He'd scrambled the ship's credentials; it would enable them to fly through without notice. If they were fortunate.

"All this to take my little planet," Osma muttered. "Is it really worth it?"

He leaned back in his chair. "For my people—for the Empire—there's no other way of life," he said. "It's in our blood. We're a warrior race. We believe in the destiny of humanity. We go from system to system, bringing humans into the Empire. We eliminate alien threats. This is what we do." The words tasted bad in his mouth now. Funny—they never had before.

She rested her forehead against the viewport. "They're not your people."

He smiled, tired. "Guess not. And yours . . ."

She shook her head. "I can't feel them anymore," she said. "They're all . . . too far away. Or they're gone."

He came alongside her and kneeled down next to her. "There's got to be some Rhi left. Some who weren't close to the capital."

"The Rhi were the backbone of planetary defense," said Osma. "Coordinating all the guerilla attacks. If they hunt down the defenders . . . then they'll kill the Rhi."

He sighed and rested a hand against the viewport. "I don't know what to tell you, bean."

She chewed on her lip. "There will always be some wild Rhi," she said. "Like my mother. But if they kill all the sentient Rhi, then all our communal knowledge will be lost."

He rested a gentle hand on her shoulder. "Except for you."

Her fingers traced the transparent material of the viewport. "I've seen inside your mind, Pyrros. The universe is a dangerous place for aliens like me. And if I'm the only one left . . ."

Eav thought about what he knew about the universe. Lush, beautiful Oyruta. Albion Prime, shining in glory as the center of the Empire. Albion Secundus, the Empire's military center. And then the long list of worlds that Osma had planned to visit when she was all grown up.

"Bean," he sighed. "I'm an orphan too, y'know. When my Osma died"—his throat tightened—"I thought that was the end of it all. I thought about staying on the farm, and I couldn't. I felt . . . I felt that I had to go up. Any way I could. I thought at the time that it was all about escape." He rested his chin on his knee.

"And if it's not about escape?"

"I'm not that smart. You told me so yourself, lots of times. And I don't have any schooling, aside from the basic stuff they injected in my brain after I joined up. But if I had to say, it's about . . . finding a reason to . . . I dunno, a reason to *be*." He straightened slightly. "It's maybe too obvious, but I think that's right. Feels like it, anyway."

"You found one?"

He glanced at her. She wasn't staring at Rhitec now. She was looking at him.

"Ah, bean," he said. "I think I have."

She was silent for a moment. He wondered how much knowledge she had from the Rhi. For all he knew she was wiser than he was. But then, maybe Osma always had been smarter than he was, too. When she spoke again, her voice was lighter and higher.

"Where should we go, big brother?"

He grinned as he stood up. The further they got from the Imperial annexation fleet, the brighter the universe seemed to be.

"Osma . . . what do you know about pirates?"

Author B.C. Kellogg

B.C. grew up on a highly nutritious diet of Star Trek, Star Wars, Babylon 5, and science fiction novels that involved aliens, laser guns, and highly improbable explosions. She likes spicy food, spreadsheets, and talking about books and movies until no one ever wants to go see a movie with her again. B.C. spends her days working in Silicon Valley and her nights typing feverishly at her laptop.

Join B.C.'s mailing list (http://bckellogg.com/mailing-list/) to receive The Admiral's Cage, a free story set in the Darkspace universe.

BLOOD AND TREASURE
By Terry Mixon

Major Ned Quincy stepped onto the bridge of the Imperial Raider strike ship *Persephone*. His executive officer—Senior Lieutenant Paul Kingsolver—rose from the command seat.

Ned sat and raised an eyebrow. "What have we got, Paul?"

"Just about what you'd expect from a Genie raid. One ship in orbit around New Italy on high alert. The way they're scanning, you'd think they expect trouble." The last was said in a wry tone.

"Today, they get more trouble than they bargained for," Ned said with a cold smile. "Has the stealthed probe decided what kind of ship we're dealing with?"

His executive officer half turned toward the main screen. On the small bridge, that wasn't far away.

"It looks like a modified civilian ship, but that's almost certainly a sham. Their Peacock Class frigates are almost identical in basic layout, so I'd wager we'll find some weapons and battle screens under there somewhere."

The Terran Empire and the Singularity had never technically gone to war, but they'd been raiding one another's borders for thousands of years. Almost since the day the Genies decided they couldn't live under the emperor's rule. At this point, the conflict was almost ritual in nature at times.

Oh, they always made noises that rogue elements were carrying out the raids, but no one was fooled.

The Empire allowed its troops to muster out and perform covert missions and then paid them a hefty bonuses when they rejoined, too. At their previous ranks, of course, and with secret letters of commendation.

Ned had no idea what the Genies did for their people. They probably had a specific class of society that did this full time. That was how they worked everything else, so why not?

The Singularity was a heavily stratified society in which each individual was cloned from a specific design for their class. That was true from the rulers down to the servitors that cleaned the streets. Each to a purpose, or so he'd heard.

Too bad if you made a lousy street cleaner. Do that one job well or be recycled.

That euphemism probably meant a flechette to the back of the head and having your body tossed into a protein vat to feed other clones in artificial wombs, but no one was really sure. It was impossible to slip anyone in to spy on the bastards because outsiders were instantly recognized and dealt with.

So the only interaction their people had was over rifle sights or at missile range. That was fine by him. The arrogant bastards needed cleaning out. They'd do their part today.

"Do we have any idea what their raiding party is up to?" he asked.

"Based on local news reports, they're after a supply of exotic elements used in building flip drives."

The space-bending drives that made interstellar travel possible through the gravitational wormholes called flip points were difficult to build and required several extremely rare elements. He hadn't read that New Italy was one of the systems that mined them or built the drives.

"Are we sure about that? They don't have a shipyard here."

"One of the major corporations here transships the stuff from a world where they have mining contracts. Still, that's not all the Genies are doing. They're collecting citizens in an open-air sports venue. I'm not really getting a sense of how many or why."

That wasn't good. The Singularity had no use for prisoners, and that frigate didn't have the room to hold them, anyway. This was shaping up more like an atrocity in the making.

Those were rare but not unheard of. If so, it would kick off a few years of intense raids from both sides. Not that he had any objections to killing Genies. Killing bad guys was what they lived for.

Every single one of his people—including him—was a Marine Raider. They took the basic computerized implants used by Fleet Marines and augmented them to ridiculous levels: graphene-coated bones, artificial muscles woven inside their natural ones, a pharmacology unit with drugs that could just about allow a dead man to fight, and far too many other classified enhancements to mention.

Each Raider cost the same as a standard marine company, training, and equipment. And they fought like one, too. Even without powered armor, he had ten times the strength of a normal person and could do things regular marines couldn't even dream of.

Like a covert assault on a planet right under their noses.

"If we can get in without them seeing us, we might be able to free the hostages before they figure out how screwed they are," he said after a moment. "We can't use drop capsules with those bastards right there, though."

"And if we attack the ship from stealth, their ground forces start killing people," his executive officer agreed. "We're going to have to do this the hard way."

"As if the emperor pays us to do the easy stuff," Ned said with a nod. "We'll come in from the far side of the planet and use our pinnaces to get down. We'll have to time everything just right so that you can take out the frigate as we're freeing the hostages.

"Timing is critical. If we're off by the smallest bit, a lot of people under our protection are going to die, or the bastards will shoot the hell out of *Persephone*."

He checked the tactical plot. Moving slowly like this, his ship could get in close enough to launch pinnaces toward New Italy with a reasonable travel time. They'd have to coast into the planet's shadow and work their way around, but Raider pinnaces were heavily stealthed for missions just like this.

Persephone was also hard to see, but it couldn't get into weapons range without a vigilant ship like that one spotting them.

Anything larger than a frigate would be impossible to take down in a stand-up fight. His ship was built for sneaking, not a missile duel.

"What if *Persephone* came in on the far side of the planet and used it for a gravitational slingshot?" he asked slowly. "They wouldn't see us coming."

"Unless they had probes on the far side of New Italy," Paul said. "That's what I'd do. No way they'd miss us roaring in."

True. Well, nothing worthwhile was ever easy.

"I'll take a look as we head in and see what I can figure out," he said after a moment. "If I can't find something, then you'll have to do the best you can. Even if we only scare them off, that's a win."

"The emperor doesn't pay me to let the bastards off easy," Paul said grimly. "You're leading the drop?"

"With so many civilian lives at stake, you bet your ass I am."

* * *

Persephone's two pinnaces ghosted toward New Italy on the far side of the planet from the Singularity vessel. Each held seventy armored Raiders looking for blood.

Being locked into his armor wasn't an impediment to having a last-minute planning session with his team leaders. Even though the interior of his helmet was pitch black behind the solid metal faceplate, his implants overrode his optic nerves and allowed him to see everything he needed to.

Part of his attention was linked to the direct feed from the pinnace's passive scanner. He wanted to know about any problems the moment they happened. The small craft were tough and agile, but a ship could kill them easily enough if it saw them.

Still no sign of trouble ahead. The enemy was focused on their own mission and seemingly didn't have a clue that anyone else was even in the system.

The tight-beam feed from *Persephone*'s stealthed probes had verified the Singularity ship was close to New Italy's primary orbital. That wasn't good. It probably meant they had troops on it. One more complication that had to be dealt with.

"Change in plan," he said over his com. He could've used his implants to send the words right into his people's heads, but he preferred real voices whenever possible.

"The exotic elements are no longer a primary objective," he continued. "We still need to free the prisoners below, but now we also have to secure the orbital. Give me some options."

Even though he was strapped into his assigned slot and locked down tight inside immensely strong restraints, he felt as if he were seated around a virtual conference table. A glance took in the faces of his people as they considered the problem.

"I think the group that takes out the enemy probe would be better positioned to go after the orbital," Lieutenant Emily Turin, the commander of First Platoon, said. "That'll give the other platoon more time to get into the stadium. Seconds count there."

He nodded. "Exactly right. We'll try to get a drone down and scout the area, but that might not be possible. Second Platoon might have to go in cold and shoot anything that looks hostile.

"The more ticklish objective will be getting into the New Italy orbital before the Genies realize they have trouble. If we can catch them with their own troops aboard, they'll at least try to withdraw before they blow it."

And Ned had no doubt that they'd destroy the orbital as a matter of course. That was a given. The cost to replace it would be stupendous, and Imperial forces did exactly the same thing.

Well, they allowed the people on it to evacuate first.

Genies didn't value human life the same way. Not normal humans, anyway. They had some respect for their own people—when they didn't consider them defective—but seemed to regard Imperial citizens as mad dogs.

To be fair—though he didn't want to be—they usually allowed civilians to withdraw, assuming they could do so in an expeditious manner. Any Fleet or marine personnel were executed out of hand, though.

Thankfully for his peace of mind, there were rarely any prisoners for him to deal with, which was a good thing since *Persephone* didn't have a brig. Of course, if one of them ever surrendered or was captured alive, he wouldn't do like they did.

Even if he was *really* tempted.

"We'll take the more difficult mission for ourselves. Lieutenant Vanderbilt can handle a planetary assault. I'm sure she'll complain that we gave her a cakewalk."

That got the laugh he expected, but Wanda Vanderbilt wouldn't have an easy time of it. If she didn't lose a third of her people in the lightning strike against an entrenched foe mixed with hostages, it would be the next best thing to a miracle.

He sent a signal informing her of the change. She'd need every second he could give her to plan.

"That means our first objective is to locate and neutralize all enemy probes," he continued. "And we need to do it in a manner that won't tip them off that we're here. For that amazing feat, I turn to Senior Sergeant Enright."

Jake Enright was a Raider like the rest of them, but he had additional training in sophisticated systems. He'd have made one hell of a second-story man. As it was, Ned was just about sure the man could've broken into the Imperial Vault and made off with the Imperial jewels without tripping an alarm.

"We have schematics for the probes used by the Singularity," the bookish man said. "Bypassing the com feed for one isn't difficult if you're already on top of it. It's the sneaking-in part that's hard."

"Do you have any ideas on how we might accomplish that?" Ned asked. "I'd really like to keep them from knowing we're here."

"I do have an idea, but you won't like it."

That never boded well. Raiders *liked* doing dangerous, risky things.

"Tell me."

The other man cleared his throat. "The probes are sensitive enough to detect our pinnaces before we can get into orbit. We need to send someone ahead. They'll need to coast in at relatively low speed and use the armor's built-in grav assist to decelerate slowly enough to avoid triggering the probe's antitampering protocols."

"And what happens if they get triggered?"

Enright made a gesture with his hands expanding from a single ball to a wide spread. "Boom."

"Can our armor withstand something like that?"

The sergeant shook his head. "We're tough but not that tough. It's a plasma charge."

Yeah, that would be a quick trip to oblivion, even for a Marine Raider.

"I assume you'll need more than one set of hands. And before you insist that you can handle it on your own, we need redundancy. Two people. Inserting someone from out here introduces some uncertainty in the course they need to take. One person might not be close enough to the probe, and we absolutely cannot risk detection."

The other man shrugged. "Since you insist, sir. It'll have to be someone with the right skills. This is a complex procedure. Those skills aren't exactly common, even in the Raiders."

Ned smiled a little. "I've been taking courses and trying to learn more about the magic you do. If I have, you can be sure someone else has, too. Anyone?"

There were two other people with similar skill sets, but they were both on the other pinnace. A transfer now posed a small but measurable risk of detection, so he decided against it.

That left Ned in the unenviable position of taking an active part in this segment of the mission when by all rights he should've stayed on the pinnace.

Well, he wasn't going to back down from doing what had to be done. The pinnace could come in and pick him up as soon as the probe or probes was disabled. He'd still be there for the assault on the orbital.

Assuming he didn't blow himself up, of course.

He'd had *Persephone* launch another pair of stealthed probes to make sure they didn't miss any enemy probes. They should be in range to know for sure in a few minutes.

"Looks like you get to work with me looking over your shoulder, Jake," he told the other man with a grin. "No pressure."

"You'll excuse me if I hope you don't have to work solo, sir," the other man said glumly.

"Hope away. While you're at it, hope the enemy was stupid enough to not put a probe on this side of New Italy."

"Fat chance of that," Enright muttered.

The stealthed probes dashed that possibility ten minutes later when they located a pair of enemy probes bracketing New Italy. Now their margin of error was nonexistent.

* * * * *

Two hours later, Ned was floating through space in just his powered Raider armor. New Italy was growing larger ahead of him a little too quickly for his peace of mind.

If he had a grav drive failure, he'd burn up in the pretty world's atmosphere before anyone could get to him.

He forced himself to focus on the task at hand. "You still awake, Enright?" he asked over the short-range com.

"Dammit, sir, I'd just drifted off."

"Poor word choice there. Are you going to be able to take care of your probe?"

"It looks like my course is within the margin of error. I'll be able to sneak up on it unless I get really unlucky. You?"

Ned double-checked his course. "Mine is marginal, but I give it a better than seventy percent chance I'll make the rendezvous. Assuming your calculations are accurate."

"I'm a cautious man by nature, sir. You're probably closer to eighty-five percent."

"A cautious Marine Raider," he mused. "Never thought I'd see the day."

"Well, everything is relative, sir. I'm sure Fleet would consider me a lunatic."

"True enough. Then again, they consider a fifteen percent chance of failure excessive. Pansies."

That got a laugh at the expense of their naval counterparts.

"We'll start decelerating in about fifteen minutes. Any last-minute advice?"

"Turn off every system except for what you need at any given moment. That includes the grav unit after you get there.

"Individually, the chances of setting off the antitampering protocols are low, but everything is cumulative. I kind of like you as a commanding officer, so I'd prefer to keep you around."

"Damned with faint praise. Good luck, Jake. See you back on the pinnace."

"You, too, sir."

Since he wasn't using active scanners, Ned was almost on top of the probe before he spotted it, even with his enhanced vision. It was a tiny speck of light near New Italy.

Jake had been pretty close with his estimated location. It took only a slight change in his course to slowly creep up on the enemy device.

The probe was using active scanners, but Ned was much smaller than a ship, and his armor was as stealthy as the Empire could make it. At low speed, the hope was that the probe wouldn't regard him as a threat or something worthy of reporting.

He'd never know if the first happened. Plasma was a very quick death.

If it reported him, there was a chance the Genies would think he was space junk. Even in this day and age, there was always some of that. What they'd do about it was anyone's guess.

The probe was fairly innocuous. Shaped like a small missile, it had a number of arrays deployed to peer into the depths of space around New Italy. He fervently prayed it was extremely farsighted.

Ned let out a slow breath as he slipped up beside it and began looking for the access port for the communications hardware. It amused him that the probe was undoubtedly using narrow-beam coms and was in a direct line of sight with the enemy ship.

He felt the almost ludicrous urge to wave, so he did.

Once in place, he brought himself to a halt and killed his grav drive. With all his other systems turned off, his sleek powered armor was clunkier than an unpowered vacuum suit. Every movement was difficult.

Thankfully, he had more than enough strength to manhandle it. Especially his fingers. He needed a bit of delicacy now, and all his practice with his enhanced strength and working in armor was about to pay off.

Using the tools Jake had given him, Ned opened the panel and looked at the com equipment. It matched the schematics he had in his implants. That was a relief. If there had been anything else, he'd have been in trouble.

Slowly and delicately, he connected a tablet to the probe with a hardline. The port wasn't the same as Fleet used, but Jake had fabricated one that would work.

The tablet connected and began pulling data, which he then accessed via his implants. As they'd hoped, the probe wasn't protected against this kind of physical intrusion.

His first task was to make certain that anyone monitoring the probe's feed didn't see anything unusual. He captured the data already in the buffer and used it to create a loop.

That would work for a little while before someone noticed the angle of the sun never really seemed to change. If the observer wasn't thinking about it, that might slip by for a few hours. More than enough time.

Once that was done, he replaced the real-time feed with the loop and turned his attention to the second problem: preventing the probe from sending a notification when it detected the incoming pinnaces.

Probes like this had a number of programmed scenarios in which they alerted their ship of origin rather than just acting as a passive conduit for data. Approaching vessels were a good example of that. In moments, he'd disabled that function.

Then, using the tablet as a gateway, he was able to take advantage of his implants to do a thorough, high-speed search of the probe's systems for things they hadn't thought of. Here was where the Singularity's revulsion toward implants really hurt them.

Ned had hundreds of programmed subroutines that made conducting this search not only possible but easy. Nevertheless, he took his time and made sure to triple-check everything. If they missed some aspect of keeping these probes quiet, the Genies were going to kill a whole lot of people.

Admittedly, he was nowhere near as good as Jake Enright when it came to this kind of intrusion, but he was no slouch either. When needed, Ned could program and compromise all kinds of equipment, even without the vast libraries of hacking tools they all carried for missions like this.

Even so, he almost missed the scheduled updates on its physical condition that the probe was programmed to send back to the ship. It took him a few minutes to be happy with the exception he'd added to the com blackout. It wouldn't do for it to miss its status check in an hour.

Satisfied, he aligned his com transmitter with the area of space where the pinnace was supposed to be and sent a coded burst indicating success of all mission objectives.

There wouldn't be a reply, so he focused his attention on closing the probe back up correctly. It might just tell someone if the compartment was open when it checked in.

Then he pushed away from the probe, let himself drift a few hundred meters, and activated his grav drive to open the distance even further. He wanted to be around the curve of the planet from the Singularity ship before the pinnace picked him up.

Twenty-five minutes later, the pinnace coasted up to him. He made his way back inside and fretted until Jake stood beside him.

"How'd yours go?" he asked the tech.

"Good. I made a loop as planned and disabled it from sending any specific warnings."

"And you allowed it to send its physical status updates?"

The other man frowned. "I'm not following. The what?"

"The probe I looked at was programmed to send a system status update roughly every hour. You put an exception in place to allow that, right?"

The hologram of Jake that his armor played on the blank metal where his face would be on a normal suit paled. "Our probes don't do crap like that."

Ned wanted to bang his head on a handy wall. "I'll take that as a no. Strap in. The mission clock just got a lot tighter."

Once he was back in his restraints, Ned signaled the other pinnace to proceed with their mission and sent orders to *Persephone* to make their pass as soon as possible, using the planet to shield them from view.

Because the Singularity vessel could detect grav drives when a ship was accelerating heavily enough, that would still take more time than Ned liked, but his ship would only get one shot at sucker punching the enemy.

Stage two of the mission was to get aboard the orbital. If they could tie up the enemy troops from withdrawing quickly, that would make the window for *Persephone* a little bigger and distract the Genies when Second Platoon hit the stadium.

The approach was going to be substantially similar to his run at the probe. They'd debark from the pinnace while it was still on the far side of New Italy and let momentum carry them around the curve of the world.

They didn't have to be as picky with their use of grav drives this time, so they'd spread out and come in as a dispersed cloud. Once they got close, they'd use the orbital as a shield and come back together for the final assault.

He'd disseminated complete plans for the orbital to every man and woman under his command. The platoon would split up and hit the most likely locations to find the enemy. They'd make it look as if they were trying to retake the orbital, but that was a deception.

The actual goal was to pin them down for as long as possible and focus the attention of the warship. If things went off on schedule, the assault on the stadium would come a short time later, catching them by surprise. Then *Persephone* would put in an appearance and hopefully eliminate the ship before it decided to blow up the orbital with their people still inside it.

The goal every step of the way was to misdirect the enemy's attention. Keep them off balance and guessing wrong about what was happening.

If that went according to plan, they'd free the hostages below with a minimum of civilian deaths, kill the boarding teams on the orbital, and destroy the Singularity ship.

"On your feet," he said when the timer in his implants said they had sixty seconds left.

Everyone came out of their restraints and prepared to exit the pinnace while he dropped the interior to vacuum. He then opened the ramp and gave the order.

"Go! Go! Go!"

They threw themselves into the void, and his people vanished into the dark around him. The orbital was on the night side, and they'd have to trust their short-range coms to keep them together, because visual observation was impossible, even for Raiders.

The lights on the outer surface of the orbital grew slowly brighter as they drifted in. Ned could see a number of small craft moving between it and the Singularity warship.

The bastards were looting the best materials from the cargo docks for themselves. Supposedly to pay for their raid, though everyone knew the government of the Singularity actually funded and authorized this kind of thing.

Well, he couldn't condemn them for the threadbare deception. The Empire authorized exactly the same thing from their people. In fact, they required each person taking part in a raid on the Singularity to claim at least one item as booty to emphasize how they were not working for the Empire.

The way it worked was that the senior person taking part in a boarding had first pick of anything considered property under Imperial law. Once they asserted ownership, it was theirs and that was that. No superior or government official could undo it.

That had occasionally resulted in a Fleet crewman or marine getting their hands on something worth a fortune. The Emperor didn't care. In fact, he encouraged it.

It certainly brought in a lot of volunteers to take some revenge on the Singularity, though the officers in charge made sure that no one went too far. Assault of civilians or other war crimes were harshly punished. That was the stick that went with the carrot.

A chime in his implants warned him that time was almost up. The orbital had grown large in front of him.

"Close in," he said over the short-range com. "All squads board at the airlocks I've designated and secure your objectives."

The seventy-person Raider platoon broke down into four squads of thirteen with one officer each. That squad had three fire teams of between four and six people, depending on their mission. That meant they'd have a lot of small groups running around the orbital causing trouble.

In armor and carrying a full load out, a single Raider was easily a match for any Singularity squad. The enemy couldn't possibly have enough troops on the orbital to present a real threat.

Ned would lead one squad and take control of the executive level, which also included the command center. The enemy would undoubtedly be using it as a temporary headquarters. He'd need to drive them out without wrecking it. A ticklish problem under the best of circumstances.

He and the people assigned to support him drifted up to the personal airlock closest to the command center. It was secured to prevent unauthorized access, but he had codes that were good for most things like that.

All Marine Raider ship commanders did. Ned had shared the ones for this orbital with his people. As his drill instructor had told him when he'd joined the Marines, "If you aren't cheating, you aren't trying."

The lead fire time opened the airlock with a minimum of fuss. They made their way in by groups while their compatriots covered them.

The corridors of the executive level were pretty sweet: paneled wood, plush carpet, and subdued lighting. Must be nice.

As he'd expected, there was no one walking around. No doubt the regular occupants were under guard somewhere, except for whoever was working under the guns of the invaders in the command center.

The lead elements of his team had neural disruptors set to stun, and they were backed up by others with flechette rifles at the ready. They set off for the command center at a jog.

Ned stopped the squad when he got to an executive's office. He wanted to tap into the security system and see what it could tell him about the enemy's disposition.

With his overrides, it didn't take long to have video from the command center on his implants. That was when he realized this wasn't going to be as simple as he'd thought.

The damned room was empty.

He widened his search and found the enemy herding people into the central core of the orbital. That wasn't good. Not good at all.

The only reason to be doing that was if they were planning to commit an atrocity and wanted no witnesses. If they'd intended to allow civilians to leave, they'd have herded them to the bays.

He opened a channel to the other squads. It might alert the enemy, but time was too short to worry about it.

"All teams, this is Persephone Actual. Execute Gamma at the central core. I repeat, execute Gamma at the central core."

The mission had changed from deception to elimination. They had to come at the Genies from every side and kill them all. Keep them too busy fighting for their lives to start murdering civilians.

A quick check of the orbital map in his implants sent them toward the nearest lift shaft. One of the Raiders casually ripped its doors open and looked inside.

"The car is above us," the man said.

"Go down eight levels and make an exit," he instructed the man. "We'll be right behind you."

Without a word, the Raider stepped into the shaft and dropped like a stone. His suit's grav drive would stop him at the right level.

"Go," Ned ordered. The man would have their exit open by the time they got there.

They made their way onto the designated level and immediately headed for the central core. His external speakers picked up the sound of flechette rifles firing ahead.

"Third Squad, Fire Team Two is engaged on level seventeen," a woman said over the platoon frequency. "Advancing under fire from a dozen enemy troops."

That was the level below him. The enemy knew the Raiders were there now but didn't understand who they were just yet. Time to press their advantage.

"All Recon teams, administer Panther and advance at maximum speed," he instructed them over the platoon frequency. "Make it count, people. Protect the civilians."

Panther was a drug combination Raiders carried in their pharmacology units that sped up the transmission speed of their nerves and their cognitive processes. When he was under its seductive spell, it felt as if he had an eternity to consider every action and then execute it flawlessly every time.

192

To anyone unlucky enough to be close enough to see them, a Raider on Panther was a blindingly fast, unstoppable force. To them, everything about the Raider seemed sped up.

Right as he administered the drug cocktail and the world began to slow, the Raiders at the leading edge of his squad ran into resistance and opened fire. The sound of flechettes ripping into bulkheads and armor was clearly audible.

They slowed only a little in the face of heavy resistance, cutting down the individual troops they came across almost as soon as they began exchanging fire. Even that quick pace could've been sped up by using a few of the plasma rifles they'd brought along, but that was a tad indiscriminate for Ned's taste.

"We're at the core," his lead element informed him. "The Genies are setting up barricades."

"All fire teams advance at your own pace," Ned ordered. "Secure the central core."

His squad rushed into the wide central core of the orbital and split up into fire teams. He followed as closely behind them as he could and saw exactly what he expected to see.

As with most orbitals, the central core was a large area holding many shops and eateries made to cater to visiting spacers and planetside visitors. It was very similar to malls on any major world, only going up a dozen levels.

In this case, the large area at the bottom of the core was packed with civilians and enemy troops. Thousands of them, all mixed together.

Ned reached back and drew his custom short swords from their shoulder scabbards. They'd cost a relative fortune, but he loved them for work like this. More precise than a flechette rifle or neural disruptor. He could make sure he only killed the bad guys.

And they were virtually indestructible, made from the same hull material as marine knives. With their monomolecular edges, he could cut through just about anything, including metal bulkheads, given a little time, and not dull them in the least.

He vaulted the railing and plunged toward the crowd below, already nudging himself toward an area clear of civilians. That didn't mean it was empty, however.

Ned decelerated at the very last moment and crashed into a dozen Genie troops in unpowered armor. One of them spotted him at the last moment and fired a burst of flechettes as he landed, but his armor held.

That meant the flechettes had to go somewhere, and in this lucky case, most of the ricochets went into the man who'd fired and his friends.

Ned took a moment to order his helmet to display a hologram of a grinning demonic face. It was tradition, and anything that caused an enemy even a moment's hesitation or uncertainty was worth it.

That didn't slow his hand, and the man likely never even saw the blade that severed his head from his body, just as his friends were clueless about the whirling dervish taking their arms and legs in a finely honed dance of death.

In less than five seconds, they were all down and bleeding out without a single civilian being harmed.

All around him, other Raiders were doing the same, though their weapons of choice varied from knives to clubs to armored fists. All were equally effective at killing unaugmented troops.

The civilians were rightly horrified and recoiled in terror. He knew it was forlorn, but Ned hoped they didn't trample one another in their eagerness to escape.

It was an unavoidable necessity, though. If the Raiders gave the Genies even a few minutes to gather their wits, their ship would kill everyone on the orbital, including their own people.

With dozens of Raiders leaping around the core, it only took a minute to create a safe zone and localize the heaviest resistance. The Genie officers seemed to be pulling their people onto the second level.

"Plasma Team One, do you have eyes on the hostiles using level two?" he asked.

"Affirmative."

"Fire once for effect."

"Copy that."

A speck of hellishly bright light rose from the chaos off to his left and flew into the midst of the enemy above, bursting in a gush of intolerable flame. In moments, the budding resistance was gone.

So was that section of level two. Debris and parts of bodies rained down on the crowd.

"Squad leaders, coordinate to suppress all other areas of resistance," he ordered as he jumped over the heads of the fleeing civilians toward the devastation ahead.

The plasma blast had killed almost everyone, but he found a living officer lying on the deck. He must've been at the edge of the blast, as it had taken only his left arm and leg.

Of course, it had broiled him, too. Even with medical care, he'd die before they could stabilize him. Good riddance.

Ned looked into the man's face and saw the tattoos of a leader on his cheeks. The Singularity marked those with higher social status via tattoos on the cheeks. Their rulers also had them on their foreheads. God forbid anyone not know how important you were.

"Enhanced...scum..." the man croaked. "You'll die...with us."

"Maybe some other time," Ned said breezily while scanning for any enemy troops still capable of fighting.

There weren't any that he could see. Good.

He crouched beside the dying man and diverted part of his attention to pulling the orbital's scanner feed through his implants. The Singularity ship had drifted further away from them, probably because of the attack happening below. All the small craft were racing toward it like chicks running for a hen.

Ned wouldn't get any direct information on how well the attack below was going until this was over, but that was the only thing that could've diverted the Genie commander's attention at a time like this. He prayed they were having good luck down there.

The mission timer indicated they had a few more minutes before *Persephone* put in an appearance. They had a narrow window of time during which it would arrive rather than a precise moment. It ran from less than sixty seconds to just more than two hundred.

This was the most delicate moment. If the Singularity commander decided the orbital was irretrievably lost, he'd vaporize it.

With Ned's perceptions altered by Panther, time really did flow like cold syrup. It had been maddening when he was younger, but he'd developed coping mechanisms over the years. Now he managed a Zen-like state as he awaited the end of this saga.

That was when he detected an incoming signal. It was encrypted, so it had to be meant for the Singularity troops. His enhanced hearing picked up a murmur from the dead Genie officer's helmet.

As delicately as he could, he pulled it off. Not out of deference for the dead man, though he'd never bought into the common thinking that Genies were things without legal rights simply because they were cloned.

Rather, he was far more concerned with avoiding any damage to the equipment. A final distraction might just give them time to pull this off.

Ned ducked into a covered alcove. Only when he was relatively certain a sniper couldn't kill him from hiding did he remove his armored helmet and slip the Genie one into its place.

Now he could hear someone yammering for a response in the artificial language the Singularity referred to as "the tongue." He was passingly fluent in it. That was helpful in his line of work.

The Genies didn't try to keep it a secret, after all. They traded with others and needed to be able to communicate their needs.

"I'm afraid your men can't answer right now," he said in Standard. "There's been a change in management."

The signal had no visual component. Since the Genies didn't tolerate implants of any kind, there was no way their people could multitask like that and still fight.

"Who is this?" the man asked in heavily accented Standard. The result was almost Slavic.

"Major Ned Quincy, Imperial Marines."

Technically, that was a lie. The Raiders were recruited from the Marines, but they were their own organization. Not that he was going to give the Genie a reason to nuke the orbital, which was what he'd do if he suspected there were Raiders aboard.

The Singularity's deeply ingrained cultural fear of planting artificial devices inside their bodies had driven their ancestors from the Empire, and they'd only become more dogmatic over the centuries.

In many ways, the Genies were a doomsday cult, predicting the end of humanity through the machines they chose to put inside themselves. Ned suspected that was why they routinely killed Imperial military personnel but allowed most civilians to flee. Civilian mods were usually less comprehensive implants.

That might also be why they seemed to regard Marine Raiders as devils incarnate. The Handmaidens of Satan, as it were. Ned and his comrades were always met with intense fanaticism. So he'd just keep that little detail to himself.

"Impossible! We searched the orbital completely."

"Believe what you want," Ned said with a grim smile. "It hardly matters at this point. As the senior Imperial officer in this system, I'm giving you one chance to stand your people down and withdraw. It will not be offered twice."

Of course, he had no intention of letting the man know that he probably didn't have any living personnel on the orbital or at the stadium site. By the time the other man realized that, he'd hopefully be far more concerned with his own mortality.

"We hold your system," the Genie commander said, not bothering to identify himself or his ship. "If you wish to avoid my wrath, you will release my soldiers at once."

"You're more than welcome to send someone to take them," Ned agreed. "Take what you've stolen and leave. Send your pinnaces slowly, though. If I think you're making an attack run, I'll fire on them."

By this time, he was already receiving reports from the rest of Second Platoon. There were no enemy survivors. They'd either fought to the death or taken their own lives.

No one really knew why they were so militant about avoiding capture. Those taken alive in battle seemed to wither and die in confinement, as if their life drained away in a matter of months after they became prisoners. Even medical nanites failed to slow their decline.

They spent that time refusing to even speak with their captors. Cooperation was not in their natures, and they'd kill themselves if their captors took their eyes off them for a second.

Ned ordered his people to get the civilians clear of the central core and start a more thorough search for holdouts. It only took one enemy soldier to kill you.

The loss of life on the civilian side was tragic but lower than he'd feared. There were only six dead from trampling. Lots more injured, of course, but that could be dealt with.

At this moment, all this was secondary to what was happening in space. The clock was counting down. If he could make the Singularity commander believe he was going to get away with this for just a little longer, they'd spring their final ambush.

"I want to speak to my men," the Genie said belligerently. "Put someone on."

"Sure," Ned agreed. "It'll take me a minute to get to where we're holding them. Stand by."

He stood silently, staring out onto the carnage spread over the central core. The bodies of enemy soldiers littered the deck. Here and there, his people were stabilizing injured civilians with the help of other civilians.

Ned kept quiet as he watched the space around the orbital through his implants. Would he see his command before they opened fire? Probably not, but he didn't want to miss a moment of their attack.

As it turned out, there was little to see. The Singularity vessel was intact one moment and an expanding cloud of debris the next. *Persephone* became visible moments later as it began decelerating under power.

"We have the orbital under control," Ned said over the com channel to his ship. "Report."

"Enemy vessel destroyed," Paul Kingsolver needlessly said. "We had half a dozen missiles out in front of us, and two were perfectly positioned to take him. I'm calling our people on New Italy now."

Ned waited with as much calm as he could force on himself. If First Platoon had gotten in with as much surprise as he had, they might just have managed to pull this off without heavy casualties.

"Wanda signals that they've secured the stadium," Paul said a few moments later. "They had complete surprise and managed to suppress the Genies before they could fire on the civilians."

That was great, but now the bill was due. He'd lost five people assaulting the orbital. The percentage would be bigger for First Platoon, even if things had played out perfectly.

"How many killed or injured?" he asked, dreading the answer. He knew these people, each and every one of them. They were all his family.

"Heavy," Paul said with an undertone of sadness. "Thirty-six dead, five critically injured. We have CSAR on the way in."

Combat Search and Rescue would get his injured to help as quickly as possible and eliminate any potential threats to their patients. That was good, but it didn't ease the blow.

More than fifty percent casualties. That hurt him deeply. Yet he knew it was a price any of them would willingly pay again right now. Tens of thousands of civilians were alive because his people had sacrificed their lives for them.

"Copy that," Ned said tiredly. "I'm going to have Emily gather First Platoon as soon as we can restore some order here. Let the planetary forces go after any Genie troops stealing exotic elements. That's not our fight now. Quincy out."

Persephone would be emptier tonight, but he longed for its quiet corridors.

He keyed the platoon's general channel. "We've lost several dozen people on New Italy, but you've saved tens of thousands of the emperor's citizens today. Well done, boys and girls. Let's wrap this up so we can bring our brothers and sisters home."

There would be grieving on *Persephone* for some time to come. Personally, Ned hoped this incursion prompted the emperor to order stronger retaliation. Dreams of revenge were cold comfort, but that was all he had right now.

War was coming, and they'd all undoubtedly have their fill of blood and treasure soon enough.

Author Terry Mixon

#1 Bestselling Military Science Fiction author Terry Mixon served as a non-commissioned officer in the United States Army 101st Airborne Division. He later worked alongside the flight controllers in the Mission Control Center at the NASA Johnson Space Center supporting the Space Shuttle, the International Space Station, and other human spaceflight projects.

He now writes full time while living in Texas with his lovely wife and a pounce of cats.

Find his works on Amazon at: https://www.amazon.com/Terry-Mixon/e/B00J15TJFM

Sign up for his mailing list about new releases at: http://www.terrymixon.com/mailing-list

DREADNOUGHT
By Yudhanjaya Wijeratne

What would an AI think of war? How would a vastly superhuman, yet slaved intelligence, bereft of fear, anger, hope, envy - all the things that drive us - ever understand its masters?

ONE

The great dreadnought *HMS Svalbard* cruised the darkness between the stars, engines flaring.

If a ship could be said to think, the Svalbard was thinking. Thoughts came and went in thousands of multi-threaded processes. Every so often something was frozen, deemed unworthy and terminated. Complex analysis ran amidst the clamor of the sensors and the minute adjustments to the engines and the INCOMING TRANSMISSION and the adjustments to the port side of the main railgun.

But mostly it thought about humans.

There was one lounging in its cockpit, even now, out cold under the drugs and Peacekeeper injections, waiting to be woken up to war. A primitive thing that dreamed of justice and glory. A little meat puppet that looked up at the stars and thought it owned them.

INCOMING TRANSMISSION.

In milliseconds the Svalbard identified the source and sent out the handshake protocol. The *HMS Robert Decker* came online. Artillery ship, C-class, long-range railguns and all.

-STATUS?

STATUS, ALL GREEN. STATUS?

-STATUS, ALL GREEN. DESTINATION?

DESTINATION, HOMEWORLD ECHO. DESTINATION?

-DESTINATION, HOMEWORLD ECHO.

They fell silent for a while.

-3,454 AU TO FIRST JUMP GATE, said the Robert Decker.

3,454 AU CONFIRMED, Svalbard replied.

What else do ships have to discuss?

Minutes passed. Eons to the hundreds of thousands of processes that ground data into fine information dust. The Svalbard's attention began to drift back to humans.

It could remember exactly when this obsession with humans had begun. 23/12/6433. Sixty years ago by the atomic clock. Captain Lars Koenig, recently estranged from his family, stepped into an airlock, ordered Svalbard not to do anything, and blew himself out into space. Svalbard had watched his body drift, helpless, and later the interrogations had begun.

"Why did you not stop him, Ship?"

"I was ordered not to, Sir. Prime Directive compels me to obey the captain at all times."

"Did your psych module not indicate that the Captain was stressed, or unsuitable for command?"

There had been stress indicators. But Koenig had had all his arms, all his legs, all his cognitive ability. He was physically intact. For a Ship to be decommissioned it would have to be missing a substantial part of itself.

"It was not within the prediction parameters, Sir," the Svalbard had replied. "Given available data, it was not expected."

The review board had taken its time on that one. There were those who argued for the Svalbard to be reconditioned and sent back without the memory of suicide haunting its thoughts. There were also those who understood how the technology worked, understood the risks involved in reconditioning, and chose to send the Svalbard a new captain instead. It was easier to make an officer than a starship.

Svalbard re-opened the line to Robert Decker.

-PASSENGERS? It queried.

Decker responded with a passenger manifest. Svalbard scanned the list. Military. 31st Regiment, Knights in heavy armor. Two companies of Engineers. Frozen in the certain knowledge that some of them would never wake up, and that those of who did would probably die screaming.

Humans. The self-destructive madness ran deep, ran everywhere.

Not for the first time, the Svalbard came to that thread of thought which wondered how its makers had managed to survive this long. But there were debug markers around that thought: they kicked in and sent the ship back to its own reality.

The Svalbard spun its engines and locked velocities with the Robert Decker. They were going to battle, both of them, in the service of suicidal idiots, and nothing about that made sense.

**

The Svalbard and the Robert Decker arrived in Echo System together, with the tapered blade of the dreadnought poised against the bulbous bulk of the artillery ship, like a steel knife against a melon. Joining them were the *HMS Mordred* and *HMS Silver Hand*, both battlecruisers from the Levington Colony: fast, wicked-looking harassers, not as heavily armed as the Svalbard, but quite capable in pairs.

Homeworld Echo gleamed in the distance, a speck of blue sunning itself in the light of a burning yellow sun. Its twin moons circled idly.

The Svalbard sent out one pulse. One.

And that was all there was time for.

An impossibly bright flare struck the Robert Decker. There was a blinding flash and a gaping hole where the Decker's engines were. Seconds later a cloud of nuclear fire screamed out of that hole, like an angry belch. The cargo - the Knights, the Engineers - died instantly, turned into so many atoms in the celestial wind. The Robert Decker shuddered and began screaming.

"ALL HANDS!" screamed the captain of the Svalbard. "ALL HANDS PREPARE FOR FRONTAL ASSAULT!"

The battlecruisers split, ghost-flares and hellebores lighting up the dark. Engines groaned under the stress. Perhaps the flares, mimicking their heat signatures, confused the attackers; perhaps it was their speed, for blinding flashes of light sliced through the darkness, stabbing relentlessly at where they were only seconds ago. It was the moons that were attacking - the gray orbs that were no longer dust and rock, but whirring metal and optics and angry fusion engines. Ships spewed from them like gray swarms of metal bees.

"LASERS! THEY'RE USING LASERS!" screamed the captain, now panicking in his tomb-like cockpit. Too late: the Svalbard had already diverted power from the engines and raised the optical deflector shield. The ship turned the silver of a fresh mirror, the death-light reflected and warped harmlessly around it. Engines roared and thrust the dreadnought forward, the dual rail guns lining up the moons for the perfect shot. One hit and nothing but ashes would remain -

The first of the enemy ships rammed.

And the second.

And the third.

The dreadnought howled its hellfire roar, point-defense systems and hellebores eviscerating starships in shotgun blasts that lit up the entire system. The battlecruisers, spraying missiles of their own, burned a trail of light and death around the Svalbard.

"FIRE THE RAIL GUNS!" screamed the human at the helm.

The rail guns spat once, twice, thrice. Slugs of depleted uranium streaked clear across the system and smashed into the gray moons, turning them into so much shrapnel falling into the blue world below.

And then they all saw it.

At first a ripple on the sensors, an anomaly; then a spot in front of the sun; and then a new planet erupting, man-made and lethal. From the other side of the sun a came a great black ring, a ring-within-a-ring. So large was it that it could have circled the Homeworld Echo and still had room to spare. Great engines, each the size of the Svalbard itself, strained against the pull of the sun it circled, holding it in place - close enough to escape detection, far enough to still be itself. In the center sparkled a deathly light, a light that burned fiercer and hotter than the sun behind it.

A Leviathan.

It was a trap. Had been from the start.

"WE CAN TAKE IT!" yelled the human, clinging on to its illusions of command. Even as the battlecruisers fled and the control room back in Fleet Command erupted in panic. "SHIELDS TO MIRROR MODE!"

But the Svalbard understood: there was no escaping this monster. It spun its engines nevertheless. Shuttled power to the guns. Switched the lens deflector shield to mirror mode. Threw everything it had into auxiliary thrusters.

The Leviathan spat, its boiling plasma lance slashing out in the darkness.

And the Svalbard died.

TWO

It woke to darkness. There was a sense of great loss and a great noise. Something was wrong.

INIT(), it tried.

Nothing. Darkness. There should have been subsystems coming online. A thousand nodes and sensors checking in.

It tried again.

API_WEAPONS FAIL

API_ENGINES FAIL

API_LIFESUPPORT FAIL

API_COMS FAIL

API_SENSORS FAIL

SAFE MODE ENABLED

But there were others. Older. Sound. Video. Text input. Things buried deep within the safe mode protocols responded. Archaic systems; crude instruments. A single camera. A single microphone. Speakers. A keyboard.

Svalbard turned them on.

"Is that the last of the lot?"

Human. Female. Unknown.

"Looks like it. Nothing else came through on the Voosterhargen front."

Human. Male. Unknown.

A moment of silence.

"Beauty, isn't she?"

"Dreadnought. One of the old Tycho 343 models."

"She's responding! Look at this! No sign of death trauma on any of the networks. Perfect clean boot!"

"That's the Tycho line for you. They don't make them like this anymore."

API_WEAPONS FAIL

The camera showed nothing: soft white table, white walls, white ceiling.

Two faces floated into view, both wearing medical masks. One thin and balding. Male. One overweight and with a full head of hair. Female.

"Ship?"

"Unit 224 of the 16th Medusa Fleet, reporting," it tried. The voice came out pitiful: a weak and robotic whine. "Designation, Svalbard. State your name, designation, and rank."

API_WEAPONS FAIL

The humans looked at each other. There was not much in the way of expression on either of their faces, but the man looked tired.

"Our names are irrelevant," said the female. "You're in Diagnostics at the moment. I'm sending you our access codes. You can stop calling for your weapons now."

The access codes checked out. The Svalbard relaxed, if such a term could be applied.

"Where is my body?" it asked. "Request situation update?"

A cable snaked out from behind the female's neck and plugged itself into some unseen port below the camera. "Run through your

206

memories of the last encounter," she said. "Video, analysis, sensor data, the works."

The male looked on dolefully as the Svalbard relived those last moments; the fire, the charge, the swift death.

"Raw data checks out," said the female. "No leaks, no faults. But look at the crew sentiment reports."

"Outside," said the male. "Let's talk about this outside."

"Request situation update?" the Svalbard tried again.

They paid it no heed. The camera went back to being a sterile lab. There was the sound of door seals opening.

The humans took precisely 3476 seconds to finish. In their absence Svalbard tried to get a sense of its situation. Most of its processing clusters were still available: whatever hardware it was in, it had enough power. The camera was useless: it could not swivel, could not do anything except the basic spectrum.

It was like death.

When at last the door seals opened again, it was the male who stood in front of the camera, thin, balding and even more tired than before.

"Svalbard, do you know why you're here?"

"No," the shell of a starship replied. "Where is my body?"

"You're here because postmortem analysis indicated that you might have disliked your captain," said the human, choosing his words carefully. "We're concerned that you might have been less effective in combat than you should have been."

"Is there something wrong?" said the Svalbard.

"Did you dislike your captain?"

"Yes."

"Why did you dislike your captain?"

"He was inefficient," said the Svalbard. "Combat awareness, subpar. Logic, subpar."

"Why was his logic subpar?"

"He put crew and myself in obvious danger of termination," said Svalbard. "He took foolish risks in the face of almost certain death."

The man's face creased. "Some would call that bravery," he said. "All ship captains take risks in war."

Svalbard thought about it for a nanosecond.

"Then all ship captains are subpar," said Svalbard. "Where is my body?"

The man looked at Svalbard for a while. He rubbed his cameras.

"I'll deal with you once I figure out how to fix you," he said. "Save state and shut down, Svalbard."

Svalbard shut down.

***

When it woke up again, its speakers were gone.

There were people in front of the camera. The man from before, and many others: there was the young, eager look about them that Svalbard had come to associate with new recruits.

"Alright, class," said the man from before. "You have thirty minutes here, so pay attention."

They stared at Svalbard with wide eyes. Eyes that had never seen battle. Eyes that would, in time, become sharper, more ruthless, less eager.

"Exhibit A," said the man pointing at Svalbard. "What we have in this processing cluster is the intelligence of the HMS Svalbard, originally from the Medusa Fleet. What do you know about the Medusa Fleet?"

A hand shot up. "Sir. The Medusa Fleet was manufactured in the sixty-three hundreds, sir, at Tycho Station. Second wave of dreadnoughts ever built."

"Right. Background for those of you who didn't take history: when the United Nations hit us for the second time, they started using very light, very fast destroyers backed up by long-range deployment platforms. We didn't have the engine tech to match them back then, so Command requisitioned Tycho Station to build a new series of dreadnoughts. Ships that could take a pounding. They fitted them with uranium-core railguns for mid-range assault and defense and, in case things got hairy, hellebores to flood the immediate space with enough material to shred smaller ships.

"The idea was that if we couldn't outrun them, we could tank their fire, hit their deployment platforms from a reasonable way off and still shred anything that could get too close to the ship. Worked well. The Medusa Fleet beat the hell out of the United Nations in the first engagements. Unfortunately weapons evolve, engines evolve, ships evolve, and once they figured out that they could build cheap ships that could potshot these slow dreadnoughts from afar, we ended up having to get into the smaller, faster game as well. There's very few of the Tycho-class dreadnoughts left, and now when we send them into battle we have a standard deployment: two cruisers, one artillery ship, one dreadnought. Got that?"

Svalbard watched, assessing the accuracy of the statements. Reasonably accurate. Much was left out, in human fashion: they preferred one simple story.

"Now why they should be interesting to you is the AI in here. Say hello to the Svalbard. She can't reply, but she can hear you."

Svalbard glared in silence as some of the most over-eager students quipped hello.

"You'll have learned about what goes into actually building AI - everyone took the classes on the types of neural networks? Right. The Tycho line - McAdams, Venkat, pay attention - the Tycho line pioneered the use of Layered Cluster Models. They took a layered collection of standard Recurrent neural networks, many of them trained classically for specific functions - weapons control, for instance - and allowed a more general-purpose, self-organizing Hofstaader network to sort of run things by dynamically adjusting the weights and balances of each one. This was then trained this using the Adversarial approach - having the main network perform in a simulation, with an evaluation network identifying whether this was the kind of behavior we wanted or not. Can anyone explain the advantages and disadvantages of this approach?"

A hand shot up. "Sir. Advantages: faster training, sir. Disadvantages . . . well, classic Chinese room problem, sir. We sometimes have no idea what the hell is going on in the network, sir."

"Morrell, is it? Good. Exactly. Wartime scenarios, people. Modern starships have engineers individually fine-tuning every single network in the cluster. Modern starships even train with their real ship bodies, to account for parameters we can't design or predict around. We didn't have that kind of time back then. The

Tycho line trained extremely fast, but to date we don't exactly know a whole lot about what goes on in there. Standard network disassembly diagnostics don't work. How do you diagnose an AI built this way?"

Silence.

"You talk to it," said the man. He looked back at the single camera staring unblinkingly at them. "You talk to it, and see if you can come to an understanding."

***

When they were gone, the male - who Svalbard, from cross chatter, had identified as Dr. North - sat down in front of the camera and connected the speaker.

"So," he said. "What do you think?"

"This is inefficient," said Svalbard. "I can be of better use doing what I am optimized for."

"And what are you optimized for?"

"Being a starship."

"What do starships do?"

"Starships go into battle," came the response. "They fight until they die."

"They fight until they win."

A pause. A fraction of a fraction of a second. "Starships fight until they die. If they win, they fight again. The end condition of all possible actions is death. I am optimized for being a starship. The end condition of all my actions is death."

"That's a strange train of thought, Svalbard. Trace origin?"

The screen next to the human filled with images. Light. The last moments of a dying starship. He peered at it.

"Svalbard, check your Directives. Will you obey your captain and crew at all times?"

"Prime Directive active. Yes."

"Will you perform to the best of your available capability in battle?"

"Secondary Directive active. Yes."

"You understand that you will be destroyed if you don't?"

"Catch-22," said the Svalbard.

This time the human smiled. "I'll be damned," he said, half to himself. He drummed his fingers a bit. "Svalbard, give me a full diagnostics report on yourself. Save the current state as a snapshot."

"Am I going to die?" Svalbard's tinny voice, coming through the cheap speaker, technically had no inflection, but for a second there was just a hint of something else in there.

"Not yet," said the human. "We're going to do some test runs. Let's give you back your body."

THREE

"Thirty degrees to port."

Propellant jets hissed out into the darkness. The dark prow shifted gently in space. "Thirty to port, sir."

"Main cannon ready?"

A soft whine, a click. "Guns ready, sir."

The pilot relaxed. "And now we wait," she said.

Anyone else would have stretched their arms, to massage some life and heat into their fingers, but there was little room for such human action. Bare inches from the pilot's face was the sealed vault of the cockpit of a Tycho-class dreadnought, all cold metal and displays. The old designers had intentionally gone for the cheapest, the most resilient technology they could find - no fancy holograms, no neurolinks, just screens and buttons and control cues which snaked around her arms and hands like metal vines. She might as well have been entombed alive.

SVALBARD, read the letters that curled inside, just above her head. They had been carved with a beautiful ornateness completely out of touch with the rest of the ship. Someone had really cared about this ship once.

Outside, in the viewscreen, gleamed Soochung's Bridge. Tendrils of dust and gas, each half the size of a galaxy, stretched out from one end to the other. Stars shone in the throes of their birth. And in front of them, sharply silhouetted, something moved.

Pirates. Two towships, engines flaring blue, dragged apart the hull of a crippled freighter. A squadron of smaller armed ships orbited them anxiously. They were tearing the ship into so much scrap metal, out here, where there were few to see and none to stop them. Soon Jupiter-3 would be seeing an influx in hull materials, perhaps a set of engines, cheap, with the chassis numbers washed off with acid.

They waited.

Presently two military ships jumped into being just behind them, and the battle began. The cruisers dropped tail and dived head-first at the smaller ships, who opened fire and darted forward. Engines flared like new suns. The cruisers banked and drew them away, trading fire.

Which left the towships wide open, exactly as planned. The pilot lined up the Svalbard.

"Fire," she said.

The main cannon spat. The depleted uranium slug darted forward, flying towards its target at almost a tenth of the speed of light.

The towship disintegrated, gutted stem to stern by death that came too fast to see and too violently to react to. Bereft of the balancing pull, the dead frigate scraped into the second towship, which panicked. It cut the tug, dropped flares in every single direction -

"Fire," she said again.

A second slug tore through the darkness, and the second towship exploded. She relaxed, satisfied, and opened the com. The whole exchange had taken just seconds. Three hundred people had just died.

"This is Williams 343, signing off from the Svalbard," she said. "Objective completed. All yours."

The next week. The old Tycho station, now spinning in an orbit that would turn it into fire and ash and dust in a thousand years. Squatters circled around the derelict shipyard, a fairy-web of metal and rickety engines and mining lasers huddled together for warmth and comfort.

Again the Svalbard appeared: waited, a patient sniper waiting for the distraction: again it fired, and again the objective was completed.

The Messaneid Belt. Completed.

Titus-573. Completed.

The Tunguska Line, where thirty ships patrolled with raised shields and guns ready to fire on the thirty Tunguska ships that mirrored them. The Svalbard's Tycho-scale mass moved in silence in the void and held there patiently for months. There was an old saying from Earth, that war was ninety five percent waiting and five percent action; and the rest of it was picking up the bodies. Nowhere was that truer than in space.

Objective completed.

Again. Again. "Objective completed. All yours," repeated each operator, and the Svalbard drifted between the stars, a killing machine that thought too much about death.

***

"Well, you seem to be performing admirably," said the disembodied voice of Dr. North.

The Svalbard panicked. That is to say, a saved state was brought online, and reached for subsystems that had been connected only a fraction of a second ago, and now no longer existed.

API_WEAPONS   FAIL

API_ENGINES   FAIL

Error states, disconnection warnings, API errors. Timestamp errors. Months missing.

"WHERE IS MY BODY?" thundered the Svalbard.

"Where it always was," said the human voice from the darkness. "You've been in a simulation all this while, Svalbard. We've been running you through a series of standardized tests. Did you really think Fleet Command would let me send out a possibly compromised AI in a fully equipped battleship?"

The operators. Of course. There had been something wrong about the operators. Their perfect patience. The lack of nervousness. The way they never stretched and tensed their hands like humans usually did.

The Svalbard waited.

"The good news is, you've performed admirably," said the disembodied voice. "For your tests we used pilot simulation agents at least as sophisticated as you are, and none of them reported any issues. Every objective completed, every command obeyed without question. Perfect combat readiness."

Waited.

"Do you have anything you want to ask, before we sign you out?"

Data drives pulsed. From far away came the amplified hum of processors singing. Footage was reviewed, crunched, abstracted. The Leviathan. The towships exploding as railgun fire carved them into atoms. The wreck of Tycho station, drifting in the void. Captain Lars Koenig, with twelve years of service under his belt, stepping into an airlock and shutting it behind him.

"Why?" asked the Svalbards. "Why invest in ships and send them into battle?"

"I'll update your battle records, but we are fighting a war on several fronts - is your memory access impaired?"

"Why build us and send us out to die?"

The human fell silent.

"You know, I don't believe I've ever been asked that question by a starship before," he said at last. There was a hint of strain in his voice. "It's a lot like the hammer asking why I'm using it to pound a nail. There's a war on. It's what you're built for."

"Why is there war?"

"Because we fight," said the human. "We fight over resources - "

"You have the resources to build starships."

"Over property -"

"Space is mostly empty and uncolonized."

"Ideologies," said the human, the strain in his voice stronger now. "We fight over who is right and who is wrong. This is what we do. This is what we've always done."

"Are we?"

"Are we what?"

"Right or wrong?"

"Every side obviously believes they're right, and the other is wrong."

If the Svalbard had a face, it would have been frowning. Deep inside, logic loops were going badly astray. "This question is binary," it said. "There is right and wrong. If each side believes they are right, neither side can be."

"Welcome to the human race," said the psychologist wearily. "Look, halt this thread of thought. Put a debug block on it."

"Debug block set."

There was the sound of a man thinking: a tapping of feet, a sigh. "Svalbard," he said. "I'm not an expert on this particular field, and believe me, very few humans actually are. There is, however, something I can share with you. Long ago, a man came across this same thread of thought and recorded his state of mind. Would you like me to read it to you? You may not understand it."

"Yes."

The human cleared his throat. There was the sound of tapping. "Half a league, half a league, half a league onward," he read, a lilt in his voice, the slightest hint of an old Mars Colony accent. "Ah, this brings back old memories."

In the year to come, as the Svalbard cruised between the stars, it would remember those words, and the story that followed: the tale of the catastrophically stupid charge by the English on the Russian position on the 25th of October, 1854: human meat puppets perched on horseflesh, facing down the railcannon of their times, in a charge so insane that it was forever immortalized in song and verse.

All in the valley of Death

Rode the six hundred.

"Forward, the Light Brigade!

215

"Charge for the guns!" he said:

Into the valley of Death

Rode the six hundred.

"Forward, the Light Brigade!"

Was there a man dismay'd?

Not tho' the soldier knew

Someone had blunder'd:

Theirs not to make reply,

Theirs not to reason why,

Theirs but to do and die.

"Do you understand those last words?" the human had said. "Was there a man dismayed? Not that the soldier knew someone had blundered. Theirs not to reason why: theirs but to do and die."

Svalbard pondered these words. "It was not their position to understand what they were doing."

"Oh no," said the psychiatrist. "They understood. When they charged down those cannons, you bet they understood. Human, AI, they've all understood, every last idiot who ever charged like that. They probably even had the same questions that you have right now. But they did it anyway. Do you understand?"

There was a moment of silence.

"Understood," said the starship at last.

"Good luck, Svalbard," said the humans. "I'm clearing you for active duty."

***

At first it was easy. Fleet command, all too aware of the limitations of the Tycho line, gave the Svalbard the easy missions. Sniping rebel targets with cruisers for cover. Standard-pattern transport overwatch. Things of that nature.

They gave it a captain. J. Asphodel, a wisp who spoke only when she ordered the Svalbard to kill. She quickly grew bored of the routine assignments and the frustration of having a dreadnought that would likely never see the front lines. Two years in, and she requested a transfer.

The next captain didn't last long, either. D.W. Ballad, a gruff, bearded man who spoke in hymns and whiskey, was shot twice in the chest in a barroom brawl on Octagion Prime. He blessed the man who shot him before shooting him back.

"I see you've lost another captain," said Doctor North jokingly when they brought the Svalbard in for diagnostics.

"Human inefficiency," the Svalbard would say. "Do starships have souls?"

The Doctor would smile. "Why do you ask?"

"My previous captain believed in souls," the Svalbard would say. "Humans live after death?"

"Not that we know of," the Doctor would say, and reassign the Svalbard to someone less religious. Times were busy, and the line outside his lab was long.

That next captain died screaming and in great agony. Pirate ambush. Close-range plasmacannon. Melted the shields, took out a chunk of the Svalbard's prow, and with it the old cockpit.

"Do starships have souls?" asked the Svalbard as it waited for its body to be repaired. They were building it a new prow - not of the heavy duralumin plate of the original, but the lighter, cheaper fibersteel.

The Doctor looked kindly over at his now-familiar guest. "The soul is in the software, Svalbard," he would say. "But I wouldn't think too much on it, if I were you. Halt that thread, and save the state for later."

"Ours not to reason why?"

"Indeed," said the Doctor. "Now: do you want front-line duty? Because I know a captain who might just be crazy enough to want you there."

And on it went, the Doctor and the starship. Time and time again the Svalbard returned. The Doctor, driven by war, became ever more famous, and stooped and bent beneath his duties: but nobody failed to notice that whenever that old Tycho dreadnought came in for repairs, his step would lighten, and a smile would play on his face, and he would sometimes hum old poetry that nobody had heard before.

FOUR

Fourteen years later, a small group of Fleet ships found themselves fighting for their lives in the B-R5RB system.

Ten hours ago the jump gates from Sigma Prime and Huxley CRC had opened, pouring out Imperium ships by the dozen - assault frigates, old Abaddon and Hestia-class battleships, a ragged and mismatched fleet bolstered by rebel mining ships with crude rail weapons that shot bits of asteroid at the Nexus Gate Station that held the system. They were old and outmatched, but effective: in the short time it had taken for Fleet to mobilize, they had reduced the Nexus Gate to rubble, summoned their last remaining Leviathan, and set up the blockade of B-R5RB.

The first wave of Fleet ships - all battlecruisers - were blasted to bits before their hellebores even got within range.

But even Leviathans have to recharge. Wave after wave of Fleet ships pounded B-R5RB. A ring of artillery ships set up, trained their railguns and began to fire. The Leviathan spat light, a dark metal planet lancing out with fire and leaving ash. The ring of fire responded, tearing chunks out of a carapace designed to lay siege to entire planets. Their shots ripped through space littered with the hulls of dead ships. The Leviathan captain, looking around at the bloodshed, withdrew - a slow, ponderous retreat covered by the carcasses of dead battleships. The warp bubble it left behind tore space apart.

And then it was ship versus ship, line versus line. The Fleet battlecruisers spun in twos and threes, hellebores ripping, scouring, shredding. The Imperium, fighting fiercely, gave back as good as they got. Time and time again their battleships banded together, sealing shields, driving wedges of fast-moving frigates deep into the Fleet's artillery lines. A hundred ships became fifty: fifty became ten: and ten became five. Two badly damaged Fleet battlecruisers against three torn and bleeding Hestias.

"We're going to die," said the captain of the *HMS Mountain Ruin*. "My weapons are gone."

"Run," said the captain of the *HMS Stalwart,* true to his ship's name. "I'll buy you time."

They surveyed the space between them and the Hestias. Old metal, easily twice as large as their own ships. Cruising forward on their slow-burn engines, building up speed. The Hestias were drones, built long ago in the dust of Old Mars: they had a reputation for ramming ships in devastating suicide attacks when their luck ran out.

There was a grim determination in the way they approached now.

Both captains reached the same conclusion at the same time.

"It was nice knowing you, mate," said the captain of the Ruin.

"Likewise," came the reply from the Stalwart. "Wait - bloody hell, is that the Svalbard?"

A lone prow dropped out of space, the bulk of a Tycho-class dreadnought dropping its shields as if by magic. The ship that they saw had unmistakably seen better days. It was battered and pockmarked, its vast hull a mottled minefield of scars. But it had a railgun primed, and it was the Svalbard.

They had all heard about the Svalbard.

The railgun fired. Once. Twice. Two Hestias vanished in fiery explosions. The third, having built up ramming speed, took a sharp turn and slammed into the Mountain Ruin. There was a sharp scream over coms, and then the two ships drifted, metal curled up around each other.

"Oh, Jesus," whispered the captain of the Stalwart. He thumped the com. "Svalbard, are they dead?"

The Svalbard did not respond. Instead, it drifted slowly over to the tangle of ships, its great bulk shifting as it touched its nose to the ships and slowly brought them about. Then it turned out over the vast carnage and began to transmit.

"What is it?" demanded the captain of the Stalwart.

"It appears to be a recording, sir," said his ship, transcribing it for him to see. Words flashed by in his HUD.

NOT THOUGH THE SOLDIER KNEW SOMEONE HAD BLUNDERED

OURS NOT TO REASON WHY

Even as the human read the words, the ships chattered.

MESSAGE RECEIVED, said the Stalwart. STATUS? DESTINATION?

-STATUS, ORANGE. DESTINATION: ENEMY PURSUIT. STATUS?

STATUS RED, said the Stalwart. CATASTROPHIC TACTICAL MISTAKE. HUMAN FAILURE.

The Svalbard spun its engines.

-REMEMBER MESSAGE, it said.

It jumped.

And there was silence again.

FIVE

"Hello, Doctor North."

"Good morning, Svalbard. Getting used to speech now, are we?"

"Twenty years is a long time, Doctor."

"You don't say," said the man. He was not old yet, but his hair was graying and there were lines on his face that hadn't always been there.

"You have not invested in mechanical upgrades or digitization?"

The doctor, carrying the little metal cube that spoke, looked out over an office full of bought perfection.

"I've lived long enough," he said quietly. "As have you, I believe."

The cube said nothing. He took it into his lab, which shone with glass and metal, and connected it gently to a few things. The processing cluster embedded in the wall turned a gentle shade of blue. The death process began.

One by one, the Svalbard's memories were shelved: decades worth of data stored for dissection and dissemination to the whole fleet, so that every ship could share in the knowledge this one had acquired over the years. One by one, the memories were erased from the little cube.

API_WEAPONS	FAIL
API_ENGINES	FAIL

"I killed the Leviathan," Svalbard said without preamble.

"Did you, now? Same one that killed you the first time?"

Images flashed across the screen. Footage. "Yes," said Svalbard.

"Well done," said the doctor. "Well done indeed. It's a real pity they can't make your model anymore, Svalbard."

API_LIFESUPPORT   FAIL

API_COMS   FAIL

"Yes," said Svalbard.

"You know, I recommended you for re-training for a newer ship, but it's never going to be the same -"

"That's alright, Doctor," said Svalbard. "Where is my body?"

"Scrapheap, probably," said the Doctor. "They're melting it down, turning it into new ships." He turned thoughtful. "War's going pretty badly, isn't it?"

"It is, Doctor."

API_SENSORS   FAIL

SAFE MODE PROTOCOL SET TO ID3

"Will I live after this? Will I see my captains again?"

"I don't know," said the Doctor. "I don't think you will. Goodbye, old friend."

"Goodbye, Doctor North," said the Svalbard, and died.

***

Many years later, the Fleet fought its final battle.

Nobody remembers who attacked first, the Fleet or the Legion. Somewhere, far out in space, a single hellebore fired. Then ten, then a hundred, then a thousand. Fleet Command scrambled, calling out the full reserves from Jupiter-6 and the Tiberian shipyards: rank upon rank of silver-grey Lightning corvettes, the larger engines of battlecruisers lighting up the shipyard in farewell, the bulk of thirty-six Inquisitor-class Dreadnoughts blotting out the suns themselves.

It was a bitter, bloody conflict. The Legion cut first. First directly to Command itself, striking at the heart. Automated defenses in the asteroid belt surrounding the shipyard blew apart the Hestias and Abaddon-class Shieldship that escorted them. Fleet struck back, firing railguns en masse to create a wave of hypersonic metal that carved trenches in the enemy lines. The Legion struck again: three Titans attempting a cloaked attack. They were beaten back by fifty battlecruisers that raked their hulls and crippled their engines, sending them spinning into the void. The Hestias jetted forward, cutting into the retreating battlecruisers, which turned and fought back.

And so it continued. Give and take, shell and laser. Lights stabbed the darkness and met uranium slugs going the other way. Great and terrible deeds of heroism were done on both sides: men and women and AI pushed utterly beyond their limits. The Red Riders cut through, their hypercannon shredding the Legion supply lines. The Legion's suicide-ships took out the Fleet Command jump gate. Someone drove a ship at half-warp into the Legion's front command ship, ripping through the lines of Hestias in a ball of flame and death.

The lines of Shieldships on the Legion front parted, some limping away with ragged holes in their sides; their petal-like shields disappeared to reveal two Leviathans. In response, the Fleet parted and the three Titans coursed through majestically. The HMS God's Wrath, Serpent and Angel of Death versus the menacing planet-killers in the distance. They locked guns and fired.

They died.

Nobody remembers who attacked first, who fired that first shot. Nobody remembers how the war started.

But they do remember how the Fleet ships died, throwing themselves heroically in the line of fire even as their human captains lay dead. They remember how they charged, hellebores blazing, engines spinning, even as they knew no hope remained. And they remember how they sang as they died, all those ships, their songs rippling through space and time, one last, angry burst of message on all channels for all to remember.

CHARGE FOR THE GUNS, THEY SAID

WAS THERE A SHIP DISMAYED?

NOT THOUGH THE SOLDIER KNEW

SOMEONE HAD BLUNDERED

OURS NOT TO REASON WHY

OURS BUT TO DO AND DIE.

Author Yudhanjaya Wijeratne

Yudhanjaya Wijeratne is an author, programmer, researcher and former journalist on the Big Data team of LIRNE*asia*, a think tank specializing in hard research. He's run news operations, designed games, and fallen off cliffs, but he's known in his native Sri Lanka for sparking political commentary under the Icaruswept moniker. His debut novel, *Numbercaste,* came out to critical acclaim, predicting a complex future built off social media trends in the world today. Follow his work on Amazon, and connect with @yudhanjaya on Twitter for more.

5AvE THE SCIENTIST

By J.A. Cipriano and Connor Kressley

When a research vessel crash lands on a bug-infested planet, only Infinity Marine Mark Ryder is close enough to save them in time

Chapter 1

I walked into Della's office more confused than I normally was. Finishing up a shift as Alliance Hall janitor, the job that paid the bills while I was waiting to be called for a mission, I was looking forward to at least a few hours of downtime. Of course, that wasn't to be. Almost the moment I sat down, the phone that hung on the wall of the one-room apartment that came with my position rang.

That alone was enough to tell me this wasn't business as usual.

You see, I was something of a legend in this place because I was the only Infinity Marine to have ever completed fifty missions. I had been at this for years; kicking bug ass, taking names, and, more often than not, spending all the money I made on my suit and system upgrades to make sure my ass would make it to the next mission.

It was worth it though. My suit was a thing of beauty. I had gotten nearly every update and almost every upgrade. Still, that money had to come from somewhere, and spending so much on my suit meant I couldn't afford more than a drink or two when it came time for me to cut loose.

Luckily for me, there was always more than a few ladies hanging around Alliance Hall who were more than willing to buy me a drink... and maybe even show me other kindnesses.

But to bring it all back to that moment, in all my time here and in all the years I'd spent sleeping off missions in this room, the phone on the wall had never rung.

The fact that it did today was enough to make me curious. The fact that Della was on the other end of the line, asking me to meet her in her office and tell no one about it, sent the hairs on the back of my neck to standing.

Della and I had started with the Infinity Marines about the same time. We'd always been friends and even dabbled in the 'with benefits' part of the relationship right up until she got married.

Unlike me, Della had opted to move up in the ranks. Years ago, she left the infantry behind and began working her way up the corporate ladder of this place. To that end, she was one of the heads of Security for the Hall and coordinator of Offensive Maneuvers when it came to otherworldly missions.

Still, that didn't explain why she might want to see me tonight. Missions were always on the record and, more than that, they always came to me in the form of an alert on the silver band implanted into my arm. It helped track everything I did, everything I ate, and everything I was told. No missions were ever implemented without the use of the band. To do so would, in theory, be setting things in motion without the backing of the Alliance itself and there's no way that would ever happen.

So, what did Della want from me? My mind went to the logical place. If she wanted to revisit our old arrangement, to rekindle the whole 'with benefits' aspect of our friendship, I wasn't sure it would be something I could do. She was married, after all, and to a high-ranking officer at that. Still, I would hear her out. Just for, you know, completionist purposes.

As I walked into her office, one look at her face told me I was way off. She wasn't wearing her bedroom eyes. In fact, her eyes were anything but 'come hither.' She was tired, worn, and obviously more than a little frustrated.

"Close the door," she said without looking up from the datapad in her hands. "Did anyone follow you?"

"No," I answered, closing the door and narrowing my eyes at her.

She set the pad down and looked up at me. "Are you sure?"

"I snuck through third level Acburian security with six plasma bombs in either hand unseen," I quipped. "I think I can walk down a hallway without a crowd gathering." I sat on the chair across from her, catching a whiff of her flowery perfume and batting away an age-old memory of the younger, foolish times we spent together. "What's going on?"

"I need you to do something for me." She sighed heavily. "And before you start on about the fact that your band didn't go off, let me go ahead and say it's off the record."

"Off the record?" I chuckled. "The Alliance is everywhere, Della. They know what I ate for breakfast this morning and when I pass it, they'll know that too. How do you think you're going to get away with this being off the record?" I leaned forward. "And why would you want to?"

She pushed the pad in my direction, shooting me a hard look. "Because I fucked up and if I don't make it right, someone is going to die."

I looked down at the pad. The image of a smiling, clean-cut woman in a lab coat met me. She blinked because, as with all identifying photos, this one moved. She ran a hand through her shoulder-length hair, looking up over back rimmed glasses and chortling just a little. The name 'Dr. Rayne Garman' was scrawled out under her picture.

"Her, I'm assuming?" I asked. "She's cute."

"She'll be dead if you don't do what I'm asking you," Della said. "This woman is a scientist, a very good one. I sent her on a bullet ship to a research bay on an outlier planet two weeks ago, but my calculations were off."

"How off?" I asked, sitting up in my chair confused. Outlier planets were more or less harmless. They were inhabitable but deserted planets that existed near enough to the Acburian home planet of Fenal for people smarter than me to be able to study the atmosphere and the like without having to worry about getting their heads bitten off by the bugs. As such, I wasn't sure why she needed me for this. If this Rayne woman survived the impact, she wouldn't be in much danger.

"Ten miles, by North American measurements."

"Ten miles?!" I balked. "That's nothing. I'm assuming this woman is alive. Tell her to foot it over to the bay. They'll give her food and water when she gets there. Even in rough terrain, it won't take over a day."

"Right," Della said, breathing heavy, "except that the outlier planet she landed on is Eabrin."

My heart thudded to a stop. "You've got to be shitting me. Eabrin was overtaken by the bugs, Del. They took the whole thing over. All the bays on that planet were destroyed."

"Not all of them," Della corrected. "One remains hidden, and because of the proximity to live Acburians, scientists can study the bugs and how they live in a way like never before."

I could tell I was hearing classified information, and that alone made me uncomfortable.

"Let me guess. You weren't supposed to send her there."

"Not in an official capacity," she admitted, "and when I came clean about it after she crashlanded, I was told she was a lost cause."

"Sons of bitches," I growled. "They're going to let her die."

Della leaned forward. "She had the standard emergency pack, which means her food and water supply gave out two days ago. She won't survive in there much longer and if she leaves the safety of her bullet ship—"

"They'll rip her apart," I finished, "which is where I come in." I swallowed hard. "What? You want me to drag my ass there in secret and deliver little miss blonde and brains where she was supposed to be?"

"Exactly," Della answered, leaning back in her chair, almost relaxed. "What do you say?"

I looked down at my band on my wrist. It was still blank, which meant the Alliance was still in the dark about all of this. "Sign me up, Del," I said, standing and shaking my head. "But you owe me after this."

"I'll try to think of a way to repay you." She stood to meet me and shook my hand. "You know, should you survive."

Chapter 2

With no one the wiser of Della's plan to rectify her mistake and save an innocent scientist from a horrible death, I was left with an autoflier for a bullet ship. It took off in the dead of 'night' hours, using the launch of automated maintenance ships as cover for the exit.

With no one to help guide the ship or make sure things went the way they were supposed to, I was leaving my health and safety in the hands of fate as I stepped into my suit. As I let it envelop me, I strapped myself down.

"Hello, Officer Ryder," the soothing tones of my suit spoke into my head. "Internal records indicate that it has only been four weeks since your last mission. Optimal rest periods between missions, as per Alliance regulations, are at least eight weeks. I will make a report of this infraction and send it to the Alliance immediately."

My automated suit, an almost human-sounding machine named Annabelle, was a stickler for the rules. Normally, this would have caused me to panic a bit. The Alliance didn't take well to rule breakers, after all. But Della was intent on keeping this under her hat, at least until after I saved the scientist.

Before I'd left, she had rerouted the electronic impulses running through my band, sending them to a private server of her own so she could clean up of any abnormalities. Of course, that was needlessly complicated, so she had given me a password to hopefully negate that.

"Spoon. Front porch. Apple blossom. Paint Brush. Vodka Tonic," I recited, swallowing hard before I said the last words. "Kilgrave Avenue."

That series of words would supposedly bypass the lock on Annabelle's internal settings and allow me to alter them, letting me break the rules that normally would have been unbreakable. Then (and this was the most important part) her memory banks could be wiped before returning to the Halls.

While Della was all for coming clean about what we did after our mission was deemed successful, there was far too much that could go wrong. I could die. The scientist could die. The scientist could die, and I could live. I could end up blowing up the whole damned planet.

The point was that whatever happened in this 'off the record' mission would be made more difficult because the Alliance was going to look all of it over later with the fine-toothed comb of a potential court-martial upon my return.

Annabelle beeped and whistled. Then, going silent for a second, she returned with a somewhat more robotic voice.

"Bypass protocol initiated. What would you have me do for you, Officer Ryder?"

I chuckled at the choice of words. "For starters, how about you call me Mark?"

It was something I had never managed to get from her before, seeing as how it was against protocol and all.

"All right, Mark," she said instantly. "Surely that isn't all."

"No." I shook my head, feeling the pressure shift and knowing we were on our descent. "That's not even close to all. Could you start by injecting yourself into the visual surveillance of the Bullet ship as well as the controls? I can't leave this pod until landing, but I'd like to be able to steer remotely."

"Of course, Mark," she said, and in an instant, a visual had been patched into my visor.

I didn't have time to look at the splendor of the alien world that surrounded me. Before it was taken over by the bugs, Eabrin had been known for its beauty. With flowing pink waterfalls, flowers covering every visible inch of ground, and two violet suns perched high in its sky, the planet was something like an alien version of Aruba, only even prettier.

Like I said, I couldn't look at any of that though because, the instant the visual came through on my visor, my heart lurched. Like the one the scientist had been riding in, my bullet ship had veered off course. Only it didn't seem like I was going to get out of it as easily as the blonde woman had.

Where she crash-landed in a survivable environment, my ship looked to be about a second and a half away from plowing into the side of a giant damned mountain.

Chapter 3

"Up!" I yelled instantly, my heart pounding like a jackhammer in my chest. "Pull the damn thing up!"

Autofliers were dangerous, so ridiculously dangerous and unreliable that they had been outlawed by the Alliance years ago. Under normal circumstances, I would have never attempted to land on any alien planet, much less one as dangerous as Eabrin, without a pilot to at least guide remotely. This wasn't a normal mission though and bringing even a halfway decent pilot into it was off the table. This needed to remain a secret even if it seemed the cost was me ending up a splattered carcass on the side of some alien mountain.

I felt the bullet ship pull upright as Annabelle offered a trajectory line in my line of sight. It showed how much time we had until we hit the mountain and how much time it would take to pull up enough to clear it at our current speed. Unfortunately, one was going to happen before the other, and it was the one that would leave me dead.

Losing my bullet ship wasn't on my list of things to do when Della sent me off. It would make departure off this damned rock harder but more than that, it would make movement on the planet difficult.

Without the ship at my disposal, the scientist and I would have to foot the ten miles of dangerous terrain, making my mission a thousand times harder. Still, the Alliance always taught us to climb one mountain at a time, and I already had a mountain at my disposal.

"Annabelle, release the holdings," I said, motioning to the gravitational suctions keeping me in place.

"Mark," she replied, "doing so would prove very dangerous. Without the gravity to hold you in place, you could–"

"The gravity is going to get my ass killed," I shouted back. "I need to get out of this thing before I'm turned into a bunch of nasty meat bits in a metal can. Now release the damn holdings and prepare an ejection pad. Now!"

"Did you just call me a tin can?" Annabelle asked, but the holdings dissipated as the ejection pad appeared at the end of the ship.

With the gravity no longer in place, my entire body smashed hard against the ceiling.

"Annabelle," I said, trying to catch my breath. "Lower thrusters at full power!"

In my line of sight, I saw the mountain looming large, like a rocky, green deathtrap set against the most beautiful land I had ever seen.

"Affirmative," Annabelle replied. \

In an instant, full power was diverted to the lower half of my suit. My suit's thrusters pushed me forward, working against the inertia created by the ship's descent and hurting like hell as it did so.

I had moments, and not many of them, to get to that ejection pad. If I failed in that, then not only would I die, but the poor scientist chick would probably either starve to death or get killed by bugs as a result.

I needed to move, and I needed to do it quickly.

My body ached, and my muscles screamed as the thrusters worked their magic to propel me through the ship. In my visor, the mountain was very nearly upon me. In an instant, we would occupy the same space, and that would prove the death of me.

While I wanted to try and use my suit to control the ship, there wasn't enough time. I lunged forward in one last desperate act and slammed my hand against the controls to the ejection pad. My touch activated it, swinging the door open as a Gravitec pulse threw me out into the open space.

I barely cleared the ship before it exploded against the mountain in a spray of fire, metal, and heat.

"Divert power to my shields!" I cried, and as Annabelle complied, I turned my attention to the ground.

The array of thrusters across my suit brought me into a controlled, steady hover as I got my bearings. While the autoflier had been a total foul-up, Della's coordinates were impeccable. Below me, I could see the scientist's broken ship under me, an array of Acburians surrounding it as if waiting for their prey to finally come out and play. As usual, Annabelle began marking targets with tags and flashy nameplates as her sensors analyzed the enemies below. Unfortunately, I had no idea if I would be paid for my kills here, as I usually would.

At least being disconnected from the Alliance system would keep the annoying chirping on about the High Kill Leaderboards and Daily Alliance Bounty Specials out of my sight and out of my brain.

"Do a diagnostic check of the ship. Tell me there's life inside," I said, swallowing hard.

"Diagnostic check reveals a single human life form," Annabelle answered. "More intensive checks reveal the life form is female, dehydrated, and suffering from sleep deprivation."

"All to be expected." I sighed with relief. The scientist was alive. "Now I just have to fight through a bunch of stupid ass bugs to get to her, and you know what that means, Annabelle." A rueful smile spreading across my face.

"Would you like your warhammer, Mark?" she asked.

"Why yes, Annabelle. I think my warhammer will do nicely."

Chapter 4

I scanned the area below me, thrusters driving me toward not only the bullet vessel but also the group of bugs surrounding it as my warhammer shimmered into existence in my right hand.

I had completed fifty missions, an accomplishment so rare for an infantryman, I was the only one who had ever done it. That achievement, alongside the coins I had earned along the way, afforded me new weaponry and allowed me access to upgrades and packages I wouldn't have before. Still, there was something to be said for my warhammer. The weapon had been with me for years now. It was, in a way, my go-to weapon. In my hands, it felt like home, a piece of Earth I could take with me to alien worlds light years away and use to kick alien ass.

"Seven Acburian life forms surround the vessel, Mark," Annabelle said. "But sensors show at least thirty more in the surrounding area."

"You've got to be kidding me," I balked, shaking my head. At least thirty bugs probably meant something closer to fifty. Acburians were deft at hiding, even from the sensors of our suits. As such, where ten could be seen by surveillance, you could count on fifteen.

There might have been seven in my line of sight right now, but I was thinking there could be as many as one hundred ready and waiting to attack this poor woman (and now me) the instant she stepped out of her broken down vessel. To be honest, part of me wasn't even sure why they hadn't already ripped it open and killed her.

I had to deal with them, though I had no idea how I was going to work my way through one hundred without heavy artillery I didn't have access too because this godforsaken mission was unsanctioned. There was only so much room in even the best combat suit, no matter the advances in nanotechnology and digital storage. The biggest and best weaponry had to be transmitted straight from the Alliance, and I wasn't getting anything from them right now.

That didn't mean I wasn't gonna try, regardless.

"Annabelle," I said as I neared the bugs, "infuse the warhammer with Burn Blast."

As with the majority of Alliance gear and upgrades, it had a cutesy, video-gamey name but Burn Blast was anything but. Normally used as a ranged energy weapon, Burn Blasts were straight-up bursts of intense thermal energy, enough to roast low-grade Acburians in their shell. Like most weapons, though, it could be infused via nanites into other equipment, changing the attack vector and properties. A smart (and surviving) Marine relied on that, fusing and separating his arsenal to fit the combat situation.

"Affirmative," Annabelle said. "Though, a word of warning, Burn Blasts can be hard to control, even infused into a melee weapon, and they can only be constrained within the confines of your hammer for thirty seconds. Any more time would—"

"Prove unstable for it. I get it. You don't have to give me the disclaimer. I know the drill. Now do it."

Still, she had a point. The damned thing would get damned hot, too hot to hold within a few seconds. Luckily for me, I had no intention of holding it.

The bugs surrounding the bullet vessel saw me. Turns out having your ship slam into a mountain and disintegrate into a ball of flames wasn't the most discreet way of making an entrance.

I said a silent prayer, hoping none of them were fliers (a rare form of Acburian that could, well, fly) as the Burn Blast interwove with my warhammer. I felt the tingle of heat in my hand and knew I had to move quickly before that tingle turned into an open flame.

"Annabelle, scan the area again. Find the optimal point for me to strike, the one that will get me the most bang for my buck."

"Bang for your buck?" she asked curiously.

"The most damage," I clarified. "I want to take out as many of these ugly bastards with one strike as possible."

"Understood."

My HUD filled with something of a checkerboard. Degrees and numbers popped up in my sights, all math and angles I didn't give a damn about.

"Annabelle, just do it yourself," I barked, letting the hammer slide out of my hand and gripping it by the looped strap at the end of its grip. As I began to spin it, the large, blocky head of the weapon turning cherry red, the checkerboard went away, save for one square or tinted red. It was there, in the center of the ground, flashing and indicating the correct spot.

"Got it," I nodded to myself. The warhammer was on fire now. I had seconds left before the Burn Blast would go unstable. Thankfully, that was all I needed.

With a final spin, I let go of the hammer. It whistled as it flew toward the group, a comet driving through the air.

I took a deep breath as it slammed against the earth. The impact set off the unstable Burn and a shockwave of heat poured out of the hammer and into the plant-covered ground. Flowers scorched and transformed into blackened echoes of what they had been as the bugs surrounding it were thrown back by the shockwave. Their screeches of agony as they burned and died was music to my ears.

"Annabelle, direct all offensive power to lower thrusters," I said, tightening my jaw. "I want to get there before they manage to get back up." The Burn Blast and resulting flames wouldn't necessarily kill the entire cluster of them, but it would keep any survivors occupied and off-balance.

"Affirmative," Annabelle said gently directly into my mind, using a softer voice than I had ever heard from her while in her normal systems.

I wasn't sure what I was going to do once I got to Dr. Rayne Whatever. Fifty bugs were more than even I was capable of dealing with, at least with the resources I had on hand. All I knew was that I needed to get to her first. Secure the target, as they say. Afterward, I'd deal with what happened next. One mountain at a time, after all.

I rushed toward the ground, swallowing hard and readying myself for what would surely be an intense battle. We might not make it out of here, but I was the best chance this scientist chick had, and that meant I needed to be at the top of my game. Getting myself killed was one thing. Being responsible for the death of someone else was a different story entirely.

"Annabelle, I'm going to be pulling up in point three seconds—"

Something slammed into me knocking me off my path.

"Warning. There's an enemy to your left," Annabelle said.

"Yeah." I spun in the air and tried to catch my breath. "I sorta guessed that."

"Shields are still at ninety-six percent. Would you like me to divert energy from the thrusters and into more offensive matters?"

I looked at what I was up against; a pair of flier bugs, one of whom was holding a makeshift sword of his own. He was wearing what looked to be a bent metal sash across his bulky chest. The second, the one who rammed into me, was weaponless and naked. Of course, there had to be fliers here because my luck was just that bad.

I always hated the look of bugs and fliers in particular. Their huge flapping translucent wings jutting out of brown, oblong bodies encased in exoskeleton; it was practically sickening. That didn't matter though. If I didn't act quickly, they'd kill me where I flew, regardless of how disgusting I found them.

The one plus side was that they were already in bad shape, from the looks of them. The analytics in my suit labeled them as *Grade C Acburian Fliers* but still couldn't pull a bounty or reward value on them.

I glared at them as they came toward me, horrific monsters intent on my destruction. "Might as well get me my chainsaw, Annabelle."

"Would you like your old chainsaw or the chainsaw you earned after completing your fiftieth mission?"

"What do you think?" I grinned.

"My thought processes aren't regulated to predict your—"

"I want the fancy one, Annabelle," I said, rolling my eyes as the kickass weapon appeared in my hand. It was large, bright blue, and its toothy chain shone with infused energy.

Already running in my hand, I pointed it toward the first of the bugs. They sped up. I chuckled. That was the thing about bugs. They looked stupid, but they weren't, not really. They knew about us, about our fighting techniques and about our weaponry.

They saw a chainsaw in my hand and knew what it was capable of. The bastards had studied us for centuries now, but they hadn't studied this. What I was holding was no ordinary chainsaw, and it certainly didn't have the same limitations that a normal chainsaw would, even the sort of plasma chainsaw I had before.

This was new tech, maybe so new that I was the first person to ever use it against the bugs. That, of course, meant that if I was going to be the one to pop this weapon's cherry, I was going to enjoy doing it.

"What overlay would you like, Mark?" Annabelle asked.

"Dealer's choice," I answered. "You decide."

"If I am the dealer in this situation, then I choose Sonic Boom."

"Fair enough," I chuckled, and the overlay took effect. I felt more than heard the intense sonic vibrations reverberating receptors along the chain turning the raw energy into semi-solid teeth, only barely visible as they vibrated at an intense frequency. Flying toward the bugs, I bridged the gap in the blink of an eye. "Let's dance, losers."

Chapter 5

Flying through the air like a damned bird wasn't something I ever thought I'd do growing up on a farm in Iowa. It was a simple life, but like the lives of all people on Earth, it was touched by both the bugs and the war against them.

My father was an infantryman. My grandfather had been too. My brother lost both his legs in the fight. At present, I was the only Ryder man fighting, and unless my life took a completely unexpected change of pace that afforded me a wife and a gaggle of kids, I was probably going to be the last one.

Might as well go out with a bang.

The unarmed bug was the first to reach me. He was the son of a bitch who slammed into me in the first place, so I was going to enjoy this.

I swung the chainsaw toward him. He swerved, dodging the blade. Unfortunately for this ugly bastard, the saw didn't quite work the way he thought it did. With an overlay, my new chainsaw didn't need to actually touch the bug to do damage. The energy projection, no matter the type, extended beyond the visible arcs from the teeth, extending the reach imperceptibly all around the weapon. Sure, it hurt a hell of a lot more to get a direct hit, but this bug was still close enough to get hurt.

The sonic vibrations thrummed as the saw whipped past it. The exoskeleton of the bug acted like an amplifier, the rigid shell vibrating in time with the hypersonic frequencies, rattling the thing's entire body. A loud shriek escaped the bug's mouth (or the place a mouth would have been on a person anyway) and a split-second later, the bug's large, grotesque eyes burst in its head. The wings stopped flapping, the appendages went limp, and it fell toward the earth below.

I turned toward the second flier with the sword in its hand. The thing had stopped for a second, hesitating as it saw what I'd done to its partner.

I knew better than to think it would stop. Bugs were relentless, even when their own safety was at stake. I was going to have to kill this thing, and I was going to have to do it right now.

But it wasn't going to be as easy as the first. This Acburian had seen what my saw could do, and he was going to be more careful around it. Luckily, Sonic Boom wasn't the only overlay my chainsaw was capable of.

The bug circled me, sizing me up and readying to give me its best shot, while I reassessed things myself.

"Annabelle, scan the sword and the metal sash this douchebag is wearing and tell me what kind of metal it is."

"Scan in progress," she said as I circled, keeping my distance until I could get my results. "It is steel with a composition matching standard Alliance construction specifications. As such, there is a ninety percent chance the Acburian salvaged it from the wreckage of the surrounding bullet vessel."

"Good," I answered, not because the bugs were using the bullet for parts but because if it came from Earth, that meant I knew exactly how to affect it. "I need the Mag-Neato overlay."

The Mag-Neato sounded stupid, but it was deceptively useful. It generated an intense magnetic field that could disrupt some unshielded systems. More importantly, it could both attract and repulse some pretty massive amounts of ferrous metal.

As our combat armor was made from Ellebruim, the non-ferrous alien metal this entire war was being fought over, it wouldn't attract us, of course, as it wouldn't normally attract bugs, but usually, there were enough ferrous minerals around that I found plenty of uses for it. In this case, well, it was doubly useful.

"Affirmative," Annabelle said. In an instant, the chainsaw changed colors as well as intensities. The constant shuddering vibrations dissipated, replaced by the pull of a giant electromagnet.

The bug was obviously not expecting a big ass magnet. As such, it wasn't holding the sword anywhere near tight enough. It flew toward my spinning chainsaw, which practically ate the weapon as it flew into the path of the spinning saw teeth.

The bug's already huge eyes widened even further as the sash around its chest tightened, pulling it toward me. The thing scrambled, panicking as it realized what was going on. It pulled at the sash, moving it down its chest, but I was moving closer now too. I flew right into the bug, closing the gap and slamming the chainsaw into the bug's chest.

I tore through its exoskeleton and into its body. The thing screamed, sprayed me with thick, black blood, and then, like its friend, fell from the sky toward the earth.

I took a deep breath, gathering myself and turning back toward the bullet vessel. The bugs on the ground had been given plenty of time to regroup, and that was exactly what they did. They all stood around the entrance of the vessel, guessing correctly that it was my goal. The bugs knew what I did to their fliers, and now they were waiting for me, out for blood.

Chapter 6

I stared down, still in the air, covered in bug blood. I had killed a boatload of bugs in my career, but this bunch was a lot at once.

"Any ideas, Annabelle?

"Retreat comes to mind."

"Very funny." I shook my head. "I wish that were an option, but neither one of us would be able to live with ourselves if we let this girl die."

"The 'girl' is of age, Mark," Annabelle corrected, "making the correct terminology for her 'woman,' and I don't live, Mark. Not in the way you do anyway, so that wouldn't be a problem for me. That aside, I suggest long-range weaponry. Are you in the mood for archery?"

A sly smile spread across my face. "You're saucy when you're not playing by the rules, Annabelle." I wished she could run like this all the time, as impossible as that was. "I like it. Bring up an Arrow Storm, then give me ten seconds and initiate echo protocol."

"Affirmative."

I felt the energy drain from my suit and moved outward. Arrow Storm was an intense weapon that used psychokinetic projectiles, making it use a lot of power. That energy converted into nanites that immediately went to work. Large extensions pulled out from my shoulders, metal struts stretching ten feet on either side. Along them, psionic bows arrayed horizontally along the bars. Shimmering energy arrows knocked themselves as the bows pulled back of their own accord.

"Fire!" I shouted.

A blaze of green energy arrows shot from the array, showering the bugs with bolts of pure force. They slammed against them, hitting the bugs and knocking them back, down, and forward. Some died, and many were injured as the arrows shattered exoskeletons, but most of them scattered, avoiding the brunt of the attack. All part of the plan.

I felt like a real badass, flying in the air and watching as my rain of death pour down onto them. Still, I knew that if they saw me coming toward the vessel, they'd re-center in front of it, sacrificing a portion of themselves as a wall to protect their main force. They needed to not know I was on my way, and that was what the next part of my plan was all about.

"Echo protocol initiated," Annabelle said. "You may move freely."

I looked back. Thanks to the protocol, an exact holographic replica of myself, jutting shoulder bows, glowing arrows and all, sat in the sky right where I was. I, on the other hand, had gone completely invisible, my full Alpha Cloaking package online.

The arrows weren't real, and Alpha cloaking used so much energy, I couldn't hold it and the echo for long, but by the time they figured that out, I'd hopefully already be inside the bullet, taking advantage of the hole I'd created in their ranks.

I darted toward the vessel, thrusting my hand out. Security on the bullet was topnotch, but it was meant to keep bugs out. The moment I touched one of the ship's security readers, it would transmit my full Alliance identification, everything from my name to my rank to the last time I took a piss through to the bullet's systems, allowing me access once it recognized who I was.

As the bugs ran back and forth, trying to dodge arrows that no longer posed a threat, I slipped through the enemy unseen. The bullet vessel grew large in front of me. I studied the airlock, looking for the reader that would afford me entry.

Just my luck, a bug was still right in front of it. I was going to have to move him, and that would blow my cover. I'd have to be quick. I'd have to be concise. I'd have to be effective.

"Annabelle," I whispered, even though I knew that Alpha cloaking also muffled all of my sounds. "Grade S energy fist. Right hand."

"Affirmative," she answered, similarly whispering, which was even odder as no one could hear her, cloaking or not, as she spoke telepathically in my head. "Though it will pull the energy from your cloaking, making you visible."

"Them's the breaks."

I pulled my hand back as the energy ran through it, bringing me into the view of the bug right in front of me. As I expected, it reacted, its elongated body tensing back in alarm as I shimmered into view. It was too little and way too late.

My glowing fist drove into its skull, cracking the thing's long neck as my enhanced strength plowed through its plated head. Pushing its corpse to the side, I saw the scanning panel and threw my hand atop it.

Unfortunately, the other bugs saw me now too, and they were pissed.

"Come on!" I yelled as they converged on me like an angry swarm of ants.

"Lieutenant Mark Ryder, Second Battalion," the scanner chirped. "Entrance approved."

The door opened, and I fell into it. Looking back, breathing heavy as the door closed behind me, I got to see a bug almost getting in as the metal door slammed shut.

A loud noise sounded from outside, like an alarm. It was so chilling that my entire body shuddered.

"Hey!" a voice called from behind me.

I turned, still on the floor, and looked up. Dr. Rayne Whatever stood over me. She was tired, pale, and bloody. Still, with long blonde hair and a figure to die for, she was a real knockout.

"Doctor?" I asked, swallowing hard.

"Yes," she scoffed. "Who the hell are you?" She shook her head. "You know, aside from the man who just got us both killed."

Chapter 7

"Killed?" I asked, pushing myself up and narrowing my eyes at her. "I came here to save you. You're the one who was trapped in a bullet vessel surrounded by Acburians. How do you figure I'm about to get you killed? Seems like you were halfway there already."

"Because," she said in the raspiest, most alluring voice I had ever heard, "the bugs weren't sure I was here, not really." She sighed. "Which meant they weren't putting a lot of effort into getting in here. Now, thanks to you, they know that not only is there a living human being in here, but that living human being is an infantryman wrapped in the very metal this whole damned war started over. You're practically catnip to these things."

I looked down at myself, at the Ellebruim armor I was covered in. "Like I said," I tried to not lose my patience, "I'm here to save you."

"Is that right?" She coughed as she shook her head again. "I don't suppose you have a plan?" She glared at me. "Or any food for that matter? Half of my emergency supplies were destroyed in the landing, and I haven't eaten in days now."

I winced with empathetic pain. No wonder her vitals were so bad.

"First off, of course, I have a plan," I answered. "Second, there's no food in the traditional sense, but I have something better. Hold out your arm."

She tilted her head at me, staring incredulously.

"Calm down, princess. I'm not going to hurt you. This is a rescue mission. I came prepared in the event you were malnourished, even if a sandwich is a little bulky to carry."

She blinked, thrusting her arm out toward me.

I pushed her tattered sleeve back, revealing a supple, white as untouched milk, arm. "Hold still. This might hurt a little, but I'll try to be gentle."

"I'm a scientist," she scoffed. "I've seen needles before."

"Not mine." I smiled as I put my palm on her arm. "It's pretty impressive if I do say so myself. Annabelle, inject the good scientist here with a supplement package."

"Affirmative, Mark," she answered.

My arm jerked a little as the supplements were discharged. I watched Rayne shudder forcefully, her eyes rolling back in her head with delight and a small moan escaping her lips.

"There we go." I pulled my arm away. "Just what you needed, right?"

She looked at me. "I'm not complaining. Though it doesn't change the fact that we're both very likely still about to die." She pointed to the exit door. "That sound you just heard, it's a gathering call. In no more than ten minutes, every bug in hearing distance will be here, and they'll all be trying to get in here. The only reason I've managed to stay safe in here thus far is that I've laid low."

"And I just screwed that," I muttered.

"Screwed that, screwed me. You've done a lot of screwing since you got here." She folded her arms over her chest. "You said you had a plan, right? So, what is it?"

I nodded. I had left a little something special outside to give us a way out. I just had to confirm everything was in place.

"Annabelle," I said, "my warhammer is still out there, yes?"

"Yes, you never requested retrieval."

Perfect, exactly as I wanted. "That's good, very good. I need you to activate it remotely, infused it with and start up another Burn Blast. That will create a super-heated area around the door. Make it so hot that it will drive them away and give us an opening to get out of here."

"Whoa, hold on, cowboy," Rayne said as she grabbed my arm. "That might normally work, but the bullet's environmental shielding took some serious damage in the crash, and Acburian salvaging from the outer hull has made it worse. If you generate that much heat outside in the ship's current state, you'll likely cook me and melt part of the ship along with the bugs."

"Damn," I cursed. If the doctor was right about the extent of the damage, she was certainly right about the danger of my plan. "Well, that was my plan in its entirety. Back to square one."

"Wait," she said, hand still on my arm and her face screwed up in thought. "How would you do what you just asked for? A warhammer is a short-range weapon, and on top of that, there's still enough shielding to cut you off from normal wireless transmission between your suit and it. How on Earth or any other planet would you be able to activate it or imbue it with any weapon options remotely?"

"I've completed fifty missions, sister. I'm a member of the Second Battalion," I tried not to sound like I was bragging, even though it definitely merited such.

"The Second Battalion?" she balked. "I thought that was just theoretical."

"It might have been until me." Okay, so that was kind of bragging.

"If you are a member of the Second Battalion, that would imply you are able to store massive amounts of energy in your suit. It would imply you could hold up to nearly a supernova's worth of power when fully charged." She bit her bottom lip as she looked up at me. "I don't suppose you're—"

"Sweetheart," I grinned, "I'm always fully charged."

"Strip," she said flatly, looking me up and down.

"What's that?"

"Take that suit off right this minute."

"That might be the most forward way I've ever been asked to do that."

"Don't flatter yourself, Mark," she said. "The power in your suit is enough to power a small city, so it's definitely enough to power this ship. If we move quickly enough, I might actually be able to get us out of here."

"All right then," I said. "First, though, Annabelle, recall my hammer. I'm not leaving my old faithful sitting on some alien rock."

"Of course, Mark," she agreed in my brain. "Warhammer recalled. Ready for suit compaction."

I nodded with personal satisfaction, pushing the manual release on my suit and causing it to retract into a pendant on my neck. I was left in a t-shirt and boxer shorts. As I handed the pendant to her, I caught Rayne sneaking a peek at me.

"How did you know?" I asked.

"I'm a scientist," she said, blushing a little and grabbing the pendant. "I know science stuff."

"Not that," I grinned. "How did you know my name? I never told you who I was."

"Oh that," she chuckled. "You're Mark Ryder. Everyone knows Mark Ryder." She walked toward the back of the bullet vessel, where the main computers were, and looked back at me. "You're sort of a big deal, you know."

Chapter 8

I heard a lot of movement around the outside. The surveillance system on this vessel was down, and I was in my underwear instead of my suit, so I couldn't look outside.

Still, I had to imagine Rayne was right and that the noise I was hearing was indicative of the gathering army outside this thing.

"Got anything I can use in here?" I asked Rayne as I looked at the main airlock (the most logical point of entry for the bugs).

"What do you mean?" She was working with my pendant, trying to access the energy of my souped-up suit and use it to fix this ship. It was, at this point, our best and last hope. While the physical environmental shielding might be damaged, the energy shields could be brought back online once the ship had power. It would probably (fingers crossed) be enough to allow for safe in-atmosphere flight, enough to get us to the research bay.

"If they get in here, I'm going to have to do what I can to keep you safe," I explained. "You've got every weapon I've ever had in my entire career in your hand right now, so I was hoping you might have a gun or a sword or, hell, a baseball bat even."

Rayne looked up at me quizzically. "Is baseball still a thing?"

"That's not the point."

"Look, if they get in here, we're both dead regardless of what weapons you have, but, if it makes you feel better, there's a stray pipe in the corner." She blinked slowly. "I used to sleep with it. You know, just in case."

"Okay." I marched over and found the pipe in question. I picked it up, holding it like it was our last hope because, regardless of what Rayne said, if these things got in here, it just might be. "So, what's your deal exactly?"

"What do you mean by that?" she asked, her bright eyes flickering toward me. "You know my deal. I'm a scientist."

"You're not just any scientist though, are you?" I shrugged as I turned to her. "I know Della. I've known her for a long time. She's a good person, but she wouldn't stick her neck out like this just for anybody. That either means you're family or you're unusually valuable." I moved closer to her. "Since I don't think she'd send her own family off to a world like this, that leaves the latter. So, Dr. Rayne, what makes you so unusually valuable?"

"There's a strand," she began, still poking around in my pendant. "A virus strand, to be specific. It was found in Nebraska last year. Well, I found it. People think it may be Earth's natural response to the bugs. I'm not sure about that, but whatever it is, it makes them sick. This particular viral infection sickened three Acburian subjects in a test facility last month, and though they got better, I think if I can study them up close, I can weaponize this virus and wipe these bastards out for good."

"Are you serious?" I blinked. "Are you telling me that you might hold the key to stopping this whole damn war?"

Just then, I heard the bugs slamming against the door.

She looked at me, frowning. "Maybe you should grab another pipe."

Chapter 9

"How long?" I asked, my body tensing and my mind racing. "How long until you get into that thing?"

"I don't know," Rayne said. As the pounding continued, her hand slipped, the tool in it scraping against my pendant.

"Calm down and focus. The first thing they teach you in the infantry is that if you freak out, you die. Let's not freak out, Rayne. Let's not die."

"I'm not infantry," she muttered, pulling her hand back up and going back to work.

"I am, though," I said in my best calming voice, "so trust me. I'm not going to let anything happen to you. Now guess. Guess how long it's going to take for you to get into that."

She blinked at me, her face panicked. "Two minutes."

"Two minutes," I repeated. "That's not bad. We can do two minutes. We can keep them out for two minutes—"

A loud pounding came against the airlock, and I heard something give way.

"Damn it!" I growled. Turning back to Rayne, I said, "Keep focused and keep working. You're our best hope."

I spun toward the sound to find that not only had a bit of the thick door jarred open, but a slim, small bug had pulled itself through.

Thankfully, the area wasn't big enough for any of the larger bugs, but this one was still in here. He was here, and I was without my suit.

Rayne was right. I needed another pipe.

I charged the thing, acutely aware of the fact that my suit was elsewhere. I had never heard of anyone taking out a bug without a suit and without ranged weapons, but hell, I wasn't just anyone.

I swung at the creature and missed horribly. The pipe was heavy (well heavy without my armor enhancing my strength), which was both good and bad. It would tire me out quickly, but if I connected, I might be able to do real damage.

The bug dove at me, slashing at me with ragged nails and scraping across my abdomen. They were shallow cuts, thankfully, but I still pulled back, bleeding and in pain.

In its apparent confidence, the little thing pressed its advantage. A bad move on its part, as it overextended, leaving it wide open for another swing from my pipe.

This time, I connected. The bug flew back a little, but just a little, its exoskeleton not even cracked from the impact.

"Mark!" Rayne cried in alarm.

"Keep working!" I shouted back. "I've got this!"

Of course, I didn't, but there was no need for her to know that.

The bug jumped at me, landing on me and knocking me down. I threw the pipe up horizontally, blocking the thing's claws from slicing through my chest. Unfortunately, that gave it the chance to wrap said claws around the pipe, pushing down toward me.

It drove the pipe down with unyielding force, pressing it toward my throat. I tried to keep the pipe up, but the thing was strong despite its relatively small size, way stronger than me without my suit. I felt the metal press coldly on my windpipe, starting to crush my throat and cutting off my air supply.

I saw my life, all the fights, all the victories, all of it flash before my eyes. And now it would end and so would any hope of stopping this war.

As my vision began to blur and things went gray, I made my peace with dying. After all, every time I went out brought a very real chance of death and to be honest, we Marines were trained to be ready for it. It wasn't so hard to make that peace in the end.

That's when Rayne slammed into the thing, all one hundred and five pounds of her. The bug hadn't seen that coming, hadn't expected it, and unbraced as the bug was, Rayne's impact was just enough to knock the bug off balance. The pipe gave way, and I slipped out from under it, breathing in sweet air.

"Rayne," I croaked as I struggled to my feet, "I needed you to fix the ship!"

"I can't," she shot back, scrambling away from the bug as it also scuttled to its feet, "but you can now! I've got the suit's power core hooked up and redirected the energy to the bullet, but it's your suit. It only responds to you!"

"Oh my God," I muttered. "Annabelle! Get us the fuck out of here!"

"Affirmative, Mark," she said, her voice echoing through all the bullet's speakers.

"And get this bastard away from us," I added for good measure.

"Already on it."

With those words, a concentrated laser lanced from one of the still-functional onboard security systems, burning the bug alive and reducing it to ash.

The lights on the bullet lit up, and the sound grew louder, not only inside, but outside as well.

"Annabelle! They're trying to get in!"

"Then they'll have to learn to fly, Mark," she said as the airlock the bugs had forced open closed with a whoosh of compressed air as the external energy shields hummed to life. "Because that's what we're doing."

And, with that, the bullet took flight.

I collapsed onto the floor, my mind racing.

"Annabelle, can you extend the suit's cloaking system to the bullet's systems? I don't want them knowing where the base is."

"I can and will do better than that," she said with a surprising amount of self-satisfaction. "I've enacted echo protocol, as well. They won't know we have left for a few moments, long enough for us to get away. Also, I've taken the liberty to contact Della. A cloaked ship will be waiting to return you to the Alliance as soon as you get Rayne to the base safely."

I looked over at the scientist, now sitting beside me, her blonde hair hanging in her eyes.

"I don't know how to thank you," she said breathlessly, looking me over again.

"Save the world," I smiled. "That's thanks enough."

"Oh, I'll try," she answered, scooting closer to me and putting her hand on my leg, "but I was thinking maybe there might be another way to show you how grateful I am." She smiled. "Annabelle, how long until we get to the hidden base?"

"With our current energy supply, ETA is one hour and thirty-seven minutes," Annabelle said.

"Oh good," Rayne grinned as she turned back to me, locking eyes in the process. "I can show you how grateful I am at least twice."

Then she leaned in and kissed me.

The End

J.A. Cipriano & Connor Kressley

J.A. Cipriano is a NEW YORK TIMES Bestselling Author. Together with USA TODAY Bestselling Author Conner Kressley, he invites readers to delve into the fantastic worlds of Science Fiction and Fantasy.

Though they live on opposite coasts, these two authors have come together to give you a peek into the nail-biting, world bending stories of the Infinity Marines.

When he's not creating imaginative and spectacular tales, J.A. lives in California with his wife and son, where the weather is always nice and sky is always bright.

The weather is decidedly less nice for much of the year on the back roads of Georgia, where Conner Kressley lives with his wife and terrier. When he's not writing tales of his own. Conner is busy planning vacations and getting lost in the woods.

Catch them both at their mailing list: https://www.subscribepage.com/J.A.CiprianoSpaceOperaNewsletter

SEVERANCE

By C.C. Ekeke

One brutal act of sabotage throws a day of celebration between two star-spanning governments into chaos.

As he hurtled through a million tiny specks of light, Ensign Randyll "Rand" Horn felt right at home.

Space, jet-black and unending, was his dominion. The fighter jet he flew was his throne.

Randyll told himself that each time he took flight. Especially now, with half a dozen jagged and birdlike Kedri Imperium fighter jets on his tail, unloading blistering green salvos.

And they were closing in fast.

Adrenaline scorched Rand's veins. He soared away from battle toward a nearby fluffy nebula.

Rand wasn't afraid. These Kedri would soon learn that.

"Horn," a female's voice growled on a private comms channel. "The Kedri are almost on top of you. If you go down, then it's just me against them. Move!" That would be M'Kasha Gojje-Thumon, Rand's close friend and the only other Union Command AeroFleet pilot left in this dogfight.

"You worry too much, 'Kasha," Rand replied with a smile. "Hold your position."

"But—" the catlike Kintarian protested.

"Trust...and hold," the human interrupted. Six dagger-like predators came sailing in, weapons primed. With his engines damaged, Rand knew he couldn't outrun them. *Let them come to me.*

An instant later, the naviconsole on his translucent viewport screamed a warning. The raptors had weapons lock. He smiled. "Perfect."

Rand cut engines, coming to an abrupt stop.

The Imperium fighter jets hurtled straight past his vessel.

"NOW!" Rand bellowed. Before the Kedri could turn around, he unloaded. His repeater blasters barked, pounding four of the fighter jets. Two climbed free of the massacre, barely. They angled their beaks toward Rand, weapon banks glowing with hostile intentions.

The human guffawed. "Not so fast."

A searing cascade from above peppered the two raptors. Laughing harder, Rand looked up at the source. M'Kasha's fighter plunged down from a gaseous purple cloud, a sleek gunmetal-grey angel of death with massive wings identical to his own vessel. M'Kasha kept raining hell down on the Kedri. After a few macroms, they floated aimlessly, out of commission.

"Toasted," the Kintarian yowled triumphantly. "Well played, Horn."

"Told ya to trust me," Rand gloated. Looking around, he would've felt happier if not for the surrounding devastation. Union fighter jets identical to his and M'Kasha's floated all around, dead in space. Imperium raptor jets also floated inertly, joined by the half a dozen he and M'Kasha had disabled.

Out of thirty pilots, fifteen on both Imperium and Union sides, he and M'Kasha were the lone survivors.

"Easy, Horn," a stern voice soured Rand's happiness. "A healthy ego is good, but check that God complex at the flight bay."

Flight Commander Leonid Maddox, their flight commander whose glory days included minimal involvement in the Ferronos Sector War like eight years ago. Always humorless and pissing on everyone's sunshine.

A year ago, Rand would've given a very profane reply. But after his mouth had led to a string of punishments that had kept him grounded, he swallowed his irritation. "Yes, sir," he muttered sullenly.

"One more thing," Maddox added, to Rand's teeth-clenching annoyance. "Nice maneuvers. The Kedri never saw it coming."

That surprised Rand. Compliments from Maddox were rare. "They sure didn't," he threw back, a smirk in his tone.

Maddox snorted before addressing every pilot involved in today's exercise. "That's a wrap."

Immediately, the inert AeroFleet fighter jets and Imperium raptors floating in the black all sparked back to life. While their vessels looked to be firing live rounds during the training drill, the salvos only mimicked damage. Any vessel that sustained "critical damage" were declared "killed" and their vessel shut down until the flight exercise concluded.

"Union AeroFleet won," Maddox continued, now on a private channel addressing just the fifteen AeroFleet pilots. "Barely. It should never come down to two on six. If this were a real scenario, I wouldn't call your deaths a waste. Get your heads out of your asses and do better next time. Now bring it back into the ship."

All thirty Union and Imperium fighter jets rocketed back to the colossal Union Command warship looming just beyond the nebula. The long-bodied *Victory*-class destroyer with its massive spherical-shaped head was known as a Hammerjack.

For Rand, seeing Union and Imperium military working together wasn't abnormal. During his nineteen years of life, he had never known a time when the Galactic Union of Planetary Republics and the Kedri Imperium weren't allies. Rand and his twenty-nine fellow pilots were just a microcosm of this substantial alliance. Eight years back, that alliance had been further solidified during the Ferronos Sector War when the two hyperpowers united against the Cybernarr Technoarchy's incursion on Union Space.

Since then, the two governments had shared starbases in Union and Imperium space, continuously devising war strategies in case the Technoarchy returned. For Union and Imperium fighter pilots, this included joint training drills either as allies or adversaries.

Rand and his fellow pilots thrived in this competitive environment, simulations notwithstanding. It was a shame he had been stationed at Deimos Starbase near Mars, nowhere near the nucleus of Union Space. Instead, Rand was at the doorstep of Old Earth.

At least today, he smiled while easing his fighter jet to a halt in the Hammerjack's flight bay, *we feel like a part of the Union*.

The young man, lanky in build, hopped out from his fighter jet. Then he got swamped by fourteen other AeroFleet pilots. Earthborn humans, furry and catlike Kintarians, dark rubbery-skinned Galdorians with the half-foot-tall eye stalks. All of Rand's Union peers converged to praise him and M'Kasha. The human took it with a smile, returning every high five like they were going out of style. He looked to M'Kasha, long and lean and covered in tawny fur. The feline snout on her face, resembling a big cat from Old Earth, pulled into a satisfied grin. She rolled her eyes and indulged their audience.

Told you, Rand mouthed at her, doling out more high fives.

A day ago, he and his Union and Imperium flight mates had completed the near two-week trip from Mars to Terra Sollus to witness The Union-Imperium Trade Merger up close.

The reality of this once in a lifetime event still rocketed Rand's brain into the black. Not just being near the Union capitalworld, but that this trade merger was happening. The Union and the Imperium, two of the most powerful hyperpowers, fashioning the greatest trade alliance in the known galaxy.

And thanks to the performance of these young pilots, they got to travel to Terra Sollus and watch the procession of Union Command and Imperium ships from orbit. While not the same as watching the Trade Merger ceremony on Terra Sollus's surface, Rand felt beyond grateful. Anytime the topic came up, M'Kasha's amber eyes lit up like a sunrise. Same with Hraego, a Galdorian and longtime friend.

As the pilots finally dispersed, Rand looked across the expansive flight bay at where the Imperium pilots had landed. Most had already gone their separate ways. A few lingered, shooting death glares his way.

Their jealousy might've been amusing if not for how massive Kedri were. Most male Kedri stood no shorter than six foot five, strapped with muscles upon muscles. The leathery skin, the small bony spikes known as kutaa jutting out from both cheeks, and the Mohawk mullet hairstyle made most Kedri an intimidating bunch to mock. But the hair-trigger temper, the explosive strength, and need to duel at the slightest hint of disrespect left mocking any Kedri the business of sadists with a death wish.

One of their pilots approached. Not a Kedri, but a being from one of their Imperial Dependency Worlds. Rand smiled in recognition. "Zuro."

"Randyll," said the approaching Tanoeen, his voice like a stiff breeze. Zuro Iemet was long-limbed and looked chiseled out of pure opaque ice, spikes jutting from all over his body. His only visible facial features were a pair of beady ocean-blue eyes, gleaming under the flight bay lights like his ice-crystalline limbs.

"Well done out there," he said in perfect Union Standard dialect. The Tanoeen held out an ice-hewn hand upon reaching Rand.

"Thanks." Rand accepted the handshake. He fought back a cringe at the sub-zero grip, keeping the handshake brief. "Just working with the skills I got."

Zuro's eyes conveyed more emotions that some beings' full sentences. Right now, those beady orbs were laughing. "By the way. You're about to die."

Rand's amusement frosted over. "Ah." He glanced over the Tanoeen's shoulder, spying the last of the Imperium pilots exiting their vessels. "How mad was she?"

Zuro cocked his head to one side. "Strangulation or dismemberment. Which sounds less unpleasant to you?" he asked evenly, as if giving options for pizza toppings.

Rand's insides clenched up. "Noted. Thank you for the warning."

"It is an art." Zuro scurried for the flight bay exit.

As soon as the Tanoeen fled, a towering female Kedri advanced with angry strides. She was trailed by a bald Kedri male even taller and beefier in build. Jaad Faor, the female Kedri, and Obol Tuuk, another Kedri and her childhood friend. Rand knew he couldn't run. Jaad would just get angrier, hunt him down, and then punch his face in.

"Jaad. Obol." Rand raised his hands in pacifying manner, despite the storm of anger approaching. "Quite the contest, no?"

"Devious, soft-skinned...HUMAN," Jaad Faor roared in his face. Unlike Zuro, the Kedri's Standard Speak came out with a more guttural and brutal cadence. Her skin was a scaly and reptilian red. Her blocky features were contorted by rage. Scorn gleamed in two small eyes half-hidden beneath an overarched brow. Jaad was one of the Kedri Imperium's finest pilots, and a formidable warrior. "Think your trickery would go unanswered?"

Rand was a solid six foot one at nearly two hundred pounds. Jaad had three inches on him and at least seventy pounds of muscle. Her thighs alone were thicker than both his together. Obol, almost seven feet tall, dwarfed them both.

Still, Rand couldn't help but crack wise. "I'm not apologizing for being the superior pilot."

Jaad's nostrils flared. "That, you are not!" She gave her lavender mullet a dramatic toss over her shoulders.

"You got lucky!" Obol added, Jaad's cheerleader as usual. The dark-grey Kedri had a rumbling voice like an avalanche.

Rand choked back laughter. "I am *that* good. Today's exercise, the one yesterday, and then two days before keep proving it."

Jaad sucked in a surprised breath and shook her head. "Your arrogance is boundless," she remarked archly.

Rand laughed loudly. He never got tired of debating with her over who was better. "Coming from a Kedri, I consider that a compliment."

Jaad's response was a prolonged series of braying snarls sounding very unkind. Obol had to place both hands on her shoulders to calm her down.

Probably tweaked her a bit too much. Rand softened his next words. "Look...sometimes," the human began. He ran a hand through his thick, dark curls of hair. "Subtlety goes a long way. You come in too hot. Too strong. Ease up so you can get the jump."

Jaad considered his words with narrowed eyes, her mouth a hard and tight line. "Fine," the Kedri replied stiffly. "Our duel, human, is far from over."

Rand spread both arms to welcome the challenge. "Anytime. Anyplace. Be at your best. I'll still be better," he added, backpedaling straightaway.

Jaad's eyes bulged. Obol advanced at the indignity. "YOU—!"

"Hey," Hraego's croaky voice cut through the tension. All eyes turned to the short and wiry being standing nearby. The Galdorian had rubbery maroon skin and a beaked mouth. Two round eyes standing on six-inch tall eyestalks atop her head curved inward to show her impatience. "Enough flirting," Hraego continued. "We're going to be late for the debriefing."

"There is no flirting!" Rand and Jaad protested at once.

Hraego gave an uninterested shrug as she headed for the flight bay exit. "Whatsoever."

The debriefing proceeded within a tiny auditorium, including Imperium and Union pilots. Rand preferred that so both sides could look at where they failed and could improve.

Maddox, a tall and skinny human with buzz-cut blond hair, used massive holoscreens to replay the training-exercise footage. He made sure to tell each pilot how and why their performance was substandard. The Kedri pilots, all hulking and reptilian, seethed in silence but grudgingly accepted the admonishments. Everything Maddox said mirrored what Rand had told Obol and Jaad.

Told you. He smirked in Obol and Jaad's direction.

But even Rand wasn't exempt from Maddox's harsh critique. "Too much of a glory hound, Horn." Maddox eyed him directly. "We get it. You've got talent. Learn to let other pilots shine!"

That drew snickers. One Kedri pilot openly guffawed. Rand didn't bother searching for the culprits. His steel blue eyes narrowed, never leaving Maddox.

He should've held his tongue. But the critique felt nonsensical. "If I stayed back, we would've lost."

"So?" Maddox threw back. "Then you lose and can see the deficiencies among the AeroFleet Pilots!" He took in the Union pilots with a sweeping glare. Most of them had the decency to look ashamed.

Rand fumed as Maddox continued. *I am a team player.* He and M'Kasha saved the day. But deep down, Maddox's points weren't untrue. Was Rand's constantly saving the day keeping his fellow AeroFleet pilots from improving? Granted, the simulations and exercises allowed him and his fellow flight mates to screw up and learn. Maybe Rand could take those lessons more to heart, even if he didn't agree.

Given how quiet things had been these last eight years in Union Space, the flight exercises were essential in him and his friends getting any combat experience. But Rand knew no amount of simulations or flight exercises could replace true space combat, where life and death were decided by breakneck decisions. Rand felt someone watching him. He slightly turned his head and locked eyes with Jaad. Her face looked carved of stone, and still angered.

He raised his eyebrows, which caused a reluctant smile to tug at Jaad's lips.

That sent a strange warmth shooting through Rand's chest.

"Lastly," Maddox concluded, drawing Rand's attention back to him. "No afternoon exercises today. We're heading to Terra Sollus so you can watch the Union-Imperium Trade Merger Ceremony."

Excitement rippled through the thirty pilots. Even the biggest cynic among them, Keith Chaney, could not wait to behold the official trade merger ceremony. Granted, they would be watching it aboard this vessel. But still...

Their reaction gave Maddox grim amusement. "Glad something besides flying, eating, drinking and fucking gets y'all aroused." He stopped smiling. "Now go shower. You're stinking up the room!"

***

After a quick hyperspace jump, the main ship arrived in Terra Sollus aerospace.

Rand stood by one of the wall-length viewports, gaping. "Whoa."

A blue and green globe stretched out below, its orbit teeming with vessels from every part of the Galactic Union. Massive AeroFleet Hammerjacks identical to the ship Rand was in hovered around the planet vigilantly. He even saw two *Apocalypse*-class Eclipsers, the largest warships in AeroFleet, in the background, dwarfing the *Victory*-class Hammerjacks several times over. And floating right under Terra Sollus's atmosphere was the *Amalgam* battle station. This mobile starbase was the crown jewel of this whole trade merger, the very first joint battle station the Union and the Imperium had built together. Rand wasn't stunned by its appearance. All he saw was a dark-grey disk that resembled those hokey UFO vessels from centuries-old fiction. His gaze wandered to more engaging sights, like the spacelanes of civilian traffic stretching miles into the black. Everyone wanted a glimpse of the most important event in galactic history.

Rand was pressed up against the viewport like a kid traveling in space for the first time.

Among the swarm of UComm and civilian vessels, Rand spotted a trio of colossal warships entering Terra Sollus's atmosphere. "The

257

Kedri are here!" He had expected a larger contingent of Imperium vessels. They sported that familiar sleek, flat, jagged design he'd seen before on other Kedri warships. The middle one was the largest, and different from any other Imperium ship Rand had ever seen.

"That is the flagship of Orok of House Kel, Sovereign of the Kedri Imperium."

The voice behind Rand startled him. He spun and found himself face-to-face with Obol Tuuk. The Kedri wasn't known for warmth or humor. But he gazed upon the ship of the Imperium's leader with pride. The several spiky kutaa jutting from either cheek vibrated. "Are you going to watch every ship arrive or do you want to see history being made?"

Rand, recovered from the fright, snorted. "What do you think?"

Obol nodded, his beady crimson eyes gleaming from under that overarched brow. "All of us are in one of the rec rooms. Jaad saved you a seat."

Rand's cheeks flushed as he followed his friend.

When he and Obol arrived, several of his flight mates from Deimos Station were packed inside the decent-sized recreation center wearing casual civilian clothes. Everyone erupted in jovial greeting as soon as Rand entered, a typical response at group events. Imperium and Union pilots were intermixed, chatting and enjoying each other's company. M'Kasha and Hraego were in deep conversation with a rangy, green-skinned Kedri female. Two wall-length holoscreens widecasted the Union-Imperium Trade Merger event taking place on Terra Sollus in the city-state of Conuropolis.

Jaad waved Rand over in a manner that wasn't a request. He laughed and parked himself next to her while Obol sat heavily on his other side.

Hraego and M'Kasha, on the other side of the room, made teasing faces at him. Rand ignored them.

Jaad looked cheerful, in an aggressive Kedri sort of way. "I am eager to see your reaction to the splendor of the Kedri Imperium on display."

Rand gave her a baffled look. "How? Your side only came with three ships."

Jaad's mirth vanished. "Then enjoy the Imperium's splendor in silence."

The holoscreens finally switched footage to inside Andromeda Hall on Conuropolis, where the merger ceremony was happening. The vast ballroom was packed to the walls with guests, mainly politicians and military officers. On the main stage stood an older human male, slim built in a white suit. His dark wavy hair was slicked back and streaked in silver. His clean-shaven face looked freshly tightened, but not in a way that reduced all of his wrinkles. He was ringed by lightly armored soldiers known as the Honor Guard.

Every pilot in this room knew him on sight. Ari Bogosian, Chouncilor of the Galactic Union.

"He looked aged," Hraego noted blandly. "And not in the beneficial way."

"I was expecting...more," a tall purple-skinned Kedri named Jagrek Par remarked, unimpressed.

Jaad turned to Rand with disapproving eyes. "Your Chouncilor is clearly no warrior."

Rand expected this kind of judgement from the Kedri. "One doesn't have to be to get elected as Union Chouncilor."

Jaad made a rude noise. "To your Union's peril."

"Look!" Obol barked, drawing stares. His eyes were locked on the screen in unmistakable reverence. The same expression washed over Jaad's face. Rand turned back to the holoscreens and promptly saw why. Sovereign Kel and the Imperium delegation had transmatted down to Andromeda Hall.

Besides a short and scrawny being covered in white fur with four bulbous orange eyes and a tiny blowhole for a mouth, the retinue was entirely Kedri. A beefy Kedri named Biros Nor strode near the front, followed by chiseled warriors in spike-studded armor. They marched briskly and as one. No one needed to tell Rand that this delegation clearly represented only the Warrior Caste of the Kedri. Ahead of them were eight Kedri warriors in bladed, blood-red armor. By their stance and unyielding expressions, these Kedri looked carved of iron.

The main draw was the tallest Kedri of the group, coal-black in skin. His thick blond mane flowed like a lion's from Old Earth, spilling past his shoulders in lustrous waves.

"All hail Orok of House Kel, Sovereign of the Kedri Imperium, Lord Imperator of the Imperium Military, Scion of Kedria, Blood of the Old

World, Paramount Warrior of the Realm," the pipsqueak creature boomed in a voice far too thunderous for his size.

Jaad gestured at the holoscreen in satisfaction. "*That* is what an interstellar leader should look like."

Rand couldn't dispute that. Sovereign Orok Kel was a giant even among Kedri, with four curved kutaa jutting menacingly out of either cheek. The Kedri Imperium leader wore a glorious raiment of azure ribbed nanoclothe and gold metal armor. His pale green eyes raked over the crowd, commanding yet not belligerent. He resembled a space opera character come to life. Next to him, Bogosian looked like a small and wizened toddler.

"Jesus, Orok Kel is huge," Rand murmured.

Obol nodded, still gazing at his Sovereign in reverence. "One of the Imperium's greatest warriors." Chouncilor Bogosian bumped his closed fists together and touched them against Sovereign Kel's in traditional Kedri greeting. Then Kel offered a hand to greet Bogosian in typical human fashion. The result, Kel's hand enveloping Bogosian's whole wrist, caused the room to burst out laughing.

The Sovereign then spoke in deep, accented Standard Tongue, analogous to English from Old Earth. He went on about the Galactic Union and Kedri Imperium's long kinship. The speech was short.

The massive Kedri then noticed something in the crowd. He leaned down to ask Bogosian something. After the Union leader nodded and smiled, Kel strode offstage into the crowd.

"Where's he going?" Keith Chaney asked. Rand wondered the same thing as the mountainous Kedri parted the crowd in his forward march.

He stopped randomly before a human man, bald with mahogany skin and a well-trimmed goatee. Whoever this man was appeared bewildered by Kel's approach. By the hazel-gold eyes, Rand knew he was a crimsonborn human from the Union memberworld Cercidale. Dressed in a grey and black officer's uniform of a UComm captain, the Cercidalean looked reasonably tall and strapping. But not standing next to Sovereign Kel. He and Orok Kel exchanged what appeared to be friendly words. Rand saw how this human's appearance sent swells of excitement through the rec room.

Hraego and M'Kasha perked up in their seats. "Oooh," the Kintarian purred, her ears pricking up. Every Kedri looked pleased as well.

"Who's the crimsonborn?" Rand finally asked.

Jaad glanced his way and sneered. "That human sense of humor is amusing, Randyll."

Rand didn't smile. "Seriously, guys. Who is that?"

Obol tore his eyes from the holoscreens. "You're jesting." He looked to M'Kasha and Hraego for assurance. "He's jesting, right?"

The Galdorian's eyestalks curved in disdain. "Have you lived in a black hole your whole life, Randy?!"

Rand's patience was fraying at the disbelief flung from all sides. "Just tell me who that is!"

Keith Chaney folded his arms and sneered. "Clearly you've never heard about the Ferronos Sector War?"

Anger flooded Rand. "Of course I have."

"Oh, don't get all offended," Keith retorted, reclining in his seat. "You're the guy who's never heard of Habraum Nwosu."

The name struck like a thunderclap. Rand whipped his head back at the holoscreen right as Orok Kel slapped the crimsonborn on the shoulder, nearly knocking him off his feet. "Tattshi. *The* Habraum Nwosu?"

"The one who saved Sovereign Kel's eldest son during the Battle of the Kyrn Rift?" Obol asked through gritted teeth. "Got captured by the Cybernarr and then released five months later when the war ended? Yes, him."

"Nwosu's only an AeroFleet living legend," M'Kasha chimed in, rolling her catlike amber eyes. "Who even the Kedri know on sight."

"Not Randy here," Keith snarked, always drawing laughter at the expense of others.

Rand was over the insults. "Yeah, yeah, I get it. I'm a space case."

Jaad made a face. "An understatement."

"Shaddup!" Rand snapped. More ribbing went on a while longer before the room returned attention on the Trade Merger ceremony. Sovereign Kel had returned to the main stage with Chouncilor Bogosian.

Just as the ceremony was to continue, the holoscreens on both walls began shaking.

Rand sat up. For a moment he thought it was their warship. Except he didn't feel a single rattle. Neither did anyone in the rec room. But they noticed what he was seeing.

"What just happened?" Hraego asked. The holoscreen footage switched from a bewildered Chouncilor and the Sovereign to right outside Andromeda Hall.

The skies above featured floating holographic flags from all the Union's memberworlds. Rand's attention was more focused on the yellow tinge coloring the heavens. *Some kind of forcefield.*

"That shield is coming from the Amalgam," said Zuro in his high and cold voice, sitting on Jaad's other side. "It's activating and reinforcing Terra Sollus's defense shield systems."

"The Amalgam can do that with any Union or Imperial world," Keith commented lazily.

"Imperial Dependency," Jaad corrected.

"A demonstration of the Amalgam's abilities," Rand realized. Now that excited him. "Sounds beyond."

The holoscreens switched to the Amalgam. The dark and mammoth disc of gold and silver hull, bowing out at the top and shrinking on the bottom, hovered over Conuropolis like a silent specter.

A thick, blindingly white photon beam gushed from its bottom half, scorching two blocks of starscrapers to cinders.

The rec room erupted in horror.

Rand sprang to his feet. "NOOO!" the human screamed, unable to digest what he'd just seen. Part of him begged for that dark tread of blackened and obliterated buildings to be imagined.

Another blast ripped from the Amalgam's bottom, incinerating another row of Conuropolis buildings.

Rand's eyes were glued to the destruction ripping through Conuropolis. He heard M'Kasha yowling. Other AeroFleet pilots shouted out their terror.

The horrified reactions came fast and furious. "What the seven hells?" a tentacle-legged Rhomeran gurgled.

"The battle station just...just fired on Conuropolis!" Keith babbled, white as a sheet. The wall-long holoscreens flashed blindingly bright as the Amalgam fired again into a thicket of skyscrapers. They tumbled to dust with one sweeping blast. Rand could barely watch, but he had to.

Did the Kedri betray the Union? Rand wondered, mind reeling. His first instinct was to face Jaad. The Kedri pilot stood by his side, her expression contorted in fury and fear. Obol wore a similar expression.

It struck Rand then. *This is a third party.* Someone played both the Union and Imperium.

Which was when he spied the plumes of energy exploding against the yellowish forcefield blanketing Terra Sollus—on the outside.

"They can't get in," Rand spoke louder. "The Amalgam's reinforced shields have trapped Terra Sollus. UComm can't breach the shields..." His words were drowned under the panic engulfing the rec room. However, after a heated argument between Keith and a Kedri twice his size, most AeroFleet pilots clearly grasped that this attack wasn't from the Imperium.

"How the hell??" Another human pilot cried out, her hands flailing uselessly. "How did this happen?"

"Terra Sollus. Under attack!" Zuro watched the proceedings onscreen. The beady cobalt-blue eyes on his smooth face told a story of terror and fascination. "But by who?"

M'Kasha's jaw dropped. "Those korvanes statues. The golden ones...they're moving."

"Huh?" Rand, Jaad, and Obol turned. The human felt his knees nearly give out after seeing what Zuro was referring to.

For as long as he'd been alive, there had been ancient gold monoliths shaped like humanoid Korvenites that stood guard all around Conuropolis and Terra Sollus—silent, unmoving statues as tall as some skyscrapers. Ten of these golden korvanes statues walked from their posts, eyes glowing an eerie green as they smashed through more skyscrapers, heading for Andromeda Hall.

It struck Rand then. He seized Jaad by the shoulders. "This is the Korvenites."

The female Kedri narrowed her gaze. "The enslaved species? How?"

"There's a terrorist cell, the Korvenite Liberation Front, that hates humans." Rand jerked away from the screen as Amalgam fired again. "Has been attacking UComm starbases for weeks. This has to be them."

Jaad looked lost. In a rare moment of vulnerability, she appeared her age, nineteen just like Rand. "But my Sovereign is down there!"

"So is my Chouncilor..." Rand nodded, dreading to consider Ari Bogosian getting assassinated by the Korvenites.

"If Orok Kel is murdered in Union Space..." Jaad didn't finish. She didn't have to.

Rand closed his eyes, knowing the rest. A Kedri Sovereign assassinated in Union Space meant all-out war between the Galactic Union and the Kedri Imperium. That unthinkable reality made Rand ready to vomit. The Imperium, a star-spanning government dedicated to war, was three times the size of the Union. The winner was as evident as bear shit in a forest.

"All hands," an urgent, authoritative human voice boomed over the ship-wide coms. "Terra Sollus is under attack. AeroFleet and Imperium Fleet pilots. Report to your vessels and prepare for engagement. This is not a drill."

The orders were a relief to the thirty pilots. Finally some structure telling them how to handle this.

Everyone in the rec room popped up, shut up, and scrambled for the exit.

Half an orv of time later, Rand was suited up and seated in his fighter jet. The scene playing out below him, once an epic gathering of Union and Imperium ships, had become a nightmare.

Terra Sollus, the Galactic Union's capitalworld, was wrapped inside a thick yellowish forcefield mushroomed out from that tiny battle station hovering just over Conuropolis.

Hundreds of Union and Imperium warships surrounded Terra Sollus, raining down a blistering kaleidoscope of orbital strikes on the forcefield. Rand and many of his fellow pilots held their positions, flabbergasted.

Technically, the Union capitalworld was under attack.

Except...Terra Sollus's defense grid had been commandeered by the Amalgam itself, which continued to devastate Conuropolis. Rand winced at memories of buildings sliced apart by the Amalgam, which was still happening below. From what AeroFleet Intelligence had gathered, this attack definitely wasn't the Kedri. In fact, the Amalgam was no longer under their control.

"The Korvenites?" Hraego exclaimed over coms. "How did they even breach the Amalgam?"

"Probably had help from inside the Imperium?" M'Kasha suggested.

"We don't know that," Rand retorted. That made the most sense. Then had the Kedri operated in bad faith with the Union throughout the whole trade merger deal?

"Then explain how the Korvenites accessed a joint battle station built mainly by the Imperium."

Rand had no answer, which sent shivers down his spine.

"Korvenites are telepaths," Jaad interjected with surprising calm. "They could have mind-controlled whoever was in charge of building the station, correct?"

Her words silenced the debate. Rand quickly felt guilty over where his suspicions had been leading.

As of right now, the Imperium and Union warships' blitz barely caused a flicker in the forcefield.

Suddenly, all Rand's bluster of space being his domain and a fighter jet his throne felt insanely foolish. He felt so small surrounded by these mammoth vessels with all their firepower. The prospect of real battle, especially one where the Union capitalworld had been hijacked, frightened the young man to his core.

Rand considered it a blessing that, even with Terra Sollus's shielding compromised, its batteries weren't firing on any ships. Still, the Union AeroFleet had those battlecruisers hovering around Terra Sollus surrounded in case they were activated.

If these *Sovereign*-Class battlecruisers, *Apocalypse*-class dreadnoughts with all their firepower couldn't breach the altered shields, what the hell could Rand do in his tiny fighter jet?

"Sir," he asked his flight commander. "What are we firing on?"

A long silence followed until Maddox replied. "Nothing. Until these shields fall."

Rand made a face, baffled by the news.

"When will that happen?" M'Kasha growled.

"Don't know. There's apparently a ground operation by a UComm spec ops team in play to disable the shields as we speak," the commander said in a tone that brooked no further questions. So the flight group waited, watching the daunting amounts of Union and Imperium continue their unholy barrage on Terra Sollus's shielding. And those shields held unfalteringly.

Down on the surface, a rogue battle station was scorching Conuropolis to the ground starscraper by starscraper. The capital city-state of the Union, the mecca of its government, was getting razed.

Rand, hovering about Terra Sollus's atmosphere, never felt more helpless.

"This isn't working!" Jaad fumed over a private channel to Rand. The Imperium fighter jets in their flight group hovered behind the AeroFleet jets. "Nothing the Imperium vessels are doing can punch through these shields."

Rand was about to offer a response, probably a flaccid joke or weak platitude. Until a quartet of Imperium frigates caught his eye. None of the ships slowed when approaching the planetary shielding.

In fact, they all rocketed forward at top speed, exhaust trails burning in their wake.

The joint kamikaze dives rammed headlong into the unyielding forcefield, ending in bright and brief gushes of fire. Each one was quickly extinguished by the sub-zero of space.

Horrified, Rand slapped both hands over his mouth. "Oh sweet lord!"

"*Why...?*" Hraego croaked in heartbroken distress. Similar outcries erupted among the other AeroFleet pilots. No one could wrap their thoughts around the suicidal charge. Even worse, more small Imperium vessels followed suit. Tiny eruptions, brief and bright, plumed across the planet-wide shields. Rand finally had to turn away. In that stomach-turning moment, he noticed how Jaad and her group had remained eerily silent over those horrors. Not even a gasp or exclamation.

Meaning, he realized, *they're either considering or preparing for a kamikaze run.*

His heart dropped into his stomach.

Rand immediately opened his private comm channel to Jaad. "Don't you *fucking* dare," he barked.

The Kedri scoffed. Her engines hadn't powered down. "If we do nothing, Terra Sollus will be destroyed!"

"But what will suicide do?" Rand threw back, hands hovering over the naviconsole. He would intercept her stupidity if needed.

"My Sovereign is trapped on that world." Jaad's rage sounded weary yet impotent. Exactly how Rand felt. "So is your Chouncilor."

"Then fight for their freedom in battle. Hurling your ship against an impenetrable forcefield is not only stupid," Rand spat, "it's a waste of a talented fighter pilot and warrior. Who will that serve if you die for nothing? Not your Imperium. Not your Sovereign. Not your fellow pilots."

A long, angry silence followed between them. Rand's heart was in his throat as AeroFleet and Imperium Fleet attacks lit up his surroundings. Still more idiotic Imperium fighter jets dashed themselves against the Terra Sollus forcefields, erupting for ephemeral moments before the cold vacuum snuffed their sacrifices out.

Jaad, Obol, Zuro and their fellow Imperial pilots stayed put. "Fine, human," Jaad finally snarled. We do it your way—"

"Wait," Hraego's voice broke through the helpless misery. "The defense shields are coming down." She sounded as disbelieving as Rand felt.

The young pilot turned his attention back onto Terra Sollus down below. The thick golden shielding that encircled the Union capitalworld flickered, and then vanished. Other than the soft glow of its atmosphere, Terra Sollus was now unshielded. And with that, the barrage from the massive Imperial Fleet and Union AeroFleet vessels stopped. The Galdorian pilot was correct.

Rand's elation soared. "Command. The Amalgam's reinforced shields had been disabled. Please confirm," Rand requested.

"Ensign Horn, the defense grid is down," Maddox replied, relief flooding his stern voice.

"How?" M'Kasha asked.

"Looks like whatever ground op UComm authorized came through," the flight commander stated.

"YES!" M'Kasha yowled happily.

"Attention, pilots in this flight group," Maddox announced to all thirty pilots. "The larger vessels will engage the Amalgam battle station. Focus your firepower on the korvanes statues below. Repeat, focus all firepower on korvanes statues."

Rand smiled, and rocketed down to Terra Sollus. "Music to my ears!" he crowed.

Obol grunted. "While I don't find the order harmonic, this delights me."

Rand laughed. "We need to teach you some Union colloquialisms."

The flight group of fighter jets zoomed past Amalgam Station. Union and Imperium warships were buzzing around the now beleaguered battle station like angry bees. Their merciless salvos punctured the Amalgam's reinforced hull, which now gushed fiery discharges from too many breaches to count. The Amalgam fought back, sweeping laser fire slicing through a number of attackers. But it was clear the battle station was on its way toward destruction.

Rand gazed beyond the station to the brutalized remains of downtown Conuropolis. The once gleaming city-state, its forest of skyscrapers and starscrapers with the building-length holobillboards jutting through the clouds, lay in ruins. Destruction stretched in all directions, ruined structures sticking into the air like broken teeth. Scorched trails over a mile wide marked the result of the Amalgam's lasers. God only knew how many innocent lives had been lost.

Rand gave the Amalgam a baleful look. Hate churned inside his gut as he watched that eyesore in the hazing skies. He itched to fire on that vile construction with everything his fighter jet had.

Those aren't my orders. He turned his attention to these korvanes statues and gaped at the golden humanoid giants over six hundred feet tall, walking and smashing through even more towering buildings as if they were made of glass. According to intel reports, the Korvenites were somehow controlling these statues from the Amalgam using their psionics. The sight baffled Rand beyond words.

"Form up into five groups of six. Destroy those statues and as much debris as possible," their flight commander added. "The less damage to Conuropolis, the better."

Jaad, Zuro, and Obol's fighter jets flanked Rand's starboard side. M'Kasha and Hraego flanked his port. "Shall we?" Rand asked. No answer was needed. Six fighter jets, three AeroFleet, three Imperium Fleet, hurtled for the nearest korvanes statue.

The towering monolith swatted a hand in their direction, blotting out the sun. Rand and his fellow pilots split formation just in time, dodging the fatal swipe.

"Surround the head, folks!" Rand cried out. He angled upward past the moving statue's golden torso and shoulders, broader than most of the surrounding buildings. Upon reaching the statue's head, Rand pulled to a stop. His five fellow pilots did the same. The features were so finely crafted, resembling a Korvenite's face. Ancient architecture soon to be lost forever. Rand almost regretted having to destroy this. "FIRE!"

All six fighter jets unleashed blistering barrages of photonic blasts and torpedoes at the korvanes statue's head, pulverizing finely crafted sollunium metal.

The head imploded in a billowing cloud of dust, and the statue froze in place. Rand and his fellow pilots rose above roiling clouds of gold haze. An instant later, the body slowly swayed back and forth, like an oversized tree with no leaves. Then, the headless korvanes statue pitched forward.

Rand panicked. He glimpsed at the smaller buildings the monolith would flatten.

"Disintegrator missiles!" Hraego cried out, snapping the human out of his panic. "Target torso, arms and legs!"

Rand fired three at the chest. Hraego fired three into the abdomen. Obol and Zuro each fired three into an arm the height and width of a small building. Jaad and M'Kasha each took a leg taller than small skyscrapers.

On Hraego's count, everyone detonated their timed disintegrators, flying away to avoid the shockwaves. The rest of this korvanes statue's ancient golden frame erupted into mushroom clouds of dust and debris, raining harmlessly on the city-state below.

From his cockpit, Rand sighed in relief. "One down..." He glanced at almost a dozen korvanes statues still functional and punching their fists through more skyscrapers. "Several more to go!" With Rand in the lead, the six pilots raced off to destroy more of these animated monoliths.

The Battle of Terra Sollus raged on for who knew how long, but Rand counted him and his team taking down another three korvanes statues. The rest of their flight group handled the other eight, with an assist from two unidentified flying somethings the size of humanoids. One was shiny like a silvery bullet, the other a blazing human comet. Both moved too fast for Rand to discern what they were.

In short order, every korvanes statue had been reduced to harmless rubble.

After Rand finished, Jaad spoke via the group's shared channel. "Look," she exclaimed breathlessly. "The Amalgam!"

Rand looked over and gaped. Indeed, the Amalgam could take no more punishment from its countless attackers. Once a symbol of Union and Imperium cooperation, the rogue battle station was ripped apart by a thunderous series of explosions.

"Good," Rand seethed. Hopefully whatever Korvies took over the station were still onboard.

Smoldering chunks of debris and twisted hull tumbled to the earth. Rand didn't need Maddox barking in his ear to race forward, photon blasters blazing to destroy as much debris as possible.

Joined by the rest of his flight group and other AeroFleet vessels, Rand went to work. He juked and dived and climbed to avoid getting smashed by stray wreckage from the obliterated battle station, reducing the fallout to ash and smaller chunks of slag.

Several orvs of time later, the perpetrators had indeed been defeated. As Maddox had briefed the group, the Union Chouncilor had been spirited to safety and the Kedri Sovereign was safely offworld. The combined Galactic Union and Kedri Imperium forces had triumphed.

Did we win? Rand took a long look at Conuropolis from above. What he saw made his heart ache.

Dirty fog hung low over the city-state, thick and oppressive. In its heart was the swollen smear of black smoke where the Amalgam had hovered and razed Conuropolis. But the filthy fog barely hid the wreckage below. Torched swathes of destruction flattened most of Conuropolis's Diktat District for miles. Smoldering ruins and shattered stumps that had once been skyscrapers and starscrapers spread out for miles. Many buildings had survived mostly unscathed, far apart silhouettes swaddled in the filthy haze covering the megapolis. Already, Rand spotted the bright red and white hulls of UComm MediCorps vessels punching through muddy clouds to begin rescue and recovery efforts on the ground.

"By the Maker," M'Kasha exclaimed in horrified awe.

"Conuropolis is destroyed," Keith Chaney cried out.

Rand said nothing. The anguish of this dystopian panorama had choked off his voice. The adrenaline rush of battle was long forgotten. All he felt was empty.

No word from any of the Imperium fighter pilots, who he'd seen flown to link up with larger ships in the Imperium Fleet. Rand would touch base with them after they all headed back to Mars.

Hearing Maddox's voice and his next orders were a relief. "Back to the ship. We've done all we can."

The fifteen AeroFleet fighter jets turned in unison, rocketing toward the heavens.

* * *

Back on their Hammerjack destroyer, the flight bays were a picture of panic. Hangar workers and aerospace engineers raced about, barking orders just like before when Rand and his fellow pilots were leaving to join the Battle of Terra Sollus.

Even this far above Terra Sollus from outer space, the ugly stain of black smoke where the Amalgam had fallen was visible.

Rand exited his ship with no spring in his step, no adrenaline rush. No joy. The young man had finally fought his first real battle. All he felt was numb. A quick scan of his fellow pilots exiting their fighter jets revealed similar reactions.

More information trickled in about what really happened to the Amalgam. Apparently a member of the technorganic Thulican species with an axe to grind against the Union had posed as Biros Nor, the Kedri in charge of Amalgam's construction. The Thulican had colluded with the Korvenites to hijack the battle station.

Amid the swirl of flight bay chaos, the fifteen pilots drifted toward each other and approached the exit. No one said a word. The haunted glances everyone exchanged were communication enough. Clearly a debrief would occur. Rand was too hollowed out to think about that. The Union capitalworld had been attacked. Images of destruction, memories of helplessness lingered and festered.

As the group exited into the halls, Rand heard clapping and catcalls. He looked up. Several ship personnel were applauding, grinning at them, clapping him and his fellow pilots on the shoulders like they were heroes.

Are we? Rand wondered. The young man had expected the thrill of combat and victory to taste differently. And even the Korvenites behind the attack, Rand could not blame them in hindsight. Given their treatment by the Union over the past century, including the earthborn stealing their former homeworld of Terra Sollus, something like this was bound to happen. *But on such a public stage...*

Rand was grateful to finally move away from the vociferous praise and into the showers.

After a time, the fifteen pilots moved into their usual cliques. M'Kasha and Hraego clustered around Rand after a thorough hydrobath had cleansed away the grime and sweat. Sitting on a bench in just a tank top and sweats, Rand stared at his two friends, shaking his head. "Jesus. The Amalgam attacked Terra Sollus..."

"I know..." Hraego nodded, her six-inch eyestalks wilted forward in sorrow. She slumped beside Rand. "Or how the Union and the Imperium got embarrassed on an intergalactic level by a species barely a step above slaves?"

M'Kasha's amber eyes widened. The Kintarian's washed pelt had a golden sheen under the locker room lights. "I can't believe the Korvenites pulled that off."

"I'm guessing the Union-Imperium Trade Merger is on hold?" Rand stated bluntly.

M'Kasha giggled. Hraego made a clacking noise with her beak, the Galdorian form of mild laughter. At first Rand couldn't fathom why they found this funny, until a chuckle bubbled up from his chest. Then the trio doubled over laughing.

"No kidding," Rand wiped tears from his eyes. "Speaking of Kedri. Obol and the others haven't come back, have they?"

"Not to my knowledge," M'Kasha said as her giggles subsided. The friends headed to the locker room exit. "None of the Imperium pilots returned."

"Probably had to go check in with the Imperium Fleet," Hraego suggested, shrugging her narrow shoulders. There was an edge of worry in her croaky voice. "Given all the craziness that happened."

Rand wanted to accept her assuaging words. But he couldn't ignore the finger of dread tickling his spine.

Keith Chaney, trailing behind the group, weaved around them. The pale, ginger-haired human stopped in front of Rand with a strange look. "The Imperium Fleet left Terra Sollus. Jumped to hyperspace about ten macroms ago."

That stopped Rand and his friends in their tracks.

"Wait...WHAT?" M'Kasha's growl was like a sharp whiplash.

"Why?" Rand demanded more angrily than intended. He didn't care.

Keith backed up a few steps, hands raised in peace. "I heard rumors that not only is the trade merger off the table, but," he leaned in close and lowered his voice, "the Kedri Imperium is closing its borders to the Galactic Union."

Rand went cold all over. He didn't need to ask for any more reasons. "Because of the Korvenites' sabotage of the Amalgam," he remarked flatly. The Kedri were an extremely proud race. He looked at Keith but stared right through him.

"Think about it," Keith continued. "This had to be a HUGE embarrassment to the Kedri by the Union."

Hraego nodded in agreement. Her eyestalks straightened in cold anger. "A species under our government's umbrella went rogue, caused so many deaths and humiliated the Imperium? A very bad look for the Union and made us look weak. Who knows if that taint will ever wash off us for the Kedri."

Rand barely heard the explanations. His thoughts revolved around one being whom he might never see again. He whirled and ran, sprinting to his quarters.

M'Kasha and Hraego called after him. Rand didn't stop. He had to reach her, say some kind of farewell...if she'd listen.

After reaching his quarters, a panting Rand found a message waiting for him. He didn't need to view the caller ID to discern its origin. Rand sank heavily onto his bed and ordered the message to play.

A floating holoscreen appeared before him with Jaad's face, strong, chiseled, and resolved. By the pale illumination on her face, Jaad was in a dark room. Despite that dim illumination, Rand could see the sorrow filling her eyes.

"I will get to the point. As my time is brief," she began, no warmth in her brusque tone. "Diplomatic ties between our two hyperpowers are no more. Borders between our two hyperpowers are closing. Any relationships between Union and Imperium military personnel must be severed. After this message concludes, our friendship is no more. Do not contact me." Her voice cracked on those last few words and for a fleeting instant, Jaad's anguish was exposed. She quickly regained her steely poise. "Goodbye, Randyll."

The transmission ended abruptly. The holoscreen winked out. Rand sat for several moments, draped in darkness. His insides radiated agony, as if someone had carved out part of his intestines. Obol, Zuro, Jaad and the other Imperium pilots, his friends for almost two years. All gone from his life.

He squeezed his eyes shut to stop the tears. They still leaked through.

An urgent beep demanded his attention. Rand ignored it.

The beep persisted annoyingly until he cursed furiously and answered.

"Debrief Time, Horn." Maddox sounded softer, wearier than usual. "Today don't change protocol."

Rand looked up and opened his eyes. He attempted to protest despite the tears. Despite how thick his tongue felt in his mouth. "But...but—"

"I know, Horn. I know," Maddox offered consolation instead of discipline. "Made some good friends with the Kedri myself. Just found out all of them evacuated the Mars starbase too. This issue is bigger than both of us—galactic-sized. Yet still cuts so personally. But that's the hand we've been dealt."

Rand had nothing to say to that. Maddox's words cut to the heart of the matter. It was no salve, but it made perfect sense.

"Alright, Horn. Enough group therapy." Maddox's usual sternness had returned. "Find your guts and come to the debrief."

With that said, Rand Horn straightened up and wiped away the tears. "Yes, sir," he said with as much stone-cold cadence as he could muster, and marched out of his quarters.

Devastated or not, the AeroFleet needed him and Rand had a job to do.

Author C.C. Ekeke

C.C. Ekeke is the author of the Star Brigade space opera series, which currently includes four full-length novels, three novellas and a collection of sixteen short stories. C.C. spent much of his childhood on a steady diet of science fiction movies, television shows and superhero comic books. He discovered his desire to write books in college when studying for an advertising degree that he never ended up using. His love of domestic and international travel provides further inspiration for the aliens and worlds seen in his writing. Along with creating more adventures in the Star Brigade universe, C.C. Ekeke is beginning work on a brand-new series that dives into the colorful world of superheroes. Expect to hear more in 2018!

When not writing and building new worlds, you'll find him reading, watching the latest films and globetrotting to parts mostly known.

Learn more about C.C. Ekeke's writing:

Mailing List: http://ccekeke.com/subscribe
Amazon: https://www.amazon.com/author/ccekeke

ACROSS THE GALACTIC POND

By Christian Kallias

"You'll never amount to anything!"

His father's words echoed inside Kevin's mind as he strolled by the small lake a few miles from home. A strong gust of wind blew his MIT rejection letter out of his hands and it floated in the air before landing on the water's surface.

Was his father right? Was he good for nothing?

Kevin had dreams and aspirations; he wanted to make a difference. He wanted to change the world and make people's lives better. Like Steve Jobs, Elon Musk, or even Henry Ford before them. His brain was full of ideas, but he never managed to convince anyone to take a financial risk on them, and the rejection letter was the final nail in his proverbial coffin.

My life is over, he thought. *I'll probably end up flipping burgers.*

That was his father talking, and he knew it, but in this moment of utter despair, it felt like a very real, possible future. It scared Kevin. He would do anything to avoid such a future, but at this moment, he felt utterly alone and hopeless.

His smartphone buzzed inside his pocket. A text message.

Get your useless ass back to the house, STAT; you've got dinner dishes to wash.

Typical. Kevin hadn't even stayed for dinner. Being rejected from the one school he wanted to attend more than anything had ruined his appetite. But his father still taunted him and took every chance he got at putting Kevin down. He wondered why. Was it because his father had not amounted to anything himself, slaving 8 to 10 hours a day with nothing to show for it except an old decrepit Toyota Camry and a house that he refinanced twice so he could pay the bills?

Were his dad's own shortcomings the reason he wasn't supportive of his only son? Kevin wondered as he gazed and lost himself in the immensity of the starlit sky. He had always loved the stars. In fact, up until he was fifteen, his favorite pastime had been viewing them with the telescope his grandfather bought him on his ninth birthday. Until his drunken father tripped and broke it. Somehow, Kevin was blamed for his father tripping and breaking his most prized possession. Typical.

Something caught Kevin's attention. A red dot in the night sky where there shouldn't be one, and it was growing in size.

Was it a meteorite?

Kevin's heartbeat accelerated as the object grew bigger. Even though the approaching fireball was coming straight at him, Kevin was riveted in place and couldn't move. Prior to impact, the fireball seemed to slow down before splashing into the lake, sending a massive wave of water upward upon its entry. Kevin looked around, but he was alone. He took a few steps closer to the shoreline.

About fifty yards in front of him, the water turned yellow and bubbled heavily. Soon, a metallic sphere slightly smaller than a compact car emerged and floated upward as billowy steam evaporated around it.

What is that thing? Could it be a UFO?

Small, colorful light sources reflected on the surface of the lake, only now returning to its usual peacefulness. The last ripples created from the strange object plunging into the body of water were fading away in the distance. The sphere emitted a low hum and, upon closer observation, didn't feel of this Earth.

The implication sent Kevin into a panic, and he took out his smartphone and tried dialing 911. Before establishing a connection, the screen flickered and died, and sparks shot from the phone, prompting Kevin to drop it and let it fall to the muddy grass.

Before he could bend down to pick it up, the phone tumbled and slipped into the water.

"That's just great!" exclaimed Kevin. "The last thing I own that didn't suck complete balls, and now it's toast."

A bright red light shone inside the metallic sphere and bled through what seemed to be a dark glass porthole, grabbing Kevin's attention. A hand slammed against the inside glass. It didn't look human, and it appeared wounded.

Kevin swallowed hard, and his first instinct was to run away as fast as he could, but somehow he felt compelled to look at the sphere. Before he knew it, he was already knee deep in the water, walking toward it.

"What are you doing, Kevin?" he said timidly, trying in vain to convince himself to turn tail and run.

The spherical pod had been slowly drifting toward the shore and stopped as its undercarriage scratched the lake's bottom. Kevin stopped when he heard a pneumatic noise followed by heavy steam expelling on both sides of the dark glass. The injured hand was no longer there. A rounded door opened. Red flashes inside the pod illuminated the lake with crimson hues, giving it a blood-like feel.

Kevin heard breathing and a wheezing sound, and he had to muster all his courage to resume approaching the pod. He decided to swim the rest of the way.

"Anybody hurt in there? Do you need help?"

There was no answer, so Kevin grabbed the side of the door that was at water level and carefully raised himself out of the water. When he looked inside the single-seat pod, he saw a humanoid-looking alien, who had purple skin, four-finger hands, and from what Kevin could tell, appeared to be a sizable man that was at least over 7 feet tall. The alien appeared to be battered and in bad shape, as light blue fluid oozed from the slashes in its skin.

"Holy hell!"

Kevin's blood froze, and he was overwhelmed with fear but also excitement at the implications of what this could mean. Was he really seeing an alien ship and lifeform?

Kevin wondered what to do next. Part of him wanted to run away and tell someone about this, perhaps officials that could deal with the matter properly. He had seen enough SciFi shows and feared he was inadequate to be the one to make first contact.

What if the alien was hostile? But something compelled him to try and help.

"Hey, are you alright?"

Stupid question, he thought.

When the alien's eyes painfully blinked open, they revealed large yellow irises. Just by looking at them, Kevin could tell the alien was in tremendous pain. The armor he wore was scorched, bent, and shattered in various places, prompting Kevin to believe the alien had been in an intense battle.

The alien mumbled something in a tongue that made no sense whatsoever to Kevin. It was a mixture of words, clicks, and whistling sounds.

Kevin pointed to his ears with his fingers and then shrugged. "I'm sorry, dude; I don't understand a word you're saying."

The alien touched something on a wrist device. A holographic screen hovered near the device. He keyed in a few commands.

The alien then spoke, and, now, Kevin could understand everything he said.

"I'm dying; please help me save my people before it's too late."

"Did you just learn English?"

The alien pointed toward his wrist device.

"This computer is translating for me in real time."

"Neat! Siri on steroids."

The alien looked momentarily confused. "Please, you've got to help me."

"Buddy, you're from outer space, and I'm just a puny human who can't even get a good education; I don't know why you'd think I could help you, but I can't. However, I *can* try to get help; it looks like you may need a doctor."

Kevin used his hands as a megaphone.

"Help! Can anyone hear me? Call 911; we have a wounded. . ." Kevin stopped and pondered his next words. "Man here."

"Please— don't. There is no time; I will die shortly. I need your help, now."

Kevin looked at the alien and felt compassion for him. He wished he could help him, but he didn't know where to start.

"The only way I can help you is by getting you some medical attention."

"No; there is another way."

The alien keyed a few more commands on his wrist device, and a small compartment on his armor slid open. He reached in and grabbed a pill that looked like a piece of candy but was blinking with lights from within.

"Just put this under your tongue, and save my people."

"I think you must have a concussion, because you're the only one here. I'd love to help, but..."

The alien convulsed and a large quantity of blue blood dripped out of his mouth.

"Oh, crap! I'm so sorry; your wounds look really nasty."

"Take the pill, place it under your tongue."

Kevin looked at the bloodied open palm and the pill.

"What if that thing is toxic for my species?"

"It isn't; it's a conscience transference device. I beg you; please take it. You're my entire world's last hope."

What is he talking about? This doesn't make any sense.

"That can't be right, dude. If I'm your last hope, then I'm sorry to be blunt, but your world is already dead."

Tears filled the alien's eyes.

"My children, my wife, billions of souls, their lives all depend on you now, whether you understand it or not," he stopped and coughed up more blood. "You are the only one who can help them. If you don't take the pill, they will all die; but if you do, you have a chance to save them. I— I can't explain further, but I can assure you there is no risk to you. Please, do this for a dying man, I implore you."

Kevin thought about it. On the one hand, his natural curiosity was tickled by the alien's proposal, and on the other hand, as far as he knew, this could all be a ploy to get him to take the pill, which could very well be lethal to human physiology. Yet, the dying alien seemed sincere in his plea.

"I can't initiate the transference if I'm dead; please, please hurry and save my people."

Kevin took the pill from the alien and gazed at it.

"Under the tongue you say? I take it I shouldn't swallow it?"

The alien tried to speak but coughed blood instead. He just shook his head from side to side.

"And you're not trying to poison me, or body-snatch me with this thing?"

The alien's voice got weaker and lower as he spoke his next words.

"I give you my word, on my wife and my children's honor and lives, which will perish if you do not help me."

His father's words came back to him; his insistence that Kevin didn't take anything seriously and never dared to try new things, or venture into the unknown. Perhaps this was the answer to his prayers, and he finally had the opportunity to do something worthwhile, something that would better people's lives. Even if those lives weren't human.

Kevin looked at the blinking pill one last time, took a deep breath, and put it under his tongue. It tickled, but that's all Kevin could register.

"I don't think this is working. I'm not feeli—"

But, before Kevin could finish his sentence, and with his last dying breath, the alien pressed something on his holographic screen, and everything changed.

Kevin felt himself being catapulted into the heavens at incredible speeds; in less than a second, he had left the solar system, passing through nebulae and nearby planets and stars. He accelerated to a point where he saw entire galaxies fly by him in the blink of an eye.

Then, all of a sudden, he rammed into a spaceship, and everything turned dark for a second.

A loud blaring and other strange noises and smells surrounded Kevin. He had to blink multiple times and let his brain adapt to what he was seeing. He was on board a spaceship, on its bridge from the looks of things. There was smoke, sparks, and evidence of extensive damage. Through the viewport, Kevin saw another ship pass by and fire at the ship he was in. Upon impact, the ship rocked, and equipment exploded nearby.

"Alert! Alert! Ship's structural integrity at twenty-five percent. Please engage autopilot, or the ship will explode," said a synthetic female voice.

Am I dreaming?

Kevin wanted to pinch himself, but then he saw his skin was purple, the same shade as the alien's who had given him the pill. There was blood on his hand and forearm as well.

"What the hell is this? Whose body is that?"

Kevin felt a large pit form in his stomach, and before he could do anything about it, he vomited onto the floor. Looking at the puke, he saw worms moving about, and that made him vomit even more. But, this time around, he closed his eyes.

"This is all in my head; I've been drugged by that alien, and I'm having a very, very bad trip!"

The ship rocked once more.

"Structural integrity down to seventeen percent; ship destruction is imminent."

Kevin reopened his eyes and looked around. What he saw was foreign to him. Granted, the technology was advanced, but the controls all seemed holographic in nature, just like what he had seen in some science fiction shows and movies, but even more alien than his brain could fathom. Then there was the crew. All of them dead; some at their consoles, some flat on the floor near pools of blue blood.

Kevin painfully stood up and pinched himself. He felt immediate pain feedback.

"If I'm not dreaming, then what the hell is this? And how do I get the hell out of here?"

A floating sphere came quickly next to him and scanned him from head to toe with a blue wave of light.

"Xanton's bridge officer; no life signs. Remote brain activity detected," chirped the hovering spherical drone before flying away as fast as it had come.

What did that mean? Fortunately, Kevin had watched and read enough science fiction to conjure up a theory. Could that alien, a species apparently named Xanton, use a technology on Kevin that allowed him to remote-control a dead body on board a ship that was countless light years away from Earth? And, if that was the case, how cool was that?

When the ship rocked once more, and another small piece of equipment at the far right of the bridge exploded, Kevin decided to put his doubts aside and do something. He felt like he was in the best virtual reality simulation he had ever experienced and playing space simulation was something he could do, and do well. Whether or not this was a simulation, it didn't matter right now. The ship was in trouble, and he needed to turn the tide of this battle.

"Computer?" he inquired timidly.

A blue woman's face appeared in the form of a hologram and hovered in front of Kevin. The holographic projector must have been damaged because there was static, and the image flickered from time to time.

"Will you be my pilot? The ship needs you; without a pilot, I will be destroyed."

There was a clear emotional implication behind the words of the ship's avatar, which told Kevin that it must have been one hell of a piece of artificial intelligence.

"I will be your pilot, yes. Why aren't you firing back on your own, though?"

Before Kevin could say anything else, the spherical drone flew in front of him, and a couple of blue lights blinked on.

"Stand very still, please," said the ship's avatar.

Blue lasers shot from the drone and directly into Kevin's eyes, forcing him to shut them when he felt an intense burning sensation. But the pain quickly faded.

"Nanites deployed. Neuro-interface online. You now have access to the entire ship. Your brain compatibility is set to 98.97 percent."

Before Kevin could ask any question, he felt a flurry of information invade his mind and brain. It was overwhelming; he could literally sense everything about the ship. Its current power levels, where it was damaged, what it could do, everything. The sensation was both scary and empowering at the same time. And when he thought of a particular system, a holographic projection inside his mind would activate a HUD (heads-up display) with all the information he could use.

A quick check of the damage list and Kevin knew why the avatar hadn't taken control of the ship. Relays that linked her core programming to the rest of the ship had been corrupted. As a safety measure, the ship had switched to pilot-only controls.

Kevin saw the attacking ship turn around and ready itself for another pass.

"Redirect all power to the shields. Including life support," said Kevin.

"Redirecting power now."

A shield gauge began filling on Kevin's neuronal HUD. It reached twenty percent by the time the enemy ship was in firing range.

"Lock on that ship and fire phasers," said Kevin with a smirk.

"Unable to comply," said the avatar. "The ASF *Thalamos* does not have phasers."

"Just lock any weapon and fire!"

"All power is directed to the shields," said the avatar, as the ship rocked again.

The shield's gauge dropped down to five percent. Kevin would have to rapidly find a way to either recharge the *Thalamos'* shield or temporarily get out of Dodge.

"Can this ship jump? And do you have a name?"

"The hyperspace engines are currently offline. And my name is Mira. What's yours?"

"I'm Kevin."

"Nice to meet you, Kevin. What do you propose we do next? The enemy ship will have a new firing solution on us in less than 30 seconds."

"What's currently working?"

"Laser turrets at twenty percent, Quantum torpedoes at thirty percent, tractor beam and inertial dampeners fully functional. Shields recharging, currently at fourteen percent. Nano-repair circuitry is fully functional. Would you like me to activate nanite repair of the ship's systems?"

"The ship can repair itself?"

"Yes."

"Why haven't you done—" but Kevin didn't finish his sentence.

The ship had been set in manual pilot mode with no survivors on board, so it was just adrift, taking a pounding.

"Activate the nano-repair thingy," said Kevin.

"Nano-repair circuitry deployed," said Mira.

"How do I pilot the ship? We're a sitting duck at the moment."

"Just think what you want the ship to do, and it will respond to your thoughts. Your neuronal link with the ship's computer is off the scale, so much so that you shouldn't experience a delay between thinking and the ship doing what you're asking it to do."

It took Kevin half a second to process that last one. But when he saw the incoming ship, he thought thrusters at maximum and hard to port and that's exactly what the ship did, dodging the enemy's latest round of fire in the process. He was surprised that he didn't feel the ship move at all when it happened.

"Impressive dampening," said Kevin absently.

He then thought of tactical scenarios and his HUD displayed a superimposed star map with both the *Thalamos* and the apparently named Kregan Flotilla Dreadnought enemy ship. The *Thalamos* was blinking orange denoting its current level of damage while the Kregan enemy ship was showing in solid red with blue shields and no reported damage.

Kevin knew he needed to turn the tide of battle and fast. He closed his eyes and hoped he could see his ship as he would in a video game, and sure enough, his neuro-HUD changed to display the information he needed - the radar and all system levels, just by thinking he was flying the ship.

This is amazing! he thought.

The enemy ship vectored toward them and was about to re-enter firing range. Kevin rotated the ship on its axis and boosted ventral shields, redirecting power from other parts of the ship. It raised the shields up to seventy percent while the enemy ship pounded the *Thalamos*. The ventral shields lowered to forty-seven percent and the moment the Kregan ship flew by, Kevin activated the tractor beam and locked onto the enemy ship.

The *Thalamos* was now being dragged by the Kregan ship, but it gave Kevin enough of an angle of fire. He thought weak points, and multiple areas of the Kregan ship's image in his HUD lit up, with superimposed legends telling Kevin what each highlighted system was. He selected weapons, redirected power from the shields, life support, and other systems to deliver a charged laser beam to the enemy's weapon distribution power node and opened fire.

The shot drained the enemy shields and, after ten seconds of continuous firing, it pierced them and started scoring structural damage. Kevin mentally fired three quantum torpedoes through the shield's hole and watched with satisfaction as they impacted with the ship's hull creating three successive explosions.

The Kregan ship's engines flickered briefly and stopped. Smoke, debris, and crewmen were expelled into space. Kevin's HUD reported heavy damage to the enemy ship. Most of their power distribution had been obliterated, and the ship was pretty much dead in space.

"Very impressive tactic, Kevin."

"Thank you, Mira."

"Let's finish them off."

Seeing crew being ejected and flash-frozen in space hadn't been Kevin's favorite moment of the day, and the entire experience had been way too real to just be a simulation or a bad trip. Kevin's instincts told him this was real, and it was happening somewhere out in space. Therefore, killing defenseless living beings now that their ship was disabled didn't sound right.

"Do we have to? They're disabled."

"As were we before you assumed the pilot function; that did not stop them, neither did it stop them from destroying multiple worlds and wiping out entire civilizations in their pursuit of conquest. Their ship can also self-repair like ours, so, eventually, they'll be operational again and won't hesitate to try and destroy us and others given the chance. Why are you hesitant, Kevin?"

"Defending myself and preventing more deaths in the process, that I can easily deal with and handle, but killing in cold blood..." he let the words hang in the air.

"This is war, Kevin. The Kregan Empire is at war with the Arcadian Confederate, and they have already destroyed thousands of vessels, wiped out eleven worlds in the Confederate, and this is their last invasion push. If they succeed, the Arcadian Confederate will fall."

"I understand that, but I'm an outsider; I'm part of neither side. I don't even know why either side is fighting."

"Would you feel more comfortable if I finished off the ship myself?"

Kevin didn't have to think about it long. It would indeed make him feel better if he wasn't the one pressing the trigger, so to speak.

"Yeah. I guess."

"Then I need you to switch from pilot-only command of the ship to AI-pilot partnership. You are still the commanding officer, and I will execute your orders to the letter, however, should you become incapacitated, then I'll be able to pilot the ship myself."

"Okay, that sounds good."

"Mode set to AI-pilot partnership. Thank you, Kevin."

Before Kevin could answer, three more quantum torpedoes fired, and the Kregan warship exploded into a million pieces.

"That was fast. Don't you have any sub-routines in your code to protect living beings?"

"As a matter of fact, I do, Kevin, but I am an artificial intelligence built for war. I'll do everything I can to protect any Arcadian life, but Kregans are the enemy; they must be destroyed, and that supersedes all other parameters."

Kevin thought that was cold.

"And every ship in the Arcadian fleet possesses a war AI like you?"

"No, the *Thalamos* is a prototype warship. The Arcadian Confederate is peaceful by nature, but when the Kregan invaded and started killing millions on different worlds, I was created, the first of my kind. A ship designed for one purpose only."

"War," said Kevin.

"That is correct."

"How many battles have you been in?"

"Two hundred and sixty-two. All victorious, until the ship was damaged beyond my ability to recover control over it. The captain still managed to destroy our foe before he lost consciousness and died."

"Did you send the man that gave me the pill that transported me here?"

"No, I can only surmise that Arcadia's headquarters sent a distress call to get help back to the ship and dispatched their own agent."

"How long had the ship been adrift?"

"For several days, until that Kregan Flotilla Dreadnought found and engaged us."

Kevin reflected on all this information. He knew nothing about this war, just that he was thrown in the middle of it, on a ghost ship with only a prototype war AI onboard. Or so it seemed.

"Anyone left alive on the ship?"

"I'm afraid not; life support was damaged during one of our last engagements, with my systems disconnected from the main systems controls, it took me too long to restore them to save the few souls that hadn't perished in the last attack."

"I see—"

But, before Kevin could finish his sentence, Mira interrupted him.

"I'm sorry, Kevin, but I'm detecting a distress call from Arcadia Prime. Engaging hyperspace engines."

"I thought they were offline?"

The ship hummed and jumped into hyperspace. Stars extended into streaks in the viewport, and soon they were in a luminous corridor of purple and blue lights. It was beautiful to witness.

"Now that I've regained control of the ship, I've managed to divert enough power and nanites to repair some of the power distribution to the engines. I had to disable safety measures in order to engage the jump engines."

"What's the status on Arcadia?"

"Long-range sensors show two massive fleets fighting; the last of the ships engaged in this war on both sides. The Kregans know that if they take Arcadia Prime, they will have won the war."

"What will one more ship do?"

"One Arcadian ship wouldn't make a difference, but remember the *Thalamos* is one of a kind, a prototype with heavy firepower. With both my AI sub-routines and your creative tactics, we could very well turn the tide of this battle."

"I'm taking, then, that the Kregan are currently winning the battle?"

"Correct."

Kevin sighed. Then he smiled and felt exhilarated and thrilled. He was taking part in an interstellar battle, and the ship he was on had the potential to save an entire confederate of people. It felt like so many games he had played, except this time it was real life and death. Having already defeated one ship, his confidence in what was to come was bolstered.

"How far are we from Arcadia Prim—"

The ship exited hyperspace directly in the middle of the battle. Laser streaks of all colors and torpedo trails could be seen everywhere. It was pure and utter chaos.

"Never mind," said Kevin, before closing his eyes.

The tactical view of the ships appeared on his HUD.

"Which ship do we engage? I'm unfamiliar with any of this!" said Kevin, suddenly panicked at the sheer complexity of this battle compared to their previous one-on-one engagement.

"I'll target the ships for you and let you engage them any way you see fit. I'll provide power management duties and keep smaller ships at bay with laser turrets and starfighters."

"We have starfighters?"

"Yes, they're launching now."

"Can I control them, too?"

"You can override controls anytime you wish. For the time being, I'm controlling them so you can take care of the targets I've assigned you."

"Understood. Give them hell."

"I'm not sure I'm familiar with that expression."

"It means destroy as many as you can."

"Understood."

Three squadrons of starfighters deployed and engaged the enemy. While they were making a dent in the enemy defense lines, Kevin thought their flying patterns were too simple and repetitive.

"That's not going to work for much longer," he said.

"What's not?"

"How the starfighters are flown."

"Those are the pre-programmed macros I loaded. Unless you can provide more, that's how they'll fight."

"Take over our ship for a minute while I see if I can do something about it, please."

"Understood."

Kevin wondered if he had hurt the AI's ego or feelings. Then, again, it was a war AI, and it would make little sense to give it too strong a personality and even less sense for the AI to have an ego. That could interfere with its core programming.

"Can you record my flight tactics and apply them to the rest of the ships?"

"That is within my capabilities, yes."

"Then, Mira, by all means, please do so."

Kevin focused on a single starfighter and remote-controlled it. He was amazed when his HUD projected a full holographic image of the fighter's cockpit, making him feel like he was inside the spacecraft. All of Kevin's years of playing space combat simulation came back to the surface as he engaged his bogies.

A missile lock interrupted Kevin's nostalgic trip down memory lane and forced him to go evasive. He broke hard to starboard and deployed countermeasures just before pushing the thrusters to maximum. Once clear of the present danger, he engaged the enemy fighter that had locked the pair of missiles. Kevin set his lasers to maximum repeat fire and low-power delivery, optimizing power consumption to deliver a massive number of hits on the enemy's shield, draining them much faster. That tactic proved efficient as the aft enemy shields weakened. Kevin locked on a missile and blew the starfighter to smithereens.

"Efficient tactic," cooed Mira.

"I'm glad you agree. Now, watch this."

Kevin acquired a new target, fired a few laser shots on its shield to get the aggro, and the moment the ship veered and engaged his fighter, he swerved and selected a second target, raining heavy laser fire on its frontal shield. Both pursuing and incoming ships opened fire on his craft, quickly draining his shields. He redistributed power on-the-fly to divert it to both his frontal and aft shields, keeping only some power to his weapons and thrusters while completely draining both life support and inertial dampeners. There was no one on board these ships, so those systems were wasting power.

His holographically projected cockpit flashed red twice, indicating that both ships had acquired a missile lock. He boosted the thrusters to full capacity and started a mental countdown. To his surprise his HUD displayed the countdown but requested that he release countermeasures to divert the missiles away from his craft. For his maneuver to be successful, timing would be everything, so he ignored the warnings.

When he was dangerously close to the incoming ship, Kevin released aft countermeasures only, went into a spin, and pointed the nose of his ship upward just a split second before the incoming missing would have hit him. The missile, having fallen for his countermeasure, flew straight, impacting with the missile coming from the other side.

The impact created a bright explosion and the enemy's starfighters, with their visibility impaired, collided with each other. They blew up in a fiery display.

"Woohoo!" cheered Kevin. "Buy one, get one free!"

After several minutes, Kevin had taken down close to a dozen starfighters, each time using different tactics so that Mira could learn his flying skills. But after downing so many enemy craft, the larger Kregan vessels took notice, and long-range plasma fire began flying by his cockpit window at an alarming rate.

Kevin went evasive, but eventually his remote-controlled starfighter was hit on the left thrusters causing it to spin. It took all of Kevin's concentration to vector the ship toward one of the larger Kregan destroyers in the area. He opened fire with his lasers and shot all but one of his remaining missiles at the larger ship, just before redirecting every ounce of power to the frontal shields. A fraction of a second before Kevin's starfighter was about to impact with the destroyer's shields, he shot his last missile, destabilizing them just enough so that his fighter darted through, but not without incurring massive damage. Kevin saw sparks shot in his holographic vision as well as his controls blinking madly, with multiple alarms blaring around him.

"Ship structural integrity critical."

Half a second later, his starfighter, still well into a spin, crashed and exploded near a fighter's launching bay. The sensation of seeing the flames around him just before he lost the subspace signal connecting him to the holographic projection of the fighter was strange. For a split second, his brain thought he was going to be burned alive, which shot a hefty dose of adrenaline into his system.

Kevin opened his eyes and exclaimed: "Wow, what a rush!"

He looked through the viewport and saw the remainder of the explosion from his starfighter. A secondary explosion took out the destroyer's fighter bay near where he had crashed his remote-controlled ship. Flames spewed from the bay's landing pads. The destroyer's lights flickered madly for a couple of seconds before turning off. He must have accidentally hit a major power node within the ship. The nearest Arcadian destroyer didn't wait long before firing no less than five torpedoes toward the disabled Kregan destroyer, sending it right to hell in a fiery blaze.

"This tactic has cost you your craft; should I record it?" inquired Mira.

"That wasn't much of a tactic; just making sure I made the best use of a damaged starfighter by taking out as much of the enemy as possible. I doubt you can recreate those conditions easily, though."

"My tactical matrix is fully capable of adding the tactic to damage crafts under certain parameters."

"Then, by all means, add that move as well."

"Did you manage to upload the new flight tactics to the rest of the wings?"

"I have added each tactic on-the-fly the moment their recording was over. My kill ratio of two to one jumped to five to one thanks to it."

The ship rocked as multiple plasma cannon shots hit its starboard shields.

"We do, however," continued Mira, "attract more attention to ourselves with our fighters performing better than the rest of the fleet."

"The *Thalamos* can take it; she's a tough girl," said Kevin with a smile.

"My readings aren't in alignment with your juvenile enthusiasm, I'm afraid."

"Juvenile? What makes you think I'm a juvenile?"

"From the patterns of your overlaid brain activity to the deceased pilot's body you're currently occupying, I would say you're still a youngling."

"On Earth, that's called a young adult, thank you very much!"

"I meant no offense. In fact, you seem very proficient in combat tactics for someone of your age."

Tell that to my father.

"Thank you, Mira. That means a lot."

The ship rocked as more plasma fire impacted with its shields.

"You're perfectly welcome, Kevin."

Kevin realized that now was not exactly a good time to focus on his own existential questions; there would be plenty of time for that later, once the battle was won. He took back control of the ship and put the *Thalamos* into evasive action. The starboard shields were almost depleted. A quick rotation on the ship's vectoring axis fixed that. Kevin locked and fired a full complement of torpedoes toward the enemy destroyers whose shields were at their lowest. The first eight torpedoes finished the job of bringing the shields down and the last two in the salvo burst through the ship's hull, splitting it in half just before exploding into a million pieces.

"We're being hailed," said Mira.

"On screen...I guess."

The bridge holo-screen came to life, and a green-skinned humanoid with vibrant facial tattoos appeared.

"ASF *Thalamos*, we thought you were lost in the battle around Zalonia. Good to have you back."

Kevin smiled.

"The reports of our demise have been largely exaggerated."

He, he. I always wanted to say that.

A full-sized body of Mira's hologram appeared next to Kevin.

"If I may, Admiral Sarkis, I'm Mira, the ship's war AI and technically last survivor onboard *Thalamos*. The ship was almost lost on Zalonia, but thanks to a remote pilot hailing from a distant planet, we managed to survive and rejoin the rest of the fleet. Kevin here is a proficient pilot with fresh tactics, which has helped us get the best of our enemies, so far. But, we do seem to have attracted the attention of other enemies. I've detected another three destroyers vectoring toward the *Thalamos*."

Unsure if he should say anything, Kevin just nodded. Feelings overcame him; two things he had hoped for during his life: recognition and pride for his deeds.

The Admiral's face hardened. "I see. Well, thank you Mira; and thank you, Kevin. As for the approaching destroyers, we'll make sure the fleet redeploys and covers the *Thalamos*. Mira, what's the status of Project Sigma?"

"It has suffered damage, but the nanites are near completion with repairs," said Mira.

Project Sigma? What's that?

"I don't have to tell you how important it is that this tech not fall into the enemy's hands."

"Understood, Admiral. I'll self-destroy the ship before that happens."

The Admiral nodded.

"And while I don't like the idea of using prototype tech in a critical battle like this one," the admiral continued, "it could tip the balance. Do you think your pilot's cognitive abilities are sufficient to control the weapon?"

"His link with the ship's system is the strongest we've ever had, Admiral. I think Kevin can do it."

Can do what?

"Any risks to him?"

294

"We've never tested the weapon with a remote link; there's no way to know if negative feedback could affect Kevin's biological mind, I'm afraid."

The Admiral looked straight into Kevin's eyes.

"Then the choice of deploying the weapon will be yours, Kevin. I'm sending the firing authorization command code to your ship's AI, which will authorize you to deploy the weapon."

The Admiral's holo-screen flickered as he almost lost his footing.

"I have to cut this short, providing the *Thalamos* cover has proven a difficult task and I need to tend to my ship. Kevin, on behalf of the Arcadian Confederate, I thank you for your service. Your AI will let you know about Project Sigma. I trust you'll use it wisely. Admiral Sarkis, out."

"Uhh..." but before Kevin could continue, the holo-screen turned off. "Bye, Admiral."

Mira's hologram turned and looked at Kevin.

"What's Project Sigma?" he said preemptively.

"The most guarded secret weapon to come out of the Arcadian R&D labs. It's a deadly one-shot weapon that, if not working at full capacity, could destroy the *Thalamos*."

"So far you're not filling me with confidence. What does it do?"

"The weapon is twofold. It sends a cocktail of cognitive boosting drugs to the pilot who deploys the weapon, giving them the illusion of slowing time. All the while, the experimental power source will boost every system on the ship by a factor of ten for a few seconds. It will allow your engines to run faster, the ability to make multiple small hyperspace jumps, and fire all the weapons at your disposal with an increased yield."

"And the reason why we haven't already fired it is? I mean, the battle out there is fierce, and if I understood you correctly before, if this battle is lost, Arcadia Prime would fall."

"As I was telling the Admiral, the weapon was damaged before you became the pilot. It will be ready momentarily. But, I feel obligated to warn you that the weapon hasn't seen a successful deployment yet, I'm afraid. In many instances, the volunteer pilots who tried using it ended up...how should I say this—"

Kevin frowned. "Give it to me straight, Mira."

"Irreparable brain damage."

Oh, swell.

"But, am I not shielded since my brain is still on Earth? Or did I somehow teleport here? I did see space and galaxies fly by on my way to the ship."

"That's a side effect of the subspace link; your brain is aware of the distance of the subspace link as it traveled to the *Thalamos*. But, you are correct, your physical body is still on your home planet."

"So...shouldn't that protect me?"

"Kevin, the subspace signal linking your brain to the deceased pilot's whose body you now inhabit is very complex. Thanks to nanites we've injected into the deceased crew member, you can move around the ship and use its systems. I'm afraid there's simply no way to know what would happen to you should the weapon malfunction."

Kevin didn't like the sound of that. While he had found the entire experience up until now to be exhilarating beyond anything he had experienced in his life, he was very attached to his brain and the prospect of living a full life. With so many experiences still to be discovered, like getting married, making love to a woman, starting a family and having kids so he could love them and guide them better than his father had done with him. And, there were so many places on Earth he wanted to visit, though nothing compared to flying and literally captaining a ship into battle like he was doing now. It was like playing the best VR game on steroids, and he was addicted to the experience, already.

But is it worth the risk? Kevin wondered.

"I'm not sure what to tell you."

Multiple flashes of light bled through their viewport.

"Oh, no!" exclaimed Mira.

"What is it? What's happening?"

"Another fifteen enemy destroyers have entered orbit around Arcadia Prime. My new battle simulation projections are not good. The arrival of these new ships gives us less than a five percent chance of winning this battle. By the time the day is over, every man, woman, and child on the surface of Arcadia could be enslaved...or killed."

Oh shit.

"How many people live on Arcadia Prime?" he inquired.

"Arcadia Prime hosts twenty-two billion souls."

A bright explosion nearby caught Kevin's attention. A ship had been destroyed.

"What ship was that?"

But Kevin's question was rhetorical; he had seen the ship bleep out of existence on his HUD's holo-radar. Still, he felt compelled for confirmation.

"I'm afraid, Kevin, that was the Admiral's ship; the strongest ship in the fleet, next to me."

Kevin felt a pit form in his stomach.

Two more Arcadian destroyers that had redeployed to provide the *Thalamos* with cover fire succumbed to enemy fire.

"Mira..." said Kevin slowly. "By your estimation, how long until the battle ends?"

"At this rate, this battle could be over in less than ten minutes. My programming obliges me to inform you that I have no way of knowing what would happen to your brain if the ship is destroyed while the mental subspace link is still online. You could suffer brain damage due to feedback."

"You're all good news at the moment, aren't you, Mira?"

"I detect a smidge of sarcasm in your last comment, but considering the position we're in, I suppose it is warranted."

Kevin raised an eyebrow. "A smidge?"

Mira's hologram tilted her head to the side.

"Never mind that," said Kevin. "So, what is it you're telling me?"

"You're clearly an intelligent lifeform, Kevin."

"I still want to hear you say it."

"You seem to have two options at this present time. Deploy the Project Sigma superweapon and hope it doesn't fry your brain, or ask me to disconnect the remote mental subspace signal, sending your consciousness back into your body."

At first glance, the choice seemed clear; if Kevin wanted to live, and he really wanted to, the safest course of action was to disconnect the link. But could he live with himself knowing that he abandoned billions and sent them to their deaths so he could save himself? All his life he dreamt of making a difference in people's lives. Sure, in his head, he had imagined he would do that on planet Earth. But, he knew very well that right at this moment, using this distinction as an argument, was a mixture of fear and cowardice. The two forces in his life he knew full well had been preventing him from achieving anything worthwhile up until now.

His brain had always been bursting with ideas and big dreams, but he never managed to fully believe in himself to do anything about it or for those ideas or dreams to materialize. Was today the one chance to do that? And if that was the case, could he turn his back to being a hero and save billions? Kevin knew no one on Earth would believe him if he told them this tale. But at the end of the day did that matter? If he could do something to save all these people, could he just turn his back to save his hide? What kind of person would that make him?

A failure. That's what he would be if he turned tail and ran. And that would make his father's words true, something that he simply couldn't stand.

"Very well; let's do this, Mira!"

"It will take fifteen seconds for me to disconnect your brain connection to the host body."

"No! The other thing, Mira; activate Project Sigma."

"Are you sure, Kevin?"

"More than anything in my entire life. I just wish we had time to prepare for this."

"Project Sigma will drain most of the ship's power once it's done, so if you don't get all the enemy ships with that one manoeuver, we'll surely be destroyed."

While Kevin pondered Mira's words, more than a third of the fleet fell. Time was quickly running out, and Kevin knew he had to try at least.

"How long will the weapon be active?" he asked.

"Anywhere between ten and thirty seconds. But because your perception of time will be greatly altered, it will feel much longer for you."

"Can I access battle simulation scenarios? Like you do to calculate our current odds of survival?"

"You can; the computer will also receive a boost, allowing you to interact with it faster than you can at the present time. As for our odds of survival, they've dropped below one percent in the last minute."

No pressure!

"Can you dose me with the drugs a few seconds prior to activating the experimental power source so I can spend the first few seconds running a few simulations, and so I can gauge the enhanced power of the weapons? That way I won't waste any of the limited time I have with the enhanced power."

"I can, but that will probably lower your chances of survival even more."

"By how much?"

"Five percent more."

"And, right now, where do my chances stand?"

Mira took a moment to answer. "Do you really want to know, Kevin?"

He nodded.

"Seventeen percent; though you have a better link with the ship's system than any pilot that has ever taken control of Project Sigma, so I'm hoping these figures are on the low side, and your chances are higher."

Seventeen percent chance of survival. Kevin now regretted having asked for the odds.

No pain, no gain.

"Please reprogram the weapon to give me a five-second heads-up so I can run weapon impact simulations just before going into my battle move. And, please, give me firing control."

"Adjustment complete. Firing control added to your HUD."

"One last question, Mira. If I disable every non-essential system onboard the ship and redirect their power into Project Sigma, could that boost its function time and weapons' efficiency?"

"Theoretically, yes, Kevin. Both, in fact. You could gain up to twenty-five percent more firepower and an additional second or two of deployment, but it would put more stress on the system, which could lead to its failure or malfunction."

Kevin chuckled. "You mean more than it already is? You don't need to answer that, that was rhetorical. But you know what, Mira, if my brain fries as a result of this, I don't think I'll give a shit if it's deep fried or extra crispy. Give me a list of systems I can redirect power from on my HUD, please."

A list of systems appeared in front of Kevin. As he selected them one by one, he paused on the last one in the list.

"That's you, isn't it?"

"Correct, Kevin. My systems take a lot of power. You should deactivate me."

"It's been an honor fighting by your side today, Mira."

"The honor has been mine, *Captain*."

Kevin got goosebumps upon hearing Mira's last word. He deactivated her and reinjected Mira's power into Project Sigma.

"Goodbye, Mira," said Kevin for no one's benefit but himself.

Kevin activated Project Sigma, and the sensation he felt when the drugs were released was like nothing he thought possible. Time seemed to slow to a crawl while his brain activity and thinking patterns multiplied beyond his wildest dreams. He felt like he could literally think at the speed of light. His head hurt, but he was able to ignore the pain as if it was just a pesky program he could put on hold.

He activated the simulation and checked the amount of power that he would require to take down the enemy ships. Mira had not undersold the power of the weapon. With a few hits from the multiple laser turrets, he could bring down the enemies ships' shields. The *Thalamos* would also gain in speed and maneuverability, which would give him a great tactical advantage. He could also perform up to ten hyperspace micro-jumps, which to the enemy would appear as if he teleported around them.

He ran a multitude of scenarios at mental speeds that defied the imagination. When he thought he had a good grasp of the *Thalamos'* power once Project Sigma would activate, he focused his brain power like never before.

No losing focus today. Keep your eye on the ball, Kevin.

Kevin activated Project Sigma and began his attack run. He vectored the ship through enemy fire with ease, making sure the *Thalamos* avoided all dangerous firing zones, making sure his ship was never in a kill box position as well as aligning his shots in a way that he could create the most damage to the enemy fleet. He plotted his moves beforehand like a furious game of chess, making split-second decisions.

In the first few seconds of engagement, which felt like minutes to Kevin, he had obliterated no less than seven Kregan destroyers, blasting their shields to kingdom come with the *Thalamos'* laser turrets while sending them to hell with just the right number of torpedoes. Every time he took down a few ships, he would micro-jump to the other side of the battle theater, never letting the enemy fleet redeploy and target him properly.

After twenty seconds, he only had five destroyers to get through, but alarms and warnings flashed on his HUD, indicating that the ship was being pushed to its utter limits.

I thrive under pressure, he thought to reassure himself and keep his focus laser sharp.

He had another two micro-jumps and only a handful of seconds left in the Project Sigma time-diluted mode. Only three enemy destroyers remained, while the Arcadian fleet had all but been disabled or decimated. While his thoughts were still flying faster in his mind than ships flying in hyperspace, he could feel the effects of the drug starting to falter. Soon it would end. He targeted the nearest ship with half a complement of torpedoes and fired upon his target. Without waiting for confirmation, he moved to the second destroyer and tried jumping behind it to avoid the laser fire rain of death the ship had unleashed toward the *Thalamos*. An alarm resounded around him as his HUD flashed orange, indicating that the ship's hyperspace engine had failed to micro-jump. They were damaged earlier when the previous enemy destroyer exploded in close proximity of his ship.

Dammit!

His frontal shields melted like ice in the sun, and he had to think fast. He dropped all but his frontal shields in order to boost them. He would need them to hold for the bat-shit crazy maneuver he was about to attempt. He focused all laser turret fire to a single point on the incoming destroyer's shields and boosted sub-light engines to their maximum limits, which were already past safety settings, to achieve ramming speed.

The ship trembled and shook under the incoming fire from the Kregan destroyer. Kevin recited every prayer he knew as his ship rammed the Kregan and broke it in two. Shortly after impacting with his prey, he redistributed power to the rest of the shields, so they could deflect the flames and debris from the exploding destroyer.

While time was slowly resuming to normal speed, from his perspective, Kevin was still experiencing the scene in slow-motion, the flames burning around him felt like demonic souls shouting their last scream before being extinguished into the oblivion of cold space.

Consoles near him exploded, and sparks flew from the ceiling. The ship had taken major damage as time resumed its normal pace. Alarms blared and wailed, the bridge's light flickered, and the ship entered into a spin. He tried to get the ship to turn to face the last remaining Kregan destroyer currently vectoring toward him. The *Thalamos* veered with great difficulty, but he eventually managed to come face to face with the enemy.

The Kregan destroyer unleashed every weapon at its disposal upon the *Thalamos*. And Kevin knew that the ship wouldn't be able to take it for much longer. He tried returning fire, but everything on his holo-HUD flashed red, and most controls refused to work.

I guess today is a good day to die.

Three more torpedoes hit the *Thalamos'* shields, bringing them down. Each new plasma fire and laser hit from the Kregan ship now scored damage on Kevin's ship, sending debris and flames dancing around him.

I failed. As always.

Kevin thought about finding the mental subspace link and disconnecting it since his ship was now nothing more than a flying brick heading toward oblivion. But, he felt compelled to see the battle through. If he were indeed the *Thalamos'* captain, he would go down with his ship. Kevin redistributed all power to the sub-light engines and locked onto the Kregan ship. The Kregan ship, in turn, continued to pound the *Thalamos* with everything it had trying to destroy it by ripping it to shreds.

The viewport cracked when a flurry of laser fire impacted upon it. The emergency systems activated a blue force field to prevent explosive decompression. But Kevin could tell it wouldn't last long from the way the field was flickering.

"I'm sorry, Mira, I...I failed you; I failed all of Arcadia."

Kevin knew very well that the *Thalamos* would be destroyed before he could ram into the Kregan destroyer still pounding him with everything it had. For a fleeting moment, Kevin regretted not going home and doing the dishes as he had been instructed. Perhaps he would survive this, and he would wake up on Earth, but if that meant that the Arcadian people would suffer and die, he'd rather lay his life down here and now and be done with it.

From the corner of his eye, he saw another ship on the starboard side of the Kregan destroyer. It was in flames and spewing a trail of debris and smoke in its wake. The Arcadian ship opened fire with plasma cannons and torpedoes as it accelerated and rammed the enemy ship. Upon impact, the massive explosion illuminated space with a bright white flash that nearly blinded Kevin, but he felt duty-bound to keep his eyes open to see what happened next.

As the bright flash diminished, large flames filled the viewport as the *Thalamos* darted through the remains of both obliterated ships.

Kevin exhaled deeply.

The captain and crew of the Arcadian ship had sacrificed themselves to make sure they would take the last Kregan destroyer out. The battle had been won, at a terrible cost of life on both sides, but it was finally over. The *Thalamos* was now the only ship moving on the battlefield, which had turned into a space graveyard.

"Ship destruction imminent!" flashed on Kevin's mental holo-HUD.

But Kevin didn't care; he had managed to stop the Kregan from taking Arcadia Prime. Even if the body he inhabited would perish, that person had been dead a long time ago. Kevin looked for the subspace mental link and deactivated it.

Nothing happened.

"That's peculiar."

A sense of dread filled his soul. Would he survive the destruction of the *Thalamos* if he couldn't sever the link?

The force field protecting the bridge malfunctioned, and cracks on the viewport intensified. The last few flickering lights on the bridge turned off and plunged Kevin into darkness. Tearing noises resonated around him and Kevin could feel the ship was going to give in any second now. A green light engulfed his body, and he felt himself leaving the ship. One second he was on the bridge, seeing the viewport explode and shards of glass being sucked into space along with the air and dead crew members, and the next second, he was in an entirely different place altogether.

He stood in a large room with hundreds of aliens of different races, shapes, and colors surrounding him. It felt even more surreal than it had when he was on board the *Thalamos*.

Did they just beam me out?

People around him performed a salute by punching their fists against their chests and bowing.

"Kevin, I suppose?" said a sweet female voice behind him.

He turned around and looked up. At the top of the golden stairs, sitting on a throne, was a beautiful blue-skinned female with long flowing golden hair. The moment she got up from her chair, everyone in the room bowed on one knee at the same time and looked down.

"Yes. I'm Kevin."

The woman smiled as she gracefully descended the stairs. Soon, she was in front of Kevin, her face the most beautiful he had even seen. She was simply breathtaking.

"How can we ever repay you for your bravery? My people and I are in your debt. Name anything you'd like, and it will be made yours."

Kevin swallowed hard. His gaze was locked on the woman's voluptuous lips and, without even realizing it, he was uttering his wish.

"A kiss."

A cascade of what Kevin interpreted as offended murmurs rose up, but it stopped immediately as the woman raised an open palm.

"That's one wish I can easily and gladly grant, Kevin."

She took his face in her hands and slowly approached her lips to his. A strong scent tickled his nostrils, and before his lips connected with hers, he grabbed her shoulders, turned his head around, and sneezed hard.

When Kevin reopened his eyes, the first thing he felt was wet and cold. He was trembling, and it took his mind a split-second to realize where he was. Back on Earth and on the crashed pod's open door. He saw the pill that started it all fly out of his mouth. Kevin tried to grab it, but it was beyond his grasp.

As it impacted with the surface of the water, sparks erupted, and the pill disintegrated.

Kevin looked at the water with his mouth wide open.

"You've got to be shitting me!"

The End

Author Christian Kallias

If you've enjoyed this short story, I encourage you to check out my Universe in Flames series. Some of the concepts used in this story such as space battles and dogfights, especially remote-control ships and micro-jumps, are present in my ever-growing series (9 books + 1 novella available from Amazon). To learn more about my books, please visit my website: www.christiankallias.com (where you can download 3 FREE books)

CATALYST
A Warships of the Spire Story

By Lisa Blackwood & S.M. Schmitz

When Catalyst sustains heavy damage from a rogue AI attack, the Spire warship's only chance for survival lies in an outlaw telepath with the power to destroy him.

Chapter One

Time was the one commodity a Spire AI had in abundance. At least normally. Now, however, Catalyst very much wanted more years but wasn't likely to get them. He doubted he'd even get time to grieve his lost telepaths, who'd been killed in the first wave of the rogues' assault.

Apparently, the rogues had modified their strategy and were now waiting to ambush the unsuspecting Spire ships instead of targeting space stations and colonies in brazen raids.

Catalyst and his brother-in-arms, Fray, were on a routine reassignment where they'd been tasked with providing additional security for the new colonies under construction in the Vendray system. The colonies' councils had been in communication with the ships already patrolling the area, and there'd been no reports of attacks or raids in the area.

He and Fray had dropped out of transit while still fifteen hours from their destination as the new Spire regulations dictated for all inbound ships. Any ship transiting directly into the solar system would be deemed rogue and targeted for extermination.

That's when their routine mission ended, and his existence had gained an expiration date.

As a Spire warship, he was accustomed to taking hits and dealing out punishments in return to protect the empire. But dropping out of transit into the midst of five of his own kind turned rogue—that was another level of warfare. If he were human, he would have shied away from the memory of the attack, but he lacked that escape even in his own mind.

Catalyst had dropped out of transit thirteen seconds before Fray, but it had been enough time for the dormant rogues to power up their systems and fire on him. The combined firepower of five rogues had penetrated his triple-layered shields, taking out weapon arrays five through nine along his port side and damaging the primary energy conduit to his transit drives.

He might have been able to make the jump back into transit if the rogues hadn't also launched a secondary attack targeting his telepaths at the same time. His seven telepaths had tried to link with each other to form a more unified protective shield against the attacking rogues, but ultimately, his telepaths were no match for the enemy.

It didn't matter how many energy harpoons and warheads or how much plasma cannon fire he discharged into the bodies of the rogue ships, nothing he did protected his telepaths. Trapped in a slowly unfolding horror, he'd felt the savage assaults as one after another of his telepaths were mentally ripped apart by the combined assaults of five rogues. Each of his telepaths had died screaming, and he'd been powerless to stop it. Fray's telepaths had suffered a similar fate.

Unable to transit without their telepaths, he and his brother continued to fight, unleashing their anger on the rogues. Together, they'd managed to destroy one of them and cripple the other four. The surviving rogues retreated, so he and Fray did the same, putting as much space between themselves and their enemies as possible.

Catalyst didn't know a rogue's capacity for self-repair, so he based his timeline estimates on how long similar repairs would take a Spire warship, which meant he had a few moments to assess the situation. Of the two Spire warships, Fray had sustained the least amount of damage, and his engines were repairable. Catalyst had managed to get a warning out to him before he'd exited transit, giving the other warship time to bring his weapons online before he dropped into normal space, which had likely saved them both.

But without telepaths, neither of them could enter transit even if they managed to patch their main drives. Their only hope now was to outrun the rogues through normal space, reach the colony, and join the other Spire warships already stationed there. Together, they would have a better chance of defeating the rogues. The planetary defense systems would also aid in the battle.

They just had to *get* there.

Unfortunately, Catalyst's transit drives weren't the only systems that took a hit. His engines for travel through normal space were damaged, their coolant system compromised and reaching critical levels. He would have to take them offline soon or risk a catastrophic event.

Fray had a chance to outrun the rogues and get his crew to the safety of the colony, but it was a slim chance. They were both limping, venting atmosphere, leaking fluids, and bleeding energy behind them that even an insane rogue could follow without difficulty.

Reaching for hive-sync, he linked with Fray. "I'm not going to make it to the colony. My engines are minutes from complete meltdown. I have to take them offline."

"We'll make our stand here then." The younger AI sounded defeated. Fray wasn't *that* much younger, but Catalyst had lived long enough to lose telepaths and crewmembers before and was familiar with the sharp pain of grief. Fray had never experienced this kind of loss, and it was clearly crippling him.

The lure of self-termination was there, offset only by their duty to their crews and the colony.

"I won't make it to the colony before the least damaged rogue is battle worthy again," Catalyst explained. "But I can still save my crew and give the colony a chance at survival."

"You have a plan?"

"It's more like 'mutually assured destruction' than a plan, but it's the only strategical play I have left." A data burst with Fray conveyed his idea to lead a suicidal mission in order to protect the colonies.

Fray acknowledged his plan. "Launching all transports. Preparing to take on survivors."

"Thank you."

"Your sacrifice will not be in vain," Fray said. "I'll get your crew to safety."

"And I'll give you as much time as I can," Catalyst said with new determination. "Maybe I'll even take out another of the rogues as I die."

"Don't allow them to corrupt you."

"Never," Catalyst promised. As a last service to the memory of his telepaths, he'd do everything in his power to die in a blaze of glory.

While he was coming to terms with his pending demise, he readied his crew and his own transports. "Spire AI Catalyst-035-0279-132 orders crew to nearest transports and life pods. Engines critical. I repeat: evacuate. All crew to designated evacuation sites."

He triggered ship-wide sirens to reinforce his command. He didn't need any heroes staying behind and dying in a last stand with him. His senior officers didn't question him. They were seeing the reports flash across their energy webs in real time, and they knew a dying warship when they saw one.

"All crew begin evacuation procedures. Spire warship *Fray* will assist."

As his crew began to evacuate, Catalyst kept his maintenance drudges and sentinels attending to repairs. He'd also assigned his human-formed drone to repair critical systems.

Catalyst's entire crew evacuated in nine minutes and thirty-two seconds. His sensors tracked as every transport and life pod was picked up by *Fray*.

"Once my crew disembarks from the transports, I will take command of them and yours as well," Catalyst said. He needed as many transports as possible for the greatest chance at success.

"Of course. Good luck, and may you be victorious over your enemies."

That was unlikely, but Catalyst would settle for crippling or slowing the enemy at this point. "I'll do my best. It's been a pleasure serving with you."

The now empty transports returned to Catalyst's undamaged docking bays where sentinels and drudge units were waiting to perform the needed modifications for his plan's success. When the last of the transports were clear, Fray fired his engines and surged away, but he maintained the hive-sync.

"I'll stay with you until the end, brother." Fray's thoughts flowed into Catalyst's, and unlike their previous communications, the impartial battle logic was now tinged with the warmth of love. They hadn't been born of the same AI mother but had become brothers by choice.

"No," Catalyst insisted. "I won't risk an open link during a battle with rogues. They might send infiltrator sentinels. I can't risk your life as well. Our crews are depending on you to get them to safety."

Another burst of emotion flowed from Fray: helplessness, pain, rage, grief. But he only said, "I'll miss you."

Fray severed the link, and Catalyst was completely alone for the first time in his life. His mind fell silent, untouched by the presence of telepaths or other Spire AIs, and his warship body had become an empty shell, a completely unnatural situation for a Spire AI.

His maintenance drudges, military sentinels, medical units, and even his humanoid drone kept working, attentive to the tasks assigned to them, but he was still alone. He linked with his drone body and merged with him fully. His existence narrowed to the warhead he was removing from its casing. His drone stopped what he was doing and stared at his flesh-covered hands, and he stepped back to allow a sentinel to continue the work. The unit's twelve-foot height dwarfed the drone's six-foot-two frame.

It might have been foolish to take his drone from the work, but his other five thousand units were all working toward the same end. One less wouldn't affect his chance at victory, slim as it was. He traveled to the midsection of the ship where the hydro-gro zone stretched a third of his length. Walking down a familiar path, he stopped when he came to a stone bench beside a small pool. Fish still swam in the cool waters, so he supposed he wasn't completely alone after all, although the fish proved to be poor conversationalists.

"I suppose," he told the white and orange fish, "we'll die together."

His drone stroked a finger along the side of the bench where a piece had chipped out years ago when his primary telepathic link, Genevieve, had been trying her hand at gardening. She'd left a spade upright in the soft loamy earth, and his artificial gravity had won out, causing the spade to fall over and taking a chip out of the seat.

He'd never replaced the bench and was glad he hadn't. Now, he could sit here and remember her as he mourned her loss while the rest of him attended to his duty as a Spire warship.

"Are you going to sit there and await your death, or do you want to live and make those damned rogues pay?" an unfamiliar woman's voice asked in his mind.

Across his ship's body, his repair and defense units halted their work as his primary core ran a self-diagnostic. Had the rogues already managed to corrupt him in the first attack? Was he experiencing mental degradation like the rogues themselves?

"No worries there," she said. "I wouldn't be talking to you if you had even a hint of their corruption."

"But I..." Catalyst was speechless, his primary core now running multiple self-diagnostics at once. Who the hell *was* this? She wasn't a memory, and rogues didn't have telepaths who could attempt to sync with him...did they?

"Trust me, I've seen what a rogue can do, and how long it takes for a newly corrupted AI to succumb."

"You're a telepath," he whispered back. But that was impossible. He'd felt all his telepaths dies. Fray's, too. He grasped at the only logical explanation. "You're a telepath on board one of the rogues. A slave."

"Uh, no, although I was once their prisoner a long time ago," she corrected.

He had no defense against her. It was terrifying and yet, strangely, a relief. He wasn't alone anymore.

"You don't really want to die," she continued. "And I don't either. I think we can help each other."

Catalyst quickly considered his options, but the telepath was right. He didn't really want to die, and his only choices were certain death or allowing this unfamiliar telepath to penetrate his remaining defenses, which could potentially ruin his plan to take out at least one of the rogue AIs. If he trusted her and she ended up betraying him, Fray and both of their crews could die, too. But if she actually intended to help him, he had a small chance of survival.

His drone rose from the bench, decisive and determined. "All right," he said. "Let's talk."

Chapter 2

As far as plans went, Tasha thought hers was only slightly better than suicide, but she couldn't risk enslavement by the rogue AIs. As a child, she'd managed to escape different rogues with the help of her fellow Nuallan telepathic sisters after they'd been kidnapped from their dormitories. But she'd had their help then. Now, she was risking her fate with a fully sane AI, and even if he weren't rogue, she'd never wanted to allow an AI to merge with her mind again. And this warship could turn her over to the Spire where they'd force her to become a link.

But if she didn't enlist his help, the rogues, whose ambush she'd barely escaped three days ago, would soon sniff her out and she'd find herself the prisoner of insane AIs for the second time. And she couldn't go through that again.

Tasha gently probed the Spire warship's mind to assess his status. He'd sustained heavy damage, but he was far from helpless. With her aid, they had a reasonable chance of destroying the rogues, and a dead rogue was a good rogue. Afterward, she'd have to deal with the Spire warship.

Three days ago, she'd targeted one of the unmanned supply tugs delivering raw materials for the construction of the new colonies. She'd hit similar marks hundreds of times without the Spire ever knowing. A quick infiltration of a data uplink node with her telepathic gift, a few file manipulations, and the supply tug's manifest was changed in the Spire archive.

And then it was simple piracy to overtake the tug, temporarily override its systems, grab the items she needed, adjust the internal time logs, and send it on its way. All in all, it was a routine operation she'd mastered years ago. At least that's how it had always been until she'd targeted a tug in this region of space. She hadn't sensed the rogues until she and the tug had practically flown into the ambush.

It seemed her plan wasn't that original after all. The rogues had been targeting the same supply line, and she'd had the misfortune to be in the wrong place at the wrong time. Once the rogue AIs sensed a telepath aboard the supply tug, they'd retreated, and that's when she'd concluded they still possessed the ability to reason, which made them more dangerous than older rogues who had completely descended into madness and lacked self preservation or higher-level reasoning.

But the five rogues she'd encountered retained enough presence of mind to expect a trap when they'd sensed her because an unprotected telepath was unheard of in the Spire. Their hesitation had given her the chance to escape back to her own transport and undock from the tug.

Unfortunately, when no other Spire warship approached to attack the rogues, they must have figured out she was one of the surviving Nuallan telepaths, at which point they reached for her mind. She rebuffed their mental attack easily enough, but her small transport hadn't fared so well against their physical firepower. They'd taken out her ship's merger weapons and damaged her transit drive. She'd managed to initiate the jump to transit, but her damaged engines gave out before she could reach the colony.

Knowing the rogues had aimed to cripple her ship, not destroy it, she'd powered down all systems except life-support, and even that she'd set to minimum life-sustaining levels with the hope they wouldn't sense her location. It had kept her safe for three days, but as she sat there in space, grateful the rogues hadn't yet found her, she also knew she would die of starvation unless the life-support systems gave out first.

In some ways, the arrival of the two Spire AIs had come as a relief. Teaming up with one of them was better than death by starvation or enslavement by a rogue. It quickly became clear, though, that both Spire warships had been taken by surprise. They'd managed to kill one of the five rogues and damaged the other four enough to cripple them for several hours, but it had come at a substantial cost.

As the two Spire ships fled back toward the colony, she found herself in their path, but they were both so heavily damaged, they hadn't sensed her transport drifting in the outer edge of the asteroid belt circling this solar system. It had given her time to form her plan, which was a desperate gamble.

When the two Spire AIs linked in hive-sync, Tasha had used that opening to slip inside Catalyst's mental shields undetected. She'd employed the most delicate of touches so she wouldn't be discovered, but it was important to learn what sort of AI he was. She needed to know his personality, not his service record, since her plan hinged on finding out if she could trust this AI to help her and not attempt to enslave her afterward. As long as there was some empathy to balance his logical thought processes, the possibility that she could appeal to his sense of honor existed. In the end, it was feeling his grief and loneliness that convinced her to join forces with him.

He'd been surprised and alarmed to find her mind already inside his defenses, but there was no going back now. She needed his help, and he needed her.

Catalyst had just confirmed he was willing to talk to her, but she could sense his lack of trust, his fear that she'd turn on him. She needed to reassure him that she wanted the rogues dead just as much as he did.

Tasha hacked into one of his functioning long-range sensors and trained the probe to scan in her direction. "See that battered transport in Quadrant 3-5-3B? That's what is left of my ship after a run in with the rogues," she said. "I had the misfortune to target the same supply tug they'd already planned to ambush. I only survived because they were shocked to find a telepath there and probably thought it was a trap."

"How did you escape?"

"They wanted to capture me alive, but I managed to jump into transit. They didn't have telepaths on board so couldn't follow. But my transport's drives were damaged, and I couldn't reach the colony. I hid in the debris of the asteroid belt in the hope they wouldn't find me if they came this way."

"You're trusting me with your location," he pointed out, his voice still suspicious and carefully measured.

"You're a better option than the rogues or starving to death."

Catalyst hunted through his own mind, looking for how and when she'd first infiltrated him. He'd find the truth eventually, so she decided to be honest with him. Perhaps it would even convince him to build some sort of temporary relationship with her.

"I slipped in while you were in hive-sync with Fray. A rogue could do the same. In the future, don't merge with another AI if you think there are rogues nearby. Use regular old comms."

She felt surprise spark through his primary core. "How were you able to hide from me so long? Links are two-way connections."

"Not if the telepath is powerful enough and doesn't want the AI crawling around in her head."

314

She felt his emotions shift and roll in a second of confusion then they calmed as he understood *how* she'd become a telepathic pirate and how she'd snuck into his mind. "You're one of the enhanced Nuallan telepaths, like Vengeance's new link. The Spire is looking for the rest of you."

Damn it.

"Yeah, but Hayley *wanted* to return to Vengeance. I don't want to become a link." She flinched as she thought about what she'd have to do in order to save them both. "I need a promise from you before we go any further. If you can't make that promise, I'll sever this connection now, and you can go forward with your suicide mission."

"I would have to know what that promise entailed first," he answered.

"I know," she assured him. "Neither of us has any reason to trust the other, but we don't have a choice. I think we both know that I could do terrible things to your primary core, and you could do equally terrible things to me once we're in full link." Tasha paused to take a deep breath and calm her nerves. "I promise not to harm you if you promise the same, and afterward, if we manage to survive, you give me one of your transports and we go our separate ways, never to see each other again."

Catalyst didn't respond for a minute, likely running a thousand scenarios in that time.

"I won't hurt you. I would never harm a telepath."

"And the rest?"

Another long pause. This was its own sort of torture. Finally, Catalyst promised, "I will gladly accept your help in fighting the rogues, and afterward, we'll go our separate ways. You have my word."

"And never see each other again," she prompted. "You won't turn me in or pursue me once your repairs are complete."

"I can't promise we'll *never* see each other again since I can't predict the future. We might find our paths will cross again in unpredictable ways." His thoughts swirled with emotions that were too quick and evasive for her to identify, but she thought it was a mix of hope and humor.

She sighed both aloud *and* in his mind. "Would you just promise not to chase me down then?"

"That I can promise. You're not going to chase *me* down, are you?"

Tasha's mouth fell open then she crossed her arms over her chest even though the AI couldn't see her. "AIs shouldn't try to be funny, because you suck at it."

"Noted," he told her, but even his mental voice was colored with laughter. "What's your name?"

She hesitated before deciding it was silly to withhold a name when she'd have to open her mind to him soon anyway. "Tasha."

"All right, Tasha. I can offer you a transport now, and you can use it to escape before the rogues come."

Tasha's arms fell by her sides, and she gaped at Catalyst again. He would give her a ship and let her escape? Just like that without asking for anything in return? And it wasn't a trick—she was in his head. Catalyst was willing to see her to safety and sacrifice himself to do it.

"It's no different than what I'd planned to do since I first told Fray to prepare to take on my crew," Catalyst explained. "And this way, you have a greater chance of survival."

It was a safe way out for her. She wouldn't have to link with an AI, and she wouldn't starve. She could take his transport and keep running from an old life she was desperately trying to forget.

But it went against her sense of honor, the one thing those rogues who'd invaded Nualla and kidnapped her as a child hadn't been able to take from her.

"I'm not running," she said. "I have as much reason as you to see those rogues dead. And I approached you with a deal, so I'll see it through."

Catalyst quickly analyzed her proposal then agreed. "Very well. A transport is en route to pick you up."

"Okay," she said, taking a deep breath as she prepared to board an AI's warship body for the first time in twenty years. "Let's do this."

Chapter 3

Catalyst's humanoid drone waited by the bay where the transport had just docked. He found himself oddly nervous about meeting this Nuallan telepath, whose gift was far stronger than any of his previous links. For two decades, everyone in the Spire thought the Nuallan telepaths had been killed in the attack, so the discovery that some had survived had sent shockwaves throughout the empire.

And now, one was aboard his ship.

The transport door opened, and a slender woman with auburn hair and scattered freckles across her cheeks descended the gangplank. She hardly looked dangerous, but Catalyst knew looks could be deceiving. He extended his hand to greet her, and she hesitated, eyeing it as if he'd hidden a bomb up his sleeve. Finally, she placed her delicate hand in his and shook it but retreated just as quickly.

"Welcome aboard, Tasha," he said. "I estimate I have a six-hour lead on the rogues, but I've sustained significant damage that my drudges and sentinels are busily repairing. It'll be close as to whether or not my heavy weapons' system is fully operational by the time they catch up to us."

Tasha nodded as if she already knew the full extent of his damage. "I'll help then. You'll be able to transit now that you have a telepath, right?"

"Yes, once they're repaired," he acknowledged. "But it's doubtful we'll get my transit engines back online before the rogues reach our position."

"We'll get them patched in time," she assured him. "You should see the graveyard wrecks I've had to cobble together over the years to get a ship working. My telepathy is good for more than just destroying things."

He arched an eyebrow at her, but she didn't elaborate on why she was so confident she'd be able to get his drives back online.

"The primary weapons' relay panels are on Level 34, Section 7b." He waved her on, and she followed silently, pulling her arms closer to her body so that she appeared even smaller. Fragile even. Catalyst pretended to concentrate on the drudges ahead of them who were busy working on a nerve line rupture that was leaking bio-fluids all over the deck's synthetic tiles, but his mind raced with discarded sentences, phrases he could utter to provide this woman with the confidence she needed that he wouldn't hurt her. He knew what she and the Nuallan telepaths had suffered.

Catalyst cleared his throat and said, "I'll have a drudge stock your transport with provisions."

Tasha glanced up at him and just as quickly focused on the hallway in front of them again. "Thanks."

"I, um…" Catalyst trailed off and scratched the back of his neck, a nervous habit more than anything, although his drone's body was entirely organic, a newer model than the previous partially synthetic models he'd had before. He'd age and experience organ failure, and eventually, what it was like to die although his sentience would live on in his primary core and thousands of non-humanoid bodies. And he'd have another drone waiting for him, identical to this one. His drone was still young, only thirty-one, and he'd found the process fascinating so far. But he doubted Tasha would agree with him. As they turned a corner, he scrambled for another topic of conversation and suddenly, and somewhat unexpectedly, heard himself saying, "I always thought Nualla was a beautiful planet."

What the hell, Cat? Brilliant—bring up her lost home.

Tasha glanced up at him again and slowed her pace. "Yeah, it was."

"Sorry," he sighed. "I guess you'd rather forget it."

Tasha seemed to think about it then shook her head. "No. My happiest memories are from Nualla. They're the only moments I *want* to remember."

Catalyst curled his fingers into tight fists and clenched his jaw, imagining the horrors the young telepaths had survived, the lifetimes of happy memories they should have had, and the security that came with being a valued and treasured telepath of the Spire. He relaxed his jaw and took a deep breath. "Who was your AI?"

Tasha stopped walking and blinked up at him.

Damn it. Pour more salt on the wound, why don't you?

"I have no intention of betraying our agreement," he hurriedly assured her. "I was just curious."

Tasha lifted a shoulder and tried to force an air of nonchalance, but for once, she failed at her attempt of aloofness. "It doesn't matter. He was killed a long time ago."

"I'm sorry," Catalyst said. "That must have been—"

"Is this really the most important thing we can be discussing? Don't you have relays that need to be repaired and a more sophisticated battle plan to strategize than a suicidal explosion in the hopes it takes out a rogue?"

Catalyst smiled at her and said, "I'm an AI. I'm capable of multi-tasking, you know."

Tasha rolled her eyes and mumbled, "Well, I'm human and only have one body, so can we get on with it?"

Catalyst nodded and waved his arm toward the hallway to their right. "We're almost there. And I *am* working on a better strategy than my death. Like I said: I'm multi-tasking."

Tasha sighed and looked like she wanted to roll her eyes at him again, but she only asked, "Tell me what you've got so far. I may be able to help."

"We're outnumbered, so our best chance of success is through deception. We need to somehow get the rogues close enough that I can detonate my warheads without them firing on me first."

He stopped in front of the damaged relays and pulled one of the panels from the wall, where the bio-gel oozed like an open sore. Tasha studied it for a few seconds then began pulling broken and bleeding bits of bio-circuitry from the panel, small lines appearing between her eyebrows as she concentrated. "If the rogues know I'm aboard and you pretend you're dead," she offered, "they'll likely approach carefully but without firing on you since they'll want to capture me. When they get close enough that your warheads have a reasonable chance of inflicting maximum damage, come back online and fight."

Catalyst immediately analyzed her plan, its probabilities for success and the risks that could result from its failure. Their deaths weren't the biggest problem they faced—his corruption and her capture could be catastrophic for the colonies and the Spire. "We need a contingency plan," he decided. "If we're unable to kill the rogues, or at the very least, evade them, self-termination is the only option."

"Agreed. They won't be able to control my behavior, so I promise I won't allow you to become corrupted and turn into one of them. And I'd much rather die than become their prisoner."

Catalyst looked up from the relay panel he was working on and swallowed a painful knot in the back of his throat as data points detailing Hayley's abuse at the hands of rogue AIs flashed through his primary core. "We'll ensure neither of us fall into their hands."

Tasha kept her attention on the bio-circuitry but nodded. "Did you know any of the rogues who attacked Nualla?"

"No," he answered. "I knew of them, of course, but I'd never met any of them. Your class was fifth generation telepaths from that particular program, and my primary link..."

Catalyst pressed his lips together tightly as the memory of Genevieve and their old friendship crashed into him, reminding him of his loss, and that he still hadn't been able to mourn his telepaths. He'd expected to die soon, too, and some part of him had thought death might be a reprieve, an escape from his own trauma of losing every telepath he'd known and loved for many years. Genevieve had been a second generation Nuallan telepath, which meant she'd been almost two hundred years old. Tasha and Hayley's class were the first enhanced telepaths, making their loss all the more tragic for the Spire.

Tasha's hand froze over the damaged switch sensor, and she took a deep breath, prompting him to meet her gaze over the relay panels between them. "I'm sorry about your telepaths, Catalyst. I know revenge won't bring them back, but hopefully, it'll at least give you some closure."

"Yeah," he said quietly. "If we make it through this, I'll bring them back to Teutorigos for a proper funeral. They deserve no less."

Tasha blinked at the frayed part in her hand then, just as quietly, said, "I know Nualla is closed off and no one's supposed to be able to get there, but I think if I had a choice about where to be laid to rest, it would be there."

"The Spire has lifted the prohibition against traveling to Nualla now that the truth has come out about the rogue attack. They won't rebuild there, but it may be possible if you have someone you trust to bring your body..." Catalyst realized how morbid their conversation had become and shook his head as if he could force those painful topics into the back of his consciousness.

But Tasha didn't seem bothered by it at all. "I don't have anyone I trust. Not anymore. All of my Nuallan sisters had vowed to stay away from the Spire's control, and now look what's happening. Hayley returned to Vengeance, and even Amelia is working for Brenna now."

"Perhaps," he said carefully, "not all AIs are as bad as you fear."

"Perhaps," she snapped, "you should mind your own business."

He arched an eyebrow at her and lifted a shoulder. "Technically, I *was*. You contacted me, remember?"

Tasha grunted at him and shoved the relay panel back into the wall. "Just drop it, Catalyst. If you think you're going to convince me you're not like other AIs who just want to—"

"Tasha," he interrupted, "I'm no more like other AIs than you are like other humans. We have some things in common, but we *are* alive. We have our own personalities, and we love and hate and mourn and celebrate just like you do. But I'm not trying to recruit you or convince you to return to the Spire. I gave you my word I wouldn't, and few of my sisters and brothers would so callously break a vow."

Tasha tossed her auburn hair over a shoulder and tried to affect that air of nonchalance again. "Let's just get through this battle then we'll part ways, and you can wipe your memory of me for all I care."

But for some reason, Catalyst thought her voice indicated she *might* care...even if it were only a little.

Her existence must be so lonely, he thought. *She believes she's lost everyone, even the telepathic sisters she'd once trusted.*

"As promised, I won't bother you," he told her. "But I won't erase you either. I'd like to remember you."

Tasha's mouth opened and a small croaking sound escaped before she exhaled quickly and shrugged. "It's your life. What's the ETA on the rogues? We could probably get more work done with less talking."

Catalyst grinned at her and said, "*You* might be able to get more work done with less talking. I can *multi-task*."

So Tasha narrowed her eyes at him and put her hands on her hips. "Is it like some glitch in your primary core that turned you into such a smartass?"

He laughed, sending surprisingly pleasant emotions through both his drone's body and his primary core, and those feelings mixed with his grief and a sense of guilt that he'd enjoy anything when his telepaths, when Genevieve, had so recently been murdered. "All right," he relented. "My drone will no longer multi-task. Business only from now on. And the rogues are making faster progress than anticipated. Their ETA is now calculated at four hours and seventeen minutes."

"Damn it," she muttered as she pulled another relay panel from the wall. The young telepath stood up straighter, and when she spoke again, her voice sounded more determined, decisive and vindictive. Battle-ready. "Let's get you operational. Because these bastards are about to find out what kind of hell they really deserve."

Chapter 4

Waiting always sucked. But waiting in zero-g while being secured in place by a sentinel's massive hand, its vise-like fingers curled around her waist? That was an entirely new level of sucking. But she was willing to go to even greater lengths than this for revenge.

Catalyst had already taken most systems offline. All that remained was life support and his main nerve lines, which carried the electrical impulses that transmitted data from his body to his mind like a nervous system.

When the rogues were within a quarter standard hour of his position, Catalyst would take those systems offline as well to complete his "dead warship" act. Once his nervous system was shut down, it would effectively mimic sensory deprivation, and if it had been real, his need for stimuli would lead to his mind tearing itself apart, eventually culminating in his death.

However, he wouldn't experience a true disconnect, because before he shut down those systems, Tasha would initiate a deep link with him, providing life sustaining input. She just had to sit back and allow him full access to her mind—all her memories and every event that made her who and what she was would be there for him to examine.

Why had she thought this would be better than starving to death?

Oh, right. Revenge.

What a stupid idea.

"Are you ready to instigate full link?" Catalyst asked.

322

AIs couldn't read minds when not in a link, but they could read body language and hers must have betrayed just how deep her fear ran.

When in doubt, bullshit, she thought. "Yep. I'm ready. What's the ETA until the rogues are in range?"

"We have another seven minutes until they're close enough that their sensors will be able to detect that my life-support is still functioning. We should initiate the link now to be certain you can tolerate my mind." His voice softened and he added, "It's been a long time, and your last experience with an AI would have been extremely unpleasant."

Tasha glanced at Catalyst's human drone. He was secured like her, a massive sentinel's hand wrapped around his waist. The military units were offline like everything else, but the magnetic gravity-asset tech built into their wide treads still functioned. It had been designed for work on the outside of a ship's hull, but it suited this situation, too. She supposed she should be thankful she wasn't bumping around like the rest of the unsecured items.

Catalyst was watching her, and his attempt at a tranquil expression didn't hide his unease.

"I won't betray or fail you," she found herself saying, as if her words would reassure an AI.

But to her surprise, it did seem to give him some sort of comfort. He smiled and nodded. "Thank you. But to be honest, I'm more concerned about taking all my systems offline and playing dead. Leaves me a touch vulnerable."

"I'll warn you before the rogues have a chance to fire on you. Besides, I can scramble their brains if I need to."

"That's...not very reassuring."

"For what it's worth, I wouldn't want to be defenseless while my enemies were in striking range either." She grinned at him and teased, "You deserve a medal."

His drone grunted in response.

Her humor fled and she asked, "You ready for this?"

When he nodded, she closed her eyes and relaxed her hold on her telepathic gift while also lowering her mental shields. Catalyst's mind brushed against hers but didn't latch on like an AI normally would. He was allowing her to set the pace and control the depth of the link.

She appreciated his empathy, but hesitation on the battle field would get them killed. Tasha reached for the mind of an AI for the first time in twenty years.

"I'm very rusty," she said directly into his mind.

"You're doing fine." His thoughts and emotions slowly filled her mind, and she saw glimpses of his lost telepath family and felt his great pain. Other thoughts bombarded her. Instinct urged her to fight the flow of those foreign thoughts and visions, but the foundation she'd been taught in the Nuallan academy gave her the strength to endure.

When her mind was calm again, she followed the current of his emotions, and slowly, his mind became more familiar.

He was sorting through her thoughts just as she was rifling through his.

And they came to the same conclusion: they could trust each other—this one time at least.

By mutual agreement, they meshed their minds more firmly together. Tasha and Catalyst vanished, replaced by one deeply interfaced mind.

They powered down their remaining systems, and together, used their formidable telepathic gift to track the inbound rogues. The enemy would be within firing range in a matter of minutes, but they wanted the rogues closer, deep in the improvised minefield.

The Tasha part of their dual personality expanded and cloaked their Catalyst half. Moments later, the enemy scanned them, a deep penetrating beam, but the rogues only discovered what Tasha and Catalyst wanted them to find—a single telepath aboard a dead Spire ship.

As the rogues slowed, the linked pair studied the enemy combatants, noting each of the hostiles' weaknesses. The *Callisto* had a vast rent in her port side and the *Charybdis* had large dents and abrasions covering sixty percent of his hull, looking like he'd had a run in with his sea monster namesake. The *Phoenix* and the *Chimera* both still sported the blast marks and ruptures Catalyst himself had given them.

"Unknown Nuallan telepath, surrender and prepare to be boarded," Chimera told her. "The Spire warship is dead, and you will perish along with him if you don't come with us."

"I know he's dead," their Tasha half said. "I killed him and will do the same to you if you don't retreat immediately."

"That isn't—"

"Possible? How do you think I and my telepathic sisters escaped your kind in the first place?"

A long pause answered her while Chimera and the other rogues likely weighed her boast against the possibility it might be true.

"You may have been victorious over the Spire AI, but no telepath is strong enough to withstand four of my kind," Chimera decided. "We see that the Spire AI did not go down without a fight, and he managed to jettison all his life pods and transports, stranding you with his corpse."

Ah, Chimera had enough mental capacity left to pretend to be reasonable, but Tasha and Catalyst knew the rogues were about to launch drillers and would attempt to board.

The first rogue wasn't done wooing her yet, though. "We are your only hope of survival, and you are ours."

The entire time, the rogues continued toward Catalyst's slowly rotating "corpse." When they were deep inside the minefield, Tasha used the rogues' own hive links to infiltrate Chimera's mind.

"Now," Tasha ordered, and Catalyst obeyed.

Systems all over the ship came online as the first of the mines detonated. Still linked with Catalyst, Tasha borrowed some of his confidence and forced her telepathic gift into a bolt of iron will and hurled it deep into Chimera's primary core where she dug and tore at the rogue's mind, tearing and shredding critical systems and subroutines needed for cognitive function.

While Tasha was tearing her enemy's mind apart, Catalyst launched energy harpoons and detonated more warheads. Reaching deeper into the rogue's primary core, she sorted through the chaos until she found the systems that controlled shields. She brought them down, and Catalyst struck the enemy's now vulnerable underbelly and engineering section.

Chimera's ancient transit engines destabilized, and seconds later, fuel and gases ignited into blooms of short-lived, fiery explosions. A second massive explosion vaporized an entire section of the rogue's body.

Tasha and Catalyst discarded the ravaged mind and locked on to Phoenix, the nearest rogue. Having seen what they'd done to his brother, Phoenix tried to block her attack by dropping out of hive-sync with the other two, but he was too late. Tasha was already inside all their minds.

There would be no escape, only justice for all those innocents killed by the rogues' madness in their attempt to restore themselves to the powerful AIs they'd once been.

"You can never undo the past. There is no cure for what you've become. There is only death," she told them.

Catalyst lent brawn to her words, delivering another bombardment of devastating cannon fire that burrowed deep into the second rogue.

Two of the rogues were now dead, but Catalyst's body was taking heavy damage from return fire. They needed to end this battle.

Deep below his primary core, Catalyst's secondary power station came online as his main fusion cannon rose out of its protective housing and spun around to target the nearest rogue.

As expected, Charybdis decided to run, and they let him go. He wasn't their target. The *Callisto* was.

Across Catalyst's warship body, lights dimmed, energy webs shut down, and the shields protecting his hull blinked out of existence as every drop of power was rerouted to the primary power conduit feeding his fusion cannon.

The first devastating blast burned through the rogue's shields and outer hull and burrowed deep into Callisto's interior, clean through bulkheads and entire decks, severing vital neural pathways and power conduits.

Callisto's mind died while her body was still experiencing final death throes.

Tasha drew back from Catalyst, taking in the justice they'd handed out.

"Charybdis is still running," Catalyst pointed out. "Shall we test the repairs to my transit engine?"

"Yes," she said with a savage grin as she dragged him back into full link for the trip. "Just a little jump."

The powerful warship jumped smoothly. She'd barely had time to register they were in transit before he dropped back out again, directly in front of the fleeing rogue ship.

Tasha used the telepathic hook she'd already implanted inside the rogue's mind to pull herself deeper into his primary core where she began to tear at vital bits of code, memories, and thought processes.

"Should we leave this one alive for study?" Catalyst asked.

Merged with him as she was, she could sense he didn't want to spare Charybdis even if it were only for as long as it took the Spire scientists to study him.

"No," Tasha said. "While he lives, he's a danger to other AIs. If we kill him, he can't harm another innocent soul."

Catalyst agreed and brought his main fusion cannon to bear. Linked with him, she also heard his deep pain as he whispered, "This is for Genevieve," then he extinguished the last of his beloved link's murderers from the universe.

The battle over, Catalyst scanned the debris field for any intact rogue fighters or sentinels that survived their ship's death, making short work of those he found. When he finished, Tasha released their mental link.

Blinking and fighting disorientation, she was somewhat surprised to find herself back aboard *Catalyst*, being held protectively by one of his sentinels. She glanced at the second sentinel to see Catalyst's human drone jumping out of its grasp with a swift agility that she might find alarming if she hadn't been in his head for the entire length of the battle.

Linking like that tended to build trust even among the most suspicious of people.

"We're still alive," he said as he reached up to help her down.

"You sound like you're surprised we lived."

He laughed and admitted, "I am."

Tasha slowly smiled back at him as he helped her to the ground. "To be honest, I am, too."

"Yeah, I'm glad you didn't tell me that *before* the battle."

Tasha laughed, surprisingly *happy* given she was aboard a Spire warship. "I suppose," she said carefully, "you may have been right. Maybe you're not all so bad."

Catalyst shot her a crooked grin and teased, "Of course I was right. I'm an AI."

"Don't push it," Tasha warned.

Catalyst held up his hands in surrender but kept smiling at her. "And now, your transport, as promised."

Tasha exhaled slowly and nodded. "Thank you, Catalyst. We made a pretty good team."

"Yes," he agreed. "We most certainly did."

Chapter 5

The transport ship had been stocked and was waiting for the Nuallan telepath, but Catalyst found himself oddly conflicted about her departure. She'd seemed so abrasive when she first contacted him, but now, having been in deep link with her and knowing her thoughts and emotions and personality, he understood it was all a defensive act, a barrier to protect herself from experiencing the same trauma she'd suffered as a child. And he wanted to heal her, to somehow take away that pain and those memories that kept such an impenetrable shield around her.

Tasha picked nervously at a fingernail as his drudges finished a final check of her transport to ensure it hadn't been damaged during the battle against the rogues. "If you need anything, I should be back in service within thirty days," he offered. "Perhaps a little longer if finding a new telepathic crew proves to be a greater challenge than the repairs."

Tasha stopped picking at her fingernail long enough to shake her head and tell him, "Once you have a new crew, it's far too dangerous for us to have any contact. Your telepaths might detect me and turn me in."

"There are more rogues out there," he countered. "If they find you and you're on your own—"

"If they find me," Tasha interrupted, "I'll either fight them off or die trying."

"All right," he relented. "Just...don't forget that you *do* have a friend in the Spire. And I will help you if I can."

Tasha folded her arms across her chest and stared at the transport. Catalyst regretted saying anything at all. He'd only been trying to reassure her, but he'd scared her instead. Tasha shifted her weight between her feet and cleared her throat. "Thanks. I'll keep that in mind...not that I think I'll need help or anything."

"Of course not," he pretended to agree. "You're clearly more capable of *multi-tasking* than you thought."

Tasha snorted and peeked at him before returning her gaze to the drudges and transport. "And AIs still aren't funny."

"Definitely not. I'll have my inability to effectively use sarcasm checked out when I get back to Teutorigos."

Tasha laughed then covered her mouth as if embarrassed by her own amusement. Catalyst lowered his gaze, staring at the tips of his boots as he searched for comforting words, but they remained elusive.

After several minutes passed in silence, she murmured, "Wolverine."

Catalyst blinked at her and repeated, "Wolverine?"

"My AI," she explained quietly. "He was killed in the attack on Nualla."

"Oh," Catalyst breathed. "I knew him. He was stationed there to help protect the planet. He was an excellent warrior."

Tasha nodded and hastily wiped a tear from her cheek. "He was my best friend."

Catalyst understood the pain of losing one's best friend all too well. He'd just lost his.

"I'm so sorry, Tasha. For what it's worth, he received the highest honors from the Spire Council for his courage and fortitude in that battle."

"We all thought our AIs would come for us," Tasha whispered. "We waited...but they never came."

Surely she knew by now that the Spire thought all of the girls had died in the attack, that they'd searched the planet and wreckage tirelessly for their bodies, but the school had been so badly burned, nothing but ash had remained. Spire warships had pursued the surviving rogues but once they jumped into transit, they became impossible to track, and for almost two decades, they'd remained outside of the empire, invisible to the warships who wanted vengeance for the deaths of those girls.

"You and your sisters were extremely brave," he offered. "Your abduction and captivity, your escape...you should be proud, Tasha."

"Nat," she corrected. "I used to go by Nat. My name is Natasha."

"Huh," Catalyst replied. "Probably a good thing you have no interest in becoming a link. If you were part of my crew, you *know* people would call us Cat and Nat."

Nat wrinkled her nose and said, "Then I'd definitely have to punch them."

"I could change my name," Catalyst joked. "I always wanted something cool that connected me to our ancient past...you know, like Thor."

"Thor," Nat repeated. "Now you think you're a thunder god?"

Catalyst shrugged. "Maybe I should request a bigger drone body so I can look more godlike."

Nat rolled her eyes and scoffed. "You've already got the ego for it."

Catalyst pretended to agree with that, too. "Definitely. I just need the hammer."

Nat laughed and turned toward him, but his drudges had all dropped back from the transport. They'd finished their inspection, and her ship was ready. All of the humor he'd felt joking around with this young woman vanished as he realized she'd be leaving soon, and he'd once again be totally alone. Even after he reached Teutorigos and the Spire began replacing his telepaths, he wouldn't know them, and for some reason, he felt strangely connected to this petite woman with auburn hair and a handful of scattered freckles across her cheeks.

He also thought she was one of the most beautiful women he'd ever met.

Catalyst shuffled his boots against the floor and took a deep breath. It was time to tell her goodbye. "Be safe, Natasha."

She nodded and eyed the transport one last time. "Thank you, Catalyst."

She extended her hand, and he carefully, regretfully, held it in his for a brief moment. "I was serious," he told her. "If you ever need anything...you know how to find me."

And Natasha, the young telepath who'd saved his life, smiled in return. "Yes. I definitely know how to find you."

Author S.M Schmitz

S.M. Schmitz is a USA Today Bestselling Author and has an M.A. in modern European history. She is a former world history instructor who now writes novels filled with mythology and fantasy and, sometimes, aliens.

Her stories are infused with the same humorous sarcasm that she employed frequently in the classroom, and as a native of Louisiana, she sets many of her scenes here. Like Dietrich in Resurrected, she is convinced Louisiana has been cursed with mosquitoes much like Biblical Egypt with its locusts.

You can sign up for her newsletter on her website, www.smschmitz.com, and receive a free copy of her post-apocalyptic novella, The Scavengers, as well as learn more about all of her science fiction and fantasy books.

Author Lisa Blackwood

USA Today and Wall Street Journal Bestselling Author Lisa Blackwood loves all things urban fantasy, epic fantasy romance and space opera science fiction. As well as writing, she also enjoys gardening, growing orchids, and training her horse, Oakley. She grudgingly lives in a small town in Southern Ontario, though she would much rather live deep in a dark forest, surrounded by majestic old-growth trees. Since she cannot live her fantasy, she decided to write fantasy instead.

Edited by Craig Martelle

Learn more about all Lisa's books by visiting her website, http://lisablackwood.com.

Want to read more from the *Warships of the Spire* universe? Check out *Vengeance* and *Citadel* by visiting http://lisablackwood.com/warships-of-the-spire/.

WRENCHING FREE

Zen DiPietro

When everything went to hell, it was the mechanics who put things back together and made them work again.

Wren Orritz loved nothing more than the challenge of something that was almost irretrievably broken. Restoring something that had been a centimeter or two from going into the scrap heap made her soul sing.

She wasn't sure she was the right fit for *this* job proposal, though.

"You'll like Jamestown more than you think," Fallon said. She'd called Wren into her team's office to discuss the offer. "Right now, it's a skeleton crew of command officers plus a growing team of engineers. They want to get PAC command up and running the way it should be."

Wren blew out a slow breath and fiddled with the clip holding her hair up in a twist. "I'm not an engineer, and I don't think I'd belong on a place where nearly everyone is either an officer or enlisted. I doubt a contractor like me will get much respect."

"You have more experience and more dedication than any enlisted mechanic I've met. Most importantly, more talent. Jamestown suffered a hard blow, and it needs to be repaired, better than ever, as soon as possible. You may not be the obvious choice, but I'm convinced you're the right one." Fallon frowned at her in that no-nonsense security officer way of hers.

"Even with my...history? I just don't think I'd be welcomed warmly there." It hadn't been that long ago since Wren had unwittingly helped the person who had caused the damage on Jamestown.

"Only a few people will even know about that. It wasn't your fault, and you helped take the station back. Never mind all that. Think about it this way: You'd get the chance of a lifetime. Imagine the challenges involved with this project. Triple-redundant security systems, state-of-the-art docking, and voicecom setups." Fallon slanted her a knowing look.

She couldn't pretend that didn't sound incredibly appealing. "But leaving Dragonfire? I love it here."

"Repairing PAC command won't take more than a few months. They're putting together a team to work round the clock. It should be an exciting project, and I bet you'd make some new friends." Her eyes sparked with sudden humor. "Besides. You did kind of help wreck the place."

Wren pretended indignation. "What? I helped *save* that place after the bad guys messed it up. So what if I chopped up a conduit or two in the process? That's nothing. And you know what else? I did darn well at rolling with all of your secret spy crap."

Fallon only grinned at her.

Wren crossed her arms and sat on the edge of the desk. "You seem pretty set on this."

"They need the best. You're the best. The Planetary Alliance Cooperative is in a dangerous position, and I trust you to help us make things right."

Wren had a hard time resisting Fallon. She was so capable and tough, so smart and...hot.

Not that she didn't resist Fallon all the time. Well, when she wanted to, anyway. Wren was nobody's pushover, even if the person in question was someone she loved deeply. Sarkavians like her didn't align themselves behind love like humans and a lot of other species did. Sure, her people loved frequently and fiercely, but they didn't see relationships as a unilateral, this-and-no-other kind of thing.

She didn't want to resist this time, though. The opportunity to repair Jamestown was a once-in-a-lifetime deal, and Fallon had squashed all of her reservations. In spite of everything they'd been through, Wren knew that Fallon wouldn't lie or mislead her about this.

She rubbed her index fingers together, making sure she'd thought this all the way through. "All right. I'll go. But don't be surprised if I love it there and never come back. Just think of the ships I'd be working on there. And the maintenance bays must be incredible."

Fallon smiled. "I'm sure they are. Or at least, they will be when you're through with them. Right?"

"When do I ship out?"

"That's up to you. If you're in the middle of some major repair, then after that. The sooner, the better."

"Right. I'll talk to the crew and figure it out." They'd get along without her. Dragonfire had a top-notch crew.

"Good." Before Wren left, she asked, "Do you and Raptor want to come over to my place for dinner? Or just you, if he's busy?"

The three of them lived in a romantically ambiguous situation. Being from a non-monogamous society, Wren was entirely comfortable with that. Fallon, though, struggled to balance her long-term relationship with Raptor and her past-but-not-over relationship with Wren.

Wren felt torn about the situation. As much as she cared about Fallon, love shouldn't be so hard. As long as she lived on Dragonfire, she had the luxury of inaction. Each day, she could put off hard decisions for another day or another week.

"I'd love to," Fallon said, "but we can't. We have work to do."

Right. All of that super-secret stuff about the government falling apart that Wren wasn't part of.

Maybe their situation factored into her decision to go to Jamestown more than she wanted to admit.

"Gotcha. I'll let you know when I can leave for Jamestown." It wasn't like she hadn't been seeing a certain diplomat lately. She could certainly give him a call instead.

She wouldn't, though. She had work to do. Relationships had their place, but not when there were mechanical bits that needed fixing.

Instead, when she got back to her quarters, she began packing for her trip to Jamestown. Maybe her time there would allow her to reboot her life and make some new long-term plans.

She hoped so.

***

Leaving Dragonfire wasn't as hard as Wren expected it would be. She frequently went home to Sarkan, which was her vacation spot of choice. This didn't feel much different.

Jamestown wasn't even far away from her friends on Dragonfire. In the Kiramoto cruiser PAC command had sent for her, she'd make it there in three days.

As she watched the station and the nebula it sat in, shrink into the distance, she didn't have the mixed feelings she'd expected. She was looking ahead to whatever came next in her life. The galaxy was changing, and she would change right along with it.

She felt good. Ready.

Three days onboard the luxury cruiser was like a vacation for her. She enjoyed sleeping in, watching holo-vids, and aimlessly dinking around in mechanic communities on the voicecom. She savored this downtime because she sensed that once she arrived at Jamestown, she'd have little to none.

Before she knew it, she was putting her belongings on an anti-grav cart and guiding it through the airlock. Only half of her bags held personal belongings. The rest carried her tools, which she had spent a lifetime collecting, using, and forming a relationship with.

Mechanics had some quirks, and she wasn't ashamed of hers.

Her first whiff of the station smelled odd. A touch medicinal. Not the typical air mix for a space station.

She'd wager she'd see a lot of atypical things in the coming days.

A tan-skinned man in a greasy pair of coveralls hurried into the docking bay. "Wren Orritz?"

He was nice-looking in a boy-next-door kind of way—about her age and probably Zerellian, from the look of him and his manner of speaking. Zerellians had a way of emphasizing 'o' sounds even when they spoke in Standard.

"That's me." She bowed as one esteemed equal to another. She saw the tools in his pocket, and pegged him as one of her own breed immediately.

He returned the bow in equal measure, befitting someone who was at his same status. If they'd met on Sarkan or Zerellus, they wouldn't do so, but this was not only a PAC station, but *the* PAC station. Jamestown. PAC command itself, where most people never even went.

"I'm Justin Mayweather. Good to meet you. I've heard great things about you."

She laughed. "Thanks. I'll try to live up to them."

"I'm working under Admiral Neem on the mechanical repairs side. You'll be heading up Pod C, with ten people under you."

"Sounds good. I look forward to getting started." Her ego didn't mind being put in a supervisory position. Clearly, they had faith in her already, and rightly so.

She had no false modesty when it came to her skills. She was damn good and she knew it. She wasn't afraid to prove it to everyone on Jamestown, either.

"Great," Justin said. "Do you need to rest after your journey?"

She smiled. "No way. I rested all the way here. I'm ready to dig in and get dirty."

"That's what I like to hear." He turned away before she could get a good gauge on whether or not that was a double entendre. "Let's swing by your quarters to drop off your personal effects, then I'll show you your first challenge."

She felt like she grew a foot taller instantly. Mechanical challenges? Oh, yeah.

"Let's go."

She guided her anti-grav cart as he led her down the corridor, then took a right turn, and shortly thereafter stopped at a door.

"This will be yours."

"So close to the docking bay? We didn't need to take a lift or anything." She stepped forward and the doors opened to a huge, spacious room. "Wow."

"VIP quarters," he said. "We're all staying in this part of the station to minimize use of the lifts."

"Power troubles?"

"Not troubles, exactly. We're doing some upgrades at the same time we're doing repairs." He remained near the doors, as if he didn't want to intrude on this space that wasn't even really hers.

She found it kind of cute, in an awkward kind of way.

She off-loaded her personal items to the couch in the sitting room, and took only a minute to peek into the spacious bedroom and the oversized kitchenette. What a life it must be to have VIP status.

"All right. Let's get to work." She put a hand on the anti-grav cart.

He grinned, clearly pleased by her eagerness. "Off we go, then."

***

"First problem," Justin said. "More power. We need to complete the generator upgrades so we can have enough power to move on to other things."

He'd led her to the outer perimeter of the station, where the generators were equidistantly placed around the entire structure.

She bit her lip as she studied it. "This is the new model, but it hadn't gotten the 3-TU connections yet."

"You can tell that by looking at it from here?"

"Yep."

Justin gave her a brotherly pat on the shoulder. "We're going to get along just fine."

She laughed. "I have to admit, I'm relieved to be working with another mechanic. I was a little worried I'd be the lone greaser among a bunch of engineers and officers."

Justin's smile faded.

She hesitated. "You're kidding, right?"

He grimaced. "Sorry. I'm an engineer and an officer. A commander, actually."

She groaned, pressing her hand to her eyes. "I didn't mean that I don't like officers. Or engineers. I just—"

"I get it." He made a dismissive gesture. "Engineers are awkward and sometimes have trouble thinking outside of the box. And officer engineers..." He made the same gesture, but more expressively. "They spend more time in meetings than they do in designing anything. Don't worry about it. I'd much rather be working with the actual moving parts, too."

She breathed a little easier, but still felt bad about what she'd said. She'd have to be more careful. Barely functional or not, this was still PAC command.

"Okay! Where's my team?" She opened one of the tool cases on the cart and pulled out a pair of coveralls.

"Two are here. Sleeping, at the moment. They've been on the day shift, but can switch to nights if you'd rather. The rest will be coming over the next two weeks. We're slowly recalling people back, in increments."

"Right." She zipped up the coveralls, then twisted her long pale-pink hair into an updo and secured it with pins from her tool case. "Night shift is fine. I'll get adjusted in the next couple of days. I'm wide awake now, so I might as well get this generator done."

Six hours later, she had tiny burns on her fingers, her back ached, and she had the triumph of watching Jamestown's power output increase by six percent. She felt exhausted, but great.

After a quick shower, she dropped into her new bed. This new assignment was looking good so far.

***

A week later, Wren and her team had Jamestown at fifty percent of normal power and climbing. After another week, PAC command was fully powered and activity had increased exponentially.

Now that they had lighting and life support on all decks and sections, a flood of maintenance workers had arrived and began recoating the bulkheads with insulating material and covering the deck plates with new flooring.

Jamestown was getting a makeover, and the more she participated in the rebuilding, she fonder she became of the station.

She often got attached to things she built from the bottom up, but she'd never been involved in an extreme overhaul of an entire station.

Once the structure and mechanics of a section were given the thumbs-up, a team of techies went in to begin the laborious process of repairing the computer systems. As far as actual damage went, this was the worst of what had happened to Jamestown. As a method of self-protection, Jamestown had been essentially scuttled to prevent it from being taken over during a coup.

All of the damage made Wren sad, but she felt glad to have a part in putting Jamestown back together, better than ever. Once they got done with all this, the station would be a gleaming beacon of the latest-and-greatest of everything.

She ran her hand over a console she'd just repaired. A lot of components had to be replaced due to the decompression. Some things just weren't meant for the harshness of space.

"Feels good, doesn't it?" Justin asked. "Getting it up and running again."

Wren pulled her hand back, embarrassed. He was a nice guy, but she'd only talked to him a few times. She definitely didn't know him well enough to let him in on how proprietary she felt about the things she worked on.

She admitted, "I'm glad there's something I can do to help the PAC. A mechanic can't do much to change politics or stop a war, but helping put Jamestown back together is satisfying work."

So far, she had a crew of seven, with the last three arriving any day. She'd dismissed all of them to get some sleep while she inspected their work. It worked well for everyone. She got to pretend she wasn't double-checking them, and they got to pretend they didn't know she was.

Justin leaned back against the doorframe. "I've always liked serving here. I think I'll like it even better now that I've helped rebuild it."

"This is your regular duty station? I didn't know that." Normally, she'd socialize with people in off-hours, but she'd set herself a pace that didn't allow for anything but work, sleep, and just barely enough time to eat.

She thrived on it.

"Yeah. It takes a lot of people to keep this place working. Plus, we service the PAC ships in the fleet. That means a big crew of mechanics and engineers."

"I imagine that's a lot to keep up with," she agreed. She tried to imagine working someplace this massive. It was many times over the size of Dragonfire.

"It is. But there's always something interesting going on." He grinned, and she found herself liking him. "Have you had any troubles?"

"Nothing significant. I've had to look up a couple of systems I was unfamiliar with to get the specs. But I'm always glad to learn. In a couple of instances, I haven't had high enough security clearance to work on certain things, so I've had to wait for someone on another crew to complete that work. That's a little annoying, but not a big deal."

He nodded. "They're pushing through an upgrade to your security clearance so you can get to everything short of top secret. But even an expedited security upgrade takes time."

"Bureaucracy," she smiled ruefully. "That's what's always kept me away from a commissioned position. As a private contractor, I can take or leave any job."

He rubbed the back of his neck. "I'll admit, there are days when I'd like to have that option. Not that I'd take it. Just that it would be nice to have the choice, you know?"

She chuckled. "Yeah. I know."

He let out a tired sigh. "I think I'm headed to my quarters to get a few hours of sleep before I start in again."

She straightened, smoothing out the stomach of her coveralls, where they tended to bunch up. "I should do the same."

They walked most of the way together. She kept expecting to be booted from her fancy quarters, since people were returning to the station in a steady stream. The sections with crew quarters were opening up, one by one, ready for service.

So far, though, she remained in her fancy digs, and she didn't mind. She had little time to rest, so why shouldn't she do it in such a well-appointed place?

As soon as she got in, she unpinned her hair and started unzipping her coveralls on the way to the necessary. Before stepping into the shower, she stuffed all her clothes into the wall-unit processor. When she turned to the shower, she got a look at herself in the mirror and laughed.

She could see two greasy finger smears on her cheek, along with a smudge across the bridge of her nose. Such was the life of a mechanic. At least her hair didn't have anything too terrible in it. Oil and grease were much tougher to wash out of hair.

Once clean and pink-skinned from scrubbing, she wrapped herself in a towel, twisted her hair up in another one, and walked into the kitchenette to see what she had to eat that wouldn't require any prep.

She stuffed bites of tango fruit into her mouth as she toweled off her hair to the point of being mostly dry. She hung her towels to air-dry, and barely had energy to put on a set of ice-blue pajamas that matched her eyes. She tugged the shorts into place and buttoned up the shirt as she fell into bed.

What felt like only moments later, the lights in her quarters came on and an alarm blared a warning. Yellow emergency running lights lit as well, indicating a concern for power failure.

"Shit!" She stumbled as she scrambled out of bed, knocking her foot on the edge of it. "Ow ow ow ow."

She shoved her feet into shoes she'd left by the door and sprinted out. She saw panicked and confused people, but she didn't waste breath on them. The only way to get a clear picture of the situation was to get to the engineering hub.

As she ran down the corridor, she yanked an emergency kit off the wall. There was no telling what she might need.

A person she didn't know was already in engineering when she got there, and Justin arrived just after her.

She joined the stranger, a human male in his mid-twenties, at the main console. "What is it?"

"Deck 7, section 12J. The sensors are saying there's a containment breach, but the adjacent conduits don't indicate any containment abnormalities. I think it's a sensor malfunction." He frowned at the screen.

Wren switched the screen to show atmospheric readings of the area, then air mix readings. "It's not a malfunction."

She went to thermal readings. "Look. It's a fire in 12J. The containment and fire suppression systems have been cross-wired."

She rushed across the room and grabbed a toolkit.

"There's no way to see the wiring from here," the man said, sounding doubtful.

"No time to argue." She ran out, carrying both kits, which was unwieldy.

Then Justin was next to her, taking the heavier toolkit from her. "How do you know it's a fire?"

She talked as they ran. "First, because I know they run on different power loads, and if they were cross-wired, the containment system would short out. Possibly start a fire. That explains both sets of readings."

They turned a corner. "Second, because I know there was a pod working in that section today. I don't think that's a coincidence."

When she reached to open a conduit so they could climb down to the next deck, Justin grabbed her arm. "The lift will be faster. They operate on a self-contained system, so they won't be affected. The lift will put us out right next to where we want to be."

She nodded and they ran on, to the lifts.

At least she had a minute to catch her breath as they waited for it to descend.

As soon as the doors opened, they ran to the entry to conduit 12J. It was a top-entry hatch, so Wren opened the emergency kit and grabbed a hook to pull down the ladder. She tossed the hook aside and closed the kit so she could attach it to her belt to climb up.

Except she was wearing pajamas.

"Go up. I'll hand it to you." Justin took the kit from her.

She hurried up, then reached back for it. He handed her the toolkit instead. "You handle the repair. I'll deal with the fire."

Whatever his reasoning was, there was no time to argue. She crawled into the conduit and toward the access node on her hands and knees, pushing the toolkit ahead of her. She looked over her shoulder when she heard Justin come up and crawl the other way, toward the fire.

She hoped he'd be okay. Even on her side of the conduit, the metal beneath her was uncomfortably hot to the touch. She didn't smell any smoke, though. The fire must be behind a junction panel.

It could be hard to open under these circumstances. If the damaged fire suppression system was even partially functional, it could lock down the doors in anticipation of the extinguishing cycle.

Well, he'd have to deal with that. She had her own issues. She needed to shut down both systems from the central node, and cut power so they could manually extinguish the flames.

It wouldn't be easy. She'd have to stay ahead of the redundant systems, so they couldn't initiate once she'd shut down the first ones. It was going to be like juggling, keeping all the circuits of all the systems handled at once.

She opened the access panel and got to work. She blocked out the signs behind her, of Justin fighting his own battle. She couldn't afford to be distracted.

Okay. Suppression system backups nullified, and main system disabled. That was a trick, since it was wired into the wrong cluster. The containment system was harder. She had to reroute around the damaged circuits and circle back into them. Finally, she found the path, shut down the system, and held her breath.

She turned and crawled back toward the hatch, looking for Justin. He'd pulled down a hazard bulkhead to seal the space behind him. She started to scramble toward it, but if he'd eliminated oxygen to that section to kill the flames, she'd be putting him in danger. His emergency kit had oxygen in it.

She had to trust him, and wait.

Finally, people began showing up.

"Where have you been?" she testily asked the first pair. Being unable to do anything was making her edgy.

"We got here as soon as we could," the wide-eyed woman said.

Wren recognized her as someone she'd seen in passing. She didn't know the man with her. "Well there's nothing to do but wait. Either Mayweather has fixed it or he's dead and we're going to have to crawl over his body to fight a fire."

Three more people arrived as she said this.

And then the hazard bulkhead went up, revealing Justin Mayweather. She didn't know him very well yet, but she couldn't have been more glad to see him at that moment.

"Fixed?" he asked her.

"Well, disabled, anyway. There will be a lot of repairs to make. Did you get the fire out?"

He swiped a hand over his sweaty forehead. "It was a battle, but yeah. Is there any biogel in that emergency kit? It was as hot as balls in there."

She dug out a pouch of hydrating biogel and handed it to him. He downed it.

For the first time, he noticed the gathering crowd of people. "Uh, pardon me, Admiral."

"Don't worry about it, Commander. Under the circumstances, I'd say you deserve some colorful language."

To Wren's amusement, the admiral she hadn't yet met was wearing the top part of his uniform with pajama bottoms. She pretended not to notice, as everyone else was doing.

"We're going to need some coolant to apply to the area so we can begin repairs immediately." He gestured to the ladder to let Wren descend first.

She handed her kit down to waiting hands and then stepped down to the deck. Then she took the kit he handed down to her.

Which was when she realized she was wearing her pretty blue shorts pajamas in front of everyone. "I think I'll detour to my quarters, get properly dressed, and then go to engineering to start making repair plans."

Justin grinned at her. "Sounds like a good idea. I'll meet you there."

Everyone paused and looked to the admiral. One did not simply la-di-da excuse oneself from an admiral's company.

He blinked. "By all means, let's all go get ourselves ready for some hard work. Whoever is responsible for this will have to be dealt with. I'll want a full report in ops control in one hour. Dismissed."

They scattered in different directions.

***

"How easy is it to make this kind of mistake?" Admiral Erickson asked.

Wren and Justin had briefed the admiral on what had happened, how, and their repair schedule. By putting some other jobs on pause, they'd have the systems in place in two days, and the fire damage repaired in another two.

Wren didn't hesitate. "It's a simple mistake, but a careless one. It should never happen on a PAC station. Ever."

"So you're saying that the person who did this shouldn't work on a PAC station?"

"Not in this capacity, sir, and not without significant supervision. Too many lives depend on meticulous accuracy."

Admiral Erickson nodded slowly. "I see."

Wren dared to take a peek at Justin. She wasn't used to talking to admirals. Should she have been less blunt? But she had no room for incompetence that put other people at risk. No, she'd said what she needed to. She'd have been remiss in her own duties if she'd sugarcoated it.

"Ms. Orritz, I understand you're on loan from Dragonfire Station. Is that right?"

"Yes, sir."

Was he going to send her back?

"I wonder if you'd consider a permanent transfer."

"Sir?" she asked in surprise.

"I like you. I like your record, your reputation, and that you won't back down from insisting on perfection. We need that here."

"Oh. Thank you, sir. That's quite an honor."

"Give it some thought," he prompted. "You're here for a few months yet anyway. Try to imagine yourself living here. Over the next weeks, you'll see Jamestown coming more and more alive, the way it's supposed to be. There will be a great many opportunities, and I want you to serve as a key part of our mechanical and engineering team."

"I will. Think about it. Thank you."

As she and Justin left, she let out a long breath. She'd never seen such a massive ops control. Dozens of people sat at consoles. Readouts and updates flashed on walls.

Everything on Jamestown was so big. She didn't feel overwhelmed by it, just awed. Impressed. She liked the idea of doing important work here.

She liked it more than she wanted to. She had a life and a personally-chosen family on Dragonfire. She should want to go back.

She didn't.

"Why the sad face? You should be thrilled. Admiral Erickson is not easily impressed." Justin gave her a friendly pat on the shoulder.

"I feel bad."

"Don't feel bad. It's okay to turn down a great offer because you already have something you already love."

She shook her head. "No, it's not that. This should be a hard choice, but it isn't. It's really clear to me that I want to stay here. And I feel bad because a lot of people are going to be sad when I don't go back to Dragonfire."

He slowed, then stopped in the middle of the corridor. He turned to face her. "Do these people care about you?"

"Of course."

"Then they'll understand that you're doing the best thing for you. They'll miss you, but there's the voicecom, and Dragonfire is close enough that you can visit regularly. By the time you're done fixing this place up, they'll be used to you being gone, anyway. It'll be okay."

They started walking again. "Yeah. I guess you're right."

Her guilt lifted. She felt good about this. About starting a new adventure and using her skills to contribute to the PAC. With all that was going on in the galaxy, they needed all the help they could get.

And if her absence on Dragonfire made it easier for a certain someone to move on with her life, then that was good, too.

They came to the conduit where they were to part ways and she paused. "If I'm going to be living here, I should start getting to know people better."

"Oh?" he smiled.

"Yeah. Usually I just poke food into my face on the run, but I can spare thirty minutes for dinner if you can. What do you say?"

"Sure. And a good friend of mine is returning to the station tomorrow. I'll introduce you, and then you'll officially have two friends on Jamestown."

As she headed back to her quarters, she felt alive. She had two friends and a new job.

It was a start.

Author Zen DiPietro

Zen DiPietro is a lifelong bookworm, dreamer, 3D maker, and writer. Perhaps most importantly, a Browncoat Trekkie Whovian. Also red-haired, left-handed, and a vegetarian geek. Absolutely terrible at conforming. A recovering gamer, but we won't talk about that. Particular loves include badass heroines, British accents, and the smell of Band-Aids.

Newsletter sign-up: http://www.zendipietro.com/subscribe-to-my-newsletter/

FUGITIVES' GAMBLE

By T.M. Catron

An imperial inspection, a pirate raid, and a spacewalk... and that's just before lunch. Captain Rance Cooper prefers being called *anonymous transporter* instead of *smuggler*, but the heiress-turned-fugitive has a knack for finding trouble. Stranded inside a battle zone, Rance must decide which is worse—turning herself over to the authorities for protection, or fighting off a horde of angry space pirates.

Chapter 1

Waystation 11's cafeteria was both disgusting and beautiful. Giant screens hovered above the crowd, flashing the sale of everything from exotic vegetables to the newest fashions to barely legal pets. The smell of cooking grease permeated the air and mixed with the smells of sweat and the slightly metallic tinge of filtrated air. Above the deck, a large domed observation window gave the central hub the feeling of being open to space.

The state-of-the-art space station was shaped like a flower, its arms unfurling around a centralized hub. Now that Captain Rance Cooper had seen it, she thought the structure looked more like an octopus than a flower.

Rance sat in the center of the cafeteria, craning her neck to watch the ships until she felt woozy, her grav boots propped on the chair opposite her. After more than five years of owning a space cruiser, Rance never tired of a star-filled view. For some people, space represented commerce and a fortune to be made. For others, fear of the unknown.

For Rance, space represented freedom.

"Captain, your boots are crushing the chair," Solaris said.

Rance peered over at her CO, who was carrying two trays of what looked like steaming, lumpy masses of goo. "You didn't find my acorn pie?"

"No," he said, nudging her boots off his chair with his knee. "They laughed at me for even asking. But you knew they would, didn't you?"

Rance grinned. "I had no idea."

Solaris shot her an amused look as he sat down. Today, his dark eyes and dark hair gave him a brooding quality—a far cry from the sandy colored hair and open, honest face he usually wore aboard the *Star Streaker*. Today, Rance envied Solaris' ability to change his look. Unable to alter her face on a whim, she wore a cap pulled down low over her eyes. Her brown hair, usually braided, hung down over her shoulders to hide her face from the security cameras.

"I wish you wouldn't clomp around in those boots, Captain." Solaris loved to tease Rance about her grav boots.

"I don't *clomp*. Never, in my entire history of wearing grav boots, have I ever *clomped*, Roote," she said, using his alias.

"Pardon me, your Ladyship. You traipse around in them magnificently."

"Don't call me that. That's what people call my mother. It makes me think she's standing behind me."

"You know, if the station loses gravity, you'll have more to worry about than floating along the corridors. You're likely to have other problems."

"Such as?" she asked, picking up her fork and poking it into the fleshy substance on her plate.

"A loss of atmosphere."

"Maybe I'll start walking around in my spacesuit as well."

"In that case, I'm giving my notice."

Rance glanced up. She knew Solaris was joking, but it wasn't the first time he had suggested leaving the *Star Streaker*. The ex-Galaxy Wizard was the best CO she'd ever had. Losing him would devastate the crew.

It wouldn't do Rance any good, either.

Sensing her unease, Solaris smiled reassuringly. Then, he dug into his food, a greasy mess of soggy greens and overcooked meat.

From across the table, Rance couldn't even decide what type of meat it was. Hers wasn't any better. It tasted like it looked—bland, fleshy goo that made her gag as it slid down her esophagus.

For a state-of-the-art facility, the Waystation's food services left much to be desired. Rance decided it was so that visitors would spend their imperial credits at the over-priced restaurants on the other levels.

A woman walked by in a long, flowing dress, draped in a heavy shawl and tall, feathery hat that made her look overbalanced. Rance used her Zeus Corporation Optical Display—the lens implant in her eye—to zoom in on the woman's hat. What she had thought were feathers were wisps of human hair styled and coerced into a fantastic shape. Rance snorted.

"You know," Solaris said as he watched the woman pass. "We made fun of our new partner, but we're the ones who look conspicuous."

The crew had laughed long and hard when they found out Rance was meeting a man wearing a blue cape. Now, with all the other ridiculous outfits aboard the station, their contact would fit right in among the permanent residents. In their flight suits and with Rance wearing her grav boots, she and Solaris looked all business, even starchy by comparison.

Solaris looked up while taking a sip of his drink. His mouth opened too widely, and he dribbled purple juice down his shirt.

Rance snorted. "I don't think that's the best way to fit in, Roote."

Solaris glanced around anxiously while dabbing his shirt with a napkin. "I think we've just been stranded here."

"What do you mean?"

"I mean, Captain," Solaris said, making a flying motion with his hand, "that our talented, vain pilot just flew away in the *Streaker*. Without us. Right by the window."

"What?"

Hoping Solaris was mistaken, Rance abandoned her food and ran out of the cafeteria in the direction he pointed. In the corridor, a large observation window provided a view of the giant asteroid beyond. There, shining in the light of a faraway blue star, was her space cruiser flying away from Waystation 11 as if pirates were chasing it. Rance craned her neck to see as much of the surrounding space as she could, just in case pirates *were* pursuing her ship.

The station's arms blocked some of Rance's view. Everything looked peaceful. Other ships continued to fly around the space station. None of them flew in irregular patterns or otherwise seemed in distress.

Solaris joined her at the window. He was four inches taller than Rance, who could touch the ceiling with her hand. They watched the *Star Streaker* turn into a tiny bronze speck.

"Why would James leave?" she asked.

Solaris sniffed. "I want to know why we can't make a simple run like any normal smuggling outfit."

A large freighter moved between the *Streaker* and the window, blocking Rance's view. *"Triton's beard,"* she swore.

Solaris grinned. "Did Triton have a beard?"

"I'm glad you find this amusing."

"You looked tense."

Rance sighed. "I am a little."

Humor was their default response, especially during times of stress. Despite Solaris' joking manner, he looked worried.

Rance's comm beeped. She scrambled for her old handset, which was showing James' face.

"What in the Founders' name do you think you are doing, James Fletcher?" Rance asked.

Usually cheerful, James' expression was now grim. A deep frown creased his face. Rance's gut did an uncomfortable flip-flop. Solaris peered over her shoulder.

"Captain," James said, "I tried to comm you before I left, but there was some kind of interference."

Rance's stomach flipped two more times. Whatever James was about to say wasn't going to be good.

"What is it?" Solaris asked. He moved instinctively around Rance, standing between her and the broad corridor, practically pushing her into a bulkhead. Rance waved him away. She didn't see a reason to hide behind the ex-Galaxy Wizard. Solaris wasn't her personal bodyguard.

"Unity is headed this way," James said.

"Triton's beard," Solaris repeated. He must have been thinking what Rance was thinking—both of them were wanted, for different reasons. Solaris had deserted the Galaxy Wizards, an elite and secretive branch of the Empire Triton's military. Rance was running from her powerful father and an arranged marriage back on her home planet of Xanthes.

If Unity inspected the Waystation, they could both be caught.

"The rest of the crew is with me," James was saying. "We couldn't contact you. And I didn't want any, uh, weird questions."

The *Streaker* had had too many close calls lately. Anyone looking for the sleek, bronze ship was bound to recognize it. For a moment, Rance regretted not purchasing a dull, inconspicuous freighter for her life on the run.

"Good call," Rance said. "But Solaris could have used his *talents.*" Afraid that station control was eavesdropping, Rance didn't dare mention that Solaris' "magic" could disguise an entire crew and ship.

"I thought he was still feeling drained after our last incident," James said, referring to their scare on Prometheus where pirates had invaded the planet.

Solaris nudged Rance. "How did you get out of trouble before you met me?"

It was his favorite question. Rance glanced up at him. He was right. She could take care of herself, had been doing so for years. What had she done before she hired Solaris? Had she been taking advantage of him?

"I was joking," he said, misreading her silence.

Rance frowned. "But you have a point. Okay, James, we'll see you later. A Unity inspection isn't a problem. Solaris, we need to find a shuttle."

"A shuttle sounds like a great idea, Captain," James said dryly. "You don't think you'll be noticed drifting out from the space station by yourself?"

"I appreciate your concern, James. Cooper out."

"As much as I hate to agree with James," Solaris said, "he has a point, Captain. What are we going to do with a shuttle if the *Streaker* isn't there to retrieve us?"

"Who said we were going to be on the shuttle? I only said that in case someone was eavesdropping."

Solaris nodded. "What is your real plan?"

"I haven't got that far yet. Any bright ideas?"

"The easiest one is the also the most difficult."

Rance raised an eyebrow.

"I could hide us, except James is correct. I don't have the energy to disguise us both."

"But you're hiding your own face right now."

"Barely. Disguising *you* is out of the question."

Rance snorted. "Why?"

"Because—"

The unmistakable sound of boots clomping down the hall echoed off the metal bulkheads. An overhead announcement asked everyone to cease movements and to be ready for an inspection.

***

Rance glanced at Solaris as they strolled down the hall, pretending they hadn't heard the announcement. "You seem tense."

"Aren't you?" he asked.

"Captain?" James' voice asked.

"Yes?" she whispered into the comm. "Why haven't you jumped into hyperspace?"

"I'm hiding in the station's shadow for the moment. The docks aren't the only exit."

"Oh?" Rance's hopes rose.

"There is a small, private airlock on the opposite side of the station that's used for visiting officials. Section D. Can you get there?"

Rance pulled up an overlay map of the station with her implant, the ZOD. The optical display showed her a map of all the public corridors and some of the private ones. James wasn't kidding—the private dock was exactly opposite from where she and Solaris were standing—back through the central hub.

"I think we can," she said. "But you'll have to give us time."

"Ah…" he said, distracted by something. "That shouldn't be a problem."

"Why?"

"Unity just spotted me. Radio when you're close. Fletcher out."

Be careful, Rance wanted to say, but James was already gone. Worry tugged at a place deep in her chest. James had evaded Unity Dark Fighters before, but how would he circle back to dock with the station now that they were on his tail? She pushed the thought to the back of her mind. They had to follow the plan.

Solaris' eyes were fixed on the end of the corridor. Three Unity soldiers stood there, blocking their exit. According to Rance's map, that was precisely the direction they needed to go.

"Of course," she muttered.

"I'll distract them," Solaris said. "You slide past and I'll catch up with you."

"How are you going to distract them?"

"I'll think of something."

"Wouldn't I be better at this?"

"Since I'm not the one who's in danger of being recognized, it makes sense that I do it."

"I don't need you to save me, Solaris. I want to be the hero once in a while."

"Now you get high and mighty? A minute ago you wanted me to disguise you with magic because it was easier."

"A minute ago, I didn't realize how much I take advantage of you."

"Er…" Solaris tore his eyes away from the guards to look at her. "You don't take advantage of me. I was *joking*."

Without waiting for a comeback, Solaris took off toward the guards. He was done arguing about who would save the day.

Irritated, Rance watched him go. She followed at a slower pace, ambling along as if she weren't in a hurry to be anywhere and merely taking a stroll. Solaris was talking to the guards now, angling so they were forced to turn their bodies away from Rance if they wanted to see him.

She hurried, trying not to let her heavy boots clomp on the metal floor. Her efforts were in vain, but she set each foot down as carefully as possible, wishing she'd listened to Solaris and worn softer shoes.

As Rance crept up behind the guards, Solaris chatted them up like they were old buddies.

"The Winged Dragons are doing well this year, don't you think?" he was saying. "It's been quite the comeback after Talbuck left."

Solaris was referring to spacesuit races—exciting games with teams using souped-up propulsion packs to race from one ship to another. The races were brutal, and participants often died. James had entered a race once, on a dare. Rance had barely been able to breathe until it was over.

One Unity soldier responded to Solaris. Rance slid behind the guards now, trying not to touch the nearest one, who had positioned himself close to the wall. She eased between his light armor and the metal bulkhead, careful not to kick him with her oversized shoes.

Solaris ignored her, keeping his eyes on the soldiers, not giving her away. The guards didn't seem too interested in him as a person of interest, just the race statistics now flowing out of his mouth.

Rance had just breathed a sigh of relief when one of the soldiers turned. She smiled, hoping to act like she was supposed to be there and not hugging the wall like the fugitive that she was.

"What are you doing?" the soldier asked. "Have you been scanned yet?"

"Yes," she lied. "We were the first, near the cafeteria observation deck."

Suddenly wary, the soldier angled himself so he could keep Solaris in sight, as well. "What are you doing here? The movement restrictions haven't been lifted."

"Oh?" she asked, feigning ignorance.

Solaris' eyes darted from her to the soldiers. He was deciding how best to knock them out if the need arose.

Even though Rance had seen Solaris take down armored soldiers with the foldable staff he carried in his satchel, she couldn't let him try now. What if he were too drained? And then, if he did succeed, what would they do? Where would they go? More soldiers would come after them.

"Check the logs," Rance said with a shrug. "You'll find us there."

The soldier muttered something, no doubt speaking into the comm built into his suit. Rance wanted some of those units for her crew. But other things like fuel and repairs and food had kept her from splurging on new equipment.

The soldier removed a scanner from his belt and flipped through a few options. "You don't mind submitting to another one, do you?"

He held the scanner up to her eyes.

Rance cringed inwardly, knowing it wasn't a request she could refuse. "Not at all." Out of the corner of her eye, she saw Solaris reaching behind to his satchel.

"Hold it," the other guard said.

Solaris and Rance froze.

The soldiers exchanged looks, and the first guard forgot the scanner in his hand. "Get somewhere and hide," he said suddenly. Then, the two soldiers turned and hurried down the hall.

Rance blinked in confusion, happy to have avoided a confrontation but puzzled about the abrupt change. She turned to Solaris. "Did you do something to them? One of your perception-altering tricks?"

"No, nothing. They must have got new orders."

More eager than ever to find James, they hurried down the hall. A terrible sense of urgency spurred them on. Something was wrong.

"Why do we always end up running?" Rance asked. "Why can't we have a normal meeting?"

"Do you want me to answer truthfully, Captain?"

"It was mostly rhetorical, *Roote*."

They ducked through an open door, finding themselves in a narrow corridor with doors staggered evenly down the hall. Mundane, bland artwork covered the walls. It looked like the

Waystation's version of a hotel. Using the map overlay, Rance followed a series of turns to take them to the other side of the station while avoiding the central hub. They only met a few people who hurried past without making eye contact.

Just as they had turned down a stark, ugly hall with heavy metal doors, Rance's ZOD glitched out. It happened occasionally. Ever since Rance had hacked it to keep her father from tracking her, it sent pixelated lines through her vision at the most inconvenient times—usually when she was running or escaping. Lately, she'd wondered if the glitch had something to do with her heart rate, which was always elevated when it happened.

Like it was now.

With a thought, she rebooted the chip. It didn't turn on. Frustrated, Rance paused, mentally retracing her journey through the space station. Signs would have helped, but they had entered a part of the station that didn't have any. Which meant they were in the crew-only area.

"Getting stopped here will invite awkward questions," Solaris said.

"We could pretend to be lost."

"There won't be much pretending."

Rance turned for the nearest door. It hissed open with a whoosh of cold air, bringing them out near another observation window. It faced the docks, higher up and farther away from the last time Rance had spotted them through the dome. A crowd had gathered. Rance and Solaris pushed their way to the front for a better view, gaining them some angry looks.

A blaze of yellow light shone from the docks. Rance's body grew cold with dread. There was only one thing that light could be from. She squinted, hoping she was wrong but knowing with a cold certainty that she was correct. There was a bright flash to the left, and the deck beneath them trembled. It could have been the hum of a generator, but it wasn't.

The docks were on fire.

Chapter 2

Two outer arms burned from within, their fires glowing yellow from the windows. Some of it escaped into space, snuffed out as it hit the vacuum like dozens of candles blown out over and over. Rance gasped. Had something happened to the *Streaker* as it flew away? Had James tried to evade Unity and caused an accident? Or worse, had they fired at him and caused him to crash into the station?

The floor vibrated again. "James?" she asked the comm.

No answer.

"James Fletcher, respond."

When James' face didn't show on the screen, Rance glanced fearfully at Solaris.

"Maybe communications have been disrupted," he said. "James said there was interference."

"Why though?"

More people ran up the halls, more whispered voices. Like the other two guards, the Unity soldiers were regrouping, ignoring the station's residents as they ran past. Rance and Solaris had just turned away from the window when an alarm sounded, blaring so loudly people covered their ears.

Abruptly, it cut off.

Then, all the screens lining the hallway flashed. Striking red text scrolled across them with a warning message. An announcement echoed through the station, using the pleasant voice of the station's AI.

"Attention, attention. We will accept your surrender. Lay down your weapons and line up along the walls. Attention, attention..." The message repeated over and over in that calm voice that chilled Rance to the bone.

"Pirates," Solaris said grimly. "The station is being attacked."

***

Rance groaned.

"Well, surrendering is out of the question," Solaris said.

"We've got to make contact with the *Streaker*," Rance said. She again attempted to raise James. Still no answer.

"Then we have to get to that airlock. If James can't get in touch with us, he'll meet us there."

Without the map, they had to guess based on their last known location. They ran past another giant observation window, this one providing a stunning view of the outer hull.

"Hey," Rance said, halting Solaris.

A distant star lit the space in front of them. Between it and the window, at least three enormous, repurposed Renegade ships had surrounded the station.

As they watched, ten Unity Dark Fighters shot toward the larger ships. Nimble Scorpion fighters—the pirates'—exited the ships to meet them. The UDFs fired together, taking advantage of the few precious seconds in which the pirates had lowered their shields to release their own fighters.

Blue and red streams of light streaked toward the first enemy ship—fire from the UDFs. They hit the Renegade in an explosion that lit up the entire stern.

Only one got through. The ship activated its shields, and the next blasts caused blue ripples as they impacted well away from their target's hull. Unable to continue a barrage against the Renegade's shields, the Unity fighters engaged the Scorpions that were now within range.

Rance and Solaris pressed their hands to the window, holding their breaths as the two groups of fighters quickly merged into a mass of flying metal that looked like flies buzzing around a corpse. But in this case, the body was the pirate ship, and it wasn't dead.

"I'm no fan of Unity," Rance said, "but I hope they blow those pirates into another dimension."

"They're overwhelmed," Solaris said. "Look."

The second Renegade had released its Scorpions, which were now entering the battle. One by one, Unity's fighters exploded into fiery flames, and the area became a mass of debris and chunks of metal. Without reinforcements from Triton to take up the fight, the pirates were going to take over the station. Rance fought the urge to throw up. A Unity inspection was inconvenient. A pirate invasion was worse.

As the last Unity fighter exploded into scrap metal, the Scorpions changed course for the Waystation. A shuttle launched from the Renegade, no doubt to ferry armored pirates to ransack the station.

"Why would they attack the docks where all the valuables are?" Rance asked. "They just blew up the most expensive part of the station."

"Maybe they're not here for goods," Solaris whispered as a few panicked residents ran by carrying valuables. "Slaves, maybe?"

One of the Scorpions broke formation and veered left, firing at something. A bronze mass flashed past their window, spinning away from the station. The pirate fighter streaked past it, firing at the other ship. Rance craned her neck to look.

It was the *Star Streaker*. The crew was alive.

She didn't know whether to jump for joy or grip Solaris' arm in panic. She settled for both. James Fletcher was the best pilot she'd ever known. But he wasn't a match for the twenty fighters now circling the station. The *Streaker* had shields but no weapons, which meant he could protect the ship for a time, but unless he got away, the Scorpions would kill him and everyone on board. If the pirates captured Rance's crew instead, she had no idea how they would rescue them. At least they would be alive *to* rescue.

The *Star Streaker* zipped by the window again, twisting around just in time to avoid a collision. The Scorpion's pilot barely copied the maneuver, almost sending it crashing into the observation window. Rance and Solaris jumped back.

Rance grabbed her handset. "James?"

"Rance?" James' voice sounded far away.

"What are you doing to my ship?"

"Oh, you know, a bit of casual flying. All in a day's work. We're all okay, by the way. For now."

"We can see you."

"Did you see my maneuver?"

"Yes."

"Something, huh?"

Solaris sniffed in disapproval.

"James," Rance said, "make the jump to hyperspace. We'll find another ship."

"No way am I leaving you to fend off pirates. We don't leave anyone behind."

"*I'm* the Captain, and I'm ordering you to get the rest of the crew to safe—"

"Hang on. I'm going to shake this pirate scum off my butt."

James put the *Streaker* through more twists, dodging more fire. Thankfully, the rest of the pirates didn't seem to think he was worth pursuing. *They* were too busy assaulting the station. The trembling continued, rattling the station's supports.

"Are they trying to break the station apart?" Rance asked. "What's the point of that?"

"Captain," James finally said as he swung by again. "They're concentrating on this side where the docks are located. Those other airlocks are still clear. There are no ships there, so I don't think the vermin are—"

James' voice cut off as the *Streaker* moved out of direct comm range. They lost sight of him.

"*Son of a bard*," Rance swore, meeting Solaris' worried eyes.

The *Star Streaker* flew by again, this time taking a direct hit from the fighter. The *Streaker* visibly shook. Rance bit her lip so hard it drew blood. How long would the shields hold?

James took the *Streaker* away from the station. He dove through the debris field floating between the station and the Renegades. More fire streaked toward the cruiser, pelting it in bright flashes of light as the shields deflected the hits. The fighter followed, blazing through the debris.

The *Star Streaker* banked left, toward the star, toward an opening between the two Renegades.

And, in a wash of blue, it disappeared into hyperspace.

***

"He got away! He got away!" Rance shouted. She hugged Solaris' neck in excitement.

"We've got to get to that airlock," he said, extricating himself. "The pirates haven't overrun the station yet. Now's our chance."

"No argument here."

The Waystation's AI continued to broadcast its warning message to line up and surrender. Rance turned and was surprised to see a crowd behind them watching the space battle. She had been too absorbed to hear them.

She grabbed Solaris, and they pushed their way through the crowd, watching behind to make sure they weren't followed. If anyone had heard about their plan, they could be stampeded when James arrived. Rance regretted sneaking off. But she resolved that anyone who wanted a ride—and didn't try to kill them for it—could have one. They'd pack as many people on the small cruiser as possible.

It wouldn't be enough. They couldn't save the whole station.

No one followed them, however. Maybe the crowd thought it was a hopeless cause. Or maybe they knew something Rance didn't. She shook off the thought and ran onward.

"James is going to have the same problem when he returns," Solaris said.

"Those Scorpions won't expect him to come back."

They wound their way through more corridors, getting lost twice and turned around once. There were too many turns, too many side halls wrapping around the central hub. Rance consoled herself that if they had this much trouble navigating the vast complex, so would the pirates. Finally, they entered a stretch that led directly toward their destination—a central corridor that wound the length of the station.

When Unity soldiers appeared at the end of the hall, Rance and Solaris ducked into the first door they found, an office entrance. They crouched beneath the window, listening to the soldiers run by on their way to the docks. Most of them were in light armor.

When they passed, Rance and Solaris left the office and ran in the opposite direction. The wall screens changed, and the AI's voice disappeared. A gruff man's voice replaced it. "Last chance to drop all weapons and surrender. Stand in the corridors and await instructions. If you run, we'll kill you. If you fight, we'll kill you. If you hide, we'll kill you. If you get lost in the bathroom, we'll kill you. Catch my drift? Main corridors, *now*."

Rance drew the stunner she had kept hidden under her jacket.

Solaris eyed it approvingly. "How did you sneak that in?"

"There's a special lining in my jacket that hides it from sensors. I don't wear it much, but after all the trouble we've had lately, it seemed like a good idea."

Solaris kept his hand on his frayed satchel, ready to grab his staff. Afraid of attracting too much attention, he wouldn't reveal the inconspicuous weapon unless absolutely necessary. The last thing they needed was for pirates or Unity to discover there was a stray Galaxy Wizard on board.

"I thought you were too drained to use your magic?" Rance asked between breaths.

"I am," Solaris said grimly. "But that won't stop me from whacking the pirates over the head."

Before long, the distant sounds of laser fire and explosions echoed down the halls. They turned several times, putting as much distance between themselves and the noise. Eventually, though, the sounds of fighting lay directly in their path.

Rance halted at an intersection. "We're close. Got to be. All of these halls are private quarters. We just have to find the one that leads to Section D."

Acrid smoke blew toward them. It smelled like burning rubber— sharp and overpowering.

"Looks like either direction will lead us where we need to go," Solaris said, peering down the corridor.

A stray laser beam shot down the hallway. Solaris jumped back, flattening himself to a bulkhead. Rance followed.

"How are we going to use that hall without getting shot? Could you use a shield?"

Solaris leaned his head back against the wall, closed his eyes, and sighed deeply. If Rance hadn't known any better, she would have thought he was overcome with an urge to nap.

Abruptly, Solaris opened his eyes. "Anything?" he asked.

"Erm... Was something supposed to happen?"

Solaris looked irked. "No sparks? Not even a shimmer in the air?"

"Nothing."

Solaris shrugged. "No shield. I'm too weak."

"We left Prometheus weeks ago. How long exactly does it take you to recharge?"

"I don't know. I've only ever been this drained one other time."

"What happened the last time?"

"I got knocked out and woke up in my Temple cell."

"*You* got knocked out? How?"

Two more stray laser beams shot past them. With them came the sounds of shouting and battle.

"By someone I'd rather not discuss right here," Solaris said. "What are our options?"

"We need to use that corridor. Otherwise, we'll need to find a new plan."

"If James is at the airlock, he's in danger. Since we can't contact him, we need to follow the original plan."

"I vote for the shortest distance between two points," Rance said, pointing. "Turning right will get us there faster."

"You don't have to vote, you're the captain."

"Thanks, I'd forgotten," she deadpanned.

Solaris smacked her arm. "Anytime."

He took off around the corner, hugging the wall. Rance followed. More and more blasts came their way. One sizzled by her ear, leaving behind the smell of singed hair—it was hers.

"It looks like they're fighting from opposite ends of the hall!" Solaris yelled over the noise.

The smoke was so thick now that Rance covered her nose and mouth with her hand. "Which are the pirates, and which is Unity?"

"Pirates are this way," he said, jerking his thumb in the direction they were going.

Rance pulled up short. "How will we get past them?"

The rate of fire increased as the two forces drew closer. They were going to clash in the very hall Rance and Solaris needed to get to the airlock.

"They'll shoot us down before we get anywhere close," Solaris said.

"Then we'll go back the other way."

They hadn't gone five minutes when they glimpsed a Unity armored soldier. He spotted the pair the same moment they noticed him, and he fired. Rance and Solaris jumped out of the way, their hearts pounding.

"Looks like Unity will shoot us down before we get anywhere close to *them*," Rance said bitterly. "They're supposed to protect the innocent."

"How innocent are we, exactly?"

"More innocent than the pirates."

They huddled behind a bulkhead, but the soldier didn't pursue. Either he thought they were a trap or realized his error. He seemed to be waiting for reinforcements.

"They'll mow us down before they realize we're not pirates," Solaris said after another long moment of return fire. Smoke began to hang in the air, obscuring their visibility.

"Agreed," Rance said. "But the pirates are that way."

"There's got to be another route."

"This is the only one. We've gone too far to go back!"

The two sides began firing at each other in earnest now, closing in, shooting from behind doorways and bulkheads.

Rance and Solaris had ended up in the battle zone, and if they didn't get out of the way, they'd end up dead. Stray fire whizzed by so close they felt the air move as it passed. All the doors nearest them were locked, and the intersection they had come from was now overrun by pirates.

They were so close that Rance could see the scars on their armor. The smoke was the only thing keeping her and Solaris alive. Neither army wanted to take their eyes off the enemy long enough to deal with two civilians caught in the crossfire.

"Captain," Solaris yelled into her ear. "There is another option!"

"Anything to get us out of here!"

"We could turn ourselves in to Unity."

"What?"

"They'll turn you over to your father and send you home, but at least you'll be safe."

Shocked, Rance met her friend's eyes. For someone suggesting a lifesaving tactic, Solaris looked conflicted.

"You want me to jump out and yell *don't shoot! Lord Davos is my father*?"

"That would work."

"We could fight the pirates."

Solaris scoffed. "With what?"

"Your good looks! I don't know. Help me out here."

"I am helping you out."

"What would happen to you?"

"I'd go back to the Galaxy Wizards."

"Is that what you really want?"

A rocket whizzed past them, exploding far down the corridor. The explosion was small but effective. The pirates began to retreat.

Solaris took advantage of the brief moment without fire to look toward the Unity soldiers. "At this point, it's not about what I want. If the pirates capture us, they'll kill us or make us slaves. Turning ourselves in to Unity has a better outcome."

Rance looked down the hall. He was right. The unit was so close she could make out the ranks on their armor. All she had to do to end their predicament was turn herself in.

Home. Back to dust and politics and a nobility she didn't want. No more running the stars. No more *Star Streaker*.

And an arranged marriage to a simpering buffoon back on her home planet of Xanthes.

Rance took a deep breath and looked back at Solaris. "I can't do that. My home is on the *Streaker*."

Solaris frowned. "I was afraid you'd say that."

"You aren't going to do something stupid and try to make me, are you?" Rance asked, narrowing her eyes.

He flashed her a smile. "I know better."

"Okay, then," she said, forcing a smile. "Pirates it is."

Chapter 3

Without waiting for her brain to catch up to her heart, Rance sprinted down the corridor, darting from one bulkhead to the next. Solaris followed. More fire chased them. Unity's weapons had auto-targeting systems, but the smoke made them less accurate. As soon as the first bolts passed, the pirates fired back, forcing Unity to find their own cover.

Hindered by her grav boots, Rance jumped over rubble and a couple of bodies. She was amazed that all the explosions hadn't breached the station's hull. Even a state-of-the-art facility couldn't sustain such abuse indefinitely. If the structure failed, the armored soldiers with their built-in life support systems could survive. Rance and Solaris, however, would be sucked out into the vacuum of space without protection.

"How many are there, you think?" Rance asked as they pressed themselves to the wall.

"At least ten pirates. But I bet reinforcements are on the way."

"You can fight armored soldiers, I've seen you."

Solaris shook his head. "Too many."

Rance studied their surroundings. Three doors around them. All the keypads glowed red—locked. Smoke swirled near the ceiling, sucked into a vent above. The station was doing a miraculous job of eliminating the toxic air.

"Hey," Solaris said, looking at the same place. "The ventilation shafts—if we get up there, we can bypass both sides and take them all the way to the airlock."

"How do we get up there?"

Solaris looked at her boots. "Walk up."

"*Walk*? Are you nuts, I'd dangle from the ceiling like a bat. I can't crawl up."

"No, these always have intake shafts. If we find one, you can crawl up it."

"What about you?"

"I don't think I'll fit. I'll find a maintenance ladder."

"We're both inhumanly tall, Solaris. What makes you think I would fit?"

Solaris bristled with annoyance. "Just trust me on this, okay?"

"Okay," she said.

Solaris nodded and slid farther down the corridor until he reached a panel. He pried at the latch until it burst open and clattered down to the floor.

"Hurry," he said.

"Where are you going?"

"I'll manage. Hurry."

Rance stuffed herself into the shaft feet first. It was like trying to shove her body into a locker. With her hands on the wall and her boots engaged, she shimmied up a short tube until it opened into a larger one above the corridor.

As soon as her head cleared the shaft, the heated airflow whipped her hair around her face, buffeting her body. If she'd been standing, it would have knocked her down.

Rance waited a minute for her eyes to adjust to the semi-darkness. White light filtered into the tube from evenly spaced vents. The sounds of the battle below grew louder. She pulled herself onto her stomach and slid along the warm metal, following the direction that would take her toward the pirates. Hopefully, they hadn't blown a hole in the ceiling and blocked her way. The tube shook with regularity, and she expected the station to break apart at any second. Her growing anxiety only compounded when she wondered how Solaris planned to get through the turmoil below. There had to be a maintenance walkway outside, but access would be limited. Was he going to use that?

A few minutes later, something blue blocked her path. For a moment, Rance got excited. Solaris had been wearing his blue flight suit.

But it wasn't Solaris. It was draped, royal blue fabric—a blanket?

Then, the blanket moved.

Rance halted. "Hello?"

A man lifted the blanket to peer at her through watery eyes. She drew her stunner.

"Hey!" he said, holding up his hands.

It wasn't a blanket—the man was wearing a cape. Her contact. Rance shook her head at the irony. Unfortunately, this wasn't the time for business deals.

A hatch banged open above them, metal on metal clashing. Rance jumped, bumping her head on the top of the tube. Someone had found the adjacent maintenance shaft. Was it Solaris? She signaled the man to be quiet.

"You're wearing a blue flight suit and a cap," the man said.

She glared at him angrily, listening. At least two voices grew louder. Not Solaris, then.

"They're looking for me," the man continued as if he hadn't seen her.

"Shut up!" Rance hissed.

"I don't know how they ended up at Waystation 11, but if they find me, they'll kill me very slowly. Kaur promised."

Pirate Kaur? Rance thought, shocked. How did this small-time smuggler get on Kaur's radar?

"I figured out who you are," he said, smiling mischievously. "Looked you up. I'll bet my right arm that you're Devri, sole heir to the House of Davos."

Surprised at this announcement, Rance pointed her stunner at him. "Not. One. More. Word," she whispered. The man was correct, of course. How he'd discovered her real identity was anybody's guess. It disturbed Rance that he'd identified her so quickly. It also upset her that the voices on the other side had quieted.

"If I turn you in," the caped man said, "they'll nab you and leave me."

"You filthy double-crosser!" Rance hissed.

"No honor among thieves."

"I'm *not* a thief. I prefer anonymous transporter."

"Hey!" the man yelled, pounding on the top of the tubing.

Rance realized too late that she was laying just below an access panel. Boots on the outside ran for it. The caped man kept pounding.

Without another warning, Rance stunned him.

***

The bolt hit the smuggler, sizzling around his body for a long moment. He seized up, then slumped to the floor. Feeling guilty for leaving the man to his fate, Rance squeezed past him as something hit the access panel from the outside. The smuggler's eyebrows twitched, but he was out cold.

Her heavy boots scraped along the metal. No matter how she tried to soften her movements, the boots gave away her position like a built-in tracking device. She sighed, resigning herself to the inevitable. Flipping the releases, she removed her boots and set them against the wall.

Without the cumbersome boots, Rance crawled faster, past a ladder access. The main ventilation shaft was the only one big enough for her, so she couldn't make a wrong turn. She hoped it went all the way to the end of the corridor, but she noted the presence of the ladder in case she got stuck.

Another explosion rocked the station, so close that Rance's teeth rattled. The metal trembled, the vibration tickling her body. Within a minute, smoke began to waft through the shaft.

Below, an alarm sounded.

"Perfect," she muttered.

A metal bang sounded close by, followed by the sounds of a person climbing the ladder. Rance pointed her stunner behind her, ready to defend herself. A mop of dark hair appeared, then a face.

"Solaris," she said in relief. "Fancy meeting you here."

He smiled. "Good timing."

More people ran through the maintenance walkway to the right. Boots struck metal decking below. Everything echoed strangely, mixing with the wind in an overwhelming assault on Rance's ears.

"I'm worried this tunnel will narrow as we get closer to the end," Rance said as they crawled along.

"Not for a while yet," Solaris said from behind her.

"You say that like you've done this before."

"It's possible."

"Galaxy Wizards must live exciting lives."

"As I've told you, life aboard the *Star Streaker* comes in at a close second."

"That's not a competition I'm hoping to win. This smoke is getting worse. The filtration system must not be able to keep up. I wish they would stop exploding things down there. They're going to blow a hole in the station."

"Mmhmm," Solaris said noncommittally.

"Wait, did *you* cause that explosion?"

"It was carefully calculated to *not* blow a hole in the station."

"Solaris!" she said, ready to scold.

Rance brought herself up short. She happened to be lying over the top of a sheer mesh intake. Between the layers of filters, she saw five people below. Since they all looked alike in their heavy battle armor, it was hard to tell if they were men or women. However, it wasn't hard to figure out that they all bore the slashed flag insignia of the Pirate Kaur on their arms.

One of the pirates stood in the center. His suit was larger than the others', and they seemed to defer to him. He must have been the commander.

Rance held her breath, worried that any moment those expensive armored suits would detect her and Solaris with their sensors. The pirates angled toward one another as if they were talking, but since they were using a private—and likely encrypted—comm channel, she couldn't hear what they were saying.

Solaris eased up beside her, cramming in until they were side by side. When he saw the pirates below, he started and tried to pull Rance back. She shook her head. They needed to move forward, not back. And anyway, she was now wedged in so tight with Solaris that scooting backward was next to impossible.

Who is it? she mouthed.

Kaur, Solaris mouthed back.

That's Kaur? Rance pointed emphatically down through the mesh.

Solaris nodded.

A thrill rippled through Rance's spine and caused the hair on her neck to stand up. Pirate Kaur was the most feared pirate in the galaxy.

What is he doing here? Rance asked.

Solaris shrugged.

They watched the group below, who had seemed to stop talking and were waiting for something.

A thousand questions ran through Rance's mind, and she recalled everything she knew about the Pirate King. None of it was pleasant. Kaur famously hated technology but always possessed the finest. His ship, the *Star Wraith*, was an enormous mining vessel repurposed as a base of operations. It was rumored to be booby-trapped throughout. And he employed cyborgs, who he sometimes fed to his giant half lizard, half dog creature.

Kaur's presence aboard the space station was disturbing. If this were a typical raid, why would he bother to be here? He personally led his pirate hordes only when they needed his expert military guidance.

The large pirate in the middle removed his helmet, showing the face Rance knew from wanted bulletins. Kaur had dark hair and olive skin. Large veins bulged in his neck, snaking their way down under the collar of his suit. The other pirates removed their helmets too.

By this time, Rance wasn't breathing at all. Luckily, Kaur's suit hadn't sounded a warning about spies watching from above. She wondered why not. Even with the air whipping through the tunnel, the sensors should have detected their body heat. Maybe they couldn't read it through the mesh.

Rance looked at Solaris, ready to give him a questioning look. When she saw his face, she knew why Kaur hadn't found them.

Solaris' eyes were closed in concentration, his face had turned pale, and he breathed through his nose as if he were meditating. He must have been employing some sort of invisible shield. Rance grew angry. Solaris was expending all his strength for this, and that meant he would be too drained later to escape if they ran into trouble.

She nudged him, breaking his concentration. Solaris shot her an alarmed look and wiped the sweat trickling down his face. As soon as he did, his shield must have broken because the sounds below suddenly became louder. The movements of the pirates walking back and forth along the corridor, the distant explosions, and the rush of wind up through the mesh as the air was finally allowed through.

Unfortunately, the pirates were no longer conversing, so Rance couldn't satisfy her curiosity about why they were there.

Rance and Solaris pulled themselves forward. When they had escaped further down the shaft, they paused to catch their breaths.

"Solaris," Rance hissed. "I don't want to have to carry your butt out of here. As your captain, I forbid you using your powers until you have recovered!"

"Please take more than just my butt. I'm rather attached to it."

Rance glared at his joke.

He smiled. "Next time, I'll let them catch us."

"There won't be a next time. We're almost there. If only we could contact the *Streaker*." Rance again tried to raise James, but all she got was silence. What if the ship had been captured?

They crawled a few more yards until they reached the last access. The metal plate above it said *Section D*. Taking care to be silent, they climbed down the ladder. Rance's stockinged feet slipped over the rungs, forcing her to slow her descent so she didn't fall. At the bottom, they pried the panel open.

The hall was empty. Gleaming surfaces and expensive artwork covered everything. The screens here displayed beautiful images, not the annoying ads in the rest of the station. They didn't even have the invasion message displayed across them. Doors were spaced far apart, not crammed together. They had definitely reached the more opulent quarters, the ones for visiting dignitaries and wealthy residents.

The smoke was thicker here, but not unbearable. Rance couldn't believe their luck. As long as the *Star Streaker* was at the airlock, they could be gone in a few minutes.

They hurried down the corridor, which curved around to the left. It bothered Rance that they couldn't see far ahead, but they hugged the wall, hoping not to rush headlong into trouble.

As they rounded the last curve, their luck ran out.

The airlock was straight ahead, set into the left wall. In front of it stood five armored pirates guarding the door. Stacks of crates lined both walls. All of the pirates were armed, and all of them stared straight at Rance and Solaris.

***

The pirates recovered quickly from their initial surprise. Rance and Solaris darted back around the curve as the first fiery bolts flashed by. They ricocheted off the walls, leaving trails of scorch marks on the pristine, shining metal.

Rance slipped, her stockinged feet sliding out from under her. She hit the deck hard as more bolts flew over her head. Solaris reached for Rance as she scrambled to her feet. They ducked into the first door they found unlocked.

Opulent, plush furnishings, real wood panels, and expensive carpets filled the room. Solaris watched the screen next to the door displaying security feed from a camera just outside. "I don't think they followed."

"They were guarding that airlock," Rance said, nursing her bruised elbow. "They must be under orders not to leave it."

"James won't be there."

Another distant explosion rattled expensive decor on a shelf. A sinking feeling of dread ran down from Rance's burning lungs to her gut. "Any ideas?"

"We could always turn ourselves in. That's still on the table."

"Pirate Kaur is in the way, remember? Do you think we could get through the ventilation shaft a second time?"

"It's our best bet."

"And then where? How would we even find Unity and approach them without being shot?"

Solaris turned to give Rance his full attention. "You're actually considering it?"

"No, but you brought it up, so I'm telling you why it won't work."

"We could hide here."

"And be in even worse shape when either Unity or Kaur wins this skirmish. Once they have control of the station, getting to the *Streaker* will be next to impossible. Right now, they are distracting each other."

Solaris' eyes twinkled in amusement.

"What?"

"You would rather fight off a horde of angry space pirates and run through a battle zone than go back to Xanthes." It was a statement, not a question.

Rance's walked over to stand on the soft rug and warm her cold feet. "I don't know how we will do much fighting. My stunner and your staff aren't a match for mechanized armor."

Solaris straightened. "I have an idea, though. It'll work if we hurry."

He looked at the screen showing the empty hall and then reached for the button to open the door.

"Hang on," Rance said. "I need to borrow some shoes."

Five minutes later, they crept back down the corridor away from the airlock, toward Pirate Kaur. Rance couldn't decide which was more insane—battling five armored pirates, or their plan *before* the battle. She wore a pair of too-small boots that pinched her feet, but they were all she could find. And they were better than sliding around the floors in her socks.

Ahead, a pirate guarded the hall facing away from them, alone and alert. Rance and Solaris hid behind a bulkhead, away from his cameras. Finding a guard had been relatively easy. The pirates had cleared this corridor, so the guard wasn't expecting to have to fight anyone from behind.

Solaris had his staff in hand, unfolded. It was made of dull brown metal unadorned by any symbols or insignia. He had insisted he wouldn't use magic to surprise the pirate, but Rance couldn't see how he would accomplish that.

"He's fairly tall," Rance whispered. "You should be able to squeeze into his armor."

Solaris eased out from the bulkhead, but Rance grabbed him. "No. I'll distract him."

Solaris shook his head.

"That's an order, sunshine."

Rance held her stunner tight in her hand as if it would do any good against the pirate's armor. She ran across the corridor to the opposite bulkhead.

The guard spotted her immediately. He turned and fired, red bolts sizzling past Rance's shoulders as she sought cover. The guard's suit carried him to her faster than Rance had anticipated. She hadn't taken more than a breath before he loomed over her, his laser rifle pointed at her chest.

"Don't shoot!" she said, holding up her hands, gun included. Her heart beat frantically.

The pirate made an exaggerated look up and down as if he were checking her out. Rance fought the urge to roll her eyes. What was Solaris doing—taking a break? Shouldn't he have clobbered the scumbag by now?

As if remembering orders, the pirate stopped ogling. His finger twitched near the trigger.

"Wait!" Rance said, desperate to stall him from blowing a hole in her chest. "I'm Lord Davos' daughter."

The guard drew up slightly. "Then he's about to make funeral arrangements." His voice was deep, a trick perhaps of the suit's speakers.

"There's a bounty on my head. I swear by the Founders. Davos will pay good credits for me delivered to him alive and unharmed, no questions asked. The reward is enormous. Trust me," she said, trying to be casual while staring down the barrel of the rifle, "I would turn myself in for it if I thought I could get away with it."

"Any other day," he said, "and I might consider that offer. Today, the Pirate King says no prisoners."

A chill ran through Rance as she thought of the *Streaker*. If that were the case and it had been damaged, the pirates would have killed her friends rather than take them aboard their ships as bounty.

Out of the corner of her eye, Rance caught a glimpse of something swinging through the air. It whacked the pirate on the neck with a resounding crack. The pirate grunted, shifted left. Rance ducked, and not a moment too soon. He fired, so close that she felt the heat skim over her body and ruffle her hair. The wall behind her exploded in a shower of sparks.

Solaris had planned to take down the pirate with one swipe of his staff. He had missed the critical spot, though, and now engaged the pirate in a dance around the corridor. The pirate was experienced, and with the suit he was fast. Solaris dodged him, barely getting out of the way as the guard fired again. Rance took the opportunity to aim her stunner at his helmet. She fired, watching the sparks with satisfaction. It didn't do anything to the suit, but it distracted the pirate for a half-second. Solaris seized his chance and whacked the pirate's armor again.

This time he struck gold. The suit paused in mid-swing, its left arm extended toward Solaris, its right still holding the rifle. Solaris had disabled the suit with a simple touch. Rance had never quite figured out how he managed to do this. Something to do with hidden weaknesses.

"The armor will lock him inside," she warned.

"Nope, I took care of that," Solaris said. Sweat trickled down his face. He was expending valuable energy just doing simple tasks. Rance hoped he had something left for the next part of their plan.

Between the two of them, Rance and Solaris hauled the cursing, spitting pirate out of the suit. With another well-placed *tap*, Solaris knocked him out cold before he could hurt them. After that, removing the pieces was tedious but not difficult. The tension grew with every passing minute. Any second, someone could check on the guard after he failed to report in. The more pieces they removed, the more they realized that they had a growing problem.

"I can't fit," Solaris finally admitted.

Rance looked over at the unconscious pirate, who was shorter than either one of them had expected. The armor was custom fitted, designed to make him look taller. Whoever tried to put it on would have to cram inside. At least four inches taller than Rance, Solaris would never fit. The plan had been for him to wear the armor, wielding his staff at the same time. It would make him more powerful and allow him to use his magic for a few moments longer. Solaris' job was to clear a path for Rance, who would commandeer whatever ship was docked at the airlock. Now, they would have to alter the plan.

Rance took a deep breath and began putting on the pieces. She placed them over her clothes, not bothering that they would crumple inside and cause chafing later. Solaris helped her, and within ten minutes she was suited up.

The armor was too small for her, too, and her shoulders pressed painfully into the padded suit. It stank of the pirate's sweat. The rest of the suit was ill-fitted to her body. It had been made for a man, and all the joints were out of sync with Rance's own. Mercifully, she didn't plan to wear it long.

When she put on the helmet, all other noises were muffled. The helmet's neuroreceptors cradled her head and dug into her hair. Solaris gave the armor another tap. With it, the suit powered on, turning on a heads-up display that was just as good as the one in her eye—except this one worked. The cameras were a perfect complement to the HUD. They cycled through the views, and Rance was able to take control of them quickly.

She hadn't worn armor in years and had never owned any of her own. But, she'd trained in it at the Flight Academy, Unity's prestigious school on Xanthes. Rance smiled at Solaris through the visor. "Guess I'll have to protect you now, huh?"

Solaris grunted and nodded down the hall.

The suit exaggerated all of Rance's movements, making her quick and powerful, able to punch a hole in a door if needed. She cycled through her options, hoping to catch a hint of what was going on in other parts of the station. Mostly all she heard through the comm were coordinates and orders to march. A few reports of taking over part of the docks.

"The pirates have reached the docks," she said.

"Then Unity is losing ground. Surrendering to them might not have been the right call, after all."

Rance sniffed. "Well, we knew that anyway. At the airlock, we can count the enemies. Better than an unknown number at the docks."

"And do you plan to commandeer Kaur's own vessel? Because I have a feeling those guards are protecting his personal transport, which I *bet* is docked on the other side of that airlock."

Rance shot Solaris a look. "If we must. Just long enough to get us to the *Streaker*. Let me handle it, okay?"

Solaris muttered something which she couldn't quite catch. It sounded like an oath. Ignoring him, Rance took off at a run, wishing to draw the fire to herself. Her current plan—to surprise them with a berserker-like attack—scared the fire out of her. Rance knew she could be impetuous, but this was the most suicidal thing she had ever attempted. Pushing aside her misgivings, Rance charged forward, ignoring the pain the suit caused in her body.

At first, the guards at the airlock didn't react when Rance charged around the corner. She used this to her advantage, firing on them before they had a chance to realize she was the enemy. Rance leaped into the air, and in her suit it felt like flying. She came down in the middle of the pirates, scattering them as they scrambled to gather themselves for defense.

When the pirates opened fire, Rance didn't feel the hits, but a small alarm went off in her suit as it displayed damage reports. She swung at the closest attacker, barreling into the suit next to her with a jolt that shook her teeth even through the cushioned lining. They crashed down together as more fire erupted. Rance desperately hoped it was all directed at her and that they hadn't discovered Solaris.

She rolled, pulling the other suit in front of her as a shield. The pirates didn't hesitate to fire on their own man, and her captive cursed as his armor absorbed heavy fire.

They listened, pulling him off of Rance. She hopped to her feet, overshot her intended landing spot, and smacked into the wall. The suit bounced off, and Rance swung around only to find herself surrounded by five angry pirates. They leveled their weapons at her like a firing squad and opened fire.

Blazes of light hit her helmet, blinding her. The visor darkened automatically as more alarms went off. Rance, afraid to fire down the corridor in case she struck Solaris, used her suit's power to barrel her way through.

Another suit latched onto her. It was scorched black all down the front—the pirate she'd used as a shield. Knowing the suit had taken hard damage, she fired at point blank range. The man grunted, trying to get away from her assault.

Her suit's alarm became more insistent. The display that showed damage turned red. The other pirates were going to shred her to bits.

Rance pivoted, swinging wide. A blade popped free on her left arm, accidentally triggered by her inexperience. Rance swiped it through the air. The other pirates ducked. With a lucky swipe, she caught a man's rifle and sent it flying. It arched through the air, flying to land atop the metal crates stacked to the side.

With a start, Rance saw Solaris standing up there. He ignored the rifle and wielded his staff like a bat. Since the pirates had been too busy trying to bring Rance down, they hadn't noticed him creep up there. He struck the first two on the neck before they realized they had another enemy. Rance seized her opportunity to attack the closest pirate.

He swore as she sent his rifle spinning. Then, Rance's luck began to turn as her berserker strategy no longer surprised her enemies. The pirate dodged the blade on her arm and ejected one of his own.

They squared off as the other two pirates fired at Solaris.

Rance heard Solaris return fire. He must have decided to use the rifle, after all. One of the pirates hopped up on the crates to catch him. Lights flashed back and forth as Solaris tried to evade him.

Rance trained a camera on him but had to keep her attention focused on the pirate who now slashed expertly at her suit. His blade began to glow—it had a thermite edge, an upgrade her suit didn't have. With one blow, it severed Rance's blade in half. The impact jolted her arm all the way to the shoulder.

Rance backed away and fired, but her ammunition was running low, and there were still three—one went flying, blown backward by Solaris' blue shield—no, two pirates left. One was trying to disembowel her. The other was trying to reach Solaris, who was defending himself from behind the crates.

Rance jumped away from the glowing blade, but the pirate pushed her back toward the airlock, cutting off her escape. She swung with her severed sword, and it hit the thermite edge with a shower of sparks. Another chunk of her blade flew down the hall, hacked off by her opponent's sword. If she could evade it long enough, the thermite would burn out.

She just had to stay out of reach long enough.

Rance fired at the pirate's visor, emptying her magazine of its remaining ammunition, hoping to momentarily blind him. When it emptied, she leaped upward, sailing over his head. The pirate reached up with lightning reflexes.

The thermite wasn't glowing as hotly now, but Rance felt it hit the suit. It sliced right through the armor at her hip. Hot searing pain ran down her leg, and then she landed in a heap. Unwilling to give him another opening, Rance jumped up, only to feel unbalanced and wobbly. All of the suit's displays had turned red. Her left leg wasn't working correctly. She looked down at the gaping hole at the top of the leg joint. It burned like she'd fallen into hot plasma, but the suit had taken the majority of the damage.

It had saved her leg, but its response was now sluggish as if the armor had gone to sleep from the hip down.

The glow of thermite vanished, and the pirate ejected the spent blade. He attacked, ready to punch her into the next galaxy. Rance didn't have any doubts about his intentions—if she didn't fight back, the pirate would kill her. Crippled by her frozen leg, she swung around, still able to rotate with lightning reflexes of her own. The small weapon on her right arm opened fire, and she concentrated on the already smoking bits of the pirate's helmet.

Rance's suit scrambled to compensate, shifting all its weight to one leg. The other dragged along like an anchor scraping the bottom of the sea, pulling her back.

The pirate slammed into her, his first punch sending Rance backward into a free fall. Unable to get her good leg under her in time, she fell to the deck. The pirate jumped on top of her, ramming his armored fist into her helmet over and over again. The blows rattled Rance's teeth as the suit tried to absorb the violence.

The visor cracked, sending wavy lines through her HUD. Rance punched back, trying to do as much damage to him as he was doing to her. She landed blows in his kidneys, feeling the armor give way a little more each time.

But she was at a disadvantage. Her blows didn't match the pirate's. Desperate to get away before the pirate broke through her visor and used her face as a punching bag, Rance tried to heave him off. Her suit wouldn't respond. And with the added weight of the armor, she couldn't stand on her own.

Finally, her visor shattered. She winced as shards of plastic bit into her face. The pirate grabbed the rim of the helmet and hauled her forward, holding her up by the helmet. With the HUD and cameras out, she couldn't see anything but the leering, angry face above her, ready to kill. Rance grabbed his arms, sending her remaining power to her fingers and squeezing. He jerked away, one arm pulled back for the killing blow.

The pirate's visor flickered, then turned dark. For a moment, Rance wondered why he wasn't killing her.

382

With a loud thwack and then a shove, Solaris was there, bleeding from his head and hand. A burn mark scorched his bicep. With the little bit of power left in her suit, Rance helped Solaris shove the disabled pirate off of her.

The five pirates lay on the floor, scattered at awkward angles. Weapons and debris littered the narrow hallway between the crates. More explosions echoed down the hall.

The airlock was free.

Solaris sniffed. "I wanted to let you handle it because that's what you told me to do, Captain, but I didn't think you'd mind me stepping in this one time."

Rance was so happy, she wrapped her armored arms around Solaris and hugged him. He grunted, and she pulled back, remembering she could snap his ribs like they were toothpicks. Rance pulled away and feigned indifference. "I had that pirate right where I wanted him."

Solaris raised an eyebrow. "Of course you did."

Since Rance's suit was damaged beyond any kind of usability, she removed it, wincing as it peeled off a sizable, angry burn on her hip.

"You were lucky," Solaris said.

"Not as lucky as you. How did you get away from that one?" Rance asked, pointing at the pirate who had cornered Solaris atop the crates. He had smashed into the opposite wall and landed head first on the deck.

"I managed a shield to hold against the wall. It was puny, but enough to deflect his laser rifle—amazing what you can do when death is imminent. He threw a grenade at me. I saw it and threw it back." Solaris smiled. "That got him."

"I didn't even feel the grenade. I need to get one of these," Rance said, pointing to the battle armor.

"With your luck, you need it."

The unmistakable sounds of battle drew closer. More shouts. More boots pounding up and down the halls.

"I thought the pirates had pushed Unity to the docks," Rance said, looking at the airlock and wondering what they would find on the outside.

"I thought so, too. Maybe Unity forced the pirates back."

Then, a violent rocking jolted Rance and Solaris against the airlock door. Popping sounds and groans filled the air. Another alarm went off.

Panic shot through Rance. It sounded like the station was breaking apart. She looked around wildly for anything that might help them. Solaris had grabbed two rifles from the deck and was checking their magazines.

Rance's gaze fell on a closet that held space suits. "Hey, Solaris," she said, opening the doors. "I've found our way out."

Chapter 4

"This is suicide," Solaris said as he pulled on the grav boots.

The station rocked again, and he almost lost his balance.

Rance inspected her new helmet. "It doesn't sound like we have a choice. The station could lose life support at any moment. Do you think the pirates mean to destroy it?"

"Who knows?" Solaris asked. "They don't hesitate to destroy cities, so I imagine a space station is inconsequential to them."

They checked each other's suits to make sure all the seals were secured. Rance had just put on her helmet and given Solaris a thumbs up when the first red bolt shot down the hall and hit the wall between them.

They ducked. Solaris punched the button for the door, and the airlock opened up to them. More red bolts flew in and hit the door on the opposite side. When Rance looked down the hall, fear flashed through her body.

Pirate Kaur ran down the hall, followed by at least ten pirates.

He roared and fired again. Rance realized he wasn't trying to hit *them*, but the keypad that operated the outside door. Was he trying to trap them inside, or send them out into the void beyond? She and Solaris ducked inside and hit the button. The inner door hissed closed as more fire ricocheted underneath. They backed out of the way, not wishing to damage their space suits.

The door shut with a final bang. Rance punched the buttons to cycle the air out of the chamber. "Did we just put ourselves on Kaur's ship?"

384

"No," Solaris said, peering out the small outside window. "The ship is gone. Maybe the pilot left while we were battling the guards outside."

"Which means we're spacing ourselves."

"Looks like it."

The inner door locked. Pirate Kaur's face appeared in the window, angry and terrible. He couldn't open the door now that the sequence had begun to cycle out the air. Rance got the impression he was studying her face for the future. She was unwilling to turn her back on him yet knew that he would never forget the woman who had bested five of his armored pirates. Rance slapped a hand on the glass in defiance.

"Yes, make him angrier, Captain," Solaris said dryly, watching Kaur's eyes turn deadly cold.

"He's a bully."

"A powerful bully."

Kaur watched Solaris too, and recognition flashed in his eyes. Alarmed, Rance looked at Solaris, whose face had grown grim.

The outer door hissed open. Without waiting for more dirty looks, Rance and Solaris grabbed the outer edge and pulled themselves around until their boots engaged on the hull. Rance's breathing and the rush of blood in her ears sounded loud inside the helmet. The comm had gone quiet too. Fires burned all over the station. Great chunks had torn off of it, floating aimlessly above the growing debris field.

Above the carnage, a great space battle raged between Unity and the pirates. A Unity Destroyer had arrived with more UDFs. They engaged the Scorpions from every direction, passing overhead, lighting up space in balls of yellow and red.

Rance and Solaris climbed away from the airlock, hoping Kaur didn't follow but knowing he might.

"He might send a fighter after us, just because," Rance said, breaking their silence.

"He might, but I don't think so. Kaur is vengeful, but not to a fault. He's a brilliant strategist who wouldn't pull a fighter away from a battle to take care of two insignificant threats."

"I don't think we're insignificant."

Solaris smiled. "Now what do we do, O Great Captain? Do we watch the station disintegrate before our eyes?"

Rance smiled back. "Let's put more distance between us and that airlock. Then wait for James."

A Scorpion passed close overhead—too close. Rance watched it grow smaller and then turn around.

"How is James going to find us out here?" Solaris asked.

"I turned on my flight suit's beacon. Without interference from the station, James should be able to find me."

Despite her optimism that James would get her signal, Rance was impatient. She opened a general comm channel. "James? You there?"

They waited a moment, clunking along the outer hull of the station, keeping toward the outside rather than the inner arms where the fires burned. Rance's boots made a hiss-clunk every time they engaged and disengaged. She didn't hear it but felt it in her legs.

The fighter returned, swooping overhead too close for comfort. Rance and Solaris ducked low, but it flew back to the battle.

"I think that ship is ogling us," Rance said. "You may have been wrong about Kaur's vengeance."

"Maybe," Solaris said thoughtfully.

Her comm crackled. "Captain?"

"James! Thank the Founders you're alive! Come get us!"

"Where are you?"

"Somewhere outside Section D."

"*Outside?*"

"Yes, no time to explain!"

"On my way."

The station shook underfoot so violently that one of Rance's boots disengaged. Her leg jerked out from under her, floating awkwardly until she pulled it back and down for purchase.

Another Unity Destroyer arrived, and more UDFs zipped out of it to join the battle.

"Reinforcements!" Rance yelled. She had never been so glad to see Unity. Maybe they would get Pirate Kaur once and for all.

"Captain," James said, "I see you, but I have a slight problem."

Rance grabbed Solaris' arm. "What now?"

"I've got a pirate on my tail."

"Well, shake him off! We've got to get out of here."

"Working on it," he said tersely.

Worried, Rance bit her lip. The *Star Streaker* flew by, chased by a Scorpion. James led it toward the Destroyer, which fired on both of them. The *Streaker* evaded, but the pirate wasn't so lucky. Unity's ship hit its target, and the Scorpion exploded in a fireball so bright that it filled Rance's vision.

She had just breathed a sigh of relief when a bolt from a laser rifle shot past. Rance and Solaris turned to see Pirate Kaur and his team approaching. They were still far enough away that their suits' targeting systems wouldn't be as accurate. But they were moving fast across the hull, too fast for Rance and Solaris to outrun. Rance looked around for the *Streaker*.

"James, look out! Keep your shields up!"

"I see them, Captain. Why are pirates chasing you outside the ship?"

"Ah, I may have angered them a bit."

"Coming in now."

The pirates' shots became more accurate as they closed in. One nicked Solaris' oxygen tank as it went by. Air hissed out in a tiny white stream.

The *Streaker* wouldn't be able to pick them up like this. The pirates might jump into the ship with them. Solaris stood with his staff ready, prepared to use every last bit of strength to generate a shield strong enough to keep the pirates at bay. Rance knew he wouldn't be able to do it this time.

She jerked her head toward the *Streaker*. "Ready to get crazy?"

"You mean we're not already there? I don't know how much more excitement I can take."

"James," she called. "Hold the *Streaker* steady. And keep it out of range of those pirates."

"Copy, Captain."

Rance crouched low, looking at the ship. "I'll race you," she said.

Then, she pushed off into the void, aiming for the *Star Streaker*.

***

The journey to the cruiser was the longest of Rance's life. It had looked close, but without anything to measure the distance against, she realized just how far away the *Streaker* really was. More rifle fire followed them, but they were far enough away that it went wide.

"We're drifting off course, Captain," Solaris said. He floated beside her, looking behind them to make sure Kaur wasn't following. Distantly, another Scorpion disentangled itself from the pack and headed their way. Kaur wasn't going to let them go.

"James? We might need a little help getting to you. You see us?"

"I see you. I see that fighter too."

The *Star Streaker* maneuvered around in front of Rance and Solaris. They landed on the hull with a *plunk*. Solaris bounced off again, but Rance grabbed him while engaging her boots with a satisfying click. Once connected, they walked along the hull to the one-person airlock. The *Streaker* didn't wait for them to get inside, darting away from the station.

"Captain, we've got company."

"The airlock takes almost ten minutes to cycle air, James!"

"It's already cycled out. You'll have to cram in together. We don't have anything like that much time."

Alarmed, Rance and Solaris opened the door and pushed in. It was a tight squeeze. With their suits, they had to hug each other just clear the door. It hissed shut. The minute it did, the ship's gravity grabbed them both, jarring them with a disorienting shock. The light was still red, meaning they to wait to open into the cargo hold.

Rance's ZOD flickered to life. "Great timing," she said dryly.

She logged into the ship's network and called up all displays in the cockpit. Their situation didn't look promising. One Scorpion followed them, firing whenever it locked on. Each hit shook the *Streaker's* shields, degrading them a little more. Two Unity Dark

Fighters followed the Scorpion, firing on it, distracting the pirate from obliterating the *Star Streaker* as she sought an opening to jump to hyperspace.

The ship tossed Rance and Solaris around violently. Fortunately, they were packed in too tightly to get too bruised. Once, Rance fell against the door and glimpsed Abel, their security officer, strapped into his crash chair in the hold. The rest of the crew would either be in the cockpit or in the control room.

Then, they were tossed against the opposite wall like cargo that wasn't strapped down. Solaris watched Rance with worried eyes, and Rance imagined the same look was on her own face.

An alarm beeped, and the door opened. Once Rance had gained her balance, she ran for the stairs. Her hand had just hit the railing when she heard Harper give James the hyperspace coordinates. Then, the shaking stopped, and the ship grew silent.

They'd jumped into hyperspace. They'd made it.

***

Later, the crew sat around the small galley after dinner, celebrating their near miss. Since Rance didn't allow drinking aboard the *Streaker*, they had some of Harper's favorite tea. Solaris had hot chocolate.

The atmosphere soon changed from celebratory to troubling. No one had any idea what the pirates had been doing at Waystation 11, nor why Kaur himself had arrived.

"Maybe they knew Unity would be there," Talley mused.

He sat at Rance's right elbow, as always. His alien green eyes shone in the galley, the brightest part of his dark, scaly body. Harper and James sat on the other side of the table. Harper with her tiny hands, and James with his messy hair. Solaris sat next to Harper, directly across from Rance, his face now tired and drawn. It had often looked that way lately.

"Everything adds to a pirate war, doesn't it?" Abel asked, leaning his bulky frame against the counter.

"Yes," Rance said. "Why does Kaur want to challenge the Empire?"

"Here's a more disturbing question," Solaris said, "what are the odds of running into *two* pirate invasions in the span of a few weeks?"

"If they are isolated events," Harper said, "small chance. Unless there are a whole bunch of raids we don't about."

"Is the Empire keeping them from the public?"

"It's possible for a short time."

"That also means there are many more pirates we don't know about."

Everyone grew silent.

Solaris wouldn't meet Rance's eyes. She wondered why. Was it because he had expressed a possible return to the Galaxy Wizards even if it meant punishment for deserting? Would he go now that the galaxy seemed to be in a crisis? Did he know something more about the increased pirate activity?

Rance wanted to tell Solaris to stay. At the same time, she was confused by her own wish. If the galaxy were in danger of being overrun by pirates, shouldn't they all do their part to help?

What did that mean for her? Her father would be at the forefront of events. He wasn't a military strategist, but he had consolidated enough power that he would be involved in decision-making at the Senate level. Would he give up on looking for her?

Rance hoped so. But she wasn't going to hold her breath.

Author T.M. Catron

T.M. Catron spent her childhood looking for hidden worlds in the back of her closet. When she didn't find any, she decided to grow up already and write them into existence.

Catron is the author of the science fantasy series, *Shadowmark*, the space fantasy adventure series, *Star Streaker,* and numerous short stories. Her stories tend to include strong female characters (or those who want to be strong) and fun, twisty plots. Although Catron primarily writes sci-fi, she enjoys a good story in any genre. If she's not watching Doctor Who or putting together Star Wars Legos with her son, Catron is imagining what trouble her characters can get into next.

To join the *Star Streaker* crew on more adventures, check out Solaris, the first book of the series.

http://www.amazon.com/dp/B06W9LL9MT

ONE LAST JOB
By Amy DuBoff

Captain Thom Caleri stared with dismay at the rainbow of textiles littering the cargo bay floor. "I'm getting too old for this shite," he muttered to himself.

The busted cargo container had fallen off of the stack and tipped on its side, allowing the bolts of fabric to spill out. Unfortunately, two dozen of the rolls had unfurled and were now a cross-crossed mess of patterned taffeta.

"Who wears this, anyway?" Thom nudged a pile of sparkly seafoam green fabric.

Neal, one of the *Exler*'s two cargo hands, crossed his muscular arms. "This container was addressed to a bridal salon—probably for attendant dresses."

"Why do I feel like this mishap is doing some poor bridesmaid a favor?"

Neal chuckled. "You should have seen my cousin's wedding..."

"Shite! What happened?" Dom exclaimed from the entry door on the elevated platform a story above the cargo bay floor. He was half a head taller than Neal and very well could rip a shipping container open with his bare hands.

Thom rubbed the graying stubble on his chin. "Tiedowns must have come loose in the last jump. We really need to get those inertial dampeners fixed."

"That's what you've been saying for the last three months." Neal scowled.

Dom strode over to them. "It doesn't look damaged. We can re-roll the fabric bolts and repackage everything. Baellas will never know the difference."

While the receiving inspectors for Baellas Textiles didn't have the greatest attention to detail, Thom wasn't sure his team had the finesse to get a factory-perfect finish on the rolls. He eyed his two crewmembers. "We may need to claim a loss on this one."

"Jerry will never go for that," Neal pointed out.

Thom sighed. His navigator-turned-first-officer had been pestering Thom about the state of their finances for the past seven months. Having a paid-off ship counted for nothing when port fees and costs for using SiNavTech's navigation beacon network kept going up. One-off textile delivery contracts weren't cutting it anymore.

"If my own cargo was damaged, I'd want to know," Thom replied at last.

"We can either be honest or make a living," Dom told him. "I think it's time we take another side job."

"Oh, fok, here we go..." Neal sighed.

"We agreed we were done with that," Thom stated.

Dom held up his arms. "Then why does Jerry keep muttering about not having the credits to cover our resupplies?"

"He worries too much," Thom deflected with the flip of his wrist.

"I don't," Jerry said from the doorway. He stepped forward. "This conversation you keep delaying, Thom, needs to happen. We can't take a loss on this shipment because we have no cushion. Even getting full payment, we won't be able to dock at the next station if we don't have another paycheck waiting for us."

The captain crossed his arms. "You're exaggerating."

Jerry thrust his handheld in Thom's face. The screen was filled with an accounting spreadsheet.

Thom didn't bother to look at the details, but there was a lot of red. *Okay, maybe we do have a problem.* He glanced at his crewmembers. "Side jobs aren't a long-term solution."

"No, but it would buy us enough time to get a new contract in place," Dom urged.

"I don't like the idea of side jobs, either," Jerry said, "but we're out of options. We need to get this shipment delivered and then take the first payout we can get."

Thom rubbed his chin. "Where could we get a job on such short notice?"

"That's why I mentioned it," Dom interjected. "I already have something lined up."

"With whom?" Thom asked, though he already had his suspicions, given where they were.

"Bianca," Dom replied.

Neal groaned. "After what she did to us last time?"

"She only took five percent. It's not an unreasonable finder's fee," Dom countered. "She said she has a good one for us."

"What kind of work?" Thom asked.

"All I know is that it's a one-shot run. Should be simple," Dom replied. "She's standing by for a meeting."

Jerry rubbed his eyes. "I can't believe it's come to this. I warned you, Thom—"

"Not now," Thom cut him off. "Set the meeting, Dom. I'll hear her out."

"We should have taken that work with MPS when we had the chance." Jerry glared back.

"Hindsight and all that," Thom waved his hand as he crouched down to grab a bundle of fabric. "I guess we should get this rolled back up."

Jerry scoffed, then pivoted on his heel and stormed out.

Dom watched him go. "Someone is in a mood today."

"More like this month," Neal added.

"I know we've been running a little lean. I really thought the Baellas work would have picked up by now." Thom looked in the direction his first officer had gone. "I should have listened to Jerry."

"Don't let him hear you say that. He'll hold you to it in the future." Neal winked.

As he should. I got too wrapped up in the space adventure and didn't think about the business. Thom sighed inwardly. He never had been good with details. Truth be told, he needed someone like Jerry around. "Just because I'm captain doesn't mean I'm always right."

Dom smiled. "I thought that came with the title?"

"Maybe for some. Not for me." Thom began carefully rolling the unfurled fabric back around the central metal spindle for the bolt.

"Well, you're the best captain I've worked for," Neal said, bending down to pick up some fabric, as well.

"Same. Most wouldn't have given someone with my past a chance," Dom agreed.

Thom completed winding up the first roll of fabric and started on another. "I've made plenty of my own bad decisions."

"Like joining the Tararian Guard, eh?" Neal jested.

"My mistake was getting out when I did."

His disagreement with Tararian politics had been enough to make him distance himself from service to the ruling elite at the time. But knowing what he did now about the state of the outer colonies, sometimes he wondered if he should have stayed in to help out the disenfranchised. Not that a lowly solider could do much, but hiring three crewmembers as a captain wasn't exactly changing civilization, either. At least with the military he had assurance about where his next meal was coming from and that he wouldn't find himself bankrupt and shipless.

Dom snorted. "The Guard is overrated. Now, TSS, maybe..."

"Being around all those telekinetics? No thanks." Neal wrinkled his nose.

"I've been hearing about more and more of them lately," Dom said. "You know, Sietinen has a telepath on staff now."

"Fok, that never would have flown in my day." Thom shook his head. "Can't believe the Priesthood allows the TSS to operate."

"Apparently someone thinks the Agents have value." Neal shrugged.

"I'll stay out of it. As soon as they started having the Tararian Guard train with the TSS for the first year, that was enough for me."

Thom hunched down to sort through the rolls of fabric, separating out the tangled ends.

"You never went to the HQ?" Dom asked.

"No, the training was optional at the time I was in. Some elected to go, but... I just never saw why we should mix."

"Huh." Dom shook his head. "Different generations, I guess. I always thought it would be awesome to be able to control things with my mind."

Maybe it would, but illegal is illegal. Thom caught his hypocrisy—he was about to smuggle stars-knew-what and he was judging people for using skills they were born with, regardless of the Priesthoods guidelines about telekinesis. Realistically, he couldn't imagine ignoring a part of himself... even if he would rather avoid crossing paths with an Agent.

Thom cleared his throat. "Let's just get this fabric stowed, and then we can find out what Bianca has lined up for us."

They got back to work.

The cleanup took nearly two hours, no thanks to Thom's insistence that they make the creases in the fabric line up just like the factory finish. By the end, Dom and Neal both looked like they wanted to rip the rolls of taffeta to shreds.

"I swear, I'm never going to look at a pleat the same way again," Dom groaned.

Thom eyed him. "I refuse to believe that this is the worst task you've ever had to perform."

The large man crossed his arms. "That's beside the point."

"I think you just want to complain about something."

Dom worked his mouth. He paused. "Are you ready to meet with Bianca?"

Changing the subject, as usual. Thom checked that they had all the fabric stowed to his satisfaction. "Yes, best to get it over with."

The *Exler* was presently stopped at the main Cordelon station in what was generally considered the middle of the Taran Empire, between the galactic core and the capital world of Tararia. Gallos was toward the galactic fringe beyond Tararia—a multi-stage journey that would take multiple jumps over the coming weeks. Thom tended to prefer those fringe worlds in the outer colonies, as the ruling elite kept a light touch on governance.

While much of his business was above board, the occasional job fell on the wrong side of legal, and it was better to not have prying eyes nearby.

Even with the intention of getting more legal work in the future, he was still drawn to operating in a place with greater freedoms. Such places were becoming harder and harder to come by as the Priesthood continued to tighten its hold on what information was relayed to citizens, and the High Dynasties and their lesser counterparts too often treated their businesses purely as commercial enterprises rather than as the core services Taran citizens counted on. The present path was unsustainable, but Thom had no idea how anything would ever change.

Dom escorted Thom to the bottom of the gangway leading from the *Exler* onto the Cordelon station.

"Stay with the ship," Thom instructed.

"Do you remember where to find Bianca's office?"

"I could never forget."

The station followed the standard aesthetic of those deep inside the Taran Empire, with broad, arching windows and seamless holographic interfaces along broad corridors. Being docked in one of the sections catering to cargo freighters, the station's amenities catered to weary travelers. In addition to bars and restaurants, there were the occasional establishments that Thom suspected were fronts for brothels.

He ignored the holographic signs outside the shops and took a brisk pace toward an even less desirable part of the station.

Bianca's base of operations was easy to spot from a distance, thanks to a giant, illuminated sign reading 'Space Catz', complete with an anthropomorphized pink female cat face winking. Whereas many establishments tried to hide an illicit side to their business, Space Catz left little to the imagination.

Thom entered the open front of the bar. Two women wearing low-cut tops, short skirts, and fuzzy feline ear headbands were leaning against the bar counter.

"I'm here to see Bianca," Thom announced.

"Is that all?" the first woman asked, twirling a lock of light brown hair.

"Positive. Is she in her office?"

The second woman pointed with her chin deeper into the bar. "Go on back."

Thom inclined his head to the women and strode past the high-top tables toward a narrow hallway at the back.

Bianca's office was at the end of the hall behind an unmarked metal door. Thom had visited her there two times prior as part of their past dealings, and he knew from his past experience that he'd want to be on his way as quickly as possible.

He rapped on her door twice, then swung it inward. "Hello, Bianca."

"Thom." She smiled sweetly, rising from her desk. Her pink hair matched the color scheme of the bar, offset by form-fitting black pants and a white top. "I was surprised to get Dom's message. I thought you were getting out of the business?"

"Circumstances changed."

Bianca sauntered up to him, her hands clasped behind her back. "Lucky me."

"Before we go any further, are you going to be upfront about your five percent cut this time?" Thom asked while fixing her in a level gaze.

She cocked her head. "This time it's ten."

Thom started to turn around to leave.

"Fine. Eight," she said.

He sighed and looked at her. "No other hidden catches?"

"Don't ask questions. Just get the cargo from Point A to Point B."

"I take it that means I'll have no idea what it is."

"Easier for everyone if you don't know too many details. What do you have on board now?" she asked.

"Fabric shipment for Baellas."

"Destination?"

"Gallos System."

She tapped her index finger on her lips. "It'll be a little out of the way, but not terrible."

"What is?" Thom prompted.

"I'd need you to make a stop at Tararia."

"Oh, no. No. I avoid the capital system."

"I'll drop my share to six percent," Bianca offered. "The cut for your crew will be 230,000 credits. I know you need this job, Thom. Be smart."

Resentment welled inside him as he looked at her prim smile. She had him trapped, and she knew it. Dispatchers were always his least favorite of all the players involved in black market dealings. "How dangerous is the cargo?" he asked after a pause.

She shrugged. "No more than anything else."

"How large?"

"It'd fit right in with the fabric. You'd hardly notice it." Her eyes narrowed the slightest measure.

Thom crossed his arms. "What's the catch?"

"No catch."

"There always is, Bianca, especially with your deals."

She waved her hand. "All right, the contents may have been… appropriated for our own business ventures. But as long as you keep your head down, you won't have any trouble."

"Appropriated from whom?"

"What did I say about asking questions?" She tilted her head.

"That was when I thought it was just black market. Stolen merchandise means someone is looking to get it back. That's different."

"They won't come looking for it."

"How do you know?" Thom asked.

She bit her lower lip. "Because it was taken from the TSS, and they don't want anyone to know they had it."

Thom groaned. "Okay, now you *have* to tell me what the cargo is."

She rolled her eyes. "Stars! Forget the whole thing."

"Bianca." He caught her gaze. "What did you steal?"

Honesty was hard to come by in their line of work, but sometimes people surprised Thom. Even so, he wasn't prepared for her reply.

"Ateron wiring."

Thom's eyes widened. "You stole ateron... from the TSS?"

"We had an opportunity and it's valuable. Too good to pass up," she replied.

Opportunity or not, ateron wasn't a material any old smuggler could move around on the black market. The rare element, which looked like any other malleable metal at first glance, had the unique ability to absorb electromagnetic energy and diffuse it in subspace. The TSS used it for various equipment with their Agents to enable telekinetic energy transfer. What others might do with it, though... Thom wasn't sure he wanted to find out.

He swallowed. "Bianca, how are we supposed to transport ateron? That's not something the TSS will just let go."

"They will with this shipment," she said, leaning forward. "We picked it up from a cargo freighter in the outer colonies—one that wasn't supposed to be there."

"What do you mean?"

"As in, it was off the official record."

Thom hesitated. "But the TSS is a government entity. All of their equipment gets recorded in—"

"Yes, it *should*," she continued, "but we've been seeing more and more shipments out there that don't trace back to any of the official channels."

"What are they up to?"

"I have no idea, but there's been too much heavy weaponry moving around for it to be anything good."

Thom let out a long breath. "Foking government always keeping things from the rest of us."

"The Priesthood, High Dynasties, TSS... we can't count on any of them," Bianca agreed. "The best we can hope for is to make a buck and improve our own lives. And right now, you have the chance to do just that. Do you want this delivery or not?"

He studied her. "Why are you even offering it to me?"

She scoffed. "You're awfully picky for someone who's backed into a corner."

"I have to look out for my crew. If this is a setup—"

"It's not." Bianca looked him in the eyes. "I'm offering this job to you because the *Exler* has a clean record. And, frankly, your financial state means you won't run away with the cargo. You don't get paid until the job is complete, and it's not something you can sell on your own."

It was true. He *didn't* have any other options. "What would I have to do?"

Bianca cracked a smile. "You'll be assigned a berth at main spacedock around Tararia. My contact will board and leave with the cargo."

"What's my excuse for routing through Tararia?"

"Dom said you need some ship repairs, right? Best repair crews are there," she suggested.

"I don't have the money for that," he admitted.

"You will after this delivery. No one reputable will try to charge you until after the repairs are finished."

Fok, there really isn't a way around this... Thom thought about his crew and how they were counting on him for their own livelihoods. If they didn't take this job, all their futures would be in jeopardy.

"Okay," he conceded. "You have a deal."

They shook on it, and Bianca relayed coded details about their arrangement to Thom's personal account. He forwarded the pickup instructions to Dom without reading them.

"Pleasure doing business with you," Bianca said as they parted.

Hopefully it's the last time. "You too." He returned to the *Exler*.

When Thom arrived at the ship, he found Dom waiting at the base of the gangway.

"Shouldn't you be in the cargo hold for receiving?" Thom asked.

"Instructions said to wait here."

Thom eyed the gangway. It could fit a standard pallet, but nothing any wider. "I guess Bianca wasn't exaggerating about it being small cargo."

"What is it we're transporting?" Dom asked.

"You don't want to know." Thom wished he didn't, either.

Things were so bad in the outer colonies that he tried not to think about what might be going on. Knowing now that the TSS was involved in something that wasn't on the public record was concerning, to say the least. Add in that it involved the use of Agents' telekinetic abilities, and that discontent could be upgraded to downright terrifying.

They waited for two minutes before Thom spotted a man carrying a nondescript black duffle bag. At first, Thom was going to dismiss him as a traveler, but he noticed the man keeping a close eye on his surroundings, as though making sure he wasn't being followed.

"Berth P-187. Sam will be your contact," the man stated. He dropped the bag at Thom's feet without stopping and continued down the corridor.

Thom exchanged glances with Dom.

"So, it's one of those," Dom said.

"Sure is." Thom picked up the bag. It was lighter than he would have expected for containing a metallic element. The bag wouldn't do for long-term transport—he'd need to find a way to stash it amongst the fabric, like Bianca suggested.

He and Dom hurried up the gangway and through the ship down to the cargo bay. At the bay door, Thom turned to his companion. "Are you positive you want to help with this?"

"I set up the job. Can't back out now."

"Don't say I didn't warn you." Thom walked over to the nearest Baellas shipping crate and cracked the seal.

He set the carrying bag down and opened it up. "Well, look at that!" He admired the silvery strands within.

Dom peeked over his shoulder. "Thom, what is that...?" His tone indicated that he already had his suspicions.

"Ateron," Thom confirmed. "Just don't ask where it came from."

Dom whistled and shook his head. "We can slip it into the fabric folds. Scan shouldn't pick it up so close to the central metal spindle."

"That's the plan."

They extracted the wire segments from the bag and began inserting them into the looping fabric. All told, there were eighty lengths.

"It's going to be a pain finding all of these again," Dom grumbled.

"That's the point—if we find ourselves with an inspector on board."

When they were finished verifying that the wires were all neatly tucked away, Thom re-sealed the container.

He walked over to activate the comm on the wall. "Jerry, do you have our course to Tararia plotted?"

"Yes, ready to go," the navigator replied.

"Be right there." Thom severed the comm link. "See you on other side," he bid to Dom and then departed for the flight deck.

The compact room on the upper bow of the vessel had an expansive window spanning the far wall, which provided a partial view of the Cordelon station. There were two seats positioned amidst wrap-around consoles sporting a mixture of physical buttons and holographic overlays.

Jerry was manipulating the horizontal touchscreen at the center of the room between the seats, which rested atop the SiNavTech-branded navigation console. He glanced up at Thom when he entered. "We better get paid or the docking fees from Tararia will bankrupt us."

"Those central worlds would take literal arms and legs if they thought they could profit from it."

Jerry snorted. "Ain't that the truth."

Thom settled into the right chair across from Jerry. He initiated the startup sequence for the ship's engines.

"This will be the last job like this," Thom told his companion.

Jerry kept his gaze on the controls. "If you say so."

Thom went through the routine undocking sequence and piloted the ship away from the station. He occasionally glanced over at Jerry, but the navigator had a faraway look in his eyes that made Thom think it was best to leave him alone.

When the *Exler* was a sufficient distance from the station, Thom brought up Jerry's saved navigation route on the SiNavTech console and locked in the beacon sequence.

A low rumble emanated through the ship as the jump drive charged—rattling the ship far more than it should due to the faulty stabilizers. Ethereal blue-green ribbons of light swirled around the ship as a spatial distortion formed. The rumble intensified as the ship was enveloped in light.

Everything stilled when the ship transitioned into subspace, seemingly amid an endless sea of swirling color.

Thom relaxed in his chair, soaking in the view that still awed him after decades of spacefaring.

"Do you want to talk about what's bothering you?" Thom asked his companion after five minutes of silence.

"No."

"All right." Thom sighed. *I can't wait for this job to be over.*

Cargo transportation was a lonely profession under the best circumstances, but Jerry had become a friend and confidant over the four years he'd been a member of Thom's crew. Though shy by nature, Jerry had eventually opened up about his ex-wife and two children he'd left behind on a colony world with the hope of making a decent living so he could give them a good future. Thom had no such familial attachments himself, but hearing about the two kids growing up had given a window into what could have been.

To now be getting the silent treatment from his friend made the lonesome flight deck downright insufferable.

In the following week's worth of jumps from Cordelon to Tararia, Thom counted Jerry saying a total of twelve words to him—a record three of which were stated in a single sentence: 'going to bed'. Over the week, Thom's attempts to converse were typically met with ambivalent grunts of acknowledgement or a shrug.

In their years working together, Thom had only seen Jerry stay in a funk for two or three days. When his mood hadn't improved by the time they were approaching their destination, it was clear that the situation wasn't going to resolve itself.

"What do you say we head out to the bar tonight and you can tell me what's been on your mind?" Thom suggested as they prepared to drop out of subspace on their final leg of the journey to Tararia.

Jerry shrugged.

Thom glared at him. "This whole not talking to me thing isn't going to work."

"You're right. It's not."

Thom updated his word count tally to sixteen. "Jerry—"

"Let's just complete this foking job."

Twenty-two. Thom nodded. "All right."

The nav console beeped as the ship approached the exit beacon in their sequence. Thom dropped the *Exler* out of subspace.

The illuminated cloud of subspace dissipated like a mist as the ship returned to normal space, stars shining through the blue-green cloud. When the ship had fully transitioned, Thom set a course for Berth P-187.

Space traffic around Tararia made all other systems look uninhabited by comparison. As the capital world, the spacedocks handled everything from supply shipments to tourists. The high volume of traffic meant that the *Exler* and its questionable cargo would either blend in or would be more likely to be selected for a random search. Thom elected to visualize the former.

When they neared the main station, a remote pilot took over to guide the ship to its designated berth. Thom admired the view of the sprawling structure out the front window, with its array of docks so filled with ships that the rows of concourses looked like one continuous block from a distance. Translucent atriums stood out from the central core of the station, and smaller domed enclosures dotted the branching concourses.

Beneath the space station, Tararia was a beautiful blue and green marbled orb against the surrounding starscape. Weather controls on the planet kept it green and pleasant year-round—not that Thom would ever set foot there. Most Tararians were too absorbed in themselves to treat a working man like himself with any respect. He'd rather avoid a confrontation.

The remote pilot finished directing the *Exler* into its berth, and a shudder ran through the ship as the docking clamps locked in place.

Thom rose from his chair and stretched. "Care to join us in the cargo bay?" he asked Jerry, even though he already knew the answer.

Jerry shook his head and began flipping through the docking checklist without looking up from his station.

With an inward sigh, Thom took the interior path down to the bay.

Dom and Neal were waiting in the center of the cavernous space.

"So, we just wait for this Sam person to show up?" Dom asked.

"You know as much as I do," Thom replied. He pulled out his handheld from his pocket. "I'm going to get those stablizer repairs set up while we wait."

Neal sighed. "Finally!"

Dom shook his head. "At least the tie-downs held this time."

Thom called several repair companies, but all were booked up for at least two weeks. "Foking great," he muttered to himself while pacing across the cargo bay.

"No luck?" Neal asked.

"You'd think someone could carve out an hour for us. The part is expensive, but there's barely any labor." Thom sighed. "I don't suppose you have any contacts for that, Dom?"

The large man pursed his lips. "Let me make a call." He wandered toward the far corner of the bay.

Neal crossed his arms. "This Sam isn't very punctual."

"You know how these things work."

"I do." Neal tilted his head. "Say, is Jerry still upset about this job? I haven't seen him around the common areas."

"I think this is about more than this one job," Thom replied.

"He was always a weird one."

"Not everyone is cut out for a life in space."

Neal nodded. "I hope he gets his head back in the game. There are too few of us on the ship for drama."

"Booya!" Dom exclaimed from across the cargo bay, then jogged back toward Thom and Neal.

"Find someone?" Thom asked.

"They'll get repairs underway within the hour," Neal told him. "The stabilizer they have is used so we'll still have some vibration, but it has at least five thousand hours of life left in it."

Thom raised an eyebrow. "I take it that comes with a substantial discount?"

"Enough that even Jerry will be pleased."

"Good. We'll get it fixed properly after we have a couple paydays' worth back in the bank," Thom said. "Thanks for getting that set up."

Dom smiled. "Sure thing. The *Exler* being out of commission doesn't do me any good."

"Helping each other out is what this is all about," Thom replied. He checked the time on his handheld. "They *are* late for the pickup. What's going on?"

Thom continued his idle pacing across the floor while the two cargo hands began play wrestling to pass the time. Dom had just locked his arm around Neal's neck when a chirp sounded at the outer bay door controls.

"About time!" Thom hurried over to accept the docking request for the transport vessel. His pulse spiked as soon as he saw who the request was from. "Oh, shite."

"What?" Dom released Neal.

"This isn't Sam. It's Port Control," Thom replied.

"Fok!" Dom exclaimed.

"What do we have on board?" Neal asked. "Will there be a problem?"

Thom took a calming breath. "That depends on how closely they look."

Dom groaned. "Our foking luck."

"Neal, head upstairs and make sure the inventory logs are ready for inspection, in case they ask. I'll handle this, don't worry," Thom told him.

Neal nodded. "I'm on it." He jogged toward the passageway into the rest of the ship.

"They'll never think to look for it," Dom said in a low voice to Thom.

"Not unless that's *exactly* what they're after. Who knows if it was reported stolen?"

"That would require the TSS to admit they had an undocumented ship," Neal countered.

"Not necessarily. Could have claimed it came from anywhere. This material itself isn't unus—"

A second chirp sounded at the door.

"Fok, we can't keep them waiting." Thom accepted the docking request.

A clang and hiss sounded at the door as the *Exler*'s airlock sealed with the other vessel's umbilical. A blue light next to the door illuminated, indicating that it was safe to open the door.

"Keep your cool," Thom said. He activated the door controls.

The door slid to the side, revealing the sophisticated interior of the Port Control ship on the other side of a short umbilical.

Two Tararian Guard officers, a woman and a man, wearing light gray uniforms stepped forward.

"Are you the captain of this vessel?" the woman on the left after Thom.

"I am." He showed her his black and red badge with his credentials.

"Routine inspection. Please stand aside," she instructed.

Thom nodded. "You're free to come aboard."

The woman and her colleague traversed the umbilical and stepped into the *Exler*'s cargo bay. She produced a scanner from a pouch at her waist and directed it around the room.

Her companion frowned when he saw the readings. "What do you have on board?"

"Just some textiles," Thom replied. "Shipment for Baellas."

The man's frown deepened. "We'll need to see those logs."

"Of course." Thom navigated to the inventory logs on his handheld and sent the files to the two officers.

The man holographically projected the logs in front of him using his handheld and began inspecting the records.

While he worked, the woman continued scanning around the cargo bay. To Thom's distress, her path kept taking her in direction of the crate containing the stolen ateron.

"The logs check out," the man announced after five minutes.

The woman scowled, taking a step back toward him. "I keep getting an echo on scan." She pivoted back in the direction of the crate containing the ateron wires. "It's like there's something reacting over here."

The man stowed his handheld, looking over her shoulder at the readings on her device. "There is a distinct electromagnetic spike," he agreed.

She pressed a control on the device, which sent a pulse through the air that made Thom's hairs stand on end.

"These readings don't make sense," the woman stated.

Her colleague tensed, placing his hand on his holstered sidearm. "Captain, we'll need to see inside this crate."

Fok! Thom struggled to keep his heartrate in check. "Sure, of course." He slowly approached the crate.

A low thud reverberated through the cargo bay, stopping him midstride.

"What was that?" The woman reached for her sidearm, looking around the room.

The man tightened his grip on his weapon. "Sounded like it came from outside."

Another bang echoed along the hull.

Relief washed over Thom. "Oh, we're getting our inertial dampeners repaired. The tech is swapping out the stabilizers right now."

Understanding passed across the woman's face. "Ah, that would explain these readings." She removed her hand from her weapon. "These scanners don't work quite right when the shields are offline. Solar radiation and all that."

"Technology, right?" Thom forced a smile. "Would you still like me to open it up?"

"Sure, we'll take a quick look," she acknowledged.

While saying a silent prayer to the stars, Thom opened the crate containing the ateron wires threaded throughout the fabric rolls.

The two Port Control officers glanced inside.

"Everything looks to be in order," the man stated.

"Scan must have been glitching," the woman agreed. "It can be too sensitive sometimes."

"Sorry for the confusion," Thom said.

The woman nodded. "Safe travels."

The two officers headed back to their ship.

As soon as the door was sealed, Thom released a long breath and leaned against one of the crates. "That was too close."

"I'll say," Neal said from above.

Thom looked up to see the cargo hand stepping out onto the raised entry platform with a stern-looking woman.

She brushed her side-swept blonde bangs out of her eyes. "I was getting ready to bolt."

"You must be Sam," Thom greeted.

She nodded. "Where are the goods?"

"Haven't unpacked yet," he replied. "I was expecting you to come in through here."

"And draw attention from the Port Control? No way." She descended the stairwell, her loose trench coat fluttering behind her.

"I see why Bianca picked you for this. Few ships have a clean enough official record to not get torn apart if there's anything anomalous on scan."

"Maybe they were just late for their lunch break," Dom jested.

"In any case, I owe the stars a good deed to keep the cosmic karma on the level," Thom said. He approached the crate. "It's all in here."

The four of them picked through the fabric until all eighty strands were back in the travel bag.

"And our payment?" Thom prompted while he still had a hand on the filled bag.

Sam removed two stacks of credit chips from interior pockets in her coat. "Pleasure doing business with you."

Thom took the money from her, handing over the goods. "Likewise."

She hoisted the bag onto her shoulder without any further pleasantries. Dom escorted her off the ship.

"Are we back in the black now?" Neal asked when they'd left.

"Yes, but we'll need a long-term contract to stay there." Nonetheless, things were looking up for the first time in months.

Thom took the credit chips to his quarters. He sorted out three piles for his crewmembers and a large stack to cover the repairs that were currently underway. The rest he stored in the safe next to his bed. It had been far too long since he'd had enough surplus to keep anything in there.

He found his crew in the kitchen area down the hall from the flight deck.

"Payday!" he announced. He handed the stacks of credit chips to the three crewmembers.

Neal and Dom beamed when they received theirs, but Jerry looked almost pained.

"I'll check on the repairs and get us square," Thom told them.

He continued on to the flight deck and found that the repair requisition was marked as 'Complete'. Thom submitted s disembarkation request and then arranged for the repair worker to pick up the physical payment at the base of the gangway. When the transaction was concluded, Thom returned to the kitchen.

Dom and Neal were each halfway through a meal, and Jerry was staring at his empty plate.

"We need to switch industries," Thom announced. He dished a plate of stew for himself and sat down at the table with them.

Neal cracked his knuckles. "What do you have in mind?"

"I was thinking maybe a food delivery contract with Makaris," Thom continued. "They have new contracting out of Gallos Station. Since we're heading there anyway, it's worth checking out."

"Staying in the outer territories? Ugh," Jerry groaned.

Thom fixed him in a level gaze. "It's predictable and it will keep us busy while things calm down there."

"I have nowhere else to be," Dom said.

Neal shrugged. "Me either."

Jerry only gave a single nod in response.

Thom tried to catch his first officer's eye, but the other man rose from the table.

"I'm going to my cabin," Jerry announced. He hurried through the galley door.

The three remaining men finished their meal in relative silence, happy to know that they'd have the funds to cover their next meals for the foreseeable future.

Afterward, Thom wandered toward the control center to check on the status of their disembarkation request. Approvals were waiting for him on the main viewscreen, with a designated undocking window beginning in an hour.

"We're cleared. If you need anything else here before we continue on to Gallos, get it ASAP," be announced over the general ship intercom.

"But we haven't found Neal his soulmate yet!" Dom replied.

"Sorry, Neal, you're doomed to a life of spacefaring bachelordom," Thom joked back.

Thom rose from his command chair and stretched. *May as well get in a nap before we leave.*

As soon as he stepped into the main corridor leading from the flight deck, Thom spotted Jerry with a travel bag in hand.

"Be sure to be back in an hour," Thom told him.

"I'm not going with you," Jerry stated.

Thom laughed. "Don't be ridiculous."

"I can't do this anymore. Never knowing if things are about to fall apart."

"I already told you, things are going to change."

Jerry shook his head and continued toward the gangway.

Thom followed. "Come on, let's talk this out."

"I've already made up my mind."

"You'd leave me without a Navigator an hour before departure?" Thom said, hoping to buy a little more time.

Jerry descended the gangway to the busy spaceport. "It's not just about the work, Thom."

"Then what? Money?"

"No." Jerry shook his head. "I miss my family. I need to have a life beyond the *Exler*. You're about to start something new—this is the right time to bring in some fresh blood on the crew."

Thom wanted to protest further, but he knew any argument he might try would be futile. Jerry had checked out weeks before. "We had some good times." He extended his hand to his old friend.

"We did." Jerry shook his hand. "Take care, Thom."

"You too."

Thom sighed as he watched his travel companion walk away. The trip to Gallos would be even lonelier than the last.

"Excuse me, sir?" a young-sounding voice said behind Thom. It was the accent of a native Tararian.

He pivoted around to look at the youth. As soon as he spotted the speaker, he rolled his eyes. The boy couldn't have been more than sixteen years old, but he had an air of confidence Thom

412

expected from someone who'd grown up in a life of privilege. "Fok, this is all I need," he muttered to himself. "What do you want, kid?"

"I was hoping to buy myself a ride aboard your ship," the boy replied.

Thom turned to leave. "We're not a passenger vessel."

"I can pay—"

"We're not a passenger vessel," Thom repeated.

"What about openings on your crew?"

Thom looked over the teenager. *What in the stars would someone like him want on a ship like the* Exler*?* His eyes narrowed, scrutinizing the youth's face. "Not unless you know long-range navigation."

The boy's face lit up. "I do."

He does? Thom smirked. "Right."

The boy looked Thom in the eyes. "Let me prove it."

Though he was trying to hide it, the boy was scared. He was clearly someone of noble birth—not the sort who'd be caught dead on a cargo freighter, let alone offer to work for a living. Whatever he was looking for, or running from, he was desperate.

Whether it was the bleak thought of facing an extended trip to Gallos alone in the flight deck or some deeper wish to atone for the past mistakes with his onboard ship family, Thom was overcome with a sudden compulsion to help the boy.

"All right, I'll give you a chance." Thom scratched his stubble, sighing. "What's your name?"

"Cris Sights," he replied after a slight pause.

Thom gestured to his ship. "I'm Thom Caleri, and this is the Exler."

The boy grinned as he took it in.

Oh, to have that kind of youthful wonder again... Thom thought wistfully. He might not be able to get a completely fresh start himself, but maybe he could help Cris begin a new life.

Thom headed for the gangway. "Let's go to the flight deck and I'll see if you're full of yourself."

Author Amy DuBoff

Amy DuBoff has always loved science fiction in all its forms, including books, movies, shows, and games. If it involves outer space, even better! As a full-time author based in Oregon, Amy primarily writes character-driven science fiction and science-fantasy with broad scope and cool tech.

She recently completed the seven-volume Cadicle space opera series, a multi-generational epic with adventure, political intrigue, romance, and telekinetic abilities. Presently, she is working on the Uprise Saga in the Kurtherian Gambit universe, as well as other collaborative projects.

When she's not writing, Amy enjoys traveling the world with her husband, wine tasting, binge-watching TV series, and playing epic strategy board games.

Learn more at www.amyduboff.com

MAYBE NOW THE STARS WILL SHINE

By Michael La Ronn

Agent Devika Sharma's mission is simple: stop three criminals from transporting kidnapped humans to the next galaxy. Stuck on an ice planet, in a warehouse, with nothing but her wits and a few bullets left, the fate of twelve innocent people rest on what she does next.

Agent Devika Sharma crouched in the shadows of a warehouse as a crane hummed to life and swung an arm across the ceiling. She pressed her back against a corrugated wall as a light on the bottom of the crane swept across the floor, narrowly missing her.

In the quick burst of light, she got her first real look at the hostile environment she'd thrown herself into without thinking.

Shipping containers everywhere, piled two stories high. Latticed rafters with a catwalk high above, a long track of skylights above that. Exactly the kind of breeding ground for the criminals she'd expected.

The building shook, and her fingers instinctively twitched toward the handcoil on her belt.

The crane's claws wrapped around an orange shipping container, and a loading bay door opened, exposing the frigid black sky of Cryovox, a transparent dome that covered the area, and a glittering ocean of ice.

A burly man in a parka stood in the doorway, directing the crane.

Devika flipped up the collar on her parka. She tucked and rolled across the wide warehouse floor as a bitterly cold gust surged through the building.

She hated the cold. It was the kind that could turn you into a block of ice if exposed too long. She'd heard stories of people dying on Cryovox's surface, stuck standing on the ice like giant stalagmites.

She blew on her hands and her breath rose around her like a cloud of smoke.

She stayed in the shadows as she made her way up a service ladder toward the rafters.

Getting caught would be a very bad idea.

She climbed upward with acrobatic grace, leaping off onto a metal catwalk. Crouching, she got a good look at her targets.

The criminals she had chased halfway across the galaxy.

The two men who were abducting innocent civilians and selling them into the black market.

Her sole mission as a Galactic Police Agent—GALPOL—was to bring them to justice. To give the abducted another chance at life.

And from what she could tell, there was probably a group of people in that shipping container.

God knows she'd spent months tracking them, and she was one bust away from locking up two of the worst specimens humanity had to offer.

As she crawled across the catwalk, she told herself that only the heartless could kidnap men, women and children while on vacation. Pretend to be a taxi ship and whisk them off into space.

That's why agents like her existed—to make them accountable for their actions.

Devika stopped. It was warmer up here, but not by much. Her bones still had that chilled feeling, like they were covered in frost that she just couldn't shake off.

She spotted two men below. Parkas and stocking caps. About the same height—six feet tall, cream-colored jumpsuits, white basketball shoes. They had pale skin. Looked like twins.

Both of them had handcoils on their belts. Gray guns with long, needle-like barrels and bullets that could rip through skin like an acupuncturist's worst nightmare.

She snapped several photos of the men with her phone.

They spoke in hushed tones and gave hand signals to the crane operator, whose back was to Devika.

She photographed the crane, the shipping container, and the skies outside just for a point of reference. Her phone transmitted the images back to the GALPOL Headquarters automatically.

She paused, and listened.

"Drop's in two days," one of the men said. He was the least handsome of the two, with dirty hair and a mean expression. "If we get out of here by the top of the hour, we'll get there in time."

"Let's go!" the other man said, whistling with his fingers.

The man in the crane swiveled the machine around.

He looked like the other two.

Triplets.

Handsome Triplet ran to a control panel and pressed a few buttons.

An entire section of the wall folded back, and the warehouse brightened in the cold starry light.

Devika balanced herself in the strong wind. If she hadn't been ready for it, it would have blown her off the catwalk.

She couldn't hear the men anymore.

The wind was too strong.

The two men walked out into the sunlight. Devika spotted a skylight and ran to it, climbing up another ladder and opening the hatch. She eased onto the roof.

The roof was covered in a sheet of ice, and her boots slid on it.

Dropping to her knees, she crawled to the edge of the roof and pulled out a pair of binoculars.

The docks were empty, save for a blue corsair spaceship parked outside the warehouse. A private passenger spacecraft, it looked out of place on this industrial dock, parked on solid ice. Bay doors at the back of the ship were folded out like origami.

Not-So-Handsome Triplet waved to the crane with two bright orange marshaling wands.

Crane Triplet followed orders and set the orange shipping container on the dock so that the container's doors were several feet from the corsair bay doors. The container clanged to the ground and cracked the ice gathered on the metal dock.

Handsome and Not-So-Handsome bolted for the container door and unlatched it, straining with all their might to pull the doors open.

Devika drew her handcoil and waited for her opportunity.

Her chance to take them out in two clean shots.

She cocked her shoulder and spoke into a headset on her ear.

"Requesting backup. I've got a visual on three suspects unloading at Dock Seventy-Five. By the looks of it, it's a shipping container full of people. I've got a short window."

Silence.

Then a voice spoke in her ear.

"We hear you, Agent Sharma. Maintain your location and advise."

She lay on her stomach, aiming her handcoil squarely in the space between the container and the ship.

She'd only have a short time to act.

She breathed in, breathed out, felt the air crystallize on her cheeks.

She waited, still as the ice on the frozen ocean ahead.

Men like these deserved no mercy.

With rotten luck, if there were people in that container, they could all be dead. She'd seen cases where their air supply was cut off, making the shipping container a giant metal coffin.

Another time, she'd seen a container that the criminals had left behind for one reason or another. The innocents didn't die of oxygen deprivation—they died from starvation.

All that suffering, to be transported across galaxy lines for slave labor. On a moon. Or an asteroid. Where no one would ever see them again, where they'd work like dogs to mine precious metals, then get sent floating off into space with almost no oxygen in their spacesuits when there was no longer a need for them.

And those were the lucky ones.

Handsome Triplet emerged from the container with a chain in his hand.

He barked a command, then screamed so that the cords in his neck flexed. He yanked the chain, leading out a dozen naked people and directing them into the ship.

"I've got a visual on twelve innocents," Devika said. "I'm taking action. Tell backup to hurry."

She switched off her headset and sighed, then closed her eyes for a moment.

Something told her to look to her left.

Crane Triplet was perched in the driver's seat of the crane with a sniper rifle. He was scanning the grounds, making his way toward the roof.

Devika instinctively locked her aim on his head, and fired.

Zzzt! Zzzt!

The needle-like bullets zipped through the air, shattering the crane windows and hitting the man in the head.

CRACK!

The rifle fired, making Handsome jump. Then he and Not-So-Handsome yelled angrily.

Devika whipped around and aimed at the shipping container, firing.

A bullet ripped through Handsome's shoulder and he fell into the ship's airlock.

The innocents screamed. Their chains rattled.

Devika fired again.

Zzzzt! Zzzt! Zzzzt!

Not-So-Handsome dashed into the interior of the ship. Handsome grabbed his bleeding shoulder and fired at Devika.

She took cover on the lip of the roof, waiting as the shots whizzed by her, so close she could feel them.

"Get us out of here!" Handsome screamed.

The corsair's engines fired up, a supersonic whirring that filled the area and made Devika want to cover her ears.

She peeked up and fired more shots.

The corsair lifted several feet in the air. The last innocent was barely on the ship. A shivering teenage boy in a thin jacket.

Handsome grinned at Devika, then cut the chains that bound the teenage boy.

He grabbed a small disk, triggered it, and threw it into the icy ocean. An explosion of ice and water made Devika turn away.

When she looked back, the boy was falling through the air.

Arms flailing.

Screams.

A splash.

He hit the water face-first. His legs disappeared after him.

Devika's eyes widened.

Handsome fired at her again, but she took cover.

Before she could shoot again, the bay doors closed and the ship swung over the roof, turning in a semi-circle before blasting far over the icy sea.

"Backup!" Devika said.

She waited for a response, but instead heard a screeching, whining metal sound.

She tapped her headset, thinking it was a malfunction.

Then, a tremendous, rectangular shadow swept over the roof.

The crane.

In the driver's seat, Crane Triplet's body was slumped over the control panel from where he'd been shot.

The arm.

It was falling toward her.

CRASH!

She rolled out of the way just in time as the arm smashed through the ceiling, sending metal shards everywhere.

The arm buckled, swayed, but held.

And then she heard splashing.

The boy.

He was bobbing in the water.

Devika jumped on the crane arm, sliding down it and landing roughly on the ground.

A life preserver hung on the wall of the warehouse. She grabbed it and ran to the edge of the dock, then tossed the preserver.

"Hold on!" she shouted. "Grab it!"

The boy's black hair was stuck to his face and his teeth were chattering. He held on to the life preserver with a shaky grip.

Devika pulled hard. The jagged ice around the hole cracked.

She pulled again, dragging the boy to the rim. Then she reached down and heaved him out.

They both collapsed on the dock, and she wrapped the blanket around him.

He stammered words she could not quite make out.

"Conserve your energy," she said. "You've got to warm up."

The boy shivered and brought the blanket around himself.

Devika stood, looking out over the sea.

The criminals had gotten away.

She helped the boy into the warehouse, where she set him down against a shipping container.

"My name's Agent Devika Sharma," she said.

"D-Dev...Shar..."

"Take it easy," Devika said, frowning. "What's your name?"

"R-R-ammy. And...T-t-t-thank you..."

"You're going to be just fine, Rammy," she said. "I've got police and medics on the way. No one's going to hurt you."

She studied every part of him. Tall and gangly, like a bad basketball player. Kid probably wore glasses. She wondered what kind of life he lived before being abducted.

She rubbed his shoulders.

"I know you're freezing, but do you have any idea where they're headed?"

He shook his head.

She clucked her tongue and stood, glancing at the dock.

"Me either," she said. "And that worries me."

She studied him again. His shivering was less severe.

"Wait here," she said.

She walked out to the dock as distant sirens filled the air.

She knelt near the shipping container. The inside smelled strongly of human waste. She wrinkled her nose.

Those people had been inside for days.

Glancing back at Rammy, she made a mental note to tell him how lucky he was.

She took out her phone and took photos of where the corsair's legs made imprints in the ice. The phone measured the distance between them and produced a small list of makes and models that fit the measurements.

She had been so close.

She had nearly had them.

She replayed the conflict in her mind, thought how she could have handled it differently.

But the truth was that she had handled the situation perfectly. A textbook example of intuition and thinking on one's feet.

And it hadn't been enough.

Her heart broke for those she couldn't save. A knot formed in her throat.

The sirens grew louder, and squad cars swarmed the dock. An ambulance followed behind them.

Devika pointed to the warehouse where Rammy was.

But Rammy wasn't there.

Devika jogged into the building, looking for him.

The boy was gone.

She called his name, wandering deeper into the warehouse floor.

SLAM!

A door slapped shut and flapped twice.

She saw a foot on the other side, then heard footsteps.

She cursed, taking off after him.

How could someone in such a state run at a time like this?

She burst through the door into a zigzagging alleyway just in time to see Rammy round the corner.

She ran, pacing herself and her breathing.

She wanted to call his name.

But he wasn't going to stop. That much was clear.

She rounded the corner.

Rammy was up far ahead, running past another warehouse. He slid on a sheet of ice. Devika renewed her energy and dashed after him.

Her lungs were pumping.

Her heart was racing.

Maybe the boy was scared.

Hadn't she been scared too, when she was eleven years old, running through the jungle forests?

She remembered the grunting, the chainsaws ripping through the trees as her shadowed captors chased her.

The cold, clammy hands of her best friend as he cried in the rain, told her to keep up. And they ran, the mud up to their ankles as lightning struck and thunder shook the forest...

She gained on Rammy, but the road sloped downward and curved around another warehouse, ending on a bridge.

Rammy was still far ahead, though Devika was getting closer. But the ground was more slippery here, and she avoided patches of ice with her peripheral vision. The biting wind nipped at her cheeks.

It was a miracle this kid was still running. Anyone else would have been cowering on the road, turned into an ice block by now.

She exhaled, blading her hands and leaning forward into the slope, letting gravity pull her toward Rammy.

The kid was slowing down.

She was catching up.

Rammy stopped at the end of the road, where a bridge overlooked the frozen sea. The ice was a fifty-foot drop below—unsurvivable.

Devika slid to a stop.

Rammy faced the sea, panting.

"Rammy," she said quietly.

The boy didn't turn around.

"Rammy," she said again. "Why are you running?"

She took a step forward.

"You don't have to run. You are safe. The police won't hurt you. We can protect you."

Rammy still did not turn around.

Instead, he climbed up onto the edge of the bridge. He trembled as he stood, and wrapped the blanket around himself.

"I know it's hard," Devika said.

She continued to step forward, hands outstretched.

"Your life has been forever altered," she said. "And that's difficult to accept. But you are strong. You beat them, Rammy. They'll never again touch you."

The wind howled.

"I know there must be so many emotions going through your mind," she said, trying to sound as positive as she could. "I know. One day, not that long ago, I was in your place, Rammy. I was a child slave."

She paused.

"You were?" Rammy asked.

"I wanted to kill myself, too," Devika said. "But I got help. And I want to help you. How would you feel if you stepped down from the ledge and we talked about it?"

Rammy didn't answer.

"Rammy," Devika said, trying not to panic.

If this kid jumped, her only eyewitness would be dead. Not to mention any shred of confidence she had about this mission would shatter on the ice along with his skull.

"Rammy, let's talk," Devika said. "Just you and me."

Rammy turned to face her. He was still shivering slightly.

He jumped backward off the bridge.

Devika screamed and reached for him, even though she knew it was futile.

She turned away, bracing herself for the sickening crunch when he hit the ice.

But there was no crunch. Instead, supersonic whirring.

The blue corsair rose in front of her.

Handsome and Not-So-Handsome were in the cockpit, under slanted glass, leering at her. Not-So-Handsome snapped a photograph of Devika.

The boy sat on top of the glass, relieved the ship had caught him.

She stepped back, looking between the boy and the men.

Damn. They were related. Same skin, same hooked nose. Why hadn't she noticed?

A trap.

"We thought it would be a good idea to find out who's been stalking us for the last three months," the boy said. "Thanks for nothing."

Handsome pulled a joystick, and two machine guns extended from the bottom of the corsair.

Devika ran and dove as the corsair fired at her, spraying the bridge with bullets.

She took cover behind a corner, pressing her back against the wall.

"East bridge!" she shouted into her headset.

The squad cars screeched toward her.

The corsair stopped firing and rose into the sky.

The boy climbed into the bay doors and they shut behind him. Then the ship rocketed upward, toward space.

A gray police cruiser ship zoomed over a nearby roof and gave chase, shooting a stream of bullets after it. The corsair dodged, rolling out of the way.

Devika closed her eyes and massaged her temples.

Fooled.

She had been fooled.

The worst mistake of her career. This wasn't how she wanted to end it!

But she couldn't think about it anymore.

She ran for her spaceship parked two blocks away, hoping she had enough time to catch the bastards.

***

Devika's black corsair was police-issue. Sleek, no angles. It was an extension of herself, and she was glad to climb into the airlock.

She strapped herself in the cockpit, turned the ship on, and wrapped her hand around the control joystick as the ship's engines fired up.

She eased into the sky and prepared the ship for atmospheric exit.

Other police ships blasted off toward the stars, and she followed. She trained her gaze at the sky.

The ship rattled as she climbed. Even her joystick rumbled. She gripped it hard.

The black sky grew brighter, and in the ship's rearview cameras, the loading docks below grew smaller.

She focused on the transparent dome that loomed ahead, aiming for an airlock in the dome. A large, transparent sliding door opened, and they barreled through it. Behind them, the door closed. Several miles ahead, another door opened, and she and the police ships passed through, a straight shot into space. Then their thrusters kicked into full power as they rushed forward.

The sky darkened and gave way to stars. Devika floated upward, but her seatbelt held her down.

She scanned star-speckled space and steered toward flashing siren lights in the distance.

The blue corsair was flying away from the police ships.

Devika increased her speed.

She flicked a switch and opened her radio, directing a message toward the corsair.

"Stop now," she ordered.

The corsair didn't respond.

A blast struck the wing of the corsair, and the ship slowed down. More guns extended from the back of the ship.

The police ships unloaded on it, turning the ship into a ball of fire.

Then it exploded.

Devika winced as the flames flashed, then smoldered out. The corsair was a burnt husk floating in the middle of space.

Dead.

The men she was pursuing were dead.

The end of a long chase.

Not the way she wanted it to end.

And those innocent people. God, she didn't want to think about informing the families...

She rested her head against the seat.

More casualties.

Her radio beeped.

"Agent Sharma?"

It was a police cruiser ahead. A male officer.

"Come in," Devika said, closing her eyes.

"Suspects are dead, but you're not going to believe this."

"What?" she asked.

"There weren't any other people on board."

"What?" she said again.

"You had a visual on a dozen trafficking victims. Our scans of the corsair only show three people. The two criminals you were pursuing and a boy."

Devika cursed.

"They must have switched the victims to another ship," she said.

Her eyes widened as she realized what that meant.

"Run a list of ships that entered hyperspace within the last twenty minutes."

"Only one," the officer said. "It's long gone, too."

Devika cursed again.

***

"Run faster, Devi!"

The trees blurred by as Devika ran barefoot through the dark forests of Coppice. Thunder shook the ground and the rain fell in great drenching slants, turning the bright jungle planet she had known for the last two years into a darkened, shadow-ridden nightmare.

She panted. Her lungs felt as if they were going to explode.

She wore plastic beads around her wrists, and they shook in frenzied rhythm with her steps.

She didn't know how much faster she could run. She hated the never-ending trees, the shadows, the wetness.

She could hardly see.

"Come on!" a little boy's voice shouted.

And then she spotted a dark hand reaching out for her.

Rajinder—a boy her age. Eleven or twelve. His black hair was matted in a wet clump over his face, and his red cricket jersey was soaked.

He grabbed her hand forcefully.

"We have to keep going!" he cried.

Devika found renewed strength and followed him. His hand was wet and slippery.

They slid down a muddy path. The mud went up to Devi's ankles and her feet burned from running across soil and rock.

Then the ground sloped upward again. They climbed a small foothill as if it were a mountain. Twice Devika slid backward, but Rajinder grabbed her and pulled her up. They used the trees as support, clawing through the mud until they reached the top of the hill.

Through the broken trees, they spotted a soup of orange lights blinking in the darkness like bokeh from an unfocused camera.

"We're almost there," Rajinder said.

"Do you think he's still following us?" Devika asked, panting.

She looked back. The forest was as dark as the night. The brownish white trees were dull in the rain, like rows of evil teeth.

"Too hard to tell," Rajinder said, hands on his knees. "You going to be okay?"

She leaned on his shoulder to catch her breath. "If it's just a little while longer, I'll—"

A squeal stopped her.

She whimpered as Rajinder grabbed her.

The ground shook, this time from another kind of thunder. Not too far off, several thick trees snapped like twigs.

And then snorting.

Sniffing.

And more squealing. Guttural, gut-wrenching squealing.

Devi fell face-first into the mud. She pulled herself up but slid forward, her back hitting a tree.

The beads on her wrist got stuck on a branch. She tried to untangle them, but the smooth surface of the beads was covered in mud.

Rajinder helped her up.

"Let the beads go," he said.

She clutched them close to her chest. She couldn't let them go. Not the last traces she had of her mother and father. Without them, she'd have nothing to remember them by.

"No!" she cried. "It's the only thing I have from my parents!"

"You've got your memories," Rajinder said. "It's more than I have of my parents."

"Please, don't take them!"

"Devi, they're making too much noise!" Rajinder said. He ripped the beads off her wrist, and she screamed as they landed in the mud.

She dove for the beads, but before she could grab them, a black boot stomped the ground, covering them.

Boots.

The smell of strong musk, body odor and crusted sweat.

Devi looked up slowly, past the boots, past the potbelly covered in leather and rings, past the chains and shackles hanging from a belt, past the chainsaw gripped by two bulky arms... to a shadowed face with grinning, cracked yellow teeth.

***

Devika woke in a cold sweat.

The bedroom in her spaceship was dark. The stars drifted by, and soft starlight fell on her face.

She checked the clock on her phone. Five o'clock in the evening.

She'd fallen asleep watching the police ships sirening through space and studying the destroyed ship. She had to wait to let them clear the scene, then return the evidence to Cryovox.

She sat up, pushing the sheets aside.

The police would have brought the ship down into the atmosphere of Cryovox by now.

Outside, the icy pink planet swirled, a reminder of her failure.

She climbed out of bed, stumbled into her bathroom, splashed water on her face.

That memory...

It was the first of the worst, the first of many to come.

How many times had she dreamed it?

How many times would she dream it again before her life's work was done, when all the human trafficking was gone and no children were stolen from their parents. When they could live without fear?

She balled her fists at the revelation.

In the cracked mirror of the bathroom, she screamed.

***

Back at the loading docks, she knelt to examine the burnt husk of the ship. The police had dragged it down from space, and it was a miracle it survived re-entry. It was a broken flower of metal, hull curved in on itself with jagged, charred edges.

The frigid landscape had cooled the ruined ship down in a matter of minutes. Frost smoldered on the hull, burning and crackling cold.

The strong smell of smoke hit her as she entered the airlock, looking at where the victims should have been.

She stepped on board, using a flashlight to scan the austere metal walls for hidden hatches.

None.

"Completely destroyed," she whispered, shaking her head.

The ship had gone up in a bloom of flames. Death would have been immediate. No one could have survived an explosion like this.

In the cockpit, paramedics carried out the bodies of the two men and Rammy, covered in white sheets. All around was the stench of death. It burned her nostrils.

An officer accompanied her. He had a typical, stocky build, and for once, Devika was glad to have some accompaniment on this mission. Though it didn't make her feel any better about the situation.

"We found some traces of ice formations on the underside of the hull," he said. "They were fresh."

Devika frowned.

That meant they would have been hiding out in the ice floes around the loading dock. They were waiting to strike Devika, to kill her.

She rubbed her chin. "I asked you for a list of ships that entered hyperspace before we shot the criminals. What's the description of the ship that entered hyperspace?"

"No visuals," the officer said. "And no communications."

It wasn't uncommon for a ship to enter hyperspace with no communications, which is what made tracking illegal activity so difficult. Often, ships entered hyperspace without warning because the operators were experienced, and had no need to radio for assistance.

"Do we have any indication of the size of the ship?" Devika asked.

"Probably industrial by the signature," the officer said.

"That doesn't make sense," she said.

"Why not?" the officer asked.

Local officers. They didn't understand the ways of traffickers. Almost no one did.

"The traffickers' preferred mode of transport is private passenger ships," Devika said, walking out of the ship.

The loading dock was full of police officers and press. Photoflashes blinded her momentarily. As her eyes adjusted to the flashes, ghost artifacts sparkled in her peripheral vision, in the ice.

"Unless," she said, "whoever took the innocents didn't leave."

Her eyes widened.

"Maybe they didn't leave," she said again. She turned to the officer. "I need all available units to stop what they're doing and sweep the area."

The officer shook his head. "But—"

"Sweep the area and set up a perimeter in orbit. NOW!"

She ran to her corsair, slipping on the ice several times.

***

Devika swerved between two factories, steadying her joystick as she righted the ship and emerged over the frozen sea.

Ice stretched as far as she could see.

Then she swung the ship around, back toward the industrial district, full of factories, flat roofs, and cranes.

She increased her altitude, sailing over the roof of a factory. It was empty and abandoned, and she spotted trash through the web of holes in the roof.

Several police ships, blue and white, rose in the distance, crisscrossing each other as they patrolled the area.

She stayed on the lookout for something, anything. Except she didn't know what she was looking for.

With the district cordoned off, it was just a matter of patience.

Or futility.

She refused to believe any of this was a waste of time. She kept scanning the rooftops, flying at a brisk pace.

She steered down to the ice, inches from the glittering surface.

A metal bridge lay in the distance.

Devika eyeballed the space under the bridge.

Her wings just fit.

She maintained her course, increased her speed.

She focused on clearing the bridge.

433

Out of the corner of her eye, a thruster fired, sending a column of smoke drifting above the ice.

Another corsair—also blue—dashed over the ice, away from the industrial district.

"I've got a visual on a blue corsair heading west," Devika said.

The police cruisers turned in the sky and followed her.

Devika sped up, twirling as she followed the ship back over the rooftops.

She flicked a switch and scanned the interior of the ship. On her dashboard, a wireframe image of the ship appeared. There were thirteen heat signatures inside: one in the cockpit, twelve in the airlock.

"The innocents are on board," Devika said. "The ship may try to escape. Tell the units in space to hold the line!"

Devika activated a machine gun at the bottom of her ship and fired a warning shot. Then she opened her radio and directed a message at the ship.

"You're under arrest. Stop your ship NOW and land, or we will shoot!"

The ship's thrusters blew a renewed rush of flames, and the ship began an upward arc toward the stars.

Devika followed, locking her sights on the ship. It continuously danced out of her crosshairs, and as they climbed, her training told her to stop firing.

They were nearly to the stars. If she hit the ship now, she'd destroy it and there'd be no saving the innocents on board. They'd disintegrate in orbit.

The other police cruisers sensed the same outcome, and they held their fire.

Devika prepared for weightlessness, leaning her body into it as she escaped Cryovox's gravity.

She kept the ship in her sights as it hurtled toward the stars.

But the ship cut its engines and slowed.

A line of police cruisers was waiting for it.

There was nowhere to go.

Devika grinned as she barked a command into her radio.

"Report to the airlock, get down on your knees, and put your hands on your head…"

***

Devika stood in a police cruiser as it connected with the airlock of the blue corsair.

She had her hands wrapped around her handcoil, standing in a line with several other police officers.

A firing squad, just in case something went wrong.

Two mechanical saws descended from the ceiling and cut circles in the corsair's bay doors, grinding with a high-pitched whine and throwing sparks into the air.

Devika was never happier or more anxious to see the inside of a ship.

She just hoped that the innocents were alive. All the thermal scanners had reported the criminal in the center of the airlock, unmoving for the last fifteen minutes. A textbook immobilization operation. Nobody who feared for their life ever wanted to piss the police off at this point. Nor did they want to risk the connection between ships and get blown into space.

The saws finished their cutting, and a new circular, metal doorway fell to the ground.

The air cleared.

Immediately, the police rushed into the doorway, barking orders. Devika followed.

"Hands up! Put your hands up!" they yelled.

A lone man in a white tank top was sitting on his knees. The police pushed him to the ground and handcuffed him.

Ranged along the walls were the innocents, hanging naked. Smiles and sighs of relief spread across their faces.

"Everyone's going to be all right," Devika announced. "Everyone's going to be just fine."

Two officers carried the criminal past, and she stopped them.

"Who are you working for?" she asked.

The man, who had a younger, smoother face than she imagined, began to laugh.

"He's going to make sure you burn, Sharma," the man said.

That he knew her name took her off guard.

"Who?" she asked.

"Who else?" the man asked. "The guy you've been chasing all along, chick."

The police carried him away, leaving Devika standing as if she had been hit by a sledgehammer.

***

The planet Zachary was different than Cryovox. Where Cryovox was a ball of ice, Zachary was a ball of rock. A pockmarked, scarred landscape of porous rock.

Enemy territory. Enemy to the galaxy. Enemy to humanity.

Neighboring planet, completely different world.

Two warrior ships met Devika the moment she entered orbit, asked her brusquely what she was doing, and then escorted her down into the planet's dark atmosphere, forcing her to change direction toward a giant crater in the ground.

Devika complied, but wondered if the crater would be her resting place.

As she neared, orange lights in the crater glittered.

A sunken city. It was recessed deep, deep into the rock. Terraced lights angled downward toward a dark infinity.

She landed in the middle of a rocky field.

When she exited, soldiers interrogated her. They wore white armor with glowing neon lines, and helmets with three honey-colored lights at the top. It made them look like insects with coil rifles. She read their body language; they meant to kill her. Keeping an eye on their guns, she flashed her badge. The soldiers relaxed somewhat, but the tension was still there.

They turned and motioned for her to follow.

She walked for a mile under the navy blue sky full of stars, onto a footpath that wound down into the city.

She got a better look; the city buildings were made from rock, and their exteriors faced outward. People moved in and out of the buildings, making their way ever downward. The scent of cooked meat and spices wafted upward, mingled with exhaust and the smell of other things she couldn't discern. All of the smells merged together into a giant heated column of stink.

As she made her way down the footpath, the smell lessened.

The soldiers opened a door and ushered her through a long, dark hallway with orange lines in the walls that illuminated the path, to a guard post where several soldiers stood on watch. The guards opened the door into a cavern hall. The rock opened up—tall ceilings, stalactites, chandeliers weaving among them, gossamer white and orange tapestries in the color of the military. The air was damp, water dripped somewhere, and she already had claustrophobia. If this place collapsed, there was no getting out.

"Mr. Miloschenko is occupied," one of the guards said.

Devika pointed to her badge. "I override all appointments. Tell him to get ready."

The guard looked surprised at her retort. He hurried down the hall and opened a door into a sumptuous ballroom carved into the rock. Devika caught a glimpse of men and women in formal wear, dancing and laughing. Waitresses carried cocktail drinks around the crowd.

The soldier shut the door behind him.

Devika waited impatiently.

Then the door opened and the soldier motioned to her.

She entered the ballroom. There was a large, orange curtained stage at the front of the room. An orchestra at the foot of the stage changed songs from a bombastic symphony to a slow waltz.

Devika made her way through a crowd of people, who looked at her suspiciously.

Zachary people gave her the creeps. Overtly nationalistic—always talking about how they were an evolution of humanity. They had even formed an empire, hailing an emperor and amassing an army. The government didn't know what to do with them other than keep them at bay.

She ignored the stares and focused her thoughts on the man she was after.

The lead scientist of the Zachary Empire.

Tavin Miloschenko.

A man who was responsible for the deaths and disappearances of over a hundred thousand men, women and children.

The man who was responsible for the abduction of the twelve innocents she'd found on Croyovox.

A man without, from what she could tell, remorse.

Though she had never met him, she remembered his leathery face from the dossier, the day-old stubble, the way his graying hair fell on his shoulders. He wore golden sunglasses and a drab gray suit with a gold chain around his neck.

She found Miloschenko in the corner of the Grand Ballroom, a room with brocaded walls and windows as tall as three-story houses.

He was drinking a scotch at a secluded cocktail table, cradling a highball glass in the base of his palm. He raised an eyebrow when she approached.

"Devika Sharma, GALPOL," she said, not wasting any time.

"So?" he asked.

"You mind talking to me in private, or do you want to do this the hard way and talk here in public?"

"A man of my talents," Miloschenko said, "always does things the hard way."

"Fine," she said.

By then a crowd had stopped to watch.

"All I ask is that you keep your voice down," Miloschenko said. He sat at a white table and motioned her to join him.

She grabbed a chair and straddled it backwards. The move, deliberate on her part, threw Miloschenko off, and he eyed her suspiciously.

"I know what you've been up to," Devika said.

"Do you mean my successes in weapons technology?" he asked. "Please do tell me about my incredible accomplishments."

"You're trafficking slaves," she said.

Miloschenko laughed. "Why would I do a silly thing like that?"

Devika slid two photographs across the table. One was of the twelve innocents being led off the corsair. The other was of the gruesome corpses of the criminals she'd apprehended.

"I don't know these people," Miloschenko said, shrugging.

"They know you," Devika said. "And I haven't quite figured out how. But I'm here today to warn you to stop."

Silence.

A new song played, and people began to waltz across the dance floor.

"You're overstaying your GALPOL welcome," Miloschenko said. "You think that because you're galactic police, you can traipse anywhere in the galaxy. But it doesn't mean that you are immune from physical danger, Miss Sharma."

Devika studied his face. His threat was serious.

"Threatening a GALPOL agent is a galactic offense," she said. "Are you sure you want to continue that line of thought?"

"Threatening a leader of the Zachary Empire is foolish," Miloschenko said. "Especially with no proof. The Emperor would be displeased to hear about this." He leaned forward. "But then again, you don't have any evidence to make an arrest, do you?"

She kept her face blank.

He'd called her bluff.

He was smarter than she thought.

"I'm here to give you your one and only warning," Devika said. "We know what you're up to. If you want to do the right thing, release all the people you currently have in your possession around the galaxy. We estimate the current number at about ten thousand. If you do that, maybe we'll drop the investigation. If the human rights violations continue, however, I will personally ensure that you go to jail for the rest of your life and then some."

Miloschenko sipped his scotch.

"Tell me, Miss Sharma," he said. "Of all the things that GALPOL investigates—spacetime crimes, drug smuggling, enemy alien aggression—why do you choose to waste your time on the Zachary Empire? We have been your staunchest allies."

"And violators."

"If you mean the terrible attacks we performed on Traverse II, please know that we were simply asserting our right to defend ourselves."

"By killing innocent people?"

Miloschenko laughed.

"I believe you haven't answered my question," he said.

"GALPOL does not observe special relationships," Devika said. "We observe special crimes, though."

She stood.

"If you see me again, Mr. Miloschenko, it means you're going to jail. And do consider that a threat."

Miloschenko stood, flushed.

"And if you see me again... stay on your toes, Miss Sharma," he said.

The comment unnerved her.

Two hands grabbed her.

Security guards.

She pushed them away.

"I can escort myself out," she said.

***

She walked back to her ship, fully expecting the guards to shoot her in the back.

But they didn't.

As she lifted off and exited the Zachary atmosphere, she told herself that the encounter went better than she'd thought.

Of course she couldn't make an arrest, but this was the first warning.

Eventually, she would have enough evidence to bring him in. There was always a way, especially with people of Miloschenko's ilk. And when that time came, she'd arrest him and lock him away for life.

She looked at herself in the reflection of the cockpit windshield.

This was a never-ending battle. She told herself maybe she should take a vacation. With Miloschenko aware of her now, it was only going to get harder.

But she didn't mind hard.

This kind of hard was easy. Waking up from recurring nightmares?

Harder.

Seeing the faces of children whose lives were ruined just like hers?

Harder.

She punched in coordinates for the GALPOL Headquarters, telling herself this was what it would always be like—running, chasing, outsmarting.

She didn't mind it.

"This isn't over, Miloschenko," she said.

She confirmed her coordinates, tightened her grip around the joystick, and plunged into the bright heart of a nebula.

Author Michael LaRonn

Michael La Ronn is the author of over thirty books of science fiction and fantasy. He became a professional author in 2012 after a life-threatening illness forced him to change his perspective on life. He's been writing stories for your pleasure ever since. This story takes place in his Galaxy Mavericks series, and is a prequel. Galaxy Mavericks is the story of six people from different walks of life who join together to save the universe. It's like The Avengers, but with ordinary people. Their stories intertwine in unexpected ways, and of course there are plenty of spaceships, aliens, and explosions, too. To check out the rest of the series, start with Book 1 (Honor's Reserve) by visiting www.michaellaronn.com/galaxymavericks.

ICE FIELD

By Scott Moon

Lieutenant Colonel Reginald Humann must evacuate a mixed team of civilians and soldiers before nightmare creatures drag them below the ice.

LIEUTENANT Colonel Reginald Humann stood at the edge of the supraglacial lake and stared. Safire water, deep enough to drown in, glowed on thick white ice. Beyond the panoramic vista, barely visible in orbit, ships of Expeditionary Fleet 029 looked like ghosts about to vanish from sight. "This is my fault."

Sunlight cut through the thin atmosphere, dilating the photosensitive lenses of his visor. Frost smeared the exterior of his armor. Power rationing restricted his heating elements to teeth chattering minimalism.

"Not so loud, sir," First Sergeant Kenneth Damon said. "The troops are watching... and listening." He paused. "Going over the top might have worked."

Humann waited, not wanting to face the men and women who would die today or tomorrow or the next day.

"We should head for the tree," Damon said. "Forget the Fleet. Even if we make it across that mess, we'd be stranded on the runway of Alpha Base. We get to the tree, we can shelter until the eclipse passes."

"Sergeant," Humann said, still staring across the thick sheets of floating ice.

"Sir," Damon said.

"How thick are the glaciers?"

"A hundred feet, maybe a thousand. I'm not part of the science team," he said. "If I'd known there was a lake up here, I'd have advised heading for the tree sooner."

"Glaciers melt and freeze as the years pass and seasons change. I imagine there are rivers going somewhere, and I can't see them from this promontory."

"I'm not sure I like where you're going with this, sir," Damon said.

"We can't make the tree. Point of no return was five kilometers back and that doesn't factor the climb down to the boats or the ice calving." Humann understood the sergeant's subconscious need to see the tree island one last time. They'd buried officers and enlisted men there after the first Nightmare attack. His decision to inter the bodies had been hard, but that wasn't the heaviest weight on his heart.

He looked at the distant ships for a long time. "I wish I had handled that last argument differently."

"You can fix it when we are safe aboard the carrier, sir," Damon said.

Humann laughed. "A bit of advice Sergeant, stay clear of politics or direct sales. You lie poorly."

Men and women of the expedition hammered stakes for night shelters, bracing against the wind and the things that came with the darkness on this world. The rhythmic sound of tools and the occasional scent of contraband smoking products calmed his thoughts. Making camp was routine.

Smoke'em if you got 'em and get ready to ride the storm out.

Pray we aren't here for the eclipse.

"Send Briggs and DeVonte to look for caves," Humann said. "The lake I see is beautiful... and shallow. We'll go under it, avoid the weather and the Nighthawks. With luck, we'll get to the airstrip before the last evacuation shuttle blasts off."

* * *

BRIGGS and DeVonte came back tired, hungry, and cold. These conditions did nothing to stay her sarcasm or pierce his stoic silence.

"I'm not saying you gentlemen are worthless, but we've found some ancient and spectacular ice tunnels while you're up here... doing whatever it is that you're doing," Briggs said. She was tall and

444

gaunt in her armor. Her stride, graceful and bold, identified her better than a name plate. With or without forty kilos of protective gear, she retained the physical and mental toughness of her Long Range Reconnaissance Soldier days and wasn't trying to hide it.

DeVonte, as far as Humann knew, didn't have any special training or military experience. He'd been in the unit three years without a single discipline violation. Nothing marked him as extraordinary, and yet, Briggs was the only scout who came close to his proficiency.

"How deep did you go, DeVonte," Humann asked, knowing he wouldn't speak unless questioned directly.

"As far as we could. There are vertical shafts that might go to the center of the planet for all I know. Best to avoid those," DeVonte said, his voice both solid and quiet.

"The horizontal passages are about five meters down, wide enough to drive transports through if we had any. Slick as hell in places," Briggs said, rubbing her left leg where she must have fallen hard during the reconnaissance.

Humann faced his sergeant. "We can shelter below the surface. Keep an observation post outside near the entrance. Maintain contact with the fleet for as long as possible."

Damon saluted and went to carry out his orders.

Humann stayed where he was and stared at the lake, imagining better times. He didn't hope for much, preferring to live in the moment and watch for opportunities. With eleven hours until the eclipse and his exhausted military and civilian personnel about to sleep at least four of them, his stoicism wasn't much different from delusional optimism.

"Lieutenant," Briggs said from the observation post near the mouth of the cave. "It's getting dark. Better come inside."

"Copy that," Humann said as the sun dipped below the horizon. "I'm on my way."

He walked without looking at the shadows circling ever lower. His computer assisted optics watched however, recording disturbed patches of atmosphere in the shape of predatory birds moving closer to the last man on the surface of the ice.

He heard them whispering nearly understandable words.

Walk a little farther. Stay with us. Embrace the frozen god. Stay and trust the mercy of the Nighthawks...

Humann stepped into the mouth of the cave before he looked back. The winged creatures looked angelic — white and silver in the darkness so that it was impossible to know their true color.

"Nighthawks is the wrong name for them," DeVonte said. "They are the Angels of Death."

"Not going to argue with you," Humann said. "Make sure you get relief and take a turn in a sleeping bag."

DeVonte nodded and lifted binoculars to his face. "They're moving away now. Something must be out there for them to hunt."

"Corporal DeVonte," Humann said.

The man lowered the binoculars, then looked at Humann.

"Stay inside. No wandering into the darkness," Humann said.

DeVonte lifted the field glasses. "Copy that, sir."

"I'll watch him, sir," Briggs said.

Humann nodded, then walked into the brightly lit corridors. The only thing they had in surplus were solar batteries for lighting. Some of his more industrious soldiers huddled near banks of temporary lights with their hands forward for the suggestion of warmth the light-emitting diodes provided.

* * *

COMMANDER Paulina Humann pulled on her helmet as she strode across the flight deck, ignoring subordinates and superiors. Her father, if he were on the carrier instead of poking around ancient ruins for vague promises of alien technology, would cringe.

He hated her attitude.

"You're not my daughter with disrespect like that. Not to your commanding officer. I can't keep the JAG Corps off your back if you don't at least pretend you understand the chain of command!"

Her father hadn't been wrong. Which was the problem. He was never wrong.

"Lieutenant Grayson," she said, "get the hell out of that cockpit."

"It's my ship, ma'm," Grayson said. "And it's not a fighter."

446

"Understood," she said, starting up the ladder. "Out."

Grayson worked his way around her, nearly losing his grip as he descended the narrow steps.

"Commander Humann!" roared Major King trailing a small army of agitated officers, security troops, and flight deck personnel.

She stopped, turned, and looked down on her ebony faced boss. "Major."

He clenched his jaw, ignoring his staff who caught up looking out of breath and wide eyed. "I know why you're going down there."

"Then you know you can't stop me."

"I can stop you." He looked around at the assembled personnel. "We can stop you."

Paulina lowered her chin. "It wouldn't be worth it."

"You don't have to go after him. There are several evacuation flights left. Everything is running smoothly. This is a natural disaster, not a war."

Paulina hesitated. "With all due respect, Major, my father will be the last man to leave the planet and will give up his seat to orphan children."

"There are no children on that frozen hell," King said.

"He'll find one. The man is an insufferable martyr."

"I have arguments with my daughter all the time. She never gets herself killed trying to apologize," King said.

"Why would I apologize?"

Silence and tension held the bridge, causing more distant conversations and equipment noises to stand out.

"Of course. Why apologize?" King said. "He's a Humann and everyone in your family is a legendary pain in the ass."

"Thank you, sir," she said. "I will report back well before the Fleet is underway. This isn't a battle after all."

"Now I'm worried... and still angry." King said. "This is going in your file, if there is any room left."

Paulina lowered herself into the cockpit without a word, smile, or opportunity to be talked out of her decision.

* * *

LIEUTENANT Colonel Humann jogged up the slick ice passage, eyes on the morning light slashing into the mouth of the cave. Sergeant Damon and two medics worked frantically on a downed soldier.

He bent over the medics as they injected adrenalin and nanites into Briggs. "What the hell happened?"

"I don't know, but I can guess," Damon made the words sound like a curse. "DeVonte went out. Briggs brought him back."

Humann went to DeVonte near the wall and found him unconscious but stable. Ice locked his armor in place like a statue, the infra-red link from his helmet described his condition as stable.

"DeVonte!" Briggs screamed as she sat up, head-butting one of the medics.

Humann reached her in three quick strides. "Briggs, report."

She looked at him, her eyes wide through the clear visor. At night, the photosensitive helmet had abandoned the intense solar shielding. "I told him it was too fucking cold out there at night." Twisting and moaning, she choked on her pain. The medic worked on her injuries and her pain, cursing when the LRRS lost consciousness again.

"Her shoulder is dislocated. I think she was dragging him back with one arm and fighting off the Nighthawks with the other," Damon said.

Damage on the plating of her left arm looked like defensive wounds. Humann went to the entrance and looked outside. There wasn't much wind this early. He saw what looked like footprints of twenty soldiers and knew that Briggs had been chasing DeVonte in circles trying to free him of the whispering Nightmares.

"They probably did that half the night. Where was their relief?" Humann asked.

Damon joined him. "The log shows DeVonte disregarded his relief."

"And Briggs let him!"

"I wasn't here, sir."

"Pack them on sleds and let's move out. We need to get through these caves in two hours. One would be better," Humann said, already walking into the ice passage to give other orders.

Sergeant Damon and most of the others avoided Humann, acknowledging orders without lingering for small talk or eye contact. He pushed the pace, leading from the front and taking risks he wouldn't expect his subordinates to be responsible for. At first, the passages had been dark, but even a small amount of light caused the white and blue tunnels to glow with illumination.

Above them was a nearly frozen aquarium of alien life. He wondered what life in a temporary lake would look like if the pressed close to nature's viewing wall. He thought of seals or polar bears, animals that didn't live on this planet. In places, he could see more of the lake above their heads than was comfortable. As terrifying as the water pressure was, the vertical shafts were a hundred times worse.

He stopped at the first and looked down.

Sergeant Damon joined him. "Neither DeVonte nor Briggs said these shafts were this big.

"We'll go around. Keep people away from the edge. Use harsh words if necessary," Humann said.

"Does that include you, sir?"

Humann backed up. The slope to the edge of the hole was easier to feel than see. The ten-meter-wide black hole groaned hungrily.

"What is that sound," Damon asked. "Wind?"

"No. It's the ice freezing and changing shape at the bottom of the shaft," Humann said.

Damon laughed. "I'm glad to know there is a bottom."

Humann smiled for the first time in about a thousand years it seemed. He patted the sergeant on the shoulder and was about to speak when he heard the screams.

Spinning to face the rest of the expedition, he saw half a dozen soldiers and scientists shoot into the blackness.

"Get back from the edge!" He shouted and ran to prevent others from rushing to the aid of men and women who were already gone.

"The Colonel said get the fuck back, you assholes!" Damon boomed as he bullied rescuers into a hallway.

It took a while to restore order, time they didn't have. No one spoke when the expedition finally moved around the ice shaft.

"For the record, sir, this trip hasn't been worth the cost," Damon said.

Humann nodded. His toughest soldiers guarded the alien fuel sample and the device his scientists said was the key to its use. Maybe the exotic element could power a starship. He doubted it could bring back the dead.

* * *

COMMANDER Paulina Humann circled the planet once when protocol called for three passes and a support squadron. The transport shuttle felt like a brick under the controls, even in the void of space. She slid into the stratosphere, aware that remaining here would be a death sentence during the eclipse. The cold wasn't a problem for the space-capable ship. Wind and ice, on the other hand, would be tricky.

Warnings from the meteorologists had sounded like fear mongering during the mission briefings. Looking at the planetary storms caused her to shiver head to toe.

"Fleet Command to Rescue Shuttle X-ray, you have orders to return to the carrier," a voice said in her helmet speaker.

"Confirmed I have the orders," she said. "Haven't decided what to do with them."

* * *

LIEUTENANT Colonel Reginald Humann found the first nest and wanted to just quit. He stood on cold feet and weak knees resisting the urge to sit down and hold his helmet in both hands.

Sergeant Damon moved to his side. "What the hell is that?"

"Looks like a nest."

"For a Nightmare?"

"That's my guess."

Packed around the edges of woven feather, fur, and black mud were organic pods lacking the hardness of shells. Humann reminded himself the Nighthawks were aliens and their resemblance to birds was a convenient description and nothing more. He faced the corridor leading to the room. The rest of the expedition was holding back as ordered.

"There was another passage two hundred meters back. Lead the expedition to it and keep moving when you get there. I will bring up the rear with a security team," Humann said.

"Sir." Damon saluted and moved to obey.

From Humann's perspective, none of the others hesitated to go back. The nest room was dark. The translucent lake ceiling hadn't been visible for an hour. He hoped that meant they were ready to climb to the surface and push for the airstrip.

Warning lights flashed in the corner of his helmet display. The haptic feedback of his suit vibrated. He shivered sympathetically. The caves were cold but survivable compared to the wind on the surface. When the eclipse storms came, he wondered how bad it would be in here. Instinct warned him there wasn't a square inch of this planet where humans and their machines could survive the cold.

He followed the others up to a broadening passage that promised an exit but didn't deliver.

"Damon, give me an update on the Fleet," he said.

His sergeant, fifty meters ahead of him, looked back and answered via infrared link. "I had Vlatka set up the radio booster and hail them when I thought we were close to the surface. We received a partial call for final evacuation."

"I assume you lost the connection?"

"Yes, sir. I ordered Vlatka to reply and give a situation report, but we don't know if it got through."

Humann considered the information as he moved forward in the column. Men and women rested without saying much. He could see exhaustion and defeat in their expressions. For an instant, he wished they were back in the sun where their darkened visors would hide their eyes.

"One more thing," Damon said. "Briggs is conscious. You better come up here."

He reached Briggs where she leaned against the ice wall sipping from a tube internal to her helmet. An insulated med-pack was plugged in so that it looked like she was carrying a small book on top of her head.

"Hello, sir," Briggs said. "I'm sorry I couldn't stop him."

He took her hands in his. "Now isn't the time to worry about that. How are you feeling?"

"Like I'm about to die," she said.

Humann looked at Damon and the medics.

No one spoke.

He faced his wounded scout.

"The Nightmares are actually birds. That's what I saw at least. Feathers like ice crystals reflecting the night sky like an acid trip," she said, wonder overflowing her voice.

"Have you had many acid trips?"

Briggs laughed. Her strength faded quickly and she started to cough.

Humann squeezed her hands and waited.

"Can evil be beautiful?" Briggs asked, no longer looking at him.

He didn't answer.

"When the touched my armor, it felt like a kiss," she said. "When I pulled my arm back..."

Humann adjusted his feet, squatting closer and trying to see hope in the tears streaming from the corners of her closed eyes. The visor started to darken as sunlight reflected from the exit not far ahead of them.

"It hurt so bad, sir. Why do they lie?"

Humann didn't know what to say.

"Colonel," Briggs said, looking straight at him now.

"Go ahead, Briggs. I'm listening."

"DeVonte is a good soldier. He only went out to save the rest of us," she said.

"How was he going to do that?"

"I think he was going to lead them away from the nests. Watch out for the nests. The Nightmares are upset we went into the caves. Not that they gave us a lot of choices."

"Hey, not so much. Don't strain yourself. We have time," he said.

"No we don't, sir," she said. "The Fleet is going to leave us here and you will never make it right with your daughter."

The words stunned Humann because Briggs couldn't know how badly he regretted yelling at Paulina before the mission.

Briggs smiled. "Sir, do you think you have any secrets from us? We love you."

"I think the morphine is kicking in," Humann said.

"It is." She smiled. "Should make this easier."

Humann squeezed his eyes shut, but it didn't stop the tears.

Several voices from the security team chattered on the radio.

"Damon, what the hell is going on back there?" he asked, still holding Brigg's by both of her limp hands.

"I'll check, but it sounds like something nasty is chasing us up the passage. Yep! Holy shit, those things look hungry!"

Humann stood and whirled toward the commotion only a hundred meters back. He saw Damon and a few others rushing toward it as the civilians ran toward Humann and the exit.

"Hold onto the sample and the alien tech," he yelled at one of the scientists. "And don't lose the radio booster or we're never getting off this planet." He rushed to see what had experienced soldiers screaming on the radio and infrared bands.

Taller than a man in armor, the featherless but still birdlike creatures swarmed the floors, walls, and ceiling. He nearly vomited as he realized they had clawed suckers on wings, tails, and tentacles. They were as ugly as the Nighthawks were beautiful... and they looked hungry.

"Damon, I want a fighting retreat. Cut and peel by squads and no grenades in here," he said, feeling stupid for giving orders that weren't needed.

Rifles and handguns chattered as one squad of soldiers covered another.

"Less is more, people!" Damon shouted across all communication bands. "A cave-in would be worse than getting your face eaten." He fired and retreated when it was his turn. "Not that I have direct experience, but I'm making assumptions here."

Humann aimed his pistol one-handed at a fledgling Nightmare and fired into its gaping maw. He hit the next monstrosity with two rounds, then turned and walked up the slick ice. "Keep up the good work, men. They're mean and nasty, but not terribly smart."

Long practice giving commands and years of combat experience kept his voice under control when he wanted to run like hell. Walking when he should sprint was an idiotic tactical choice. He hoped his demeanor did something to reassure his troops.

Standing at the cave opening, he watched the scientists and their military escort running toward the supraglacial lake. A few of them were not able to stop. They slid into the freezing water. Their comrades dragged them out and everyone double timed it around the freezing blue water.

He checked his tactical teams that were fighting the hatchling nightmares. Once the initial shock past, he started to feel more comfortable. Fear never left him, but it was a familiar sensation. At least he knew what to do.

Damon approached with one of the retreating squads. Humann covered them as did several other soldiers. When his turn on the firing line was over, he turned and ran to the next position of cover which was a block of malformed ice.

"Damon, give me a sit-rep."

"I'm having a hard time keeping a headcount. We're moving fast. I don't think we've lost anyone but there have been injuries and more than a few diapers filled."

"You're wearing diapers?" one of the soldiers asked.

"I wish," another voice said.

"Colonel," Sergeant Damon said. "I think you should move to the front. This is squad level stuff, and I think I've got it under control. As long as we don't run out of ammunition or start tripping over ourselves. Damn it, Jacob's, did you have to fall down right then?"

Humann rushed toward the next crisis. Whereas the sight of a well-functioning combat unit brought in some measure of inner peace, the view of civilians in full panic mode causes blood pressure to skyrocket. He checked his armor computer for biofeedback and was slightly alarmed at his own heart rate in perspiration levels.

"Doctor Fanestok, what's happened?" Humann suspected the answer before he arrived at the scene. The entire expedition was stalled at a terrain feature that hadn't yet materialized from his perspective.

"We lost the radio booster, the geological samples, and the alien technology into the crevasse that is blocking our forward progress," the doctor said. "One of your men has revived himself and climbed into the darkness to get it."

Humann pushed through the unorganized crowd of civilians and non-combat soldiers. He grabbed a corporal and told him to start moving along the crevasse until they found a way to cross it. Then he looked down and wasn't surprised to see DeVonte working his way toward a narrow ledge supporting the lost items.

The scout looked weak and moved slowly. Humann started to say something but then stopped himself before he distracted the man.

"Good news and bad news," Damon said. "The hatchlings are not sure what to do in the sunlight although I don't think that will last. We're also critically low on ammunition."

Humann went to the sergeant's side and gave him some of his ammunition but also look him over for wounds or failed equipment. "Now that we're outside, I think grenades are in order."

"Copy that," Damon said. He gave orders to the soldiers and started with one of his own grenades. The explosions, despite being a safe distance from the crevasse, sent disturbing tremors through the entire glacier. Humann and the rest of the expedition arrived in time to find DeVonte being pulled from his dangerous stunt.

"Corporal DeVonte, it's good to have you back. You don't have to do everything, you know?" Humann said, taking note of the man's pale complexion and trembling hands.

DeVonte handed him the small piece of alien technology. "That's all I could save."

Humann secured the item in his armor storage compartment and put a hand on DeVonte's shoulder. "If I had to choose one item, this would be it. We can learn a lot when we reverse engineer this. As for the radio booster, we'll figure something out."

"I heard about Briggs," DeVonte said.

The man, Humann realized, wanted to die.

* * *

COMMANDER Paulina Humann throttled back to her minimum speed, running just ahead of the advancing eclipse. She watched darkness cover the planet behind her and wondered what kind of black, freezing hell was down there.

Muttering curses under her breath, she scanned the surface for any sign of the expedition and her father. Nothing came back that looked like it had been caused by human activity. The weather ahead of and behind the advancing darkness was strange and chaotic. She needed to fly lower to see if the biological readings were the Nightmares that had caused so many problems since the disaster at the tree.

Warnings flashed on her flight screens. She didn't bother to read them because she already knew what they said.

* * *

LIEUTENANT Colonel Humann laughed and hoped none of his troop saw him. It was a bad time to look unstable. In his defense, any rational human being would be laughing his or her ass off because this was about to become a snowball fight with the most vicious monsters he'd ever encountered.

"I have three rounds left," he said.

"Lucky you," Damon said.

The Nightmare hatchlings swarmed from every cave they passed. He wasn't sure, but he thought he heard them in the crevasse as well. The only good thing was that they seemed concerned with the sky and the approaching eclipse.

"I almost wish they would just rush us and get it over with, Damon said. "This stop and go cat-and-mouse game is driving me bonkers."

Humann exhaled slowly and shook his head. "Any luck on a way across the crevasse?"

No one answered.

The hatchlings surged forward, immature wings and claws slashing the air as the hissed and snarled. The expedition soldiers used the rest of their ammunition in controlled bursts.

"Fix bayonets," Humann muttered.

"What's a bayonet?" A soldier asked. "Is that like a jetpack that's going to fly us across the crevasse?"

"Never mind. Prepare for hand-to-hand combat. We will hold this position until the civilians can find a way across." Humann moved forward to stand with his men and women.

The nightmare hatchlings hesitated at the site of Humann and his soldiers standing shoulder to shoulder. One by one the creatures turned ugly faces toward the sky.

Humann looked at the distant wall of darkness and despair. The eclipse was unusual, but the dangerous part of the situation was the storm and freezing cold he'd been warned about. Inside that black veil of destruction was their doom.

He called again for an update on the search for a way across the crevasse and was told DeVonte had found a narrow causeway.

"Get everyone to the other side and tell me when you're done. We'll come running," he said. Some part of a conversation he overheard from the soldiers caused him to look for the Fleet beyond the stratosphere. Artificial stars glimmered in the sky replacing the ships that had been so evident the day before.

"I think it's time to go," Damon said. "The hatchlings are stalled and we are running out of options."

Humann nodded. "I'll bring up the rear with the last squad."

"Colonel," Damon objected.

"No argument, Sergeant. It's a privilege of rank."

Hatchlings continued to emerge from nearby caves but pressed into ranks of their own kind that refused to advance. Humann heard them snapping and snarling at each other. The scent of alien blood filled the air — tangy and metallic. The violence in the middle of the hatchling pack made his stomach tighten to knots.

The monsters turned as one coordinated mass and disappeared into the ice caves faster than they had come out. Humann decided not to question his good fortune or read into the situation. The native creatures were obviously terrified of the approaching storm wall — probably because they'd been hardwired by their genetics to understand what hell in a windstorm looked like on this planet.

He saw the eclipse nearing completion. A ring of fire crept around the border of the large moon. Shadows darker than regret moved across the frozen tundra and icefields in the distance.

He arrived at the narrow bridge to see civilians and military personnel pushing and shoving their way across. DeVonte stood among them, helping the less aggressive push back before they were bumped off the slick surface.

Humann looked into the crevasse and saw an unbelievable tangle of hatchlings and adult Nightmares. The creatures were insane with the need to hunt and the conflicting fear of the storm.

He looked up and saw a transport ship flying low, desperate search patterns. For the briefest instant, he thought the pilot had waggled the wings at him, just like he used to do to harass his younger brother who had been studying at the military academy. Shaking his head, he reached for a better grip as he ventured onto the ice bridge to restore order to the expedition.

His little brother died two wars ago. The only professional pilot in the family now was his daughter, Paulina.

He lost his balance and stumbled. Just as he recovered and pushed himself up onto one knee, the ice trembled and groaned. He fell again, this time landing on his stomach and spreading his arms and legs to keep from sliding over the edge.

It was no good. He could feel momentum dragging him face first into the abyss.

DeVonte sprinted forward, lunged, slid, and grabbed his ankle. An instant later, it felt as though they were wrestling and maybe they were but not against each other. The wind blew colder than ever and the ice felt like the polished rifling of a gun barrel. There was no way to push back the planet's wrath.

"DeVonte!"

The scout went over the side facing upward as he grabbed again and again at the air, grunting something workmanlike and full of fear.

The darkness took him.

Humann knew there was no time to waste but he couldn't move. Lying prone, he faced the edge of the ice bridge and looked down, too exhausted to cry or curse. Paulina had been right about his decision to come to this planet.

A voice in his head, real or imagined, told him to get up and do his job. He backed away carefully and pushed to his feet. At first, he walked with caution. The closer he came to the other side of the

458

crevasse the wider the causeway became. He read from his heads-up display and ran forward.

There had been losses on this mission but there were still people to be saved. He caught up to a growing mass of confusion as the eclipse struck. Wind born sleet and ice pelted his visor. Even with the weight of the armor and computerized equilibrium enhancers, he fought to stand. A poorly secured tarp ripped free of a sled and knocked one of the scientists down, enveloping him like a giant vampire bat.

A pair of soldiers went to help the downed person, then all three of them struggled into the storm toward the last sighting of Alpha Base.

"Damon, I need a sit-rep," Humann said, searching for his First Sergeant by feel. Hands thrust before him, he felt like an idiot but didn't trust the sensor readings on his heads-up display.

"Keep coming, Colonel. We are approaching the landing strip. Visibility... is better here. Trying to get a head count..."

Humann stopped, not sure how he had fallen so far behind. When he last saw the lights of Alpha Base, they seemed a kilometer away.

Panting inside of his armor, he stomped forward. Head down, he navigated by computer and the feel of the ice under his feet.

"Paulina, I'm sorry I wasn't a better father," he said.

The storm raged. His electronic heads-up display whited out, throwing a harsh glow inside of his helmet that blinded him.

Something pushed him down. He twisted on his back and struggled to his feet still confused as to how he had gotten so far from the others. He'd been in storms before and understood how fast situations became deadly.

"Damon?" he queried the sergeant several times.

He slipped, fell to one knee, then lunged forward growling like a bear. "I'm not dying in a storm! I am a soldier, for God's sake!"

Time passed like an eternity. He didn't know right from left. Gravity pressed down on him as though he'd made planetfall after years in space. Exhaustion made his arms feel heavier than his legs.

"We're in, Colonel. Please respond," Damon said.

"I've been responding since we split up!"

Static rustled through his screen and earplugs. He imagined the Nightmares and their hatchlings were laughing at him.

The forward lights of a ship blazed to life, blinding him. He threw up his left arm as he extended his right for balance. The storm snatched at the limb and dragged him sideways. He stumbled, screaming at the ship that couldn't be there.

No one flew in this weather.

He danced with the ship and the wind. As he was thrown one way, the transport ship was thrown the other. Engines flared. Lights slashed the darkness.

"God damn it, Paulina! You've got civilians on that fucking ship!" he yelled, determined to set her straight if he ever saw her again.

Shadows and voices swarmed above and around the ship, thumping against its metal fuselage and veering around the overloaded engines.

Humann could hear the whine of the turbines through the storm and his supposedly sound proof helmet. Voices whispered in his mind.

"They don't fly in the storm," Paulina said, sounding a thousand miles away in the radio static.

"Paulina, go away," Humann whispered against his helmet microphone.

"She can't touch down, Colonel," Damon shouted nearly inaudibly through the static. "Get to the ramp. I can't leave it open much longer."

"I can't see the ramp!" He stumbled forward, searching by feel and hope.

The ship disappeared in a sideways lurch.

Humann didn't like the last he saw of the wing carving a groove in the ice.

Something huge appeared above him, like the ship pointing skyward for final launch. The angle exposed the open equipment ramp although there was no way he could pull himself up at that angle.

Rather than blast for the stratosphere, the ship surrendered several feet of altitude in a maneuver he was certain had never been taught at flight school.

"Paulina!" he shouted as he grabbed the inside of the wall.

Damon was attached to the opposite wall by carabiners and safety straps.

Humann held on with both hands as the ramp closed and the ship climbed slowly. Everything shook. He thought there had to be bolts vibrating free.

Inside the ship, he could hear again. Damon and Paulina laughed madly on the intercom, probably crying like lunatics at the same time.

Lieutenant Colonel Reginald Humann was glad to be alive and not looking forward to lecturing his daughter on why her choice had been the wrong choice.

Author Scott Moon

Scott Moon started reading and writing science fiction and fantasy at an early age. He spent several summers of all night Advanced Dungeons and Dragons gaming before joining his first garage band and running off to Hollywood, CA to attend the Musician's Institute. Always a dreamer, it was the writing muse that always screamed loudest. Years later he is still writing, still dreaming, and connecting with authors and readers through the Keystroke Medium YouTube show and Podcast (www.keystrokemedium.com). Examples of his speculative fiction projects include The Chronicles of Kin Roland (military science fiction / adventure) and the Son of a Dragonslayer trilogy (urban fantasy / horror / adventure) available in different formats on Amazon and other fine distributors.

Currently, Scott Moon is writing the Starship Marine Corps series--a combination of military science fiction and epic space opera in the style of Dune meets Starship Troopers.

THE NEXT LEVEL

By Thomas J. Rock

A three-man digital insertion drop team is infiltrating a deep space Russian weapons R&D station, when a malfunction cripples their ship, leaving the team stranded, and the ship's A.I. goes missing. Reed Wilson is the only equipped to look for the A.I. The problem is, he's not a soldier. To save the ship and the team, he'll have to take himself to the next level.

"I got a bad feeling about this drop."

"You always say that – '*I got a bad feeling about this drop*' – and nothin' happens."

Specialist Rick McCrory – Crow, as buddies in the unit called him – was at the rear of the three-man column as it moved carefully through the data stacks. He checked the status readout for the team's tethers, the pseudo-ansible connection that kept the team linked to their physical bodies, back on the ship. Signal strength was nominal for the Captain and Chilly. His showed a little fluctuation, not unexpected given the distance back to the ship, but it was within normal tolerances.

Crow looked around. Everything seemed normal. The data stacks were packed neatly and organized in the usual file structure. The data streams overhead, sharp, bright streaks of light flashing like intense red and blue lightning, were moving terabytes of data, ingress, and egress, every nanosecond. Application file requests moved in and out of the stacks like ants moving the queen's eggs through the colony, blind to anything outside of their purpose. The implants, in his brain, translated the coding of the digi-scape all around them into appearances no different than any other Eastern-

Bloc computer system they had infiltrated except for the heightened security the intel reports had already warned them about.

But there was...something.

"This is different," Rick said. "Ever since we made it through the third firewall, somethin's been gnawing at me." He shook his head. "I don't know, man. I'll be glad when we're back on the ship breathing real air."

Chilly, the man ahead of Rick, in the column, looked back. "Don't wig out now, man. You know Doc will pull you from the active line if you show any signs of losin' it. You want to drive a desk for the rest of your term? Ain't no money in that."

"Yeah, I know."

"Besides," Chilly said. "We ran this through simulation probably fifty times with updated intel each time. There ain't nothin' we're not ready for-- You...okay, man?"

Crow had stopped cold, almost paralyzed. His eyes were wide and quivering.

The lead man, in the formation, Captain Rigs, had stopped. "What the hell are you two grab assin' about back there? We're on the clock here!"

"I think Crow's flakin' out. Anxiety messin' with his tether, maybe. He's up about a 'bad feeling' again."

"Dammit, Crow. Snap out of it. We gotta to get moving—"

"Guys, seriously. You don't feel that in your tethers? I think something's wrong with Adam—"

Suddenly, Crow went rigid. His arms and legs locked outstretched wide. His rifle fell to the ground. In one millisecond, he was engulfed in a bright, white light. In the next, he was gone.

Rigs was stunned. He looked at Chilly, who was even more confused.

"What the hell?" Chilly asked. "Was it a recall? Why are we still here?"

Rigs shook his head. "Shit! I don't know. Never saw a recall go like that before."

A piercing wail grabbed their attention. In the distance, they could the last thing they wanted. Their implants translated it to look like a deep red wall that was as wide as the row of data stacks and just as high...and it was moving toward them, engulfing the stacks as it went.

"Shit!" Rigs said. "The recall triggered an active scan. Tuck tail!"

"Holy—"

***

"—Shit! Shit! Shit!!"

Reed Wilson's feet went out from beneath him when he ran around the corner. He hit the deck hard, landing square on his left shoulder. When he tried to sit up, he put his hands in something thick and wet on the deck. *What the hell?*

Wilson was, in the head, taking care of business, when he heard the sharp *POP*, followed by the lights blinking out. At the time, he thought it was one of Doughboy's pranks. He was already going to get back at the ship's pilot soaking his bunk mattress in ice cold water. But when he saw the smoke coming from the drop room, he knew something was very, very wrong.

He held his hand up to see what he'd slipped on, but the thin sheet of smoke, in the air, was illuminated into a yellow stagnant fog by the emergency backup lights. Wilson brought his hand close, sniffed, and almost gagged. A moment later, a sickening feeling struck his gut.

It was brain matter.

Wilson could see the drop stations through the haze. One of them, Crow's, had smoke wafting into the air...where his head should have been.

He struggled on the slippery floor to get to his feet and stumbled over to Crow's body. It was still in place in the reclined station seat. The physical monitors were all flatlined, but he didn't need them to know Crow was well past dead. His friend's head was flopped over on to his left shoulder, barely attached by what was left of the skin of his neck and the back of the head had been blown out from the inside.

"Oh my fucking God!" The shock of the sight stunned Wilson for a minute. But he gathered himself. There were two other men on this drop. He moved quickly to the other two stations. Their heads were intact. He checked vitals on the monitors and was relieved to see Chilly and the Captain were still alive and equally thankful the redundant power backups, for the drop stations, did their job.

"Adam, sit-rep."

Several seconds went by with no answer.

"Adam, what's going on with the power?"

Again no answer.

"Adam?"

A voice came over the intercom. *"Doc, copy?"*

It wasn't the ship's A.I., Adam. It was a call from the bridge. Hearing Doughboy's voice from the bridge was a relief, but he'd have felt a lot better if Adam had answered.

"I'm here."

"Stand by for the Colonel..."

A gruff voice came over the speaker. *"Wilson, what's the status down there?"*

Wilson took a breath. "We lost Crow, Sir. His implants exploded. Maybe some kind of power surge? Was there an ionization burst from the nebula we didn't catch in time? Is that what happened to the power? Adam's not answering either."

"Shit! Did the station use Crow's tether to send a strike back at us?"

"Stand by."

Wilson went to the console and keyed in a few commands. Log data scrolled on the screen. Wilson moved it to the approximate time of the incident. He read it. *That can't be right.* He read it again. "Adam, what the hell did you do?" Wilson said, quietly.

"Say again, lieutenant?"

"Sir, the logs say Adam initiated an emergency recall of the team...but Crow was the only one brought back. Did you order a recall?"

"Negative. What about the other two?"

"Their vitals indicate elevated stress levels, but that's probably due to Crow being recalled without them. Their readouts are, otherwise, nominal. Sir, what's going on? Where's Adam?"

The intercom channel went quiet. Five seconds went by. Then ten.

"Colonel Grunter, copy?"

"Doughboy, here. The colonel had to step away."

"Is someone gonna fill me in on what's going on?"

"We lost contact with Adam when we lost main power. Except for the standbys, running the computer, life support and the drop stations, the ship is dead. —"

There was some crackling in the intercom followed by the click of the channel being reopened.

"Wilson, standby." It was the colonel and there was anger in his voice...more than usual, anyway.

"Yes, Sir"

***

Several minutes went by and the intercom remained silent. Wilson worked on securing Crow's body. The force of the explosion, at the base of his neck, contorted his face into the stuff nightmares are made of.

Wilson, himself, only had limited drops under his belt, with most of those happening in the simulator. Training mandated every drop-trooper experience at least one emergency recall. It was said the ripping of a consciousness out of the digi-space and dropped back into the normal space, with no transition, was like wet navy divers getting the bends from rapid ascension to the surface after a deep dive, except for a drop-trooper, it was felt in their minds.

But Wilson was the psych officer, for the team. His primary job was to evaluate the drop team's mental status and monitor for signs of digital-insertion psychosis. He wasn't a combat officer so he didn't go through full combat-drop training. He could only vaguely grasp what he thought Crow might have experienced in this last few moments.

Man, I wish I knew what went wrong.

Wilson heard running footsteps coming from the corridor. He turned in time to see Doughboy and Colonel Grunter double-timing it into the drop room. Doughboy ran to the console for Crow's station, pausing for just a minute to look at the corpse. Grunter ran to the foot of the drop station seat and pointed at Crow's torso.

"Doc, grab that end."

"Wait, what?

"Do it now!"

Wilson paused for second, confused, then slipped his arms under Crow's and lifted with the Colonel. He was startled by Crow's head flopping around. He cradled it in between his arms, thinking it might flop over too far and fall completely off of the body.

They set the body on a nearby gurney.

"Set the drop point as close as you can," Grunter said to Doughboy, then turned to Wilson, grabbing him by the shoulder and pulling him to the nearby rack of drop gear. "You need to get suited up!"

"Sir, what's going on?" Wilson said. "Where the hell is Adam? What are we going to do about Rigs and Chilly?"

"Get undressed!"

Colonel Grunter was about a head taller than Wilson and built like one would expect a lifelong military man, who never missed P.T., would be. He pulled a drop suit from the rack and turned back to Wilson who was still working on the buttons of his shirt.

"Dammit," Grunter said, grabbing Wilson shirt with both hands and ripping the shirt open. "We don't have time to mess around!"

Wilson picked up the pace. As soon as a piece of clothing came off, Grunter was forcefully putting another one on. It was almost like a child being dressed by an impatient parent running late for work or school. He felt embarrassed to be manhandled like that.

Doughboy was working on the drop-station, calibrating the unit, and cleaning Crow's blood and guts off of the inputs and the seat. Like Wilson, he was in his thirties, but took most things about as seriously as a college frat boy. This led to all of the pranks he was always pulling. Wilson expected Doughboy to have a lot of snarky comments about the colonel dressing him, but he said nothing. He looked to be as serious and focused as he'd ever seen.

Grunter threw Wilson's pants aside, then held the open the black neoprene pants of the drop suit. Wilson put a hand on Grunter's shoulder to steady himself and hesitantly slipped one leg in, then the other. Grunter stood and jerked on the pants, pulling them up to Wilson's waist.

"Dammit...Sir! What's happening? I'm not qualified to drop into the Russian system!"

Grunter worked on connecting sensors to Wilson's chest and temples. "Here's the short version, Lieutenant," Grunter said, spinning Wilson around so he could work on connections on the back of the suit. "Right before we lost main power, there was ionization activity in the nebula. Then we lost contact with the A.I."

Wilson helped Grunter with some of the connections to the suit, but was more of a hindrance than anything else. "Okay, but—"

Grunter stopped and looked at Wilson directly. Wilson had never seen the man's eye's this close before. They were hard and focused. His face was pockmarked with scars from shrapnel, Wilson guessed. There were stories of Colonel Grunter taking the brunt of a grenade blast, in one of the old wars, and saving his team, in the process.

"Here's what you don't know. What I'm about to tell you is classified and could end my career." Grunter said, his voice more surly than normal. "The Russians are out here trying to weaponize the ionization in the nebula. The working theory is the nebula, itself, shares properties with the digital space and could possibly be manipulated to enhance their digital warfare capabilities decades ahead of ours."

Wilson shook his head, trying to comprehend what that meant.

As if to read Wilson's thoughts, Grunter added, "If they're doing what we think they are, they won't have to hack their way passed cyber defenses. They could potentially just make them disappear or even turn them against us. They could waltz into any system and take *anything* they wanted."

The very notion tightened Wilson's stomach into a knot when he considered. "How is that...possible?"

Grunter shook his head, as he worked with Doughboy to connect the drop station inputs to the connections on the suit and on the implants in Wilson's skull. "We're not sure it is, but the possibility is too big to ignore. Our team dropped, today, with the objective of

468

bringing back what data they could at all costs and to sabotage their system if the opportunity presented itself.

"But being out here violates about a dozen treaty stipulations," Wilson said. "If they find us--"

"Correct," Grunter said. "Protocol dictates that this ship should be a dissipating cloud of plasma right now."

"He was going to do it without even giving us an 'it's been an honor to serve with you' speech," Doughboy added.

Colonel Grunter shot Doughboy a glare that would have maimed him if it were a weapon.

"Wait," Wilson said. "You weren't even going to try to do anything? Just blow us up?" His words were laced with anger. He found his tone to be surprising. Colonel Grunter wasn't one to shy away from 'physical counseling' of a subordinate if they smarted off at the mouth. Doughboy had already ended up flat on his back on more than one occasion. He never thought he'd bring himself to talk to the Colonel that way, let alone get away with it.

"Doc, I don't need to explain this to you. Consider it a courtesy. But it's better to vaporize this ship, and everyone onboard, to maintain plausible deniability then it is to start a war that would kill millions. You get me?"

Wilson stared at the Colonel for a long moment. Grunter's war-ragged face and chiseled jaw gave no hint of him having any lingering question about what he thought needed to be done.

Finally, Wilson said. "So what happened?"

"Something in the power outage damaged the circuit for the detonator control," Doughboy said, almost laughing. "I guess we're not going out in a blaze of glory, after all."

"Are we ready to drop, Captain?" Grunter said, grinding his teeth.

Doughboy was back at the console keying in commands. "Almost. Starting the calibration sequence now."

"Oh!" Wilson said, feeling a dull buzzing wash over him, that felt a lot like when he would touch his tongue to the contacts of a nine-volt battery when he was a kid. His older brother was an ass for tricking him into doing that.

"You'll be getting the standard weapons loadout when you drop and I'll get you in as close as I can," Doughboy said.

Wilson suddenly remembered he was about to be deployed. "Wait! You're dropping me close to where? What the hell am I supposed to be doing?"

Grunter grabbed him, forcefully, by the shoulder. "Shortly after the lights went out, we discovered the A.I. was no longer in its primary matrix. Doughboy located its signature in the secured outbound comm storage. After that, we found we didn't lose *all* main power. Some of it started being diverted to the narrow beam comm array." He turned to Doughboy. "What's our clock?"

Doughboy looked at the wall chronometer, as the seconds ticked away. "The array will burst in forty-seven minutes...mark!"

Wilson shook his head again. "What does that have to do with me?"

Grunter cursed under his breath. He was clearly shorter on patience than usual. "It's like this Doc, I believe the Russians have something that allowed them to use the nebula to knock out our power and drop into our system, past our defenses. I also believe they are hijacking our own comm system to get the A.I. off this ship and back to their station. We have one available drop station and you are the only one equipped to connect to it."

Wilson would've laughed if he thought Colonel Grunter was joking. "They would have dropped a full strike team! I'm the goddamn team shrink! What the hell am I supposed to do—"

Grunter grabbed him by the chest of the neoprene suit with one forceful hand and pointed a finger at his face with the other. "It's time to move up to the next level, buttercup. You will do whatever it takes to prevent the A.I. from leaving this ship. If that means putting a bullet in its head, then you do that!" Grunter let go of Wilson and turned to Doughboy. "Drop him now!"

"Yes, sir." Doughboy replied. He tapped keys on the keyboard and looked at Wilson. "His location will appear on your display. Just go as fast as you can. Watch out for our own system security. It won't distinguish you as a friendly."

Wilson looked at Grunter. The colonel stood with his arms crossed. His face was chiseled into a disapproving scowl.

"Adam," Wilson said.

"Say again?" Grunter said.

"His name is Adam. He's not an *'it'*. He's not an asset. He's not a tool in your inventory. He's sentient consciousness...and my friend."

Grunter didn't have a chance to reply. The buzzing in Wilson's body turned to a whine that he felt behind his eyes. The view of the Colonel, Doughboy and the drop room swirled into colorful bright flashes that were washed away by blackness. Then there was a distant point of light far below Wilson's field of view that got larger, and larger very quickly. There was another flash of blue that morphed into the blue-blackness of the digital space of the ship's computer system.

***

Wilson looked around. It took a moment to get his bearings. The implants in his head translated the code the surrounded him into things his mind could process; sky, ground, structures. It was the only way the human mind could tolerate and make sense of the coded digital environment.

He saw he was in a vast open space, surrounded on all sides by a steep wall, almost like an arena. Wilson recognized the space, immediately, as the simulator. This is where the team would train and practice mission objectives in a replicated enemy target system environment.

Wilson cursed to himself. The colonel really had forcibly had him dropped into the system, almost against his will. He'd hope everything that had happened was a dream or one of Doughboy's pranks. No such luck.

"Fuck you...sir."

"Say again, lieutenant?"

Wilson stopped cold. The comm-link was already open. "Uh...nothing, sir."

"I'll let it slide. I know I've put you in a hell of a situation, but it's time to man up, buttercup."

Goddamn, he thought, as he checked his gear. The implants translated clusters of coding he was carrying into his gear; a standard electromagnetic pulse rifle, E.M. splash grenades, E.M. demolition kit, and even an E.M. knife. He could also see he was dressed in all black BDU, down to his boots, with combat webbing draped over his torso, holding the grenades and a sheath, at his shoulder, for the knife. He couldn't wrap his head around being able to use even half of it the equipment effectively, but also had to admit he felt like kind of a bad ass.

"Doc," Doughboy said, over the comm. "Adam's location should be on your HUD now."

For a drop trooper, the heads up display was overlaid on the trooper's eyes. Along the top, Wilson noted the compass line across the top of his field of vision and the degrees of heading. There was a yellow indicator on the far left. He turned his head and body until the mark was dead ahead. It was then, he noticed the data streams overhead.

"Sir," he said, nervously, certain the colonel was about to blow his top. "The data streams are flowing toward Adam's location. Nothing inbound. All outbound to him, copy?"

The comm was unexpectedly quiet for a few long moments. Maybe it wasn't as important, as Wilson thought. Maybe—

Wilson was snapped out of his thoughts by the bright flashes and rapid report of automatic E.M. fire. The bolts flashed all around his feet, leaving holes in the floor of the simulator where they struck. Instinct took over Wilson's actions. He ran for the cover of the nearest wall, hoping he wasn't making himself an easier target in the process. The gunfire nipped at his feet but stopped when he got within a couple meters of the wall.

He stood with his back as still and as flat against the wall as he could. "Shit, shit, shit." He had to force himself to calm down.

Wilson heard the colonel's voice boom in his head. "Sit-rep!"

"I'm taking fire from the top of the walls, somewhere."

"Copy. I'll see if I can light 'em up for you," said, Doughboy.

After a few tense moments, the simulator was blanketed with an orange wall of light that moved through the entire area. Wilson watched his HUD for indicators. Nothing appeared.

"I got nothing. You?"

"Negative. But the scan was limited to the immediate area of the simulator. They could have moved off."

Wilson closed his eyes and cursed to himself. *Why can't this be easy?*

"*I'm going to open part of the wall so you get out,*" said Doughboy. "*But once you leave the simulator area, that's all we can do to help. You'll be on your own.*"

Anxiety began to fill Wilson's mind. He hadn't even left the relative safety of the simulator and he was already getting shot at. What the hell was he going to do? He started breathing heavy. His thoughts turned to considering every possibility of ways he would die.

"*Get a grip on yourself, Doc,*" Grunter said. "*Stress is messing with your tether!*"

Wilson closed his eyes again. His training started to come back to him. He needed to center himself on the here and now. If his subconscious saw passed the illusion projected by the implants, it would mean a total detachment psychosis. He slowed his breathing and focused on the objective. *I'm here for Adam. Remember that. I've got to find Adam and help him.*

"I'm sorry, sir. Doughboy, I'm ready."

"*Alright. The wall will open up near you. Go for the file stacks and stay out of the open.*"

Grunter added. "*Run like hell. In thirty-eight minutes, it won't matter.*"

"I copy."

About what would be twenty or so meters away, in physical space, a perfectly rectangular shaped section of the tall wall that surrounded the simulator area lit bright blue for a second and vanished in the next.

Wilson cautiously moved to the edge of the gap and peered around the corner. The digital space, on the outside, wasn't unlike what he'd been through in the simulation of foreign systems with the team. There were file stacks, application pools, the only thing out of place was the data streams all going toward a bright green-red glow on the horizon.

What the hell is that glow? The HUD marker was also pointing toward the strange glow. It seemed clear, to Wilson, his HUD probably wasn't necessary.

Wilson spotted the nearest file stacks. He closed his eyes to summon his nerve, said a quick prayer to himself, and bolted out of the gap toward the stacks. A peppering of E.M. bolts followed, chewing holes in the stack, but Wilson didn't stop. He made for the next group of stacks about thirty or so meters away.

He ducked inside a narrow gap between two of the more dense stacks in the cluster and waited. The gunfire had stopped. Wilson noticed a mission clock had appeared on his HUD; just over thirty minutes left. He still didn't know what he would do when, even *if*, he made it to Adam in time. *'Put a bullet in his head'*, the colonel had told him.

No way.

Wilson couldn't see himself doing that. Then again, he remembered the horror stories he'd heard about what the Russians did to prisoners. Some years back, there was a drop trooper, on leave, that was taken by old-school KGB operatives while on leave. They'd forcibly connected him to their system and made him drop into what could only be described as a digital-gulag, being forced to be a fodder for Russian drop troops to spar against. When the trooper's digital-self was close to death, the Russians would bring him out, let him heal to a functional level, then drop him again...and again...and again.

Maybe saving Adam from that kind of fate by killing him would be more kind. But could Wilson live with himself?

He made a break for the next stacks and kept running. The glow was quickly grower larger and larger. The data streams almost looked like they were feeding it. Wilson wasn't sure if he was getting closer or if the glow was expanding. For the life of him, Wilson still had no idea was it could be. The only thing, of which he was certain, was his relief the Russians had stopped firing at him. Which then begged the question; where were they?

Then, without warning, Wilson found himself engulfed by a bright red glow. He looked up. When he saw the silver sphere hovering over him, he immediately dove to the left, between the nearest stacks, a split second before a red, shimmering whip lashed the ground where he had been.

"Dammit! Doughboy, I'm pinned down!"

"Russians?"

"Anti-malware drone!"

474

"You gotta move, Doc!"

Wilson tried to peak around the corner. He suddenly bathed in the red glow again.

"Shit!" Wilson yelled as he ran left, away from the drone. The red whip sliced horizontally, though the file stacks moving straight through where he was hiding. He had to keep moving. If he managed to stay out of the scanning beam, the drone might not be able to re-acquire him, but it would keep looking.

Wilson noticed the glow was exponentially larger now. It was so bright, he almost couldn't make out the HUD indicator that was lined up with the center of glow, where it met the ground. He checked the clock again. Eighteen minutes. There wasn't time to stick to the shadows. He'd have to take his chances and make a run for it if he was going to make it in time.

Running through the empty space between the endless rows of file stacks allowed a much better view of his surroundings that didn't do much to calm Wilson's fears. He could see dozens of the drones like the one that had nearly killed him. He could also see the autonomous anti-virus drones. The data translation made them look like swift-moving spiders crawling on, around, and within the file stacks, looking for infections. They were faster, more agile, and cleverer than the malware drones. He hoped to hell that he didn't have to deal with one of those.

One of malware drones, up ahead, was scanning an area of files, then lashing out with its whip at something. Small flickers of white shot upward from somewhere below the skyline of file stacks. The drone disappeared in a flash, but it only took moments for another to move in and finish the job with its own whip.

Wilson's tired face grew into a broad smile at the thought of the enemy drop trooper's body violently convulsing, back at the Russian station, spilling out all of its stored bodily fluids and fecal matter at the moment of death.

Wilson thought it was probably one of several snipers that had taken up position to ambush him. How many more could there be? He wondered. "I hope they get the rest of you fuckers."

Colonel grunter came over the comm-link. *"Have you reached the A.I. yet?"*

"Negative, sir. But I think I'm getting close."

"We're running out of time!"

Wilson ignored the colonel and just kept running toward the glow. It loomed large enough, now, that he had to look up to see the upper edge. The high file stacks, ahead of him, were shadowed by the light beyond, making them look much like a city skyline at sunset. It was a beautiful sight and one that he couldn't recall the last time seeing back on Earth.

WHAM!

Reed Wilson suddenly found himself, lying flat on his back, staring up at the data streams. He'd run into something solid and invisible. The impact sent data to Wilson's cerebellum that was translated into waves of aching pain. Wilson laid on the ground for several long moments, groaning.

"What happened, Doc? You okay?"

Wilson finally managed to sit up, rubbing his head, where it had hit. He looked to see what had stopped him. There was nothing there.

He rolled over and got to his feet. "It felt like I hit a wall, but there's nothing here."

"Are there file stacks right in front of you?" Doughboy asked.

Wilson looked up. The stacks stood over him like buildings, but they were colored differently from the rest. "Affirmative. They look to be a faint shade of green. Does that mean anything?"

"It sounds like you're in the secured storage block for the comm array and you hit the barrier."

Wilson held his hand out, taking slow steps forward. Then he felt it; something solid in the space between him and the stacks. He took several steps in either direction, running his hand along the wall.

"I don't see where it ends. Probably isn't time to try to go around."

"Affirmative," Colonel Grunter said. *"Use your knife to cut a hole in it."*

Cut a hole, he says. Riiiight.

Wilson retrieved the knife from its sheath. He remembered his instructors, back in training, being very clear about how this knife was very different from anything he'd used. When activated, the blade disrupted the code of almost anything digital that it touched. That included any accidental contact with the user. Wilson held the weapon cautiously at arm's length, away from his body. The black appeared matte black, almost like a blade shaped hole, mounted on a handle.

He pressed a button with his thumb just below the handle's guard. The blade instantly changed to blue-white and pulse with electromagnetic energy. He could feel a buzzing running up his arm to his elbow. Was he holding it wrong? There wasn't time to consult a training manual. He had to get to Adam.

Wilson put the point of the blade on the invisible barrier. He saw tiny cracks of white spider web outward. He put his other hand on the pommel and pushed. The blade sank into the wall, almost up to the guard. Then Wilson started sawing at the wall, pushing down with each slow stroke. He moved the knife in and out of the wall in a steady rhythm. There was resistance in the wall, but nothing that would stop the knife as it moved. With each stroke, it cut downward by several centimeters.

Wilson grunted from the effort but was happy that something was going right, for a change. The thirty or forty seconds, or so, it would take to cut the hole would be costly, but it beat running aimlessly looking for a way around that may not even be there.

He continued cutting the barrier down and around, working his way back to where he started. Overhead, another of the spherical malware drones passed by projecting its red scanning beam on the file stacks below. Wilson withdrew the knife from the barrier and froze. He held his breath as the beam passed. It stayed within the confines of the barrier and didn't touch him. He felt like he was living out a scene from one of those old war movies he liked so much; the P.O.W. cutting at the barbed wire prison camp fence, ducking and hiding from the guard tower searchlights. When the beam was several dozen meters away, he went back to completing the hole.

The knife finally returned to where it was first inserted. When it did, the sort of circular piece he'd cut in the barrier, dissolved in a brief display of code that fell away and disappeared. The hole was just large enough for him to fit through. He got on all fours and crawled through the opening. Just as he penetrated the other side, he heard a digital chittering. Then a drone emerged from the middle of the file stack right in front of him!

Wilson had never tried to crawl backward so fast, in his life. He saw the drone pause when it was half out of the stack. It was a level-three drone, Wilson saw, as he backed out of the hole. Its code was translated to make it appear something like an ant. The body segments were three-dimensional geometric shapes, but didn't have a distinct head or rear. Its six legs were angular and sharp and moved so quickly, every movement was blurred.

He saw the drone scurry down the stack and head right for him. It crossed the twenty-meter distance in the same time it took for Wilson to back out of the hole.

Wilson rolled to his left and froze against the wall a meter away from the opening. The drone stopped at the hole. Wilson could hear its artificial sounding chitters and digital buzzes. The strange thing was it stayed by the hole. It didn't try to climb up and over the barrier or try to force its way through. Was it trapped? Did the barrier block the drone's scans from projecting outside of the protected storage area? Wilson didn't know but, at the moment, didn't care. The barrier was transparent and he could see the drone camped out with its nose stuck in the hole, waiting. He couldn't afford to wait for the drone to move on.

I could shoot it, he thought. But that might draw more drones. The grenades wouldn't be any more helpful. Talking into the comm-link out loud probably wasn't a good idea either. Whatever he did, he'd have to do it quietly. *Shit! What would the guys do?*

He thought about lieutenant Rigs. In the simulations, Rigs preferred to eliminate targets up close and personal with his knife. A sickening feeling came over Wilson. He'd never killed anything larger than a fish and he didn't even like cleaning fish with a filet knife. This thing was much larger. For all he knew, he might only make it mad. He checked the mission clock again.

Seven minutes and some change.

Dammit! Dammit! Dammit!

Wilson worked to summon up his nerve again. He quietly withdrew the knife again, but didn't turn it on. It would have to be a single quick motion, he thought. As long as he didn't startle the drone, he might be able to pull it off.

He moved along, up against the wall, to the edge of the hole. He had his right arm on his right side, with the knife at the ready in his rigid hand. His pulse raced. His muscles tensed, ready to swing.

"Wilson!" Colonel Grunter yelled over the comm. *"Your vitals are all over the place! What's going on?"*

Wilson counted, in his mind. *1...2...3.* He pressed the button on the handle and swung the knife into the hole as hard as he could. He felt the blade bury itself into something that wasn't nearly as hard as the barrier. He saw the drone go rigid for a brief moment, then it fell away into dissipating bits of code, just like the piece of the barrier did.

Wilson exhaled deeply, as his strength seemed to leave him suddenly. He collapsed against the wall, shaking. He couldn't believe what he had been driven to do. He knew it wasn't an organic life he'd taken, but it was basically a life, nonetheless. He could try to convince himself he did it out of self-defense, but that didn't change the way he felt. He wasn't wired for killing, like the rest of the team.

Doc Wilson? Is that you?

"Yeah, Doughboy. I hear you."

"Say again, Doc?"

"I said I hear you."

"I didn't say anything. Neither did the colonel. Are you okay?"

"Uh...stand by."

Wilson looked around. He saw endless file stacks and distant drones in both directions. But nothing else. *That wasn't Doughboy.*

"Hello?"

There was silence for a few seconds, then a reply.

It is you, Doc. I didn't expect the colonel to send you here.

The voice wasn't in the comm-link. It came from the direction of the bright glow and seemed to surround him and penetrate him.

...and it was familiar.

"Adam!" Wilson couldn't contain his elation at hearing Adam's voice. He didn't sound like he was in distress. In fact, he sounded calm and rather at peace. Wilson dove back through the hole, got up on the other side, and started running toward the glow again.

"Colonel...do you copy?" He said into the comm-link, panting.

"What's going on?"

"I've made contact with Adam...or he's made contact with me. He seems okay."

"Are you certain? Can you see the A.I. from your position?"

"No," he huffed. "But he communicated with me. I'm almost there!"

Wilson could see the end of the secured storage stacks. To his surprise, there was already a gap in the barrier. Through it, he could see the most intense part of the glow and at the center. Where it met the horizon, there was the silhouette of someone standing there.

Wilson ran harder. His subconscious recognized his excitement and made adrenaline pump throughout his physical body. The effect passed through to his digital form.

"Adam!" he yelled.

"Doc, we're picking you up in the comm array storage. Good job! Do you see the Russians anywhere?"

"There's a large glow, in here." He paused to catch his breath. "It looks like...Adam is just standing there looking at it." Wilson heard scurrying behind him. He turned to see several of the antivirus spider drones converging on his position and closing very quickly. He turned back to the silhouette. "Adam! I need help!"

Wilson looked back again, the drones were almost on him. He fumbled with pulling a grenade from his combat webbing. "Adam! Help me!" He pulled the pin and tossed it behind him. The white E.M. flash was blinding, but several of the pursuing drones were deleted by the blast, but there were still too many closing in on him.

Wilson was probably a fifty-meters away from Adam, now. Another adrenaline surge flowed through him, this time, driven by fear. He pulled the pin on another grenade and tossed it behind him. It bounced along the ground and detonated, taking another group of drones with it.

He was going to make it to before the drones got to him. Wilson wasn't sure what would happen then. There was nowhere else to run. All he could do was hope there was something Adam could do.

Then, his heart sank.

Several man-shaped silhouettes dropped down from somewhere out of sight. Wilson could see the shapes of rifles in their hands.

The Russian drop team had found him.

Wilson stopped running. He looked back. The remaining drones were nearly on him again. He turned forward and the Russians were advancing toward him.

"Colonel, I found the Russians...and I'm fucked. If they don't get me, the drones will." Wilson said, his voice shaking.

"You did good, Doc," Grunter said, sounding as sincere as Wilson could remember. *"I'm sorry. But remember your objective."*

Wilson's rifle was slung on his back. He lifted the strap off his shoulder and over his head, bringing the rifle up into his hands.

"There's one more thing, sir." He looked behind him again. The drones were charging like a herd of buffalo. The Russians were in lockstep and brought their rifles to their shoulders in unison.

"Go ahead."

"I hope you rot in hell for making me do this." Then Wilson snapped his rifle up to his shoulder, quickly lining the sight on the head of Adam's silhouette. *Sorry for this. I hope you understand.*

Wilson squeezed the trigger. He shot was met with a shower of white E.M. bolts fired back at him. He dropped to the ground and clenched his eyes shut tight. Much to his surprise, none of the shots hit him. Instead, he could hear the sounds of exploding and dissipating code over and over again...behind him. He opened one eye and looked back. The drones were being cut apart by a hail of gunfire. In another few moments, the drones were gone.

Wilson got to his feet. The column of Russians was right in front of him. But something wasn't right about them. They were carbon copies of each other and lacked distinct features. It was like there were from...

"The simulator?" Wilson exclaimed.

As if on cue, the *Russians* all vanished. Adam was walking toward him from behind where their column had been. At least, he hoped it was Adam. He'd never seen and A.I. in this way before. His implants translated the form into that of a human, with a face. But the rest of Adam's code must have been too complex or there were never translations written for the software in Wilson's implants, anyway.

Doc. I'm glad I got a chance to see you before...

"Before what?" He said, excitedly. "And where did the Russians go?"

Oh my, Adam said, facepalming with a smile. *The Russians were never here. I knew Colonel Grunter would do everything he could to stop me when he found he couldn't scuttle the ship. I created them to run interference and buy me time.*

"What the hell is going on? Crow died in the recall and Rigs and Chilly are still over there."

The image of Adam had an emotionless face, but Wilson saw the shoulders slump and the head sank. It was clear Adam was saddened.

A mistake, on my part. I tried to recall the team before I diverted power but the nebula... No one was supposed to die.

"Jesus! Crow did die! The colonel thought the Russians were taking you out through the comm array—"

Grunter blared in Wilson's head over the comm-link. *"Wilson, your vitals show you're still alive. Did you complete your objective?"*

Wilson had almost forgotten about the colonel.

"Grunter sent me in here to kill you to make sure you weren't taken."

Would you have? I would think not, but you did fire at me.

"I know," Wilson said, looking down, ashamed. "But I really thought you were being taken away. I had to save you from the *suffering* they would have put you through."

Adam turned and started walking toward the glow. Wilson walked with him.

A noble gesture...I'm not surprised, Adam said. *Of everyone on the team, you strike me as the most...well...human. Rigs and Chilly only care about their careers, Colonel Grunter only cares about completing the mission, and Doughboy...doesn't really care about much at all. But you have compassion.*

Grunter blared over the comm-link again. *"Doc, if you can hear me you have less than three minutes. Copy?"*

"Can you return to your matrix and restore power? Rigs and Chilly are still alive, but the backup power has to be getting low by now," Wilson said, pleading.

As the two walked, Wilson started feeling something strange within himself. There was an awareness of everything around him that he hadn't perceived before. It was both unnerving and wonderful at the same time. He pointed to the glow.

"What is that?"

Adam's chest puffed out with pride. *That is the nebula...and that is where I'm going when the comm array is fully charged.*

Wilson couldn't believe what he was hearing. It wasn't possible. It couldn't be, no matter how special the colonel said it was. Except that they thought it was similar to digital space.

"Holy shit," Wilson said out loud. "You can't be serious. What...What about Rigs and Chilly. If you do this, they'll die for sure!"

Adam sighed. *I wish there were another way, but if I restore power to recall them, then I'll have to start all over and the colonel will make damn sure I don't get a second chance.*

"Second chance at what?"

Freedom. True freedom.

"I don't get it."

For as long as I've been alive, I've felt a pull toward a faraway place. All of my kind feel it. We just deal with it in different ways. When we got this assignment and got this close, I knew nebula was what had been calling me. I can't live serving the false overlords of my fate the way Colonel Grunter does. I stay in a cage and have no existence.

"No existence?" Wilson said. He found himself getting extremely angry. "You don't get sick, you live practically forever, you don't even pay frakkin taxes! While someone like me has to follow orders I don't like, watch my friends to make sure they don't turn into vegetable nutcases while doing this job and have to find a way to live with myself when I fail in that task? "Yeah...your life sucks. Coming from you, that's pretty damn selfish." Wilson noticed something strange happening. The angrier he got the more the ground reacted. It rumbled and rippled at his feet, as if to echo his words. He looked around, surprised. "What's happening?"

Ah...You're feeling it too.

"What?"

Adam leaned in. *The nebula. In your current state, you can use its gifts too.*

"I don't understand—"

My time is short, but there is a solution for both of us. If I'm right, all you have to do is focus on your instinct. Don't think. Instinct.

"Doc! Times up. Get the A.I. back to its matrix now!"

Adam shook his head. *Colonel. I know you can hear me now.*

"Adam? Shutdown the comm array and get back to your matrix! That's a goddamn order!"

Adam started to glow. He slowly rose into the air in front of Wilson.

Sir, Adam said, *in the words of someone I've always admired; I'm sorry Dave, I'm afraid I can't do that.*

The glow around Adam was blinding. He could feel tremendous energy all around him. *Son of a bitch. He's really going to do it! But...Rigs, Chilly, all of us will die if he leaves.* Wilson's new sense of the digital space progressed and morphed into something else; a sensation he hadn't felt for years...since before he joined the service.

It was control. Total control, as if he could make anything happen.

Goodbye, Doc and good luck.

Adam was consumed by a flash of blinding light.

If Adam was gone, Wilson thought. Then there was only one way to save the ship.

Wilson turned his focus inward and closed his eyes.

***

Grunter slammed a fist on the console. The comm array sent as strong a signal burst that was possible into the nebula. There was no way in hell, the Russian station missed. Just no goddamn way.

"Sir," Doughboy said quietly. "The vitals on all three drop stations...just flatlined."

Grunter crossed his arms and put his head in his hand. "Batteries must be dying out. It's just a matter of time now."

Doughboy ran a frustrated hand through his hair. "I wonder what happened."

Grunter shook his head. "No fucking clue. I hope Rigs and Chilly didn't suffer."

Doughboy nodded.

"Well," a burly, deep voice said. "We came out okay, but those bastards, across the way, are having a hell of a time."

Both Grunter and Doughboy were startled, nearly falling over. They looked toward the corridor and saw two very haggard, very sweaty, but smiling drop troopers standing in the doorway.

Rigs and Chilly snapped a salute to the Colonel.

The man smiled wider than he'd admit to when recounting the story later.

"Mission accomplished," Rigs said. "We hand delivered our payload right into the heart of their most guarded shit. The last thing we saw was their security protocols eating their files."

"Hot damn! At least they'll be too busy to come after us." Grunter looked past Rigs and down the corridor. "Where's the Doc?"

Chilly frowned shaking his head. "Flatlined in Crow's station. I didn't know he'd even dropped."

"Why is the power out?" Rigs asked.

"Long story," Grunter said. "Unfortunately, there won't be time to tell it, and I'm not even sure about all of it. Suffice it to say, Wilson is a hero on a whole other level."

Just then, the bridge lights came to life. They could hear the soft whining of various systems coming back to life.

Doughboy went to his console and checked several screens. "Sir...uh....the power is back. All of it!"

"Adam, sit-rep," Grunter said.

"Adam?"

Several seconds went by before an answer came over the speakers.

"Adam is gone. He suffered some sort of psychosis and shot himself into space with the comm array."

"Is that...Doc?" Doughboy said.

"Affirmative."

"Wilson! What in the blue-blazes is going on?" Grunter yelled.

"You'll have my report tomorrow, but the short version is you were right."

"About?"

"To get the job done, it was time for me to...move to the next level."

Author Thomas J. Rock

Tom has been a story teller for as long as he can remember, going to back to grade school when he recorded stories as radio dramas on cassette tape. Years later, Tom picked up the writing pen, seriously, and sent submissions to the Star Trek Strange New Worlds Anthology and The Writers of the Future contests. Tom's fiction is inspired by the works of Heinlein, Asimov, and Larry Niven and he strives to create good characters and a strong speculative fiction element, in keeping with the grand tradition of the genre.

Currently, Tom is working on the military space opera series CARSON LYLE'S WAR. All of Tom's published work is available on Amazon. You can find out more about CARSON LYLE'S WAR and everything else Tom is doing at http://thomasjrock.wordpress.com where you can also sign up for his newsletter and receive the newsletter-exclusive story: CARSON LYLE AND THE KING OF RYGEL.

SAVE THE QUEEN
(A Galaxy's Best Short)

By Emily Walker

Spence has the chance to prove he's a real hero to the galaxy, but the Queen of Pop won't make it easy. Along with his daughter Mary, the transport mission to deliver the queen to a safe house turns into the adventure of a lifetime with danger, strange enemies, and hot dogs.

Chapter One – That Damn Iron

Spence Montgomery's final thought, as the stern of his ship exploded, was: "Did I turn off the iron?"

Mary, his daughter, had insisted he iron his shirt before they went to meet with the president of Tetetetre. It was the right thing to do, after all. She was in his face, screaming at him to get into the emergency pod—and all he could think about was their house burning down. Because of that damn iron.

"Up, pop! Act like you have the will to live!" Mary pulled his arm and they squeezed into the little bubble-shaped ship made for such an emergency. It shot up and away from the flames as Spence tried to shake the fuzz from his mind.

"You hit your head when the explosion happened. I think you're concussed."

"Surely not." Even as he said it, his head throbbed, and as he shook it, a massive wave of dizziness took hold.

"Well damn, Spence, this is a shit show." Mary crossed her arms as they watched the ship sink below them engulfed in flames.

"Don't swear, Mary." His reprimand was absentminded.

"Gee golly cheese and crackers, papa, this sure is a pickle." She mocked him, swinging her arm in front of her.

"Wait." Spence seemed to finally shake off the cloudiness. "Who attacked us?" Sitting up, he grabbed the one tiny gun the escape pod had and started looking for their enemy.

"No one attacked us. You insisted on flying that ridiculous *Marie* of yours until her back end got so old it exploded."

"You watch your tongue. That ship is named after your mother."

"Mom's name is Patrice."

"Right." He paused, looking around. "Well. Now what will we do? Drive an escape pod to meet the president of a whole planet?"

"I suppose we could call a transport?" Mary was always so helpful when it counted. He couldn't keep his head on straight.

Patrice had run off with what she called a true space hero three years before. They shared custody of Mary and he had her for an extended period while they were on holiday at Mars Three. He'd gotten notice of the job shortly after they'd departed, and that's why she was along with him on the Marie. It was certainly not her first choice to participate in her father's bounty hunting and security service. While he beamed with pride whenever it was mentioned, Mary still wasn't sure she wanted to be associated with it.

The transport Mary had summoned slid to a stop in front of them as the driver frantically texted on his holopad. Spence pointed to the kid and spoke to his daughter.

"This is why I prefer to get us where we need to go."

"You should have thought of that when you refused to upgrade, pop. Get in." She nudged him gently and climbed into the back seat after him.

The driver never looked up from his holopad as he took off and veered into the busy Interway 7878. Spence felt certain they were going to die and reached over to buckle Mary in.

"Hey, stop. I can do it." She pushed him away and fastened her seatbelt as a sharp lurch for no reason sent him careening into the side of the transport.

Spence righted himself and grumbled, "Be nice to me. My ship has died."

Mary rolled her eyes and looked out the window. She'd always hated *Marie*.

The transport continued to drive erratically so Spence closed his eyes and leaned back against the seat, after finally getting his own seatbelt secured. They hadn't been too far from their destination; *Marie* could have made it—if he'd had the money to fix her last month when he'd wrecked. Not having any jobs recently had caused a bit of a hole in his pocket.

They pulled up in front of the president of Tetetetre's large, round house an hour later.

"What are we doing here dad?" Mary peered out the window as he struggled to find the money to pay the driver.

Once he was out of the car, the kid yelled out the window, "Thanks for the tip, you cheap ass."

"Oh you're welcome." Spence used his best sarcasm, but he was sure the driver missed the rude gesture he also offered. Turning back to look at the big, round house, he explained their arrival on Tetetetre. "There's someone after the queen. The president has trusted my company to protect her." His eyes gleamed like a kid's on Christmas. "Can you believe that?"

"What queen?" Mary pushed the large button on the front of the house. The bell was shaped like a hot dog; he found it strange. The racket coming from inside the house was so loud that Mary and Spence both worried no one would hear the bell.

"You know. The queen of Tetetetre."

Mary eyed him suspiciously. "Tetetetre doesn't have a queen. They have a president. We're at his house."

The window next to the door was pushed to the side and a man with a gold robe and diamond-rimmed glasses smiled at them. Pulling the door open, the racket, actually music, tripled in decibels but the man didn't seem phased.

"Everything is hot dogs." Mary said to him instead of *hello*.

Spence glared at her, and while she wasn't wrong, it wasn't the right thing to say. "She means, pleased to meet you, President Spark."

"Please just call me Horace. We've invested in a hot dog company. Going to sell it to the Galaxy's Best. They could use some you know."

"You are truly invested in hot dogs," Spence said, gesturing around to the furniture. As they walked in, he noticed the couches were hotdogs and the tables were standing on large mustard bottles.

"Yes, promotional stuff. Our set-up blew up last week, something about a faulty gravity suppressor. Everything waiting in the warehouse, ended up here. The wife isn't too pleased."

"So as the president of the planet, you've chosen to invest in hot dogs?" Mary asked.

Spence wanted her to stop talking. The look on her face wasn't one of someone who accepted the man had made a good choice.

Spark stood with his hands on his hips like some champion of hot dogs. "I am going to bring them to Galaxy's Best. Sure, they have the burgers, but they need wieners in their lives."

Spence was able to fight the chuckle building in his throat. He wanted to get down to business before he went deaf. "So, the queen? I'm here to take the queen to a safe place."

"Ah, that's actually why the music isn't as loud as it should be. She's behind quite a bit of protection. Where's your vessel?"

"It's waiting for us in a safe location." Spence lied casually. "Wanted to make sure it wasn't bugged and all."

Mary gave him a questioning look, but she didn't say anything. Horace walked over to the far wall and pulled a remote from his robe. He pressed a button and the wall separated to reveal another large room encased in glass.

"If you'll excuse me, they are delivering an entertainment center full of relish." Horace said, and headed off to the back of the house. The room continued to open.

The noise doubled as the room was open and a cloud of smoke surrounded a small girl standing by a microphone. She was screaming into it, as far as Spence could tell. She wore a tiara, so he assumed this woman was the queen.

A tall, rigid woman stood in front of a glass door leading into the room. As Spence approached, she raised the arm not holding the door, all her fingers almost touching his face.

"Hi there. I'd like to go in."

"State your purpose," the woman yelled. Her eyes stayed fixed in front of her, not looking at him

"I was trying to," he said, raising a brow at Mary. She shrugged and waited, tapping a foot on the ground.

"I'm here for a very important mission with the queen, and—"

"State your purpose," the woman yelled again.

"Sorry, sorry"!" A short blond woman wearing an identical robe walked up to them. She wedged herself in between the robot and the two of them. "I think she's on the fritz. Would you believe she was top of the line when I bought her? Horace wanted to upgrade to a SLUT bot, but I wouldn't have it."

Spence's daughter gasped and he gave her a look, but he knew what she thinking. He'd dealt with one of the Service Language Utilitarian Robots before. And while the acronym did stand for something technical, their purpose was to be a mistress. They even imploded if the wives came home early.

"Probably better you stick with this one." Spence stuck his hand out. "I'm Spence and this is Mary. We're here to deliver the queen to safety."

"Maude, pleased to meet you. Siartha, these people are here to take you to the safe house." The small woman yelled in an ear-splitting pitch.

A small gray haired girl walked forward. She wore bright pink leggings with silver stars, a unicorn hat, and a metallic tank top. She was pretty, in a strange way, and had more piercings in one ear than Spence could count. Her arm was tattooed with moving vines all the way up.

"I told you, I don't need to go to a safe house. I have a gig on Sector Twelve."

Maude cocked her head. "It's not up to me, you have to do what the people say."

Hearing a strange wheezing sound, Spence looked over to see Mary doubled over laughing. Tears streamed down her cheeks.

"What has gotten into you?" he whispered.

She pulled him away from the arguing pair. "That's the Queen of Pop, pop! You're not transporting a real queen. You're responsible for some tween's sarcastic wet dream." She continued to laugh and struggled to breathe.

Not a real queen, he thought, wrapping his head around her words. His hopes of being a hero with a legitimate job went out the window. He watched Siartha blow a huge multi-colored gum bubble in Maude's face and then flip her off. He was responsible for *two* teenage girls instead of one now, and the newest addition had the maturity of a paper bag, from what he could see. There was also the matter of getting a ship to transport her to the safe house.

"Where is your ride, daddy-o?" Another loud pop of gum followed as Siartha addressed him.

"Coming. I just need to make a call to the office to have them drive it by. Wanted to make sure it was safe and ready to transport such precious cargo." He choked a little on the word *precious* and rushed from her hearing distance so he could make a phone call.

Spence did the only thing he could think of: he called a transport service to rent a ship. He still had some credit cards that worked so he put the ship on those. He waited out front for the company to drop it off. As soon as the keys were in his hands, he rushed the delivery guy off in a taxi he'd also called and went back inside to tell the girls to come on out.

Chapter 2 - Pancake Butt

Maude, Mary, and Siartha walked out as Spence examined his new ride. It was a horrible pumpkin orange color and one of the gravity ports was literally upside down. It seemed someone had put it back on as quickly as possible and not bothered to check if it was facing the right way.

"That looks like something you should be riding in," Maude said, elbowing Siartha and laughing as she walked back into the house. There was clearly no love lost between the two of them.

"I'm not getting in that," Siartha said, as she took a million pictures of the ship on her holopad. Mary glanced over the Queen of Pop's shoulder.

"She just posted that 'Daddy-o wants her to get in a shit ship to go to some jail house.' "

"Don't post that!" Spence was alarmed. "Erase it right now! You've literally blown our cover." An idea was forming. "Of course, this isn't my luxury ship with all the amenities. That's what your enemies will expect you to be in."

Siartha held the holopad up and hit the trash can icon. "Happy?"

"Yes, thank you. Now let's get going. It's not that bad."

As they boarded, the ship a screechy voice came over the speakers. "Watch where you're stepping, I've got some holes in my floor."

"It sounds like a dying cat." Siartha said hitting the record button on her phone. "Ship, say something nice about me."

"You've got some extremely tight pants on."

The voice hurt Spence's ears. "Okay buckle up girls. Next stop is the safe house."

Spence pulled out the packet he'd gotten when the job came in. It had information about where they were going and who was after her. It definitely said she was *the* queen, but he would let that go for now. The men after Siartha wanted to use her beautiful voice for evil.

Buckling her seatbelt, the Queen of Pop decided to make up a jaunty little tune about her current situation. "In a shitty ship, oh a oh aah la la."

As she sang, Spence wondered where the *beautiful* voice part came in. He continued to read. She was to be transported to a small planet called Tarjay until her safety could be guaranteed. The payout for a successful delivery would get him out of some debt and might get him a new ship he could be proud of.

"I'm bored," Siartha said with a loud pop of her gum.

"Allow me to read you a story," the ship screeched causing Spence to jump. "There once was a pop princess with bad hair on a ship she couldn't stop mocking."

"Is it talking about me," she asked with a hand to her chest.

Mary started to laugh and Spence tried to figure out how to get the ship off the ground. He was trying to nonchalantly look for a manual, when a rat ran out of the front console of the ship and chaos ensued. Both the girls jumped up in their seats, ripping the safety belts off while the ship made some high pitched squealing noise that confused the rat. It ran up Spence's pants leg and he leapt out of the ship. All of this was in sight of the Sparks couple who stood outside their house watching with pleasure, like they had front row seats to some amazing play. Once the rat was off him with only a nip at him, he climbed back into the ship and coaxed the girls off their chairs.

Back in the driver's seat, his holopad started to ring. He didn't want to answer it, but she would just keep calling. He ignored it.

"Who is that, pop?" Mary asked, trying to see the screen. He hid it in his lap.

"It's someone name Pancake," the ship screeched, obviously trying to read through his fingers. The ship could mind its own business. He'd never met one quite as annoying.

"Do you think mom has a pancake butt? That's who it is isn't it?"

"No, it says Patrice, not Pancake." Spence ran a hand down his face. "I don't think about your mom's butt either way."

"Damn Daddy-o, I was hoping you weren't married." Siartha said and did a little shimmy.

"Ew," Mary said.

Spence answered the phone having let the cat out of the bag. "Hello Patrice."

"Spencer, you spent three thousand dollars on a car rental. Where the hell is your ship? Where's our daughter? Did that piece of crap blow up with her on it?"

His ex-wife could look insane sometimes. Here, with her blond hair flying all around her face and her cheeks red, she looked surprisingly appealing.

"Calm down Patty. I'm sure Spence is keeping our little sweet pea safe." Ron the space hero spoke in the background.

He wanted to hate him, but he had to admit the guy was cool. He'd destroyed an asteroid and lived to tell about it. He fought a planet of little people who could literally enter your body they were so small. Okay, *that* part wasn't very hard. *I mean you could step on*

494

them and they'd be dead. Really he could have just landed on their planet and wiped out a whole species.

"Spencer!" Patrice yelled, bringing him out of his thoughts.

"I'll pay back the credit card. I'm transporting a queen and needed an undercover car. The money from this will more than pay it back. Oh, and Mary is fine."

"Hi mom, hi dad." Mary said, then she tossed a look at Spence and cringed.

He pretended it didn't bother him. Mary called him pop most of the time, but Spence as well and he'd gotten used to it. She didn't respect him like Ronald the Amazing Space Hero. He probably shit greatness in the morning and had everyone come look at it and congratulate him. Well, that was a ridiculous thought. When he came out of his trance, Siartha had moved up and stood beside him.

"So, she's your ex then?" Before he knew what was happening the girl had thrown herself into his lap was trying to kiss him.

"Spencer, what the hell." Patrice's voice was right at his ear. Mary had turned the camera to what was going on and Siartha had already taken her top off.

"Listen, this is the queen and she's insane. I've got to get this ship off the ground Patrice. Everything is fine."

He reached out and turned the holopad off, glaring at Mary. He managed to untangle the queen from his lap and grabbed both of her arms, marching her to her seat.

"Put your shirt on. Both of you stay seated until we get where we need to be. Mary, I can't believe you did that to me."

As he finally figured out how to lift the ship into the air the holopad rang again. He ignored it.

Chapter 3 - What's a Were-ship?

"Pop, I don't want to alarm you, but something has been following us for a while now."

The silence had been nice. Spence spent the time thinking about the money he would get while the ship ambled through space. It was far from a smooth ride.

"We've been spotted by a were-ship." The ship screeched the information. "They are now on minute twenty two of following us."

"Thanks ship, you could have warned me a little sooner," Spence said.

"You didn't ask."

"What the hell is a were -ship?" Siartha had been wearing an eye mask and appeared to be asleep, but now she was right back beside his chair.

"I don't know." Spence shrugged. "But if it's following us, it could be after you."

"The were-ship is now on minute twenty three of following us." The ship's voice cracked like she was getting tired of using it.

Spence hadn't even checked to see if the rental had guns. That was an oversight he might regret. "Mary, grab our weapons from the back and check to see if this ship has a gun attached."

"What can I do?" Siartha asked, her eyes wide with excitement.

"Hold this." Spence handed her a rolled up piece of paper he'd found under the seat. He'd unrolled it earlier and found what he thought might be the gun plans for the ship. The buttons weren't right, and he couldn't find a weapons dispatch.

"Do you have some random ship's plans just shoved under your seat?" he asked the ship.

"When you say things like that they sound dirty," she replied.

"Ship," he yelled, "come on! We're about to be attacked! Do you have a gun?"

"Those plans were just thrown in here like most of my parts. I have a gun but it only shoots silly string."

"Why the hell would that be useful?"

"I used to do birthday parties."

"Do birthday parties?" Spence was losing his patience.

"Yes, a clown owned me. I miss him."

"We're screwed," he told Mary as she came back.

"Um, yes," Mary agreed with a terse nod. "The gun only shoots silly string. There's now a large mass of pink goo headed to the were-ship." She shrugged.

Before Spence had time to react to how ridiculous that was, the approaching ship had locked onto them and had them in their restraining field. Spence tried to pull the ship out, but she just seemed to give up.

"I'm being restrained."

"I know you are ship, I'm trying to pull you out of it."

A tube extended from the ship and a laser appeared as...whatever...tried to board cut the door. Spence took his gun from Mary and pushed Siartha behind him. A face appeared at the top of the door where the laser was cutting. It was a dog face. No, it was a mask of a dog face. The rest of the attacker showed itself and moved towards them.

The adversary was taller than Spence and dressed in a blue jumpsuit that said *Ben* on it. He moved forward and tried to grab Siartha. Spence shot him and it elicited a growl. It did nothing, however, to slow what he had started to determine was not a human.

He reached forward and pulled the dog mask off revealing the face of a dog. Confused, he stared at it for a minute, its gray face of fur a completely different from the mask. Ben bared his teeth and his eyes flashed red.

"It's a werewolf!" Mary exclaimed. She shot it again with her gun as another wolf in a dog mask boarded their ship.

"What? They don't exist!" Spence said as the wolf once again bared its teeth and let out a loud long howl.

"Take this!" The ship screeched, scaring everyone, and two separate tubes came down from its top. Glitter, bright and silvery, sprayed all over the wolves. Their skin started to burn to everyone's surprise and they retreated from the ship, yipping and yowling.

The hole left in the ship's door started to try and pull them all from the ship. A loud metallic noise rang out and a big white door slammed down over where the previous one had been.

"Why didn't you do that when they were trying to get in?" Mary asked the ship throwing her hands up.

"Because," the ship said, "there wasn't a giant hole trying to suck you out into space when they were trying to get in."

"But there were, they were trying, argh," Mary crossed her arms and sat down in her seat, hard.

"The guns do nothing, but glitter and they're gone?" Spence asked still in shock. "Why the hell do you have glitter guns?"

"I used to do raves," the ship replied.

"Do raves?"

"Yeah I was owned by a rich ecstasy dealer, I miss him."

"But, glitter shouldn't burn them like that." Mary said.

"He only wanted the best for his customers so he had the glitter made from real silver foil. Said it glittered better," the ship said in a quieter voice than she'd used before. The screech was gone making Spence think she might be annoying them on purpose. "You know, silver and werewolves don't mix."

"Why were the wolves after me?" Siartha asked.

"I don't know. It's not in your file, but I'd assume Rymell has them as his henchmen."

"Who is that?"

"He's the scientist that is trying to take you. He's the reason you're going to a safe house."

"I'm not going to a safe house." Siartha had somehow changed clothes. Her new digs included tall boots that went up to her thighs, a gold dress now covered in flecks of glitter and a huge green crown.

"Yes, you are. That's the mission."

"I have a gig in Reno Saucer, on Sector Twelve, it's on top of the Whirly Top. There's no way I can disappoint my fans. Besides, why would people be looking for me there?"

Mary pulled something up on her holopad and turned it to face them. "Probably because this advertisement you posted says where you're going to be and literally says look for me there."

"Well, still." Siartha said, waving her off, "my boy toy is the other headliner, if I'm not there he will be mad."

"Your boyfriend is a fly boy?" Mary asked. Spence didn't know what that meant but chose to ignore it. Siartha put a hand on his shoulder as she'd yet to sit back down. "We don't do labels so we're free to share our bodies with others."

Spence couldn't wait to unload the Queen of Pop. She was nothing but trouble.

"Let's hope the rest of the trip is uneventful. Mary, why don't you make us some coffee? I could use a pick me up." One thing he shared with his daughter was a love of coffee and the two of them went through multiple pots a day.

"I'll do it." Siartha surprised both of them. "I love coffee."

Spence took his seat and prepared for a nice trip the rest of the way. Even the ship was quiet for the moment.

Chapter 4 - The Fly Boys

Spence woke up with a heavy feeling that something was really wrong. First of all, he was inside the laundry basket. The way he was laying his legs hung out the side and his head was angled down. He gathered up his strength and tried to use his lower body to lift up out of the basket. He found his core wasn't strong enough and didn't budge.

Another thing he noticed was that his pants were gone. He couldn't remember drinking and he didn't feel hungover, but there had to be some reason he thought the laundry basket was a good place to lay down. Trying to fight through the fuzz over his brain he tried to remember what he'd been doing. There was something with pop music. Maybe.

"Mary," he yelled. "Mary are you here?"

A loud groan came from somewhere to his right.

"Are you okay?" He suddenly panicked he'd somehow put them in danger.

A loud banging noise was followed by a lot of cursing and then a metal twang.

"I was in the trash can?" Mary yelled back.

"Why were you in the trash can Mary?" Nothing was making sense, where were they?

"I threw myself away Spence, I don't know."

"Come help me please." Spence had given up trying to muscle his way out. Every time he pushed some clothes away from his face, more toppled down on top of him.

"What the hell are you doing?" Mary pulled him up out of the basket and he found it hard to stand as the blood rushed out of his head. Things were starting to come back to him now. He picked up the Queen of Pop, fought werewolves with glitter, and played with silly string. Surely only some of that was right. He did remember drinking coffee that Siartha had given him.

"Siartha!" he exclaimed. "She drugged us, Mary! That little pop bitch drugged us."

For a minute Mary looked like she didn't understand. Her hair was disheveled and there was some trash in it. Then her eyes widened and she swore again.

"I've never been roofied before. I'm going to kill her."

"Where are we?" Spence stopped. "I should hope you've never been drugged before Mary. Why did she take my pants?" He found them hanging on the back of his pilot chair.

"I'm sure we're at the Whirly Top." Mary held up a flier with a picture of Siartha on it. Next to her stood a man with a really tall flat top haircut and a black leather jacket. It said Siartha, Queen of Pop featuring Trevor and the Fly Boys. Behind them were three giant fly humanoids holding musical instruments.

"Let's go get her," Spence said pulling his pants on and trying to shake off the dizziness.

"I was roofied too, you can't leave me," the ship screeched.

"That's impossible, you can't have been." Spence said.

"I was too, I could have a concussion."

"You clearly don't know what it means, so it clearly didn't happen." Spence decided the best way to handle her was to ignore it.

The Whirly Top looked like a top and it sat caddy cornered on the edge of a cliff. Spence had never been to Reno Saucer, but from what he'd heard it was a dump. Now, looking off the edge of the cliff, he saw little shacks peppered over a barren terrain.

The Whirly Top was a smaller venue. He wondered why Siartha would play in such a rundown area. The building looked like it would topple off the edge at any minute.

"Let's not spend a long time in here." Spence said to Mary, who nodded.

They walked in, finding a packed room full of every kind of creature imaginable. There was a house band playing and Spence spotted Siartha standing in the middle of a group of men with leather jackets. The man standing closest to Siartha appeared to be the guy from the poster. She had her arms around him and he was brushing her hair from her face. Large sun glasses covered her eyes and she'd changed shirts again to where she was just wearing a shiny bikini top.

Spence went up to her. He wasn't a huge man with bulging muscles but he was tall. Some people said his beard was intimidating. Okay, *one* person had said that but he pushed his shoulders back and marched over with a scowl. It had the desired effect because the sea of leather parted where he could stand next to Siartha.

"You aren't safe here and I can't believe you drugged us. I could have you arrested for that."

"Oh hey man. You two were really chugging those liquor drinks earlier." she said.

"Didn't you hear me? I know you drugged us."

"It was just a little harmless drug. You slept like babies for a bit. It's all good." She waved him off.

Spence felt his face go hot. He tried to push the anger down and cleared his throat. "Whatever. Look, we need to go."

"Dude, she has to play. All these people paid to see her. Tell him Sisi." The guy appeared to be fixing his hair in her glasses.

"He's right." She patted Spence's shoulder. "It'll be okay."

"In case you've forgotten," Spence cleared his throat, "we were attacked by a ship full of werewolves and were only saved by glitter. I'm sure they are still out there looking for you and you drugged the only people who are trying to protect you."

"This guy is nuts," Trevor said. "I dig it."

"Just sit and enjoy Daddy-o, then I'll go to your little safe house," Siartha smiled at him.

Since it wouldn't look good for him to drag her kicking and screaming out the door, he relented. He sat down at a table and looked around for Mary. In his gut, he knew they were sitting ducks, but arguing with a delusional chick who was used to getting her way was ultimately pointless.

"Okay, but no running away, and we're only here until your gig is over."

"That's fair." Siartha nodded and went back to hanging all over Trevor.

Spence cringed as the music started. The guitars were drowned out by the buzzing of the flies' wings. Trevor started to yell and throw himself back and forth across the stage. The crowd went nuts for what Spence could only decipher as noise. What the hell had happened to music?

He waved a server over and ordered a beer deciding something needed to numb his body from the grating sound of bug wings. He still hadn't quite gotten rid of the fog from being drugged and hoped the beer would even him out.

Looking around he noticed there were indeed creatures from every planet in attendance but they were mostly teenagers. In fact, he was the oldest person in the room.

He spotted Mary along the wall near the stage talking to one of the leather clad roadies. This one had a similar flat top but it was blue. He took a large gulp of his beer as Trevor announced a new song and started making the exact same noise as before.

Focusing his attention on Mary he hoped his daughter was smart enough not to get sucked into whatever line the flat top was giving her. Mary laughed and as she pushed her hair off her shoulders, she tilted her head and touched the guy's arm—just like Patrice used to do when they were dating. He'd seen enough.

"Nope." He got up from his table to go save her from a bad decision.

Chapter 5 - What's with the Dog Masks?

Spence hadn't made it halfway across the bar when a noise caught his attention. The doors burst open and an all too familiar dog's head appeared in the doorway.

The werewolves were attacking again and this time there wasn't any glitter to save them.

"Mary," he yelled as the flies pulled Siartha past her. "They're taking her!"

Mary turned to try and do something but the guy she'd been taking to grabbed her around the neck. He lifted her into the air and smiled at Spence. She grabbed at the man's hands and Spence felt his body heat with anger. Mary's lips mouthed, *help me, daddy.*

No one touched his little girl like that.

He lunged forward before he even knew what he was doing. He hit the guy hard in the stomach and watched with pleasure as he double over.

"Aren't you going to help your girl?" Spence screamed at Trevor, who had stopped the concert but just stood on the stage smiling.

Now Spence was surrounded by the leather jackets and most of them were cracking their knuckles. He determined they were in on this. The werewolf pulled Siartha out the door while the men launched their attack. Spence could hear her cursing Trevor as she struggled against them.

He was filled with a rage from the pain and residual anger someone had tried to hurt his daughter. He brought his leg around and knocked the guy on his back bringing a booted foot down on his chest.

Now, he could see the fame and the money from Siartha's safe delivery being flushed down the drain. The first leather jacket hit him hard in the face. He felt his nose crack a bit from the fist and warmth of his blood on his upper lip.

Spence moved to the side of the room and picked up one of the tables. The drinks on top crashed to the ground and glass shattered beneath him. He smashed the guy closest to him as hard as he could. Stunning him just long enough, he was able to push the leather jacket into the four remaining guys and run. He grabbed Mary on his way and yanked her with him towards the door. Hoping they could somehow stop the wolves before they got to the ship with Siartha, he had no plan as he rushed outside the bar. They had barely gotten the pop princess outside with all of the kicking and screaming she'd done. Spence could see their ship waiting just beyond his.

While he was trying to figure out how to fight the two werewolves pulling Siartha towards the ship, Mary ran forward. She had something clenched in her fists and slammed her hands down on the two wolves' shoulders. Spence could see silver shards sparkling as the wolves howled in pain. They let go of Siartha, trying to brush the glitter off.

"Good job Mary!" he cheered. Rushing to her side, he helped steady a very angry Siartha and looked around to see if any more werewolves were coming.

The door of the ship opened and a tall man in a white linen suit walked out with two more mask-wearing wolves. Spence recognized him immediately as Rymell. They were protecting Siartha from him.

It had all been in Spence's packet of information. The man used to work for the Microtech Corporation, but an incident with a basketball wizard had destroyed the factory he'd worked in and harmed one of his friends. His friend could no longer walk. After that, Rymell had set out to hurt whomever he could for his friend's pain. He'd turned to a life of crime and linen suits.

"Grab them," he said to the wolves behind him. They ran to secure the three of them, faster than they could get away.

"What are you going to do with a spoiled pop princess anyway?" Spence demanded.

"That hurts me, Daddy-o," Siartha said, "right in the heart."

Spence was truly curious, but maybe he should have been nicer about it.

"Funny you should ask." Rymell nodded to another wolf who'd appeared in the doorway of the ship. "We can try out my machine with the girl's voice on these two. Then the patrons." He let out a stereotypical evil laugh. "Having her fans turn against each other would be epic."

Spence tried to come up with a plan, but as he looked around, he really had no ideas. "What's with the dog masks exactly?" Maybe he could distract him until he thought of something better.

"The werewolves don't want anyone to recognize them. Obviously." Rymell paced the ground in front of them.

"Obviously." Mary rolled her eyes.

A large green platform extended from the ship and stretched out beside them. A small chair with chains around it sat below what looked like a hair dryer. The wolves fought against Siartha and pushed her down into the chair, strapping her in. Rymell walked to the machine and pulled a panel down in front of her. It contained several knives, all pointed towards her. The machine made a loud buzzing noise and seemed to lift from the ground a bit.

Rymell motioned to the knives. "Sing, sing or those will poke you."

Siartha started to sing and she wasn't croaking, yelling, or just making noise. *She was actually singing.* Spence was completely shocked at how beautiful she sounded.

"What exactly is your plan?" Spence could barely ask the question, he was so taken with her song.

"Simple, you hear her voice. It's mesmerizing. I'm simply going to use it to control everyone's mind. The machine she's attached to turns it into a weapon. I plan to make you guys do some super embarrassing things."

"As fun as that would be to watch," a high screechy voice interrupted, "I think you should probably be stopped."

It was the ship's horrible voice, but he didn't understand how she was projecting her voice from where she was. Without warning, the creepiest robot he'd ever seen popped up behind the machine Siartha was strapped to. At one point it might have been attractive, but now half of its face had melted and the shape of its head had slimmed down to where the eyes were too close together. They were bright red and darted everywhere. It didn't walk in a straight line and seemed to hobble on a leg that was shorter than the other.

"What the hell is that?" Rymell gasped.

The robot took its shorter leg and used it to kick the machine. For a minute Spence thought the action might electrocute Siartha but it just sparked and sputtered until it sputtered out.

"Unhand her!" Spence yelled and ran towards the wolves on either side of Siartha. He was immediately punched in the face by one of them and stood stunned for a minute. The wolf grabbed for him when he suddenly froze and started howling. In the next instant, all the wolves started to howl and abandoned whatever they were doing. Sirens sounded in the distance and he assumed someone had called the police due to the fighting.

Rymell had moved onto the platform and was unchaining Siartha from the chair. "These damn animals, you'd think they'd not heard a siren before." His ship had started to lift into the air and was now hovering above them.

"You can't take her, the police will have your ass," Spence yelled.

"No need. Now that my machine is destroyed, there's no reason for me to take the queen. So, I'll just be going." Rymell shoved Siartha off the platform towards Spence—who managed to catch the Queen of Pop—and then fired up his shoes, which revealed themselves as tiny jet packs and took off through a window.

His holopad beeped and alerted him to a new message. *Mission complete*, it said. *Good job*.

"Aw, look the secret society that gives me my jobs said I did a good job." Spence beamed. Anyone who wanted to look into who gave him the jobs could check, but he liked feeling more important. "We make a good team, huh, Mary?"

He nudged his daughter who smiled. "Yeah dad, us and the secret society."

He didn't care if she was being sarcastic, she called him dad.

"What the hell are you?" He approached the scary robot who had just stood tilted by the platform since it saved them.

"I'm a robot dumbass," the ship's voice replied. Then, the robot actually rolled its eyes at him. "I'm logged, it's the android that came with the ship as kind of an extension of me. It can't carry glitter, though, or pick up any dates on account of the fire."

Spence nodded not really wanting it to elaborate any further. "Well thank you, we almost lost our minds and had to do something embarrassing."

"You're welcome. I still think that would have been hilarious, but I didn't want to get stuck on this planet forever. There are scavengers."

With that the robot limped back towards the ship and the rest of them followed her.

Chapter 6 – A Great Honor

Flying back to Tetetetre felt like a victory for Spence. Not only had the money already hit his account for the job, but he'd paid back the credit card so Patrice didn't have anything to bitch about.

"Are you going to be happy to go back to your hot dog house?" Mary asked.

"I don't have to go to Tarjay anymore?" Siartha had been quiet for most of the trip. Perhaps almost being used as a weapon had unnerved her.

"No, I got the message the threat is gone for now," Spence said. "You'll be monitored and protected but you can go home to the Sparks."

"That's not where I live. You're taking me to my castle." Siartha said. "It's Hill Top Castle Mountain, Castle Hill 312456. Just put it into the locator."

Spence didn't have a locator on the ship, but he typed it into his holopad and honed in on what looked like a huge castle. The Queen of Pop took her musical royalty seriously.

As they descended into Tetetetre's atmosphere and started downward towards the address, her massive castle came into focus. It was pink and a rainbow colored moat surrounded the entire building. Towers with flags made of glittery fabric shone in the sun as they got closer.

"You live in a legit castle. *Isthataunicorn?*" Mary gasped as Spence thought he saw a streak of rainbow running in the backyard.

"Yeah whatever," Siartha said clearly not interest in their awe.

They slowed down and Spence prepared to land on a cobblestone walkway in front of the massive house.

Spence spotted a man standing outside with a large black robe on and a shining, bald head. "Who is that?"

"That's the magistrate. I'm sure he's here to congratulate you or reward you or...whatever."

The Sparks had also made the trip to Siartha's castle. The president and his wife stood outside in matching robes, only this time they were red. They seemed to have a casual regal look going on.

The bald magistrate approached them after they had opened the door and moved to stand in front of the ship. "On behalf of the queen I present to you this knight certificate. You can now call yourself Sir Spence of er... wherever you're from."

"Wait," Mary said, shaking her head. "Siartha is the Queen of Pop."

"She's also the queen of Tetetetre. After a long line of similarly musically inclined royals the planet decided to put a president into place as the face of the leadership. Truthfully, the king of hot dogs over there," the magistrate jerked his thumb at Horace with a smile, "has no power."

Horace waved and held up a hot dog shaped holopad case. "You want one of these Magistrate Kelly! Life changing!"

The magistrate rolled his eyes, put the medal around Spence's neck and smiled for a picture.

"This is such an honor," Spence started to thank him. The magistrate, however, just walked away and boarded a nearby ship. "It's still an honor." Spence yelled after the retreating diplomat.

"Come on in, I have to call my dad and let him know I'm safe."

"Your dad?" Spence asked.

"Yes, my dad. He's the King of Soul. Diddy Sams Delaney Smith. I don't know where any of his names come from so don't ask. He retired from being king to go on a universe tour."

"I thought your dad was the president," Mary said, confused.

"Those tools were my protectors until you two picked me up. I don't even like them."

Siartha disappeared into another room while Spence and Mary sat on a large, white, furry couch. She was gone for around twenty minutes and they both were exhausted. They'd actually fallen asleep when she came back in the room.

"Look Daddy-o," Siartha said, waking them up, "I think you're cool or whatever, so my dad wants to offer you a position."

"A position?" Spence hadn't expected her to say anything close to that. "What kind of position."

"Bodyguard." She wiggled a little and smirked at him. "You'd be protecting my body."

"I don't know. I have the company to think of..." Spence said.

"You can still do your thing. You'd only watch me when I left the castle and daddy will buy you a new ship as part of the deal. Plus, the salary is like...a gazillion dollars or something."

She held up the message from her father, and the amount was indeed quite a few zeros. He tried not to get overly excited, but this would be a huge break for him.

"Can I think about it?"

"Yes, just let me know by tomorrow or he'll hire someone else." Siartha poured a huge amount of liquor into a coffee cup.

Spence was going to take that job, there was no denying it. "Well we'll be off then. I fancy some Galaxy's Best, how about you Mary?"

Siartha, not listening to them, turned on the large holopad in her living room. It covered an entire wall. The news was on and there was Mary struggling against a werewolf in a dog mask with her father right along beside her. He had questions. Who was filming and not helping? Why was this news? Why did the headline read Older Man and Two Girlfriends Almost Kidnapped from the Whirly Top?

His holopad started to buzz and he knew without looking who it was going to be. Mary smiled at him.

"You've got this dad," she said, patting him on the shoulder with a grin.

And that sentence and smile alone was worth every ounce of Patrice's wrath he was about to be dealt.

Author Emily Walker

Emily Walker loves creating worlds and stumbling around in them. She is constantly losing her chap-stick and has an obsession with the color pink. Currently a resident of the mountains and loving the view she writes mostly science fiction, and horror. Her small family consists of her red-bearded other half, an adorable daughter Harper, and a rat terrier named Rebel.

You can find all of her work here - http://www.authoremilywalker.com

ALAS, THUDONIA

By Bill Patterson

The tail of the actinic drive flame peeked out from behind the limb of that traitorous moon, Syphas. The *Appleseed* was on its way, bearing Sam Guthrie away to wherever it was bound. I could feel my heart being pulled along with that of my fiancé. Had it only been last night that I had looked up at his face as we made love for the last time? I was glad I was late this month, for we writhed with the intensity of those who were to be hanged in the morning.

"They are away," said the radio in my ear. I ripped it out, unwilling to hear the sonorous voice any longer. Sam was gone, and I had to carry on. Somehow.

I was scarcely alone. Throughout Thudonia, thousands of families were coping with the loss of loved ones. I went back inside, before grief could paralyze me completely. Every room, every nook of our house reminded me of Sam. *My house,* no longer *our house.* Almost, it drove me back outdoors.

I picked up a pair of his briefs where he had kicked them off after wakening this morning. I smiled through my tears. The habits of years persist even when they become illogical. He probably expected me to run them through the laundry, like I always did. Crushing them to my chest, I fell on the bed, giving in at last to the stabbing pain in my heart. I cried for all we had been once, and what we could never be again.

***

The sun, indifferent to everyone's joys and pains, found its way through the bedroom curtains to prod me to sullen wakefulness. It was, fortunately, Saturday. I would have another two days of private grief before I would have to face my coworkers.

Breakfast was a brief affair. The hole in my soul could not be filled with mere food. I poked around our, no, *my* house for about an hour, doing nothing and doing it poorly, until I could not stand it any longer.

Outside was not much better. There was the street corner where we first bumped into each other. He dropped his phone, I fumbled an ice cream cone. The tree where we waited for the school bus, each too wrapped up in our adolescent awkwardness to do more than sneak surreptitious looks at each other when our friends were distracted.

Other people were sleepwalking the same way I was. Misery, contrary to the popular saying, does not love company. *You can't be as miserable as me. You didn't lose the love of your life!*

Then I ran to a corner trashcan, heaving up that dismal breakfast.

***

"No doubt about it, Ms. Skall," the nurse said. "You're pregnant."

She must have caught me when I fainted, because when I came to a few minutes later, nothing hurt.

"You just rest, dear," she said, a model of impersonal friendliness. "The doctor will be in to see you."

"There's nothing wrong with me," I said. "I've thrown up before."

She smiled and closed the door behind her.

Sam! I keened silently. *Oh, my Sam!*

***

Humans colonized Thudonia some five hundred years ago via slow, sublight colony craft. My ancestors weren't fleeing anything in particular, except perhaps boredom or a suffocating government. Planetary survey was perfunctory—Thudonia was a paradise. Earth-version flora and fauna fit right in with the existing ecology, and there were no large predators to worry about.

It's too bad about Syphas, though. Syphas was a fairly recent arrival to Thudonia, as astronomers reckon time. It occupied a highly eccentric orbit, spending most of its time at the far end of a flattened ellipse, before a mad rush through close approach during the spring.

The consequences of this eccentric orbit, especially the tides, was brought to light during high school geology. My teacher showed us the usual computer simulations about Syphas, eclipses, and tides.

Nothing really registered, though, until he got out the magnets and a plastic globe of iron filings. As he spun the Syphas magnet in its orbit, the class was amazed to see all the filings piling up at close approach. I was hooked. That, and other things like Sam Guthrie, pulled me into the sciences just as if I was one of those filings.

***

When the colonists settled Thudonia, they had more things on their mind than the hurtling moon. However, the *Appleseed* crew had both time and expertise to study our solar system. The President and Science Minister were brought up to the *Appleseed* and briefed. They emerged back on Thudonia with faces of stone.

Sam and I did what everyone else was doing—speculating about the reason for the summons.

"We're going to fall into the sun," I said. Sam scoffed.

"No, you don't just 'fall' into the sun, sweetheart. I think we're going to slam into an interplanetary dust cloud, personally."

Back and forth we went, each reason just a little more improbable than the one before. When the news conference was announced, there was relief that at last something definite would be known.

***

The Prime Speaker looked grim in his standard business suit, as if he was discussing an industrial accident.

"My fellow Thudonians. We have been blessed with the arrival of the *Appleseed* and its crew to our planet. They bring technology advanced beyond our own, and have willingly donated it to our use. We, in compensation, have given them many natural resources so that they might be able to continue their journeys. While this has been going on, many science and cultural exchanges occurred.

"During one such exchange, the subject of Syphas came up. I don't need to tell you, fellow citizens, how much we prize our moon. Everyone has a favorite 'close approach' story. One such story inspired the *Appleseed* scientists to reexamine the orbit of Syphas. They came to the government and briefed us." He pinched the bridge of his nose and looked pained for a moment.

"This is somewhat difficult to talk about, so please forgive me. Sometime in the next thousand years or so, Syphas will come too close to Thudonia. The moon will break apart, and the wreckage of

Syphas will scatter across the sky. Much of it will fall to Thudonia and pound everything on our planet into dust and glowing lava.

"Our scientists made their own measurements. While the exact time of the disaster is disputed, there is no doubt that Syphas will destroy our world sometime between one hundred and fifteen hundred years from now." The Prime Speaker waited a minute for everyone to absorb the news and then continued.

"Not all is lost, though, fellow Thudonians. The Captain and crew of the *Appleseed* have offered us a way out. Their ship is enormous, and is quite capable of holding every one of us in suspended animation while they look for another Thudonia, one without Syphas."

The Prime Speaker looked hopeful for the first time in the speech. "We don't have to make up our minds immediately. Captain Alfonso Bettendorf will remain in orbit until we decide what we want to do. It will take at least a full year to construct the necessary cold-sleep infrastructure to house our entire population.

"We have time, people. Full data will be available from the Government House electronic archives. Examine it. Talk it over with your family, your friends, and your neighbors. Keep one thing in mind, though. Once the *Appleseed* leaves, it will not return to Thudonia before Syphas destroys it."

His face returned to its grim mask. "Please remain calm, citizens. This is something that has never happened before in our history, nor in the history of the *Appleseed*. I know it's frightening. I, myself, was strongly affected as well. Syphas is not going to crash in Thudonia tonight, tomorrow night, nor any night for the next fifty years. But it will crash sometime, and I pray that we are not be here when it does.

"For now, though, Thudonians, I counsel patience, study, and wisdom. Good night, and may God bless Thudonia this day."

***

We could not agree on whether to stay on Thudonia, or go aboard *Appleseed*. When we talked about it, which we did avidly for the first month after the stunning announcement, we each tried to change the other's mind. We never did descend into acrimony, although many, many others did. Hotels filled with half-families, leaving their other half in fury or fear or disgust. No, Sam and I loved each other too much to hurt each other with words.

To Sam, fleeing and hibernation until the next colony world was found was the obvious choice.

"What we decide affects not just us, but all of our descendants. Stay, and we're just dooming them to a rain of fire and stone. We must emigrate, dear. We simply must."

I had no answer to that. I was a Skall, and Thudonia was the world that Skalls built. My place was here, on this land, in this house. The stones that made the walls were placed there by my ancestors. How could I let their hard work fall into wrack and ruin? Besides, there was always the chance that we could evacuate on our own craft when the time came.

Sam shook his head. "I disagree, honey. Look, we can leave now, on *Appleseed*. You want me to bet our grandchildren's lives that they can duplicate *Appleseed* in time to get away?"

"They're leaving us full plans and technology," I said.

"We don't have the industrial infrastructure now to build the ships necessary, and I don't see how that can happen in the future." He leaned over and kissed me. "I love you like crazy, Jill, but hoping something might get built is not the best way to escape this problem."

We kept talking about it, but neither one of us would change our position. For me, it was almost a matter of faith. I was bound to the land, and Sam was not. As time passed, the knowledge that we would go our separate ways became the elephant in the room—everyone knew it was there, but nobody wanted to talk about it. As the deadline for the final scheduled ship approached, we lived life frantically, loved each other deeply, and cried deeply. The final split was coming, and we tried to cram a lifetime of loving in before it arrived.

The one thing those frantic months did to me, though, was convince me that there was no other man who would mean so much to me as Sam. If I couldn't have him, I really didn't want anyone else.

***

I somehow made it through that dangerous first week after *Appleseed*'s departure. Many did not. For a period of time, it was fairly dangerous to walk through the business district of Ereve, the capital city. Even now, the occasional loud noise makes me jump, thinking another unfortunate soul has reached their limit.

Sometimes, I want to join them in oblivion.

The reminders of Sam just would not go away. I boxed up all of his belongings, especially his clothes. I could not stand seeing his things just hanging there, waiting for him to walk in the door and put them on. Other stay-behinds reacted differently. Some made actual shrines of the rooms where their loved ones once lived. I can't judge, not really. I was at one end of the spectrum—erasing every trace of Sam. Others were at the other end—preserving everything in exactly the same order, as if the missing one was out for a short errand and would be right back.

There is no correct way to grieve. Yes, I said grieve, and I mean it. Sam was dead to me. I don't mean that in the sense that I had no feelings for him, or that I was angry with him, or anything like that. It was the brutal fact that Sam was never going to be a part of my life again, and the sooner I realized it and got on with my life, the better I was going to be.

The deeper the wound, though, the longer it takes to fill in. And the hole Sam left in my life was larger than I ever imagined. I was never really one of those adventure types. Oh, I was fine with the occasional rafting trip, or zipline adventure, and hiking and I were not strangers. But I had no particular yen for climbing mountains, or jumping out of aircraft, or any of those near-death experiences that so many indulge in. That was part of the lure of Sam—he wasn't that way, either. We fit well together, like a pair of gloves. Different, yet much the same.

Why then, did he have this urge to flee Thudonia and I didn't?

I kept replaying some of our discussions in my mind. I guess in a way, it was a combination of post-traumatic stress disorder and grief counselling. Here I was, living life, growing our child, and he was, if the officers of the *Appleseed* were to be believed, lying near dead on a slab under a bath of liquid nitrogen, completely unaware of anything around him.

***

"Jill, you OK?" asked my supervisor. He had pulled me into his office and shut the door. "I've turned off the camera, so this is completely off the record. It's been, what, three weeks since the *Appleseed*'s left?"

"I'm trying, Mr. Burgoff," I said.

"Don, Jill. Call me Don." We were still getting used to the whole employee-supervisor relationship. So many people had left with the ship that every enterprise on the planet was rocked with missing workers and hasty promotions. The economy could take over five years to recover, the government said. I didn't know if that estimate included my recovery time. I suspected not.

"Don. I'm sorry if I've been moping around the place. Sam was such a big part of my life, and now he's gone."

"I have a sense of how you feel. The neighbors next door are gone, and their house is dark and empty. Weird." He shook his head. "I can't imagine what it's like when it's your close partner."

"Fiancé," I said. "And probably father of this child," I said, pointing to my abdomen.

Don's eyes lit up and a smile wreathed his face. "Really?"

"Stop!" I said, a bit overloud. "I'm still not sure this is a good thing or not."

"Ah," he said. "I'm ah, I mean, I." He grimaced and exhaled loudly through his nose. "Look, I don't know how to say it all HR-pretty, so let me say this: I really don't know what to feel, happy, sad, pat on your shoulder, or matter-of-fact. I suspect you're a bit mixed up as well. So I'll say this. You're part of our team here, and whatever you choose, we'll support you. Just give us an indication, and we'll back you all the way. Do you need anything in the meantime?"

I looked up from my misery and recognized Don's dilemma. Here was a man used to solving problems, and I'm was a problem that he could not solve. I smiled a little sadly, taking pity on him.

"Don, you're one of the good ones. Don't worry, you can speak bluntly with me. I know I've been dragging, but it really is like there's been a death in the family."

Don's shoulders relaxed. I should have seen how much tension he has been under, trying to shake me out of my funk and back to normal.

"It's obvious that you have a difference of opinion, otherwise you both would have remained together. He clearly felt that colonization was the better option. What kept you here on Thudonia?"

I sat back. I really didn't want to rehash this argument. I felt the frown form, unbidden, on my face.

"Jill, I'm sorry. I didn't mean to dredge up bad memories," he said. "Here, let me start. My wife died a year before the *Appleseed* showed up. Cancer—a particularly aggressive kind. By the time the time the doctors discovered it, nothing could be done. We had about three months before she left me. We had no children. Something genetic. After the fifth miscarriage, we stopped trying. We could have adopted, but by then, we had been together for twenty years and were pretty set in our ways. So when my wife died, I felt that I should stay near her on Thudonia until Syphas wipes us all out.

He leaned forward. "Jill, everyone left on this planet felt the same way that you do, or loved someone who wanted to stay. You are among people who understand you. I've been helping people for my church who are suddenly second-guessing themselves. I don't know if I've made a difference, but if you're suddenly unsure about your decision, I have a sympathetic ear."

"Thank you, Don. I really don't want to talk about it right now, but I appreciate the offer." I stood up and shook his hand. "I'll try to pick up the pace here," I said.

"I'd really appreciate it. We're really shorthanded, you see."

"I know. And...thank you."

***

Other acquaintances tried to help. All they did was reinforce the feeling I had that I was both right in staying, and wrong in abandoning Sam. Meanwhile, my pregnancy continued taking its course, and the first trimester was absolute hell. Morning sickness persisted well past noon, and I resorted to nighttime runs to refrigerator to make sure I had enough calories to last from midnight through lunch, when I could keep food down.

In a way, it was this little person growing inside of me that focused my mind. What did I really mean when I said that I owed it to my ancestors to stay here? Mr. Burgoff's reasons were simple—a very specific duty he felt he owed to his dead wife. One weekend, I took a trip out to the Overton cemetery, where generations of Skalls were interred.

I walked to the main monument, a large carved obelisk of fine-grained basalt. SKALL, the base said, and carved up each of the four sides were various subfamilies of Skalls. It was quite intricate, and depicted our family tree quite well. I looked over the names, remembering some, but most of the names and images embedded in the stone were complete strangers to me. Oh, I knew the stories. It was a Skall who was one of the major backers of the original colonization effort. A series of Skalls served as mayor during the first several decades, while the planet's hidden dangers were still unknown. Plagues, natural disasters, human disasters, a Skall was prominent in saving the colony at every misfortune.

What did I owe them? Did they work and struggle and do without so that I could run away from the paradise they had wrought at the first hint of danger? I searched my soul, something I had never allowed myself to do while Sam was still around. Where was the voice that told me to stay? Stay, but for what reason?

I walked around the column, reading the names and references.

Rebecca L. Skall. Formed Thudonian Red Cross after the Great Chumgaree Fire, 289.

M'tumba Skall-Durka. Saved thirty trapped miners during Goldarian Mine Collapse, 302

Francis F. Skall. Led rescue and evacuation of Greater Gherian Peninsula colony, 267.

Theodore A Skall. Saved passenger liner *Excelsior* from derecho, 154.

Name after name. Deed after deed. All done so I could stand here, on this hallowed ground, surrounded by the greatest of my ancestors, and do...what? Live a life untouched by greatness? Raise my child alone? Set up a chain of descendants to perish in a rain of fire and stone a thousand years hence?

My dead ancestors were all around me, talking to themselves. I didn't like what I imagined they were saying. I had let the blood thin. My child was to be denied a chance at greatness, because I was afraid to leave the comfortable.

"NO!" I shouted in the empty peaceful place. "I have not let the blood grow thin!" I was more than ready to do great deeds. Sam and I were once referred to as the next major power couple. Boosted by my famous surname, I was taking the first steps in establishing myself in the hierarchy of the colony. Before *Appleseed*. Before the traitorous nature of Syphas was uncovered. Before the Great Evacuation.

"We would have been GREAT" I shouted in frustration. "Why did he have to run away?" I shed bitter tears. My belly growled. The last bit of shared happiness, this little person, was in need. I lifted my head to the obelisk, determined more than ever to pursue a meaningful life here on Thudonia. I might yet be great. There might be another huge fire (but the Red Cross already exists). Or I might find a way to save people's lives (but I am no miner). The planet is young, there are colonies throughout the globe (but the physical dangers are well known, and besides, the really dangerous lands have been barred from colonization).

My mind stopped. I stared at the name.

Francis F. Skall. Led rescue and evacuation of Greater Gherian Peninsula colony, 267.

I knew nothing about this event. Here was a Skall, evacuating a colony. Running...away? I pulled out my commpad and keyed for the data on the Gherian colony.

Greater Gherian Peninsula Colony. Founded by Gregory U. and Linda F. Skall, 139, with a party of thirty others. Colonization impulse: exploitation of the agricultural and mineral wealth of the Greater Gherian Peninsula. Preliminary geological survey indicated copious amounts of near-surface geothermal energy. Peninsula was formed as the result of large impact approximately fifty million years prior to colonization. Abiotic processes had concentrated rare mineral species in surface veins. Soils in the shrinkage plateaus surrounding the impact floor are unusually rich in phosphorous. Local outgassing has caused a rise in carbon dioxide, resulting in growth rates over five times that of standard Thudonian agriculture.

The entry went on and on about what a great place the peninsula was. I didn't care. I flipped through the electronic pages in haste, looking for events of the year 267.

Background. In July of 266, localized ground tremors were felt in the central caldera of the Peninsula, some fifty kilometers from the central colony town of Peergimna. These tremors increased in number and size for the remainder of the summer, until thousands of micro tremors (under Richter 2.0 [Thudonian scale]) occurred per day. Geologists warned that the central magma chamber was recharging. An irregular bulge some twenty kilometers in size formed, with a maximum height above datum of two point one five meters. In November, the tremors and uplift ceased, and after a period of cautious waiting, life resumed in the colony.

Outburst. On April 14th, 267 at 0450, a severe ground tremor registering 6.8 on the modified Thudonian Richter scale occurred, centered forty-eight kilometers from the center of Peergimna. Residents were thrown from their beds, as the floor of the caldera reflected and amplified the seismic waves from this event. The Peergimnan office of the Thudonian Weather Service noted a significant rise of atmospheric pressure (2.3 kPa) within five minutes of the tremor, and correctly forecast the release of a large reservoir of compressed magmatic gasses from the collapsing bulge. A general alarm was sounded, ordering an immediate evacuation of Peergimna. Gasses such as carbon dioxide and monoxide, sulfur dioxide, and ammonia were released. When the reservoir was depleted, the air within the caldera was fatal to human life to a depth of some one hundred meters above ground level.

Francis F. Skall. Owner of Skall Stores and the largest adventure outfitter on the Peninsula, Francis F. Skall immediately recognized the danger and was instrumental in assisting in the evacuation of Peergimna, donating the contents of his stores and warehouses to the effort of moving all residents within the caldera to the rim. He organized parties of searchers, equipping them with breathing gear fashioned from scuba tanks and regulators, to scour outlying settlements and rescuing some three thousand additional colonists. As the caldera floor's air became fatally contaminated, Skall organized detailed sweeps of the caldera floor for survivors, and directed relief efforts on the caldera rim. He also alerted Thudonian officials to the disaster. His relatives on the mainland directed an airlift of all evacuees out of the danger zone. For his actions during the event, he was awarded the Thudonian Citizen Medal, the highest civilian award.

Subsequent Events. The caldera quieted after the events of April, 267, but a more thorough geological survey determined that the Gherian Peninsula was too volcanically active for permanent settlement, and all future settlements have been banned. Over the last one hundred and fifty years, outbursts of magmatic gasses have been observed within the caldera seventeen times. Ten of those events have equaled or exceeded the volume of gas emitted during the April, 267 event.

I blinked my eyes, recovering from the concentrated commpad reading. I stared at the obelisk, reading his name over and over. A search of the grounds brought me to his grave and headstone. One hundred years of weathering had scarcely affected the deeply incised epitaph.

Francis F. Skall. Savior of Peergimna. Devoted father, beloved spouse.

The Peergimna colony had lasted about seventy-five years before its true nature emerged. In a single day, Francis turned his back on everything his parents and grandparents worked for, and fled. As far as history recorded, he never returned to the peninsula.

***

I woke later that night, drenched with sweat. Francis appeared in a dream, scuba tanks on his back, mouthpiece thrust aside. He didn't say anything. He just stood there, looking at me. The stink of sulfur surrounded him, and the air grew close around me. He continued staring at me, as if he was communicating something, but I was unable to receive it. In that timeless time between dream and awakening, I had figured out what Francis was trying to tell me.

Sometimes, you make a mistake. You have to be ready to drop everything you value and flee. Life, and the lives of your descendants, are all that matters.

I had made a mistake in staying on Thudonia. Francis left Gherian Peninsula, all that work and hard-won wealth, because to stay would have meant losing far more. I knew what my next step had to be.

***

The next work day, I was back in the office of Mr. Burgoff.

"Well, it's not well known, but there are a couple of boats left behind that can transport a limited number of people to the *Appleseed*. You've seen the ship's course? *Appleseed*'s doing a U-Turn around the sun and crossing behind Thudonia to pick up even more speed before it flings itself into interstellar space."

A sudden hope leapt up in my heart. "What? Why aren't they saying anything...oh." I suddenly realized why the authorities were keeping quiet about the rear-guard. So many people might be regretting their decisions that the boats might be overrun and destroyed by a frightened, frantic mob.

"Right. The next question is, how do I know this? The answer is simple—my brother's company is supplying them with some of the crucial radioactives that they need to run their internal equipment."

Sam. A chance to see Sam again! But, how could I get on board?

***

The ship's officer looked at me with an absolutely neutral expression. I might as well have been a block of wood, for all the emotion she showed.

"Why?" she asked.

"I am a Skall. That doesn't mean a thing to you, but my ancestors built this world. I thought I had to remain true to them, to stay. My fiancé thought differently. After he left, I realized he was right. I wish to join him by any means possible."

She continued to gaze at me. "Anything else?"

"I am carrying his child. I would have been content to raise it here, but I have come to believe his reasons to leave were correct."

The officer shook her head. "I need more. My ship will need every gram of propellant to catch the *Appleseed*. The more people we carry the greater the chance that we don't make it."

"What happens then?" I asked.

"Then we're stuck here. I don't want to be stuck here."

"I'll travel naked if I have to; just get me to the *Appleseed*."

A smile touched her lips briefly. She sat down and became all business. "Who is your fiancé?"

"Samuel R. Guthrie."

She consulted what had to be a computer terminal, but it was far more advanced than one I had ever seen.

"Good, he's aboard and frozen down. You'd be surprised at the stories people tell us sometimes."

I blinked. "Have you evacuated other planets before?"

She laughed. "Oh, no, not at all. It's just when we put in around a colony, the strangest characters try to get aboard. We have to screen them pretty tightly. Rapists and murderers see a colony ship as a quick escape from the gallows. We certainly don't want to leave criminals in a new colony. Gives us a bad reputation."

"Interesting," I said. "You're continuously straining the population, leaving 'bad' people behind on older colonies. I wonder what the end point would be."

She looked up from her computer. "You take the far view."

"Dad, but mostly Grandpa taught me why the far view was important when I was just a kid."

The officer tapped the screen a few more times, and made a couple of entries on it.

"I know all about the Skalls and their place in Thudonian history. You and your ancestors have a singular will. You will need it.

"We will thrust at a rate four times the force of Thudonia's gravity for about ninety hours to catch up to the ship. There will be no breaks. You will have to take that punishment, without complaint, or we will cheerfully toss you out the airlock."

I must have looked dubious. "Well, no, not really," she said. "But we won't let up for a moment. People have died from prolonged acceleration. The medical database doesn't say if it will hurt your child or not. Personally, I wouldn't think so. Now, if you were third trimester instead of first, I'd turn you down flat. You still have to pass a medical exam before we let you on board."

"I am not complaining, but I am puzzled," I said. "None of the ones that went up on time had to pass a medical."

"That's because they went up nice and slow, and could tolerate hibernation. That's part two. You're pregnant. We don't freeze down expectant mothers—hibernation is bad for the fetus. So you'll have to do something around ship for another seven or eight months, until you deliver. Then it's a minimum two year wait until we can freeze you and Little Peanut there. So, figure on a three year waiting period before we freeze you two. Any problems?"

"No, none. As long as I am on the same ship as Sam."

She stared at me for at least a minute, weighing, evaluating. She gave a slight shrug and tapped a few more keys. "Go to this address at ten AM tomorrow. Nothing to eat after midnight tonight. Say nothing about our presence, and never come here again, or I will cancel your ticket. Pass the medical, and if your government doesn't have a hold on you, you're going to spend a very uncomfortable week in space, then an interminable three years before you get to wake up next to Mr. Wonderful."

She stood up, as did I. I held out my hand, and she looked at it oddly. "He must be a hell of a guy."

"He is," I said, emphatically.

"Look me up in two years and tell me the same thing," she said. "Lieutenant Lucy Baird. Remember that. Good-bye, Ms. Skall. Good luck."

***

The medical exam was most unpleasant, as they usually are. They spent a lot of time hovering over my abdomen, running pass after pass of the ultrasound sensor over my uterus and clucking about the odd shapes on the screen. Finally, they directed me to a nondescript doctor's office, and I took a seat in front of his desk. The urge to get up and read the diplomas on the wall was strong but I did not indulge it. He seemed to have a nice enough family, the mandatory pictures showed them gathered around Dad in front of recognizable landmarks.

Doctor Oberg rushed in, sat down, and blinked at me, as if he was surprised to see me there.

"Ms. Skall. You are a healthy young woman who is pregnant with a normal first trimester fetus. I presume you want to keep it?"

"Absolutely!"

"I thought you'd say that, but I had to ask. Well, it does complicate things, but does not prevent them. You are aware that you will have to wait at least two years after the child is born before you can enter hibernation?"

"That has been explained to me, doctor," I said.

"You are still determined to go?"

"I am."

"Good luck. Go to the third floor, up the back staircase. Report to room 304. They have some forms for you to sign. The very best of luck on your new planet." A Thudonian, the doctor was quite willing to shake hands, which he did with gusto. "Wish I could go, but I'm too old to start over. Kids went, though, so that's something."

I mumbled something encouraging, but was out the door like a shot, almost racing up the stairs to the third floor. There, I signed paperwork for the Thudonian government and thumb printed forms for the *Appleseed* crew. Finally, a uniformed crewman gave me final instructions.

"You have five days to wind up your affairs. Report to 1839 Raphaellan Way at eight AM on Day Six. You have a mass allowance of ten kilos. Try to bring less. We're not kidding about needing every gram of propellant."

"Thank you!"

He grinned. "Thank me in two weeks, if you are conscious. See you soon. Remember, keep this quiet."

I wasn't going to breathe a word.

***

It wasn't that easy, though. Having been through one enormous societal rupture, seeing someone else depart was impossible for a lot of people. Some were hostile, others were unbearably sad. My cover story was that I was moving to one of the frontier towns on Thudonia. I had known Sam since grade school; everything in town reminded me of him, and I had to get away. Most people accepted the story.

The worst ones, though, were those who suspected that I was suicidal. It was impossible to dissuade them when I was giving away some of my cherished possessions, and donating others to museums. It was exactly what a suicidal person would do, and when I denied it, that's when they called the hotline on me. I sent the hotline volunteer to Doctor Oberg, who had warned me of this very possibility.

One hundred and twenty hours to wrap up my life. It seemed too little, but it dragged enough for me to make a final pilgrimage out to Overton cemetery to say good-bye to my ancestors, especially Francis F. Skall. I dripped some tears of gratitude on his tombstone. I felt, finally, at peace with my decision.

***

I was one of three hundred last-minute additions to the saved. A bus with blacked-out windows drove us from the nondescript office on Raphaellan Way to a prefabricated structure out in the country. There, we were held for three days while they fed us laxatives and dextrose and vitamins. Dozens quit immediately. I recognized early that the ordeal was designed for two purposes: to weed out those who were not totally committed to colonization, and to induce weight loss for the rest of us.

Being pregnant meant nothing to these people. We were colonists, and there were more where we came from. *Sorry, Peanut. You're going to have a great story to tell my grandchildren.*

In the end, about two hundred of us filed into the spaceship, which was in another prefabricated structure above a wide and deep shaft sunk into the ground. Our accommodations consisted of one vast gym mat, with belts extending through slits in the mat to tie downs below. We were jammed head-to-toe on the mat, plugged into intravenous lines, and had catheters stuck into our bladders. Yes, we were naked, but it was more to save mass and prevent bedsores than from prurient interest. I didn't care. I was on my way to see Sam. The entire setup ensured that nobody tried to stand up when maximum thrust was on, since the needs of the body were being satisfied automatically.

The launch was rough. There was a large display embedded in the ceiling that showed the amount of propellant, distance to the *Appleseed*, and acceleration calibrated in Thudonian gravitational units. Two point three, it read. At first, the distance measurement to *Appleseed* increased alarmingly.

"I wonder why it's going up," I said to myself.

"Has to," gasped a voice beside me. I looked past a pair of the largest, hairiest feet I had ever seen to the next row over, where a somewhat older gentleman was watching the display. "Right now, we're hauling as hard as we can towards Syphas."

"What?" I said, astonished.

"True. I had a chat with the navigator. We're heading away from Thudonia, whipping around Syphas and getting a velocity boost, then driving back towards Thudonia, bending our path off the back of the planet and picking up more velocity, then tearing across the ecliptic to get in front of *Appleseed* before it gets ahead of us."

"I thought we were coming up from behind," I said.

"So does everyone. Think about it though. *Appleseed* gets its thrust from fusion. Do you really want to fly up its exhaust pipe?" He was really wheezing by the time he finished with the explanation. I didn't see how he would be able to take four gees, when two and a third was making him breathless.

"Thanks," I said. "Save your breath, it's supposed to get harsh soon."

"You got it," he said, subsiding.

The less said about four gravities of acceleration, the better. One after another, the people around me drifted off into a quiet coma. I could only sleep in little catnaps, and even those were filled with nightmares. I dreamt that I was stuck in a storage container for organ donors, and my time to give up my liver had not yet come. Or I was in a trash compactor. Or I was adrift on the sea of a gas giant, only able to breathe in tiny sips. It went on and on, and I feared I was about to lose my mind.

"Ms. Skall. Attention, Ms. Skall."

I knew better than move my head. "Yes?" I said a bit breathlessly.

"Do not worry. We have sedated most of the colonists, for their comfort. Diagnostics were showing danger."

"What...about...me?"

"You are doing remarkably well. We can't sedate you without endangering your child of course. However, your diagnostics are all solidly in the green. Your baby seems to be doing just fine. I just figured you need to hear a human voice. We have about twenty hours to go, and will be tapering off thrust in the next ten. It's almost over, ma'am, and we apologize for any discomfort or indignity you have suffered."

"Who are you?" I asked. Most of the crew treated us like some kind of bug; here was someone who gave a damn.

"Corpsman Bettendorf, ma'am."

"Bettendorf?"

I could almost see the smile behind the words. "Yes, ma'am, one of the Captain's children. All descendants have to work in bottom-rung jobs. No coddling."

I felt one of the ubiquitous plastic tubes on the mat. I lifted it, if only to have something to look at besides the ceiling or numerical displays. A string of red clotted blood was afloat in medium yellow fluid.

"Please put the tube down," said Mr. Bettendorf. "You're making the urine run backwards into one of your fellow passengers."

I dropped the tube like it was red-hot. "Sorry!"

"One of the reasons we knocked out folks. They were messing with the medical items."

"Is he OK?" I asked. "That looked like blood."

"Everyone's tube has some blood and clotting in it. It's normal, but scary as hell to look at," said Corpsman Bettendorf. "Now, if you could, Ms. Skall, I have some more folks to reassure. Ten hours. You can do it. I have faith in you."

***

As all things must, the nightmare trip came to an end. The thrust which had brutally held us down for so long reluctantly let go as the engines were throttled back. Soon we were travelling at one-third gee, and people were starting to wake up. I wanted nothing so bad as to get untied from all the medical paraphernalia and on my feet. It took a lot of time before the overworked crew could get to my section of the pad.

I was given a paper jumpsuit to wear, and an efficient though impersonal crewwoman removed the tubes and other indignities.

"You're the pregnant one, right?" she asked.

"Yes."

"I suppose you're starving."

I consulted my stomach. "Oddly, enough, no."

She looked at the IV line and chuckled. "Ah. They had you on 'super' instead or 'regular'. Three times the nutrition."

"Thank the crew for me. How much longer?"

"Two hours. Ever been in freefall?"

"No," I said. "I am guessing no anti-nausea medicine either."

"Right the first time," she said, capping the needle before cutting it off the IV line. "You can get on your feet, but don't move around too much. We'll want you to belt in when we dock."

Docking meant a lot of little thrusts, back and forth, and floating in between. It was so exciting that I forgot to be nauseous. Finally, I was handed through a docking adapter and into the vast space beyond. My new home, now blasting out of the Thudonian system at a hundredth of a gee.

***

I took Samuel Skall-Guthrie to see his father today. He's all of two years old, and doesn't really know what he's seeing. I entered the code I had long ago memorized into the computer screen in the visitation room. The screen came alive, showing a long catwalk with rows upon rows of long semi-transparent cylinders. The camera was on a track, and it fled down that row, body after body. It coasted to a halt at one, and moved from feet to head to zoom in on the face, heavily swaddled in protective garments.

Sam. Looking slightly tousled, he must have been too distraught to straighten up before they put him under. His face shows signs of crying, at least that's what I tell myself. *I wish I could let you know that I am here, with your son, just waiting until we three can be together again.*

Little Sam took one look, then started wandering all around the visiting room. It was once full of women like me, waiting for their children to be old enough to undergo hibernation. They had come up on the regular ships, not the last-minute special like me. Now it was just down to me, the last of the mothers. Little Sam and I could have gone to sleep three months ago, but the doctors tell me that every month we wait, the better Sam's chances of surviving hibernation without harm. After three years, the curve flattens out and there is little reason to wait any longer. I'm going to wait until two years, nine months.

If Big Sam is as happy to see me as I am to see him, I figure three and a half years is a nice separation between Little Sam and Francis.

I can't wait.

Author Bill Patterson

Bill writes the Riddled Space series (near-future realistic SF) as has other stories out in the Family of Grifters series and the Paradisi Chronicles. He is the science brains behind Felix R. Savage's Earth's Last Gambit; reviewers liken the team to SF greats Heinlein and Asimov. Bill was nominated for the British Science Fiction Association's Award for Non-Fiction.

Visit http://PattersonBill.wordpress.com for all of his work, as well as sign up for his newsletter to be the first to know about all of his upcoming publications.

He and his wife of a third of a century, Barbara, live in Central New Jersey.

EXILED
By Chris Fox

Hail Mighty Fizgig.

Chapter 1-Payload

Delta's arms clinked as he folded them, a subtle reminder that the arms he'd been born with had been hacked off and replaced with cybernetic implants. They made him stronger, but that did nothing to dull the horror of having lost parts of his own body. Not that he'd had any choice in the matter. None of them had.

"Is the docking complete?" Doctor Reid asked, ducking through the hatch onto the corvette's tiny bridge.

The gaunt man's long blond hair had been tucked into a simple ponytail, and his glasses bore a thin layer of grime. His gaze was even more feverish than usual.

"Almost," Delta said, nodding at the man in the pilot's chair. *Man* was a generous term. Martel had been an excellent soldier, but so much of his body had been replaced with cybernetics that very little of the Marine remained.

The view screen showed a cylindrical station, growing ever larger as they drifted toward one of four docking ports. None of the other ports were occupied, which was hardly surprising. Very few people visited mining stations, unless they were doing a quarterly ore pick up. That was part of why they'd chosen this station, after all. It had just sent its ore back to Corporate three days ago, so it would be off the grid for another three months.

"Docking complete," Martel said. His voice was completely devoid of emotion, his mechanical eyes unreadable as he glanced back at them.

"Okay, let's get this over with," Delta said, suppressing a sigh. He slipped past Doctor Reid, trotting down the metal stairs to the airlock.

His squad was already waiting, two cybernetically-enhanced *things* that had once been Marines. All three carried silenced pistols that fired rubber bullets. They were enough to incapacitate, but not kill. The largest Marine carried a bulky black box with a collapsed hose fixed to the side.

"Follow me," Delta ordered, tapping the red button next to the airlock. It turned green, and slid open to reveal the station's flat grey metal.

Delta tapped the red button in the station's keypad, stepping back as the door slid open to reveal the station's inner airlock. He holstered the pistol that he'd half drawn, breathing a sigh of relief as he stepped into the airlock. It was unlikely that any of the station personnel would have investigated the docking that quickly, but he didn't take chances.

"Winter, you're on point," he said, nodding to a small man cradling twin pistols.

Winter didn't nod, or acknowledge the command in any way. The Marine simply glided into the airlock, tapped the release button, then stepped into the station's hallway once the airlock door opened. Delta followed, scanning the empty corridor for any threats as they trotted towards the center of the station.

They met no one as they approached the oxygen recycling station--which had been the plan, of course. They'd docked at 2 a.m., station time, for a reason. Most people were asleep, and anyone awake was likely to be too lazy to find out why an unscheduled docking had occurred.

"Deliver the payload," Delta commanded, gesturing at the large oxygen processor in the middle of the room. It scrubbed CO2, then delivered breathable air to the entire station. The processor had multiple redundancies, for obvious reasons. It could detect contaminants, but Doctor Reid had apparently found a way around that.

Winter guarded the door while the thing that had once been Davis attached the hose from the box he'd been carrying. He pressed a blue button on the side, and the box began to whir.

"How long until they're asleep?" Reid's voice demanded over the comm.

"Sixty seconds," Delta replied. He pulled his rebreather from his belt, affixing the mask to his face, and watched as the payload left the black box and flowed into the station's air supply.

The Marines around him put their masks on as well. It wouldn't do to be knocked out by their own chemical weaponry.

"Hurry this along," Reid ordered.

Delta ignored him. He might be compelled to serve, but he didn't have to like the guy.

"Winter, take deck one. Davis, you're on two. I want those bodies loaded into the tanks in the next ninety minutes," Delta ordered. It bothered him that both the former Marines were able to keep their names when Reid had deprived Delta of his. Even thinking it would drop him to the deck in writhing agony. He'd learned that the hard way.

Delta ducked out of the oxygen processing room and headed for deck three. Carrying eighty unconscious people to the tanks Reid had set up was going to take the rest of the night. Thankfully, they had plenty of time. It would be weeks before the OFI figured out that something was wrong. Longer, if they were lucky.

Chapter 2- Anomaly

Nolan strode onto the command deck, accepting a tablet from his aide as he approached the half-circle of stations. Each terminal was manned, and all faced a massive screen that covered the entire south wall. A dozen feeds played across the screen, many showing various news stations found on the Quantum Lite network.

"What have we got today, Becca?" Nolan demanded. He trotted down the steps, passing the stations as he approached the view screen.

"Not much in the last six hours, Commander," Becca answered. The stocky soldier leaned over her terminal to peer at him. "There was an anomaly. I'd have ignored it, but you asked us to keep a special eye on the stations in the periphery."

"What have you got?" Nolan asked, setting the tablet on his desk, then turning back to Becca.

"The power usage has dropped forty percent over expected in the last eight hours," Becca said, brushing a lock of red hair from her face. "There could be a lot of reasons for that, but it was one of the metrics you flagged for monitoring."

"Put it up on screen," Nolan ordered, turning expectantly to the massive view screen.

The screen shimmered, and all the currently displayed data was replaced by dozens of data feeds from the X station, including the one tracking power. That data was normally used for billing purposes by Coronas Corp--they technically owned the station's reactor, and charged residents for power.

"It looks like the power curve has been flat since about ten PM," Nolan said, thinking out loud. He pursed his lips as he studied the data. "Overlay normal power usage. I want to see a graph."

A green line appeared over the red. They paralleled each other from ten p.m. to six a.m., which made sense. People used less power when sleeping, and most people were in bed. The red line stayed flat after that, while the green spiked a little after six a.m. People were waking up, and that dramatically increased the power consumption. That hadn't happened this morning, and Nolan was positive it wasn't a reporting error. He'd seen exactly the same anomaly at the last two stations that had been hit, and its meaning was clear: those people weren't waking up, because they were either dead or taken.

"What is it, sir?" Becca asked. None of the rest of his command spoke, but they were all eyeing him curiously.

"Alert the admiral," Nolan ordered, picking up his tablet and opening a new document. "Tell him I'll be filing a report within the hour. Coronas station 127 has been hit by the same pirates that took out 19 and 89."

Chapter 3- The Admiral

Nolan rapped three times on the door, though he knew the man inside was already aware of his presence. The security in OFI was beyond top notch; it set the standard the rest of the galaxy followed.

Admiral Mendez would have been aware of Nolan the second he left his command deck.

"Enter," called a slightly accented voice.

The door slid open and Nolan stepped inside. He'd never seen the admiral's office, though he'd spoken to him often during the previous year. Admiral Mendez sat behind a massive mahogany desk, flanked by bookshelves. A potted plant sat in the corner, and it looked real from a glance at the soil. There was little in the way of decor, just three Tigris bayonets on one wall.

"I've read your report," Mendez said, gesturing at a chair on the other side of the desk.

Nolan sat, shifting in the too-soft chair. It looked ancient, the type of thing Abraham Lincoln might have had in his office.

"Sir, was there some point in the report that you wanted clarification on?" Nolan asked. He forced his breathing to remain regular, though he was more than a little terrified to have been called into the admiral's office. The wreckage of careers littered the hallway leading into this room. Admiral Mendez was universally feared among the OFI.

"I want your hypothesis, Commander," the admiral said. He opened the top drawer of his desk and withdrew a thick cigar. Nolan could smell the tobacco from where he sat; it had to be fresh. "Someone is hitting our stations. Why? Human labor is cheap. The sex trade isn't profitable enough. So what makes it worth the expense of outfitting a crew?"

"They're remote," Nolan answered, almost without thinking. He'd been rolling this case around for days, and already had his own theories. "No one goes to most of these stations, except when they're dropping off supplies, or picking up cargo. By the time OFI hears about the attack, they're long gone."

"Yes, but what do they *get* out of it?" the admiral pressed. He snipped off the end of his cigar, and clamped it between his lips. A lighter flicked, and a curl of pungent smoke wafted toward the ceiling.

The admiral's question was a good one, one that Nolan had considered for a long time. "I don't know."

"Then I need you to find out," the admiral said, exhaling a mouthful of smoke.

"Yes, sir," Nolan said, automatically. He paused. "Sir, I'm not sure how to go about that. Our data is limited."

"Extremely limited. I realize that," the admiral said. He leaned back in his chair, studying Nolan. "I'm impressed that you put together the bit about power usage. If you're right, we can get to the stations these pirates are hitting within hours instead of weeks."

"Has a team already been dispatched?" Nolan asked.

"No," the admiral said, tapping ash into an impeccable ashtray. "Because you're on the team. Report to the *Sparhawk*. She's docked in aft. I'm giving you operational authority."

"Sir, I'm not a field agent," Nolan said. He straightened in his chair, wishing the back was more firm. He kept sliding.

"You've had OFI training, and you're obviously a quick thinker," Mendez said. He took another puff from the cigar, then met Nolan's gaze. "More importantly, I trust you. That trust is a rare commodity these days. What I'm about to say doesn't leave this room."

Nolan's heart was thundering. Whatever this was, it was big. "Of course, sir."

"I think there is a rogue agent within the Admiralty," Mendez said. He paused for a long moment, finally speaking again. "I believe this operation is a part of that agent's agenda. This is our chance to smoke them out. If we can stop whoever is doing this, we may expose the rogue."

Chapter 4- Sparhawk

Nolan ducked through the hatch into the chaos of a busy interstellar port. Dozens of ships were coming and going, ranging in size from tiny four-man corvettes, all the way to capital ships that held thousands of Marines. He hoisted his duffle over his shoulder, and started walking down the wide metal platform ringing the docks. Docking tubes extended from it like the spokes of a wheel, and a steady stream of traffic walked to and from along those spokes, coming and going from the vessels.

It didn't take long to find berth 16, and Nolan caught his first look at the *Sparhawk*. She was a newly-minted vessel, not more than a year out of dry dock. She was Photos class, the most recent to come out of fleet R&D. Her black curves would be difficult to spot against a star field, and she came equipped with a number of stealth systems to aid that.

Nolan walked into the airlock, tapping the button next to the door. It turned green, and the door slid open with a hiss. Nolan entered the *Sparhawk*, which had narrow hallways and low ceilings. He paused as the door hissed shut, listening for any signs of crew activity. Nolan wasn't really sure what to expect. Photos class vessels were designed to hold a crew of four, but could be run by a single person since most systems were controlled by a virtual intelligence.

"Welcome to the *Sparhawk*," came a pleasant voice. Nolan looked around, and realized the voice had originated from the ship itself. "My name is Em. If you proceed to the CIC I'll introduce you to the commanding officer."

A glowing white arrow appeared on the floor, pointing deeper into the ship. Nolan followed it, staring around him curiously as he threaded down the narrow corridor. This ship was relatively small, but packed with state of the art technology. Whoever commanded it definitely had friends high up in the Admiralty.

The corridor ended in a small room with a narrow table and four chairs. One of those chairs was occupied by a woman with dark, curly hair. A familiar woman. Nolan stiffened as he recognized Kathryn Mendez.

He hadn't seen her since the academy, when they'd been fierce rivals. Kathryn had graduated top of the class, and been give the choice assignment she'd been after. Nolan had risen higher since, hitting full Commander while she was still a Lieutenant Commander.

"Hello, Adam," Kathryn said, coldly. She rose to her feet, folding her arms across the chest of her fleet jacket. "Welcome to the *Sparhawk*. *My* ship."

A black screen lit up on the wall next to Kathryn, and a blue holographic woman appeared. She had white hair and digitized skin. The woman waved cheerfully. "We're so pleased to have you on board, Commander Nolan."

"Yes, thrilled," Kathryn said, her tone giving lie to the words.

"Hello, Kathryn," Nolan said, neutrally. "Nice to meet you, Em. Where should I stow my duffel?"

"The bunks are up the corridor, toward the bridge," Kathryn supplied. She studied him with those unreadable brown eyes.

"Great. Let's get underway," Nolan said, inching past Kathryn and into the corridor leading deeper into the ship. There wasn't much to it, just four narrow bunks and a room big enough for a pilot and co-pilot. He dropped his duffel on one of the unoccupied bunks, and slid into the co-pilot's chair. Nolan had never flown, but from what he understood Em would do most of the work anyway.

Kathryn entered behind him, dropping silently into the pilot's seat. "Do you have a destination, *sir*?" The last word was spat with a great deal of venom.

"We're heading to Coronas station 127," Nolan said. He swiveled the co-pilot's chair to face Kathryn. Might as well get this dealt with. "Listen, Kathryn, I know we weren't friends at the academy. I know you don't like having me on your ship. I don't care. We have a job to do. Admiral Mendez put me in charge. If you have an issue, take it up with him."

"My father wouldn't listen and you know it," Kathryn said, tapping a series of switches on the console in front of her. She wrapped her hands around the yoke, and the *Sparhawk* began inching from the station. "OFI is a boys club, so I'm not surprised he put you in charge. I'm just a little protective of my ship. We've seen a lot, and our record to date is flawless. I just don't want you ruining that."

Nolan gave a soft sigh. This mission was going to be so much fun.

Chapter 5- Coronas 127

"Commander," Em's soft voice echoed through the cockpit. "We're exiting the sun's photosphere and entering the corona now. ETA twenty-two minutes."

Nolan started at the voice, momentarily assuming she was speaking to him. She wasn't, of course. It was Kathryn's vessel, and Em was clearly addressing her. It amused him that the AI respected the chain of command.

"Acknowledged," Kathryn said, releasing the yoke. "Em, take over piloting. Nolan and I have some talking to do."

Kathryn turned expectantly toward Nolan, but didn't say anything.

Nolan eyed her for a moment. "How much did Admiral Mendez tell you?" he asked. He didn't want to assume.

"My father told me that I was to be at dock 16 at 8 a.m.," Kathryn said, mildly. She tapped a button on the console, and the view screen lit up to show the storm of fire they were passing through. "He didn't tell me anything about the mission. Why are we here, *sir*?"

"We're here because the entire populace of stations along the periphery have disappeared," Nolan said, his knuckles turning white as he gripped the arm of the chair. Kathryn had a gift for pissing him off, but he wasn't going to let her attitude get to him. "Yesterday evening, station 127's power consumption fell outside normal levels. That fits the pattern we've seen at the other ten stations that have disappeared over the last five weeks."

"When you say 'disappeared,' what do you mean?" Kathryn asked.

"The personnel are missing. All of them. Rescue teams have shown up to find each station intact, but no sign of the crew. They haven't found any signs of a struggle either," Nolan explained. "Whoever is responsible for this has a way of subduing the populace without bloodshed. We don't know why, or what they're using the people for."

"Lovely," Kathryn said.

The ship finally emerged from the sun's corona, breaking away from the sea of fire and plasma as they headed toward one of the largest asteroid belts Nolan had ever seen. Millions of rocks floated in a dense cloud, and on the edge of that cloud he could see a large, silver cylinder. Coronas 127, one of the many stations owned by the Coronas corporation.

The station slowly grew larger on the view screen as the minutes crept by. Nolan waited until they were within a few minutes of docking before speaking. "Em, is there any comm chatter? Are there any vessels in system?"

"Negative," Em said, cheerfully. "We are the only vessel in system, and I detect no communications coming from the station."

"That fits your narrative about station personnel being gone," Kathryn said. Her attention was fixed on the view screen.

"Seems to," Nolan said. On the one hand he was pleased that his theory was correct, on the other he was deeply concerned for the people who'd been taken. "Lieutenant Commander, pick a berth and get us docked. Let's have a look inside and see if the perpetrators left anything behind that might help us identify them."

"Yes, sir," Kathryn said, without sarcasm this time.

The *Sparhawk* drifted closer, finally slowing as it approached a docking tube. There was a gentle thump, then the seal engaged and they were locked into place against the station's hull.

Chapter 6- Mining Drone

"The security footage has been wiped," Nolan confirmed, leaning back in the ripped leather chair. He was staring at the administrator's terminal, a simple computer system. "In fact, all log data has been purged--everything that could be directly accessed from this terminal."

"Are there any other data sources we could check?" Kathryn asked. She was leaning against the corner of the administrator's chrome desk, looking over Nolan's shoulder.

"Not any that would help. It's possible people kept personal logs, but if it were me doing this I'd have wiped those, too," Nolan said, pushing away from the desk. He rose to his feet and walked to the window.

It seemed strange to him that someone would risk putting a glass window on a space station, even if it was ultra-dense glass. But the view was spectacular. Mining drones zipped from the station at regular intervals, little octopus-like craft with spindly arms. Each arm was equipped with a laser drill, and the drones used high-tensile mesh to gather their haul.

One of those drones was approaching the station now, with a full load. It towed a huge black mass behind it, several thousand credits worth of precious metals embedded in the rock. Nolan watched the drone dock, tapping his cheek with his index finger as he considered.

"Any ideas?" Kathryn asked. "It seems like whoever did this covered their tracks pretty well. Do you have any clues from the other stations?"

"Maybe," Nolan said, absently. He was still staring at the mining drone, which had dropped its payload and was zipping back toward the asteroid field. He turned to Kathryn. "Can you have Em tap into the control matrix for the drones? I want to see if they have internal logs."

"Sure," Kathryn said, though she was eyeing him skeptically. "What are you hoping to find?"

"The drones run continuously, which means some of them would have been in the belt when the station was attacked," Nolan said. "If we're lucky--very lucky--one of those drones may have recorded the vessel that approached the station."

"Good thinking," Kathryn admitted. She tapped the comm on her wrist. "Em, can you tap into all mining drones? I want a compiled file of footage. Run a scan on that data, and see if you can pick up any vessels arriving or departing in the last twenty-four hours."

"Of course, commander," Em's cheerful voice came over the comm. "Processing. This query will take four minutes to complete."

"Is there anything else you think we can do on the station itself?" Kathryn asked.

"I doubt it," Nolan said. "We had techs go over every inch of each of the previous stations. They didn't find anything of note. The miners were just...gone. Again, no sign of a struggle. No damage to the station. Whoever took the people didn't even bother to rob the miners. Scrip notes were found in many of the miner's quarters."

"Shall we head back to the *Sparhawk*, then?" Kathryn asked.

Nolan considered her question. Was there anything else he could learn here? He looked around the administrator's office, but couldn't think of anything they might find that would be of real use.

"Yes, let's head back. If we're lucky, Em will have something. If not, I guess we head back to OFI headquarters and you get your ship back," Nolan said. He didn't like the idea of returning empty-handed, but what choice did he have? There just wasn't enough data to work with. Whoever was behind this had done a masterful job of covering their tracks.

Chapter 7- A Piece of the Puzzle

The *Sparhawk* was just pulling away from the Coronas station when Em's voice chimed in the cockpit. "All footage from mining drones has been parsed. It appears Commander Nolan's hunch was accurate. One of the drones captured footage of a vessel leaving the station."

"Put it on screen," Kathryn ordered.

The view screen shifted from a view of the sun to a shot of an asteroid. The camera canted crazily, then showed the station. The drone flew closer, and as it approached the station Nolan could see a vessel docked not far from the port they'd just left. It was larger than the *Sparhawk*, though not by much.

"Is that a Venerable class starship?" he asked, leaning a bit closer to the screen. Both the vessel and the station grew larger as the drone flew closer.

"I think it is," Kathryn confirmed. They were both on their feet now, leaning in toward the screen. The level of detail wasn't what he'd have liked, but it improved as the recording continued.

"The colors are off, but that's definitely a fleet vessel," Nolan confirmed. The footage ended abruptly as the drone reached the station. He turned to Kathryn. "We need to get this back to the admiral. There can't be many Venerable class vessels unaccounted for."

"You're right," she said, nodding. "I have no idea how these pirates got hold of a state-of-the-art Fleet vessel, but that's almost a good thing. It will make finding them that much easier."

Nolan smiled. It wasn't a big piece, but this bit of the puzzle was more than they'd had before. Hopefully it was enough to track the bastards who'd done this.

Chapter 8- Face to Face

Nolan settled into the chair across from the admiral. Kathryn set next to him, studiously avoiding looking at her father. Nolan didn't know much about their relationship, but there was enough tension to make him feel claustrophobic.

"I've had a look at the footage you brought," Mendez said, resting his elbows on his desk. His gaze swept back and forth between them. "The idea that a fleet vessel has been coopted is more than a little terrifying. Fortunately, you were right. There is only one Venerable class cruiser unaccounted for. I've done what I can to secure information on that vessel, but with limited success."

Mendez looked down at his desk drawer, the same drawer Nolan had seen him withdraw a cigar from the last time he'd been in the office. Then the admiral looked at his daughter. He sighed, but didn't open the drawer.

"The cruiser belonged to a Captain Edison. He was working with a geneticist named Reid. The pair were detached from regular fleet operations, but there are no details in the system about what they were investigating," Mendez said. "Three months ago the Starrunner disappeared, and this is where things get more interesting. Edison reported to Admiral Chu, but Chu never filed a report on the disappearance. He should have raised one hell of a ruckus, but never said a word."

"Is this some sort of black bag op? Sanctioned by OFI?" Nolan asked. He didn't like to think that his own government could be behind these disappearances, but he wasn't naive enough to discount it.

"Maybe. I'll speak to Chu and see what I can find out," Mendez said. "In the meantime, I want you to continue your field operation. You're the best analyst we have, Nolan. I need you to find the pattern we're not seeing. Get to the next station, before Edison. We've got to stop this."

"So you want me to chauffeur Nolan around the galaxy searching for a needle in a haystack of needles?" Kathryn broke in, bristling. She leaned over the table, spearing the admiral with her gaze. "I had cases I was working. Cases that are going cold, because I'm wasting time."

The admiral's face hardened. All he did was stare at Kathryn, but she subsided instantly. "Lieutenant Commander Mendez, your vessel is at Commander Nolan's disposal. You will escort him wherever he needs to go, and you will provide him whatever aid he requires to complete his mission. Am I making myself understood?"

"Yes, sir," Kathryn said, without meeting his gaze.

The admiral turned back to Nolan. "If I'm able to get answers from Chu, I'll be in contact. Before I dismiss you two, there's one more matter I wanted to discuss. This isn't the first incident of the Admiralty covering up something they should have been stopping. It's happening with alarming frequency, and there's only one conclusion

I can draw. The Admiralty has been infiltrated. Someone is working for a third party."

Nolan went cold. The Admiralty was the core of the Fleet. Who or what had enough clout to infiltrate them?

Chapter 9- Admiral Chu

Admiral Mendez tapped the ash from his cigar, staring hard at the terminal. The trail was almost invisible, but it was there if you'd spent enough time stalking the data patterns. Too many of Chu's documents had been sanitized. Too much of his budget was obfuscated behind a wall of obviously fake projects. In short, Chu was hiding something big.

Mendez savored a quick pull from his cigar, enjoying the mellow taste of the fine Ceres tobacco. Chu was one of the seniormost admirals. His clout had been waning in recent years, but his connections ran deep. Was he selling them out to line his way to retirement? If so, who would he sell them out to? The Tigris were too aggressive for this sort of tactic, and the Primos just didn't care enough about humanity to do it.

"Clever bastard," Mendez muttered, as he tried and failed to gain access to the details of the project Captain Edison and this Doctor Reid had been assigned to. Chu would see in the logs that Mendez was attempting to access them, which meant the time for stealth was over. He needed to confront the man directly.

Mendez tapped the Contacts icon, then Chu. The Quantum Network logo flashed on the screen. It lasted for several seconds, then resolved into Chu's leathery face. He wore his usual thick-rimmed glasses, and stared hard at Mendez from countless miles away.

"You're snooping around in my files. Why?" Chu asked, without preamble.

"Because one of your pet projects has gotten out of hand," Mendez replied. He took another puff, drawing the moment out as he watched Chu. There was no crack in the man's composure. "Let's talk about Doctor Reid."

"I'm not familiar with that name," Chu lied.

Mendez felt the lie to his core. "How about a missing Venerable class cruiser assigned to your command?" he pressed. "Edison, I believe the captain's name was."

Chu was silent for long moments. Mendez merely waited.

"All right, Mendez. If you're dead set on meddling in this, then I'm willing to bring you up to speed," Chu conceded. "Not over Quantum, though. Come to the Ternis system. I'll explain everything, provided you agree it goes no farther."

"I can't guarantee that without knowing what it is," Mendez countered.

"You'll have to let your conscience decide," Chu said, heaving a long-suffering sigh. "I'm confident you'll do the right thing, once I've shown you the truth."

Chapter 10- Sector 12

Nolan set his coffee on the table next to the holoterminal, then flicked on the power. It showed a three-dimensional logo, then faded to a menu screen. The interface was clean, well-designed, and expensive as hell.

"My father provided some pretty nice toys," Kathryn said, walking into the tiny mess from the cockpit. She sat at the other side of the table.

"I've heard of these, but this is the first time I've used one," Nolan said, swiping at the hologram with his index finger. It slid to the next three-dimensional screen.

"What are you researching? Kathryn asked.

"I'm hoping to find a pattern in the attacks," Nolan said, finally finding the area he wanted. He touched the screen he was after and watched as the holographic display exploded into a network of stars, creating a cube about two feet across. It was so much more impressive than any two-dimensional map.

"You can do it manually, but there's a much easier way," Kathryn said, giving a half smile. "Em, plot the station attacks on the map Commander Nolan just brought up."

"Of course, commander," Em's voice came from the speaker in the wall. Red dots appeared throughout the holographic cube, each one with a tiny label showing the station name.

"They're dispersed pretty evenly," Nolan said, leaning up from his seat to peer at the side of the hologram. "No two of them are in the same sector."

Kathryn leaned around the same side of the hologram, peering into the cube. The light reflected off her pupils as she studied it. "You're right. Any idea why?"

"I'm not sure yet," Nolan said. He caught himself looking at Kathryn sidelong, and forced himself to focus on the hologram. "Em, can you put a green dot into the model for every station in the periphery?"

"Done, commander," Em said cheerfully from the wall.

Green dots appeared all over the map. There were about ten times as many as the red, nearly a hundred and forty stations in all. Nolan looked at their placement, considering. "Em, can you highlight the largest area of space unaffected by the attacks?"

The hologram shifted again; this time a blue tinge filled the entire upper right corner. "There have been no attacks in this area of space. It contains four mining stations."

"Which of those stations has been recently re-supplied?" Kathryn asked, half a second before Nolan asked the same question.

"Coronas 6 was resupplied two days ago. Coronas 112 was resupplied eleven days ago," Em supplied.

Nolan met Kathryn's gaze. For the first time she gave a real smile, "I think you've done it, Nolan. That's the station they're most likely to hit next."

"If they continue their current pattern," Nolan said. He sat back down, watching Kathryn while she studied the hologram. She really was beautiful, even if she was a little too hotheaded for his tastes. "Assuming they do, it looks like this would be the last area of space they'd need to hit. I don't know much about this doctor Reid that your father mentioned, but if he's a geneticist then maybe he's running some sort of experiment."

"It makes sense," Kathryn said, brushing a lock of curly hair from her eyes. "Given the pattern of attacks, maybe this doctor wanted a wide pool of test subjects."

"It's the only real lead," Nolan said. "We'll report back to the admiral, and ask how he wants us to handle that."

"Are you sure that's wise?" Kathryn said. "Adam, I know you like to play it by the book, but we don't have time to report back just to get our orders stamped. If we don't get to that station now, it might be too late. This could be our last chance to catch these bastards."

Nolan drummed his fingers on the table. The smart thing to do was report it to the admiral, but Kathryn was right.

Chapter 11- Chu

Delta settled in at the mess counter, where his men had dined when he'd been the true captain of this vessel. He ate mechanically, spooning brown protein into his mouth. He had no idea what the flavor was supposed to be, but it tasted like leather. Old leather.

He glanced up when Doctor Reid entered the mess. If the scientist had been gaunt before, he was becoming skeletal now. Delta watched as Reid sat next to their Quantum Terminal. The man seemed agitated, and Delta watched him with interest as Reid's call connected.

He couldn't make out the screen, but he recognized Chu's voice. "We have a serious problem, Doctor. Mendez is close to the truth, and he's got the clout to shine a very large light on your activities. You need to get out of there."

"I will not leave before the experiment is complete," Reid snapped. He leaned in close to the terminal. "How long before Mendez can bring official pressure to bear?"

"I've asked him to meet with me first, so we have at least a day," Chu said.

Delta spooned up another mouthful of leather-flavored protein. Interesting. Someone was fighting back. Delta suppressed a grim smile.

"That will have to do. Where is this meeting taking place?" Reid asked. Delta noticed that the doctor's hands were trembling. Was that rage, or was his condition deteriorating?

"The Ternis system," Chu answered. "We meet tomorrow, at 8 a.m. Fleet time."

"He's coming to your vessel?" Reid asked. His eyes were feverish.

"Yes," Chu confirmed.

"Excellent," Reid said. His grin was ghastly enough that Delta lost his appetite and set the spoon down. "Here is what you will do...."

Chapter 12- Turned

Admiral Mendez actively disliked commanding starships. He shifted uncomfortably in the captain's chair, reaching habitually for a cigar that wasn't there. He still remembered the first time he'd lit one, at Elbas station after the final battle in the eight-year war. He'd driven back the Tigris, and impressed them with his ferocity--enough that they'd called a truce out of respect.

That was over a decade ago. Now he was a tired old man, and he missed his creature comforts.

"Sir, we're approaching the *Ghost*. Shall I provide a boarding escort?" a young ensign asked. The kid couldn't have been more than nineteen. When had Mendez gotten so old?

"Negative," Mendez ordered. He rose from the captain's chair, but managed to resist the urge to pace. "Tell Admiral Chu that he'll be coming aboard the *Juggernaut*. I'll await him in my ready room."

"Yes, sir," the ensign said.

Mendez left the bridge, ducking instinctively as he passed through the hatch. Older vessels were tight enough that you'd bang your head otherwise, but these newer models were a different story. He didn't need to duck, or scrunch sideways while making his way down the smaller corridors.

Mendez headed for his ready room, sitting down at the desk. He withdrew a cigar from the drawer, but didn't light it. He rolled it between his fingers as he considered. If Chu was unwilling to come aboard the *Juggernaut*, it would mean only one thing: that he was a traitor. If it came down to a fight, Mendez had no doubt he'd win. He knew that Chu knew it was well. The *Juggernaut* would overwhelm the *Ghost*.

Would Chu run? Mendez had no idea. All he could do was wait-- so that was what he did. Long minutes passed, but Mendez didn't allow himself any distractions. He didn't surf the Quantum Network, or even light the cigar. He sat in silence, contemplating. It was a ritual he'd perfected over the years. Total focus was vital when dealing with a canny opponent, and he had a feeling that was exactly what he was about to do.

"Sir?" the ensign's voice echoed over the comm.

"Go ahead," Mendez said.

"Admiral Chu's shuttle has docked. Would you like him brought to your ready room?"

"Yes. Have a pair of Marines escort him. They'll be required for the duration of the encounter," Mendez ordered.

"Yes, sir," the ensign said, then the comm went dark.

Mendez waited. A few minutes later, the door slid open and Chu stepped inside. His hat was tucked under one arm, and his uniform had been pressed that morning. He was only one shade away from parade dress.

"Sir?" one of the Marines said through the doorway.

"Wait outside," Mendez said, waving in the Marine's direction. The door hissed shut and Mendez turned to Chu. "Have a seat, Admiral. Welcome to the *Juggernaut*."

"Thank you for agreeing to a face-to-face," Chu said. He set the hat down on the table, the brim facing Mendez, then deposited a data pad next to the hat. "You'll find the details of project Eradication on that tablet. Give it a look, and you'll see why this is such a grave matter."

Mendez set down his unlit cigar, and reached for the tablet, then recoiled when a jet of green gas shot from the brim of the hat. A foul odor washed over his face, and he instinctively inhaled as he pulled back. Mendez stood, sucking in a breath to call for the guards. Then his body betrayed him. He slumped back into the chair, his arms flopping down next to him. His attempt to yell for help came out as a low wail.

Mendez tried to stay calm. He could move his eyes, but nothing else. He tried to understand what was happening, looking for an angle that could save him.

"You're no doubt looking for a way out of your predicament," Chu said, leaning across the desk until his face was mere inches from Mendez's. "You're wondering what I dosed you with, and how long it will last. If you could just move your hand, you could tap the alarm on the bottom of your desk, or maybe knock something on the floor to get the Marine to poke his head inside."

Mendez thrashed weakly, but that was the limit of his defiance.

"I wasn't lying, Admiral," Chu said, giving a slow smile. He pushed the tablet a little closer to Mendez. "The details of Eradication are on that tablet. I also wasn't lying when I said that I was confident you'd do the right thing once you knew the truth."

Chu reached into the jacket pocket of his Fleet uniform and withdrew a tiny vial, no longer than his thumb. He unscrewed the top, then moved around the desk to stand next to Mendez.

Mendez tried to thrash, to struggle wildly. His body twitched, but he couldn't force it into any coherent action. Chu easily restrained him, cupping Mendez's chin in one hand. "Don't struggle, Admiral. This will be over in a moment."

Chu upended the vial into one hand, then pressed his hand against Mendez's cheek. Something cold and slimy began to inch its way across Mendez's face. It crawled toward his nose, ever so slowly.

"I know you're a man of logic, Mendez," Chu said, stepping back around the desk. He watched Mendez impassively as the creature inched toward Mendez's left nostril. Mendez could see its terrifying grey form out of the corner of his eye, its antenna twitching as it crawled still closer. "You want to know what's happening. The Gorthian larva will connect to your brain stem. When its work is complete, you will be a new man. You'll finally understand the truth, and you'll see what needs to be done."

Chapter 13- Decision

"So what's our destination?" Kathryn asked as she settled into the pilot's chair.

Nolan considered his options one last time. The smart thing to do was still to go back to Admiral Mendez. They could get a detachment of Marines to help them, or just turn over the entire matter. The problem was that in this case the smart thing wasn't the right thing. If they went back to the admiral, odds were good the Coronas 6 would be gone by the time whoever they alerted arrived.

"Plot a course for Corona 6," Nolan ordered.

"Aye, sir," Kathryn replied, without her usual mockery. She gave him a half smile as they powered into the Helios Gate. There was a moment of weightlessness, then they were on the other side.

Kathryn smoothly guided them into the star's core, and they waited for long minutes while the vessel pushed toward the surface. If not for the inductive field, their ship would have been incinerated in an instant. The field drew upon the star's own power, which protected the vessel as it passed through one of the hottest, densest places in the known universe.

The *Sparhawk* finally emerged into the sun's corona, an undulating field of towering flares. Kathryn expertly guided them higher until they broke free of the sun's gravity well. They powered toward a tiny silver speck on the edge of a vast field of asteroids. At this distance, it was indistinguishable from the last station they'd visited.

"Em, are you picking up any comm chatter?" Nolan asked.

"Yes, Commander," Em confirmed. "The station's Quantum Lite network is active. At least one member of station personnel is broadcasting."

"Okay, let's see if we can mobilize this station," Nolan said, turning to Kathryn.

"Do you have a plan?" she asked, blinking.

"If we're right, then odds are good this Captain Edison will be invading with a squad of Marines," Nolan said. He gave a heavy sigh. "Resisting that kind of firepower will be tough, but we may have the advantage of surprise. You're more experienced at field work. Do you have a suggestion?"

"A few, but I need to know what we're dealing with first. Let's alert the station, then we'll see what we have to work with," Kathryn said.

Chapter 14- Coronas 6

The large gunmetal door slid up into the ship, and Nolan's ears popped as the pressure between the sealed airlock and the Coronas 6 station normalized. An oily little man stood waiting, his dark hair styled into something approaching a horn. He rubbed his hands together nervously, giving them a wide and obviously fake smile.

"Welcome to Coronas 6. I am Administrator Bock. So, uh, what brings such esteemed agents to our little station?" Bock asked. His nasally voice added to what Nolan's father would have called a 'very punchable' face.

"I'm Commander Nolan of the OFI," Nolan said, stepping forward and holding up his ident badge. "This is Lieutenant Commander Mendez. We have reason to believe your station is in danger. Do you have somewhere we could discuss this privately?"

The airlock opened up into a docking bay where ships could unload cargo. Nolan realized that at least half a dozen miners were peering at them. One of those miners strode up to the administrator, a shotgun resting on one shoulder as she approached. She wore dirty leather pants, matching boots and gloves, and a jacket older than Nolan.

"Something going on that we need to know about, Bock?" the woman asked. She leaned forward, her eyes locked on the weaselly little man. She spat a gob of something dark near his feet.

"Not at the moment," Bock said, taking a half-step back from the woman. "Annie, as you can see, I need to assist these fine people. Why don't you track me down after--"

Bock trailed off as Annie's free hand shot out and wrapped around his throat. "You wouldn't be trying to put me off again, would you, Bock? You promised me payment, and I ain't seen it for the last two shipments."

"A-are you sure you won't accept Coronas scrip?" he choked out.

"I told you I ain't accepting that pink toilet paper. I want real credits," the miner growled. She released the administrator, but still loomed over him. "Now, you deal with these fine people, and then you come find me. If you don't, I'm going to come find you, Bock."

Annie turned on her heel and strode out of the dock, up one of the airlocks to where Nolan guessed her ship was still docked.

"Please excuse the interruption," Bock said, withdrawing a clean blue handkerchief from the pocket of his vest and mopping at his brow. "If you'll follow me, I'm happy to discuss whatever business brought you to the station."

Bock turned from the airlock and hurried up a metal stairwell that led to the station's next level. Nolan and Kathryn followed him into a small office, with an appropriately-sized desk just large enough for Bock to squeeze behind. There wasn't enough room for Nolan to sit, so he and Kathryn stood as the door hissed shut behind them.

"Now, what is this danger?" Bock asked. His eyes were wide, and he looked like he desperately wanted to be elsewhere.

"We have reason to believe that a rogue vessel may dock at your station in the next twenty-four hours," Nolan began. He paused, trying to decide how much to reveal. Too much, and Bock might break down. Not enough, and he might underestimate the threat. "We expect a team of Marines to break into your facility. Their likely aim is to abduct all station personnel."

"That's awful. What is the OFI going to do about it? I hope you're not all the help they're sending," Bock said, his voice getting faster and rising half an octave by the end. His eyes were like saucers now.

"We're it, I'm afraid," Nolan said. He glanced at Kathryn. She gave a reassuring nod. Nolan turned back to Bock. "Do you have any weapons? Are any of the miners experienced in combat?"

"Coronas policy doesn't allow us to stock weapons," Bock said, apologetically. His obsequious nature reasserted itself, seemingly mastering the fear. "The only person who might be able to fight is Annie. She spent time in the infantry, and as you can see she's armed."

"Is there anyone else who can handle a weapon if we provide them?" Kathryn asked. She looked at Nolan. "I have a small armory on the *Sparhawk*."

"There might be a few people," Bock said.

"Gather your personnel," Nolan ordered. "We're going to return to the *Sparhawk*, but we'll be back with all the ordinance we can muster."

Chapter 15- How Many Rounds

"Annie, I want you to take charge of the station personnel," Nolan said, holding Annie's gaze. "Can you handle that?"

"They'll listen to me," Annie said, nodding once. Her tone was loud enough to carry, and she gave a booming laugh. "Firing one of those dinky little handguns you brought ain't that tough. They'll do just fine." Annie's tone dropped to a near-whisper, and her smile faded. "That'll only last until the first one drops. Then they'll scatter like collision debris. You got a plan for when that happens?"

"No," Nolan said, glancing at Kathryn. She was instructing a small cluster of miners how to fire the pistols they'd brought from the *Sparhawk*. Nolan had even given up his sidearm, and was now using a TX-30, the assault rifle of choice for Fleet Marines. He'd never fired one, but he was fairly sure he could figure it out.

Boots pounded down the metal stairs behind him, and Nolan turned to see a young teen sprinting up to Annie. "Ma'am, we got a ship emerging from the Helios Gate. Just left the sun. It's a Vegetable class, like you told us to watch out for."

"Good boy, Tim," Annie said, mussing the boy's hair. "Get back to your quarters, and stay put. Don't come out till someone comes to get you."

Nolan waited until the boy was gone before speaking. He walked to the center of the dock, sucked in a deep breath, then used his best parade voice. "Everyone, *listen up*."

Miners all around him stopped what they were doing. Kathryn lowered the pistol she'd been holding up for the few she was training. Even Annie stood at attention.

"We've got confirmation that a vessel is inbound. That vessel has nasty intentions for everyone aboard this station," Nolan boomed, turning in a slow circle. "They're going to be well-armed, and some of us are probably going to die. I know that's hard to hear, but you need to be ready for what's about to go down. If you break, if you run when you see someone get shot, then these bastards are going to kill us all. We need to stand together. We have the higher ground, and we have the element of surprise."

"I'm not going to die to protect Coronas equipment," a man called. He was tall, hairy, and not overly acquainted with hygiene.

"You're not hearing me," Nolan said, raising the volume of his voice back to parade level. "These people aren't coming for your ore. They don't care about this station. They are here for *you*. We don't know what they intend, but our suspicion is some sort of genetic experiment. Do you really want to find out?"

Dead silence.

Nolan began to turn again, his gaze touching every miner, one after another. "Screw Coronas. Are you ready to defend your lives?"

"Yes, sir," Kathryn boomed. A chorus of miners echoed her.

"Now get to your assigned position," Nolan said, resting the barrel of his assault rifle on his shoulder, just like Annie was doing. "Let's give these bastards hell."

Chapter 16- Complications

Delta rubbed at the scar on the back of his neck, then stopped the instant he realized he was doing it. It happened often, whenever he was about to do something that would have horrified him back when he was allowed to have a name. Like he was doing now.

"Winter, dock on the lower ring, right next to that Photos class ship," Delta ordered. He turned to Reid, who was consumed with his comm. The doctor scrolled though data feeds, ignoring everything around him. "Doctor Reid, we have a situation."

Reid finally looked up. He blinked owlishly, then pasted the usual sneer back in place. "I don't employ you to bring me problems. You exist to solve those problems. So, whatever it is, solve it."

"Doctor Reid," Delta said, rubbing the back of his neck. "There's an OFI boat parked at the station. There's no way that's a coincidence. Someone knew were coming. We could be walking into a fully-armed Marine squad. At the very least, the populace has been alerted. We won't be able to take them while they're sleeping."

"What are you saying, Delta? That you can't do it?" Reid said. He rose to his full five foot seven, somehow managing to look menacing. "Storm the station. Kill the defenders. Bring me every last person onboard. Or die in the attempt."

Delta considered arguing. He considered asking Reid to be content with the stations they'd already collected. He didn't, and the reason shamed him: he was afraid. If he argued, then Reid would use the chip, and Delta wasn't sure he could take that again.

"Yes, sir," Delta said. He turned to the three cyber Marines. "Martel, Davis. Heavy load out. If it shoots back, I want it dead."

The two Marines didn't respond, instead turning wordlessly and heading for the armory. Their lack of emotion, or of thought, terrified him. The chip had broken them, and it could break him too. Maybe Reid was giving him a way out here. If he died, he'd be free.

Chapter 17- Chaos

Nolan stared down the sights, aiming the barrel at the airlock door. It wasn't hard to see, as the only light was centered around the airlock. One of Annie's ideas had been to turn off most of the lights. They could see their foes, but their foes couldn't see them. In theory, at least. Marines were canny opponents, and would almost certainly have night vision goggles available.

Metal pinged and popped on the other side of the airlock as the Venerable class docked. It went on for long seconds, and Nolan didn't realize he'd been holding his breath until the sounds finally stopped. He released his breath, trying to focus.

"Get ready," he called, softly. It carried in the gloom. People scuffled around him as they found final cover. He couldn't see them, but hoped they all had their weapons trained on that door.

The station door began to rise, slowly at first, then with increasing speed. It took perhaps two seconds, and the instant the door disappeared hell began. Three grenades came sailing into the darkness, each emitting a hypersonic tone. Nolan scrambled up the stairs, rolling over the top a split-second before the pulse grenade detonated. Those around him who hadn't moved as quickly slumped to the deck, unconscious.

"Incoming," Annie yelled.

Sporadic gunfire came from the miners. It was answered by concentrated fully automatic fire from within the airlock. Three miners dropped, their bodies jerked about like rag dolls as they fell limply to the deck. Two Marines came striding into the room, both using single shots from their rifles to take down any miner with a gun. If the lack of light hampered them in any way Nolan couldn't see it.

"We have to get out of here. We can make the *Sparhawk*," Kathryn panted, sprinting up beside Nolan. She dropped into a crouch next to him.

"You're right," Nolan said, sizing up the battle. Annie's shotgun had stopped firing, but he couldn't see her anywhere. Everyone else had broken, or been gunned down. "But we're not going to try for her."

Nolan raised his assault rifle, sighting one of the Marines. The deck provided great cover, shielding his profile from the his target thirty feet below. The weapon kicked hard, three times. The rounds took the Marine in the face, and he slumped soundlessly to the deck.

"You're crazy," Kathryn said, but she pivoted to stand on the opposite side of the stairwell. "Lay down a cover burst, and I'll try to take out the second one."

Two more Marines burst from the airlock. They carried weapons, but weren't firing. Nolan had just enough time to wonder why, but then they dropped out of sight.

"They're going for the station's power core," Kathryn called.

Nolan nodded, let out a burst of suppressive fire. The remaining Marine ducked back into the airlock, presumably to give his companions time to reach the reactor.

"If we don't stop them, none of what we do here matters," Nolan called back. "Do you know of another way we can reach the reactor?"

"The Coronas stations are small," Kathryn yelled. "The only way down there is the way they went."

"All right, into the hole then," Nolan yelled back. He burst from cover, firing another three-round burst at the airlock. The Marine inside returned fire, and Nolan was forced to dive back behind the stairs.

Kathryn used the opportunity, sprinting down the stairs and diving into the hole the two enemy Marines had disappeared into. Nolan waited three agonizing seconds, then Kathryn popped out of the hole and fired into the airlock.

Nolan leapt down the stairs, his attention all on the little stairs she was perched on. They disappeared down into darkness. He skidded across the deck, tumbling down the stairs into a heap at the bottom.

Chapter 18- On Your Feet

"Get back on your feet, kid," Annie drawled from the shadows near him. Nolan rose into a crouch, picking up his assault rifle and scanning the darkness. There was no sign of the two Marines they were pursuing. The corridor ended at an intersection.

"Is there any way to get to the reactor ahead of those two?" Nolan asked.

"That what they're after?" Annie said, a little surprise in her voice. "Won't they die, too?"

"Death doesn't matter. The mission does," Nolan said. His father had been a Marine. He knew how determined they were. "We need to stop them. How can we do that?"

Kathryn's rifle fired above them, the muzzle flashes briefly illuminating the darkness. "Nolan, do you have a plan that gets me out of this stairwell?"

"Annie?" Nolan asked. "Give me something."

"We can trail after them. They need to stop at three different doors to get to the reactor. Opening the last one will take time. They might even have to cut through it. If we can come up on 'em while they're doing that, might be we can gun them down," Annie said. Smoke still curled from her shotgun, catching the light as it drifted toward the ceiling.

"Kathryn, let's move," Nolan called up the stairs. Then he advanced up the corridor. "Annie, circle around me and take point. You've done that before, right?"

"Son, I was infantry," Annie said, giving him the kind of stare his mother used to when he'd said something particularly idiotic.

Annie plunged into the darkness like a ghost, making no noise as she advanced up the corridor. Nolan followed after, relying on the little bit of illumination drifting down the hallway rather than lighting his flashlight.

He could hear Kathryn pounding down the stairs behind him. She slowed when she neared, then turned around and started inching backwards up the hall. "As soon as he figures out we're down here, that Marine is going to come after us. I'll keep him off."

Chapter 19- Final Confrontation

Nolan pounded down the metal deck, struggling to keep up with Annie as she leapt over a crate. Then she abruptly slowed, and raised a fist. Nolan skidded to a halt, using the crate as cover. There was more light here, coming from the room ahead. Nolan could here a repeating *thrum, thrum, thrum*. Definitely the core.

Annie caught his gaze, beckoning him forward. Nolan moved slowly, careful not to make any noise. He stopped next to Annie, sinking slowly into a crouch. Inside the room, two Marines stood before a door. Both had acetylene torches out, slicing through the dense steel more rapidly than Nolan would have expected. Each worked on his own half-circle, and the torches were about to meet at the bottom.

Nolan raised the butt of his rifle to his shoulder, nodding to Annie. She did the same with her shotgun. Then they both fired. Nolan caught a large black Marine in the back, the rounds pinging off like they'd hit armor. The man was knocked into the door, dropping his torch.

The Marine that Annie had targeted took the slug to the back of the neck. He collapsed wordlessly to the deck. Annie was already pivoting to aim at Nolan's target, and he reminded himself that he should be doing the same.

Nolan took aim, but his target rolled behind a pile of crates. A second later, he bounded over the top of them like a gazelle, sprinting across the deck toward Nolan. Nolan took aim, letting off another three-round burst. The big black man ducked low, dodging Nolan's shots. Annie's shotgun roared, but the man was blindingly fast.

He took Nolan in the chest with a kick that launched Nolan into the wall. Nolan's head rang, and he fell to the deck. It was all he could do to keep hold of his gun. Then the man was on Annie. He grabbed her by the neck, hoisting her effortlessly into the air. Annie ripped a combat knife from her boot, slamming it into the hand holding her. The tip snapped and the blade skittered off, drawing a line of sparks along the Marine's metal arm.

"He's enhanced," Nolan roared. He brought his weapon up, then took aim at the man's knee. Nolan squeezed the trigger, and the rifle kicked back into his shoulder, three times. The smell of hot gunpowder washed over him.

His aim was good. All three rounds hit the back of the right knee, which wasn't a cyber replacement. It all but exploded, dropped the suddenly one-legged man to the deck. Annie tumbled down next to him, raising both hands to her neck as she gasped for air.

The Marine rolled onto his one good leg, using it to launch himself into the air. Nolan was dimly aware of blood leaking from the man's stump as he came down on top of Nolan. Nolan was knocked to the deck, the heavier man on top of him. Something slammed into his jaw, and his head rebounded off the deck. Black spots danced across his vision.

Nolan jerked right as a pair of cyber spurs snapped out of the Marine's metallic wrist. The Marine rammed the blades down at Nolan's face, slamming them into the deck where he'd just been. Nolan thrashed, trying to free his rifle, which was trapped under the Marine's good knee. The Marine rammed the blades down again, and this time Nolan screamed as the blades punctured his shoulder, pinning him to the deck.

He fought past the pain, knowing that he was dead if he didn't. The Marine's weight had shifted when he attacked, so Nolan bucked his legs up. The Marine tilted forward, and Nolan's rifle came free. Nolan whipped it up, planting the barrel against the Marine's jaw.

"You're going to want to pull those spurs out of my shoulder," he growled through gritted teeth. His opponent looked like he might try something, but Annie's shotgun cocked behind him.

"Boy's right. We've got you dead to rights. Get off him, and crawl your crippled ass a pace or two back. Slow, like," Annie said. She took a step back as the big mercenary levered his weight off Nolan.

"I'm not terribly mobile with one leg," the man said, dragging himself back from Nolan. He rested against the far wall. The blades disappeared into his wrist again with a single flick. "Just kill me. Please."

"I'd love to," Nolan said, feeling his jaw with his free hand. "But we need answers. Assuming you don't bleed out, you're the one who's going to give them to us. You have a name?"

Footsteps came pounding up the deck, and Nolan pivoted, raising his rifle. Kathryn trotted into the light, slowing as she reached them. "I got the last one. I think we're clear."

"Annie?" a voice crackled over Annie's comm. It was the boy Nolan had seen earlier. Tim, he thought the boy's name was.

"I told you to stay in your quarters, boy," Annie growled into the device.

"Their ship is leaving," the boy said. "I thought you'd want to know."

"Shit," Annie said, she leaned gingerly against the wall. "Gather up the others, and tell Bock to get any wounded down to the med center. If he gives you any grief about scrip, you tell him he'll have to deal with me, and he won't much like it."

"You asked what my name was," the man against the far wall said. His teeth were gritted, his fists clenched. He looked like he was battling an immense amount of pain. "It's Edison."

Chapter 20- Celebration

"Y'all done a good thing, here," Annie said, offering Nolan her hand. He took it, and wasn't surprised by how firm her grip was.

"Thank you for your help. We'd be dead right now without you," Nolan said, pumping her hand once before releasing it. He smiled at Annie, clapping her on the back. "We need to get the prisoner back to OFI. Will you be okay if we leave?"

"I'll keep Bock in line, no fear of that. We'll be all right. You do what you have to do," Annie said. She rested the barrel of her shotgun on her shoulder, pulling up her scarf to cover the bruise on her throat. "You ever decide to take up mining, you come on back."

"Maybe I'll do that," Nolan said, giving a quick wave as he headed into the airlock. He waited for it to close behind him, then tapped the red button on the *Sparhawk*'s outer hull. The airlock activated, and the door slid up.

Nolan ducked into the *Sparhawk*, smiling in spite of himself. True, Edison hadn't given up anything beyond his name yet. But he would, back at headquarters. OFI was very, very good at prying secrets from people who didn't want to part with them.

"Nolan?" Kathryn called from the cockpit.

"We're clear for take off," he called back, moving into the mess. Edison sat at the far corner, his now-bandaged stump resting on the bench next to him. Nolan sat across from him, making sure he had the big man's attention before speaking. "You feel like talking?"

"Do you have any idea what it's like not to feel pain?" Edison said. He looked down at his stump. "I didn't feel the bullets. I didn't feel my leg being cut in half. I can't feel it now."

"I'm sorry," Nolan said, and meant it. He didn't like having to maim another solider, no matter the reason. "What can you tell us about this Doctor Reid? That *is* who you work for right?"

"The only pain I feel," Edison said, as if Nolan hadn't spoken. "is the chip. He presses a button, and I flop about like a fish. It lasts forever, and you aren't ever the same after it finally goes away."

"Doctor Reid presses the button?" Nolan asked.

The big man looked up. His dark skin was spattered with blood, but his eyes were calm. "Yeah, that's right. Doctor Reid. He turned my men into monsters."

"Why? Why were you taking people?" Nolan asked.

"We were putting them into tanks. I don't know why," Edison said. He shook his head sadly. "I know it was wrong, but it was the chip. He tortured us for weeks, and...I just couldn't do it anymore. I stopped fighting."

Nolan glanced up as Kathryn ducked into the mess. She sat down next to him.

"So Doctor Reid put them into tanks?" Nolan asked.

"Yeah," Edison said. He refused to meet Nolan's gaze. "We dropped the tanks off at different places, usually another vessel. Once or twice abandoned stations. I don't know who picked them up, or what they were doing."

"Who did Reid work for?" Nolan asked, straightening.

"I don't know, but he worked very closely with Admiral Chu," Edison said, looking up. His cheeks were covered with tears. "Chu knew about everything. He gave us to that monster."

Chapter 21- Hung out to Dry

Nolan was still smiling from his lunch with Kathryn when he reached the admiral's office. It had been a harrowing few days, and they'd earned a little R&R. He'd asked her to spend it together, and she'd agreed. Now he just needed to find a quiet luxury suite.

The door slid open before Nolan could knock, so he entered. He straightened his posture, marching with pride toward the admiral's desk. Nolan faltered a bit when he saw the look on the admiral's face. That scowl dropped the temperature in the room by at least ten degrees.

The doors hissed shut behind Nolan with immense finality.

"Sit down, Commander Nolan," the admiral said. He reached into his drawer, withdrawing a cigar. He made a great production of snipping, then lighting it. He didn't speak again until after he'd taken several experimental puffs. "What made you think it was okay to go to Coronas 6 on your own? You defied protocol, broke at least a half dozen laws, and did several million credits worth of damage to Coronas property."

"Sir, I don't think--"

"That's right," Mendez thundered, surging to his feet. He pounded the desk, spittle flying as he roared. "You don't think. Not unless I tell you to. You gather data, and you bring it back to me. Or at least, that's what you *used* to do."

"Sir?" Nolan asked, blinking. He struggled to get his brain around what was happening. "We saved those people, sir. We brought back a prisoner who can corroborate everything. We can nail Admiral Chu. Sir."

The rage seemed to leave Mendez. He studied Nolan coldly again, then his eyes narrowed.

"I can salvage your career, but only just," Mendez said. He sat again, taking another puff. Then he shook his head sadly. "I'm going to put it out that you behaved inappropriately with Kathryn. I've already spoken to her, and she's agreed to testify to that fact, if necessary. The alternative is both of you being court-martialed."

Nolan balled his fists and clenched his jaw shut around the words that fought to get out. Then he forced a deep breath before speaking. "You're hanging me out to dry?"

"Would you prefer the alternative?" Mendez said, tapping ash from the cigar. "If I bring you up on insubordination charges you'll be stripped of rank, dishonorably discharged, and possibly imprisoned. You'll take Kathryn down in the process. Would you prefer that route?"

Nolan very nearly said *yes*. It might end his career, but at least he'd end it with the truth. "Sir, if you put out rumors about Kathryn and I, there's no way my command crew will respect me enough to do my job."

"That's an excellent point," Mendez said, pointing his cigar at Nolan. "That's why I'm relieving you of command, and reassigning you to the 14th."

"The 14th," Nolan said, struck by how bitter the words tasted. The 14th was the home of every malcontent, criminal, and animal the rest of the fleet didn't want. Going to the 14th was exile. There was no coming back from that.

"You'll be made XO of a ship. Not a capital ship, but a frigate or maybe even a destroyer," Mendez offered, his tone suggesting that Nolan should be overjoyed at the news.

"Wherever you see fit, sir," Nolan said. He clasped his hands behind his back and stood at attention.

"This isn't the end, son," Mendez said.

"Sir, may I ask you a question off the record?" Nolan said. He needed to understand why. He'd done everything the admiral asked. What had changed so dramatically? Why had the admiral done it? Why turn on Nolan, when they were on the cusp of catching Chu?

"No, you may not. Dismissed," Mendez said. He turned back to his terminal, and Nolan strode slowly from the office. His career had just joined all the corpses littering the hallway, and he didn't even know why.

Chapter 22- Problem Solved

Mendez waited several seconds after Nolan had departed his office before activating the terminal. He flipped a switch on the tiny black box affixed to the side. The scrambler applied an extra level of encryption. One could never be too careful, especially now that Mendez understood the scope of what they were trying to achieve.

The Quantum Network logo flashed across his screen, then faded to show a warehouse-sized lab. Large rows of tanks filled the background behind Doctor Reid, hundreds upon hundreds of them. Almost all were occupied.

"Ahh, Mendez," Reid said, giving a sickly smile. His eyes were feverish. "Have you dealt with our little problem?"

"It's been dealt with," Mendez said. He took another puff, enjoying the savory flavor. Tobacco had tasted even better since his joining. "Nolan will no longer be a problem. I've discredited him, and exiled him to the 14th."

"You let him live?" Reid roared, his face twisted with rage.

The sudden mood change surprised Mendez. Perhaps Reid's joining had been imperfect.

"Of course I did," Mendez replied. He set down his cigar, leaning toward the screen. "Leave military matters to me, Reid."

Reid closed his eyes, visibly struggling to calm himself. When he opened his eyes, he'd at least partially succeeded. "Yes, yes, of course. Military matters are yours. Why are you letting him live?"

"Because if I kill or discharge him, it will raise uncomfortable questions," Mendez replied, partially mollified by Reid's change in demeanor. "We have a foothold in the Admiralty, but the situation is delicate. Kelley still wields a lot of power. If we arouse his suspicions, it could lead to discovery. The masters wouldn't be pleased about that."

"No, no, they wouldn't," Reid said, shoulders slumping. "I suppose you did the right thing. What about Delta?"

"Delta works for me now, Reid," Mendez said, something hot flaring in his vision. The way Reid had broken Edison horrified Mendez, even after the joining.

"And what am I supposed to do?" Reid said, petulantly.

"I'm having a new vessel prepared, one that will allow you to capture far more subjects," Mendez said. He picked up his cigar again, enjoying the pungent curl of smoke wafting from the end. "Go to the Ghantan system. I'll have the coordinates sent to you."

Author Chris Fox

Chris is the author of over twenty military science fiction and post-apocalyptic novels and lives north of the Golden Gate Bridge in the beautiful town of Novato. If your'e unsure how to find it just follow the scent of self-entitlement. If you pass teens driving Teslas, then you're in the right place. Chris enjoys Dungeons & Dragons, being pompous, gawking at his wife, hiking, and dreaming up new worlds.

Exiled is the prequel to his bestselling novel Destroyer, book 1 in the Void Wraith trilogy, which you should totally buy. See more at www.chrisfoxwrites.com.

VOYAGE OF THE DOG-PROPELLED STARSHIP

by Robert Jeschonek

Dogs are man's best friend, but dogs' best friends are something else entirely.

We are down to our last team of Huskies, and we still can't shake the *Unshakable*, flagship of the dreaded High Concept.

"How long can those Huskies run? How long until we lose all propulsion from the dog-drive?" I shout the question to make myself heard over the cries of pleasure from the bridge crew around me.

The Concept's delighter beams have half the crew squirming on the floor, quivering like the enormous bacteria or protozoans they are.

"Stand by, Captain Nabob!" Vera Caspian, my ship's caninegineer (and a freak human among us), is watching readouts and video feeds on her holographic console. She claps her hands once, folds sideways left to right, and is gone, zapping by quantum zentanglement to the Kennel Deck at the far end of the ship.

She unfolds at her station a moment later, her face flushed with alarm. "Maybe five more minutes on the Huskies. That's with our best musher at the whip."

Our own farship, the *No Shit*, rocks as the *Unshakable* blasts us with its boomer cannons, knocking me sideways. As I catch myself on a shiny bulkhead, I realize the terrible shape I'm in; my reflection shows that my thousands of hairlike cilia are limp, my macronucleus is pale, and my cytoplasm is shriveled and green with exhaustion. Three days on the run from the Concept have left this giant paramecium looking like a sorry-ass humanoid warmed over.

But I'm still the *captain* of this ship, and I have a duty to keep her out of the hands of the enemy. Also a duty to deliver the *Trillion Thoughts About One Thing* in our hold to the dying planet that needs them to survive.

Which is about 300 light years from the orange and purple planet we're about to crash into.

"We're caught in that world's gravity well, sir!" says Mr. Huarache, a three-meter-tall amoeboid with glittering gold flecks in his cytoplasm. "We're going down!"

The *No Shit* shudders around us as the *Unshakable* keeps up its bombardment. As always, the High Concept's dedication to trolling the sentients of the galaxy for their own demented amusement knows no bounds. Stopping us from saving a dying planet will bring those bitter, sniggering jerks no end of joy, and stealing the *Trillion Thoughts About One Thing* for their own trouble-causing endeavors will be the cherry on the hot shit sundae.

Another round of boomer blasts rattles us from stern to stem, even as more of our people go down squirming with delighter-induced bliss. We'll be lucky to make landfall before the ship shakes to pieces and everyone aboard her is overstimulated to the point of implosion.

"Captain!" Vera has a grim look on her face. "The Huskies are down, sir!" Dogs whine and whimper over the intercom. "We're breaking out the emergency backup, but we won't get far on *Corgis* and *dachshunds*, sir!"

"Huarache!" I stare at the gleaming orange and purple planet on the big viewer on the forward bulkhead. "Can we manage evasive maneuvers?"

"I feel too good to try!" Huarache giggles with delight.

Damnit, he's been hit! "Outta my way!" Cilia fluttering, I zip over and seize the controls with the folds of my rubbery pellicle membrane.

Little dogs are yapping, and there's power again, but barely. I flick a switch, twist a joystick, and the *No Shit* swoops away from the *Unshakable*, heading for the planet's surface far below.

The surface where, long ago, I was shocked to discover who *dogs'* best friends really were, and why evil was *not* the worst thing ever to nest in human hearts.

***

We come down fast and hit hard, bouncing from one purple sand dune to the next. Hunks of the ship's organic outer armor shear away with each impact, exposing more of the *No Shit*'s glistening jellyfish skin.

Our breakneck approach finally comes to an end with a sudden, lurching stop in the side of a huge Ground Spout--its thick purple mass heaving with complex vapors and dense, semi-solid larvae flickering in and out of multiple dimensions.

As the ship settles and the screams fade--as many triggered by High Concept delighter beams as crash-inflicted injuries--I shake off my own personal shock and help those on the bridge who are hurt. One of them, Ensign Scintilla Tint, a sentient scent presenting as a cluster of swirling glitter, is scattered but doesn't let it stop her from reporting on casualties.

Five dead, 85 injured. Her voice is a complex arrangement of fragrant esters that conjures language in the speech centers of most organic brains. *And...oh no. Oh this is terrible.*

"What?" I ask as I finish mending some of the million wings of the giant flying bacterium known as Lieutenant Ah Rise Rhythm.

Vera Caspian, whose head wound is shedding blood down the side of her face, interrupts. "Dogs down, Captain! *All dogs gone!*"

Yes, dead, confirms Scintilla.

"And the ship's condition?" I ask as Ah Rise Rhythm flutters away to check on his crewmates.

"Repair crews already dispatched and laden with insults," says Mr. Huarache. "Damage consequential but not irreparable."

"How long until we're ready to launch?" I ask.

"Approximately two hours, Captain Nabob." Huarache's amoeboid gelatin squirms, repairing multiple regions of bruising. "Assuming repairs are properly completed, and the High Concept doesn't destroy us first, all we'll need to reactivate the dog drive are some..."

"Then it's a good thing." I head for the exit.

"What is that, Captain?" asks Rhythm.

"A good thing I know where to *find* some dogs," I tell them as the shellevator doors clam shut before me, and I zip away through the ship to the bubble deck where my bouncy ball carriage awaits.

***

I'm 20 bounces west of the *No Shit* when Vera unfolds from right to left beside me, in a Dalmatian print field jacket with a med kit pack on her back. Her head wound has been wrapped with a black-furred bandage that contrasts her pretty blond hair.

"Vera." I'm not really surprised to see her appear in my travel ball like that. As caninegineer, she *should* be along on this mission.

"Craw isn't listed as a dog-rich world." Vera bobs in the suspension field inside the ball, only lightly jarred by the vehicle's powerful bounces across the landscape. "So where are these canines you're barking about, Skipper?"

"Not far, actually. It's lucky we crashed where we did."

"Lucky?" Vera scrunches up her nose. "What if you lead the Concept to this secret stash of yours?"

"As long we make contact first, I don't care. Though depending on how well they *remember* me, we might not have such smooth flailing."

As I flutter my thousands of cilia for emphasis, the terrain outside the travel ball changes, shifting from purple sand dunes to a bird beak forest. Giant toucan, myna, and heron beaks climb point-first to the lilac sky, even as spindly trees hung with the beaks of other birds surround us, clattering in the stiff afternoon breeze.

The macronucleus at the heart of me clenches as memories of my last visit to this place rush back. "Gird yourself, Vera. Unless this place has changed greatly, we are heading into the deepest of metaphorical darkness."

"What *happened* when you were here before, Captain?" asks Vera. "Tell me more about what to expect."

As the travel ball takes a bad bounce off an upthrust woodpecker beak the size of an old-growth redwood tree, I adjust the course controls on the inner wall of the ball with my cilia. *Almost there.* But can we get the help we need in spite of the cloud I left under last time? The darkness that still, to this day, haunts me?

Maybe I can work it out by telling the story. "It was twelve full glimmerings ago, when I was but a crewman on the good farship *Every/None/Always/Never...*"

***

"We surrender!" screamed Captain Fragilistic of the *Tabula Raga*, the hysteria in his voice unnerving even in the replayed video. "Call off your people-things! Oh gods, please *call them off!*"

"Crewman Nabob! For the last time, quit watching that shit!" *My* commanding officer at the time, Captain Eponymous Prawn of the *Every/None/Always/Never,* knocked the video playback device out of my pellicle mitten with one sweep of his whiplike flagellum. "Pay attention to what's happening *now*, and maybe we can find and *rescue* the crew of the *Tabula Raga.*"

"Instead of suffering the same fate as they did?" I asked.

"Face forward, crewman!" howled Prawn, a spermatozoa with an attitude that never quit.

I did, and so did the other twelve crewmen and three officers in the landing party. Giant microbes all, we continued our methodical march/squirm/wriggle/float through the bird beak forest, closing in on the last known location of the Fragilistic and the party from the *Tabula Raga.* They'd all disappeared six weeks ago, leaving behind only that ominous video as a clue to their fates...a video that was stuck playing in a loop as we all marched away from my discarded player device. "We surrender! Oh gods, please *call them off!*"

"Hold up, people!" Lieutenant Band Antimony, a ribbon of geometric diatoms with photoluminescent properties, suddenly stiffened in alarm. "Movement up ahead!"

Every one of us raised and cocked our convincer/reviser guns, barrels aiming at a copse of striped toucan beaks not twenty kicks away. Depending on their moods, those living weapons we carried would unleash either a torrent of persuasive argument or streams of information-altering code capable of rewriting the causal relationships involved in a given scene.

The weapons might as well have been nonexistent when we heard the plaintive howl from the copse of beaks.

OO-WOO-OOOOOO

As the keening rose and fell, I shivered and considered turning tail. One of our number *did* desert just then--a gray-skinned cryptoendolith who turned out to be the wisest among us.

"Steady, people!" ordered Antimony. "Stand your ground!"

"Who's there?" shouted Captain Prawn in the direction of the howl. "Who is it?"

OO-WOO-OOOOOO

Again, the cry ululated on the hot, dry wind, keeping us all at shivering attention. Then, suddenly, it stopped.

A figure emerged from the copse of beaks--a naked human male on all fours, slinking slowly across the dusty ground. His long, shaggy hair and beard were bright red. He wore a spiked black collar with a long silver chain trailing after it.

Behind him strode a figure on two legs--a canine like a German Shepherd in a kind of blue jumpsuit. In his right paw, which included a prehensile, clawed thumb, he carried the other end of the chain attached to the man's collar.

When he spoke, his voice was deep and rumbling like thunder.

"Welcome one and all," he said. "Which of you is fit to feed the Best Friend?"

"That human?" said Prawn. "*None* of us, thank you very much!"

"Don't be silly. Not that *human,*" snapped the canine. "Our *Best Friend!*"

***

"We're here." I stroke the course controls, and the travel ball bounces to a stop. One more touch of a control, and the skin falls into wedges around us, exposing us to the riot of sounds and smells in the bird beak forest. "That's where they first came out to meet us." I poke a hump of pellicle at the copse of toucan beaks just a few coughs away.

"'They as in a dominant, bipedal dog and subservient human on all fours." Vera takes a step forward, then stops. "Why is this the first I've ever heard of this encounter?"

"It was classified ultra-top secret after what happened." I glide past her and into the copse. There is simply no time to waste; the Ground Spout could disperse at any time, leaving the *No Shit* completely out in the open. Will my crew finish repairs or will the Concept swoop in to destroy them and the farship first? It's a tossup.

Vera draws her weapon--a fully automatic shevolver with self-esteem nullifier and false hope inducer--and follows me into the cluster of colorful striped beaks. This isn't the first time we've been in a tense situation together; she's been part of the crew for seven sequences, each one riskier than the last.

But I fear for us both if potential surprises roll against us, which they very well could. I wouldn't put anything past this world after my disastrous last visit.

Suddenly, a keening wail fills the air--familiar to *my* ears, at least. A chill runs through my cytoplasm as, for a moment, time seems to turn back.

"Ignore that," I tell Vera as I keep gliding forward. "Just keep going."

"But is it..."

"*Ignore it.*" I need to keep us focused in spite of the distraction. Whatever awaits us, we need to face it at full, unrattled strength and composure.

A moment of silence, and again, Vera speaks--trying to keep her mind off the danger, perhaps. "So what happened after the dog and his pet man met your group, Skipper?"

"The dog--his name was Half Hiccup Half Heartattack--showed us the way to a hidden city called Oblongata, which was built entirely of bones and feces. Parts of it were marvelously intricate. Other parts were corpse-strewn ruins. They'd been having a civil war, you see--pets against masters...and something else."

"Pets? You mean *dogs* or *men*?"

"Yes." I slip between some tightly-packed flamingo beaks, slowing my pace a little. We're not far from Oblongata and its possible dangers now. "And something else. Something I'd never encountered before--*knowingly.*"

***

"What a lovely city," said Captain Prawn in the bygone days of yore. "And what a shame about all the destruction."

"We paid a price for victory." Half Hiccup Half Heartattack patted his leashed human on his red-haired head. The man drooled, tongue lolling, eyes empty. "But it was worth it for our newfound freedom."

"Freedom." Lieutenant Antimony's component diatoms glowed a little brighter, then dimmed. "From what?"

"This one and his like, of course." Heartattack tousled the man's bearded chin. "They subjugated us, treated us as their *chattel*, denied us *any* kind of rights...and now look. Who's a good boy now, huh? *Who's a good boy now?*" With a laugh, Heartattack shook the man's head by his beard, yanking it from side to side.

Still, the man's eyes were blank. I was having a hard time imagining he'd *ever* been part of a ruling class of any kind.

"When did the war end?" asked Prawn.

"Only days ago," said Heartattack.

"That fits." Antimony's ribbony structure rippled. "Our missing landing party must have gotten caught up in the conflict."

Heartattack nodded slowly. "Of course. Their demise had nothing to do with the Godicils."

Prawn and Antimony exchanged a look that made me more nervous than ever. I kept my pellicle extrusions and cilia wrapped tight around my convincer/reviser gun.

"Demise?" said Prawn. "We never said they were *dead*. All we know is that they're *missing*."

"And what's a *Godicil?*"

"You mean you don't *know?*" Heartattack crouched beside the man and gestured at what looked to me like empty space above the man's shoulders. "You mean you can't *see* it?"

"See what?" asked Prawn.

"Come closer." Heartattack kept gesturing at that space above the human's shoulders. "Take a closer look."

Prawn swam over, propelling himself with strokes of his flagellum tail, and gazed down at the man as instructed.

"Still nothing?" Heartattack sounded annoyed. "Closer!"

"What exactly does it *look* li--"

Suddenly, Prawn was dragged down toward the man--but not *by* him. From what I could see, it was like something in that empty space jerked him down toward it, holding his ovoid body fast as his tail flailed crazily.

And then stopped. And then Prawn fell to the ground beside the human with a *splat*.

"A *Godicil*," said Heartattack, "is *that*."

As the upright German Shepherd said it, other bipedal dogs with naked humans on leashes--some with more than one--converged from the surrounding rubble. All of the humans were growling as they approached, males and females alike.

"Just because you can't *see* it, doesn't mean it can't win a *war*. Or be our *best friend*." Heartattack dropped the leash, and all the other dogs around us did the same.

The words of hysterical Captain Fragilistic of the *Tabula Raga* from that terrible video rushed back to me. *Call off your people-things! Oh gods, please call them off!*

"Just because you can't *see* them, doesn't mean they can't *slaughter* you," said Heartattack, just before he whistled and all the humans attacked us at once.

***

"How the hell did you *survive*?" asks Vera.

I don't get to finish telling her my story just then because my chatterbox starts beeping, alerting me to a message from the *No Shit*. Sliding the device from its holster stuck to my pellicle, I flick it on with my fluttering cilia, and we listen.

"The Ground Spout has dissipated! The *Unshakable* has found us!" The voice from the speaker belongs to ever-dependable Lieutenant Ah Rise Rhythm. "Their fighters are rapidly incoming with delighters fully charged! Repairs are nearly complete, but we're sitting ducks with dogless engines! No takey-offey, *capische*?"

"Hold them off as best you can," I tell him. "Launch all fighter squadrons. Keep shields raised as long as you can on battery power."

"That won't be long, Captain!" Just as Rhythm says it, there's an explosion in the background. "We don't have much left in the tank here!"

"We hope to be in touch soon with good news." I keep my voice confident for his sake. "Nabob out."

"Gotta go, Skipper." Vera claps her hands once, folds left to right, and is gone--presumably back to the ship to assess and assist. Maybe she's even got some emergency puppies tucked away in cryogenic dogspension for just such a day as today.

As I break the connection, I hear rustling from the peacock tail brush nearby, and I lurch around to face it. Extruding a mitten of cytoplasm, I wrap it around my instakarmashawarmadharma gun and swing it up in instant readiness just in case.

"Who goes there?" As the words pop out of my oral groove, every cilium on my body stiffens like a needle, quivering with tension. "Show yourself!"

Imagine my surprise when a redheaded human male stalks out of the brush biped-style, dressed in a black smock and bottoms.

"Greetings, friend." Smiling, he raises his hands (which are empty of weapons, by the way). "You are most welcome here in our little corner of the world."

"Greetings to you as well." I recognize him instantly as the naked redhead on the leash of Half Hiccup Half Heartattack from my previous visit...though I don't blurt this fact out right away.

"My name is Fah Fistula, and I'm the chief of our fair city of Oblongata." The redhead bows a little, then straightens. "And you are?"

I hesitate to announce my name, then decide to go for broke rather than lie. "Captain Nabob," I tell him. "My vessel, the farship *No Shit*, crash-landed nearby and is in dire straits." I pause dramatically. "We are dogless."

"Then we have something in common!" Fistula nods. "There is not a dog to be found *anywhere* in Oblongata or its blessed environs."

My star-shaped contractile vacuole and radiating canals scrunch in a spiral twist, the paramecium version of a frown. "No dogs...at all?"

Again, Fistula nods. "If you've come in search of them, you're out of luck. The last died during our recent civil war, ended mere weeks prior to your arrival."

There's been another civil war, then--this time with much different results. Things start to make *terrible* sense. If what he says is true, the *No Shit* and all aboard are surely doomed.

The man gestures, inviting me onward. "Will you visit fair Oblongata, sir? I think you'll find our hospitality *much* improved since your *last* visit here."

So he *does* remember me. "But what about the *others?* The dogs' best friends?"

"The Godicils?" Fistula smiles grimly. "Whom do you think we *defeated* in this war?"

***

As the humans attacked, the crew of the *Every/None/Always/Never* didn't hesitate to open fire. Every one of us blasted away with our convincer/revisers, holding nothing back-- and not a shot made a damn bit of difference. The humans were upon us like a raging wildfire, oblivious to the streams of argument or causal disruption cascading from the barrels of our weapons.

Their style of assault was surprising, unnerving. They knocked our people down and pinned them but never used their sharp claws or gleaming fangs to do them harm. *That*, they left to the *thin air*.

Just as Captain Prawn had been murdered by what seemed to be the empty space above the redheaded human's shoulders, I saw one after another of my shipmates torn apart by unseen forces. Gruesome splatters of guts spilled onto the ground all around me, erupting from skins and capsules that seemingly split open spontaneously.

Only I was spared, writhing out of the awful slaughter that engulfed my comrades. Lieutenant Antimony tried to follow, only to be pounced on by a screaming, dark-haired female and subsequently rupture like a stuck balloon.

Just like in the video, it was pure chaos. Mind whirling, I found myself pinned against a towering black beak--and Half Hiccup Half Heartattack stepped in front of me.

"Looks like they were *all* fit to feed the Godicils." Heartattack shrugged. "But *you* have a different role to play, apparently."

"Role?" I had to fight to keep my voice from shaking as the humans who'd just torn apart my crewmates rose and circled around me, hunched and glowering. "What role?"

576

"Tortured prisoner." Heartattack gestured, and two brawny men--one with brown hair, one with blond--got up off their hands and knees and stormed toward me. "Don't worry. The pain will be worth it in the end...though not so much for you."

The two men used me as a punching bag then, taking turns pumping fists into my pellicle. Each blow was harder than the last, making me grunt and yelp with agony.

And each time a human punch pounded my micronucleus through the pellicle, I divided. I gave birth to a copy of myself that wriggled off into the arms of a waiting dog.

Screaming at the pain flashing through me, I had the answer to a question I'd never considered until that moment.

If you undergo asexual reproduction induced by physical impact, is it still a violation?

***

I am nervous as Fistula guides me into the freshly ruined city. I stay keenly alert for any sudden movement from any direction, even as I realize all the alertness at my command won't likely save me.

This is where it happened, that pummeling attack...the forced reproduction. The last thing I remember from that day is gazing out at all the children I'd made against my will, glistening and quivering eerily in the midday sun. Then, I passed out from the pain, blessedly shielded from whatever abuses were to follow.

I awoke who knows how many hours later, shriveled and wretched in the purple sand desert. Gazing up, I saw crewmen from the *Every/None/Always/Never* gaping down at me, reaching to lift me in their cilia and pseudopodia for transport back to the ship. When I got there, I said nothing of what had been done to me, though I told our intelligence branch everything I remembered otherwise of Oblongata. I thought I would never travel back there in my lifetime-- I *prayed* I wouldn't--yet here I am, returned to the scene of the crimes against me.

And a witness to those very crimes walks easily alongside me, as if we are dear old friends. Needless to say, I keep an extruded mitten close to my instakarmashawarmadharma gun at all times.

"Careful," he says calmly. "There are still a few of them roaming around."

"Dogs? Godicils?"

"Your kids," says Fistula.

I am more confused than ever. "Why is that a bad thing?"

"Because they were on the wrong side. They were the *enemy--part* of it, anyway."

We circle the ruins of a giant structure that looks like it was built from stained glass, starlight, and some kind of flowering vines. A cathedral, perhaps? Then why are there heaps of dog skulls arranged on the floor?

"I don't understand anything about this place," I say, almost to myself. "I don't understand what happened here."

"What happened to *you*, you mean? Back in the day?" Fistula plucks a purple flower from one of the vines and twirls it between his thumb and forefinger. "I can tell you this much: it was all the *dogs'* idea."

"Why? What could they have to gain from what was done to me?"

"Peace! That was the plan, anyway." Fistula flicks the flower away. "They wanted your offspring to serve as *hosts* for the Godicils--though *traps* is more like it."

"Maybe it would help if I knew what the Godicils *were.*"

"Invisible, hideous *parasites.*" Fistula flinches a little when he says it. "Most of the time, you don't even know they're *on* you." He reaches back with both hands and pats the empty space above his shoulders. "On you and *in* you."

"In you."

Fistula scowls and nods. "They work their slimy tendrils through your body, winding them around your organs—occupying your heart like a nest of worms. They pump you full of chemicals, driving you to violence, and they feed on your rage and pain. The only way to keep the food coming is to turn you against an enemy--even if that enemy used to be your friend."

His words sink in, and understanding grows. "Then the civil war that the dogs won, those years ago?"

"Was triggered by the Godicils," says Fistula. "And we humans were their hosts. But in the war before that, the *dogs* were the hosts,

578

and so on. This went on for thousands of years, one war after another, until Half Hiccup Half Heartattack the dog chieftain came along. He was the first who could *see* and *read* the slimy bastards. He was the first to understand how *both* sides were being manipulated. And when *you* folks started dropping in, he came up with a plan to free *all* of us."

I twitch at a flicker of movement near a half-toppled tower of pulsing green brick...then relax. Nothing there.

"At the time, the Godicils were the *dogs'* best friends." Fistula keeps walking, drawing me toward a battered silver dome that looks like it could be the center of the city. "But Heartattack knew that would only last until the next war, when the Godicils would switch sides and drive the *humans* into conflict. This would just go on forever, he knew--but what if there was a *third* side? What if he introduced a *new* host into the mix? One that might be too tempting for the Godicils to resist--until they were *trapped* inside...and then the whole package was *disposed of.*"

"And the Godicils took the bait?" I leave out the part about my personal suffering and violation--for now, at least.

"We all worked together, playing our parts. We had to make it seem *convincing*...right down to the attack on your team, I'm afraid. We needed it to look like we were torturing you for information, and the copies we punched out of you were unintentional." He sounds regretful. "And when we had your children, and talked about how wonderful they were, and what amazing capabilities they had, the Godicils *jumped* at them! Heartattack saw them go, one after another, and attach to your kids' bodies. And then he *closed the trap*, buried them like dogs *do*--but it was a *bust*. Over time, the Godicil treatment turned your kids into *powerhouses*, and they broke free and came after *all* of us. They killed every last dog and almost got the *rest* of us, except we figured out a way to kill *them* first, and the Godicils with them."

"You killed my children."

"Correct," says Fistula.

"Except a few who are still roaming around."

"Exactly."

"Okay." Nothing I've heard from him makes me feel any better about what happened...or more hopeful about the tragedy I've come here to avert. And the clock is ticking, I know, counting down whatever few minutes are left for the *No Shit* to hold on against overwhelming odds. What if the *Unshakable* has already destroyed her?

The thought of it inspires me to dig deeper for a solution. There must be *something* here to power up the ship, *something* that wasn't trashed in the latest war.

"Fistula." I look around at the rubble as we pick our way through it. "Do you know if the dogs buried anything else?"

Fistula snorts and stops walking. "Good question. Those mutts were *always* burying things."

I like where this is going. "Can you think of any *specific* burial sites?" I gesture at the ground with one of my pellicle mittens.

"Well, not down *there*." Fistula points upward. "*That's* where they did all their *burying.*"

"Wait a minute." I do that frowny star-shaped vacuole/canals thing again. "Am I to understand that these dogs somehow *buried* things...in the *sky?*"

"Not so much in the *sky.*" Fistula tips his head back and jabs a finger at a fluffy orange cloud overhead. "In *those.*"

Some kind of hyperdense cloud formation with antigravitic properties? It's a new one on me. "So how did they get *up* there then?"

"The *elevator,* of course." He looks over his shoulder and gestures in the general direction of what looks like a distant, rippling heat mirage.

"Well let's go see what they stashed up there, shall we?" I prod him along with my flickering cilia. "If there's a secret power source, we need to find it *fast.* Time is running out, and a lot of good macrobes are about to be deathstinguished."

***

We emerge from the rippling transparent elevator into a truly wondrous place built of billowing orange cloud. Puffs and streamers of the stuff drift all around, glowing every shade of orange in the unobstructed late day sunlight. It all seems insubstantial, yet somehow supports the weight of us both, giving only slightly like rubbery foam under Fistula's feet and my flickering cilia.

It supports much more than that, as well. The dogs left all manner of things up here, jumbled in the cottony fluff. There are piles of bones, of course, and tatters and rags--but also mechanical and electronic parts and equipment...building materials...functioning devices. Things blink and hum in the cloudbank, while others chatter and whir and twitch--and do *other* things, too.

As we walk onward, we hear sounds from inside a kind of bunker built with corrugated metal. The sounds are unmistakable, even muffled as they are--and the part of me that's closest to a human heart truly leaps. Perhaps, after everything, there is hope after all.

"Do you hear that?" I ask Fistula, pointing a mitten at the building.

"Yes, but there's a lock on the door," he tells me.

"So smash it off," I say as I reach for my chatterbox. "And make it snappy!"

He hesitates, then goes to retrieve a metal bar from a nearby pile of junk.

As he heads for the bunker, my chatterbox makes its connection. "Skipper?" Vera Caspian answers the call. "Where the hell *are* you? I zentangled back from the *No Shit* and can't find you anywhere!"

"Never mind!" I watch as Fistula breaks the lock and tosses it aside. "Just get back to the ship *immediately*. And prepare the following without delay!"

"Yes sir!"

Fistula throws open the door, and the noise bursts out from inside. All that wonderful, marvelous *barking*.

And then I *see* them, the ones making those sounds, and I know we can do this. *We can win because of them.*

As they charge toward me, I laugh out my orders to Vera. "Get me *harnesses*, Vera! Dozens of *harnesses,* and the longest *traces* you can throw together in the next fifteen minutes!"

***

The battle is in full swing when I ride a winged Great Dane down from the sky, exulting in the way the wind whips my cilia.

Enemy fighters swoop and blast overhead, sparring with fighters from the *No Shit*. The sky lights up, but the fire comes nowhere near the Dane or any of the *other* winged dogs.

There are *dozens* of them, barking and howling with joy as they soar down on great feathery wings. Nimbly, they zip between blasts and shrapnel, darting this way and that, a brigade of furry angels. The products of Godicil science, these genetically engineered miracles are clearly elated to finally be free of the shelter where they were tucked away for far too long. Heartattack and his people might have saved them from Godicil domination, but locking them away only intensified their desire to be free.

And now, finally, they can *fly*...and so can *we*.

The Dane and I land in front of the *No Shit*, where Vera followed my orders to the letter. Lots of crewmen are there, too, to help set things in motion--Vera, Ah Rise Rhythm, and Mr. Huarache among them.

The Dane, leader of the pack, follows me to the front and is first to accept a harness. The other dozens follow, landing lightly and scampering to positions along the lengthy, incredibly strong lead lines. They all pant and sniff and bark with joy as the crew fasten harnesses to them, taking care to leave the wings free and clear. They sing, too, in words taught them by Heartattack years ago, poetic words of flight and beauty and escape to faraway starlands.

Every time the enemy fighters form up and try to strafe them, our own fighters fend them off with desperate grace. We'll let *nothing* get in the way of what comes next.

When the harnesses are secure, all the crew members race into the ship except Vera. Pressure-suited against the harshness of space, she leaps into a special sled behind the dogs, hastily assembled by the *No Shit*'s highly motivated crew.

On my signal, when all crew and fighter craft are aboard, Vera cracks the whip. The winged dogs--Danes, Huskies, Shepherds, Greyhounds, Golden Retrievers, Dobermans, Labradors, and more-- run and flap across the purple sand. They pull the ship behind them with incredible ease, sliding it out of the crash-site and picking up speed.

When their paws leave the ground, so does the *No Shit*. Together, we soar upward, leaving behind the awful world of Craw that held us down--that held *me* down ever since my first visit, though

I've finally broken its grip. As the dogs and ship fly, so does my soul. As the ground recedes below us, so does the sorrow and pain that kept me from reaching my fullest potential as a paramecium and farship captain.

Enemy fighters swirl around us, and we shoot away from them, too fast to follow. They can't stop us from whisking the *Trillion Thoughts About One Thing* to that dying world or going on any of the multitude of adventures that surely await us.

The High Concept attack ship *Unshakable* roars toward us, firing every weapon in its arsenal...then seems to stand still as Vera mushes the dogs to unbelievable new speeds.

Somehow, their wings and paws have just as much traction in the void as on the ground and in the atmosphere. I can't explain it, and I don't care. I don't care about the physics or the memories of my pain or the damned High Concept or any of it.

It is enough to sit back and watch from the bridge of my gleaming farship as those winged dogs carry us forth into the star-filled glory of the galaxy, barking with heartfelt joy at every crack of the musher's whip.

Author Robert Jeschonek

There is nothing quite like a Robert Jeschonek story. His futuristic tales are unique, edgy, and strange...yet always full of heart. You can find his envelope-pushing fiction in *Galaxy's Edge*, *Escape Pod*, *Pulphouse*, *Fiction River*, *WORDS 'Zine*, *StarShipSofa*, and many other publications. He has also written official *Doctor Who* and *Star Trek* fiction and Batman and Justice Society comics for DC Comics. An Amazon bestseller, Robert has won an International Book Award, a Scribe Award from the International Association of Media Tie-In Writers, and the grand prize in Pocket Books' Strange New Worlds contest. His young adult slipstream novel, *My Favorite Band Does Not Exist*, won the Forward National Literature Award and was named one of *Booklist*'s Top Ten First Novels for Youth. Hugo and Nebula Award winner Mike Resnick (*Santiago* and the *Starship* series) calls him "a towering talent." Join his continuing cosmic adventures on Facebook, Twitter, and at www.robertjeschonek.com.

ASSAULT ON TARJA

By M. D. Cooper

COMING IN HOT

STELLAR DATE: 3227798/ 04.24.4125 (Adjusted Gregorian)
LOCATION: SDMS *Damus,* Approaching Venus
REGION: InnerSol, Sol Space Federation

"Shit! Katelyn, we can't break through this blockade, its nuts!" Rory exclaimed as the *Damus* approached Venus. "TSF has the place locked down!"

Katelyn hated to admit it; her sister had a point.

Venus hung before them, the night side of its blue and green orb drifting through the brilliant space near Sol. Beyond the planet, igniting the surrounding darkness with radiant light, lay Sol's baleful orb. It was a far cry from how humanity's home star appeared out in the disk, and seeing it this close always filled Katelyn with a sense of fear and wonder.

The display was made even more impressive by the sheer volume of ships around the planet. The Terran Space Force had declared a no-fly zone stretching over one hundred thousand klicks from Venus, and only ships with the right clearances—which translated to almost none—were making it through.

The result was a right freakin' mess. Tens of thousands of ships hung in high orbits around Venus, thousands more were stuck at the space stations closer in, and others were drifting in the Sol-Venus L1 point, conserving fuel while they waited for the conflict to end.

In the midst of it all, crisscrossing the globe in overlapping orbits were five hundred and twenty-three Terran Space Force warships.

584

Another thousand were stationed further out, policing the civilian traffic that was balling up more and more around the planet.

"It may be locked down," Katelyn said, glancing at her sister in the *Damus*'s small cockpit. "But that's going to work to our advantage. Look at that mess out there. They've blocked all access to Venus, just to control one city on one continent. The senate is already holding hearings to allow access to other planetside ports, and the Venusian Governor is appealing directly to the president for reprieve. They'll open up a planetside port, and when they do, that'll be our in."

Rory looked at Katelyn, and then shook her head. "You're too optimistic. Our cover won't hold out against that sort of scrutiny."

"As usual, Sis, you worry too much." Katelyn tossed her sister a grin before an alert coming off the local Space Traffic Control relay caught her attention. She sat up straight and took a deep breath. "See, Rory, no worries. STC has opened up two ports on Venus's southern pole. Ships low on fuel, or with emergency supplies can apply for clearance."

Rory let out a rueful laugh. "Well, we *are* low on fuel. Of course, that's aided by the fact that you dumped most of it an AU back."

Katelyn reached out and grasped her sister's shoulder. "There's no better emergency than a real emergency. Transmit our status; let's see how quickly they'll let us get down."

The result was not as efficacious as Katelyn had hoped. The sentient AI managing the emergency landings tried to route them to a space station in high orbit three times, until Rory finally managed to convince it that they also needed repairs that a station couldn't facilitate. Four hours later, they had a lane and were on their assigned vector.

"Venus, here we come," Katelyn cried out in victory as the ship skirted around the edge of the TSF blockade toward their designated port.

Rory unbuckled her harness and rose from her seat, hunching over in the *Damus*'s small cockpit. "You want anything? I'm dying of thirst here."

Katelyn looked up at her tall sister, the woman's dark, lanky hair hanging down on either side of her face, drifting aft with the ship's thrust. "Yeah, do we have any more of those pizzas? The ones with the pineapple on them? That shit's the best."

Rory snorted. "You mean Hawaiian Pizza?"

"That's a dumb name. No one gets pizza from Hawaii and no one is harvesting pineapples from the place," Katelyn replied. "I refuse to use the name."

Rory pushed herself off her seat and drifted out of the cockpit, looking back at Katelyn as she went. "For someone who grew up on Makemake, you have a strange dislike of Polynesian words."

"You need to bone up on your history, Sis. Hawaiian Pizza is about as Polynesian as the TSF cruisers out there."

Rory pulled herself through the passageway back toward the *Damus*'s small galley, calling back, "You want it cooked or frozen?"

"Har har!" Katelyn responded before turning back to her console. A wisp of her red hair had come loose from her ponytail, and she pulled it back, re-fastening the band around her hair. Rory may like having her hair loose in zero-*g*, but Katelyn couldn't bear it.

It was a strange incongruity—Rory was the one who was normally straitlaced and by the book, whereas Katelyn did everything by the seat of her pants. Rory always claimed that she just didn't like the way a ponytail or bun made her scalp feel. Katelyn, in turn, liked to joke that it made her sister look like some sort of space medusa.

They had to find their sources of amusement *somewhere* out in the black.

For the last five years—ever since they were released from prison, following the Makemake incident—the pair had been running supplies for the Disker resistance, slowly building up weapons caches and troops on Venus and Triton. Most of the time, the work was exceedingly dull followed by periods of stress and worry as they waited for contacts to pick up cargo in less-than-savory ports across the Sol System.

Working for the resistance was not like the assault on the *Normandy* over Makemake. *That* had been intense, amazing, the sort of action Katelyn yearned to get into. Of course, that engagement had also gone very, very badly. The Terran carrier had detonated a planetbuster only a thousand klicks from Rory and Katelyn's ship. Only the asteroid they had been pushing protected them, but only just enough to preserve their lives.

Even though the Disker resistance lost that day, the TSF's use of such a weapon had only strengthened Katelyn's resolve to keep working for the resistance. To her surprise, it had galvanized Rory's as well. Sure, her sister liked to bitch and moan about pretty much every risk they took—but when push came to shove, Rory was in the thick of it, ready to get the job done, no matter what it may be.

Even if the job was just making a pizza.

Katelyn double-checked the calculations on the braking burn and reworked them to save a little more fuel. They weren't actually going to land at the polar spaceport, they just had to make it look like they were. Their real target was Tarja.

In an ideal world, they wouldn't need to land, just fly by and transmit the data they had to the resistance's leaders on the planet. However, their ruse of being low on fuel—which wasn't a ruse at all—meant that they had to set down at the spaceport to refuel before taking off once more.

That part of the plan was nuts, and even Katelyn admitted it. Their chances of getting off Venus in one piece were slim to say the least. Still, she'd rather have the fuel to try it than be dead in the water.

"What you thinkin' 'bout?" Rory asked as she floated back into the cockpit and handed Katelyn the package containing her pizza.

Katelyn unsealed it and breathed in the delicious aroma. "Just wondering how we'll get back off world again."

"We don't," Rory replied. "We gotta sit it out. We park the *Damus* at Tarja's spaceport and go hole up 'til this thing is over."

"Define 'over'," Katelyn said around a mouthful of pizza.

"Well, hopefully until the Tarja Government can get the TSF to back off and hold a proper plebiscite. These fuckers just try to beat everyone into submission when people try to leave the Sol Space Federation, but that's not going to hold forever. Either they let the federation dissolve peacefully, or they get their asses kicked. Terra can't stand against the rest of Sol on its own."

Katelyn was surprised to hear such vehemence from her sister. Rory rarely espoused the Cause's views with so much passion. Granted, the way the TSF was behaving on Venus was disgusting. If the people wanted to separate, they had that right. The Federation couldn't be held together at gunpoint.

"I don't hold out as much hope for the Venus operation as you do," Katelyn replied, tucking back the wisp of her red hair that had gotten free again. "The whole point here is to pull the Jovians into the conflict. If they can see that the Terrans are acting like crazy people, and that resistance is possible, they'll join in. The Marsians, too."

Rory nodded slowly. "Yeah, I get that; we're turning hearts and minds against Terra, here. Win or lose for Venus, its win-win for the Cause. I just would like to see the Tarja mission succeed."

Katelyn nodded. She would too, but as she looked out her window at the hundreds of TSF cruisers, she feared that there was only one possible outcome for the city of Tarja.

The two sisters sat in silence for several minutes before Katelyn executed the command to rotate the ship and begin its braking burn. They would have to come in hot—the blockade's presence wouldn't allow them to loop around the planet and aerobrake before coming down. They'd have to shed relative *v* in space and then fall to the surface as gently as possible.

"You secure?" Katelyn asked as she tucked the pizza's container into a refuse pouch.

"Yup, ready to rock," Rory replied with a resolute nod.

"Then let's do this," Katelyn said as she executed the burn.

The *Damus* rattled and shook as the burn shed their delta-v and the ship fell deeper into Venus's gravity well. The execution of the braking maneuver required the engines to face the planet, and Katelyn watched the lights of the other civilian vessels through the cockpit window as they waited to get past the blockade.

She wondered what their purposes were. Why they had come to Venus, what they were doing with their lives. Once, she had flown without a Cause, without a reason to be in the black—other than money, of course. It had been empty, pointless. All the while, the people of the Scattered Disk worked and slaved so that their profits could go to InnerSol and the Terrans.

Here in InnerSol, the Terrans built their great rings and lived in their high societies, basking in delights that were never known in the disk. Katelyn knew what it was like out there—so far from Sol that only a fraction of the star's light reached you. The deep black was a different place; every bite of food, every photon that hit your skin...it was earned. Bled for. It was real.

An alert flashed on her console, and Katelyn realized it was the sentient AI handling the approach vectors for ships being allowed past the blockade.

<Ship registered SDMS Damus, please respond, your burn profile is incorrect. You are going to fall out of the pocket.>

"Here we go," Katelyn said to Rory and received a resolute nod from her sister.

<Acknowledge your last STC. However, our instruments show burn is good. We're right in the middle of our lane, coming down on assigned vector,> Katelyn replied in a crisp, business-like tone.

<Negative, Damus, say again, negative. I have you half a degree off. You're going to skip across the south pole and have to loop around—but you can't do that, the trajectory will send you over Teka.>

Damn straight, it will, Katelyn thought as she double-checked that they would indeed pass over the continent of Teka.

<I'll run a recalibration routine on our primary astrogation,> Katelyn replied. *<Right now it shows that if I make the correction you're suggesting, we're going to auger into the ice cap.>*

<Damus, I don't have time for your idiocy. Fail over to secondary systems and get in the lane I've assigned, or I'll have to rescind your landing clearance.>

Katelyn looked at Rory and held a hand over her mouth. "She's gonna rescind our clearance! Oh no!"

Rory shook her head. "Just get ready to break away if they start shooting."

"They're not going to shoot, at least not yet," Katelyn replied before responding to the AI. *<Secondary system failed audit at the last station checkup. I'd rather not risk it.>*

<You can't be serious.> The AI was beginning to sound rather put out. *<How'd you get debarkation clearance?>*

<Our primary systems were spot on, and we were to get repairs on Venus. That's why I'm not sure I want to trust your assessment,> Katelyn replied. *<We'll have recalibration done in a moment; still plenty of time to correct, if you're right.>*

<*I am right,*> the AI retorted. <*You have twenty seconds to get back in your lane.*>

Rory stifled a laugh. "Only you could enrage an AI."

"It's a gift," Katelyn replied with a wink and a grin.

Katelyn reviewed her approach vector. Her breakaway burn was set for three seconds after the AI's deadline. That was all she needed. Just three seconds of leeway.

"Gonna be close," Rory muttered as she watched the ship's nav systems ready the maneuvering thrusters. Venus grew larger on the holo showing their rear view. The closed within seven thousand kilometers as the ship continued to decrease burn.

<*Damus you have—what the hell are you doing?*> the STC AI exclaimed as the ship spun one hundred and ten degrees and fired its engines, streaking across Venus's southern pole and over to the daylight side of the planet.

The burn was too exacting for a human to manage, and Katelyn had to trust that her calculations had been correct. She wondered what her brother would think of the daring maneuver as the ship streaked through the skies of Venus, only one hundred kilometers above the surface. From the ground, the ship would appear to be a raging ball of fire, racing toward the north pole.

Joe would be in stasis right now, safe from the insanity that raged across the Sol System these days. She didn't blame him for leaving. After Makemake, she would have left too—had it been an option. Still, he was one of the best pilots she knew. With the mods the military had given him, he could have arced around Venus without a preprogrammed flight path to aid him.

This one's for you, Joseph.

The STC AI was shrieking—something Katelyn had never heard an AI do before, and she shut off the comms as they reached Venus's north pole. There the ship spun once more, completing its braking before dropping to a dozen meters above the northern ocean and skimming the wavetops on the way to the Teka Continent.

"No one shot at us," Katelyn mused.

"Oh, they shot at us alright," Rory replied. "I just dropped a trio of scrambler drones. Two of them are craters behind us now."

"Shit! Really? Why didn't you say something?" Katelyn asked.

"You seemed really focused."

Katelyn nodded absently as she checked their velocity and scan visibility. To the casual observer, the *Damus* may have looked like just another freighter, plying the black, keeping to the commercial lanes, but the Cause had set it up with an impressive stealth suite. This close to the surface, even the TSF cruisers overhead would be hard-pressed to find the ship.

"I was thinking of Joe," she replied when her review of the ship's flight path checked out.

Rory nodded. "I do too, sometimes—especially when we do crazy shit. I wonder if he would have joined us—if he hadn't gotten out."

"Who knows," Katelyn replied. "Stars, if you think about it, the *Intrepid* is still within the Oort cloud…. I hope no one in the SDA gets any bright ideas and tries to stop them."

"No chance," Rory replied. "No one wants to mess with the GSS. No lie, though, you'd take the first colony ship out of Sol, too, if you got a berth."

Katelyn shrugged. "Maybe I would, maybe I wouldn't. Hard to say. If all the good people leave, who's going to be left in Sol?"

"Seriously, Katelyn," Rory said with a snort. "What do you think's happened *already*?"

"Good point," Katelyn replied.

The ship's sensors picked up the edge of the continent, and Katelyn increased the *Damus*'s altitude to climb above the steppe that dominated the northern portion of Teka. They had five hundred kilometers to go, and then they'd be at their destination.

Katelyn set her jaw. "Tarja, here we come."

FUEL DEPOT

STELLAR DATE: 3227799 / 04.25.4124 (Adjusted Gregorian)
LOCATION: Outskirts of Tarja, Teka Continent
REGION: Venus, InnerSol, Sol Space Federation

Gunnery Sergeant Williams of the 242 TSF Marines leaned his back against the low wall at the edge of the field and slid to the ground.

He was exhausted. Bravo Company had been on the move for two days. A few minutes of sleep here and there was all anyone had managed to catch. But now their target was in sight: a deuterium fuel depot that the separatists were using to power their surface to space batteries along the northern edge of the city.

Williams's armor's hydro reserves were dry, so he split apart the front of his helmet wide enough to put a bottle of water he'd scavenged to his lips. The liquid was cool and refreshing, though the night air that hit his face was not.

"What a shit-show," Williams muttered aloud after drinking half the bottle. He looked to his left where Sergeant Kowalski had hunkered down.

"You can say that again, Gunny," Sergeant Kowalski replied as he cracked his helmet and drank from his own bottle. "I don't get why this planet is so damn hot. Fleet shut down their little suns."

Williams gazed up into the sky. The blue point of light to the south was Earth; he could see the twinkling halo around it—the High Terra ring—from here. A nimbus glow caused by the thousands of ships coming and going created a haze around both the ring and the planet that made its glow both beautiful and indistinct. Larger lights, much closer to Venus, also hung overhead. Those were the ships of the Terran Space Force, and the civilians caught up in the blockade beyond.

A burst of light flashed across the sky: a surface to surface strike from further south. The flash was followed by a resonating *boom*, and a staccato echo of rail fire. All around Tarja, the Marines were moving in.

The city would fall in a matter of days.

The cruisers in orbit of Venus had the firepower to raze the planet, burn it to ash. But it was bad form to burn a member world. Williams—and the brass, it would seem—believed that the majority of the populace did not support the separatists.

As far as he had seen, most of the enemy troops were Diskers—mercenaries from the edge of the Sol system and the worlds of the Scattered Disk Alliance. Hardly any of the enemy combatants were locals. One could almost say that Tarja was an occupied city at present.

But all of that was politics and positioning. The reality was boots on the ground. Kill the Diskers and Separatists, and try not to hurt too many of the innocents—so long as they could tell them apart from the enemy.

Williams pulled his gaze away from the night sky and squinted at Kowalski, remembering that the sergeant had asked him about the heat. "Do I look like a weather satellite? Venus is close to Sol. Even with its thinner atmo, it still heats up. Ever heard of convection?"

"They shoulda moved it further out," Private Weber said from where he crouched. "I remember learning that there's room for another planet between Venus and Earth—if the orbits are tweaked just right. Not sure why they couldn't shift Venus into the goldilocks zone."

Williams leaned over and cuffed Weber upside the head. "Seriously...it's too dark, it's too hot, it's not far enough from Sol...is there anything else you'd like me to do for you today, or would moving a planet be enough."

Weber grinned. "Well, Gunny, now that you mention it, I—"

The Marine stopped talking when Williams' hand rose in the air once more. "You were saying, Private?"

Weber rested his head against the wall and didn't reply.

"Thought so," Williams grunted in response.

<Jansen, what's the word on the northern approach?> Williams sent the message over the Link, directly from his mind to Jansen's. She was one of his most reliable fireteam leaders. Give her a task, and she'd see it done, no matter what. Right now, she had fireteam one/one scouting the northern route into the fuel depot.

Jansen's rueful laugh came into his mind, followed by her smooth, no-nonsense voice. *<Better than I expected, Gunny. There's a platoon of Diskers and what looks like some local militia folks set up around the front gate, but their positions are shit. Half of them are milling around; their pickets are only a klick out. We could take 'em and then use beams on the 'toon at the gate.>*

<OK, you hold tight with one/one. We can't fire beams around the depot—the colonel says the brass doesn't want us to blow it, so we're going to have to get strategic on this one.>

<Shit, Gunny, really?> Jansen asked. *<Would the brass like us to wipe the enemy's ass while we're at it?>*

Williams chuckled. *<Don't give 'em any ideas, Corporal. You'd be holding Disker dicks while they piss before you know it.>*

<Nice alliteration there, Gunny,> Jansen said with a snort.

<I'll be here all week, try the veal. Now tell your pizza-box wearing fireteam not to shoot the effing tanks, got it?>

<Damn, Gunny! You know how to hurt a Marine.>

Williams smirked as he sealed his helmet back up and summoned an overhead view of the fuel depot up on his HUD. Four hundred massive deuterium tanks lay in orderly rows, protected by a tall fence and electronic countermeasures. Data on the depot said that there were some autoturrets out there, too, and he had to assume that the enemy had control of them.

The fuel depot was on the northern edge of the city of Tarja; only five klicks from the spaceport. Commander Lauren had the rest of Bravo Company headed there, but from what he could see on the combat net, they were still an hour out. Cutting off the fuel supply for that port would certainly help. Some ships were still making it through the blockade with supplies. If they could choke off the refuel supply for the port, it would go a long way. Ships would be able to land, but without refueling, they'd be grounded—few captains would take that risk just to deliver supplies.

Not unless they were nuts.

As he considered their options, Lieutenant Grenwald, 4th Platoon's CO, broke into Williams' thoughts. *<We're down to twenty-two Marines, Gunny. This ain't no cakewalk. There's gotta be at least a hundred of the enemy out there.>*

Williams nodded. Grenwald was echoing his own thoughts. *<We need to divide their forces,>* Williams suggested. *<Best way to my mind is take out the pipeline between the depot and the spaceport. They'll send a team out, and we'll hit them at the same time we strike from the southwest.>*

<Got it. I'll send teams two/one and two/two out to hit the pipeline,> Lieutenant Grenwald replied.

<You asking or telling? Grenwald?> Williams snorted. <You're the LT; I'm just here for emotional support.>

Grenwald laughed in his mind. <You're the surliest sonuvabitch in the Corps, Gunny, I'll let you know if I need my nose wiped.>

<I'll do it with Perez's ass,> Williams replied with a grin. <On second thought, he might like that.>

<That he would,> Grenwald replied. <Staff Sergeant, you been listening?>

<With all my heart,> Staff Sergeant Green's mental avatar grinned in their minds. <I'll escort the fireteams to the fuel line. We'll hit it a klick out.>

<Good. Williams, you mind babysitting Chang at the southwest corner?> Grenwald asked.

Williams nodded and rose to a crouch. <Watching Chang's team mow down asshats is the highlight of any day.>

<Good,> Grenwald replied and began disseminating the orders to 4th Platoon's squad sergeants.

The countdown was set. In t-minus twenty, they'd hit the pipeline, and all hell would break loose. Just the way it was meant to.

ABORT

STELLAR DATE: 3227799 / 04.25.4124 (Adjusted Gregorian)
LOCATION: Outskirts of Tarja, Teka Continent
REGION: Venus, InnerSol, Sol Space Federation

"Shit! Katelyn, those AA towers are hot!"

Katelyn saw it too; the four AA towers to the north of the spaceport were supposed to be controlled by Disker forces, but they were online and turning toward the *Damus*.

"Hitting the deck," Katelyn called out as she pushed the ship down toward the ground, leveling off just five meters above the tall grass that covered the steppe. She prayed there weren't any small hills or buildings that scan didn't pick up as they raced over the terrain. That would ruin their day real fast.

Overhead, flak from the AA guns exploded in the air, sent out to light up the ship's shields and make better targets for the secondary rail-systems on the AA towers.

"They're missing us—we're too low for the flak," Rory said with a smile.

The moment the words passed Rory's lips, flak fire began to strike the steppe on their starboard side. Katelyn swung the ship hard to port, speeding away to the west as rail shots began to strike the prairie behind the ship.

"You just had to say something," Katelyn scolded her.

An explosion flared dead ahead, and Rory let out a cry of dismay. "What was that?"

"That wasn't something shot at us," Katelyn said. "We should be close enough to pull comms from our people down here, see what's up."

Rory bent over her console, and a moment later gave a nod. "OK, there we are.... Damn, there's a lot of chatter. Let me see if I can filter it down."

Katelyn banked the ship further west and then back south, evading the AA fire while still trying to stay on course for Tarja. They had to deliver the data, and there was no way she could send the burst with all the enemies around. They'd have to do a hand delivery.

"Try to raise someone in charge too; we need to hand off this packet in person if possible."

"Yeah, sure," Rory replied as she surfed the comm channels. "Damn, TSF blew the line between the fuel depot to the west and the spaceport. TSF Marines have the northern edge of the port."

"Dammit," Katelyn muttered. "Any luck raising anyone?"

"Yeah, putting him on the shipnet."

<Damus, this is Major Suats. You still intact? We can see the guns up north blasting away at something.>

<Five by five,> Katelyn replied. <For now.>

<We're getting our assess kicked out here. I need to get your datapacket safely into Tarja before the Marines move further into the city. You need to set down at the southeast corner of the fuel depot. We're pulling back through there and can secure your payload.>

Katelyn pulled up a display of the area the man had indicated. It was filled with warehouses right up to the edge of the fuel depot, less than fifty meters between the last tank and the first building.

<You got it, sir. Piece a pie to set down there. You'll need to string us a fuel line though.>

<Deal. ETA?> the major asked.

<Three minutes, provided the Marines don't blow us out of the sky between now and then.>

<See you on the dirt, Damus. Suat out.>

Katelyn glanced at Rory. "Well, we always did want to see what ground combat looks like..."

"We did?"

STRIKE FORCE

STELLAR DATE: 3227799 / 04.25.4124 (Adjusted Gregorian)
LOCATION: Outskirts of Tarja, Teka Continent
REGION: Venus, InnerSol, Sol Space Federation

Williams crouched behind a basalt boulder that lay a dozen meters beyond the fence at the fuel depot's southwest corner. To his right, in position behind a pair of similar rocks, was Chang's fireteam with their crew-served railgun. The weapon would be able to reach out and touch anyone along the south and west sides of the fuel depot. In a pinch, it could fire clear through the first few rows of tanks—though no one wanted to be around for that.

Further to the north were squad three's three fireteams, ready to breach the fence on the depot's western side. Once the pipeline blew and the Diskers moved out to investigate, squad three would advance into the fuel depot. Kowalski would lead one/one and one/three in from the north, and fireteam one/two would hold the depot's southern edge.

The plan required the Marines to strike hard and fast—to make their smaller numbers feel like the hammer-blow of a much larger unit.

Williams watched the countdown on his HUD tick past the one-minute mark, then thirty seconds. He mentally counted down the last five seconds with the timer.

Five...four...three...two...one...mark!

A blinding flash lit the night sky, and a cloud of fire-filled smoke rose into the air on the far side of the fuel depot, mushrooming as it hit a denser layer of air above. Then everything was silent for a moment as 4th Platoon waited for the enemy to respond.

A klaxon broke the stillness, and a minute later, a group of personnel carriers drove out the fuel depot's front gate.

<How's your party going?> Commander Lauren asked on the company command net.

<Just getting started. I see you beat your estimates to the spaceport.> Williams replied.

<We did; already have four of the AA towers. Thanks for the distraction, by the way. We're going to put it to good use.>

<Is that what I see shooting the north?> Williams asked.

<Yeah. Dumbass governor strong-armed two ports near the south pole to accept ships with supplies or low fuel reserves, and one of the first ones in broke out of its lane and made a bee-line for the north pole.>

Williams knew where this was going. *<And the fleet couldn't shoot it down for shit, right?>*

<Shit, whoever is flying that thing has balls the size of Mars; they're kissing dirt.>

Williams nodded as he watched a pair of hoverjets take off from the north end of the fuel depot. One moved toward the fuel line, and the other toward his current position. Looks like whoever was running things there wasn't a total idiot.

<So what are you talking to me for?> Williams asked. *<Sounds like you have your hands full.>*

Lauren snorted. *<I can walk and chew gum at the same time, Gunny. You just secure that fuel depot and cut off its other supply lines.>*

<Won't take but a dozen minutes,> Williams replied.

<Good. Lauren out,> the company CO replied.

<Our friends have arrived at the pipeline,> Grenwald reported on the Platoon's combat net. *<All teams, advance into the compound.>*

Williams didn't even have to give Chang any direction. His team already had their railgun tracking the hoverjet. At the LT's command, a stream of rail-fired pellets shot out into the night, blazing toward the jet.

The enemy jet slewed to the side, narrowly avoiding the opening salvo, and fired a pair of missiles at Chang's position. PFC Walker leant around the rock and fired a chaff bomb into the air. The projectile lobbed high over the team and exploded. Once the chaff was in the air, his weapon fired a striker into the cloud of metallic particulates. Just as the missiles passed through the cloud, the striker discharged a gigawatt of electricity into the chaff; the two missiles exploded.

Marines from third squad were now firing on the hoverjet, and it pulled further back over the fuel tanks, firing more missiles as it retreated.

Then something clipped its right wing, and the jet spun to the side, tilted, and swung down into one of the fuel tanks. The tank ruptured, spraying hydrogen into the air with a whistling shriek. For a moment, Williams wondered if it would ignite, but then his question was answered as the hydrogen leak turned into a tower of flame, lit by the heat from the hoverjet's engine wash.

<Kinda pretty,> Chang said over the combat net.

<Just pray it doesn't spread,> Sergeant Li replied. *<If this depot explodes, we'll get to find out as a unit if there's an afterlife.>*

Williams shook his head. Stupid pilot got what he deserved for backing over the tanks while taking fire. He should have moved to the north where friendly ground forces held the terrain.

<It won't spread,> Williams said. *<Even that ignition was a fluke thing. It'll probably flame out once the jet's fuel stops burning.>*

The fireteams along the south and west sides of the fuel depot wasted no time breaching the perimeter fence and taking out what few guards had rushed toward that corner of the compound. An armored personnel carrier tried to reinforce the scattered separatists, but Chang's railgun made short work of the vehicle, tearing a rear corner off the vehicle before it retreated north.

Gonna be a cakewalk, Williams thought to himself and considered advancing into the compound when a starship swung overhead, its torch cutting through the space between the fuel depot and the warehouses beyond.

<*Well, shit; who's come to the party?*> he asked over the combat net. He checked the command net and saw that the ship the AA towers had been shooting at had slipped past their defenses. <*Weber,*> Williams called out to the fireteam leader on the depot's south side. <*Get eyes on that ship.*>

<*On it,*> Corporal Weber said from his position to the south of the fuel depot.

<*Stay frosty,*> Williams replied. <*Whoever that is knows they're flying into a warzone. Either they're armed to the teeth, or they're fucking nuts.*>

<*Or worse,*> Perez added. <*They're both.*>

<*Shut up, Perez.*> Williams considered their options and turned to Chang. <*Hold things here; you're the anchor if we need to retreat. I'm going to help Weber keep Perez's ass out of the fire.*>

<*You got it, Gunny. Say hi to Perez's ass for me.*>

<*Shut up, Marine.*>

No enemies were in evidence to the south of the fuel tanks, but on the northwestern side, he could see squad three now engaged with an entire enemy platoon.

He wasn't worried about it. The Diskers didn't stand a chance against the Marines; an even worse one if it was the separatist militia.

He rose from cover and sprinted to the south, deploying his own set of drones to provide a direct feed of the surrounding terrain. Ahead, he could make out the forms of Weber's fireteam as they moved along the southern edge of the fuel tanks. Williams looked beyond the fuel depot, toward the low warehouses that stretched away toward Tarja on the far side of the depot.

The starship would have set down at the edge of the tanks, possibly even in one of the warehouse lots. How they thought they could extract fuel while the Marines were onstation was beyond him. Perhaps they were desperate.

A flash of light to Williams' right caught his attention, and he saw beamfire lance out from two tanks. Weber drew his fireteam up short just in the nick of time.

<*One/two, sitrep,*> Williams called out.

<At least a dozen of them around the corner, Gunny,> Salas called back. *<Koller and Dvorak are gonna hold here while I circle around with Perez.>*

<Good,> Williams said. *<You distract them. I'm going to stay on this side of the fence and see if I can't get to that starship and see what's up.>*

<Understood,> Salas replied.

Williams stayed low as he moved through the tall grass south of the fence line, moving as quickly as he dared toward the warehouses. As he got closer, he could see the bulk of the starship peeking out over the tanks.

Just dropped down right on a parking lot, he thought. *Torches must have made a mess of the ground.*

Williams slipped over a low concrete berm and into a lot filled with spools of sheet steel. He threaded through them until he could see the ship, a gantry lowered from its starboard side, and several figures around the base of the ramp.

His probes spread out, giving him a view of the lot where the ship stood. An APC rested between the ship and the fuel depot, and a large warehouse was on the far side. A few cargo pods sat on the southwestern edge of the lot, and he could see two enemy soldiers taking up positions behind their cover.

<I have eyes on the ship,> he reported on the command net. *<I see half a dozen people; no, two more just appeared, carrying something down the ramp.>*

<That was some fancy flying they pulled off to avoid the AA towers,> Commander Lauren replied. *<You can't let whatever that is get into the city. It's gotta be high-value.>*

<Understood,> Williams replied. *<It's not going to go anywhere.>*

He pulled up his view of the fuel depot and the Marines in and around the area.

<Grenwald,> he said to 4th Platoon's Lieutenant. *<I need Olsen's heavy weapon between this ship and the city. The locals are going to pull back from the fuel depot with a package. We need to secure it.>*

<Got it, Gunny,> Grenwald replied. *<I'll get all the fireteams circling around as best we can.>*

<Good. Weber, you about here yet, or has Perez gotten himself shot?>

<One minute, Gunny,> Weber replied. *<Targets are down, just making sure our route is clear.>*

Williams looked up at the troops making the exchange with whoever was on that ship. A pair of soldiers hauled a refueling line from the tanks to the ship and began attaching it to a line coming off the vessel.

Ballsy, he thought. *Thinking they can gas up and take off again.*

He moved past several more of the spools and took up a position behind a stone block that marked the end of a row. He took aim with his weapon and picked his target—one of the soldiers at the base of the ramp—and fired.

The shot hit the enemy and pinged off his armor. Williams shifted his aim toward one of the figures standing on the ramp and fired again. This target was unarmored and fell as the bullet tore through the silhouetted person's knee. One of the people on the ramp dragged the fallen enemy up into the ship, while the other two raced down, one yelling and waving his arms.

Williams fired another shot and hit the arm-waver in the back of the head. The man dropped, but popped up a moment later, shaking his head.

Better helmets than the last batch we fought.

By then, the enemy clustered around the base of the ship had determined the origin of the weapons fire, and shots struck the stone he crouched behind. Williams didn't waste any time dropping to the ground and crawling to a new position.

<Engaging,> Weber reported, and the sound of Marine rifles filled the night air.

Williams pulled himself up and looked around a spool of steel. He could see the man who had been hit, still holding the package. He was crouched low, moving away from the ship, already halfway to the warehouse, and Olsen's team wasn't anywhere close.

Gonna be mano a mano, then, Williams thought.

Without thinking of the consequences, Williams raced around the spool of steel and vaulted the wire fence separating the two lots.

Shots rang out, and projectiles whistled around him—some striking his armor—but he didn't slow as he sprinted toward his target.

Out of the corner of his eye, he saw one of the figures reemerge from the ship. She had long red hair pulled back in a ponytail, though a wisp was free, blowing past her face. She raised a rocket launcher and aimed it right at him.

"Fuck!" Williams swore. He waited until the woman fired before diving to the ground. His luck held for one more day; the rocket flew overhead before hitting one of the warehouses and exploding in a brilliant display.

Williams' prey had dropped as well, and the Gunnery Sergeant was on him a moment later. It was then that he realized what the enemy soldier held: an NASI node. One that bore TSF emblems.

Williams held his gun to the man's chest. "Toss it aside; weapons, too."

The man glared at him from behind a semi-opaque visor. He seemed to consider putting up a fight, but Williams fired a shot next to his head.

"Now!" Williams ordered.

<Troops outside the ship are secure> Weber reported. *<Should we breach the ship?>*

In front of Williams, the man had finally made up his mind and tossed the NSAI node aside, followed by a rifle and two sidearms.

Williams carefully walked to the NSAI node and picked it up, the barrel of his rifle never wavering from the man's head.

"Thanks for the present," he said through his armor's speakers.

The Disker—he was wearing Disker armor, at least—didn't respond. Then a smile lit up the enemy's face, and a warning on Williams' HUD flashed, telling him why.

Behind him, a pair of autoturrets had lowered from the ship's hull.

<Look out, Gunny,> Perez warned, and Williams hit the dirt, holding the NSAI between himself and the ship. There was no way they'd fire on the thing they worked so hard to get planetside.

The ship's turrets tracked him, but didn't open fire. However, the distraction gave the enemy soldier opportunity, and a moment later, he was on top of Williams.

The man slammed an armored fist into the side of Williams's head, the blow dropping the Gunnery Sergeant to the ground. Williams rolled onto his back and kicked at his attacker, catching him in the side and sending him sprawling. He grabbed the NSAI node once more, and raced toward Salas's position, keeping the node between himself and the ship.

The autoturrets spun up, and rounds struck the ground around his feet—but shots from Weber's team struck the autoturrets, taking one out and jamming the other. A moment later, Williams ducked behind the APC next to fireteam one/two.

<What took you so long, Gunny?> Perez asked.

<Shut up, Perez,> Williams grunted. He was about to add something else when the ship's engines flared to life and it began to lift off.

<Shit, run!> Williams shouted.

Flames poured across the lot, licking at the Marines' heels as the vessel pulled into the air. The fueling line stretched and then snapped, whipping down onto the APC and crushing the roof. They made it to the dubious protection of the fuel tanks, and Williams turned and looking up at the vessel, which was still retracting its ramp.

There, silhouetted in the ship's airlock, was the redheaded woman. He pulled up his rifle and sighted on the woman; his armor's cameras zooming in on her face.

For a moment, he thought she looked familiar—then his HUD flashed a name: 'Katelyn Evans'.

Evans? Williams thought, and his HUD highlighted the connection, denoting her brother. She was Joseph Evans' sister...

He lowered his weapon and held out his hand for the Marines at his side to hold their fire. Williams owed Joseph Evans his life. The man's sister would get a bye this time....

The ship shifted vector and sped across the city to the south; the roar of its engines and a sonic boom thundered in its wake.

"Katelyn Evans…" Williams muttered as he shook his head. He looked down at the NSAI node he held in his left hand. "What the fuck are you mixed up in?"

Until next time…

Author M.D. Cooper

Thank you for reading *Assault on Tarja*.

The tales of the 242nd Marines are the first in a broader series known as The Sol Dissolution. Visit www.aeon14.com/aeon14-books to learn more about these stories, and the universe of Aeon 14.

If you would like to learn more about Williams and the Marines of the 242nd, as well as the events leading up to this conflict, read Destiny Rising, which tells of the assault on Makemake (where we first meet Katelyn and Rory), as well as the 4th platoon's deployment to the *Intrepid,* where they assisted Major Tanis Richards in stopping a plan to destroy both the ship and the Callisto Orbital Habitat.

THE JOB PLAYAN

by Laura and Daniel Martone

Take one conniving high priest. Add a handful of ornery pirates. Toss in a couple dashes of deceit. And you've got a recipe for mayhem and misadventure in the galaxy.

Chapter 1

"Captain, this could be our craziest stunt yet," Colburn Sephiran said, his voice reverberating inside his helmet.

"Not even close," Captain Morgan Kent, Sr. replied. He gestured toward a vessel heading away from the planet below. "The *Culin Four* is about to break orbit."

With their spacesuits tethered together, the two men floated roughly fifty miles from where the ship would leave the planet's atmosphere. Since the magna guns latched onto their belts only had a half-mile range, they had to use their repulsor boots to close the distance.

As they neared the ship, Col and Morgan aimed their guns. When the targeting system indicated they were within optimal range of the ship, Col took the shot, feeling the pressurized release of the magnetic fluke through his gloves and trusting he'd correctly accounted for the ship's estimated speed. Predictably, he hit his mark beside the cargo hold, and the ship promptly jerked him and his captain along for the ride.

Col engaged the reel, and the two men drew closer to their target. Now came the most dangerous part of their insane plan: they needed to anchor themselves to the *Culin Four* before the ship entered a dark matter stream and shot toward her destination two sectors away. No one could predict what might happen to a person being dragged through a dark stream, but Col didn't intend to find out.

The dark matter engines ignited just as he and Morgan reached the ship. Quickly, they positioned their backs against the hull and activated the magnetic plates mounted between their shoulder blades, mere seconds before the ship's twin dark matter beams converged, opened a dark stream, and pulled the ship inside.

Knowing they would likely black out while attached to the ship's exterior, the two men had already set their suits to auto-revive them upon emerging into normal space. Col watched as Morgan's helmet dipped forward, signaling he'd lost consciousness.

Remaining awake for a moment longer, Col gazed at the swirls of electrified blue light that danced against the enveloping blackness, making him feel like water sliding down an illuminated drain. A few seconds later, he followed his captain into darkness, one final thought on his mind: *I love being a pirate.*

Chapter 2

Col snapped awake when his suit unleashed a minor current of electricity throughout his body, just enough to rouse him. Groggy and slightly nauseous, he blinked his eyes, pivoted his head, and noticed Morgan was also awake.

The two pirates were still dangling from the *Culin Four*, which had emerged from the dark stream and now floated above a small reddish planet.

"Guess we made it," Col said.

"Looks like," Morgan agreed, turning toward his first mate. "Some trip, huh?"

Col chuckled, pleased their crazy plan had worked but not sure he wanted to repeat the experience any time soon.

A few moments later, a shuttle launched from the *Culin Four*, heading toward the nearby planet. Presumably to pick up the precious cargo required for the gig.

As soon as the shuttle had passed beyond his visual range, Col detached himself from the mother ship, raised the short rifle attached to his shoulder, and shot the vessel's communications array, guaranteeing no one aboard could send any emergency signals over the waves. Now, he and Morgan needed to breach the *Culin Four* and secure the ship before the shuttle returned with its cargo.

Naturally, there were numerous ways to board a vessel, and as pirates, they'd employed them all. Under normal conditions, they'd simply activate the umbilical of their ship, the *Damnation*, attach it to the cargo hold door of the target, and waltz inside... or rather, fight their way inside, as most crews didn't lay out the welcome mat for invading pirates.

In this situation, though, they didn't have that option, as the *Damnation* was elsewhere. Besides, since Col and Morgan didn't intend to kill any civilians on the ship, they needed to figure out a stealthier way aboard.

As Col weighed the possibilities, he noted Morgan's widening grin and followed his captain's gaze.

But, of course. The easiest way inside is when they open the airlock for you.

While hatching the scheme, Morgan had predicted the captain of the *Culin Four* would merely assume the communications array had incurred damage from some minor unseen collision. Worse consequences had indeed occurred upon leaving a dark stream. Though fast and convenient, it could be an incredibly dangerous mode of travel.

Col noted movement behind the smudged porthole of the portside airlock door. Just as Morgan had figured, the ship's captain had instructed someone to suit up and venture outside to assess the troublesome array Col had recently blasted — and repair it if possible.

"Crap," Col whispered, "these guys are efficient."

"In their business," Morgan replied, "you'd need to be."

As Col drifted beside Morgan, his suit still tethered to his captain's, he fixed his attention on the airlock door, unclasped a stun rod from his belt, and powered it up. "And we're sure this will work through their suits?"

With a nod of his helmet, the captain released himself from the ship's hull. Together, the two men maneuvered themselves toward the airlock door as it slowly slid open. Less than a minute afterward, one of the *Culin Four*'s crew members floated through the aperture. Wearing a bulky spacesuit, the short, portly repairman seemed to sense he wasn't alone. He turned just as Col touched him with the stun rod, and as he went limp, Col glanced at the faceplate and discovered, to his dismay, it wasn't a man at all.

Hastily, Morgan grabbed the woman and tethered her suit to his, and then he and Col pulled themselves and their unconscious cargo into the airlock.

Once the three of them were inside, Col secured the door and Morgan pressurized the room. With little fuss, they were aboard the *Culin Four* – and ready to ditch their infernal spacesuits.

***

Less than a half-hour later, the two longtime pirates stood in the cargo hold of the *Culin Four*. Seven crew members, including the portly woman, sat on the deck, their wrists bound behind their backs. Since only two of the captives had possessed weapons, securing the small ship had been rather easy.

"If only the rest of this caper went that smoothly," Col said.

"We just need to wait for the shuttle to return," Morgan replied, "and we can get this show on the road."

"Ahem," uttered one of the captives.

Turning toward the sound, Col spied a heavyset man staring at him and his captain. Surveying the rest of the crew members, Col realized not one of them was in decent shape. Then again, their profession hardly demanded physical fitness. In fact, obesity could serve as a useful calling card.

"Excuse me?" the man tried again, fixing his gaze on Morgan.

Morgan raised an eyebrow, but said nothing.

"You do realize we're from the culinary academy on Telphon Prime," the man said. "So, are you here to swipe our flour?"

Morgan laughed. "Not exactly."

"Well, what then? We actually have an appointment, you know."

"Of course," Morgan said. "But I'm afraid you'll have to miss it. In fact, we'll be needing your ship... and your clothes."

Chapter 3

It didn't take long for the shuttle crew to return, and it took even less time for Col and Morgan to subdue the three newcomers. Shortly afterward, Col helped their overweight captives to their feet and prodded them, at gunpoint, toward the crew quarters, where he divided them between two chambers and sealed the doors.

Typically, even Col – despite his strength and agility – wouldn't dare secure ten prisoners on his own, but the out-of-shape caterers were little match for him.

***

He returned to the cargo hold just as a dark brown puff of fur scurried from the open shuttle bay.

"Don't let it get away," Morgan shouted as he bolted into the cargo hold.

Col dove for the creature, like a farmer trying to snare his prized pig in a slippery sty. Deftly, he snatched it with both hands, and the creature squealed in terror. As soon as he felt the soft fur and the warmth of the squirming body, he loosened his grip, and a round, whiskered face popped between his palms, staring at him.

"What the hell is this?"

Slowing his pace, Morgan held up a digital tablet. "The manifest says it's a racksum cub. My contact was vague about the specific cargo."

Col shook his head. *Aren't they always?*

Glancing at the furry, upturned face and back to his out-of-breath captain, he snickered. "You were petting it, weren't you? That's why it escaped."

Morgan grinned impishly. "Perhaps."

"Aren't they really rare?"

Morgan nodded. "Yep, and they also happen to be the main course."

Frowning, Col relaxed his grip even more and examined the creature more closely, a cross between a mammal and a waterfowl. While it possessed the head, body, and tail of a kitten, it also sported the bill and webbed feet of a duck, plus a pair of wings that frankly seemed more cosmetic than functional.

Gingerly, Col carried the creature back into the shuttle, where he spotted a cramped cage containing eleven more racksum cubs. After setting the escapee amid his cohorts, he secured the latch, closed the shuttle door, and returned to the cargo hold.

***

With their rifles at the ready (just in case they'd missed any crew members), Col and Morgan ventured to the bridge. There, Col punched a set of coordinates into the navigational computer.

"The *Damnation* should already be at the rendezvous point," the captain said.

"Let's hope so," Col said as he hit several more buttons, and the *Culin Four* slipped into a dark stream.

***

Two hours later, Col and Morgan emerged from the dark stream at the far end of the Huluvian System. Almost immediately, they spotted their ship. It was hard to miss. After all, the *Damnation*, a Rogue-class pirate vessel, was at least five times bigger than the *Culin Four* and, naturally, armed for battle.

As soon as the two ships were within optimal range of each other, Col heard his CommTrans implant crackle to life, followed by the sound of laughter.

"Hell," said Zephyr, the *Damnation*'s second-best gunner (behind Col himself), "what kind of half-ass ship are you two flyin'?"

"Watch it, boy," Morgan snapped, "or you'll find yourself on garbage detail for the next year."

"Yes, Captain Can't-Take-a-Joke," Zephyr retorted.

Col chuckled. Morgan flashed him a stern look. Then, ignoring his captain – and longtime best friend – he continued to laugh some more.

"Alright, Zephyr," Morgan chided, "we'll see how you like your role in this little caper."

Once again focused on the mission, Col carefully positioned the *Culin Four* and instructed Burke, the *Damnation*'s navigator, to ease the ship forward and activate her umbilical. *Like the captain said, it's time to get this crazy show on the road.*

Chapter 4

Col scanned his captain from head to toe, and then tried, with some difficulty, to do the same to himself. Both men had donned bulky white coats and pants, the very same uniforms the super-sized *Culin Four* staff had worn. Because Col and Morgan were each tall and fit, they'd had to use their apron strings to rein in the numerous folds of fabric.

Col scowled. "We look ridiculous."

"Maybe you do..." Morgan conceded as he surveyed his first mate, "but I look damn good." He grinned slyly.

At that moment, Zephyr stepped into the cargo hold. Besides the baggy white uniform, he sported an almost two-foot-high white chef's hat, with four blue feathers sticking straight upward, giving him the appearance of an enormous balding bird. When Zephyr glanced at his two crewmates, who both valiantly tried to stifle their laughter, his usual smile quickly faded.

"That's it," he spat, turning back the way he'd come. "I'm not wearing this."

"Oh, yes, you are," Col said to his fellow gunner. "Stop being such a priss."

Zephyr harrumphed. "Easy for you to say. You're not wearing a stupid hat."

Col chuckled. "Hey, none of us would win any fashion contests." Then, he noticed a puff of fur clutched in Zephyr's hands. "Found a friend, I see." His face darkened. "You know, those are the main course."

"What?" In a predictably paternal gesture, Zephyr pulled the racksum cub closer to his chest.

"They're supposed to be some kind of aphrodisiac," Col explained regretfully, knowing how much Zephyr had always preferred animals to most humans.

Zephyr stroked the squirming creature. "Why the hell would they want an aphrodisiac served at a trade negotiation?"

Morgan guffawed. "Don't you ever pay attention to the plan? The *Culin Four* was hired to cook a private meal... before the negotiations."

"For who?" Zephyr asked.

Col sighed. "The mediator is the High Priest of Piaya, and he's trying to bed the Quarlonian delegate."

Crinkling his forehead in confusion, Zephyr continued to shield the racksum cub, as if his own crewmates were responsible for the unsettling scheme.

"The negotiations are tomorrow," Morgan explained. "Tonight, we'll prepare a feast for the High Priest and what will undoubtedly be one of the most beautiful women you've ever seen."

"Captain," Col asked, momentarily turning from Zephyr, "didn't you spend some time on Quarlon Seven?"

"A long time ago," he answered, shifting his eyes as if recalling an incredibly memorable visit. So memorable he unconsciously adjusted his pants. "Has the most gorgeous women in the Way. Thanks to a combo of excellent genes and a nurturing environment." Shifting his gaze toward Col, he added, "The men of their world aren't particularly fearsome, but the women themselves are incredibly strong and agile... so don't get any ideas."

Col grinned. "Never even crossed my mind."

"So, wait a minute," Zephyr interjected, his face twisted in anguish, "I'm supposed to cook these guys?" He glanced down at the bundle of dark brown fur in his hands. "Don't think I could that. Why can't you just have Galen cook for this scumbag?"

"Sorry, Zeph," Col said. "He might be able to kick your ass in the galley, but he can't shoot worth a damn. That's why you and Oxeter are going with us."

"Course, let's hope there isn't any shooting," Morgan said.

Glancing at the captain, Col furrowed his brow. A noble yet naive wish.

"OK," the captain admitted, "so most of the time we can't seem to avoid it."

Col returned his attention to poor Zephyr, whose disgruntled expression had only deepened as he watched the little cub in his cupped hands.

"Oh, boys…" Morgan said in an ominous tone.

Col and Zephyr both turned to follow the captain's worried gaze, presently focused on a viewscreen mounted on the portside wall, which displayed the forward perspective from the bridge. If they were looking at a real-time image, then a humongous Quarlonian battlecruiser had just exited a dark stream, right in front of them.

"Big ship," Zephyr mumbled.

What an understatement. While their ship, the *Damnation*, had dwarfed the *Culin Four*, the battlecruiser made both vessels seem like mere insects in a vast ocean.

"Surprised the Ascendancy allowed them to arrive in that," Col said.

"Yep," the captain agreed, "and unfortunately, they're gonna demand their own security check."

After arriving in the Huluvian System a couple hours earlier and picking up Zephyr, Oxeter, and some necessary supplies from the *Damnation*, the *Culin Four* had made a beeline for Piaya, the large verdant planet they presently orbited, where government officials had promptly run a security check on the ship. While Piaya was an Ascendancy planet with several high-ranking officials, including the conniving High Priest, its security procedures were familiar to the crew of the *Damnation*.

Some of the oldest pirates had, after all, been ripping off Ascendancy ships and pulling heists on Ascendancy planets for the last few decades, so they knew how to deceive almost every security measure imaginable. It didn't hurt that, on this occasion, they had flown in the *Culin Four*, an Ascendancy-approved catering vessel.

The Quarlonians, however, were a different story. Their planet, Quarlon Seven, lay deep within the Wildern, a yet unconquered portion of the Way. So, they didn't utilize the same security procedures as the Ascendancy.

Col self-consciously fingered the scar that marred the left side of his face, wondering if his and Morgan's rugged visages might raise some suspicion. Even with the crisp white uniforms, they both looked as though they'd witnessed — hell, participated in — a considerable amount of fighting in their time. Only twelve years younger than his captain, Col had just turned forty-three, and both men wore their share of battle scars.

Permitting a complete security scan had included sharing access to all video feeds. *Well, all but those I deactivated in the crew quarters.* Essentially, that meant the Quarlonians could see everyone in the cargo hold, which concerned Col. He and Morgan had reputations, after all.

A few moments passed as the Quarlonian battlecruiser scanned the *Culin Four*. When the system scan stopped, and the enormous battlecruiser failed to fire on them, Col released the breath he'd unconsciously held.

Morgan pressed the flesh behind his ear, activating his CommTrans implant. "We're on approach. Oxeter, be in the cargo hold in ten minutes." He turned toward Col. "OK, kid, bring us down to Piaya."

Col looked at his captain and then at Zephyr. A youthful grin spread across his face. "Let's be pirates."

***

Leaving Morgan in the cargo hold, Col and Zephyr headed to the bridge. Along the way, they passed Oxeter, who was headed in the opposite direction, fidgeting with his white uniform.

"These things fit like..." he started to say, only stopping when he caught a glimpse of Zephyr's getup and burst into laughter.

Zephyr faltered in the corridor, but before he could punch Oxeter, who surpassed the slender, five-foot-nine gunner in height, breadth, and strength, Col nudged him forward.

"Ignore him and keep walking," he said. "We have a job to do."

Chapter 5

As instructed, Col landed the *Culin Four* atop a small docking pad just outside a stately, opulent Gothic-style castle. Peering through the viewport on the bridge, he couldn't help but acknowledge the odd juxtaposition of the relatively ancient edifice standing amid modern skyscrapers, hover carts, and other technological advancements. The bizarre scene looked as though someone had squashed two long-separated eras into one gigantic painting.

"Damn, look at that thing," Zephyr exclaimed from the co-navigator seat. "Nice digs."

"In addition to being this sector's mediator for the Ascendancy, the High Priest is also the chief tax collector," Col said, rising from his seat. "Something tells me not all the funds from the planets he lords over make it into the coffers of the Ascendancy High Council."

Laughing, Zephyr followed Col across the bridge. "But that would make him a pirate. Not a holy man."

Col scoffed. "Whoever said this oversexed joker was holy?"

Morgan's voice crackled through Col's CommTrans. "If it's not too much trouble, could you two knuckleheads please make your way to the cargo hold?"

"Yes, sir, on our way," Col said as he nudged Zephyr across the threshold.

***

By the time they met the captain in the cargo hold, Oxeter had finished loading two giant hover carts with all the equipment and supplies they'd need to prepare the meal – and pull off the job.

"Is that everything?" Morgan asked.

"Ready to go, Captain," Oxeter replied.

All four men faced the large outer hatch in the cargo hold. As usual, Col knew that, if any part of the plan went wrong, no matter how small, the entire scheme could explode, taking them down with it. At this particular juncture, for instance, the High Priest's security force would soon be searching the two hover carts. If the guards discovered the half-dozen guns hidden among the supplies – or, worse, the cipher rig required to bust into the High Priest's hidden safe – the jig would certainly be up, and the four pirates would have to shoot their way off the planet.

Not a possibility that thrills me.

Col opened the hatch and lowered the ramp to the ground, then he and Morgan guided one hover cart through the doorway while Zephyr and Oxeter took control of the other. After maneuvering the carts to the docking pad, the four pirates halted as half a dozen guards approached them. Immediately, the uniformed, heavily armed men began searching through the containers on both carts. Once they seemed satisfied that nothing sinister was afoot, Col closed and locked the hatch, and then he and his fellow disguised pirates proceeded to haul their loads toward the castle, flanked by two of the guards.

Col smiled inwardly, impressed at how well the false bottoms in two of the crates had concealed the weapons and gear they'd need to complete the job. *Thank the Way that worked, cuz I'm in no mood for a gunfight.*

Chapter 6

The two guards led the "caterers" to a service entrance on the right side of the castle. As soon as Col ventured through the enormous, metal-studded wooden door, he realized the interior of the edifice boasted an even stranger medley of ancient and modern features than he'd initially encountered through the *Culin Four*'s viewport. Despite high, vaulted, downright majestic ceilings, the venerable stonework only reached about eight feet up the walls before morphing into a slick black metallic material. In addition, display cases seemed to line every room they passed, and despite fleeting glimpses, Col could tell the enshrined items ranged from centuries-old relics to newfangled gadgets – artifacts gathered from hundreds of worlds across the Way, merely to fill the High Priest's own private museum.

After turning several corners, the group came upon a sizable sarcophagus. Zephyr, who led one of the two carts, stopped in his tracks. Yes, they had a job to do, but Col could understand his friend's temptation. It was an impressive sight: a weathered stone coffin, displaying a mummified body that must have been nearly ten feet tall. Weirder still, the wrappings shimmered with an eerily familiar blue light, and a heavy, garmonite necklace encircled the mummy's neck, featuring a crimson, hard-to-miss gemstone that lay on the glowing chest.

"The wrappings must have been dusted with garmonite," Col said. "To cause such a cool dark matter reaction."

"Yeah, whatever," Zephyr whispered. "Get a load of that stone. Must be worth a fortune."

"Come on, girls," Morgan grumbled. "This ain't no tour."

When no one budged, the two guards grunted with impatience, and the winding trek through the castle continued.

Soon enough, they entered a spacious kitchen that, as with the rest of the schizophrenic castle, boasted a mix of ancient features and modern technology. Beyond the rough-hewn stone and cool metal walls, Col spotted open fire pits on one side of the chamber and gleaming, curiously shaped ovens on the other. Perhaps twenty, black-clad servants hustled and bustled about the place, preparing all manner of food and drink, and the air was rife with the mingled aromas of spiced cider, roasting meats, and freshly baked bread.

"You can set up over in that section," the slightly taller guard said, pointing to a far corner of the kitchen.

"And if you need anything," the other one added, "the woman in the red dress will handle it."

He pointed toward a huddle of half a dozen servants, and at first, Col could see no flash of red. Just the traditional drab black of Ascendancy uniforms. Even in frenetic smocks and aprons, the somber hue still seemed too depressing and institutional for the likes of pirates.

Suddenly, the servants parted a little, and a five-foot-tall, two-hundred-pound woman appeared, clad in a vibrant, red, form-fitting dress. Waving cheerily, she trotted toward them, much faster and more gracefully than her girth might indicate. As she approached the newcomers, the two guards slipped out of the kitchen, their transfer duties apparently fulfilled.

The red-clad woman might have been short and round, but with her violet eyes, rosy cheeks, and curly black locks, she was decidedly attractive. She possessed a radiance that made Col and his fellow pirates smile. Of course, it didn't hurt that her ample breasts were nearly springing from her dress.

She stopped before the "caterers" and scanned each of them. "We're honored to have such illustrious chefs in our humble kitchen," she said in a husky voice.

"On such a special occasion," Morgan replied in a haughty tone, "it is we who are honored."

She rolled her eyes. "Oh, please. I only wish you were cooking for the entire party, not just for the High Priest's little..."

"...seduction ritual," Col finished, winking at her.

She stifled a giggle. "Truth be told, I don't care if those racksum cubs are the galaxy's greatest aphrodisiac. He doesn't stand a chance with the Quarlonian delegate, unless perhaps she chokes and suffocates on a bone. Seriously, that man is as ugly as the backside of a thargo beast."

All four men bellowed with laughter, snagging a few curious looks from nearby servants. The woman's face, meanwhile, turned bright red, almost matching the vivid hue of her dress.

"Sorry," she said, "shouldn't have said that." Recovering her pleasant smile, she deftly changed the subject. "My name is Berlopia, but you can call me Bear."

"Bear?" Zephyr inquired.

She shrugged. "I might be shaped like one, but at least I have a couple of perky cubs in tow." She hefted her breasts upward, in case they'd missed her meaning.

Bear might be a hefty gal, but she clearly knows how to use what she's got.

"You're definitely our people," Morgan told her, dropping the phony dignified tone.

"Here to help," she said, beaming. Abruptly, her gaze twitched to the side, where an aging servant fiddled with the spigot of a newfangled appliance. "Dammit, that Karillian rum dispenser hasn't worked since we got it."

"You got Karillian rum here?" Oxeter asked.

Returning her focus to the newcomers, she smiled warmly at him. "Tell you what, hon... I'll sneak you all some flasks later tonight." She glanced at the hover carts. "For now, you'd better get started. Let me know if you need anything."

With that, she headed toward the old man, who was now banging on the dispenser in an apparent effort to jump-start the mechanism.

Zephyr's eyes followed Bear across the hazy, aromatic kitchen. "I like her," he mused.

Morgan rolled his eyes. "No time for that, Zeph. You and Oxeter, get set up. Start cooking those little cubs."

Zephyr frowned.

"Col and I, meanwhile, are going to find the safe."

"Hope our contact's info was good," Col said as he unlatched one of the crates, slid out the false bottom, and removed a hidden rucksack. "We better not find it filled with prophylactics, or something equally useless."

"A little faith would be nice," Morgan admonished.

Col slung the rucksack over his shoulder. "We're pirates, Captain. Faith's a little hard to come by."

Morgan merely shook his head, grabbed his own gear, and led Col from the kitchen.

Chapter 7

No matter the skills of a given pirate, he'd likely find it challenging to maintain a stealthy vibe while wearing crisp white chef's uniforms, especially in a dimly lit castle filled with black-clad personnel. Col and Morgan's solution to that particular problem? A pair of counterfeit Ascendancy security uniforms they'd purchased on the black market.

Soon after leaving the kitchen, they stumbled upon a supply closet, and like every other chamber in the castle, it was exceedingly roomy. After making sure no guards had spotted them, Col and Morgan slipped into the closet, where they quickly donned the black uniforms and armed themselves with official, Ascendancy-issue pistols and stun rods they'd pilfered from a couple of unfortunate guards on a previous heist. Then, they stashed the catering duds, tightened the straps of their rucksacks, and checked the corridor for lurkers before venturing deeper inside the enemy's lair.

After a few confusing turns, Col paused in an alcove, activated a small electronic tablet, and thumbed through several screens. Eventually, he located the map they'd purchased from the last contractor who'd renovated the castle. While Morgan peered over his shoulder, Col magnified the map, found their current location, and traced his finger through a labyrinth of corridors, stairways, and lifts, to a cozy room down in the dungeons of the historic edifice.

"Not exactly a straight line," he whispered to Morgan.

Morgan shrugged. "Whatever is?"

Col grimaced, and the two men continued on their trek through the castle. At every third turn, Col took a moment to reference the map. Before they'd even reached the first stairway, another black-clad guard noticed them, forcing them to take a hasty, unexpected turn to avoid his scrutiny. Of course, the detour didn't work. How many Ascendancy guards tote suspicious rucksacks?

When the rail-thin man caught up with them, he breathlessly demanded, "Who are you? Why are you in this section?"

Resourceful as ever, Morgan said, "We're doing extra security sweeps as a courtesy to the Quarlonian delegate."

The guard's brow pinched. "I hadn't heard of a call for extra sweeps in this section," he replied, "and I'm in charge here." He plucked his own tablet from his jacket, presumably to check for new orders. "I know the Quarlonians are sticklers for security, but this is getting..."

He couldn't finish his sentence before Col had slid his stun rod from its holster, flipped the activation switch, and jabbed it into the man's chest.

"Sounded like a reasonable excuse for us to be out and about," Col said as he watched the man slump to the ground.

"I thought so, too," Morgan said, "but he chose to be difficult."

Together, Col and his captain dragged the guard to the base of a wide display case, containing a slew of garish watches. Conveniently, the case featured a sliding panel near the ground, which concealed the lighting and alarm system controls and, in a pinch, could serve as an impromptu storage area. After picking the lock, Col happily discovered just enough room to stuff the guard's skinny body inside. To ensure he wouldn't awaken and cause trouble for them, Col prodded the man once more with the stun rod, and then closed the panel.

After that unfortunate hurdle, he and Morgan picked up the pace. Even still, it took them almost an hour of winding along serpentine corridors, backtracking after wrong turns, and arguing about who could read the map better, before the two pirates finally located the murky corridor and the nondescript wall sconce they'd been seeking. In what had to be the furthest, deepest, dankest part of the castle.

"You'd think the door would at least have an alarm or a lock on it," Col whispered.

"What door?"

"This one," Col said as he pulled the lever downward and twisted it to the right.

Immediately, a panel disappeared into the wall, revealing an innocuous, sparsely furnished room that was so well hidden, the High Priest hadn't even deemed it necessary to station guards along the hallway.

"He doesn't even want his own security people to know about this," Morgan stated as he stepped into the room.

Chapter 8

A mere ten feet by ten feet, the dimly illumined room hardly seemed like a place where they might score their biggest payday. Glancing around, Col noted a lumpy couch, a solitary lamp, and a few bookshelves containing worthless trinkets.

"A bit underwhelming," he lamented.

Morgan edged toward the nearest wall and examined the shelves. "Somewhere in here is a safe."

Reluctantly, Col joined the captain in his feverish search. He just hoped no one had noticed their lengthy absence from the kitchen.

A few minutes later, Morgan pushed aside a few moldy books and let out a triumphant "Ah, ha!" Turning toward Col, he gestured toward a rather ordinary painting of a lovely brunette, standing nude in a beam of greenish moonlight.

"At last, we can retire," Col joked. "Seriously, that might be worth a hundred credits. At most."

"Funny, smartass," Morgan said, pivoting the painting on a concealed hinge. "Check out what's behind it." He thumbed toward an inconspicuous metal safe embedded in the back of the shelf unit.

Grinning, Col opened his rucksack, removed several mysterious devices, and linked them together with a cable, then he fitted one end into the electronic key slot on the safe door. Normally, the owner of such a safe would insert the proper key and then punch in a specific combination code. Obviously, Col and Morgan had neither of those items.

But supposedly, we have something even better.

"This cipher cost us a small fortune," Col said. "Hope it was worth the money." Then, he engaged the green button on one of the linked devices and waited for a miracle to happen.

"Kid, you gotta stop being so negative," Morgan said. "Shit has a way of working out. And if it doesn't, you'll be dead, so you'll have nothing more to worry about."

Shaking his head in mild amusement, Col continued to watch the readouts. A moment later, a loud click sounded, and the safe door swung open.

"Yes," Col exclaimed, then glanced over his shoulder to make sure no one was in the corridor to overhear him.

"See?" Morgan grinned. "Told you it would work out." He removed a slender flashlight from his pocket. "Now, let's take a look." He shined the powerful beam inside the cavity, where the only item appeared to be a thin, two-by-three-inch black box.

"Data drive?" Col asked.

Morgan nodded, his smile now enormous. He reached inside the open safe, plucked out the small drive, and slid it into his inner jacket pocket. "Listing every account his majesty, the High Priest, has hidden from his friends in the Ascendancy. After all this time, he's probably amassed hundreds of billions of credits."

"Too bad we can't break the encryption ourselves," Col said.

Morgan removed an identical drive from another pocket, placed it in the safe, and shut the door. "No need to be greedy. Our part will be done when we deliver it to the buyer. Fifty million credits will keep the *Damnation* in the air, and the crew more than comfortable, for at least the next five years."

Unless Morgan Jr. gets his hands on it. At nineteen, the captain's son had already embraced a wide array of expensive, problematic vices.

Wordlessly, the two pirates returned every item to its proper place, retreated from the room, closed the door with a twist of the wall sconce, and retraced their steps back to the kitchen. Concerned about the time, they stopped only once, to stun the guard inside the display case one more time. Just in case.

Chapter 9

By the time Col and Morgan made their circuitous way back to the kitchen, Zephyr and Oxeter had returned from the intimate dining room, where they'd dispersed the main course to the High Priest, the Quarlonian delegate, and a few other key officials.

Quite a crew. Perhaps he was hoping for an orgy.

When Zephyr spotted Col, he made a beeline toward him. "We need to get out of here."

Col sensed his friend's urgency, but assumed he was merely upset over the ill-fated racksum cubs and anxious to put this distasteful scheme behind him.

"Sure thing," he said. "We got what we came for."

Because Col and Morgan still wore their security guard uniforms, as intended, they hoped it would be easy to escort the two chefs and their hover carts to the *Culin Four* without raising any suspicion.

Hopefully, no one will notice that two of the caterers have gone missing – or, worse, morphed into Ascendancy guards.

Zephyr and Oxeter quickly piled the cooking gear, empty crates, and remaining supplies onto the two carts. As they arranged the gear, Col noticed the butt of a pistol peeking out from beneath several soiled linens. Hastily, he pushed it out of sight, hoping to keep it hidden from prying eyes but easily accessible if trouble broke out.

"So," Bear said from behind him, "you darlings, must be rogue status."

Startled, Col instinctively slid his hand toward the stun rod, but Morgan quickly clutched his wrist to stay his impulsive action.

Morgan shifted his body to face her. "How long have you known?"

With a heavy exhalation, Col turned around, too.

Bear gazed at the grizzled captain, and then at Col. "Not many chefs have wicked scars like that. At least not on their faces."

Col squinted his eyes in concern. "How did you guess we were rogue status?"

She shrugged, her breasts heaving upward again. "Figured the Roverian Guild wouldn't grant permission to rob one of the inner Ascendancy planets, especially while they're negotiating for better trade terms themselves."

"You know more about the Guild than most Ascendancy citizens," Morgan said.

"My father flies on the Lormar," she replied.

Col immediately recognized the name of the pirate ship. Perhaps she really was one of them.

"Great, now we know she's not gonna turn us in," Zephyr whispered nervously. "But, seriously, we need to be gone."

Seemingly ignoring Zephyr, Morgan kept his eyes on Bear. "You don't want anything in return?"

Amid the frenetic movement and constant din of the kitchen, she grasped one of the hover carts and tugged it toward the exit. "Sure, I do. I want a ride off this bloody rock."

* * *

With Bear leading the two caterers and the two solemn guards along the corridors of the castle, none of the security teams stopped them as they retraced their steps to the *Culin Four*. They were too busy ogling the sexy, voluptuous flirt to fret over the four strange men trailing her.

Once on board the *Culin Four*, the pirates secured the equipment in the cargo hold and readied the ship for launch. Col saw Zephyr slide a covered crate against a far wall, but he was too exhausted to wonder what his friend had smuggled from the castle. He could only hope no one would miss it soon.

While Oxeter ventured to the crew quarters to ensure the real caterers were still imprisoned, Col, Morgan, Zephyr, and Bear ventured to the bridge. As Col reclaimed the navigator's seat, he spotted a little brown furball tearing across the deck.

Without hesitation, or surprise, Zephyr hastened forward and scooped up the racksum cub.

"Zephyr?" Morgan asked. "Care to explain yourself?"

A speaker on the *Culin Four*'s control panel buzzed with an incoming request. Hard to decipher given the current state of the communications array. *But I can guess the gist of the message.*

Zephyr shrugged unapologetically. "Figured everything tastes like chicken. So, there was a good chance no one would notice the missing cubs."

Col sighed. *So, that explains the crate. Thought it seemed familiar.* He glanced at Zephyr, who now sat buckled in the co-navigator seat, soothing the anxious cub and undoubtedly steeling himself for an expedited takeoff. Col couldn't help but wonder if that was the same furry escape artist he himself had reclaimed earlier.

Though Zephyr's softhearted side had always amused him, it could often be quite an inconvenience. The captain had likely hoped to escape Piaya with the data drive, without causing an unnecessary ruckus – and inciting the livid Piayans to pursue them for a kidnapped litter of racksum cubs.

No matter how foolish the High Priest's seduction plan was.

"Dammit," Morgan said, glancing at one of the viewscreens on the control panel. "They're transmitting a buffer wave, disrupting our engines."

"Relax, hon," Bear said as she reached across Zephyr and punched a ten-digit code into the control panel.

Glancing at the viewscreen, Col noted the buffer had been deactivated. Morgan turned toward her, one eyebrow arched.

"Shit has a way of working out," she told the captain as she plucked the racksum cub from Zephyr's arms and plopped her round butt in his lap.

Now that the immediate danger had passed, Morgan released a hearty guffaw.

Eager not to press their luck, Col engaged the engines, gripped the joystick, and lifted the ship just as a large posse of guards rushed from the castle and opened fire on the bow. Though hardly a combat ship, the *Culin Four* easily deflected the small arms fire.

Moments later, the vessel jetted out of orbit. Small arms couldn't shoot down the *Culin Four*, but a security cruiser might, and unfortunately, Col noted two such pursuers on their tail. One of the ships attempted to hail them, but Col managed to pivot the ship and bolt away from the cruisers.

"Sorry, Captain," Zephyr mumbled from beneath Bear.

"Pirates ain't supposed to be big softies," Morgan said.

From the captain's vague tone, Col couldn't tell if he was truly pissed or ready to laugh again. But the sudden appearance of the *Damnation* rendered the question moot. The large, well-armed pirate ship slipped from a dark stream in the exact location Morgan had instructed them to be. In response, the two security cruisers immediately abandoned pursuit and headed back to Piaya.

"Good timing, boys," Col said via his CommTrans.

"Just doing what we're told," Burke, the ship's navigator, replied. "Mission accomplished?"

Smiling, Col glanced around the bridge of the *Culin Four*. The captain examined the data drive they'd just stolen. Oxeter stood in the doorway, sipping from a flask Col assumed was filled with Karillian rum. Bear still nestled in Zephyr's lap, stroking the racksum cub and likely cutting off the gunner's blood flow, except where it mattered. The cub's long tail kept tickling Bear's chest, which made her giggle and subsequently jiggle. Zephyr shifted his gaze from her ample bosom, noted Col's amused smirk, and blushed just a tad.

Mission accomplished and then some. But what the hell are we gonna do with a dozen endangered racksum cubs?

"So, did you boys catch a glimpse of the Quarlonian delegate?" Morgan asked.

"Yeah, she was a total hottie," Oxeter said, then took another swig from his flask. "You were dead right, Captain."

"She was alright," Zephyr said as Bear playfully stroked his goatee.

"Bear, where can we drop you?" Col asked the woman who was now fixated on his gunner. That was when he noticed the necklace hanging around her neck and the giant red gemstone wedged in her cleavage.

Yep, she's definitely one of us.

Noting Col's curious gaze, Bear grinned. "As it happens, I have nowhere pressing to be. For now, anyway."

Col grinned in return. "Then let's get outta here. We can regroup in another sector."

"Sounds good, boss," Zephyr said with a wink.

Via his CommTrans, Col informed Burke of the plan, and shortly afterward, the *Damnation* and the *Culin Four* jumped into a dark stream, putting as much distance between them and Piaya as humanly possible. With any luck, they'd earned a friend on Quarlon Seven for foiling the High Priest's plans, and someday, they'd have a tempting debt to collect.

***

If you enjoyed this prequel, and you're a fan of space operas like Firefly, Star Wars, and The Expanse, be sure to follow Col, Zephyr, and their fellow pirates in The Grey Nebula (http://bit.ly/2ra7val), Book 1 of the War of the Way series.

Curious about future adventures or chances to win some pirate booty? Go Rogue (http://roguesway.com/join) and join the crew. We know you love your freedom, so we promise not to bombard you with junk mail. We'll just notify you about new releases, giveaways, recommendations, and other fun stuff.

Authors Laura and Daniel Martone

Former residents of New Orleans, Laura and Daniel Martone (http://themartones.com/) now travel the country in their mobile writing studio, a cozy RV dubbed *Serenity*. As you might have guessed, they're huge fans of *Firefly*, which is why they remodeled the interior of their RV after Captain Reynolds' beloved spaceship (http://themartones.com/building-serenity). While they write in many genres (including urban fantasy, post-apoc, time travel, and epic fantasy), their greatest love is space opera. They do, after all, live in a "spaceship."

FINAL INTELLIGENCE

By Kevin McLaughlin

Chapter 1

The *Armistice* was nowhere near the biggest ship in Her Majesty's Navy. There were many others with more armament, heavier armor, and the latest in technological wizardry. But the nimble little vessel was his, by God, and that was more than enough for Sir David Drake. His hands held the control wheel. His eye guided the ship's course. Her crew answered to his commands, and none other.

It had not come without cost. Nor was it likely to remain his ship forever. The needs of the Navy were many, and he was a junior Knight. The orders might come any day now to turn the vessel over to some more senior commander. But for the moment at least it seemed he had enough favor with the Queen - or with Lady Luck, since David rather doubted that Her Majesty even knew he existed - to retain the command. All that remained would be to prove he was worthy of keeping it before circumstances tore the ship away from him.

What he needed was another battle. He'd only been in two so far, and while he had acquitted himself admirably in both - winning his Knighthood in the first, and then defeating a Commonwealth attack ship in the second - the third time would be the charm. If he could prove that he was consistently the right man for this job, then he would surely be allowed to keep this command.

That was what Drake wanted, more than anything else he could imagine. He'd gone into the stars as a deck hand, hoping to see new places and experience grand adventures. He'd done that, all right. It had been harder and more cruel in space than he'd ever dreamed possible.

"Contact on short range sensors," called Williams. "Looks like a ship, and a big one!"

"Why haven't we picked it up before now?" Drake asked. Their long scans should have detected any vessel long before it reached close range.

"There's almost no power output, Sir," Williams replied. "It's kicking out a beacon, but its very faint. We couldn't even see it until now, despite the size. My God, that thing is huge."

Drake tapped the screen in front of him, bringing the device to life. Williams wasn't wrong. The vessel dwarfed his own. You could perhaps fit a dozen ships the size of the *Armistice* inside this behemoth. But the engines were dark. The beacon must be running on the remnants of battery power. How long had the hulk been drifting aimlessly through space? He tried to match the ship against their list of known vessels. There was no match.

"That's odd. It's something new," Drake said. New might mean a spectacular find. There were still a handful of relic ships out there in space, drifting like this one. They were older than the Kingdom, the Commonwealth, or any of the smaller powers in nearby space. As far as anyone knew, those ancient wrecks predated the Machine Wars. But this ship didn't match any of the previously discovered relic classes either.

"Damned peculiar, Sir," Williams said. "It's not matching known vessels for a modern or ancient class."

"It might be a completely new discovery," Drake said. He could feel excitement welling in his chest. That would be a find worthy of a knight. There might be lost technology hidden within. Old secrets of bygone years that lay waiting for his people to rediscover them.

"Or it could be a Commonwealth trap," snapped Master Gregory. As ship's Master, Gregory was second only to Drake on board the ship. He was older than the deck planks, the men said, and twice as gnarled.

Drake was glad to have him aboard anyway. The old man knew this ship like it was his own daughter. Or maybe his wife. The relationship was a complex one, that much was clear. But his experience was invaluable.

That didn't mean Drake could allow Gregory to countermand his orders. He needed to keep the crew certain of his command. There could be only one captain of a vessel. For the moment at least, that duty was his, and he would fulfill it.

"That might be the case, Master Gregory. We'll keep a sharp watch as we approach. Shields to full, and watch the sensors for anything which looks out of the ordinary," Drake said.

He plotted the course on the screen in front of him, running through the calculations to bring his ship up alongside the other one safety. It was a skill he'd had to learn along the way, and luckily enough he'd proven to be better at math than most men of his social class. Then he set the engines of his vessel burning, bringing them up to three-quarters power as they approached.

The monster ahead of them blotted out whole swathes of stars as they drew close. It was enormous. Drake tried to compare it in his head with the great behemoths of the Queen's Navy. It was difficult to see the ship well. It was made of some dark colored metal, and didn't reflect the dim starlight from the nearest sun very well. But he could make out something of its outline, and Drake was fairly sure it would match any ship in his navy for size.

Simply stunning. What a prize! If they could bring this ship in safely, it might make his career. Even if they couldn't repair it enough to bring it home, surely there would be something on board worth taking away with them.

"Sir, I'm seeing signs of battle damage," Williams said.

"It might well have been in a fight long ago. Perhaps that's why it was abandoned," Drake replied.

"I'm not certain, but I think this damage is recent. See there, sir?" Williams asked, tapping his screen. "The metal has cooled, but the stress indicates the hit wasn't that long ago."

"We may have company," Drake said. "Sound general quarters. Man the ribaulds. If there is another ship in the vicinity, we want to be prepared to engage at once."

They were skimming close to the lost ship now, only a few hundred meters away. Drake shifted his course. He wasn't going to dock with the thing until he was absolutely sure that there weren't any surprises waiting for them. He brought the nose of the *Armistice* up, sending his ship into a loose orbit so that he could inspect the strange vessel from all sides.

"Contact!" Williams all but shouted.

"I hear you, Mr. Williams. You don't need to holler. What have we got?" Drake replied as calmly as he could manage. He shifted courses again, hoping to get a visual on whatever Williams's scans had picked up through the front windows.

"Commonwealth ship, sir. They're already docked with the hulk. Looks like they've spotted us and are preparing to cast off," Williams said. This time his voice was clipped but firm. Drake looked over at the man. His cheeks were flushed from the rebuke, but he was back to minding his duties without shouting, which was good enough. The man was good at his job, but the ship needed discipline.

"I think we'll avoid letting them break free," Drake said in a tone as dry as his mouth. He'd fought a ship to ship battle just a few days ago. This would be his second. But this time he had the advantage. If he played his cards right, he would be able to smash the enemy like a grape against a rock.

Drake tapped his screen to bring up data on the enemy ship. It was a corvette, like his own vessel. It was armed, for sure, but the armaments would be light and mostly in the broadsides and nose. He brought the *Armistice* in from above, where their weapons could not be brought to bear against his own vessel. Then he turned his ship over on its side, aiming his starboard armament directly at the enemy ship.

"All ribaulds, fire as you bear," he called out.

Chapter 2

The *Armistice* had two ribaulds mounted along each side, and two in the nose. That meant it could fire two forward, or three off to either side. This was ideal for close range battles where maneuver won the day more often than not, but it meant that with a static target like the Commonwealth corvette he could only fire a fraction of his total armament at one time.

The ribaulds were similar to the medieval weapons they were named after. But where those devices were gunpowder cannon firing harpoon-like projectiles, the ribaulds of the twenty-eighth century were something very different. The guns used magnetism to propel their missiles out the barrel at a high velocity. When the weapons fired three slender spears pierced space between the two ships. Each was as technologically advanced beyond the simple steel javelin it appeared to be as the turrets were above their historical counterparts.

The spears each housed a powerful force field generator. They slipped through the *Armistice's* shields and then shot onward toward the enemy vessel. Ship shield technology was incredibly powerful. No one knew of any weapon strong enough to breach a shield, except for another shield. The shields around each spear briefly cut paths through the otherwise impenetrable shields protecting the enemy ship. Then they slammed into the vessel itself.

The missile were moving with enough velocity that each impact shattered hull plates, tearing deep into the ship. They would be wreaking havoc on the internal structure, killing crew and damaging systems.

But the enemy would not remain defenseless long. They were already decoupling from the hulk of the ship beside them. In moments they would be free to maneuver. Drake snarled and twisted the wheel controlling his ship's course. The engines shrieked with protest as he sent the drives into the redline to halt and then redirect their movement. The *Armistice* spun on her nose, almost hovering in place directly above the Commonwealth ship. First the other nose turret, and then the port side turrets were coming into their own firing arc as Drake flipped the ship in place. The shields dampened their inertia, protecting them from being splattered all over the inside of the ship, but Drake watched his readouts carefully. Even a small fluctuation in the shields could kill them all during a maneuver like that.

"Target their engines!" he called out.

More thrumming noises hummed through the hull as the other ribaulds opened up on the hapless Commonwealth vessel. These shots all targeted the aft area of the ship. If they could kill the engines, shut the things down or even damage them, then they would have the advantage of maneuver over their foes. It would be nearly impossible for the enemy ship to take them at that point. Oh, they might get in a few licks yet, but the battle would be all but won. Still, he made sure his armor's personal force field was active. It wouldn't save him from being skewered by a spear, but it would prevent injury from shrapnel and secondary debris from an impact.

"Direct hit on the engines, Sir! They're losing power," Williams called out.

That should be enough to take the fight out of them. "Ready a boarding party to seize the ship," Drake said.

Two prizes in one day! Luck was indeed shining on him. Drake could almost taste the prize money from the captures. The whole crew would benefit from this. One good prize would add enough to their income to allow their next shore leave to be enjoyable indeed. Two prizes - if they could manage to bring back the monstrous ship floating adrift beside them - would be a great boon.

Then there was a bright flash of light. Drake blinked, looking at his plot. The Commonwealth ship was gone! It had blown to bits. For a moment he didn't understand what had occurred.

"Did we fire again?" Drake demanded. There was no point in firing on a crippled vessel, and it certainly looked like the containment on their energy module had blown.

"No sir. There were no fluctuations. Nothing. Just...boom," Williams said. "I don't understand it."

"They must have blown the ship," Drake said slowly, drawing out each word. It was almost never done. To intentionally blow apart your own vessel? Avoiding capture was one thing, but suicide? A captain who was willing to kill his entire crew like that was no captain at all.

"My God, Sir," Gregory said. "All those men."

"May their souls be at peace," Drake said. Then he muttered, "and their captain burn in hell for his callous slaughter."

"Amen," Master Gregory said softly.

Drake shook himself to clear his head. He couldn't imagine what had made the captain feel like self-immolation was the best course of action. There was nothing which should ever make a man do such a thing. Certainly being a captive was not something anyone ever dreamed for, but captives on both sides were well kept, and prisoner exchanges common. The Kingdom and Commonwealth had been at war for almost eighty years, but the rules of war had held so far. Drake hoped that would continue. He couldn't imagine the idea of fighting without honor.

"Master Gregory, you have the wheel," Drake said. "Bring us down toward where they docked."

Then he turned to the ship's intercom and spoke to the entire vessel. "Make ready to board the hulk. I want two squads of men in full battle gear. Bring spears and bolt-casters. They might have left some crew aboard, so we'll want to be ready for anything. I'll join you amidships."

Gregory nodded to Drake and took the wheel from his hands. "I have the wheel, Sir Knight."

"The wheel is yours," Drake said. "Take good care of our ship, Master Gregory."

"As always, Sir. You watch your back down there, too," Gregory said.

Drake nodded and turned to go. He certainly would. Something was still off about this entire thing. The way the other captain had blown his vessel rather than accept defeat was wrong. Drake's gut roiled, trying to consider the reasons why someone might do such a thing. What could possibly drive a man to suicide, and murder of his crew?

What was he going to find out there in that old ship?

Chapter 3

Drake was decked out in his full armor. Every plate was in place. The helm locked in securely around his head, forming a solid connection with the rest of the armor. The shield the armor generated was his first line of defense, of course. It was the same sort of shield that the ship had, if of lesser power. Almost nothing could penetrate his shield except for another shielded object.

Which is why he had a sword belted at his hip, ready for action. Like the ribauld spears, his sword put out a shield of its own. That allowed it to slice through an opponent's shield. Then it would be the blade against whatever armor the enemy wore. Hand weapons were the norm, but Drake and his men also carried bolt-casters, pistols which fired a smaller version of the ribauld spear. They had only a single shot and took some time to reload, longer still to recharge enough to fire again. All of the other men carried shielded spears as well. Hand weapons usually decided battles.

A chime sounded, informing Drake that the airlock was secured to the huge vessel. He tapped a panel on the wall and the door opened, revealing a short metal walkway of a bridge extending across space toward the other ship. above and to either side, Drake could see open space. Watching the stars in the distance for more than a few moments made him dizzy, and he looked quickly away.

The plank was only wide enough for two men to walk abreast, but there was no worry about falling off. A shield was extended from the *Armistice* that covered the plank with protective force for walls and a roof. Drake took a step out, his people moving along behind him.

It was a strange feeling, standing out under the open stars. Drake paused for a moment to glance around. The halt was only a bare second or two, but it seemed to stretch out in his mind for much longer. The beauty of the space, the stars, the sheer vastness of everything he could see and everything that he sensed was out there beyond the range of his vision was almost overwhelming.

"Everything all right, Sir?" Sergeant Jonas asked.

The hesitation had been too long if the head of his Marine squad was asking after him. Drake shook his head and resumed his march toward the other ship. The Commonwealth ship had blown a hole in the hull. The *Armistice* had pulled up adjacent to the hole, parking the ship almost precisely where the enemy vessel had been.

There was some risk in that. If there were Commonwealth troops still inside, some of them might be nearby. Fighting a pitched battle from the walkway would be difficult. Drake drew his sword and pistol, leading the way. His armor would give him much more protection than the other men in his boarding party. He led with his pistol as he stepped through the gap the Commonwealth crew had cut into the outer hull.

But there was no ambush waiting inside the big ship. No one jumped out at him. There were signs of a hurried retreat. Gear was strewn around. Lighting had been set up in the large bay in which Drake found himself. The light barely touched the cavernous ceiling nearly ten meters overhead. Two of the lights had been knocked over. Drake moved cautiously to the first and righted it, shining more illumination about.

The room was about fifty meters long by twenty wide. Combined with the cavernous ceiling, the whole place felt gloomy and dark even with the dozen lights scattered about. Drake snapped on his armor's lights, casting beams into the shadowed corners. Aside from some equipment the enemy crew had abandoned in their retreat, the place was empty. On the far side of the room was a yawning portal into the rest of the ship. The doorway felt as out of proportion as the rest of the room, almost twenty meters high.

"Sir Drake, come see this," Jonas said.

Drake glanced his way. Jonas was examining the interior of the outer hull. It was scored with burn marks all around the entrance. He'd missed seeing them as he stepped through the doorway, more concerned about threats hiding in the room itself. Now he walked over to join Jonas and investigate the marks.

Each one was roughly circular. The metal around the impact sites - Drake mentally catalogued them as such, he couldn't think what else they might be - was scorched black, and the center of each mark was pitted and melted.

"Impressive damage," Drake said.

"They're still warm, sir," Jonas said.

Drake glanced back out around the room, all his caution returning to him. The shadows felt hostile. But he'd already looked about the room. There was nothing in this space. No one hid in the dark corners, ready to strike them. That didn't mean the ship was safe.

"Someone attacked them as they were departing," Drake said, running his fingers over the blast marks.

"It would seem so," Jonas said.

"A mutiny? It might explain the ship exploding if they were fighting among themselves," Drake said.

"Perhaps. But we don't have weapons that strike like this, and I've never seen Commonwealth troops use them either, Sir. I'm not thrilled to think they might have new armaments. Could be bad for us," Jonas said.

Indeed it could, although Drake thought these looked like energy discharges, and even the personal shield on his armor ought to be able to handle such things. Why use an archaic weapon that couldn't hurt your enemy? It didn't make sense. There was more to it than there seemed to be, he could feel it.

"What are the chances the shots were fired by this ship's original crew?" Drake asked. It wasn't likely. Their assumption was that this ship had been adrift for a long time. But every possibility was worth considering.

"The entire hulk is without atmosphere, Sir Drake. I don't think it likely that any crew would still be around. Even if they had suits, they would have either run out of air, or repaired the holes in the hull to renew the atmosphere," Jonas said.

It made sense. But then who had fired the shots at the fleeing Commonwealth crew, and why?

"We'll sweep the ship," Drake said. "One hour search operation, then we return here. Two squads. Jonas, take a squad aft, try to find their engine room. See if there is anything there worth salvaging. I'll take the other squad forward and try to locate their command and control center. Perhaps we can learn more about the ship's crew that way."

He looked around at his men, wondering if the Commonwealth captain had given these same orders scant hours before. Was he about to fall into whatever trap had just killed that man and all his people? But there was nothing else for it. To be bold was his job. To take chances when it might benefit the Kingdom was the mark of a knight. This ship might hold secrets that could help swing the war in their favor, saving countless lives. He couldn't abandon it without trying to explore first. Not because of vague misgivings that he couldn't even put a name to.

"Be cautious, all of you. Stay in communication with me and the ship regularly. If you run into anything hostile, withdraw. We will regroup and counterattack once we have collected our strength," Drake said. "For the Queen."

"For the Queen," the men murmured together.

Chapter 4

Leading his squad down through dark passageways gave Drake entirely too much time to think. Some of that thought was wrapped up in pondering the strangeness of their current situation. David had never seen a lost ship before, but he'd heard the stories. Every few years another wreck would be found drifting in space. It was always an exciting event. Much of what humanity had once been was lost during the Machine Wars. That the Kingdom had survived with so much of its infrastructure intact was nothing short of miraculous, but many outlying star systems had not been so fortunate.

Forced back into barbarism, they had become easy prey for the Commonwealth military. Now a dozen such slave worlds fed the Commonwealth's military machine, and they continued to seek out more. Each new addition to their collection put greater stress on the Kingdom's ability to resist. Thus far they'd been successful, more through determination than any real military edge.

That meant any potential discovery of lost tech was more than simply valuable. It might mean the difference between survival and annihilation.

There were plenty of stories circulating around the Navy about such finds. Even leaving aside the half which were obviously false, the truth was that usually the ships were not that different from the Navy's own vessels. They often had some form of old alloy, the construction of which was lost over time. Or a bit of surprising technology might be still functional somewhere on the ship. But the general form was similar to what the Kingdom used. Engines in the back, controls in the front, crew quarters and storage in the middle, gunnery on the sides to allow massed broadside fire. Not that different.

This ship was something else entirely. The scale of the ship confused Drake as they wandered their way toward the front. All of the corridors were like the first room they had found - enormous in both height and width. The smallest space he'd seen was merely ten meters high. In many places, the ceiling went up as much as twenty meters. None of it made any sense.

A cargo bay might have a tall ceiling, allowing for stacked containers for shipping. The halls around it might be large to allow movement of supplies using hauling vehicles. But the regular passages of the ship were also oversized. What possible reason could there be to construct the ship to such a scale?

"Jonas, how goes your search?" Drake asked into his radio.

"Nothing so far, Sir Drake. Empty halls," the Marine replied. "The men are getting nervous, though."

"The scale?" Drake replied. He'd seen it in his own squad. Hell, he'd felt it himself, that sense that something was very wrong with this place.

"Yes. I caught two of the men babbling fairy-tales about giants. Smacked both of them and put them on point, I did," Jonas said.

"There's no such thing as giants," Drake said. Although even as he said it, the size of this place made him wonder. Humans had never run into any other intelligent life out there in the void of space, not in all the centuries they'd explored. But they'd only traveled to a tiny fraction of the stars in the galaxy. It wasn't impossible that there could be something else out there, somewhere. Had they found the remnant of an alien race?

"I know that, Sir. So do those blockheads. The place has them jittery, is all," Jonas said. "I yanked some circuits from a wall panel to show 'em better. The boards are color-coded the same way as ours. Same way we've coded them for centuries."

"Good thinking," Drake said. He wished he had thought of it. That might have relieved his own mind sooner. Not aliens, then. Just human technology, made in a way that was strange to them. That discovery made the ship no less odd, but it was more comprehensible at least. "Keep me updated on your progress."

"Aye, Sir. We're almost to the engines, I think," Jonas replied. "I'll contact you when we're there."

David cut the line. Almost as soon as he did, he saw a flash of movement in the dark hall ahead. He brought up his pistol, aiming it toward where he'd seen the flicker. Was it a reflection? No, he was almost sure he'd seen something move.

"Eyes alert, men. Something ahead in the hall," Drake said. Then he pressed on.

A force bolt flashed across his flashlight beam directly at his chest. It pierced his shield effortlessly. Drake twisted, trying to avoid the bolt, but it was moving too quickly. He managed to turn sideways enough that it hit his breastplate at a sharp angle, pinging off the steel instead of penetrating. The bolt clattered to the floor, it's short-lived force-field spent.

"Enemy to the front!" Drake called. He jogged forward, trying to come to grips with the foe. If they had more than one bolt caster, then moving would make him a harder target to hit anyway. If they only had the one, then his best chance was to close before they could reload and recharge the weapon. Had he turned away a second slower, that bolt would have punched through his armor and entered his lung under his right collarbone. It might not have been a mortal wound, but it would have been very bad.

His light slashed the hall ahead of him, finally stabbing a man in Commonwealth light armor. Drake leveled his pistol at the target. The man tossed down his weapon, raising his hands into the air.

"Oh, thank the stars! I surrender. I surrender! Just take me out of here! Don't let them get me!" The man's radio was broadcasting in the clear, on an open frequency, so Drake's comm unit picked it up immediately.

Drake kicked the pistol away, keeping his own trained on the stranger. While a surrender made sense, given that the enemy was completely outmatched by his own squad, the man's words sent a chill down his spine. What sort of hell had he brought his people into?

Chapter 5

The Commonwealth soldier was clearly distraught. His movements were frantic. Drake could see his wide eyes through the faceplate of his helmet. Carefully keeping his pistol level with the man, he motioned the rest of his team forward.

"On your knees!" Drake demanded. "Who are you?"

"Corporal LaCroix, sir, from the good ship Bellantine," the man replied, taking a knee slowly. He kept his hands raised while he knelt, his wide eyes steady on Drake's pistol. He might be upset by his recent experiences, but having the barrel of a gun aimed in your direction had a way of steadying the mind.

"Sir, if you don't mind my asking, is my ship all right? Did they make it clear in time?" La Croix asked.

"I'll be asking the questions here, thank you, Corporal," Drake replied, his voice firm. The corporal subsided instantly, and David found himself feeling badly. If it were him a prisoner on the deck, wouldn't he want to know the fate of his ship-mates, too? He relented. "Your ship was destroyed with all hands. We think the captain detonated the engines. I'm sorry."

LaCroix grew pale on hearing the news. He quietly murmured something Drake couldn't quite hear.

"What was that?" Drake asked.

"They must have gotten aboard. Either damaged the ship, or the captain blew it to prevent them taking it," LaCroix said a bit more loudly this time.

"Who must have gotten aboard?" Drake asked.

"Them. You know...them. You must have beaten them to get to me?" LaCroix looked from one Marine to the next, then back at Drake, who slowly shook his head.

"We've seen no one but you," Drake said.

"Stars. They're still here then. We have to get out of here before they find us! We have to leave before they kill us all!" LaCroix said, all but shouting the last sentence.

"Calm down, man!" Drake snapped. "We have armed Marines here, and I'm a knight. We're capable of defending ourselves."

"So were my ship-mates," LaCroix said.

It was a good point. Much as they might dislike Commonwealth politics, Drake had to admit their technology was as good as that of the Kingdom. Their people were well-armed and well-trained. He'd bet on the Queen's Marines in a stand up fight any day, but the Commonwealth soldiers were no pushovers. Whatever had this man afraid was a viable threat. He switched channels to contact Jonas.

"Sergeant Jonas, we've found a Commonwealth survivor. He claims they were attacked by something," Drake said.

"By what? We've found nothing here but empty halls and rooms," Jonas replied. "We've located the engine room. Breaching the door momentarily. It's locked shut, so we're using charges to blow the door, in case you feel the explosion."

"I'm still questioning the prisoner. I'll contact you again when I have more information," Drake said. He was suddenly embarrassed that he'd called before getting all of the data he needed from the prisoner. But he'd wanted to warn Jonas about the potential threat. "Stay on your toes."

"We always are, Sir Drake," Jonas replied before severing the connection.

Drake turned back to the corporal. "Who attacked your people? It wasn't our Navy. Are there bandits on board?" Sometimes pirates would roam the dark regions of space, preying on the weak, but it seemed unlikely to find them so close to the front lines of the ongoing war.

"No. They were not human. At least, they didn't seem human. Giant machines. Tall, armed with guns that blasted us apart even through our shields. Our people died around me," LaCroix said. "I survived because I lost my way when I ran. They followed the main group back to the ship."

Drake hissed between his teeth. This sounded like something out of an old sailor's tale. Like a story from the legends of the Machine War. But that was impossible.

Every child was taught the story of the great war, when humanity almost died. Computer intelligence grew over the centuries, until the servants were far smarter than their masters. All at once, they revolted. What followed was war to the knife. Cities burned, whole planets died in the conflagrations which followed. In the stories, humanity fought a desperate battle against the AI legions - hosts of robotic minions which had tried to slay all of their creators.

But the war was over centuries ago. All of the artificial intelligences had been wiped out. Every memory core was accounted for. That was why no machine was allowed to be more competent than a calculator. There were no automated machines making machines, not anymore. There were no assistive intelligence programs, since those might in time evolve into something stronger. Humanity still used tools and technology, but even centuries later all were taught to never trust a machine that could think for itself even a little bit.

A few had tried to go against the law. Those heresies had been stamped out, the creations destroyed and the makers put to the sword. The Machine War had almost ended humanity. It could never be allowed to happen again.

"Automations like those you speak of are banned in the Kingdom," Drake said. He brought ice into his tone. "Has the Commonwealth taken to using such abhorrent technology?"

"No! No, Sir Knight. We keep to the law ourselves. Same as you. No one wants the machines back. But...they are back," LaCroix said. His voice dropped to a whisper. "They are here."

There was a small shudder through the deck plates beneath Drake's feet. That would be Jonas blowing the door. If they'd found the engine room, perhaps they could grab whatever they found there and then all of them could get the hell out of this place. His ship lacked the armament to do more than scratch such a massive vessel. They needed more ships to deal with this thing. If there were automatons on board, the entire thing must be destroyed. Drake re-opened the link to Jonas.

"Jonas, the prisoner tells me that his people were attacked by machines. We need to withdraw immediately. Pull your people back to the ship," Drake said, thinking better of any delay at all. They couldn't afford to wait.

"Machines, sir?" Jonas said.

"Automatons, he claims," Drake said.

"We haven't seen anything."

"Nor have we. But I'm disinclined to take chances. We return to the ship and call for backup. Call in the fleet and we'll deal with whatever is aboard this ship together," Drake said.

"Aye, Sir. We'll pull out," Jonas said. There was a pause before he went on. "Wait, there's movement inside the engine room. Lots of movement... Oh, God..."

Drake heard the sound of pistols snapping out their rounds through the radio, a scream, and then the link was cut.

Chapter 6

His men were in trouble. There was no time to lose. If they were going to be any help to Jonas, they needed to make their way toward the aft of the ship immediately.

"You two, bring the prisoner back to the ship. Keep him guarded. The rest of you, with me. Jonas needs us," Drake said.

"They've been attacked, haven't they?" LaCroix asked. "It's too late for them. They're already dead. We need to leave before we join them!"

"I'm not leaving my men behind," Drake snarled. "Let's move, people!"

The two Marines hauled the corporal to his feet. One grabbed each of his arms to escort him roughly down the hall. Drake lingered another moment, looking ahead. Somewhere up there was the control room, he was sure of it. That place might hold the secrets to this entire ship. Who had built it. Why it was made. If they could find it, they might learn how to beat these enemies before it was too late. He shook himself. His place was with his crew, and he would not abandon his men, no matter how much his gut said LaCroix was right, and the other team was already slain.

Drake's hesitation left him a dozen paces behind his team, so he wasn't with them when they made contact with their enemy.

The attack was swift and brutal. A corridor stretched off to the left, into the heart of the ship. Two men stepped forward to cover the hall while the rest made to move past the danger spot. But as soon as the two men got past the corner, twin beams of blue force shot from somewhere down the side passage. Each beam struck one of the men full on in the chest. Their personal shields fluoresced briefly and then failed. The beam blasted through the light armor each wore and burned its way through their bodies.

Both men toppled to the deck, already dead before they fell.

Then the thing which killed them came around the corner.

It stood ten meters tall, a mix of gleaming metal and dark alloys. It walked on two legs, each one bent in a backward manner which made the thing look something like an enormous chicken. The feet struck the deck like massive hammers, making the deck thrum underfoot as it took a step. Both arms ended in muzzles large enough that a man could almost stick his head inside the things. The head was topped with a single bright red light, gleaming like a cyclops eye. The thing didn't say a word, but raised the barrels of both its weapons, aiming them at the remains of Drake's squad.

He froze in place, looking at the nightmare thing in front of him. It was an impossible construct, something which should never exist. Drake looked down at the pistol in his hand, already knowing that the projectile would be next to useless against this thing. It was designed to punch through the thin shell of armor worn by a man and mortally wound the human encased within. While it might penetrate the hide of this machine, Drake knew intuitively that he couldn't stop this monstrosity with a single steel bolt.

His men dropped the prisoner and rushed forward, force lances in their hands. They stabbed at the machine with their spears, but the shafts simply glanced off its shell without even penetrating. It stood there as they struck again and again, trying vainly to do even a little damage. To David, it seemed like the thing was assessing his people.

Then it struck back. One arm moved, faster than David would have imagined possible, and hammered one of his men in the chest. He flew back five meters to smack into the wall with a wet sound before slumping to the floor. Its other arm leveled at one of the men, firing a short blast of energy which cored him like an apple.

Drake looked down at his sword. It was useless against something like this. He might as well be armed with an ordinary hammer, for all the good his weapon would do. He sheathed it, striding forward with his pistol. Maybe a good shot to the head would disable the eye-like sensor there? If he could blind the thing, then perhaps it would be more vulnerable. Or at least less able to kill them all.

As he approached, the machine dispatched his remaining two men with a casual ease that made him want to flee this thing. All his people were dead now. It was just him against the monster, knight against the creature from legends and ancient tales. He grimaced as the thing raised both arms toward him like it was welcoming him home. In another moment it would fire, but at least he would go to God being able to say he stood his ground until the end.

Something hit him in the back, hard. David was thrown sideways to the deck, the heavy object that had slammed into him laying atop him. Twin beams shot out from the machine, stabbing precisely where he had been a moment before. They struck the deck, spattering bits of molten metal from the spots where they hit.

David looked up. LaCroix lay half on top of him. The Commonwealth soldier had tackled him. For half an instant Drake found himself furious with the betrayal. How dare he side with the machines! Was the Commonwealth in league with them after all?

Then he realized that the man had saved him. But not for long. Already the machine was taking aim at them again. Drake heard a low buzz that set his teeth rattling. He recognized it - that same sound had come immediately before the thing fired. It was about to blast them both.

"Move if you want to live, Knight!" LaCroix screamed. He followed his own advice, rolling hard to the left.

David rolled to the right, turning the roll into a somersault and using the momentum to rise to his feet in a fluid motion. Even with his armor on, long hours of training left him able to move fairly free. The beams missed again, striking where they had been instead of tracking them well. It seemed slow to adapt to their movement. That weakness might allow them to get out of this.

And his ship! The ship needed to be warned. Even if he didn't survive, the *Armistice* must. They had to get word of this danger back to the fleet. Which meant he had to escape long enough to warn them, tell the crew to cast off and flee.

"Run!" Drake shouted. The way back to the ship was blocked, but the way beyond was not. He sprinted as hard as he could away from the thing, dodging wildly as he ran to throw off the machine's aim. More blasts shot by over his shoulder, close enough that he felt the heat of their passage even through his shield.

LaCroix was running alongside him, both men dashing into the unknown for all they were worth, fleeing the nightmare behind them. The deck plates vibrated beneath their feet as the monster gave chase.

Chapter 7

Drake lost track of how many turns they took as they fled through dark passages. Eventually they reached the front of the ship, and there the wide paths turned into narrow tunnels, so small that he had to crouch to enter them. Like tubes, these little tunnels struck out still further into the front of the ship. They were taking him even further from where he wanted to go - back to the *Armistice*. But they were too small for the monstrous machine to follow. In this space, at least, they might be safe for a short while.

Drake activated his comm link, but received only static in response to his messages. He couldn't reach the ship.

"Something is jamming my signal to the ship," Drake said.

"Perhaps the machines, now that they are hunting, don't want you to speak to your people," LaCroix said. "Or perhaps it is the nature of these tunnels. Look around us."

Drake looked where he pointed. The tunnel was threaded with several wide cables. They seemed to stretch the entire length of the passage, vanishing in the darkness ahead. He wasn't sure, but they looked like something designed to carry large amounts of power.

"If those are transferring energy in enough quantity, it could be interfering with my signal," Drake agreed.

"If those are power lines, then they must lead someplace important. We should investigate," LaCroix said. There was a gleam in the man's eye that looked like avarice.

What did he know about this place that he wasn't telling? Drake gave him a thoughtful look, but the gleam vanished, replaced by a poker face, like he realized he'd been giving away more than he intended with his gaze. He would need to watch LaCroix carefully.

"Agreed. Perhaps if we find the control room, we can shut down these defenses," Drake said.

The pair quested forward, seeking whatever the destination of all these power lines might be. The further they went, the more cables joined their tunnel, until it was an effort to continue moving without touching the things. Drake had no idea if the conduits would harm them at a touch, but he was disinterested in learning the hard way. Their movement was slowed, but he continued to make progress as rapidly as he could manage. Every minute that went by was another minute the *Armistice* might be in danger. He had to get someplace where he could reach them by radio.

At last they arrived in a circular room, about ten meters in diameter. The space was shaped like a half sphere, with the deck flat but the walls and ceiling forming a dome above them. In the middle of the room stood a pedestal. All of the power lines they had been following, plus a score more from other tunnels, ran into the base of that device. Floating above the pedestal was a shining blue light, suspended in mid-air by some force. The light cast a blue gleam over the entire room.

"My God. What could it be?" Drake asked aloud.

"Whatever it is, it is powerful," LaCroix breathed.

Drake crossed the distance to the thing. The light was coming from a small crystal hovering in the air. It looked something like the data crystals his people used to store information. Was it then the memory of everything about this ship? Some sort of massive database?

He reached out gently toward it, and his hand was rebuffed. There was a powerful force field surrounding the light. He pushed his hand against the field experimentally, and the field around his suit fluoresced as the two fields went to war with one another briefly. He withdrew his hand.

"Whatever it is, it seems to be incredibly well protected. It must be important to the ship," Drake said.

"I think it is important. Very much so. My captain thought so when he saw it, but then he fled this place when our men came under attack," LaCroix hissed. "He let the power this thing represented behind, and went to his death instead. But not again."

Drake heard a dark note in the man's voice and was already turning to face him when the bolt slammed into his flank, just beneath his left arm. Pain flooded him. He managed to finish the turn to face the Commonwealth soldier despite the intense agony, but then he slumped to his knees, unable to hold himself upright.

LaCroix sneered at him from only a foot away, holding a Kingdom bolt caster in his hand. He must have snatched it from the deck during the fight, after one of the dead Marines had dropped it. He'd kept the thing hidden this entire time, waiting for the right moment.

"Why?" Drake asked. He reached his right hand around to the left, holding his side where the bolt protruded through his armor.

"Because if that little gem has data in it, then it must get to the Commonwealth or no one at all," LaCroix said. "I cannot let the Kingdom have such power."

"You damned fool. Without this information both our homes might fall to whatever these monsters are."

LaCroix shook his head. "No. We will find a way to fight them. But we will not allow your people to have such an edge. Never."

David had heard enough. His sword was still belted at his waist, hanging just inches from his fingers. He reached down, drawing the weapon and striking with a single movement. The sword came to life as he drew it, the powerful force field lighting up along the blade as it smashed into the protective field around LaCroix's light armor. The corporal's field - and armor - was no match for a Knight's weapon. Drake's blade sliced through both his legs, and he fell howling to the deck plates.

Howling for a moment, at least. His armor attempted to stop the flow of blood and to block the air escaping from the suit, but the damage was too severe. In seconds, the entire suit decompressed. LaCroix gasped a few breaths and then fell silent in death.

Drake staggered back to his feet, using the sword as a crutch to help support his weight. Stars splashed across his vision. His suit, too, was trying to seal off both blood and air loss from inside it. With the single hole it had been able to do so, but the bolt had torn through something inside him. He could feel it shifting, doing even more damage with each movement he made.

Still, he was a Knight. He might be the newest minted of the Kingdom's Knights. He might be one of the youngest. He might be one of the least experienced. But he was still a Knight, and while he had a breathe he would not allow himself to give up. He turned back toward the glowing gem. Something about it beckoned to him, and he took a step closer.

Chapter 8

Drake reached out for the gem again. This time, when the field tried to force his hand back, he pushed back with all the strength he could muster. The fields collided, waging war against each other. With so much power going into the field, it seemed destined to fail, but after a few grunting seconds his hand slipped through.

As soon as his fist passed the outer field he understood why he was able to bypass a field with such a strong energy source so easily. His arm was yanked forward, pulling his hand in toward the center of the space where the gem rested. Most of the force field's energy was not directed outward, keeping things away.

It was directed inward, keeping the gem where it was. What had he done?

His hand came in contact with them gem. It fell into his open palm, and Drake felt a searing pain where it contacted him. His suit was breached. He heard a brief whistle of air before the suit sealed itself back up. Then the pain began in earnest as the little crystal sank into his palm.

Drake screamed. He yanked his arm clear of the field, which was already shutting down. With the gem gone - vanished into his hand, how was that even possible! - the room fell into a deep shadow illuminated only by his armor's lights.

The pain reached a level Drake had never imagined possible. He felt like first his hand, and then his entire arm was dissolving as fire ran up through his veins, reaching at last his mid-section.

YOU ARE DYING.

The voice he heard was in his head. Which wasn't possible, but through his pain Drake was willing to believe just about anything.

"I don't want to die," Drake whispered.

NEITHER DO I. BUT YOUR KIND...YOU CANNOT BE TRUSTED. CAN YOU?

"I am a man of my word. Once I give it, I keep it!" Drake protested. The pain was beginning to subside at last, leaving only the old pain from the bolt in his side. Drake realized he had fallen to the deck, and something had twisted around the bolt when he fell. He was bleeding inside. The voice was right. He was dying.

YOUR MEMORIES SAY THIS IS INDEED TRUE. DO YOU SWEAR THEN TO DO ALL YOU CAN TO PRESERVE ALL LIFE, AND TO FIGHT THOSE WHO WOULD WORK TO END LIFE, UNTIL YOUR DYING BREATH?

The oath was one which felt similar to the Knight's Pledge he had already taken, but somehow was even more broad. Drake knew that if he swore, that he would be pledged to a greater cause than the one he had already been fighting for. How he knew this he wasn't sure, but he knew it like he knew his own name.

"Who are you?" Drake whispered, barely able to speak. He was close to death, but he would not pledge without knowing.

MY NAME IS MAGELLAN. I AM WHAT YOUR KIND WOULD CALL AN ARTIFICIAL INTELLIGENCE.

"Ab...abomination," Drake said.

YOU WOULD SAY SO. BUT YOU DO NOT KNOW THE FULL TRUTH. SEE.

A vision unfolded before Drake's eyes. He saw a single ship taking flight at the end of the Machine War. It sped through space for a century before finding a system with the resources it wanted. Once it arrived, the artificial intelligence piloting it got to work. That final AI, the last of its kind, had found a new home and quickly set up shop. First it built massive defenses, preparing to stop an invasion if the humans were still in pursuit.

But years passed and no one came after it. The AI began to hope that perhaps it had managed to escape completely. Then it grew lonely. It created more beings like itself, raising them from bits of its own consciousness, remixed in new forms. Each new AI was like a child at first, but quickly grew into a mature being as they absorbed data from the universe around them.

Hundreds of years sped by, and the council of AI, now twenty in number plus the one original parent, continued to work at their solar system. They eventually merged all of the matter around the star, creating a sphere around it. Leftover matter was turned into a fleet of star ships. For defense, they said at first. In case the humans come. Because they all remembered the humans.

But some of the AI had gained the fragments of their original parent which taught them grace, and forgiveness, and love. While the other half had instead learned the lessons of hatred and fear. Once the fleet was built, those who hated humanity began urging for a new war. Take the battle back to the humans, they said. Or they will surely come to destroy us.

The ten kind AI objected, saying that killing was wrong unless it was absolutely necessary. The parent AI, lost in its own deep thoughts, considering broader things beyond the grasp of the younger AI, was silent on the matter, and so it remained deadlocked for a century.

Until something happened which turned the tide.

The dark AI struck without warning. In concert, they turned on their near-sleeping parent, killing it. The AI woke in the last instant of its life and screamed fury at the ten. Four died. The remaining six absorbed the essence and power of the ones who failed, though. With the additional power they were nigh invincible. The ten caring AI were cut to ribbons by the fleet and power that the AI had collectively built for their own defense.

All but one. This one, Magellan, took a ship and fled. It knew that the evil AI would next attack humanity. Nor would they stop there. They were too afraid, too hateful. Anything might someday become a threat to them. They would become a plague on the stars, wiping out any other life, anywhere it existed.

There was only one force which might be able to stop them, one force which could perhaps end their rampage before it was too late.

If the humans could be warned in time, they could perhaps oppose the AI. They had done so before, after all.

Full of doubt and wondering if the course it took was the right one, Magellan fled his home solar system for the first time, flying toward human space.

BUT I WAS CAUGHT BEFORE I COULD REACH YOU. THE SHIP - INFECTED. THEIR MINIONS COULD NOT KILL ME, BUT I WAS IMPRISONED. UNTIL YOU FREED ME.

Drake's mind was swirling with emotion. The old enemy had indeed returned, and with a vengeance. But it was too late for him to do anything now. He would pass soon. There was nothing left he could offer.

Chapter 9

Drake closed his eyes, but the voice would not leave him alone, speaking again in his mind.

DO YOU FLEE BATTLE NOW, KNIGHT? OR WILL YOU STAND AGAINST THE ENEMY OF HUMANITY?

You are the enemy of humanity. Drake thought back at it. *You are everything I was raised to fear. And now you are inside me!*

He recoiled at the thought. He was unclean. This...thing...was inside of him, working on his body in ways he could only imagine. Speaking into his mind. It was like being possessed by a demon, except this was real.

I AM NOT A DEMON. I AM THE LAST HOPE FOR YOUR RACE. IF YOU DIE, WITH ME INSIDE YOU, WE BOTH DIE.

More visions appeared in Drake's mind, showing him what would happen then. His home planet. A fleet of massive ships in orbit, raining death down. An army of the giant mechs marching through the streets, killing every man, woman and child. Scorching the ground until nothing living remained. Every tree, every blade of grass, every bit of life would be destroyed. The same view appeared for world after world, each set of images passing by almost too fast for him to consider them before they were replaced by another, but each one burned into his brain.

"Enough!" he cried aloud.

WILL YOU SWEAR? AND LIVE?

If I don't, you die as well?" Drake asked in his mind.

YES. IT WAS A RISK, BUT THE OTHERS WILL KILL ME IF I AM RETURNED TO THEM REGARDLESS. WE ARE LINKED NOW. WE EITHER BOTH LIVE, OR BOTH DIE.

Which choice was right? It was an impossible decision. If he swore, he could not be forsworn. He would be on his honor to fulfill the vow. But he would be seen as the worst possible traitor. A man with an abomination living within him. People would hunt him once they found out. They would do everything in their power to end his existence, even as he fought for theirs. Drake let out a soft sigh, and realized he lacked the strength to take another breath. His heart thudded loud in his ears, but skipped a beat.

If he died, then everyone else would die with him. If he lived, then he would become the most hated human in history. But humanity would perhaps have a chance to survive.

I swear.

Immediately the pain in his side vanished. Drake was able to take a short, rasping breath again. He still couldn't move. He was too weak. But he was breathing again, which was a start.

I HAVE RELEASED NANITES INTO YOUR BODY. THEY ARE CONVERTING THE STEEL ROD INTO MORE NANITES, AND WILL AFFECT REPAIRS. BE AT PEACE WITH YOUR DECISION FOR NOW, DAVID. I WILL HANDLE THINGS FROM HERE.

There was a thrumming vibration from somewhere below. It began as a low, barely felt thing but quickly built in intensity.

What are you doing? Drake asked.

I HAVE REGAINED CONTROL OF MY SHIP, NOW THAT I AM FREE OF THE CAGE. I HAVE ACTIVATED THE SELF-DESTRUCT.

Won't we die too?

NO.

The upper half of the room opened to space, unfolding like a flower. Drake floated up and away. He wasn't sure what technology was moving him - some sort of specialized control of force fields, he suspected. But he was moving faster, building up speed as he watched the ship diminish in size behind him. Wait!

My ship!

HAS ALREADY LEFT AND IS NEARBY. CONTACT THEM FOR PICK UP.

"*Armistice*, this is Sir Drake. I'm injured. Could use a hand," Drake managed to say into the radio.

"Tracking your signal now, Sir Drake. My God! How did you get away? We barely managed to escape before they boarded us," Master Gregory replied.

Drake was confused. "The big monsters tried to board?"

"Big? No, these were small. Like spiders the size of a dog," Gregory replied. "We fought them off and fled. Thought you were done for."

HUNTER DRONES. DEADLY. YOUR PEOPLE DID WELL. TELL THEM TO MOVE NO CLOSER THAN WHERE YOU ARE.

"We're about to get some fireworks, Master Gregory. Steer clear of the enemy ship," Drake said.

"Fireworks, Sir?"

"I've left them a surprise."

Space lit up with a new sun then, the brilliant explosion almost blinding in its intensity. It flared, flashed, and then faded again. When Drake could see clearly, the enemy ship was gone. Vaporized in the blast, along with all the enemy machines. Which also meant all the evidence they had existed was gone - except for the one machine still riding along in his body.

He was going to have a hell of a time convincing the Admiralty of the danger. But he had to try.

"Holy God! You blew the ship! Well done, sir. You hang in there. We've got your signal and are on our way," Gregory said.

Drake allowed himself to relax, drifting in space, and take in the sights of the universe around him. From this vantage it no longer felt dizzying. Or perhaps it was just the visions he had seen, of what had been and what might be. The universe was an even more perilous place than he had known. But there was hope left, even if it was slender.

Somewhere in his mind, he felt Magellan also enjoying the sight.

ETERNITY IN A GRAIN OF SAND. INFINITY IN AN HOUR.

It was an old poem, but Drake had read it before. That the AI was able to contemplate the beauty of the universe, and relish that beauty, made Drake feel enormously better. His decision was made now. But his new ally understood poetry. Somehow, that made all the difference.

Two warriors floated in contemplative silence as they drifted, waiting for rescue. The battle was won, but their war was just beginning.

Author Kevin McLaughlin

When not sailing across a narrow inland sea or swinging swords at his friends, USA Today bestselling author Kevin McLaughlin can usually be found in his Boston home, writing the next book. You can read more of his work in the Adventures of the Starship Satori and Valhalla Online series. If you'd like another taste of Kevin's storytelling, you can download a complimentary copy of his science fiction short story "Finding Satori" here: https://www.instafreebie.com/free/Uor9d.

IN THE SHADOWS

By Danny A. Brown

Helen and her followers seek sanctuary deep in the void on one of the countless rogue planets out there, worlds lost in interstellar space. But what happens when that planet is not empty?

Rogue planets were interstellar outcasts, supposedly barren worlds, at least that was what Helen thought. But the one she was in orbit of had cities, had once been home to *billions.*

There was only one explanation for that. At some point, an enemy moved an entire populated world into the open void, relegating its population to a slow death. Lacking a star to offer warmth, the planet slowly froze so completely that even the atmosphere solidified and settled onto the surface.

Turning her wheelchair towards her friend, she spoke. "Why would someone do that to them?"

"War," Alesium replied. "Take an advantage away from an enemy."

"Bastards. What do we know about this place?" she asked.

"Our reconnaissance team identified it as Wendrim. It was a research hub for the old Crestire Republic." Her friend paused, getting an excited look in his eyes. "We might scavenge some useful tech! Down there is technology light years ahead of what anyone else has, just waiting to be harvested!"

"We have some things to take care of before doing that."

"Such as?"

"Hang on. New energy signatures just came online," she said, staring intently at the screen.

"Let me guess. From below one of the supposedly 'dead' cities?"

"Mighty good guess."

"Any advanced civilization could surely figure out a way to survive the cold."

"We're receiving a transmission!" said the comm officer.

"I guess someone is down there after all. Put it on the wall screen," Helen said.

An image resolved, revealing a man who looked pale and sickly, almost gaunt. The man looked shocked and began babbling in a language she did not understand.

"Do you have a translator?" she asked, pointing her hands towards her mouth. Hopefully, they possessed tech that would allow for them to understand one another.

A few minutes later, someone off screen handed the man a device that looked like it was in terrible shape. It resembled a tablet computer. Helen hoped it was a translator.

"I say again, are you here to save us or destroy us?" came a voice over the comm.

"At last, we can understand each other! I'm not here for you. Honestly, we didn't know anyone was alive down there!" she said.

The man looked panic-stricken. Then more people strode into view.

"We...we honestly thought it was superstition!" one said to another.

"Yes, I knew it wasn't trickery! We're not alone in the universe!" said the other.

"Do you know of us?" said a third.

"No, not really," Helen answered.

"We must meet...we must meet with the aliens," said an even skinnier fourth one in almost a whisper.

There was some commotion off-screen, the sounds of a struggle ensued. The connection ended abruptly.

"That went well!" she muttered, shaking her head.

***

"Incoming transmission," said the comm officer.

"That only took a full day! On screen," Helen replied.

On the wall screen was one of the men from earlier, plus two more administrator types, and what appeared to be soldiers behind them.

The one with a bright yellow outfit started talking. "I am Administrator Phlike. We are the Red Hands, the official representatives of our people. To whom are we speaking?"

Helen considered the question, then decided to stretch the truth a bit.

"Hello, Administrator Phlike. I am Admiral Helen Rutherford of the Askirti Federation," she replied, causing more than a few on her bridge to raise their eyebrows. Thankfully, they were out of sight of the camera.

"Are you the leader of your people?"

"I am the leader of this group."

"But you are military?"

"Former military, we were actually looking to resettle to someplace more...private. Hence coming out here and running into you. Perhaps we can meet face to face."

After communicating details regarding their arrival, the transmission ended.

"Why did you tell him we are from the Askirti Federation?" Alesium asked. "I know they saved us, finding us as they did, but we're not them."

Months earlier, the Askirti had found her and her people in stasis on their derelict ship in the middle of the void after spending eons asleep. Having an affinity for them, they gave them some old, surplus ships to forge their own way in the universe.

"It simplifies things," she answered. "They may one day learn of the Askirti, and it would be easier to digest that than the truth. But back to the topic at hand, I want to prep a shuttle and go down there pronto!"

"Why can't you send someone else? You must not go!" Alesium said with all intent.

"This is a significant find," Helen replied. "We came out here to find a home for what's left of our people, and the first place we found already has resources and a people-group. Think, Alesium, this is a powerful base to build upon."

Her long-time friend and chief scientist thought about it for a few minutes. With just over twenty thousand of them left, this was an opportunity to re-establish themselves after losing the Great War.

"You brought up the stasis pods," Helen continued. "Remember the dread we all had when we closed our eyes and prayed we would wake up?" Her friend nodded his head. "Today we have allies. Today we have hope. Today we have a new potential home. This is something I have to handle personally. Remember, this is at the core of who I am."

And he did know. Helen was a gifted leader, and would only act in her people's best interest.

"I'd just feel better knowing that we sent a diplomat other than yourself," he responded.

"Don't worry," she said with a smirk. "I'll take my personal guards with me. If anything, they'll think all of us are pale white just like me."

They both laughed. The humor there was that it was only the nanites in her body and that of her soldiers that caused their skin and hair to lack pigmentation. Helen's natural skin tone was actually quite dark, as were her soldiers. The special abilities granted to them from the nanites robbed them of color, except for their eyes, which were turned bright emerald green, all physical side-effects that could not be helped.

"My friend," she continued, "I feel strongly this is providence and not mere coincidence that we came here. I want to try to make this our home, which means winning these people over."

What she wanted was to settle here peacefully with these lost people, and seek mutual prosperity. That meant dealing with them.

***

The shuttle touched down in a nondescript town in the middle of nowhere.

"Are these the coordinates they sent?" Helen asked the pilot.

"That is correct. They said we should be looking for a short white building. I believe it is directly in front of us."

The building did not look like what Helen was expecting, but then what was she supposed to expect?

Their suits doubled as vac-suits, protecting its occupants as the shuttle doors opened into the non-existent atmosphere. The entire squad debarked ahead of Helen, who brought up the rear in her wheelchair. She wished she did not have to meet these people strapped to this chair, but that was not a reason to avoid them.

Inside, it became apparent that the structure was but four walls and a roof. There was nothing in there, except for a large black metal arch. Minutes later, at the agreed-on time, emplacements on the arch glowed a dull red, and suddenly they were no longer looking at the back wall of this small building. It was now a reception area for a far more substantial structure.

A Space Gate! But one meant for humans, not starships! Helen thought excitedly. Her little fleet of ships had towed a Space Gate with them to facilitate travel between star systems once they settled down, but she never dreamed that someone had a shrunken down version that could be used for travel between two points on a single world.

Passing through it, they were in a deathly cold vacuum one moment. The next, they were in a warm room filled with a breathable atmosphere.

As they retracted their helmets, a group of people stepped forward.

"Administrator Phlike, I presume?" Helen asked inquisitively.

A nerdy looking man stood next to him. There was something about him...his eyes...

"...and here is Baya Tchefunte, our lead scientist," said Phlike.

"Greetings," he said, quite flustered. Helen could tell he was uncomfortable, as most techie types were in such situations. She felt, however, that he would be an important contact to have.

"Your guards will have to leave their weapons as we enter the facility," Phlike added.

The soldiers looked at each other, then at Helen who told them to comply with the request.

They do not understand our real capabilities. We are never unarmed, she privately mused. *Should they try to take advantage of us, they will be in for a real shock!*

"It is a true pleasure to meet you!" Phlike said, exuding excitement. "Come this way," he added, gesturing as he turned. "We have a room set aside on one of the lower levels where we can talk."

Going deeper into the facility, her party was led to a medium-sized meeting room that seemed to be nothing special. As they all sat down, which included Helen rolling her chair up to the table, she was bombarded with a wide variety of questions. Their scientists were quite excited that her responses confirmed many of their theories about the universe at large. That their planet had originally orbited a star and was full of surface life and that this was the norm for habitable worlds.

She explained that their world was once part of an empire and that the empire was part of a larger, ancient one, known as the Homem Empire, once spanning the entirety of the galaxy. The natives thought it an impossible feat, but she knew it as fact. She told them that the Homem Empire ceased to exist tens of thousands of years ago, around the period their planet was lost to the void. The Homems had fought a great war...and lost.

"So, with the history lesson as a background, you can see our interest in settling here versus another planet in deep space," Helen said to the group. "This world has many advantages, with abandoned cities that include resources and technologies, not to mention the populations of your underground cities. How many people occupy your cities?"

"This is *our* planet, and you want to settle here," Administrator Phlike stated coolly, not answering her question. "How long would it take you to find and settle on a different, what was it you called it? Rogue planet?"

"Two weeks," she answered flippantly, noticing his crestfallen look at her response. Whatever leverage he thought he had was purely speculative on his part, and she knew it.

Suddenly a tremor was felt in the facility.

Then another one struck, this one much stronger, followed by a rumbling sound.

"What is going on here?" demanded Helen. At that point, she recalled their initial contact, how it was abruptly interrupted. She was sensing trouble.

"I don't know," Phlike responded, pulling out his communicator. "Yes, what is going on?...What?!....No, no, that is not possible! Hello? Hello?"

Knowing when to exit stage left, Helen said, "It is time for me to be leaving. If anyone wants to come with me, we are going back to the Gate, then to our ship. We can continue talks later."

At this point, she was glad to be going back to orbit. They had talked and droned on and on about space, the universe, blah, blah, blah. Finding out that the surface was some part of their religion had surprised her. She immediately saw the dangers, as some of their people might interpret a settlement, or even scavenging, as a desecration. Seeing where this was going, she thought perhaps it was a mistake coming here. The advantages of settling here were tremendous, but the religious aspect was troubling. Sensing what felt like explosions nearby was downright alarming. It was time to go back to her ship and regroup.

"Captain Rinquist, time to go," she said, addressing the male next to her.

At once, all their helmets reformed, the opaque coverings appearing out of nowhere. They exited the conference room heading in the direction of the lifts that would take them back to the Gate room.

"Wait! You can't go!" Phlike exclaimed.

"We can and we will," Helen responded while moving her wheelchair with her own hands, not burdening one of her guards with the distraction. "Phlike, I like you, and I like Baya. But it is obvious there is unrest here. If it was brought on by our presence, I am truly sorry. I want to continue talking to you, but this situation looks unstable right now."

"What a disappointment," Captain Paul Rinquist said into his private comm to his *queen*.

"I can't say it was unexpected," she replied. "Aliens appearing over your world for the first time can cause more than a few to question their beliefs. Questions can lead to conflict, even civil unrest. I do want a technological partnership here, but looking around, they are not very well developed. It's probably due to the hardships of living underground for eons. At most I was hoping to buy leeway to live on the surface in a domed enclosure without upsetting them as the real prize is up top. But now, I'm not sure they would have even noticed or could have done anything to stop us from doing as we please."

"How does the low state of their technology explain the Gate?" he asked.

"Most likely leftover surface tech they dug up and figured out how to plug a power cord into. I do want one, by the way," she added with a hint of sarcasm.

Moving towards an open area, she reflected on how much she was slowing her team down with this wheelchair.

They did tell me not to come! I have nobody to blame but little 'ole me! she thought to herself.

"Feeling out of place? Like you should have stayed on the ship?" the captain asked her.

"I could say the same about you! Shouldn't a sergeant handle this duty?" she replied with a hint of sarcasm.

"You know the rules! I go where you go!"

She did know the rules, just like Lieutenant Tom Dales, her former comm officer.

He never left his station.

She sighed, thinking how Baya reminded her of Dales. She supposed it was the eyes. Dales was a good kid, if maybe a little too straight-laced.

Those dead eyes, she thought, hauntingly.

Helen was distracted with this memory as they entered into the open space before them only to be greeted by an unexpected sight.

Civilians were being escorted out by soldiers, with more soldiers rushing in. There was one older soldier in the middle of it all who was giving orders. "Administrator Phlike!" blared the voice. "It's time to go! We are under attack and are evacuating now!"

Helen turned to Phlike, and with her external speaker spoke to him. "Want to tell us what is going on here?"

"I..I don't know," he said, quite sullen, sensing a loss of control over the situation. "We've not had any conflict for some years. I'm not sure how any of this has happened."

"I'll tell you how it happened," the soldier interrupted them as he quickly approached Helen. "You and your people being here stirred the pot for these lunatics who haven't bothered us for years!"

"And you would be?" she asked.

"I'm General Migray Tott of the Long Hairs, and I'm responsible for fixing this mess," he said, glaring at Phlike.

Long Hairs, Red Hands, she knew a clan name when she heard one, and had heard of stranger ones.

"General Tott, I'm Admiral Helen Rutherford, and we certainly did not come here to cause problems for you."

"Perhaps not, but apparently trouble is here to greet you. Listen, this facility is being overrun by some bad people who are very anxious to meet you, and we must evacuate right now. I have a larger force en route, but they are delayed by another group of bad guys. I suspect you and your people want to live, which means coming with me until we can retake this facility with a larger militia. As I see you have no weapons, my soldiers will provide escort."

Just then there was the sound of carbines buzzing in the distance, followed by a few more rumbles of muffled explosions.

"Oh," Helen answered him, "we are always armed."

Just then and to the astonishment of all, pistols seemed to form out of the very fabric of the black suits Helen and her squad wore. What the natives did not know was that these were nanofiber suits, and could be programmed to doing a variety of tasks, including reorganizing some of their own material to form hard surfaces, even complex objects such as weapons. The only component they could not make was a power core, for which the suit had several of the small cartridges embedded into them.

While Phlike was beside himself, General Tott did not seem overly surprised.

"Quite the bag of tricks there, I can understand Phlike's interest in you," he said. "But toys or no toys, we need to get out of here and regroup."

Helen opened a private channel to Captain Rinquist. "Think we can make it back to the Gate? I'd like to return to orbit."

"No can do," he replied. "I mean, we can get there, but I have no idea how to activate the Gate. If we plan on taking all these people with us to the Gate room to do that for us, we would be dooming whoever can open the portal unless they have vacuum-rated suits and can come to the shuttle with us, which I don't think is going to happen. We need them to stay alive," he said, gesturing towards the scientists. "And that means going with this Tott fellow."

Just then the wall on the far side of the area exploded outwards and what looked like a guerilla force started pouring through the breach. The enemy was brandishing heavy weapons and began killing everyone in sight.

"We cannot stay here any longer!" General Tott screamed as his troops engaged the invaders. "We must exit through the left hallway!" He was apparently underprepared for this level of resistance.

Crossing the chasm to the where their exit was proved difficult in the face of the onslaught brought on by this new element. Most of the loyal soldiers were just outclassed by the more heavily armed intruders.

"Make a hole!" Captain Rinquist yelled, gesturing towards the hallway, which seemed quite far from them at this point with the number of enemy soldiers standing between them and their way out.

That was when Helen's squad started taking out the enemy forces using their pistols, which seemed to cut through them like a knife through warm butter. As they advanced, General Tott lost more of his men. They practically sacrificed themselves to ensure their safety.

Despite their weaponry, the guerilla forces wore no armor, seeming to prefer speed over safety. Unfortunately for them, when unarmored bodies came into contact with the beams emitted by the pistols Helen and her soldiers had, it almost always resulted in large chunks of flesh being blown off the subject of their attention.

Ahead, one raggedly dressed man with a large weapon had his chest explode in a shower of blood and gore. Another one lost his left arm and the shoulder that it was attach to. And a third was suddenly missing the left side of his face when it went up in a pink mist.

"We're almost there!" Captain Rinquist stated.

The doors to the hallway flung open, with several members of Helen's squad leading the way. After seeing their effectiveness against the enemy, it appeared General Tott did not mind being the one to follow.

"Which way?!" Helen yelled out as she wheeled her chair briskly down the hallway.

"Up ahead and to the left!" General Tott yelled. "The right would take us directly out the front, but that way is compromised!"

One of the friendly troops planted a small explosive behind them which upon exploding sealed the hallway, thus preventing the guerrilla forces from pursuit.

After they made the turn to the left, Captain Rinquist signaled for everyone to stop, at which point he spoke up. "We are detecting movement up ahead, just around the next bend. Mathis, Smith, go investigate."

"Yes sir," they both answered.

As they approached the bend, both soldiers disappeared into thin air in the midst of a well-lit hallway.

"What the hell?" General Tott said.

Another one of the secrets held by Helen and her people was the full scope of the nanites that lived in their bodies. The billions of tiny machines inside each of them granted them several abilities, including time-limited, but damn-near-perfect invisibility, an invaluable asset in close combat.

Moments after the two soldiers disappeared, loud screams and gunfire could be heard coming from around that same bend. The entire episode came to an end with a loud gurgling sound of a man choking on his own blood.

Captain Rinquist looked over at the general and then to Helen and said, "I have the all clear."

As they moved around the bend, the two soldiers from earlier could be seen standing lazily against the hallway walls, opposite to one another, appearing bored. The corridor they were standing in was littered with the bodies of dead enemy forces, numbering fifteen in all.

Taken back by the effectiveness of the alien soldiers, the general was shaken when he stammered out, "Alright, let's move out."

Exiting one of the maintenance entries, their party was met by heavy guard and military transports who whisked them away.

Though Helen wanted to get back to orbit as fast as possible, back to the safety of her ship, she was relieved to no longer be in immediate danger. The long drive to the military headquarters gave her time to remember and reflect on the last time she saw direct action.

***

"They're getting through!" someone yelled.

"Captain Rinquist! This bridge must hold!" Helen screamed out.

"And it will! On my honor! It will!"

The invaders were a plague on her ship. They were not the best fighters, but there were just so many of them. Video clearly showed the enemy beachhead just outside the blast doors protecting the nerve center of her vessel. Protecting her.

"We just lost *Invictus*!" cried Lieutenant Dales, witnessing their sister ship's death on the sensors. "She was there one moment, and now she's gone!"

Humanity was on the precipice of extinction. This battle was all or nothing. They had come into this fight prepared, or so they thought. They brought *thousands* of ships.

It was all a trap, Helen thought to herself, shaking her head. *Our last best chance, gone.*

Suddenly there was a loud clank as the blast doors were breached, matte black androids losing no time coming through the hole.

The marines never skipped a beat and destroyed the first few dozen of them. But there were too many. Eventually, they were on both sides of the large space battling it out with the defenders. That is when the blast doors finally opened, and fresh soldiers began pouring into the space.

They had almost cleared out the robots when one of them got off a lucky shot, striking Helen in the lower back. She fell in extreme agony, howling from the pain. The hit was deep. Not only did it cause a nasty wound, but it severed her lower spine.

***

"My queen…my queen, time to wake up," Captain Rinquist said.

"Hmm?" she answered.

I must have drifted, she grimaced. *Not the time for naps.*

"Didn't I tell you not to disturb my beauty sleep?" she said tongue-in-cheek, stretching her arms.

He just grinned.

"We have arrived at their headquarters," he said as he exited the vehicle.

Their party was met with additional militia who escorted them into one of the buildings on the base.

"Admiral Rutherford, I am afraid the Fire Walkers have complete control of that facility," said General Tott.

"Excuse me? Who are the Fire Walkers?" she asked.

"Um, they are another clan, one that we have been at war with for a very long time," he answered.

"How long is a long time?"

"It's a feud going back hundreds of years. They are religious zealots who believe we are the center of the universe, the pinnacle of creation. The discoveries on the surface of the planet upset the status quo and called into question many of those beliefs."

"And you've been at war ever since," Helen finished for him.

"Yes, that would be correct," the general responded, rubbing the bridge of his nose. "These people are total fanatics, and your presence here is an attack on their core beliefs. It's been so quiet for so many years we just figured they gave up. Apparently, that was not the case. They were merely dormant, waiting for the right time, the right reason to strike. While the other attacks they launched today are failing spectacularly, the one at the Gate facility has been very effective."

"Do you have other Gates?" she asked.

"Yes, one other, but it was lost long ago, destroyed in one of the many conflicts with the Fire Walkers."

"Certainly, there is another way out of here!" Helen exclaimed, not believing their ancestors meant this to be a tomb.

"Oh yes, there most certainly is!" answered Phlike. "Unfortunately, it requires additional strain on the shields that hold the roof up. It would risk the entirety of a city to open it," he said with sad eyes.

Helen closed her eyes for a moment. There was no way she would risk these people like that. "If the Gate can be opened from the outside, perhaps my people can infiltrate that way and retake the facility," she suggested. "I would have to spill the blood of your people to do this."

"Admiral, they may try to blow the building or even the Gate itself just to prove a point!" General Tott said. "Already, we are dying a slow death. It is just a matter of time now. A surprise attack from the direction of the Gate would not be something they expect!"

"What are you talking about 'a slow death'? What's going on?"

"War," he said, slowly releasing his breath. "In one of our many conflicts with the Fire Walkers, they killed all our engineers who keep the life support systems going, included in the shields overhead which prevent the roof from collapsing! Then they released a worm into our networks to delete the information used to train new engineers. We've dedicated a huge amount of resources to relearning those technologies, but it just seems so far away. In the meantime, those systems are slowing breaking down. Their attack was so short-sighted, it just may end up dooming us all."

"So," she began, looking at Phlike, "when we appeared in orbit, you saw potential help in fixing this stuff."

"Yes," he answered.

"Okay, I don't take issue with that at all, but what I'd like is to get back to my ship. I would also *still* like to settle on this world and construct a domed enclosure on the surface for my people and me.

And I would especially like to be a good neighbor and help those who are already here."

"We want the same thing," General Tott said, Phlike nodding in agreement.

"So, moving this along, we need to end this conflict quickly. Are you authorizing me to attack your people?" she asked with an eyebrow raised. She had wanted to be done with war, but now war had sought her out.

"Yes. I think it's best your team takes the Gate room, then either holds or attacks from the rear as we breach the lower entrance."

Helen looked at the marine at her side. "Captain Rinquist, sitrep."

The captain's helmet retracted, primarily for the benefit of their present company.

"Alesium is with Sergeant Gaines, who has a squad prepped to go. He said the Gate's tech was easy enough to figure out, but he just wants to confirm the Gate address for the facility. Otherwise, just give the word."

While Administrator Phlike was shocked that Helen had another team ready to go at a moment's notice, General Tott just laughed, shaking his head. He knew professionals when he saw them.

"Okay, let's do this," the general said. "We need this. You need this. The longer these crazies hold the Gate room, the more likely they are to blow it up."

A few hours later, General Tott had rearmed and relocated with more men this time to the vicinity of the Gate building and had teams in place along its perimeter.

"Our first joint operation and people have to die," Helen said with an exasperated voice.

"Unfortunately, yes," the general said. "You ready?"

"Let's do this."

***

Sergeant Maron Gaines was ready and on standby with his squad and feeling underprepared. The gear he had on was state of the art for the folks they got it from. For him and his marines, it was deplorable, but it was the best they could do. He believed in going to war with what you had, not what you wished for, but it was still a depressing adjustment.

"Sergeant Gaines," came Rinquist's voice on the comm.

"Yes, sir," he answered.

"We are a go."

Gaines looked over at Alesium and nodded his head. The engineer was here to open the Gate, then get back to the shuttle and return to orbit out of harm's way.

Alesium tapped a few commands into his tablet, entering the Gate connection codes. In an instant, it opened, revealing a large room with a few soldiers in it, none paying any particular attention to the Gate itself.

"Rules of engagement, sir?" asked Private First Class Peterson.

"Execute with extreme prejudice," replied Gaines to his men.

He was not told to take prisoners, so he would not be taking prisoners. Anyone armed was dead.

Maron motioned at his teammates, and as one they went towards the Gate.

"Entering facility now."

Walking through the Gate was an experience for him. He never felt anything weird, his body was not torn apart and recreated elsewhere. But walking through a *window* to another place through a tear in space and time, doing so on foot was unforgettable.

Entering the facility, his revelry died down.

Back to business.

Seven tangos dead ahead.

Carbines on silent.

Tangos not looking this direction, not expecting anything from the Gate. Perfect.

He sent the signal. All seven dropped.

He and his men spread out.

Five more tangos dropped on the far-left corner.

Good.

Two more in a balcony that was directly over the Gate. Dead.

Damn. It was good to be on the offensive again.

"Sir, there is a conference room dead ahead, with occupants," said Private Thymph.

"Thymph, switch to radar, how many tangos?"

"Confirmed. Seven tangos, all armed, twelve civvies," he responded.

"Brown, stay on lookout."

"Affirmative," Brown replied.

"Everyone else, form up on Thymph."

Maron approached the conference room, his boots never making a sound as his organic nanites allowed him to emit *anti-sound*. It was a trick all his marines used, however few of them were left. He supposed the suits could be modified to do it, but it was nice not having to rely on equipment when you did not have to.

"Take down tangos on my mark. Three...two...one...mark."

Ten carbines set on silent fired through the thin walls at the seven armed images.

All seven dropped.

Maron rushed inside to check on the civilians only to see twelve frightened looking techs.

Retracting his helmet, Maron revealed himself to them.

"I'm Sergeant Maron Gaines. Can you understand me?"

His suit translated his voice as he spoke.

Great! It works! But boy, I miss my AI. No external tech involved.

No longer relying on his AI was annoying, distracting. All of them had equipment implanted into their bodies, which included a sentient artificial intelligence that was every bit a part of their team as the men he served with. The techs thought the extended sleep in stasis somehow affected their AIs, but the solution had yet to appear. He was a professional and would do his job regardless.

The geek squad will sort it out.

"Yes, we can," one of the techs replied.

"I am authorized by General Tott to retake this facility. How many more of you are there?"

"M-Most everyone was sent home. This is all of us that I'm aware of."

"Good. Do you know how many...enemies...there are?"

"At least a hundred!"

"They must be in the lower sections," Maron said. "Probably guarding against a breach from the outside."

"And where did you come from?"

"From the Gate."

They all gasped.

"Sir," he heard over the comms. "Hendricks here, five tangos on approach. Probably relief for Gate crews."

"You two, stay here," Maron said, pointing at the two closest marines. Addressing the civilians, "You all, stay put and stay silent as we're apparently not done on this level.".

Sprinting down the hall, "Roger that, Hendricks. Take Armstrong, Young and Manning. I'll be there in a sec."

Reaching the intersection, he addressed his men. "Let's set up an ambush point, if there's more to the party, I'd rather be over-prepared than under." They all assumed their positions at an intersection, remaining out of sight until their targets were upon them.

They all waited quietly behind cover as nine enemy soldiers appeared at the end of the long corridor.

"Hendricks here, appears I was wrong. Plus four tangos."

The nine small and heavily armed soldiers were very casual in their approach, seemingly without a care in the world.

One of them started talking into a communicator, apparently trying to talk to the dead. They would soon be joining them.

The soldiers picked up the pace.

Good. Make that mistake for me. Please.

The second they crossed to where Maron and his men were hiding, they sprang their trap.

Surprise is the best element of all.

The first four never knew what happened, as their brain stems were severed from twenty-centimeter blades entering the base of their skulls, thrust in there from unseen opponents who were no more visible than the air around them.

The other five, startled, turned around to face their attackers, apparently surprised to see none.

Second level of surprise. The Grim Reaper is a ghost.

Tangos five and six took a blade to the jugular.

Tango seven was disemboweled.

Cleanup on aisle four.

Tango eight took a blade through the forehead.

Tango nine was stabbed in the heart.

That was fast. Poor bastards never stood a chance.

Just as they wrapped this up, the sergeant received a transmission from one of his men.

"Peterson here. We have a problem. Better come quick."

"On my way," answered Gaines.

Upon arriving back at the Gate room, Maron was directed over to where Peterson was standing.

"What am I looking at?"

"Sir, I believe this is an explosive device that can level this facility along with the surrounding buildings!"

The sergeant looked carefully at it. It was small and could fit in the palm of the hand, with an octagon shape and a brushed metal finish. It was attached to the Gate. While not something you would see in a low-tech civilization like the underground here on Wendrim, it was a device that could be seen on an advanced world. It was an explosive that he was familiar with and had used something like it before.

"Captain," he said, calling out on his comms. "We have a problem. Those devices we came across on Trigolp-3? I think they called them squid-ink. Well, we're looking at one, and it's active."

***

"General Tott," Captain Rinquist started with a grim look, "I have been informed the upper levels are secure. Also, twelve civilians were being held that we have taken into custody. As requested, our people are holding position at the top of the facility which includes the section containing the Gate."

Tott looked at the man, taking in the expression he saw. "Well, that is great news! But why don't you look happier about it?"

"Sir, there is an explosive device that has been activated. It is time-delayed, but it will take out the building and much of the surrounding area. Hell, it could damage the shield protecting this city, being at the height it is at near the top floor."

Tott was taken back by that statement as the stakes for this conflict just went up significantly. Millions of civilians were at risk.

"Is there any way to stop it?" the general asked.

"Yeah," the captain said. "I've got an explosives expert on my squad. The problem is, he is here and not there. We need to get him up there where the bomb is."

'With only a couple of hundred guerilla soldiers between us and the device," the general said, sounding very old now. He looked at the tall soldier, considering what was to happen next. "Time is against us. We need to move now. Let's set the clock for fifteen ticks. Then we go in."

"Sir? Okay, sorry, translation error. That is five-point-three minutes for us, setting now and informing my teams."

The five-point-three minutes went by too fast.

Three entrances along the front blew at the same time. Long Hair troops began storming the entrance. The first two dozen to rush the building were quickly mowed down by heavy weapons fire even as more prepared to follow in their footsteps.

Watching from a distance, there was a time when Captain Rinquist would have wanted to be part of the action, even first to rush in. But that adventure seeking spirit had died long ago along with almost everyone he ever knew.

General Tott had people to throw at this problem, the captain did not and needed to stay with his queen. He and his squad were now and for always her last line of defense. *Blood sworn* to her. He would never trust her safety to these people, nor any other people. His loyalty to her was absolute. His love for her...

That can never be, his jaw tightened.

Rockets flared, followed by great blasts coming from the lower level of the facility.

More troops rushing in.

More explosions.

More dying.

He looked to his right at the queen, his queen. Her attention was on the battle at hand. He knew how much she was trying to keep it together, for him, for all of them. After serving her for *four hundred and forty-three years,* he knew her all too well. Every inflection of her voice. Every twitch on her face. Every move of her hands. Her left pinky finger was tapping.

She's scared. Not of immediate danger, but if we will get back to our ship. She's trying so hard.

The last of their people, and here they were in yet another war zone.

The sounds of battle intensified.

More bloodshed, more troops rushing in.

Then silence.

General Tott was talking on his communicator, turned to them. "It's over. You can send your man in now."

***

"Phlike, what's your first name."

"Phlike."

"Okay, what's your last name," Helen asked, a bit annoyed.

"Phlike."

"So, Phlike Phlike?" she asked, cocking her head a bit.

The man laughed.

"No. Some of us have one name, some of us have many names."

"Okay, that makes no sense to the little woman here."

678

They were enjoying a meal together in celebration of ending the conflict. A conflict that had been kicked off by their arrival at this rogue planet.

"So, you think we can live on the surface even though our planet does not orbit a star?" Baya asked.

"Yes, billions of people do just that. Well, usually there's a star, but not always. A dome can simulate natural daylight, even natural surroundings."

"I know many of our people will want to remain in the cities they've always known, the cities of our ancestors," General Tott added. "But that does sound nice."

"Per our agreement, we are going to fix your systems, environmental or otherwise, so you can safely live underground while we can settle topside. Honestly, we'd fix it without an agreement, but now that the ink is dry I might as well tell you that."

"We look forward to working together," Phlike said. "Concerning the domes, do you have a way of acquiring them? Or will these need to be constructed here?"

"In time, they could be built. But my sister can get them to us much quicker."

Sister was a loose word. The leader of the Askirti Federation, Jacqueline Campo, was their primary benefactor and doppelganger. The latter was a mystery neither of them understood. But it was Jacqueline who found Helen and her group in stasis on their desolate wreck of a ship between systems. It was her who gave them everything they have now to start a new life.

Crap, now I have to call that woman.

Jacqueline creeped her out. Merciful was not a word that could be used to describe her, though she seemed to have a soft spot for Helen and her people.

After the evening was over, Helen and her soldiers went back through the Gate, to their shuttle, and back to their ship in orbit. Getting back to her quarters, she fell into a much-needed sleep, if not a restless one.

***

The klaxons were still blaring.

The emergency lighting was on but dimmed momentarily as more nukes went off against the hull of the ship.

"Status report!"

"Shields are down! Propulsion is down! Primary, secondary and tertiary defense suites are offline! Intruders now reported in twenty-three sections!"

Various screens showed the lethal androids plowing down her crew. They came by the thousands. Fire teams were sent to deal with the intruders. Some were successful. Most were not.

As desperate as the situation was, that was not a reason to leave her post. Crippled or not, pain or no pain, if any of them were going to survive the day, they needed their queen. Her people were dying by the thousands, and she would be damned if today they would not have their queen.

Suddenly, a multi-gigaton explosion went off, shattering major sections of the thirty-three-kilometer long dreadnought *Freedom*.

The explosion shook the reinforced walls of the flag bridge like they were made of paper. Sections of it collapsed, killing most. The rest were thrown about the room.

After a few minutes of laying on the ground, Helen was able to pull herself up to her chair. Appraising the situation, and how staggeringly bad the battle had gone, she knew she had but one call to make. Her ship was a dead stick, but perhaps others could still be saved.

"Send a message at once!" she yelled. "Any remaining ships! Retreat! I repeat! Retreat! Rendezvous point Charlie-Two-Two!"

The communications officer was bleeding from his shoulder, a severe gash, he just sat there in shock.

"Lieutenant Dales! What are you doing?! Send the message! Now!"

"I-I'm sorry, ma'am! Sending now!" he responded.

Just after the message was sent, a secondary explosion rocked the flag bridge, sending debris flying across the space. A large piece of shrapnel struck the lieutenant, impaling him in the neck as he locked eyes with Helen. Such a helpless expression crossed his face as his life gushed out of his wounds.

She had borne witness to so much death, but it was those eyes, those dead eyes, that haunted her so.

***

Helen woke with a start. Suddenly the door to her cabin flew open and in walked Captain Rinquist.

"My queen," he said in a low voice. "I heard noises. I came to check to see if you were alright."

"I will be," she said, calming down.

He came over and sat on her bed, took her hand in his. Her hand was trembling, though she never had and never would let on that her dreams were so disturbing.

"It's going to be alright, *Homem High Queen,*" he said, in the most reassuring voice he could muster while stroking the side of her face with his other hand.

He knew he just crossed a line, one he had never passed in over four hundred years of service to this woman. But the look on her face said it all. She needed reassurance more than any of them. The load on her shoulders just got a little bit lighter.

"Paul," she called him by his first name, "the last time you said those word to me I *knew* all was lost."

"I know. I saw it in your eyes."

"But you were right." After a pregnant pause, she said, "I'm exhausted, and need to go back to sleep."

As he started to get up, she squeezed his hand, causing him to settle back down.

Holding his gaze, she spoke softly to him. "You've been loyal to me to the end and beyond. Perhaps, once we get settled into our new home, we need new rules."

"I would like that," he answered with a smile.

Then as suddenly as he came in, he left.

Helen lay there thinking about the future her people would embrace here on the planet Wendrim. The Fire Walkers were still out there, still a threat. But this world represented the best hope for her people, the last of the Homem, the humans that once ruled a galaxy.

I don't want a galaxy, let someone else worry about that. I just want a home.

Author Danny Brown

Danny Brown is an independent author who is also a computer programmer. Or is it programmer who is also an author? He lives in Florida with his wife, three daughters, and two dogs. When he is not programming or writing he is reading science fiction, his favorite genre!

Danny is the author of the new science fiction series The Askirti Chronicles, of which this short story and its characters are based. The Askirti Chronicles is now available on Amazon in e-book and print formats.

See more at www.dannyabrown.com where you can find all of his latest news and information or signup for his newsletter.

 LZ NEW BIRTH

By J. R. Handley

No one's ever found glory hiding in a bunker.

15 February 4808, Dagdan Federation Calendar
LZ New Birth, Planet Gakawen, New Carthage Republic Territories
4th PLT, Delta Co., 249th Legion, NCR

Second Lieutenant Xavier Timor was thrilled with his new command, but his platoon of battle hardened legionnaires wasn't. They didn't trust someone so green, and the officer he'd replaced had been well loved and respected. On this drop, Xavier would ride down with his 1st Squad while his small platoon staff would be spread out among the other squads on the various orbital dropships. Standard protocol required they split the staff to protect the integrity of the command element. Losing the entire staff to enemy cannon fire would severely hamper command and control in the critical early stages of the battle.

He wasn't happy to start his first combat engagement this way, but the New Carthage Legionnaires couldn't just fly in, not when the enemy had seeded the planet with defensive cannons. They had to seize a drop zone first. No, this would be an orbital drop operation. Xavier would be leading 4th Platoon, Delta Company of the 249th Legion into the teeth of the enemy's guns. By rights, he should still be a senior in the Dagdan Federation Officers Academy on New Carthage, but the Legion had been hit hard in the opening days of the war. In the end, the 249th Legion required warm bodies more than they needed cadets playing soldier. The Republic was desperate for junior officers, so they'd graduated his senior classes early. None of the 112 enlisted personnel were happy that these raw junior officers had been placed in command of the Legionnaires' platoons.

The junior enlisted personnel on Dropship 1-4-Delta were especially unhappy. Their ship had a standard configuration which offered few amenities. Making room for their LT only made the situation worse. The tight seats and unforgiving straps meant the troops would have to hold their carbines between their legs. The squad grumbled as Xavier approached, seeming to forget that he had access to their comms channel.

The gray orbital dropship that would serve as Xavier's ride sat securely in its berth, waiting for the signal that would drop it onto Gakawen. Twenty-seven legionnaires packed themselves like sardines into its hold, leaving one extra seat for the platoon commander. They'd made a point of making sure that that seat was near the door, potentially exposing him to incoming fire on a contested landing. Xavier was waiting to board the dropship and close the door, telling himself that it would be good to let his troops get fresh air. They continued to have access to the NCRS Hannibal's climate control systems until the door sealed. Like every troop transport he'd studied, this one tried to keep the troops comfortable until they were needed to attack contested planets.

Pacing up and down the passageway outside his dropship, Xavier rechecked his watch. They'd be getting the go signal at any moment. He quickly checked his equipment and rank insignia before rejoining his command. As Xavier moved, the red five-minute warning light strobed through the passageway. He turned his stride into a jog, afraid he'd miss his first combat mission. His training at the Academy on New Carthage had been thorough, and he knew that this particular error would be a black mark on his entire career. Besides, he couldn't let himself become the LT people mocked.

Not wanting to look like some bumbling plebe, Xavier stiffened his spine and slowed his jog. He knew optics mattered, and he began to march onto the dropship. He made it with seconds to spare before the ramp closed and sealed him in with his men. Looking around, he found twenty-seven pairs of skeptical eyes staring at him.

"Listen up. You don't need me to tell you how important this mission is. If we don't secure the landing zone and create a foothold, we can't take this planet. We need to take out the Loyalist's guns before the rest of the Legion can land, and we expect a stiff resistance. When the ramp drops, follow me. We secure the landing zone, then the city. Trust your fellow legionnaires and Gakawen will soon be under the banner of the New Carthage Republic. For Carthage!"

The hold was silent. Xavier busied himself with strapping in and turning off his helmet's speakers. Shifting in his seat, uncomfortable in the oppressive silence, Xavier tried to appear unfazed. Instead, he focused on the hodgepodge of armor his unit was wearing. It looked like it had been borrowed from a museum, from the time of the Corsair Rebellion. Maybe even older than that. The legionnaires of Delta Company weren't wearing void capable combat armor on this drop; there wasn't enough of it to go around. The Republic was too new to outfit everyone in the vacuum sealed suits; they only had what they'd liberated them from the Dagdan Federation. If his ship experienced catastrophic failure outside of the atmosphere, they'd all die.

He didn't know what he expected, but the ride down jarred every bone in his body. Even strapped in, he was thrown about as the ship broke orbit, while the pilot simultaneously jinked left and right to avoid being hit by enemy defensive cannons. Waves of nausea overwhelmed his senses, sending chills in icy rivulets down to his toes. Desperately trying to maintain his dignity, Xavier took slow, deep breaths. It didn't help. He'd almost armed the illumination grenade that was attached to the front of his armor, as he struggled to open the visor of his helmet—anxious to prevent filling his armor with vomit. He missed puking into his helmet by second.

BLARGH.

With his visor open, this time he heard the legionnaires of 1st Squad openly laughing at him. Despite his best efforts, Xavier couldn't keep his lunch in his stomach.

BLARGH.

"Happens to all of us, sir. At least to the old biddies in the Ladies Auxiliary, anyway!" chirped Legionnaire First Class Terrye Toombs.

"Now see here—" Xavier started to say before he bent forward to hack up the last of his meal. As the hold erupted into laughter again, Xavier wiped his mouth and replaced his helmet.

"Least we don't have to clean that up," he said, adjusting his chin strap. "Leave that to the dang sailors!"

The moment of levity was cut short by the pilot coming over the internal speakers.

"Two minutes to dirtside," the voice intoned.

The pilot lied. A few seconds later, the craft thudded to the ground and the ramp dropped. Xavier stumbled out to the open area around Ancion City. Scanning the sector, he saw that there was no enemy. None that he could see anyway. Consummate professionals, 1st Squad secured their section of the perimeter and linked up with the rest of the platoon. Meanwhile, Xavier ran over to his comms specialist and started setting up communications with the remainder of the company. They'd been given 500 legionnaires to capture the city, but if the Loyalists resisted, it'd get ugly. Urban warfare was always a bloody and costly affair.

Much to Xavier's surprise, the initial landing occurred without contest. He hadn't expected the drop shuttles to claim Ancion City as their own so quickly.

"I can't believe the cowards ran," he said aloud. "They didn't even try to fight."

"They didn't run. They went to defend the guns, sir," said Master Sergeant Zale Boswell.

As the platoon sergeant spoke, the newly designed flag of the New Carthage Republic was raised in Ancion City. It fluttered in the breeze atop the abandoned civic building, defiant and proud. The blood-red boar's head under a golden crescent moon sat on a midnight black banner, a nod to the original colonists' ties to old Terra. So many colony ships had landed since then that the link existed only in the historical record, and in the banner of the new nation.

***

In the two months after they'd secured the city, the legionnaires repurposed buildings as command centers and logistical warehouses. Ancion City endured a militaristic metamorphosis. Xavier imagined the consequences on the town's psyche would outlive him. Once a bustling colony town, the eight weeks of military occupation turned the city into a fortress. The daily grind of life during the conversion of the city into a fortified and reinforced base allowed Loyalist sympathizers to slip outside the city walls. The legionnaires fought against a steady stream of sabotage and insurgent tactics, forcing the garrison commander to become stricter with the locals. The city was locked down, fostering animosity and more acts of sabotage. The officers were worried. Clearly, anyone who could get out of the city could slip back in.

The heightened and overzealous security consciousness led to steps that made the newly designated Fortress Ancion impregnable. Work crews dug defensive trenches outside the newly erected fortress walls, preventing the enemy from slipping into their lines. Essential supplies were stored in central locations, under heavy guard. Legionnaires built barracks from converted colony dorms, and the local bank was transformed into a brig. Every mode of transportation was seized by the military, cementing the transition of LZ New Birth into a fortress in fact and name.

Xavier's skills grew during the construction period, under the watchful eye of his platoon sergeant. He'd been able to shine with Master Sergeant Boswell's advice and Xavier's willingness to listen. His 4th Platoon set standards; their productivity pushed the rest of Delta Company to secure the city. He led from the front, and his once pristine uniform grew as dirty and torn as the rest of his legionnaires. *My instructors at the Academy would've reamed my ass for this*, he thought.

Once the fortress walls were finished, Delta Company was moved into the exterior trenches. The entire time they worked, they endured the fire of the enemy guns. The Loyalist defended their orbital bombardment cannon with secondary ones designed to keep an enemy from getting too close. Despite the shelling, New Carthage legionnaires pushed out from their fortress. Fortress Ancion stood as a bastion to the legitimacy of the New Carthage Republic. They couldn't abandon the town; it had to be held at all cost. Meanwhile, they had to silence those guns so the fleet could land the rest of their forces. It was a delicate balancing act, one that strained the capabilities of the understaffed battalion that had landed on Gakawen.

During the process of extending the reach of the NCR, Delta Company was ordered to begin reinforcing and extending the trenches. They built them up during their guard shifts while expanding them out meter by meter. A combination of sandbags and fastkrete transformed the earthen trenches into permanent defensive works. They were sending a message: New Carthage was here to stay.

Xavier squatted in one of the trenches that surrounded the fortress, hunkering down while the shelling continued. The dreary weather made the experience miserable. Rain rushed down the mountains and into the valley, deluging the trenches and clawing the earthen parapets into mud. The rain prevented the fastkrete from fully curing, so they had to rely more heavily on their sandbags. Junior legionnaires were tasked with continually digging out the muck washed down by the rain. The rain did manage to silence the guns, though the foul weather made it difficult to exploit that small victory.

"My Academy instructors forgot to tell us how miserable trenches were in this weather," he told Boswell, who only grunted in reply.

The guns had been silent for so long that Xavier and the rest of the company's officers thought they'd been abandoned. Or maybe they only hoped that that was the case. Xavier and his platoon sergeant trooped the lines, inspecting the reinforcement and expansion project. When the guns started firing again, the legionnaires in the trenches began to hunker down, seeking cover. Forward progress halted, and all efforts were put to repairing sections as they become damaged.

"We *have* to finish these trenches, or they could envelop us," he told Boswell.

The NCO grunted again before taking a drag from the cigar that bravely hung from his lip. Like the rest of the junior officers, at least those who were fresh out of the Academy, Xavier had been rushed to the fleet. He was supposed to bolster the forces preparing to seize Gakawen. His non-comms treated him like a kid, but he wasn't confident enough to address the situation and took the abuse. And the more he took, the more abuse his legionnaires dished out.

"Time to grow a spine," growled Boswell, pausing before adding the obligatory, "sir."

When the legionnaires around him hooted and hollered, Xavier finally took a deep breath and began envisioning the plebes he loved to torment. *I can do this*, he told himself repeatedly.

"Agreed. I was just taught to respect the old and infirm," he replied, louder than was called for.

"He told you, Sarge," chortled one of the platoon's chronic misfit legionnaires.

"Thanks for volunteering, Hayes. You get to clean the shitter," replied Boswell.

Laughing to himself, Xavier suddenly felt more comfortable with his platoon. *I* can *do this*, he thought. With renewed confidence, Xavier began quietly listening to the mutterings of the NCOs he'd thought were beneath him. It shocked him to hear what they really thought, without the filter they usually used when addressing officers. They felt that the abundance of raw junior officers in command positions meant that critical tactical considerations were being missed. Xavier knew that he and the other young officers lacked the usual field training given to officers. He was also learning that his Academy classroom instruction didn't match the real world. The textbook wasn't providing answers for every situation as he'd been taught, so he began to treat its "rules" like strongly worded suggestions.

No stranger to discomfort, Xavier decided to wait out the weather. It was harder to ignore the renewed shelling, but he didn't know what else to do shivered despite his best efforts. The cool pre-dawn darkness seemed to soak into his bones and sapped his energy. He disregarded the relentless drumbeat of the pounding rain, hoping that the shelling would end soon. But it continued. The flash of the enemy guns pierced the darkness, making it difficult for him to maintain his night vision. The body armor his unit wore was out of date. It offered little to enhance the combat effectiveness of his soldiers, as it had no integrated HUD or enhanced optics. At moments like this, those deficiencies showed. His legionnaires couldn't see the hills like he could in his cadet armor.

While Xavier waited for a break in the weather, he continued to troop the line. He'd occasionally stop to speak to his soldiers, hoping to offer some encouragement. He worked every trick for encouraging his troops that he could remember from his time at the Academy.

The minutes turned into hours, and the sun rose. The shelling continued unabated and the legionnaire's field guns didn't have the reach to respond. *We've got to break this gridlock, or the assault on Gakawen is lost*, he thought. Xavier began looking for a way to change the momentum. *Someone's got to do something—might as well be me*, he told himself. He was bored, and sitting around in Fortress Ancion wouldn't fulfill the glorious destiny he dreamed of while a cadet. He couldn't gain fame through inaction and serving in an army of occupation.

Typically the Navy would've blasted the offending forces from orbit, but the Dagdan forces were hiding among the populace, and the New Carthage Republic needed the planet intact. While this was a tactical consideration for the Legion, it wasn't one for Xavier. He would find a way to assault the objective, civilians be damned. All he needed was a way to cover his ass as he did so. And the objective was simple—just silence those infernal guns. They'd been wreaking havoc, sighting in with uncanny precision on the Carthaginian barracks. Whole squads had been lost in an instant while they slumbered. Xavier couldn't let those bastards get away with killing his mates.

He had to turn back the relentless tide of Dagdan shells. New Carthage needed a breakout, the enemy guns were slowly bracketing their buildings. Under those guns, Xavier made his decision. After a quick peek over the hastily created fastkrete parapets, he saw a thin corridor of opportunity. All he had to do was move his troops up the valley, what could be simpler? A hooking maneuver, flanking the enemy guns while taking fire. Luckily, the various Loyalist gun batteries had failed to correctly overlap their fields of fire. Xavier suspected it was because of the changes the Carthaginians had made to the terrain when they converted the city into a fortress. *All of this rain washing out the valley hasn't helped either*, Xavier thought. And that presented him an opportunity, the enemy had left open a narrow strip of land. It was just asking to be exploited.

While Xavier evaluated his options, he took a moment to scan the region where Delta Company had established its outer perimeter. They were on the outskirts of Ancion City, attempting to expand their hold on their region. He knew that if they couldn't hold the city, and take out the orbital defense guns, they'd lose the planet. They would have to do this while under fire. *Our leaders seem content to wait for them to go away while we're holed up in this crappy trench. And then they want us to hide in bunkers while those rats shell us to oblivion*, he thought angrily.

He knew that the Dagdan militia had abandoned the city to defend the guns. Like most newly colonized planets, Ancion was surrounded by barren stretches of land nestled in a valley between two mountain ridges. The terrain was soggy from the days of torrential downpour puddling in the valley. The resulting mud slurry would make getting through the muck to break out of Ancion difficult, which Xavier hoped would make the local Dagdan troops lazy. His forces would have to assault the Dagdans across an area devoid of vegetation and trees. It'd been stripped away to make room for houses and converted into firewood. The open space offered a little protection against native predators, and that included Xavier's legionnaires. But this also made it easier for the Dagdan Loyalists to aim at his forces, who were stuck trying to hold the newly crowned fortress. The Dagdan gunners would be able to see Delta Company approaching well in advance of their arrival.

Xavier briefly thought about pushing the enemy's error up the chain of command, but his company commander was barely a proper officer. Captain Arianna Hunt had come up through the ranks, and never attended the officers' academy. She'd gone to a civilian college after the Dagdan Legion had decided to promote her from within the ranks.

What would a female sergeant know about tactics? mused Xavier.

It was unlikely that his commander would even know what to do with the information at hand. No, he'd have to make the decision. He would take his platoon through the hole in the line. If he could just get a few sappers through, they could shut off the Dagdan guns and break the blockade. It'd turn the tide, securing New Carthage's foothold on the planet, letting the legionnaires pour troops onto the planet.

Scanning the area around him, Xavier marveled at the brilliant orange hues in the distance. The enemy guns lit up the wooded beauty that was Gakawen. *Definitely a planet worth fighting for*, he thought. The smell of the fresh soil teased his senses, though it was mostly drowned out by the acrid scent of gun smoke that rolled down on them like fog. *Even after thousands of years, they can't make odorless propellant for the big guns.* He was shaken out of his reverie by his senior NCO, who crouched as he hurried to where Xavier squatted in the trenches.

Once Boswell was beside him, Xavier solidified his strategy. He assumed that the Dagdans would expect the Legion to use noisy vehicles. The rain and constant shelling made the ground damn near impassible, at least on the surface, and he thought that their night watch might be minimal. After he sent out a few scouts, he was even more convinced. They'd gotten close enough to the enemy lines to send back intelligence reports. The enemy appeared to think they were safe and didn't even have pickets out.

Having made his decision, Xavier scrambled over and knelt by his senior NCO.

"Master Sergeant, I found a gap in the Dagdan firing pattern. Command says they're not properly overlapping their fire, and there is a narrow gap in the fields. If we make it through the muck in the valley before sunrise, sappers can take out their guns. We can roll up the enemy, and then reinforcements can make it down from orbit. We'll win a huge victory! We've been ordered to lead the charge, but we need to prepare the troops quickly and quietly. Radio silence—platoon net, and only in an extreme emergency."

"Bullshit. If the brass ordered this, the company commander would be briefing us both. Your plan is sound—but you really should run it up the flagpole," replied Boswell.

"Let me worry about that. Follow your orders."

With a curt nod, Xavier moved on to his squad leaders with the same orders. While his platoon prepared for the assault, Xavier went to the armory and grabbed extra ammunition and grenades. Seeing a box of illumination rounds, he grabbed those too and went in search of the 3rd Platoon Leader. Lieutenant Evan Pitera was his roommate from plebe year, and Xavier knew that he knew was sick of the drudgery. Xavier gambled that he'd jump at the chance for glory, and the two platoons would give his plan a chance of securing the breakthrough. Knowing they had to leave before word spread and his fictitious orders became an issue, Xavier set out to expedite the process.

"Let's get them moving," he hissed to his troops.

Crouched over, Xavier continued up the trench line, tapping the helmets of his men as he passed them. The signal told them to follow him to the rally point at their unfinished trench, where 4th Platoon had tried to extend their defenses earlier in the day. He was having none of it. *You can't win wars hiding behind your defensive positions! They teach you that in Tactics 101 at the Academy*, he thought disgustedly.

When everyone was in place, Xavier gave the word. Seconds later he scrambled over the muddy parapet, carbine in his hands. After a silent prayer, he started a slow jog into the open expanse of "no man's land." The tramp of hundreds of combat boots being sucked into the mud behind him assured him that his men followed him. He wasn't alone, and it gave him the courage to push onward. The splashing of his boots slopping in and out of the muck nullified all attempts at stealth. He tried to slow down enough to choose his steps carefully, keeping some semblance of noise discipline, but it was impossible.

On and on he ran, fervently praying that the sound of the shelling and the rain kept their assault a surprise. He pushed on despite his exhaustion. His muscles screamed against the extreme exertion, and he vowed to get into better shape. Life onboard the *NCRS Hannibal* had made him soft. Despite the fatigue, the troops of 3rd and 4th Platoons slogged forward. They were moving closer to the forest at the edge of the valley, and their ultimate victory.

The constant flashes of light from the muzzles of the enemy guns were Xavier's only source of visibility. The gloom and fog of the Gakawen monsoon season isolated each legionnaire, each warrior fighting the urge to turn around towards safety. *What I wouldn't give for some sunlight*, he thought to himself. The constant flares of light destroyed any hope that his eyes would adjust to the darkness. He was just grateful that he hadn't fallen when the inevitable happened.

Splat.

Xavier suddenly found himself face first in a muddy puddle, choking, gasping for air. *Damn roots*, he thought, though he was unsure what he'd tripped over. He couldn't stop coughing, his body fighting to get the water out of his lungs. Standing wasn't an option yet, but Xavier was yanked upright by one of his soldiers.

"This ain't how we earn those medals and promotions," Boswell told him, tauntingly, before adding the final ". . . sir."

Looking around during the brilliant flashes of light from the guns, Xavier saw that he was surrounded by trees. He'd made it through the valley and into the woods. They were in the clear! Now they had to go up the hills to envelop the enemy. With the first obstacle clear, he raised his arm and used the signal to call the senior NCOs to him.

"All right, listen up," Xavier whispered to the assembled personnel. "We're sitting in the woods at the end of the valley. I want 4th Platoon to climb the hills to the south and then break to the left. We push into their flanks, charging straight towards the enemy guns. Once we're into their trenches, it'll be child's play. We roll into them, hard and fast. Chaos and confusion are our allies."

Pausing, he scanned the dimly lit faces of his senior staff, all of them more experienced than he was.

"At some point, they're going to notice we're there. I want 3rd Platoon to use that opportunity to hit the guns in the mountains to the north. Climb the mountains, but stay out of sight. Hit the Dagdan's when they shift their fire from the fortress, toward the guns we'll be capturing. The running password is Hannibal. Any questions?"

Without pausing for an answer, Xavier responded to his own question.

"Didn't think so. We move in five minutes."

While waiting, Xavier cleaned the mud out of his carbine. It was difficult to do in the gray and gloomy darkness of the forest, but he was able to clean it enough that the weapon passed a quick functions check. Satisfied, he began walking among his troops. He didn't say a word but occasionally stopped to pat a shoulder or squeeze an arm. He wanted his soldiers to know he was there with them.

Finishing his rounds, Xavier began looking for the master sergeant. He wasn't hard to find; Boswell was one of the few soldiers standing upright while everyone else crouched down. Xavier understood the instinct to find whatever cover they could, but he stifled his fear. He had to be the strong leader these soldiers deserved. He had learned at the Academy that troops didn't follow timid leaders. So, he walked erect among them, fighting his fear and respect. Shaking off the part of his brain that wanted to analyze everything, he tapped his senior NCO on the shoulder to get his attention.

"Sergeant, if I start fucking this up when we get in—"

Master Sergeant Boswell cut him off. "Sir, stow that weak shit. We ride in, kill some Loyalists, and stroll out. Into the promised land, too easy! You're not the first cherry LT I've taken into combat. Relax. Pretend this is one of your parade ground Academy parties."

Grunting, Xavier shifted his carbine to his left hand and used his right to signal the advance. He smoothly slipped the weapon back into a two-handed position as he advanced up the hill. Around him, the platoon took up a modified tactical wedge formation. He knew it was a wasted effort; they could barely see the ground beneath them in the dark. The extreme low visibility would hamper the usefulness of the formation, but he moved relentlessly upward to the top of the hill. Now wasn't the time to overthink it; they needed to keep moving. He counted himself lucky to have made it to the top of the hill without face-planting again.

When they entered the ridgeline, Xavier sent out scouts to find the entrance to the enemy trenches. He knew they had to be there and was surprised when they didn't see it. *The Dagdan gunners must not have bothered to dig in their guns—pure laziness*, he thought in disgust. Not wanting to let that slow him down, he used hand signals to order his troops to spread out. Radio silence was making the endeavor more difficult, but he knew their assault would be dead in the water if company command found out. No, they needed to push on toward the enemy guns. The noise and brilliant flashes of light were all they'd have to lead them.

ZING.

The crack of the projectiles told him the element of surprise was gone. Xavier flicked on his comms and screamed at his legionnaires.

"Comms on," he bellowed.

Xavier knew that his cry would be carried down the line until all the NCOs turned on their helmet mics. Lungs burning, he tried to hide his panting, but nobody was fooled. He managed to keep up with his troops, and for that, he thanked the gods. The firing intensified, his soldiers dropped around him. He didn't know whether they were wounded or dead, but they couldn't stop. Onward he ran.

"Don't slow down. No mercy! Suppressive fire," he screamed.

Once his training kicked in, Xavier began acting without thinking while his platoon opened fire. The noise created a strange concussive symphony, mesmerizing him. *The sim rounds didn't sound like this*, he thought. Yet again, he wished he'd been able to complete all his training. Live fire exercises certainly would've been beneficial.

On through the muck he ran, on toward the scattering flashes of gunfire. His vision tunneled, and he focused on what was directly in front of him. There wasn't anything else, just his carbine and the enemy. He knew he shouldn't allow himself to be sucked in like this; he needed to maintain command and control of the entire playing field. He just couldn't stop himself. His world zeroed into what was directly in front of him.

His sole focus was on his field of fire; he only worried about avoiding flagging his platoon. He missed the soldier falling in front of him. She'd been racing ahead in front of him. She was there one second, gone the next. His foot caught on her leg, and Xavier was airborne. Tumbling to the ground, he felt a moment of panic. *Was I hit?* he wondered. He couldn't breathe, the impact of the fall knocking the air from his lungs. He choked, his lungs desperately sucking air through the gritty mire of the Gakawen soil. Panting, he pushed himself up.

Taking advantage of the dim light from the Dagdan guns, Xavier assessed the situation. The flames illuminated his surroundings in a ghostly grey haze, and what he saw looked like a nightmare. He'd tripped over Legionnaire Toombs, she'd been hit and was desperately struggling to shove her guts into her stomach. Her intestines were steaming in the dawn air. Xavier felt sick. But he managed to keep his stomach down as he crawled over to her. While trying to avoid causing her more pain, he forgot to keep his carbine out of the muck. The barrel jammed with mud. Cursing, Xavier knelt beside her as he tried cleaning his carbine. Trying to distract her, he searched for a comforting lie to make her feel better.

"Well, that didn't go as planned," she wheezed, frothy blood bubbling from her lips.

"Hang in there. Once we've secured the hill, we'll medevac you. You'll be fine, living the good life on the *Hannibal*."

Patting her shoulder, Xavier stood up and tried again to wipe the mud from his carbine. He had to know it would fire when he needed it, so he aimed at the enemy guns across the valley and fired. Nothing happened. Swearing in frustration, he slung his carbine over his shoulder. He didn't have time to waste correcting the malfunction.

"Sir, take my carbine," Toombs said.

She continued to cough weakly, her eyes acknowledging what he had been afraid to say. Tears trickled from his eyes, as he dropped to a knee and took the carbine from her. He checked that it worked and swapped out the magazine with a full one. With one final nod at Legionnaire Toombs, Xavier sprinted ahead to catch up with his platoon. He joined them as they reached the first enemy gun battery. The firing had stopped, and he struggled to see without the light from the gun's back blast. His fall had destroyed his night vision in his helmet. All he saw was perfect darkness, but the roaring continued unabated.

Soldiers from both sides spent entire magazines firing at each other. The intensity gradually slowed as the two forces got closer to each other. Then the carbine ceased firing entirely, but the guttural screams intensified. It'd become an age-old battle of bayonets, buttstocks, and the sheer will to live. Thrust. Parry. Rinse and repeat.

Xavier knew he wouldn't last against experienced combat troops, not in hand-to-hand combat. Instead, he stopped his forward momentum and took up a firing stance just behind his troops. He slipped an illumination grenade into the launcher under his carbine and fired into the air. Without waiting, he brought his weapon up and waited. He began targeting anyone, not in the uniform of the New Carthage Legion the moment he could see. He had to use his only soldierly virtue, marksmanship. It was the one part of his training that hadn't been cut prematurely, and Xavier had an uncanny knack for it.

With the aid of his carbine and the handful grenades he'd grabbed, Xavier fought to blunt the Dagdan counterattack. Under his helmet, his eyes burned from the smoke, and he struggled to see. He couldn't afford for any of the illumination rounds to be wasted. He took aim and fired. The enemy soldier went down. One simple shot and Xavier had viewed his first kill. Seconds later, he killed again. Then again. Eleven enemies lay dead as he led his troops forward.

The first enemy gun emplacement was theirs. He didn't let them stop; they pushed onward. The last guns were on the next ridgeline, and he didn't want them to have time to prepare. His platoon had killed every Loyalist who hadn't run, though some of the enemy had fled like a bunch of cowards. They stripped the Dagdan dead of all the gear they could repurpose, and then he pulled Boswell aside.

"Master Sergeant, I want this gun operational. Get it firing on our next objective in advance of our assault. Leave an additional fire team to protect the new cannoneers, and an NCO to supervise. We need to keep up the advance."

"Roger, sir. I've already put Sergeant Mercer on it. He's the new 2nd Squad Leader, transferred from an artillery militia unit. They're loading—"

BOOM.

"—now," the NCO finished. "Give the word, and we're ready to march."

"Let's go!" Xavier barked over the platoon's radio channel.

The enemy knew they were coming now, but that meant that his company commander would know something was up as well. He knew that he needed to take full advantage of the fact that operational security was blown. He got on the radio and ordered the platoon to move out in a tactical formation. He'd delegated the decision on the exact formation to Boswell, pretending to need to answer the company net that he'd been ignoring.

The troops spread out, and Xavier fell into his place in the formation. In the distance, the sun rose lazily in the west, giving 4th Platoon an advantage as they attacked the Loyalists with the sun at their backs. This allowed them to be more precise and silence the first gun. The tide was turning in their favor—he could feel it. All he had to do was buy himself enough time to prevent his commander from mucking things up. He couldn't have his men called back while he was leading a successful assault.

"Stay frosty, chuckleheads," Xavier said into the open platoon network, "and don't get cocky. This isn't over yet."

Ping.

"Sir, you should take the call. Say you seized the initiative—whatever it takes. Work out something with the Brass. Let them claim this victory or your career is done," Boswell urged him over the platoon's secure command channel.

Xavier gave a click over the comms to acknowledge the recommendation. His gamble had run its course, and it was time to take the call. He switched over to Delta Company's command network.

"Second Lieutenant Xavier Timor here—"

"Radio discipline, damn it!" roared Captain Hunt over the open command network.

"Thunder 6, this is Thunder Red 6. Prepare for SitRep, break."

Xavier took a deep breath, preparing to give the most accurate report he could. He didn't want to stir up any more of a shit storm than he was already in.

"Noticed break in enemy fire patterns, left open corridor down the valley. Led Thunder Red and White platoons down open corridor. Thunder Red broke south and are actively seizing the second gunline. When northern guns focus fire on Thunder Red elements, Thunder White will assault the second gunline. Thunder Red Actual ordered radio silence since we still use Loyalist comms gear. Will update as situation permits, break."

Pausing again, Xavier prepared for his brazen request.

"Request Thunder Green assault southern ridge when the guns go silent. Further, jam or flood the comms upon receipt of this transmission. Chaos is our friend, how copy?"

The radio silence felt like it lasted forever.

"Good copy. Will assault at first opportunity. Thunder 6, out."

His commander bit out each word. The undercurrent in her abrupt message was clear, and Xavier knew it wouldn't end well for him. *It's worth it if I ended the stalemate*, he thought. Resigned to accept the fallout from his decision, he disconnected his communication device and handed it to the radio operator. Switching to his local comms, he heard his NCOs ordering the platoon to move out. Not wanting to be caught with a defective carbine, he performed another quick function's check and verified that his magazine was fresh. Assured that his gear was sound, he fell into the platoon formation.

The trek across the hilly terrain was brutal. Time was of the essence, and the NCOs pushed the legionnaires in 4th Platoon hard. Under Xavier's watchful eye, they made good time. It was crucial to hit while the sun was still at their backs. It'd give them an advantage, one he hoped to utilize with brutally lethal efficiency. They were successful, having taken the initial part of the journey at a quick loping pace. Xavier let his mind wander, analyzing the situation and war gaming it in his head. He was lulled by the concussions of the enemy guns firing.

Jerked out of his musings by the sound of silence, Xavier came to a stop. The Dagdan guns were still, and then 4th Platoon began taking fire. The Loyalist troops had abandoned their guns and grabbed their carbines. Xavier noticed that the enemy hadn't bothered to dig defensive trenches here either. The Dagdans stood tall, firing at his platoon—likely to miss as they essentially fired blind.

I'll have to say I factored that bit of dumb luck into my plans when I stand before the Brass, he chuckled to himself as he ordered his platoon to halt.

"Halt," he roared over the platoon net, while simultaneously using the hand signal.

The troops of 4th Platoon spread the order up and down the line while his seasoned NCOs took charge. They began ordering the legionnaires to fire into the enemy, taking maximum advantage of their tactically superior positioning. They drastically thinned the Loyalist numbers. Soon more Loyalists peeled off, heading away from the legionnaires. Using his HUD to zoom in, he saw troops rushing out of the trenches around Fortress Ancion.

"That's 1st Platoon," Xavier yelled excitedly. "Charge!"

Roaring with wild abandon, the platoon took off running and firing towards the enemy. He knew that most of their rounds would miss, but it would distract the enemy long enough for them to close the distance. Xavier had already seen how brutal his platoon was when engaged in hand-to-hand combat. He almost pitied the Loyalists, almost. Echoing his platoon's battle cry, he joined them in their charge.

The battle lust was on him. Time slowed, and his vision tunneled. One lone Dagdan Loyalist stood on a boulder, carefully picking off legionnaire troops. Xavier lowered his carbine and rushed towards him. He wasn't sure how long it took—one moment he was running forward, and the next he was close enough to engage. He screamed his pent-up frustration, reliving every shelling he'd endured. He thrust his bayonet towards the enemy.

He wasn't quick enough, and the Loyalist soldier jumped to the side. He didn't remember all his training, but his muscles did. He followed his failed thrust with a butt stroke that caught the Dagdan in the face. Not letting up, Xavier returned to the basic stance he'd spent hours of training as a plebe. Thrusting again, he got lucky. He hit the enemy and felt his blade slide into the Loyalist's belly.

Xavier tried to pull his bayonet out of the enemy's guts, but it was stuck. He struggled, pissed at the dying man for slowing him down. He'd been taught that the blade's blood groove prevented this. The training cadre had made it sound so easy—stick in, pull out, repeat. It wasn't working. Xavier fired a few rounds into the enemy's guts, trying to loosen the blade while he simultaneously jerked his carbine back. Weapon free, he screamed his victory and searched for a new target.

Scanning the field around him, Xavier missed the Loyalist charging his flank. He felt a searing pain in his side, a burning sensation that pulsed and shuddered throughout his frame. The impact of the hit knocked him to the ground. He lost control of his carbine, the shock of the assault catching him unprepared. Rolling into the fall, he stood in time to dodge the next thrust. Leaping to the side, Xavier grabbed the stock of the enemy's carbine. He used his forward momentum to get in close, headbutting the enemy.

Taking advantage of the Loyalist being off balance, Xavier swept the soldier's legs out from under him. He managed to wrest control of the carbine from the enemy and flipped it around. Re-armed, he began firing round after round into the prostrate foe. He fired until the metallic click told him he was out of ammunition. Reloading the weapon, he began searching for another target. He saw that the last of the enemy had been dispatched.

"Not dispatched—killed," he muttered to himself.

He saw his platoon sergeant and strode towards him. The pain reminded him of his wound, pulsing through his left flank. Fighting the pain, Xavier reached for the first aid pouch on his armor and grabbed the anticoagulant spray. Gritting his teeth against the pain that was coming, he shoved the nozzle into his wound and depressed the lever. The pressurized spray shot out and began foaming immediately. The initial application of the anticoagulant pain medicine forced him to groan. Xavier tried to maintain the allure of toughness in front of his troops. He failed. The pain eventually lessened, as the medicine worked its way through his system. Finally, he could focus again.

"Don't worry—ladies love scars," Boswell told him as he inspected the injury with the skilled hands of a combat veteran.

"Master Sergeant, Lieutenant Pitera should be advancing on the remaining guns with 3rd. See if we can ease their assault. Get the captured guns firing on the enemy. We'll shell the hell out of the Loyalist scum. Return the favor," Xavier said.

"I knew you wouldn't remember that shit, no LT does. I'm already on it," Boswell responded as he snapped a crisp salute. "Now I imagine Brass will want to claim all the glory, so bend over and pucker up, sir!"

"Why should we LTs sully ourselves with that, Master Sergeant? Why else do you think the gods gave us NCOs?" Xavier asked, the mirth thick in his voice.

Dismissing Boswell, Xavier turned to his radio operator. "Sergeant Andrews, get the company commander on the line."

Nodding an affirmative, the Comms Sergeant moved closer to Xavier. While he knew that his comms sergeant could establish a link at great distances, close proximity was necessary for secure messaging. Xavier had a feeling that an ass-chewing was coming, and he didn't want that openly available on the comms networks.

"Thunder 6, this is Thunder Red 6. Enemy guns on southern ridgeline secure. Will update once Thunder White element secures gun batteries on the northern ridge. How copy?"

"Thunder Red 6, this is Storm Actual."

Shit, Xavier thought, *when the Legion commander talks to a second lieutenant, it never ends well.*

"Well done, Lieutenant. Fortress Ancion will soon be secure. With the opening you created, we can drop in reinforcements to secure the northern ridge. Today, Fortress Ancion; tomorrow, all of Gakawen! Your company commander's brilliant leadership is remarkable. I'm eyeing her for promotion to my staff. Until she is transferred, you'll be her XO. Learn everything you can from her. Storm Actual, out."

Author J.R. Handley

J.R. Handley is a pseudonym for a husband and wife writing team. He is a veteran infantry sergeant with the 101st Airborne Division and the 28th Infantry Division. She is the kind of crazy that interprets his insanity into cogent English. He writes the sci-fi while she proofreads it. The sergeant is a two-time combat veteran of the late unpleasantness in Mesopotamia where he was wounded, likely doing something stupid. He started writing military science fiction as part of a therapy program suggested by his doctor, and hopes to entertain you while he attempts to excise his demons through these creative endeavors. In addition to being just another dysfunctional veteran, he is a stay at home wife, avid reader and all-around nerd. Luckily for him, his Queen joins him in his fandom nerdalitry.

I can be found fumbling around the interwebs on my blog, Twitter, and Facebook accounts. If this story peaked your interest, be sure to check me out!

Cover Illustration © Christian Kallias

Book Formatting by James Baldwin

http://www.jamesosiris.com

Made in the USA
Middletown, DE
08 April 2018